PRAISE FOR
OLIVER PÖTZSCH

✦ ✦ ✦

"Swift and sure, compelling as any conspiracy theory, persuasive as any spasm of paranoia, *The Dark Monk* grips you at the base of your skull and doesn't let go."
— Gregory Maguire, author of *Wicked* and *Out of Oz*

"Oliver Pötzsch has brought to life the heady smells and tastes, the true reality of an era we've never seen quite like this before."
— Katherine Neville, best-selling author of *The Eight* and *The Magic Circle*

"In this subtle, meticulously crafted story, every word is a possible clue, and the characters are so engaging that it's impossible not to get involved in trying to help them figure the riddle out."
— Oprah.com

"Oliver Pötzsch takes readers on a darkly atmospheric visit to seventeenth-century Bavaria in his latest adventure. With enough mystery and intrigue to satisfy those who like gritty historical fiction, *The Dark Monk* has convincing characters, rip-roaring action, and finely drawn settings."
— Deborah Harkness, author of *A Discovery of Witches* and
... ight

"I loved every page, character ... 's *Daughter*, an inventive histo... century hangman's quest to sav... ...self."
— Scott Turow

"An atmospheric mystery with more twists and turns than a medieval labyrinth . . . Great stuff!"

—Paula Brackston, best-selling author of
The Witch's Daughter

"Oliver Pötzsch has hatched a narrative redolent of Alfred Hitchcock's best romantic thrillers, replete with mind-boggling ciphers, distinctive villains, secret societies (exotic yet historically accurate), and other pleasures both sensual and cerebral."

—James Morrow, author of *The Last Witchfinder*

Books by Oliver Pötzsch
The Ludwig Conspiracy
The Castle of Kings

THE HANGMAN'S DAUGHTER SERIES
The Hangman's Daughter
The Dark Monk
The Beggar King
The Poisoned Pilgrim
The Werewolf of Bamberg
The Play of Death

The CASTLE of KINGS

♦ ♦ ♦

OLIVER PÖTZSCH

Mariner Books
Houghton Mifflin Harcourt
Boston   New York

First Mariner Books edition 2017

Text copyright © 2013 by Ullstein Buchverlage GmbH, Berlin

Maps copyright © 2013 by Angelika Solibieda, cartomedia, Karlsruhe

English translation copyright © 2016 by Anthea Bell

The Castle of Kings was first published in 2013
by Ullstein Buchverlage GmbH as *Die Burg der Könige*.
Translated from German by Anthea Bell.
First published in English by Houghton Mifflin Harcourt in 2016.

www.hmhco.com

Library of Congress Cataloging-in-Publication Data
Names: Pötzsch, Oliver. author. | Bell, Anthea, translator.
Title: The castle of kings / Oliver Pötzsch ; [English translation ... by Anthea Bell]
Other titles: Burg der könige. English
Description: Boston : Houghton Mifflin Harcourt, 2016. | "The Castle of Kings
was first published in 2013 by Ullstein Buchverlage GmbH as
Die Burg der Könige"—Title page verso.
Identifiers: LCCN 2016010281 (print) | LCCN 2016020973 (ebook) |
ISBN 9780544319516 (hardback) | ISBN 9780544317888 (ebook) |
ISBN 9780544944473 (pbk.)
Subjects: LCSH: Couples—Fiction. | Peasants' War, 1524–1525—Fiction. |
Germany—History—1517–1648—Fiction. | BISAC: FICTION / Historical. |
FICTION / Mystery & Detective / Historical. | GSAFD: Historical fiction.
Classification: LCC PT2676.O895 B8713 2016 (print) |
LCC PT2676.O895 (ebook) | DDC 833/.92—dc23
LC record available at https://lccn.loc.gov/2016010281

Printed in the United States of America
DOC 10 9 8 7 6 5 4 3 2 1

Once again, for Katrin, Niklas, and Lily.
My castle.

What would I be without you?
Emperor Barbarossa,
As ancient legends tell,
Waits hidden in his castle
Under a magic spell.

Great Barbarossa never died,
But lies there to this day.
He is content his time to bide
Till fortune comes his way.

And with him sleeps the glory
Of German lands, it's writ,
To come back, says the story,
When those above see fit.

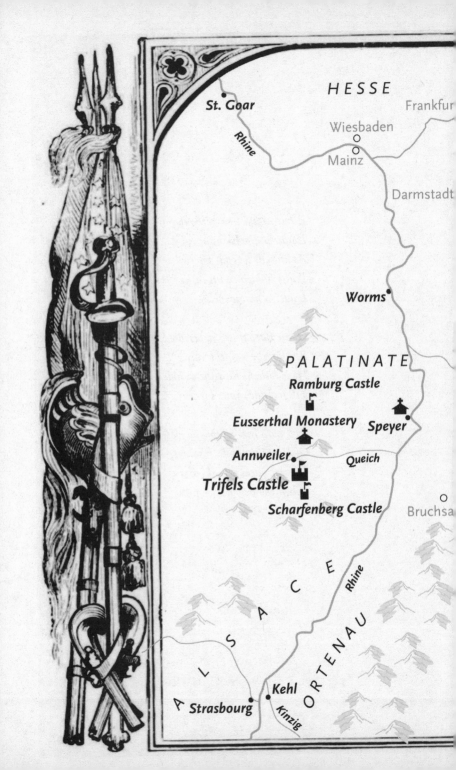

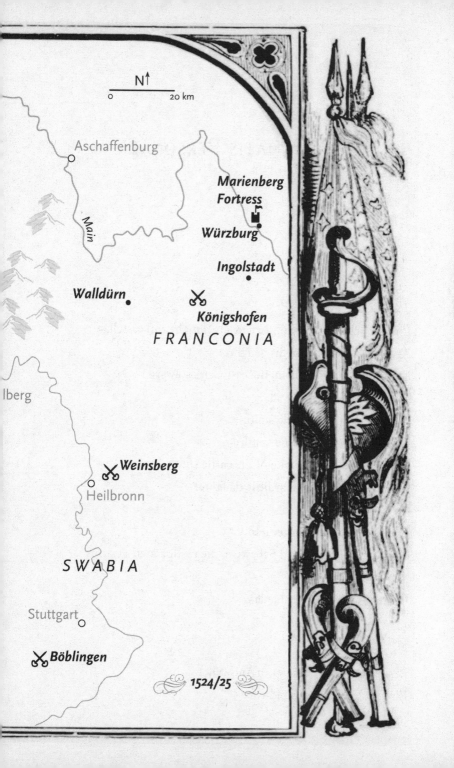

N

0   20 km

Aschaffenburg

Main

Marienberg Fortress

Würzburg

Ingolstadt

Walldürn

Königshofen

F R A N C O N I A

Iberg

Weinsberg

Heilbronn

S W A B I A

Stuttgart

Böblingen

1524/25

Dramatis Personae

Diethelm Seebach, landlord of the Green Tree Inn

Nepomuk Kistler, tanner

Martin Lebrecht, ropemaker

Peter Markschild, woolens weaver

Konrad Sperlin, apothecary

Johannes Lebner, priest

Shepherd Jockel, leader of the peasant band of Annweiler

SCHARFENBERG CASTLE

Count Friedrich von Löwenstein-Scharfeneck,
  lord of Scharfenberg Castle

Ludwig von Löwenstein-Scharfeneck, his father

Melchior von Tanningen, minstrel

OTHERS

Rupprecht von Lohingen, ducal administrator
  of Neukastell Castle

Hans von Wertingen, robber knight in the Ramburg

Weigand Handt, abbot of Eusserthal monastery

Barnabas, a procurer

Samuel, Marek, and Snuffler, mountebanks and cutthroats

Mother Barbara, vivandière and healer

Agathe, innkeeper's daughter, prisoner of the procurer Barnabas

Caspar, agent on an unknown mission

HISTORICAL CHARACTERS

Charles V, emperor of the Holy Roman Empire
  of the German Nation

Francis I, king of France

Queen Claude, wife of Francis I

Seneschal Georg von Waldburg-Zeil, military commander of the
Swabian League

Götz von Berlichingen, robber knight and leader of the Black Band

Florian Geyer, knight and leader of the Black Band

Book One

DARK CLOUDS

MARCH TO JUNE 1524

· 1 ·

Dᴵᴅ ᴛʜᴇ ʙᴏʏ ᴡʜᴏsᴇ ɴᴇᴄᴋ the hangman was fitting the noose around look any older than Mathis? Probably not. He was trembling all over, and fat tears ran down his cheeks, smeared already with snot and grime. From time to time the lad let out a sob; apart from that he seemed reconciled to his fate. Mathis guessed that he was about sixteen summers old, with the first downy hair growing above his lip. The boy had probably been proud of it, and had used it to impress the girls, but now he would never go chasing girls again. His short life was over before it had really begun.

The two men beside the boy were considerably older. Their shirts and hose were dirty and torn, their hair stood out untidily from their heads, and they were murmuring soundless prayers. All three stood on ladders propped against a wooden plank that had suffered from wind and weather. The Queichhambach gallows were massive and solidly built, and all local executions had taken place here for many decades, though recently there had been more and more of them. The last few years had brought winters that were too cold and summers that were too dry. Plague and other epidemics had afflicted the countryside. Hunger and oppressive feudal dues had driven many of the peasants of the Palatinate into the forests, where they joined bands of robbers and poachers. The three at the gallows had been caught red-handed poaching, and now they were about to pay the price.

Mathis stood a little way from the gaping crowd that had assembled to watch the execution this rainy morning. The hill where the gallows stood was a good quarter of a mile from the village, but close enough to the road leading to Annweiler for travelers to get a good view. Mathis had been delivering some horseshoes ordered by the village steward of Queichhambach from Mathis's father, the castle blacksmith at Trifels, but he happened to pass the gallows hill on the way back. He had meant to go on along the road—after all, this was his day off work, and he had plans of his own—but when he saw all the people standing in the icy rain, their faces careworn and intent, waiting for the execution to take place, his curiosity won the day. So he stopped to watch the hangman's cart taking the three prisoners to the place of execution.

By this time the hangman had put up the ladders beneath the gallows, dragged the three poor sinners over to the plank, and placed the nooses around their necks, one by one. A deep silence fell on the crowd, interrupted only by the boy's sobs.

At the age of seventeen, Mathis had already seen several executions. Most of the victims had been robbers or thieves condemned to be hanged or broken on the wheel, and the spectators had applauded and thrown rotten fruit and vegetables at the terrified creatures on the scaffold. This time, however, it was different. There was an almost vibrant tension in the air.

Although it was already mid-March, many of the fields lying around the hill were still covered with snow. Shivering, Mathis watched the crowd reluctantly parting to make way for the mayor of Annweiler, Bernwart Gessler, as he climbed the rising ground along with the stout priest Father Johannes. It was obvious that the pair of them could think of better things to do on a cold, wet, rainy day than watch three gallows birds dangling from their ropes. Mathis suspected that they had been sitting over a few glasses of Palatinate wine in a warm tavern in Annweiler, but as the duke's representative, the mayor was responsible for jurisdiction in the region, and now it was his task to pronounce sentence. Gessler braced himself against the rain blown into his face by gusts of wind, held his black velvet cap firmly on his head, and then climbed up onto the now empty hangman's cart.

"Good people of Annweiler," he said, turning to address the bystanders in a loud, arrogant voice. "These three fellows are guilty of poaching. They are nothing but robbers and vagabonds and have lost the right to life. Let their death be a warning to us all that the anger of God is terrible, but also righteous."

"Robbers and vagabonds, are they?" growled a thin man standing near Mathis. "I know that poor devil on the right, it's Josef Sammer from Gossersweiler. A decent hard-working laborer, he was, until his master couldn't pay him no more, so he went off to the woods." He spat on the ground. "What's the likes of us supposed to eat, after two harvests wrecked by hail? There's not even beechnuts left in the forest. It's as empty as my wife's dowry chest."

"They've raised our rent again," another peasant grumbled. "And the priests live high on the hog at our expense—come what may, they make sure to get their tithes. See how fat our priest is these days."

Stout Father Johannes crossed to the ladders beneath the gallows, carrying a simple wooden cross. He stopped at the feet of each man and recited a short Latin prayer in a high, droning voice. But the condemned men above him might have been in another world already, and they simply stared into the void. Only the boy was still weeping pitifully. It sounded like he was calling for his mother, but no one in the crowd answered him.

"By virtue of the office conferred upon me by the duke of Zweibrücken, I command the executioner to inflict their rightful punishment on these three miscreants," the mayor proclaimed. "Your lives are hereby forfeit."

He broke a small wooden staff, and the Queichhambach executioner, a sturdy man in baggy breeches, a linen shirt, and a bandage over one eye, took the ladder away from under the feet of the first delinquent. The man struggled for a while, his whole body swinging back and forth like an out-of-control clock pendulum, and a wet patch spread over his lower body. As his movements became weaker, the hangman tugged at the second ladder. Another wild dance in the air began as the second man dangled from his rope. When the executioner finally turned to the boy, a murmur ran through the crowd. Mathis was not the only one to have noticed how young he was.

"Children! You're hanging children!" someone cried. Turning, Mathis saw a careworn woman with two snotty-nosed little girls clinging to her apron strings. A tiny baby cried inside the rolled-up linen cloth that the woman had tied to her back. She did not seem to be the boy's mother, but nonetheless her face was red with anger and indignation. "A thing like this can't be God's will," she screamed, giving vent to her fury. "No just God would allow it."

The hangman hesitated when he saw how restless the spectators were. The mayor turned to the crowd with his hands raised. "He's no child now," he rasped in a voice used to command. "He knew what he was doing. And now he will get his punishment. That's only right and just. Does anyone here dispute it?"

Mathis knew that the mayor was in the right. In the German states, young people could be hanged at fourteen. If the judges were not sure of the age of the accused, they sometimes resorted to a trick: They let the boy or girl choose between an apple and a coin. If the child took the coin, he or she was considered to know the meaning of guilt—and was executed.

In spite of the mayor's clear words, the people near Mathis were not to be intimidated. They gathered more closely around the gallows, murmuring. The second hanged man was still twitching a little, while the first was already dangling as he swung back and forth in the wind. Shaking, the rope still around his neck, the boy looked down from the ladder at the executioner, who in turn stared at the mayor. It was as if, for a moment, time stood still.

A voice rang out suddenly, "Down with those who exploit us! Down with the duke and the mayor who let us starve, who watch us go to rack and ruin like cattle! Death to all who rule us!"

Bernwart Gessler gave a start. People shouted and bellowed. Here and there a cheer was raised for the three poachers. Gessler looked around uncertainly, trying to see who was cheering and inciting the crowd to rebellion.

"Who was that?" the mayor demanded, shouting to be heard against the noise. "Who's impertinent enough to challenge the authority of the duke and his servants as ordained by God?"

But the man he was looking for had already disappeared among the crowd again, although Mathis had managed to catch a fleeting glimpse of him. It was the hunchback Shepherd Jockel, who had ducked down behind a row of women to watch what happened next from that vantage point. Mathis thought he saw a faint smile on Jockel's lips, and then a couple of peasants blocked his view of the man.

"Down with those damn tithes," yelled someone else, not far from Mathis, a thin old man leaning on a stick. "The bishop and the duke are fat and healthy, and here you go hanging children who don't know where their next meal is coming from. What kind of a world is this?"

"Quiet. Keep calm, good people," the mayor ordered, raising his hand in a commanding manner. "Or there'll be a few more of you on the gallows here. Anyone who wants to dance has only to say so." He waved to the bailiffs who had been waiting beside the hangman's cart, and they moved threateningly toward the crowd with pikes in their hands. "But nothing will happen to anyone who goes to work as he should. All of this is God's will."

Here and there loud cursing and muttering could still be heard, but it gradually ebbed away. The storm of indignation had died down; not anger, but fear and force of habit had, as so often, won the day.

Finally, there was only a slight murmuring, like a gentle wind blowing over the fields. The mayor straightened up and gave the hangman the sign.

"Let's get this over with."

With a swift gesture, the hangman took the ladder away from under the boy's feet. The boy twitched and struggled, his eyes popping out like large marbles, but his death agony did not last long. After a minute at the most, the twitching stopped, and the boy's frail body went limp. Lifeless, he looked even smaller and more fragile than before.

Still murmuring, the crowd dispersed. Surreptitiously, people were still talking to one another, but then they all went their own ways. Mathis, too, turned away. He had seen enough. Feeling melancholy, he slung his empty bag over his shoulder and hurried toward the forest.

There was something waiting for him there.

"Off you go, Parcival! Get the scoundrel!"

Agnes looked up at her falcon as he plunged down on his prey like an arrow from a bow. The crow, an old and rather bedraggled bird, had flown a little too far from its flock and was an easy victim for the saker falcon. The crow noticed its pursuer only at the last moment, and it doubled back in the air so that the falcon shot past it. Parcival flew in a wide curve and regained altitude, coming down on the crow once more. This time his aim was better. As a ball of brown and black feathers, blood, and flesh, the two birds went into a spin as they fell toward the field below. One last flutter and then the crow lay dead among the clumps of frost-hardened mud. The falcon perched triumphantly on its body and began plucking its feathers with his beak.

"Well done, Parcival. Here's your reward."

With a chicken leg in her hand, Agnes approached the pecking falcon, while her little dachshund, Puck, jumped around the bird, barking with excitement. Parcival did not deign to give the dog a glance. After a moment's hesitation, the saker falcon flew up and landed on the thick leather gauntlet that Agnes wore on her left arm. Satisfied, he began pecking small pieces of meat off of the chicken leg. But after a little while Agnes put the leg away again so as not to over-feed her falcon. She admired Parcival's upright bearing and proud gaze, which always reminded her of the eyes of a wise old ruler. The falcon had been her dearest companion for two years now.

Meanwhile, Puck had put up another flock of crows in the freshly plowed field, and the falcon rose for another hunt. The rain had stopped, and the wind had driven away the low cloud, so Agnes could admire her bird flying in all his splendor.

"Get to work, lazybones!" she called after him. "You'll get a nice juicy bite of chicken for every crow, and that's a promise."

While Agnes watched the falcon spiraling higher and higher into the sky, she wondered what the earth looked like from up there—her father's castle on the Sonnenberg opposite, rising on a sandstone rock among beech, chestnut, and oak trees; the Wasgau, that gigantic wooded area of the Palatinate, with its countless green hills; the fa-mous cathedral of Speyer that for miles around marked the center of the world as Agnes knew it. When she was a child, her father had once taken her to the distant city with him, but her memory of it had faded long ago. Ever since Agnes could remember, her playground had been the former imperial citadel of Trifels, the little town of Annweiler just below it, the villages of Queichhambach and Albersweiler, the landscape around them. Even though the castellan, Philipp Schlüchterer von Erfenstein, did not like his sixteen-year-old daugh-ter to roam the forests, meadows, and marshes, Agnes used every free hour to take her dog and falcon away from the castle that often felt too cold, damp, and lonely for comfort. Just now, as winter was com-ing to an end, it was still dismally cold on the Trifels, while down in the valley the first young shoots of spring were showing.

By now, the falcon had reached the requisite height of almost three hundred feet. He shot down like a bolt of lightning into the flock of crows, who fluttered apart, cawing loudly. But this time they all escaped him. The little predator caught himself up only a few yards above the ground and spiraled up to dive down once more. The flock surged like a black cloud.

Agnes had been given the brown and white speckled falcon as a nestling by her father, and she had trained him without any help. It had taken her months of hard work. Parcival was her pride and joy, and even her usually morose father had to admit that she had done a good job with his training. Only last week the farmers of Annweiler had asked him, as castellan of Trifels, whether Agnes would fly her falcon over their fields to drive the crows away. This year there was a real plague of them. They ate the last of the seed corn in the ground and scared away the larks, chaffinches, and blackbirds that were often the only kind of meat the poor people tasted.

Parcival had just come down on another crow. Caught up together, the two birds plummeted toward the field below, and Agnes ran over to protect her beloved falcon from potential attacks. Crows were crafty birds, and they would often combine in mobbing a predator to get rid of it. And indeed, the flock was coming menacingly close, and Agnes felt anger rise in her, just as though she was protecting her own child. She threw a few stones, and the birds turned away, cawing.

Relieved, Agnes lured Parcival to her with the gnawed chicken leg again. She would leave the dead crow lying in the field to deter the rest of the flock. It was the seventh that the falcon had killed today.

"Come along, little one. This will taste much better, I promise you."

Parcival stopped pecking the crow and flapped his wings in excitement. But just as the falcon was about to come down and perch on her glove, a mighty roll of thunder shook the valley. The bird turned and flew into the nearby wood.

"Damn it, Parcival, stay here! What are you doing?"

Apprehensively, Agnes looked up to see if a storm was about to break, but there were no black clouds in the sky, only gray cloud cover. Besides, it was only March, much too early for a summer storm. So what did that clap of thunder mean? Well, whatever it was, it had upset her falcon so much that Agnes was in danger of losing him forever.

With the yapping Puck beside her, she ran to the little wood. As she did so, she looked around, trying to work out what could have made that noise. About half a mile of field and vegetable gardens, still with patches of snow lying on them, reached from here to the little town of Annweiler. Beyond, the castle mound rose in the soft afternoon light, surrounded by a broad belt of sloping vineyards and freshly plowed fields.

Agnes thought. Could Ulrich Reichhart, master gunner at Trifels and usually drunk, have fired a shot from one of the three pieces of artillery that the castle still had left? But gunpowder was expensive, and moreover, the sound of the shot had come from the opposite direction.

The way her falcon had flown.

"Parcival! Parcival!"

Her heart thudding, Agnes ran toward the outskirts of the forest, which were densely overgrown with hawthorn bushes. Only now did she think of something else that might have caused that thunderous crash. There had been persistent rumors lately of robbers in these parts. The Ramburg, one of the many hideouts of robber knights in the Wasgau area, lay only a few miles away. Could its commander, Hans von Wertingen, really have ventured to go marauding so close to her father's castle? Thus far the impoverished nobleman had made only the roads unsafe, and even then usually under cover of darkness. But maybe he and his men had found that hunger now had the upper hand, and with it came the urge to rob and murder?

On reaching the outskirts of the forest, Agnes cautiously stood still and looked back at the little town, with the castle mound towering behind it. It would certainly be more sensible to run up to the Trifels, to warn her father of the possibility of an attack. But then, presumably, she would never find her Parcival again. Even when trained, falcons were shy birds. The danger of his disappearing forever into the wilderness was great.

Finally she pulled herself together and hurried on into the oak wood. Immediately dim light surrounded her; the dense branches, already putting out the first buds of the coming spring's leaves and flowers, let hardly any sun filter through. In fall, the tanners of Annweiler came to this part of the forest for their tanning bark, but at this time of year the place seemed deserted. People out collecting firewood had searched the frozen ground a few weeks ago for wintry twigs and acorns, and now you might have thought that the forest had been swept clean. Agnes was glad to have Puck at least for company, even if the little dachshund was unlikely to be much help in the event of an attack. When the few branches and twigs that she trod on cracked, it sounded like bones breaking.

She trudged farther and farther into the dark forest. There could be no question of moving fast; her way was often barred by ramparts of muddy earth and prickly hawthorn thickets. Once again, Agnes thought how lucky it was that she had put on her brown leather doublet to go hawking, not the long fustian dress that her father liked so much. The thorns would have torn that expensive garment to shreds by now. Burs and small twigs clung to Agnes's fair and always untidy hair; thorns scratched her freckled face.

"Parcival?" she called again, but the only response was the angry *chirrup*ing of several blackbirds. Although she usually loved the silence of the forest, it suddenly seemed to her oppressive, seeming to stifle her like a thick blanket.

All at once she heard a familiar sound to her right. Agnes heaved a sigh of relief. It was clearly Parcival, trying to attract her attention. Young birds of prey that flew by daytime often gave that characteristic cry when they were begging for food. Sometimes the noise could be a real nuisance, but today it sounded as sweet to Agnes as the music of a lute. And now she also heard the little bell that hung from his foot to lead her to him.

Agnes hurried in the direction from which the falcon's cry and the sound of the bell had come, and a clearing in the forest opened up ahead of her. In the slanting sunlight that fell into the space, she saw an ivy-covered sandstone ruin that had probably once been a watch-tower. Only now did she realize that she knew this place. There were many towers of this kind around the Trifels, since the district had once been the heart of the German Empire. Kings and emperors had built their castles here. Now only a few songs, and the remains of walls like this one, overgrown with moss, bore witness to the former glory of this tract of land. Agnes stood there as if caught in a dream, and a shudder ran through her. Swathes of mist drifted over the ruin, and there was a curious smell of something rotten in the air. She felt as if she were looking into the distant past. A time that seemed as familiar to her as her own, and yet was as dead as the stones all around.

Once again she heard the falcon cry. Keeping in the cover of a broad tree trunk, Agnes searched the clearing and finally saw the bird on the branch of a stunted willow that had taken root in a crack in the ruined walls. She laughed with relief, and the magic moment was over.

"So here you are, you—"

Agnes stopped when she suddenly saw the figure of a man in the clearing. He had been hidden behind several large rocks, but now he came out of hiding, bending low. In his hands he held a kind of large tube, and now, with a groan, he put it down on a rock.

Agnes clapped her hand to her mouth to keep herself from screaming. Was this one of the robber knights or footpads she had heard so much about? But then it struck her that the way the man moved was curiously familiar. When she looked more closely, she also recognized his well-worn leather jerkin, his sandy hair, and his finely shaped features.

"My God, Mathis, how could you give me such a fright?" Shaking with fury, Agnes came out into the clearing, while Puck, yapping happily, jumped up at the young man and licked his hand.

Mathis was just under a year older than Agnes. He was tall, but sinewy, with a broad back and well-developed muscles on his upper arms, the result of his hard work at the anvil.

"I might have known it was you behind that infernal noise," Agnes said, shaking her head. But her anger was increasingly giving way to relief on finding that no robber had been lying in wait for her. In the end she couldn't suppress a smile. "Anywhere there's a smell of sulfur, the journeyman smith from Trifels won't be far away, am I right?" She pointed to the tube, which was almost the size of a man, lying beside Mathis on the rocks. "I can see it's not enough for you to drive your own father and mine to white-hot fury, you have to go scaring my falcon and all the creatures of the forest half to death. Shame on you."

Mathis grinned, raising his hands in a gesture of deprecation. "You think I ought to have fired it off up there in the castle? The Trifels may be a decrepit heap of stones, but that's no reason to blow it sky-high."

"You mind what you're saying, Mathis Wielenbach."

Agnes kept her voice low and cool, but Mathis was not to be intimidated. He was almost a head taller than she was, and her anger seemed to have no more effect on him than it would have on a wall.

"My humble apologies, Your Excellency." He made a deep bow. "I quite forgot I was speaking to the daughter of the venerable castellan. Is it permitted for me to approach you at all, young lady? Or aren't you allowed to talk to such a dull-witted fool of a vassal as me?" Mathis pulled a face that made him look as if he were indeed simple-minded. But suddenly his expression darkened.

"What's the matter?" asked Agnes.

Mathis took a deep breath before, at last, he replied quietly, "I was over in Queichhambach just now when they hanged three poachers. One of them was no older than me." He shook his head angrily. "It's going from bad to worse, Agnes. The people are eating husks and their seed corn, and when they're so desperate that they hunt in the forest, they end up on the gallows. What does your father say to all that?"

"My father didn't make the laws, Mathis."

"No, he can go off hunting cheerfully himself while others have to hang for it."

"Good heavens above, Mathis!" Agnes looked at him, her eyes

blazing. "You know very well that my father keeps not just one eye closed to poachers but both of them when he's out and about in his forests. As for what happens in the jurisdiction of the mayor of Annweiler, there's really nothing he can do about that. So leave my father out of this and don't keep criticizing him all the time."

"All right, all right." Mathis shrugged his shoulders. "Maybe I shouldn't have such conversations with a castellan's daughter."

"You shouldn't have such conversations at all."

For a while neither of them said anything. Agnes folded her arms and stared truculently ahead of her. But soon her wrath evaporated; she had known Mathis too long to be genuinely angry with him for saying such things, even if she wasn't going to let him run her father down. A few years ago the two of them had still been playing hide-and-seek in the castle cellars; not until last fall had their meetings become less frequent. Agnes had been looking after her falcon and spending the long winter evenings in the castle library, while Mathis spent more and more time with men who preached liberty and justice. He sometimes went too far, thought Agnes, although she herself had a great deal of sympathy for many of the peasants' demands. However, it wasn't for her or her father to change the conditions of their time; only very great lords could do that—princes, bishops, and, of course, the emperor.

"What are you doing with that thing?" she finally asked, in a more conciliatory voice.

"I've been trying out a new kind of gunpowder," Mathis began solemnly, just as if there had never been any quarrel between them. "Seven instead of six parts of saltpeter, as well as five parts of sulfur, and some charcoal made from young hazel wood." He reached for a little bag on the ground in front of him and let the dark gray substance trickle through his fingers. "And this time I've made the powder more granular. That way it will burn faster and be less inclined to clump together."

Agnes rolled her eyes. Firearms were Mathis's great passion. She would never understand what he saw in those noisy iron tubes.

"Someday you'll blow yourself up along with the gunpowder," she said reproachfully. "I just can't think what's so great about the racket they make and the stink they leave behind. It's . . . it's downright un-chivalrous, that's what I say."

Mathis smiled. "That's what your father told you, am I right?"

"So what if he did? Anyway, he wouldn't like you stealing one of his arquebuses from the arsenal." She pointed to the metal tube lying on the rock, still smoking slightly. "Because that's where it came from, you might as well admit it."

Shrugging his shoulders, Mathis turned back to the gun and began filling it carefully with powder. He pushed the tiny grains to the very back of the chamber, and finally closed off the tube with a leaden ball the size of a walnut. There was a hook fitted to one side of the gun, which Mathis now jammed into a crevice between two rocks so that the recoil of the explosion wouldn't make the arquebus fall to one side. Agnes had already seen her father's men do something similar, except that they stuck the hook of the gun into the eyelets provided for it in the merlons of the castle battlements. These arquebuses were old-fashioned weapons, but more modern technology cost a great deal of money and was hardly known here at Trifels. Mathis made fun of such ignorance.

"Old Ulrich never noticed me borrowing the gun," the young smith muttered as he carefully tipped powder into the flash pan. "He was so drunk that I could simply fish the key to the arsenal out of his pocket. I hid it here the day before yesterday—I finally had the gun-powder ready today."

"Are you out of your mind?" Agnes shook her head incredulously. "That's theft, Mathis. What do you think my father will do to you if he notices that the gun is missing?"

"For heaven's sake, he won't notice unless you tell him. Anyway, what would your father do with this rusty old arquebus? Put the Turks to flight, maybe?" By now Mathis was ready. He took a match out of his pocket and fitted it into the place intended for it. "The cas-tellan should be glad I'm putting my mind to such things. If we don't soon have one or two new falconets standing on the castle mound, he might as well pelt any future attackers with rotten cabbages."

Agnes sighed. "You know as well as I do that there's no money for such things. What's more, I don't know who'd attack us here. Not the Turks, anyway."

"Maybe not the Turks, but . . ."

Mathis stopped when little Puck suddenly began growling. The dachshund bared his teeth and stared at the other side of the clearing, his coat bristling. As Agnes turned, she felt goose bumps cover her arms. She heard noises, and not pleasant ones. The snorting of horses, followed by the clink of weapons, and the low, deep voices of several men.

Almost at once, four horsemen appeared beyond a hawthorn thicket. They wore shabby hose under stained leather jerkins. Hunting knives and crossbows the length of a man's forearm hung at their horses' sides. One of them, an unusually tall man, was also equipped with an old-fashioned breastplate and a round helmet, and a mighty broadsword hung from his belt. This giant had a large black mastiff, almost the size of a calf, on a long leash. The animal growled ferociously at the two young people.

"Well, well, who have we here?" murmured the man in armor, while his dog, panting and with bulging eyes, strained at the leash. "Here we go looking for a great clap of thunder, and all we find is two little farts."

The other three men laughed, but the man in armor, who was obviously their leader, silenced them with a peremptory gesture. Distrustfully, he let his eyes wander over the clearing, and finally he turned to Agnes.

"Are you two here alone?"

Silently, Agnes nodded. There was no point in lying to the man. It was true that she had never seen him before, but she knew from his appearance that this must be the gigantic Hans von Wertingen. In times of peace, only knights might carry two-handed weapons like his broadsword, even if they were now roaming the countryside to rob and murder. Moreover, Wertingen's huge dog was notorious far beyond Annweiler. It was said that the animal was trained to attack human beings and had torn children to pieces. It was not for Agnes to say whether that was true, but in any case the animal was more than awe-inspiring.

"Did the thunder deafen you, eh?" Hans von Wertingen growled. "Speak up. What are you doing here in these forests?"

"We . . . we're simple tanners from Annweiler, out looking for young oaks," Agnes replied hesitantly, keeping her eyes on the ground. "We need fresh bark for our tanning pits. Forgive us if we disturbed your hunting, noble sirs."

Mathis looked at Agnes for a moment in surprise, and then imitated her. Clearly he, too, had realized what would happen if Hans von Wertingen knew who actually stood before him. As a nobleman's daughter, Agnes was an ideal hostage—and holding hostages to ransom was a good way for robber knights to rid themselves of their financial difficulties.

"Oh yes? And this tube?" Wertingen mockingly indicated the arquebus lying on the ground. "I suppose you use it for peeling bark off trees, do you?"

"Found it here ourselves, noble sir," Mathis replied, assuming a simple-minded expression. "It's all old and rusty. We don't know what it's for neither."

"Ah, so you don't know . . ." Hans von Wertingen examined the two of them suspiciously. When his glance fell on Agnes's falconry gauntlet, a look of recognition suddenly dawned on his face. Agnes flinched and cursed herself for not taking the glove off earlier. It was too late now.

"Of course," the knight said, pointing to Agnes. "I know who you are. Blonde, dressed like a boy, freckles . . . You're the crazy girl with the falcon, daughter of the castellan of the Trifels, aren't you?" Grinning, he turned to his men. "A woman hunting with a falcon. Did you ever hear the like of it? Well, I think we'll have cured you of that notion by the time your father pays the ransom we'll demand. We'll look after this little pigeon well, eh, men?"

The other three laughed, and Hans von Wertingen, pleased with himself, stroked his tangled beard. His long black hair was matted, his face red and bloated by cheap brandy. Agnes knew many stories of famous knights, once celebrated in song by bards, whom the misery of the last few years had turned into ragged vagabonds. Her father had told her that the Wertingens themselves had once been a highly regarded family. They had risen to be ministers of the emperor's domains, but then their income from letting out land on lease dwindled more and more as their debts increased.

Agnes looked at this dirty, verminous man on his rickety horse and knew at once that she could expect no mercy from him.

"Get hold of the girl," Wertingen ordered in his harsh voice. "You can send the boy to the devil for all I care."

Whinnying, the horses moved into a semicircle around the two captives.

Puck ran over to the shouting men and circled them, yapping. As he did so, the little dog took care to stay clear of the big mastiff that was growling at him and tugging at the leash.

"Did you ever see anything like it?" Hans von Wertingen was laughing so hard that his battered armor clinked slightly. "A puny little cur attacking my Saskia. The creature's as crazy as his mistress. Go on, Saskia, get him!"

He let go of the leash, and the monster fell on Puck like a black demon. It all happened so fast that Agnes didn't even have time to scream. The mastiff's fangs closed on the dachshund and tossed him into the air like a wet rag. Next moment Puck was lying in front of his mistress with his throat bitten through. He uttered a last hoarse yelp, and then the little bundle of fur went limp.

"You . . . you murderer! You damned murderer!"

Crying out, Agnes ran at the knight, who was still laughing, and flailed at his legs with her gauntlet. Hans von Wertingen gave her a kick that sent her slipping backward, where she hit the back of her head on a rock. Sharp pain shot through her, and for a moment everything went dark before her eyes.

"Stupid girl," Wertingen said. "Shedding tears over a wretched mongrel like that. Never mind the dog, tell us where your falcon is. He'll be worth a good sum. Talk, or else . . ."

"Don't make a move, you bastard!"

In her pain, it took Agnes a moment to grasp the fact that it really was Mathis who had spoken those words. When she rose from the ground, groaning, she saw the smith's son standing beside the arquebus, with a burning fuse held just above the flash pan in his right hand. The metal tube was still lying on the rocks, aimed directly at the four men.

"You swine have just as long as the fuse goes on burning to get away from here," Mathis warned them. His voice shook slightly, but his eyes were firmly fixed on Hans von Wertingen. "Or even your own mothers won't recognize your stinking corpses."

For a few seconds, everything in the clearing was so still that only the hiss of the burning fuse could be heard. Then Hans von Wertingen began roaring with laughter again.

"A stupid little peasant threatening me with a gun." He mopped the tears of mirth from his eyes. "Mind you don't burn your fingers, lad. What did you load that infernal device with—acorns?"

"With a leaden ball weighing six ounces and a good pound of the best granular gunpowder. Enough to send at least one of you to hell any day."

Hans von Wertingen's laughter stopped abruptly, and his three men, too, now seemed considerably less sure of themselves.

"So it *was* you firing that shot just now?" the knight murmured suspiciously. "But how is that possible? It would take a highly experienced landsknecht just to load the thing. And granular gunpowder's expensive, that's for sure."

"Half the fuse is burned," Mathis pointed out. "You don't have much time left." He raised the gun, this time aiming it straight at Wertingen. "So get out of here."

"You . . . you windbag of a . . ." It was visibly difficult for Hans von Wertingen to control himself. At last he spat grimly on the forest floor. "Devil take it, you don't fool me. I'll be bound that thing's not loaded at all. Get him, men!"

But the three robbers sat on their horses and did not move.

"I said get him, damn your eyes. Or I'll shove that arquebus up your fat asses with my own hands."

This threat was enough to start the men moving at last. They trotted their horses toward Mathis and Agnes at a menacingly slow pace, with a murderous light in their eyes.

When they were only a few paces away, a mighty clap of thunder shook the clearing. It was as loud as if the whole world were coming to an end in fire and smoke.

Agnes flung herself down on the hard ground, and out of the corner of her eye saw one of the men fall from his horse, as if struck down by a divine hammer. His torso was a mass of red. The castellan's daughter felt something wet on her face, and at the same moment a fine rain of blood began drizzling down on her.

Thick black smoke poured from the mouth of the arquebus.

Agnes cried out in horror, while horses and men fell into panic nearby. Deadly fear came over her. What had Mathis done? There was no going back after this. The robber knight's men would undoubtedly kill them both now. Agnes desperately tried to crawl away into the bushes at the edge of the clearing, but her legs refused to obey her. After the gun had been fired, all sounds seemed muted and far away, as if her ears were wrapped in thick wool. The huge mastiff had crept under an overhanging rock, whimpering; two of the horses had thrown their riders and were galloping away, whinnying loudly. Only Hans von Wertingen still sat firmly in his saddle, his face red with anger and stained with blood.

"You'll pay for this!" he shouted, beside himself, reaching for the mighty two-handed sword at his side. "The hell with a ransom. Philipp von Erfenstein can have his daughter back—head, arms, and legs one by one."

Roaring furiously, his broadsword drawn, he made for Agnes where she crouched, frozen, in the middle of the clearing. As if time had suddenly slowed down, she saw the knight riding toward her, step by step. The air was full of the clink of metal. The blade of the sword was already coming down when Agnes suddenly felt a hand on her shoulder. It was Mathis, hauling her aside at the last moment.

"We must get away from here! Can you hear me?" he shouted into her ear, his voice muted.

Agnes nodded, as if in a trance, but then she thought of something. "Parcival!" she cried frantically. "I can't abandon Parcival."

"Forget the falcon, our lives are in danger! Look, that bastard is coming back."

Mathis pointed to Hans von Wertingen, who had turned his horse and was galloping back toward them.

Desperately, Agnes looked around, but she could see no sign of Parcival anywhere in the devastated clearing. At last she struggled up and ran into the forest with Mathis. They could hear the snorting and whinnying of the horse behind them.

"I'll get you yet, damn it," Hans von Wertingen called. "Stand still, and perhaps I'll be chivalrous and show you mercy."

"Chivalrous!" Mathis gasped as he pulled Agnes on by her hand. "A moment ago he was going to quarter us."

They stumbled through the bushes, over hollows in the ground and moldering branches, panting with fear, until the sound of whinnying died away behind them. At last Agnes stood still and listened. Her hearing seemed to be intact, apart from a slight ringing in her ears. Relieved, she realized that the knight could not follow them through the thickets on his horse.

"We'd better hide," she whispered. "Then he's sure to ride past us."

"You're forgetting the mastiff. She can smell us." Mathis made her go on until they reached a small brook winding its way through the forest. "If we wade along this stream for a while, the dog may lose track of our scent."

Still out of breath, they scrambled down into the cold water, which came up to their knees. Agnes clung to Mathis's doublet with her right hand and did her best not to think of the pitiful bundle of fur that only a few minutes ago had been her dear, cheerful little Puck.

They followed the current of the brook downstream. Once they thought for a moment that they heard a dog barking, but it was too far away to be dangerous. Agnes was staggering rather than walking, and she had lost her gauntlet long ago. She stumbled and fell on the bed of the stream but hardly felt herself graze a knee. The terrible end of her beloved Puck, the loss of her falcon, the man's bleeding torso—all these images haunted her mind simultaneously. She staggered on behind Mathis until they finally clambered out of the brook. They made for the castle mound, moving in a wide arc around it. Tears ran down her face, and again and again she suppressed sobs. The day that had begun so well had turned into sheer nightmare.

Only when they had reached the fields around the castle, and the Trifels towered strong and gray above them, did Agnes know that they were in safety.

There was still no trace of her falcon.

Not far away, in a hut in the forest, the old midwife Elsbeth Rechsteiner threw a log on the fire and watched blue flames lick around the wood. A large pot on a tripod simmered over the flames, hissing slightly. The smoke had difficulty finding its way through an opening in the roof of reed thatch, and so the little cottage was full of it.

Elsbeth thoughtfully stirred the pot. A few pale flowers and birch leaves floated in the liquid it contained. She had jumped when she heard the bang a few moments ago and murmured a quiet prayer, although she had no idea what had caused the noise. But these days, the forest that had been her home since childhood seemed a dark and dangerous place. Like an evil being that would reach for her with its branches and twigs when she wandered for hours along overgrown game paths. More and more robber knights and bandits went about their nefarious business in these parts, emaciated wolves and wild boar as big as bears had become a plague, and famine even changed many a usually peace-loving villager into a wild beast.

But if Elsbeth's hand shook now as she fed the fire with dry twigs, it had nothing to do with robbers, wild beasts, or that loud explosion; it was because of the three men sitting at the well-worn little table behind her. She had known them all for many years, but until now they had always met in secret in a cellar under the church of St. Fortunatus in Annweiler. Their sudden arrival here, in her cottage, showed Elsbeth how serious the situation was.

The enemy was back.

For some time they had all sat there in silence, with only the warning cry of the jay outside to be heard. Only now did the midwife turn to the three men.

"And the news is true?" she asked, with a lingering touch of doubt in her voice. Elsbeth was now over sixty. Age, hard work, and worry had dug deep lines in her skin. Only her eyes still shone as brightly as in her youth.

One of her visitors nodded. Old age had left its mark on him as well. The hands enfolding a beaker of hot herbal brew were bent with gout, his face furrowed like a freshly plowed field. "They're on the road again, Elsbeth," he said, "there's no doubt about it. My cousin Jakob saw them in Zweibrücken, where they searched the archives, but I don't suppose they found anything. Who knows where they'll be riding now? Worms, Speyer, maybe Landau . . . It won't be long before they're here in Annweiler."

"After all these years." Elsbeth Rechsteiner sighed and stared into the flames, her eyes clouded. She was cold in spite of the fire, the frost of March lingering in her old bones. "I thought they'd given up," she went on at last. "It's so long ago, and we've kept the secret so well. Is all the terror to begin again?"

"Believe me, they won't find anything," one of the other two men said reassuringly. He was younger, and his dirty leather apron showed that he had made haste here from his place of work. "The traces are well blurred. Only the Brotherhood knows about them. And none of us will talk, not a single one. I'd stake my life on it."

Elsbeth Rechsteiner laughed softly and shook her head. "How can you be so sure? These men are clever, and as cruel as bloodhounds. You know what they broke last time. They know no mercy. They'll search everywhere, people will talk out of fear, and in the end they'll find something. Either with you or with me."

"Remember what you promised, Elsbeth. Remember your oath." The old man put his beaker down and rose, groaning. "We came to warn you, but that does not release you from your task. If the secret is to be well hidden, better here than in the city." He gave the other two men a sign, and they walked to the door together. Only there did the old man turn once more. "We have sworn to keep the secret until the day comes at last. So many generations, and they have all kept silent. Nothing can release us from that promise."

"And suppose the day has already come?" Elsbeth Rechsteiner asked quietly, as she stared into the fire. "Suppose this is the time to act, at last?"

"It is not for us to decide that, as only God knows." The old man raised his stained hat. "Thank you for the hot brew, Elsbeth. May heaven protect you."

The three of them turned away in silence and left her hut. Their footsteps crunched on the twigs that covered the forest floor and slowly died away.

Elsbeth Rechsteiner was left alone with her fears.

Silently, Agnes and Mathis climbed the steep path up to the castle. They had rushed here from the clearing. Agnes's heart beat rapidly and sweat stood out on her forehead. Again and again she saw in her mind's eye the man's shattered, bleeding torso and heard the shouting of her pursuer. She knew that she had only just escaped death. By this time she had calmed down enough to imagine, at least, what her father would say about all that. Not only had she lost her falcon, Parcival, not only was little Puck dead, they had also had to leave the arquebus behind. If Philipp von Erfenstein found out that Mathis had stolen the gun, he would fall into one of his notorious fits of rage. Agnes did not think that her father would hand Mathis over to the mayor of Annweiler, but he was still in danger of imprisonment or even exile.

"Maybe that experiment in the clearing wasn't such a good idea," Mathis muttered beside her. He too was visibly downcast. He shivered slightly and was as pale as death, a pallor that stood out even more against the marks of soot left on his face.

"Not such a good idea? It was the most stupid idea you ever had!" Agnes exclaimed. But she was too badly shaken to be truly angry. "I'd think that explosion was heard all the way to Rome," she went on, a little more calmly. "We can think ourselves lucky that even more such ruffians didn't turn up."

"At least there's one ruffian fewer." Defiantly, Mathis pushed a lock of sandy hair back and wiped the soot off his face. Once again it occurred to Agnes that the journeyman smith was not really handsome in the usual sense of the word. He had broken his nose many years ago in a scuffle, and it had been slightly askew in his finely formed face ever since. His eyes were dark, and their expression was usually gloomy. Since early childhood, there had been something angry and hot-tempered about Mathis that had always made him interesting to Agnes.

"I should think your father would be proud of me if he knew about it," he grumbled.

"I think he'd more likely beat the living daylights out of you, so you'd better make sure he never finds out. That second explosion could have made him suspicious already. After all, he knows how you like playing with firearms."

Mathis snorted contemptuously. "If he wasn't so pigheaded, what

I know could be worth gold to the castle. I . . . I really just have to talk to him about it some time . . ."

"The Trifels doesn't need any help, or at least not from a simple journeyman smith," Agnes interrupted him roughly. "So forget that, before you drive my father to white-hot fury."

With an anxious presentiment, she looked up at the weathered castle on the rocks where her father had been castellan for many years. The Trifels was enthroned on a mighty sandstone wedge that towered, like the nave of a great church, above the surrounding forests. Tall rock formations rose on three sides of the castle to fifty feet high, hence the meaning of its name, the Three Rocks. Only to the east did a sloping plain lead to the castle, protected on that side by walls, although they were falling into ruin. The Trifels had once been an impregnable fortress, but those days were long gone. The entire castle was becoming more and more of a ruin, and Agnes knew that Mathis was right in his critical assessment. But she also knew what her father, who had been brought up in the ways of chivalry, thought of firearms—nothing at all. And as castellan he would never listen to advice from a vassal only seventeen years old. Philipp von Erfenstein was too proud and too obstinate for that. Moreover, there was no money to spare for plans such as Mathis had in mind.

Soon they passed the northern wall of the castle and the well tower, standing a little to one side and linked to the main castle building by a crooked covered bridge. A well-trodden path, just wide enough for a cart, led along the wall to the front gate of the castle. It almost seemed to Agnes that the tall, massive building were eyeing her distrustfully—like a mighty animal blinking wearily before falling into a slumber that would last for centuries.

"Suppose we simply told your father the truth?" Mathis suggested hesitantly. "After all, Black Hans was going to abduct you. Erfenstein should be glad we were armed and killed one of Wertingen's ruffians. And I wanted to talk to him about the arquebuses anyway. The arsenal is in a truly dreadful state, not to mention the rest of the defenses." He pointed to what had once been a tower, although today only its foundations were left. "If something isn't done soon, a single fierce storm will bring everything here tumbling down. Yes, and over in Eusserthal the clerics are enhancing the beauty of their monastery daily." Mathis's voice rose. "Only last year they had a new bell cast. Paid for by their hungry serfs."

Agnes herself had been against it when the new Eusserthal bell was consecrated with pageantry and at great expense last summer. The local peasants had been fobbed off with a little alms. Mathis, who had watched the casting of the bell closely, lending the master bell-founder a hand now and then, stayed away from the ceremony of consecration. In the following days he had secretly met with several strangers to the district in the forest.

"What's the matter with you, Agnes? Dreaming again? You know, I worry about you when you gaze into space like that."

Agnes started as Mathis's voice brought her back from her thoughts. He sounded much less certain of himself than he had an hour or so ago. In spite of her anxiety she couldn't help smiling.

"What about it? Would it be so bad for me to dream?"

"As long as all you dream about is me." Mathis grinned so broadly that she saw his teeth flash white. Next moment, however, a shadow fell over his face. "You're probably right. If we tell your father about stealing the arquebus, he'll skin me alive."

"Of course he won't skin you, you idiot. Who'd make him his beloved swords and daggers when your poor sick father can't do it anymore? Wait and see. I'm sure things will turn out all right." Agnes spoke encouragingly, although secretly she was thinking hard about exactly what she ought to say about the incident. What would she do if Philipp von Erfenstein questioned her directly about the missing arquebus? Lie to him? The castellan knew his daughter too well and would probably see through her at once. All she could really do was pray for her father to never notice that the gun was missing.

Sighing, she pressed Mathis's hand. "You know I'll always stand by you. All the same, what you did is theft, Mathis. What were you thinking? And now the precious arquebus has fallen into the hands of Black Hans." With a groan, she felt the back of her head where she had struck it on the rock in the forest clearing. "However that may be, I can hardly hide this bump from my father. And he's sure to ask about Puck and Parcival. So, one way or another, I'll have to tell him what happened. And that when he has so much anxiety because the peasants can't pay their rent these days." Thoughtfully, she wiped away the last traces of soot from Mathis's face. "We'd better leave the arquebus and your strange experiment out of it, or there'll be another misfortune. You yourself know that my father can explode as easily as your wretched gunpowder."

But as they finally reached the narrow path up to the castle entrance, Agnes gave him a conspiratorial wink. As usual, the iron-clad wooden gate was wide open. The old man-at-arms, Gunther, his leather doublet stained with the small beer he drank at midday, dozed in a little niche to the right of it. His slightly bent halberd was leaning against the wall beside him like a broomstick. Nowadays gray-haired Gunther, together with the gunner Reichhart, who was usually drunk, and two other guards, made up the entire garrison of the castle. When Gunther saw the castellan's daughter coming, he jumped to attention.

"Good day, mistress. What luck did you have out hawking?" The watchman, grinning, chewed on a toothpick he had cut for himself, but then he looked at Agnes with concern. "But where's your falcon? And why is young Mathis looking as gloomy as a month of Sundays?"

Narrowing her lips, Agnes shook her head. "It's nothing to worry about, Gunther." Turning to Mathis, she whispered, "It may be better if I go to see my father on my own. Otherwise he'll think you've been dragging me into mischief."

Mathis nodded, but then asked quietly, "What about the arquebus?"

"Trust me, I won't tell him anything."

Once again, Agnes briefly, pressed his hand and then, watched suspiciously by Gunther, stepped into the bailey, or outer courtyard of the castle, which was entirely deserted. Only a few cackling geese ran over ancient paving stones sprinkled with muck and droppings; otherwise there was an almost uncanny silence. The tower and main dwelling, built of reddish stone, rose thirty paces into the air above Agnes, overshadowing the courtyard. On the left was the so-called Knights' House, a half-timbered building on the edge of the abyss below. It had once been handsome, but it was now in poor repair, and the roof leaked. Beyond it were a few decrepit sheds and the domestic buildings.

Feeing heavy at heart, Agnes climbed the well-worn steps to the small upper courtyard of the castle and slipped into the drafty, sooty kitchen while she wondered what to do next. She was so deep in thought that she didn't notice the cook, Hedwig, until she was right in front of her. The stout old woman was stirring a pot of pea soup. Concerned, Hedwig looked out from under her cap and stopped stirring.

"What's the matter, child?" she asked sympathetically. "You look like a ghost." Agnes had known Hedwig all her life, so it didn't bother her that the cook sometimes treated her like she was still a little girl.

"I'm tired, that's all," replied Agnes, her voice cracking.

"Have some of this pea soup, then, that'll be sure to do you—"

"Good heavens, why can no one in this castle see that I simply want to be left in peace?" Agnes snapped. "Is that so hard to understand?" At the same moment she was sorry she had spoken so roughly.

In surprise, the cook put down the bowl she had been about to give Agnes. "All right, all right," she muttered. "I only wanted to help. Maybe you should lie down for a little; you're all agitated." She gave Agnes a mischievous smile. "That happens, you know, when you get to be a woman, with the blood surging in your veins. You feel hotheaded. You and Mathis haven't by any chance been . . . ?"

Seeing Agnes's reproachful glance, Hedwig stopped short and went on stirring her soup. But Agnes thought she still saw a slight smile on the old cook's face.

Without another word, but with her heart beating fast, Agnes climbed the steep stone spiral staircase to her own room. Wearily, she let herself drop on her bed, closed her eyes, and tried to forget the incidents of the day.

But the thunder of the arquebus still echoed in her ears.

A few miles away, a falcon soared high in the air, among scraps of pale cloud. His wings beat wearily, some of his tail feathers were broken, and soon he would be forced to come down to land. But the deafening danger still lay in wait down there, that mighty, heart-rending thunder that had startled the little falcon so much that he was now far off course, somewhere in a district with which he was unfamiliar. He could not hear the cooing sounds of his mistress's voice, or see the flickering lure she always used to bring him back to her.

He was alone.

As his wingbeats became weaker and weaker, the falcon let himself come closer and closer to the ground as he flew in wide circles. Among the many green, brown, and white dots beneath him, his keen eyes had seen a box-shaped structure in the forest below that vaguely reminded him of his home. He made for it, and was soon coming down to perch on the sill of an open window. The falcon fluttered, called for his mistress, squawked as he had learned to do since he was a chick, and at last helping hands were reached out to him. But not the soft, familiar leather of the gauntlet that usually received him.

Other hands took firm hold of his plumage.

"Surely I know you," said a surprised voice. "Who sends you to me? God or the devil?"

Something was placed over his head, and the darkness before his eyes immediately made the falcon keep still. He stopped fluttering.

Then the hands drew him into a crackling, comfortable warmth.

The game had begun.

· 2 ·

On the Trifels, 21 March, Anno Domini 1524, early evening

WHAT MAKES THAT BASTARD THINK he can touch my daughter? I'll have him drawn—drawn and broken on the wheel!"

Philipp Schlüchterer von Erfenstein had jumped up from his stool and was pacing in front of the fire on the hearth, red in the face, his wide black coat, trimmed with fox fur, swinging out behind him. His two hounds looked up wearily from the nap they had been taking, then lowered their heads again to the warm boar's pelt near the fire. They were familiar with their master's outbursts of anger and knew that they passed as quickly as a summer storm.

"Even as a youth, Wertingen was worthless," Erfenstein went on, snorting angrily. "Acted very unchivalrously at tournaments and wouldn't own himself bested in single combat. I don't like to think what he'd have done to you." The big man shook his head, and for a moment Agnes could see genuine anger in her father's face. Today there were gray strands in his once black hair, the result, not least, of sorrow and care. Long ago the knight had lost his left eye in a battle, and the scarred socket had been covered by an eye patch ever since. That and a dueling scar on his left cheek made him look grimmer than he really was. Since his wife's early death, Philipp von Erfenstein had cared for his only daughter like a mother hen—although, luckily, there were enough hiding places at Trifels for Agnes to get away from her father's scolding. Now that she was a young woman, his protective instincts had, if anything, increased. Like many men who become fathers at an advanced age, he took particular care of his daughter.

"You haven't told me yet what you were doing in that part of the forest." The broad, sturdy, giant of a man turned to his daughter, his forefinger menacingly raised. "There are riffraff of every kind around the place—you know that."

Agnes kept her eyes lowered, shifting uneasily back and forth in her chair. Her father had already been lecturing her for a good half an hour in the great hall of the castle. Twilight was beginning to fall outside, and long shadows lay in the huge room with its high ceiling supported by a series of weathered columns. Threadbare tapestries and faded carpets hung on the walls, giving only a faint idea of the magnificent designs they had once shown.

Philipp von Erfenstein had spent the whole day down among the cottages and peasants' houses, collecting their meager rent. As a result he was in a bad temper, and news of the attack on his daughter was the last straw. Agnes had decided to say nothing about the fight and the dead man for fear of upsetting her father even more.

"Was I wrong to go looking for Parcival?" she couldn't help saying, however. "You know what my falcon means to me, Father. We can be glad that Mathis happened to be near. He . . . distracted the attention of the robbers so that we could get away."

"He distracted them?" Her father looked at her distrustfully with his one remaining eye. "How did he do that? Not with one of his stinking pots of fire, I suppose? When I was down with the peasants I twice heard a loud noise like a clap of thunder. That wasn't by chance your friend Mathis distracting them, was it?" He raised a threatening finger again, as his voice rose louder. "I've warned the lad a dozen times to leave that devilish stuff alone. He should be forging swords, not meddling with such unchivalrous weapons."

"He threw stones at the robbers and then ran away." Agnes was doing her best not to look her father in the eye. "We heard the thunder ourselves. It will have been over one of the neighboring castles," she murmured, fervently hoping that the castellan would leave it at that.

After a moment's hesitation, her father accepted the excuse. "Very well," he growled. "I'll tell Mathis I'm grateful when I get the chance. That doesn't alter the fact that the boy should leave gunpowder alone. That fellow isn't fit company for you anyway," he said, pouring himself a goblet of wine from a pewter jug. "Mathis may have rescued you this time, but in general he's a troublemaker. Goes around with Shepherd Jockel, that rabble-rouser. What the devil is he thinking? God has given us all our proper stations in life. Where would we be if everyone did just as he fancied?" He drank deeply and slammed the goblet down on the mantel. "Such things didn't happen under the old emperor. Fellows of that kind were strung up, and no shilly-shallying about it."

"Times have changed, Father," Agnes replied, holding her hands out to the fire on the hearth. Although the logs were crackling and hissing, no real warmth spread through the large hall. "Mathis says the peasants are worse off than ever. Their children go hungry, they're heavily taxed, and they can't even hunt and fish. Only this morning the mayor of Annweiler had some more poachers hanged, one of them a young fellow no older than Mathis. The nobility and the church take more and more money—"

"The church takes what it's given," Erfenstein roughly interrupted her. "Why do those peasant simpletons fall for the letters of indulgence? Giving the priests money for the forgiveness of their sins, and the sins of their forebears into the bargain." He shook his head angrily. "Luther was in the right of it when he denounced such nonsense. But he's little better, encouraging the peasants to rebel." Angrily, he threw another log on the fire before continuing. "And who thinks of us knights? Our treatment at the hands of the high nobility is shameful. Yes, in the old days, under Emperor Maximilian —God rest his soul—our opinions and our fighting force were worth something. But no one cares for anything but money now that his grandson Charles is emperor. Money and landsknechts . . . we're supposed to provide those great gentlemen with fighting men as well. When I think how it was at the battle of Guinegate with his Imperial Majesty . . ."

Agnes kept quiet and let her father's tirade wash over her like gentle summer rain. Although she loved him dearly, it was hard for her to bear his melancholy swings of mood. Ever since the death of Emperor Maximilian a few years ago, Philipp von Erfenstein had thought the empire was going to the dogs. After a tough struggle, the German electors had decided in favor of Maximilian's grandson Charles, son of the king of Spain, to succeed him. With the Spanish connection, the Holy Roman Empire was now the largest power in Europe, even if it was ruled by an emperor whose residence was on the other side of the Pyrenees and who spoke not a word of German.

The sound of a door squealing stopped Philipp von Erfenstein in mid-monologue. His steward, Martin von Heidelsheim, stuck his head in around the door.

Heidelsheim, who was rather delicate in appearance, wore a broad smile on his face, a smile not entirely reflected in his cold eyes. He had been administrator of the castle's business for over ten years now, and he was responsible for Erfenstein's financial affairs. However, the pale and studious man, who always walked with a slight stoop, was beginning to feel that his position was beneath his dignity. In his little office over in the Knights' House, Heidelsheim often simply stared out of the window, bored, and spoke to the wine in his goblet. He was only in his mid-thirties but he gave an antiquated impression. Only when Agnes crossed his path did his spirits seem to revive slightly.

"Forgive me for disturbing you, sir," Heidelsheim murmured, his eyes fixed on Agnes. "But the list of the annual rents that you gave me . . ."

"Yes, what about it?" Erfenstein growled. Noticing the direction of his chamberlain's gaze, he made an impatient gesture. "Go on, Heidelsheim. My daughter is old enough to know about our financial affairs now. After all, she'll be the wife of the castellan one of these days, won't she?" He winked at Martin von Heidelsheim, who cleared his throat noisily.

"Well, as I said, the list . . ." the steward went on. "It looks incomplete. The rents of the Neueneck farm and the house down on the castle acres are missing. And the toll collected for the Bindersbach Pass is very low this time."

Erfenstein sighed and rubbed his unshaven chin. "The peasants have no more to give," he said. "Last winter was the hardest in memory. Poor devils, they've even eaten their own seed corn, and many of their children are almost starving to death. And now that Wertingen —damn him—makes the pass unsafe, merchants often look for other ways to go. That's why the payment from the toll is low."

As if in silent reprobation, Heidelsheim raised his eyebrows. "I don't have to remind you that the duke will demand his share in spite of all that. Those gentlemen won't be pleased if—"

"Where the devil am I supposed to find the money if there isn't any?" Erfenstein burst out. "Do you think I should join the ranks of robber knights like Hans von Wertingen, eh?"

Martin von Heidelsheim did not reply. He let his eyes wander over Agnes until they finally fixed on her neckline. Her breasts had grown a good deal larger in the last year, and Heidelsheim seemed to relish the sight of them. Feeling uncomfortable, Agnes turned away and pretended to be warming her hands at the fire again.

"I'll talk to the ducal administrator at Neukastell," Erfenstein finally grumbled. "I'll get him to grant us a longer deadline. The estates of the other knights hereabouts must be in similar difficulty. The peasants are discontented everywhere. We can be glad if there are no uprisings like the one in Würtemberg a few years ago."

"Well, I've heard that the Scharfenecks at Löwenstein have even given the duke a gift this year." Heidelsheim's lips stretched in a narrow smile. "One of those pocket timepieces that are being made in Nuremberg these days."

"Ha! Everyone knows that the Scharfenecks are cousins three

times removed of the elector's family. They don't need money from their peasants, they have only to drive a cart to court in Heidelberg and load up gold there by the sackful." Erfenstein laughed bitterly and stared out of the window at the milky landscape, where the sun was slowly sinking in the west. "Only last year those gentlemen had their castle extended, while the likes of us have to watch out for our own rafters falling on our heads. The whole world is out of joint, it's not just the peasants who are disaffected."

Martin von Heidelsheim cleared his throat. "If I may make a suggestion, honored castellan? To the best of my knowledge there are still some guns in the armory that could be melted down. Bronze and iron are valuable, especially in restless times like these. We might get a good price for the metal."

"Melt down the guns?" For a moment Erfenstein looked at his chamberlain in horror. "Have we come to that?" Then, hesitantly, he nodded. "But you may be right, Heidelsheim. I don't have enough men to defend this castle anyway. And maybe any money we can make will at least buy enough wood and tiles to repair the outer bailey." He turned to the door through which they reached the dwellings in the tower. "Wait here a moment. I'll discuss the matter at once with the master gunner. I'd like him to go through our stock of weapons with you in the next few days."

Agnes froze. If old Reichhart inspected the armory with the steward, Mathis's theft was sure to be discovered. Feverishly, she tried to think of ways to divert her father's mind from the idea, but he had already left. Instead, Martin von Heidelsheim was still staring fixedly at her. For a while there was no sound but the crackling of the logs on the hearth.

"I'm glad the two of us have the chance of a moment alone," said the steward after a while, in an ingratiating tone. "We ought to talk much more often, don't you agree?"

He came closer, with a playful smile, and sat down beside her on her father's stool. She instinctively moved a little farther away. Heidelsheim smelled of overcooked onions and his musty study.

"We . . . we've known each other so long," he went on hesitantly, running his tongue over his thin lips. "I remember you as a little girl, always asking me for something sweet to eat. Do you recollect it?"

Agnes nodded in silence. She had in fact gone to see Heidelsheim now and then in the past, knowing that he kept sticky-sweet quince cakes in his chest. On those occasions the steward had always patted her on the head, and sometimes on her little behind as well. Even then his body odor and insinuating ways had repelled her.

Heidelsheim went on, his eyes twinkling. "Well, you're older now, more mature, and your father has already dropped . . . er, hints to me quite often."

"What hints?" Agnes sat up very straight. "Explain yourself, Heidelsheim." She felt her disgust increasing by the second. All the same, she tried to maintain her composure.

Martin von Heidelsheim drew the stool a little closer to her, and laid his hand on her knee in a familiar manner. His fingers moved up to her lap like little spiders. "Remember, you're sixteen, Agnes, you'll soon be seventeen. Other girls of your age have married long ago. You should be looking around for a . . . suitable husband yourself. I have some ideas on the subject . . ." He grinned suggestively.

Agnes leapt to her feet, all her fears about the armory and the stolen arquebus suddenly forgotten. Could it really be true that, behind her back, her father was planning to marry her off to Heidelsheim? She knew her father had been looking for a bridegroom for her for some time. So far she had put up with his efforts in silence, for one thing because she knew that she would not be able to refuse to marry for much longer. Her father was hoping for a worthy and above all prosperous successor to his fief, but he couldn't possibly have meant Heidelsheim—or could he?

"I think you are taking the wrong tone with me, sir," she said. "Just because you could stroke my hair when I was a little girl, it doesn't mean that I'm about to fall into your arms now."

Cool as Agnes appeared outwardly, her thoughts were racing. She still could hardly believe that Heidelsheim had just made her a proposal of marriage, perhaps even with her father's consent. The whole situation was so absurd that she thought for a moment of simply storming out of the hall.

The steward raised his hands apologetically. Obviously Agnes's outburst had taken him by surprise. "You . . . don't have to make up your mind right away," he stammered. "Maybe in a month's time, six months' time if you like . . ."

"You are dreaming, Heidelsheim. I shall never decide in your favor. A scribbling clerk like you is beneath my dignity."

Suddenly a sharp, almost threatening expression came into the steward's face. His skin looked even more waxen than usual. "Be careful what you say, Agnes von Erfenstein." he hissed. "I am not just anyone. I come from a highly regarded family in Worms. You may be the daughter of the lord of Trifels Castle, but that doesn't mean you can treat me like . . . like dirt." He had risen to his feet and was looking at her challengingly. "When will you high and mighty noble folk realize that your time is over? Just look at your fine father. Feudal lord over two dozen stupid peasants who can't even pay him their rents." He uttered a mocking laugh. "This castle is nothing but a heap of moss-grown stones, and all that's left of Erfenstein is the old stories of feuds and tournaments long ago." He took Agnes's hand in his cold, clammy fingers. His tone of voice was suddenly low and familiar. "You must decide where you are going, Agnes, into the past or the future. In a few years' time no fine young fellow will want an old maid like you. Other girls are betrothed far younger. People are already beginning to gossip, they think you are . . ." He smiled awkwardly. "Well, they think you're a little strange. So what do you think?"

Agnes tore herself away and looked at Heidelsheim, her eyes flashing with hostility. "How dare you speak to me like that? I am not your strumpet. I shall tell my father what you've just said, and then you'll be sorry."

Heidelsheim dismissed that with a malicious smile. "Oh, indeed? Do you think your father will find a new steward to join him in this place? A castle falling into disrepair around him, a place that the duke wrote off long ago? I know Erfenstein is looking for a knight or a baron to marry you, but believe me, he can be glad I'm here and have taken a fancy to his penniless daughter." A pleading expression suddenly came into his eyes. "Agnes, don't you understand? I want only what's best for you."

Heidelsheim approached her, his arms outspread, but Agnes brusquely turned away.

"Find another woman for your bed, sir," she said coolly. "You are as dry and tedious as your balance sheets."

She was about to hurry out of the hall when she suddenly felt Heidelsheim's sticky hands on her throat. The steward was pulling her to him with all his might. Her dress tore with an ugly sound, her shift and the swell of her breasts coming into view above her bodice. Agnes struggled and shouted, but Heidelsheim clapped one hand over her mouth. He seemed to relish her resistance now. They fell to the floor together. The steward bent over Agnes, his lips passing over her breasts as his stinking breath rose to her nostrils.

"Agnes," he breathed. "You don't understand. I . . . I love you. I've always loved you, ever since you were a little girl."

Petrified by fear, Agnes felt the steward's right hand move slowly down to her private parts and stroke them mechanically. Stammered words came to her ears, but all she could really hear was the thudding of her heart. The penetrating stench of onions and the groping fingers between her legs almost made her faint. She felt Heidelsheim's wet, rough tongue on her throat, like a slug. When he briefly shifted position to raise her dress farther, she managed to get away with a lightning-quick movement and ran for the steps down to the kitchen.

"Agnes, wait! You must believe me. I . . . I'll look after you. You're making a grave mistake."

Martin von Heidelsheim jumped up to pursue her, but Agnes slammed the door in his face. She heard his yell of pain with satisfaction, and then ran down the stairs, past the fat cook, Hedwig, and the surprised servants, and out into the upper bailey. Blind with haste, she stumbled past the granary and a dilapidated shed, until at last she was standing on the foremost rocky peak of the Trifels—a narrow wedge pointing, like the bow of a mighty ship, to the nearby hills to the south. A cool evening wind blew through her hair, and the leaves of oak and beech trees rustled far below.

Agnes looked around with a hunted expression, but Heidelsheim did not seem to have followed her. Her heart was beating wildly, a caustic flavor crept up her throat and made her retch. Briefly, Agnes closed her eyes to calm herself down, and then she tried to understand what had just happened. In shame, she was clutching her torn linen dress together over her breasts while a sense of cold spread through her limbs. Should she tell her father about the attempted rape? Heidelsheim would probably claim that he had accidentally fallen, bringing her down with him. She had just imagined the rest of it, he would say, a hysterical girl who was known to be prone to fantasies. She thought of what Martin von Heidelsheim had said to her.

Do you think your father will find a new steward to join him in this place?

Agnes swallowed and tried to hold back her tears. She kept thinking of Heidelsheim's cold, nimble fingers, his wet tongue on her skin. Her father couldn't possibly want her to marry such a monster. But presumably Heidelsheim was right in what he said. Philipp von Erfenstein should be glad to have a steward to look after this ruin at all. Although he had been installed as castellan by Emperor Maximilian, her father had shown not the slightest economic talent for running the place over the last two decades. He was very good at fighting, drinking, and telling stories of the old days, but Philipp von Erfenstein needed a sharp-witted steward like Heidelsheim, at least for the more prosaic tasks of administration. No doubt her father would appease him and maybe even lay the blame on her. Furthermore, hadn't Heidelsheim said that her father had already thought of marrying her to him? She instinctively thought of the conspiratorial glance that he had exchanged with Heidelsheim. All the same, Agnes couldn't think that Philipp von Erfenstein would really give his daughter in marriage to a stinking, dry-as-dust clerk. If she must marry, let her husband at least be a knight, or one of the lower ranks of the nobility, not the steward at Trifels Castle. In her dreams and sleepless nights she thought of only one man anyway, a certain man kissing, caressing, and making love to her.

But he was both very near her and yet as far out of reach as the moon.

Shivering, Agnes rubbed the goose bumps on her bare arms. The rags of the white dress with the close-fitting bodice that she had put on to please her father were fluttering in the wind. She sat down on a fallen beam and stared into the twilight. In the fading light of the sun that had just set, she could see a number of other castles enthroned on the surrounding hills like weathered stone giants. Neuscharfeneck, Meistersel, Ramburg, and next to that Scharfenburg Castle and the Anebos. They had all once been fortresses, protecting Trifels when kings and emperors still had their residence here. But that was long in the past.

Now and then Agnes thought she heard droning and quaking deep within Trifels, as if the castle had briefly awoken from sleep. It sounded like someone quietly calling to her. At such moments she felt very much alone, for she knew that she was the only one who sensed that disturbance around her.

As she sat huddled up on the rotting beam, looking out at night as it fell, another sound suddenly came to her ears. It was very quiet, but she recognized it at once. In sudden agitation Agnes got to her feet and let her gaze move over the surrounding fields and woods that now lay entirely in the darkness.

It was the familiar cry of her falcon.

Head bent like a dog driven into a corner, Mathis stood in the middle of the smithy while his father swung the bag of gunpowder back and forth before his eyes. The fire glowed faintly, and only a little dim light fell through the window, which was covered by thin leather stretched over it. It was enough light, however, for Hans Wielenbach to have seen what was in the bag.

"How dare you bring this stuff into my house?" Wielenbach shouted. "A smith like you. Do you know what'll happen if it catches fire? Do you?"

Mathis ducked as his father swung back his arm to hit him. All the same, he couldn't avoid the sturdy smith's hand, which struck his cheek. Gritting his teeth, Mathis rubbed the place, which was already reddening. Then he straightened up again and stared defiantly at his father. The day when he would strike back was not far away.

"Didn't I forbid you to meddle with that devilish powder? Didn't I say I wouldn't have it here? Speak up!"

"Leave him alone, Hans," Mathis's mother said mildly. She and little Marie stood to one side by the anvil, and she was rubbing her eyes, which were red with the smoke. They both wore gray smocks smudged with the ashes of the hearth. The famine of the last two winters had left the cheeks of Mathis's eight-year-old sister pale and thin, though Agnes found a piece of meat now and then for Marie and her brother. Even so, the Wielenbachs were better off than many others in this neighborhood.

"He won't have meant any ill by it," Martha Wielenbach went on soothingly. "Did you, Mathis? I expect you found the powder somewhere or other."

"He was playing about with it. We could all have been blown sky-high, and he knows it."

Shaking with fury, Hans Wielenbach was still holding up the bag of gunpowder. His face was careworn with work and grief, and the deep lines on it made him look far older than he really was.

Mathis remained obstinately silent. In the confusion in the clearing, he had quickly hidden the little bag under his doublet so as not to lose it. It had taken him weeks to make the gunpowder, stealing out at night to scrape the walls of the shaft in the castle privy in order to get the saltpeter he wanted from the mud that contained urine. Then he had repeatedly mixed the powder with vinegar and dried it again, to get it into a granular form. Should he have left the result of all that hard work behind in the clearing? He had brought the bag home, only to run straight into his father's arms.

Hans Wielenbach swung his arm back again to strike a second blow. Little Marie whimpered and pressed close to her mother.

"Don't, Father!" she begged. "Don't hit him."

This time Mathis had made up his mind not to flinch. The times when he had run away from his father in tears were long past.

"Do you know what will happen to your mother and me if they find you with this powder?" His hand came down heavily on Mathis's left cheek, but his son hardly moved. "They'll hang us, that's as sure as *amen* in church," raged his father, and another blow landed in Mathis's face. "Now, of all times, when everyone's talking of rebellion and the peasants are demanding what they call justice in every village, my son has to go running around with a bag of gunpowder. You ungrateful . . ."

His arm went back again, but this time Mathis caught his hand at the last moment and braced himself against it. Hans Wielenbach stood still in surprise, and beads of sweat ran down his broad forehead as Mathis forced his father's arm aside, inch by inch, like a heavy tree branch. They faced each other head to head, both about the same height.

"And yet . . . it's true," Mathis gasped, his face flushed with rage and effort. "The peasants are eating their own shoes while the clerics live high on the hog in their monasteries. Isn't it only right for them to take what belongs to them? Take it by force if need be?"

From one second to the next, all the life seemed to go out of his father; his strong hand slackened, and he stared blankly at Mathis. A severe coughing fit shook him. That cough had come more and more frequently in the last few years. Hard work at the forge demanded its tribute, particularly when he was agitated. He had already had to take to his bed a couple of times, unable to go on working.

"Then . . . then it was really you shooting in the forest, wasn't it?" the smith finally croaked. "Very likely with those rabble-rousing friends you always go around with." He shook his head and took a step back. "My son a rioter, burning and murdering in these parts. Have you killed a man yet? Has it come to that?"

"Curse it, it . . . that wasn't it." Mathis could have kicked himself for talking to his father about the peasants and the clergy. Why did the old man have to be so irascible? He was always egging him on to say things that Mathis would rather have left unsaid.

"Stop it, for goodness' sake, you two fighting cocks!"

Martha Wielenbach came between the two of them and took her son in her arms. "You're too hard on him, Hans. How is the boy to understand you if you do nothing but beat him? What's more, you have good reason to be proud of him. He knows almost more than you about the work of a smith, and he's only seventeen. And the bell-founder who was over at the monastery in Eusserthal last year praised Mathis for his skilled help in casting the bells, too."

"Well, so he may understand something about casting metal and making artillery and rifles," said Wielenbach, who had by now calmed down a bit. He pushed his sparse red hair back from his forehead and cautiously felt the bag of powder with his large, callused hand. "And the lad can mix gunpowder like a damn alchemist. But can he forge a proper sword? No, he can't."

"Because pretty soon no one is going to need a sword anymore," Mathis protested defiantly, pointing to the mud-stained bag of gunpowder. "This powder will change the world. Who will want knights, crossbows, and spears if he can blow a hole in the defenses of any castle with a hundred pounds of gunpowder?"

"Don't let his lordship the castellan hear you say that," his mother warned, patting him on the shoulder. "Your father's blows will be nothing to what you can expect then. No more knights?" She shook her head. "Such nonsense! There have always been knights. Princes, knights, peasants, and the clergy—the world is made up of all of them. And mind you, don't let Agnes hear any of your inflammatory talk. What is she doing these days? I haven't set eyes on her for ages."

"Yes, where's Agnes?" cried little Marie. "I want to play dollies with Agnes again. She hasn't been to see us for so long."

"We . . . were in the forest together today," replied Mathis uncertainly. "With her falcon." He had made up his mind not to mention their encounter with the robbers to his parents. The atmosphere at home was tense enough as things were.

Martha Wielenbach smiled. "I'm glad to hear that. You and Agnes used to spend so much time together, but these last few months . . ."

"They're not children anymore, Martha," her husband said. "It's better for them to go their separate ways. Agnes is the daughter of the lord of Trifels Castle, and Mathis is only a journeyman smith. Where is that going to lead?"

Mathis looked at his father, his eyes flashing. "Don't we all have two arms, two legs, and a head to think with?" he replied defiantly, and suddenly his voice sounded like a preacher's. "Doesn't a human heart beat in every one of us? God has made us all equal, so why should she be better than us just because she is the daughter of the castellan of Trifels?"

"Hear that, Martha?" cried Hans Wielenbach. "That's the kind of thing that lousy shepherd whispers in his ear. You know who I mean, the hunchback from Annweiler with his treasonable talk."

Martha groaned. "That's enough, you two. There's barley broth been simmering over the fire in the living room for an hour now. Marie is hungry, and as for you, Mathis . . ." She took the bag of gunpowder from Hans Wielenbach and pressed it into her son's hand, lowering her voice as she spoke to him. "You'd better scatter this stuff out on the fields as soon as you can, and then there'll be an end to it. Promise me. But for God's sake, get far enough from the smithy first."

She looked at him gravely, until at last he hesitantly nodded. Then she gave him a pat on the shoulder and closed the door behind him.

After the heat of the forge, the cool, damp evening air felt like a wet cloth on Mathis's face. But the sudden silence in which he was alone did him good. Anything was better than another minute with his furious father, who just couldn't understand what Mathis was talking about.

Mathis blinked to accustom his eyes to the twilight and then turned to walk away. The smithy was on the eastern side of the castle, right beside the outer wall. A muddy path led alongside the wall and then branched off to the left, where it passed over the steep ramp and then went down to the fields. Although it was already the middle of March, a great deal of snow still lay on the castle acres, where seed corn had recently been sown, and the expanses of snow were ghostly white in the fading daylight. Beyond the fields stood the black forest.

With the bag in his hand, Mathis walked along another path past the fields and finally turned off it into the forest. He thoughtfully weighed the bag of those precious gray-black grains in his hands. Maybe the sensible thing would really be to do as he had promised his mother and throw the gunpowder away. He thought of the robber's blood-stained torso, his screams, and all the blood around him. It was the first time he had seen what the mixture of sulfur, saltpeter, and charcoal could really do.

Ever since Mathis, as a little boy, had watched traveling entertainers shooting colored rockets into the air in the Annweiler marketplace, he had been fascinated by gunpowder. In secret, he had leafed through books about firearms in the library of Trifels Castle and had laboriously taught himself to read with the help of the colorful illustrations. At first Agnes had helped him with the difficult passages. Later, Shepherd Jockel had taken to pressing thin, cheaply printed pamphlets into his hand, leaflets speaking of the oppression of the poor, of that brave professor of theology Martin Luther, who had set himself up against the pope and the emperor and for the peasants who for centuries had gone obediently like lambs to the slaughter.

Hidden in the pigpens next to the smithy, Mathis had spent endless hours poring over those pamphlets, deciphering them word by word. They were in the German language, leaflets such as the *Reformatio Sigismundi*, produced on the newfangled printing presses now to be found in large numbers all over the empire, and distributed to the people. Much of what they said was familiar to Mathis—the description of poverty and famine, the daily injustices large and small. His father, who brought up red spittle when he coughed, and his skinny little sister were all the examples he needed of how want and hard work could wear some human beings down, while others lived in luxury. Once again the memory of that boy dangling at the end of a rope haunted Mathis's mind. Under the gallows this morning, it had looked for a moment like the peasants might rebel, but then fear and the usual old routine had won the day yet again.

Deep in thought, Mathis entered the dark forest that fell gently away downhill to the west, and took out the little bag. Hunchbacked Shepherd Jockel had told him that a new age would soon begin, an age in which the clergy and the nobility would be swept away by God's holy anger, and simple folk would be able to live in freedom. Secretly, Mathis had wondered whether Agnes and her father would be among those swept away. Philipp von Erfenstein was sometimes irascible, but on the whole he was a just and kindly castellan, and Mathis had spent almost his entire childhood with Agnes. They were like brother and sister—and they would never be more than that to each other, for after all, she was the daughter of the lord of a castle, and he was only a smith's son.

Although he was already seventeen, and a good-looking young fellow in the bargain, Mathis had never yet felt drawn to any of the girls in the town. A few hurried embraces in the hay, a few kisses, that was all. Mathis did not have the money to get married, and in addition, no sensible woman would want to move up to the castle mound with him and live next door to a drafty, godforsaken ruin of a castle.

And then there was something else: every time he touched one of those girls, he saw the face of Agnes before his mind's eye. It was like a curse. When he had seen her again today after a long time apart, he had felt almost faint. He loved her mass of tumbling blonde hair, all her little freckles, and the tiny lines around her nose when she wrinkled it in annoyance at something or when she was buried in her books. Even as a child he had admired her skill in reading and writing. To him, the letters of the alphabet were restless spirits, and he had difficulty in catching and holding them fast.

Mathis shook his head and took a deep breath. Shepherd Jockel couldn't possibly have meant Agnes and her father when he talked about the end of the ruling classes. The elector and the bishop, yes, and maybe also fat Abbot Weigand of Eusserthal monastery, but not Agnes.

He put his hand in the bag with its stinking contents that had caused death and destruction today. The grains ran through his fingers like poppy seeds. He gazed gloomily at the darkness of the forest, when he suddenly heard the call of a bird not far away.

The cry of a falcon.

Mathis pricked up his ears, and the screech came again. Could it be Parcival? Had he returned? Quietly, he put the bag of gunpowder back under his doublet and went farther into the forest. He would think about his promise to his mother later; the priority now was to find the falcon. If he brought Parcival back to Agnes, he was sure she would be able to smile again—and then everything would be the way it used to be.

On tiptoe, he stole through the trees in the direction from which the screech had come. The ground underfoot was slippery and uneven, but all the same he tried to avoid stepping on broken twigs and dead branches. He knew from Agnes how timid saker falcons were. A single crack and the bird would fly away again. Once again he heard that high-pitched sound, almost a lament, but this time much closer. And now he could also hear the familiar ringing of a little bell. So he was on the right track. As Mathis pushed aside a low-hanging branch of a beech tree, he saw the elfin figure of Agnes among the trees. She was standing in a little clearing, an outcropping beyond which the slope fell steeply away to the valley. In the moonlight, she looked in her white dress like one of those magical beings his mother used to tell him stories about. She was holding the fluttering bird on the leather glove she wore, and talking to him in a strange, soft language.

"Abril issi' mays intrava, e cascus dels auzels chantava . . ."

"Agnes," Mathis whispered, taking a few steps forward. "So here you are. I might have known."

Agnes gave a start, and only after a moment did she smile in relief. "What a fright you gave me, Mathis. I thought it was Wertingen's men again." Cautiously, she raised the little saker falcon in the air. He obviously felt comfortable on the glove. "Look, Parcival has come back. I heard his call all the way from the Dancing Floor Rock."

"I heard him too; that's why I'm here." Mathis stroked the falcon, who now had a leather hood over his head and was perfectly calm. "You were talking to him in a foreign language. What was it?"

"Oh, just a few scraps of Occitanian, the old language of bards and kings. I picked it up from the books in the Trifels library. I think Parcival likes it. It calms him—that and the hood." Smiling, Agnes ran her hand over the leather helmet that made the falcon look like a miniature knight. "I put it on him because he was beside himself," she explained quietly. "Poor fellow—that loud bang probably scared him into flying all the way down to the plain of the Rhine. Look, two of his tail feathers are broken. I'll have to mend them." Cautiously, she searched the falcon's plumage for any other injuries, and suddenly stopped in surprise.

"What for heaven's sake is that?"

She felt Parcival's right leg and finally drew something small and glittering off it. A ring. In the pale moonlight it shone gold like a ducat coin. Its upper part was beaten into a flat surface with something etched on it. Mathis took the ring and held it in front of his narrowed eyes.

"It's obviously a signet ring," he said at last. "But what a strange seal. It shows the head of a bearded man, that's all. Where exactly did you find it?"

Agnes took the ring and rubbed it thoughtfully in her fingers. "It was on his leg, quite firmly fastened there with a bit of twine. It can't be chance. If you ask me, someone fixed it to his leg on purpose."

Mathis laughed. "On purpose? Agnes, really! There are plenty of thieves who steal rings from people's fingers, but attaching a golden ring to a falcon's leg? I've never heard of anything like that before."

"I know it sounds odd, but is there any other explanation? Parcival can't have put the ring on his own leg."

"Maybe he just got married?" Mathis grinned broadly, but Agnes just glared.

"Very funny. Why not try to work out what all this means instead of laughing at me?"

"I think . . ." said Mathis, but suddenly he stopped when he heard a horse whinnying. The next moment they caught the muted voices of several men.

Not again, he thought. *Dear God, don't let it be Wertingen and his men out for revenge.*

He held Agnes's hand firmly and put a finger to his lips. It was not unusual for horsemen to be out and about in these parts, even after dark. Except that the sounds came from the forest, not from the road leading up to the Trifels. What would travelers be doing in this deserted part of the woods? Mathis felt his heart beat faster.

Silently, he pointed to a hollow in the forest floor, overgrown with prickly brambles. Agnes understood his gesture, and together they crawled into the damp dip in the ground, taking the falcon with them. They could already hear the thud of horses' hooves.

Only a little later the shadowy outlines of half a dozen men appeared, leading their mounts on a short rein behind them. The animals were sturdy ponies loaded with all kinds of items, although Mathis couldn't see exactly what in the darkness. And he could see only the vague shapes of the men themselves from the hollow in the ground. They were whispering excitedly to one another when one of them suddenly hissed. He was the only man in the group to be sitting on his horse, a large creature prancing nervously up and down. He wore a cloak with a hood that he had drawn down over his face.

"Keep still, for God's sake," he whispered. "It's not far now. All we have to do is—"

At that moment the falcon uttered a cry.

It was only a short screech, but enough to make the men listen intently. The one at the front stopped in his tracks and looked around the clearing. He was only a step away from the dip in the ground, his heavy breathing clearly audible. In alarm, Mathis glanced at Agnes, who was moving her lips in soundless prayer and stroking Parcival's hooded head.

"What the hell was that?" asked the man directly in front of them. "Did the rest of you hear it? That cry clearly came out of the ground."

"Yes, there's witchcraft abroad near the Trifels," said a second figure just behind the first. "Could be evil dwarfs wanting to lure you into their caverns, or the Emperor Barbarossa himself." The man chuckled, and his companion nudged him hard in the ribs. "Maybe you just awoke him?"

"Devil take it, stop this nonsense! It's bad enough freezing our balls off here by night. I can do without your stupid horror stories." The man shrugged. "It was probably an owl. Although . . ."

"What's going on up there?" hissed the man on the horse, obviously the leader of this strange group. "Go on, and no dawdling! Or must I make you get a move on?"

Grumbling, the troop began to move on, until finally they were out of the young couple's field of vision. Only the leader lingered for a moment longer in the clearing, looking slowly around. Mathis thought he could see the man's eyes shining under his hood. At last the stranger dug his heels into his horse's sides and trotted after the others.

Mathis and Agnes stayed where they were for a little while, lying rigid in the hollow. At last Agnes cautiously sat up.

"Who were they?" she asked.

"I don't know." Mathis crawled out of their hiding place beside her, pulling bramble thorns out of his doublet. "Maybe Hans von Wertingen and his men? It was too dark to tell. But judging by his voice, he could have been the leader in that hood. And the horse was black, like Wertingen's."

"Do you really think Wertingen would venture so close to my father's castle?" Agnes asked incredulously.

"We annoyed him very much, to say the least. Maybe he wants to see whether the castle is well guarded by night, or if attacking it would be worthwhile." Mathis lowered his voice. "You ought to tell your father about this, in any case."

"Oh yes, and what am I supposed to say?" asked Agnes, with a mocking frown. "That I was out in the forest with you after dark, where he's expressly forbidden me to go? And all that after, only this morning, you went off with one of his arquebuses . . ." She stopped, and struck her forehead.

"What is it?" asked Mathis, baffled.

"The arquebus! I entirely forgot. Heidelsheim and the master gunner are going to inspect the armory in search of some weaponry to be melted down to make money." Agnes bit her lip. "If they see that there's an arquebus missing there will certainly be questions. Father suspects that you've been playing with fire again anyway."

"And he's not the only one." Mathis's face darkened. "Your father, my father, old Ulrich Reichhart, and now that windbag of a steward into the bargain. Anyone might think the whole of Trifels was in league against me." He angrily kicked a fallen tree trunk with mushrooms growing all over it. "Damn it, I ought to have left the rusty old thing where it was."

"And then I'd be in the hands of Wertingen now, and my father would probably be setting fire to half the Palatinate in his fury." Agnes stroked his cheek, and Mathis felt a wave of heat surge through him. "I have you to thank that I'm not, Mathis. It takes a lot of courage for one man to face four robbers."

"Nonsense," he muttered. "Anyone else would have done the same. And besides . . ." He stopped and looked at Agnes's dress. Only now did he notice its torn bodice.

"What happened to you?" he asked. "Did you get caught in a thicket just now?"

"Ex . . . yes, that was it." Her glance wavered slightly. "A pity, but a dress can be mended. Unlike other things . . ." she added darkly. She beckoned to him to follow her. "And now let's go home. We can think all this over tomorrow."

Mathis walked after her. As he put his hand to his right side, he suddenly felt the little bag still hanging from his belt. *Damn it, the gunpowder! And I promised Mother to throw it away . . .*

But on the spur of the moment, he decided not to get rid of it just yet. The stuff was simply too expensive to be scattered over the fields. He would bury it behind the house, where his father would never find it.

Furthermore, he might yet need it someday.

Half an hour later, Agnes was lying in the canopied bed of her bower, staring up at the wooden paneling overhead.

She had taken the still restless Parcival to the falconry down in the castle courtyard. The little bird was screeching and fluttering wildly back and forth on his leather leash, and only when Agnes gave him a large piece of raw pigeon did he slowly calm down. Something that she could not do after the day's events.

Her eyes wandered to the door of the room, which she had locked, for safety's sake, after her dreadful experience with Martin von Heidelsheim. Her room was plainly furnished with a chest roughly put together by a joiner for her clothes, a stool, and one of the few tiled stoves in the castle that could be heated. All the same, in winter icy drafts came in through the windows; their thick bull's-eye glass had broken several years ago. The old head groom, Radolph, had covered the spaces with leather as an emergency meas-ure, since there was no money to spare for new glass. The only other personal possessions that Agnes had were some books that she kept in another chest under her bed, and she cared for them as the apple of her eye.

She carefully drew a well-worn tome with its thick parchment pages out from under her bedstead and began leafing through it. Although this book had always soothed Agnes in the past, this time she was still strangely on edge. Her heart was thudding so much that it hurt her rib cage. Finally she put the book down and tossed and turned in bed restlessly. She kept thinking of this morning's explosion, of Heidelsheim's attempt to rape her, of the strange men with their heavily laden horses in the Trifels forest, and of the ring.

Most of all she thought of the ring.

It was lying on her chest of clothes beside the bed, hard and firm as a pebble. Now she picked it up and examined the golden seal more closely again. It showed the head of a bearded man, and that was all. No name, no initials, not even a date. The gold had a dull shine with tiny scratches all over the surface, as though the ring had been worn for a very long time. But that very simplicity was what made it so remarkable. Agnes could almost believe that she was holding one of those magical rings she had read of in old tales and legends.

How in the world had Parcival come by that ring?

Agnes was sure that someone must have tied it to the falcon's leg. But why? What was the point of putting a ring on the leg of a bird that happened to fly near you? A gold ring at that, surely worth many guilders.

Unless the owner of that ring knew whose falcon Parcival was . . .

With her mind busily at work, Agnes sat up in bed. Was it possible that someone had sent her a message in the shape of the ring? But what message?

The warm gold slipped through her hands like a small animal. The ring felt good. She put it on her finger and it fit perfectly, like it had been made for her.

Sighing, Agnes lay back again, pulled the warm woolen blanket up to her chin, and closed her eyes. As her blood pulsed beneath the ring, she slowly calmed down. Her heart beat more slowly, and, after only a few minutes, she was asleep. She had a confused dream of falcons and crows, of an explosion that sounded like thunder and streams of blood pouring over her torn white dress. Yet all those impressions suddenly vanished. As Agnes, murmuring, felt for the ring on her finger in her sleep, images came into her mind like waves that carried her away and washed her up on the shores of a distant land. The dream visions that she saw were clearer and more powerful than any others she had ever known.

That was the night when she saw them for the first time . . .

◆ ◆ ◆

Soft music, swelling more and more until it echoes in her ears like a peal of bells. Chimes, hurdy-gurdies, and shawms, full of the laughter of many people and the rhythmical stamping of dozens of feet. A minstrel singing an old and familiar song.

"Under the linden tree, on the moorland, there we made a bed for two . . ."

Agnes looks up. She is in a great hall with tables on a dais and men and women in long, brightly colored robes sitting at them. They are robes such as are shown in her book on falconry—wide and easily slipped on, and the men wear multicolored close-fitting hose under them. The hair of the guests, both men and women, is worn long, and many have a circlet of silver or a wreath of flowers on their heads. They hold heavy goblets of chased metal in their hands, from which wine splashes onto tables stained with meat juices. Four servants carry in a roast swan to the sound of loud acclamation. In front, musicians stand by the open hearth playing a tune that goes around and around in circles, like a carousel.

"Under the linden tree, on the moorland, there we made a bed for two . . ."

When Agnes looks around, she is surprised to find that she recognizes the hearth, the pointed arches of the windows, the seats in niches along the walls, covered with valuable furs, the stone sculptures grinning down at her in mockery from the ceiling above.

This is her father's castle, Trifels.

Furthermore, it is the real Trifels, the imperial castle. Not the gloomy ruin she knows, with the wind whistling through it and swallows and pigeons nesting in the holes in its walls. Emperors and kings meet here, the music plays constantly for dancing, knights ride out from this place to great battles. Agnes feels a great longing; how happily she would stay here, as if the other Agnes in the bleak pile of stones with its drafty holes and tumble-down walls were nothing but a dream.

Maybe, she wonders, this is reality?

Agnes is just about to test the idea by touching one of the women crowned with flowers, when a young man suddenly steps into the hall. The guests fall silent. Unlike the other men, the newcomer wears a shirt of chainmail reinforced at the elbows and shoulders with iron plates. A long sword hangs by his side; he seems a little unsure how to handle it and seems unused to its heavy weight. The guests drink to him, and he bows with an uncertain smile. As he does so, the point of his sword knocks over one of the goblets on the table, whereupon soft laughter breaks out.

Then a broadly built gray-haired man steps up beside the younger one and raises his hand. He gently takes the young man by the arms and presses him down until he is kneeling on the floor. The old man takes the young man's sword and touches him with it on the shoulders, as he speaks strange words, words that remind Agnes of a magic spell.

"Better a knight be than a squire . . ."

The youth has a thin, almost ascetic face, like the face of a young monk. His hair is pitch-black, his eyes shine like two green pools.

Suddenly he looks at Agnes, smiling. It is the smile of a boy on the verge of manhood.

"Under the linden tree, on the moorland, there we made a bed for two . . ."

Agnes feels a shudder run over her scalp, and something stirs deep within her. She smiles back, awkwardly, and raises her hand in greeting.

Then the vision blurs. The youth, the old man, and all the others disappear in a mist, until there is only the empty, cold Knights' House before her. A sudden gust of wind extinguishes the fire on the hearth. Sparks swirl and whirl in a circle, faster and faster, until they form a blood-red circlet.

A ring . . .

◆ ◆ ◆

Agnes awoke with a scream, her forehead and her nightgown drenched with sweat. It was a moment before she knew where she was. This was her bedchamber, her bower in Trifels, her father's castle. All was dark and still except for an owl hooting in the distance. It must be the middle of the night.

Agnes shook herself, trying to return to reality. This was not the first dream of the castle that she had ever had. Especially as a child, she had often dreamed of it, and even then she had dreamed of knights and ladies. But this dream had been so real that she could almost smell the people she had seen in it. Their sweat, the fragrant resinous wood of the tables, even the logs burning on the hearth—it was as if she had only to go downstairs and find it all just as it was in her dream.

Sighing, she lay back on her pillows. Why couldn't she live in a time as colorful and rich in stories as that dream of hers? Why couldn't castles be what they once were? Sometimes life seemed to her as gray as a faded picture in a tattered old book. Nothing happened now; everything seemed to be standing still.

But then Agnes thought of everything that had happened to her on the day just passed. She thought of the ring again. Had that been merely a dream as well? She felt her finger until she touched the gold. Only then did she close her eyes again, falling into a deep and this time dreamless sleep.

So she did not hear the chopping, hauling, and hammering sounds that came softly from the forest and through her open window.

About thirty miles away, in Speyer, where the bishop had his residence, the secretary Johannes Meinhart was still poring over the records in the scriptorium of the chancellery late at night.

There were a couple of legal cases, just concluded, to be filed away in the archives, and, as usual, the handwriting of the assistant city clerk was so poor that Meinhart had to write out half the minutes of the proceedings again himself. The secretary sighed softly as his pen scraped over the thin parchment. He was an ambitious young man on his way up in the world. It was rumored that the Imperial Supreme

Court would soon be moved back to Speyer, and anyone who hoped to be recommended for higher employment there often had to do a few hours of overtime work. In addition, Meinhart confessed to himself that he liked these hours after darkness had fallen. He was all alone in the chancellery then, with no company but a heap of old parchments and the candle burning merrily away. At home there was no one but a shrewish wife and five whining children; he preferred the rustling of the files.

Meinhart was just concentrating on a particularly complex case of the reallocation of a debt when a slight sound attracted his attention. He sat up straight and listened. There it was again: a squealing and rattling as though the wind had blown one of the windows in the room next door open. Meinhart frowned.

But there's no wind blowing, he thought.

The secretary felt the hairs stand up on the nape of his neck. In the Retscher house nearby there had been another haunting only a few days ago; the maidservant of the patrician Landau had heard heavy furniture moving about in the room above her, but when she went to look, the room was empty. Had the ghosts moved here to the Speyer chancellery?

"Is there anyone there?" croaked Meinhart, his voice as thin as a sheet of paper.

He rose to his feet, and was just on his cautious way to make sure that all was well, when the door of the scriptorium flew open so suddenly that the draft swept all the parchments off his desk. Meinhart's scream was stifled when he saw who had just entered the room.

It was the devil in person.

The secretary shuddered. No human being's face could be burned as black as that. In the light of the wildly flickering candle it gleamed like polished ebony, with white eyes rolling back and forth in it. Apart from that, however, the stranger looked very human. He wore doublet and hose, and an expensive fur-trimmed coat over them that had probably cost as much as Meinhart's entire wardrobe. In addition the man didn't limp. Nor did he smell of sulfur. Trembling, Meinhart took a step back. If the black-skinned stranger wasn't the devil, he was still an odd fellow, and he probably had no business being in the Speyer chancellery at this time of night.

"What do you want?" Meinhart managed to say with difficulty, but he kept his composure.

The stranger sketched a slight bow. "Forgive me for disturbing you so late, Master Secretary," he said with a foreign accent, yet with all the elegance of a fine gentleman. "I could not be here any sooner. It is a long ride from Zweibrücken. I bring a letter from the duke."

With a fluent movement he brought out a sealed document from under his coat and handed it to Meinhart. The secretary opened it and read the letter. Then he looked at the other man, startled.

"You're to have access to *all* the records?"

"I am sure the council of Speyer will not turn down this little request from the duke of Zweibrücken. Especially as I really need only a few specific files." The stranger adjusted his coat in such a way that Meinhart had a glimpse of a curved sword under it, a weapon more common among the heathen Mussulmen. Where in the world did this man come from?

"I just need information about a particular place," explained the stranger. "There should be an old castle called Trifels in the Wasgau area. What do you know of the country around there?"

Johannes Meinhart frowned. It was a long time since anyone had asked about that old fief. They said the castle was nothing but a ruin now, and its castellan a drunken old sot. So why would the stranger take an interest in it?

"Well, once Trifels was at the center of the empire," the secretary began hesitantly. "A mighty imperial palace surrounded by a number of fortresses. Several German rulers had their residence there. Emperor Barbarossa lived at the castle from time to time, and his son Henry went out from Trifels to fight the Normans. But that's all long ago." Meinhart ventured a cautious smile. "Of course, there are some who say that old Barbarossa still sleeps under the castle mound, and will awaken again when danger threatens the German Empire."

"Indeed? How very interesting." The stranger seemed to be thinking for a moment, and then he went on. "I need all the information you have about that castle. The building, its past, the surrounding countryside. Hamlets, villages, towns. Everything you can find. And now."

Incredulously, Meinhart shook his head. "But that's impossible. The records are not in particularly good order. And it's late, and my beloved wife—"

"Have you forgotten the duke's order?" The black-skinned man came so close to Meinhart that the latter caught a sweet, exotic fragrance, something like incense. "I am sure the city council would be most displeased to hear of a mere clerk refusing the request of an imperial prince. Speyer is powerful—but as powerful as that?"

Meinhart nodded, perhaps dazed by the sweet fragrance. "I . . . I'll see what can be done."

"Do that, and hurry up about it. Or must I tell the duke?" The stranger dropped into the chair behind the desk and waved Meinhart away with an impatient gesture.

His heart thudding, the secretary disappeared into the room of archives next door, where he began feverishly searching among the countless shelves that covered the walls. At least that took him away from the strange, black-skinned man who must come, if not from hell, at least from a country very close to it.

It took three whole hours for Meinhart to collect everything worth knowing about the Trifels and its surroundings. There was far more than he had expected. Satisfied with his work, and relieved, he finally returned to the study with a mountain of files under his arm. The stranger was still sitting in the chair at the desk like a dark monolith. He had closed his eyes, but as Meinhart approached him they suddenly opened.

"Well? Did you find the records?"

Meinhart nodded industriously. "That castle is far more interesting than I knew. A pity, really, that the present castellan lets it go to wrack and ruin. Even the seals show that the most influential ruling houses have been competing for that part of the country for long years. The Salian Franks, the Hohenstaufens, the Guelphs, the Habsburgs . . . I wonder why . . ."

"I didn't request you to put questions, only to find me information. Thank you for your efforts." The stranger snatched the files from the hands of the surprised secretary and made for the door.

"But those are valuable papers," Meinhart called after him. "At least give me a note saying you received them."

The stranger turned once more. When he smiled, his teeth shone white as moonlight. "I do not think that will be necessary," he replied. "Or have you forgotten the duke's orders? I am only acting on his behalf."

And he was gone, like some uncanny creature, leaving Meinhart to wonder whether the man had not, after all, been one of those ghosts of which there was so much talk in Speyer these days. But then his glance fell on the ducal letter still lying on his desk. Well, if he had been a phantom, then he had been sent from very high places.

Once again Meinhart studied the few hastily written lines, and then looked at the broken seal of the duke of Zweibrücken. In his fright he hadn't really studied it earlier.

It showed the head of a Moor with his tongue sticking out.

What in the world . . . ?

Cursing, Johannes Meinhart ran to the window and peered out into the night. Directly below him, a shadow scurried over the forecourt of the cathedral and disappeared among the houses. The secretary thought that he heard a faint, almost imperceptible laugh.

With a slight shudder, Meinhart closed the window and decided that the last few hours had been only a dream.

Which at least spared him a number of uncomfortable questions.

· 3 ·

Annweiler, 24 March, Anno Domini 1524, late morning

MATHIS COULD SMELL THE TOWN long before he saw it. When the wind came from the west, the stench was particularly bad, and it always took him some time to get used to it. The sweetish smell of rotten meat mingled with dung, the smoke of wood fires, and the acrid vapors of the tanbark made by boiling the bark of oak trees. It was the smell of Annweiler, and Mathis liked it because, after the silence of existence up near the castle, it promised noisy, colorful life.

His way had taken him over the castle acres, and then steeply downhill through the woods, along an old carters' track that was hardly used these days. It met a broader road that was sometimes knee-deep in mud. At last, when Mathis had passed a bend in this road, which was still icy in many places, the little town of Annweiler appeared ahead. Smoke hung like a great gray cloud above the houses that were surrounded by a fortified wall, already falling into ruin here and there. A small stream drove a great many millwheels and sparkled like silver in the morning sunlight. The town church was just ringing its bells for the end of mass, and soft laughter and the sound of voices drifted over to Mathis. He took a deep breath and then threw the heavy bag of carpenters' nails and axe blades over his shoulder and made haste toward the gate.

Mathis was extremely glad that his father had given him permission to go to Annweiler. The old man had kept him toiling hard in the smithy for the last two days. There had been nails to make, as well as horseshoes, knives, and several tools. Mathis had done all he was told to do without complaining, so that his father would have no excuse to forbid him this little outing. After a few quick spoonfuls of barley pottage to break his fast, he had finally set off this morning.

Diethelm Seebach, landlord of the Green Tree Inn in Annweiler, had sent the Wielenbachs a large order. It was a good two weeks ago that Mathis had managed to persuade his father to let him deliver those valuable wares to the town himself. The fact that this was a Sunday did not seem to surprise Hans Wielenbach, but Mathis had taken good care that the order was ready the evening before—even if that meant the sacrifice of his day off. After all, he had been personally invited by Shepherd Jockel, an honor that still made his chest swell with pride when he thought of it. True, Jockel had already talked to him about the distress of the peasants' lives before, but they had generally been on their own then, and out in the open fields. This was the first time that Mathis was to take part in one of the secret meetings in Annweiler.

In spite of looking forward to it, he was also afraid of being found at the meeting and handed over to the town bailiffs. Mathis didn't like to think what his father would say about that, not to mention what the castellan of Trifels Castle would say.

After another quarter of an hour, he had finally reached the stone archway of the outer gate and saw a few carp swimming peacefully around in the cool water of the town moat. A bored watchman was sitting on a bench beside the gate, letting the spring sun shine on his face.

"Hey there, Mathis," the bailiff grunted, picking his nose without any inhibitions. "How's your old man? I hear that cough is still troubling him."

Mathis nodded and tried to answer with composure. "Thanks, he's not doing too badly. At least he's well enough to unload work enough for three onto me." Grinning, he held up the heavy bag, making its contents clink. "Nails and axe blades for mine host of the Green Tree. I'm to deliver them to him. Seebach is finally going to mend his roof."

"Then you'd better hurry. That inn looks like it'll fall down if I so much as sneeze."

The watchman bleated with laughter and then opened the small door in the right-hand wing of the town gate to let Mathis in.

"Greet Agnes for me," the bailiff called after him. "I saw her doing well with the crows a few days ago. There really aren't so many of those pests about now." He chuckled. "Well, except on the gallows hill. They always have good pickings there."

"I'll tell her when I see her." Mathis turned around once more, and then, with his heart beating fast, went along the alleyway full of dung and refuse to the millstream. The smell of leather and tannic acid was so strong here that it enveloped him like a cloak. Soon he saw the artificial channel, with a dozen millwheels creaking as they turned in its murky waters. Some of the tanners were washing the leather they had made in the stream, and then hanging it up on wooden frames to dry in the sun. A few grubby children laughed as they sailed toy boats on the water, others helped their mothers to scrape skins.

Mathis thought how fine a place the Free Imperial City of Annweiler had once been. Hundreds of years ago, Emperor Frederick of the house of Hohenstaufen himself had given it the right to mint coins. But like Trifels Castle, Annweiler was now forgotten, and the city of the old days was little more than a large village owing tribute to the duchy of Zweibrücken. The town wall and the houses were falling into disrepair. For a long time now, rich merchants had avoided its muddy alleys, preferring to trade in Speyer and Worms.

As Mathis walked along beside the millstream on his way to the inn, his thoughts were on Agnes. He hadn't set eyes on her these last two days. There had been too much work to do, and whenever he was going to take a break and go up to the castle, his father thought of something else. Mathis kept expecting the castellan to summon him because of the stolen arquebus, but it seemed that he hadn't yet noticed its absence. And Agnes herself hadn't come to see him since that strange incident in the forest. On the evening when she found the ring on her falcon's leg, she had seemed to him curiously withdrawn.

Still deep in thought, Mathis finally reached the inn that lay beside the town wall, at the end of a narrow alley. Like the other buildings around it, it was a whitewashed half-timbered house that had once been imposing. But now the whitewash was flaking away, and the house stood slightly askew, as though a stormy wind had blown at it too hard. The Green Tree was one of the town's three taverns. As it was close to the millstream, it was mainly frequented by tanners, who made up the largest guild in Annweiler, but a few of the more prosperous weavers and clothworkers sometimes went there to do business. A tall linden tree with a wide canopy stood in a small square outside the inn, giving it its name.

After Mathis had knocked cautiously a couple of times, the door opened just a crack, and the fierce face of Diethelm Seebach appeared. On recognizing Mathis, the landlord nodded in relief.

"Oh, it's only you," he said. "I thought it might be the bailiffs paying me a visit on account of the tax on ale. The mayor's raised it again, damn his eyes, and I'm not paying. He can take me to court, and we'll see what comes of that." Impatiently, he waved Mathis in through the door. "Come along, Jockel said you'd be here. The others are waiting in the backroom." He cast only a casual glance at the bag that Mathis handed him, and then put it down in a corner. "Ah, yes, the nails and axe heads. I quite forgot. I'll pay you later. First I'll introduce you to the rest of them."

Diethelm Seebach led Mathis through the low-ceilinged, stuffy bar that was only gradually filling up now that the church service was over. A couple of toothless old men sat dozing over a jug of wine. The muted sound of voices came from somewhere. When Seebach opened the door to the backroom, the voices were suddenly clear and distinct. Mathis looked at a room where more than a dozen men sat at a large,

weathered oak table, arguing heatedly. He recognized some of the
tanners, as well as Martin Lebrecht, the ropemaker, and the rich
woolens weaver Peter Markschild. Even the apothecary Konrad
Sperlin was present—a little man with spectacles and a faded cap, one
of the few in Annweiler who could read and write.

But above all, Mathis found his eyes drawn to Shepherd Jockel.

He sat stooped at the end of the table, a wiry man with long black
hair that he had tied back in a braid behind his head. His sinewy torso
moved nervously back and forth. He had a small hump on his right
shoulder, and it made him look a little like an evil-minded court
jester. With his sparse beard, torn linen shirt, and shaved calf-hide
hose, Shepherd Jockel looked like a beggar compared to the tradesmen around him. All the same, the other men fell silent when he
spoke.

"I was walking over near Eusserthal Monastery last week," he began. His voice was quiet and yet penetrating, like the music of a flute.
It was his weapon, and he knew just how to use it. "I was grazing my
sheep there; you know there's not much for them to eat this year. And
all of a sudden an aroma rises to my nostrils—the smell of salt meat,
of roast meat, of sausage and bacon. I must be dreaming, I tell myself." Jockel laughed, and it sounded almost like the laughter of a
child. But then a cutting, almost menacing note came into his voice.
"I look through one of the monastery windows, and I see the clerics
carrying in the dishes to be served to their fat abbot, platters piled
high with meat, more than the likes of us ever see even at the parish
fair. Beef from *your* cows, pork from *your* pigs, while you yourselves
don't know how you'll survive through next winter. And on the gallows there hangs a child whose only crime was to have shot a deer. I
ask myself, is that right and just? Tell me, friends, is that right and
just?"

The tradesmen murmured together in agreement. They were so
spellbound by Jockel's speech that only now did they raise their heads
to see Diethelm Seebach and Mathis standing in the doorway.

"This is Mathis," said Seebach in paternal tones, noticing the men's suspicious glances. He clapped the young man on the shoulder. "Son of the castle smith up at Trifels; of course I'm sure you all know him. He—"

"What would we want with this young pup?" the tanner Nepomuk Kistler interrupted. Kistler was a gray-haired old man who sat on Annweiler council, representing his part of the town. His voice was deep and used to giving orders; he had worked for the interests of the community for decades. "This is men's business, Diethelm. What's more, who's to say the lad won't run straight off to the mayor to tell him about this meeting?"

"Kistler is right," put in Peter Markschild, the woolens weaver, also a member of the town council. His puffy red face showed that he had probably drunk a jug or so of wine already. "A crazy idea, inviting that boy here. Throw him out, Seebach."

"The boy stays here. I invited him myself." Shepherd Jockel's voice was low and soft, but the weaver reacted with a start all the same.

Mathis remembered how shrill that same voice had sounded a few days ago on the gallows hill at Queichhambach. The shepherd really did have a gift for bewitching men with words.

"But . . . but . . ." stammered Peter Markschild. "What are you thinking of, Jockel? That lad could endanger us. If he goes to the mayor, then . . ."

"Then what can he tell him? That a number of honest men meet at the Green Tree every Sunday and talk to each other?" Jockel shook his head. "We've let those who think themselves our betters intimidate us for too long. We can't be forbidden to talk."

With a thin-lipped smile, he gestured to Mathis to take the chair beside him. Once again, Mathis noticed that Jockel had only three fingers on his right hand. The other two, those you had to raise when you swore an oath, had been chopped off by the duke's executioners years ago, because even then he had kept company with rebellious peasants. "Mathis here is a clever fellow, as I know," Jockel went on. "Trust me, he'll be useful to us yet."

Blushing red, Mathis sat down beside the shepherd, who clapped him on the shoulder.

"The boy knows what's said up at the castle, and he'll keep his ears open for us. If the duke or maybe the bishop of Speyer is planning anything against us simple folk, then the castellan of Trifels Castle will be one of the first to know. And soon after that we'll know too. Won't we, Mathis? You'll be our little mouse."

Mathis nodded, and shifted uncomfortably back and forth on his chair. A bit more than a year ago he had met Shepherd Jockel for the first time, down in the meadows of the Wingertsberg valley with his flock of sheep. They had met perhaps a dozen times since then. Jockel had been the first to tell him about Martin Luther, a scholar and former monk who had translated the Bible from Latin into German and who had been preaching for years against the sale of indulgences. Only recently, clerics had been about in Annweiler itself, promising people the forgiveness of all their sins in return for money.

In his gentle, flattering voice, Jockel had told Mathis about the growing injustice in the empire, the way taxes were always rising while the clergy and the great nobles lived in luxury. At other times he had denounced the serfdom that enslaved the peasants and didn't even allow their children to marry without the feudal lord's permission. Even when peasants died, their widows had to pay death dues to the knights, counts, and dukes.

Mathis was not the only one to whom Shepherd Jockel talked like this. Over the years, the journeyman who traveled the valleys and clearings of the Wasgau in a shepherd's hut on wheels, taking his flock to pasture, had gathered an increasingly large community around him. Recently, many of the citizens of Annweiler had fallen under his spell. Sundays in the Green Tree had become an established meeting point for malcontents. With the excuse of taking a morning drink, they secretly argued about religion and politics there.

"We were just speaking of the way the mayor of Annweiler has raised interest on the grinding of corn again," Jockel said, turning to

Mathis. "Soon the peasants will get no flour at all, but they'll still have to pay. What do you think, Mathis? Should we put up with this any longer?"

Mathis felt the older men's eyes all resting on him, and the blood shot into his face. "We ought . . ." he began hesitantly, "We ought to send the emperor a petition. I'm sure he doesn't know about all that. After all, he can't want his subjects to starve to death."

Jockel inclined his head, seemingly deep in thought. As the same time, his hump moved like an animal breathing. "Appeal to the emperor, hmm . . ." he began quietly. "Not a bad idea. But there's something you may not know. It's a long time since the emperor had any say in the running of the empire. Even good Emperor Maximilian's word didn't count for much, and his newly elected grandson, Charles, is even less influential. He sits somewhere at the other end of the world, where the Moors live. To the best of my knowledge, he's a spoiled young man who doesn't even speak our language."

A few of the men laughed, and Jockel continued, with a smile, "No, it's not the emperor who rules us. The electors have divided up the country between themselves, handing parts of it over to their dukes, counts, and bishops. And they in turn give presents of land to their knights and barons, who make merry and go hunting. While the peasant, the ordinary working man, is right at the bottom of the pile and has to bear the expense for everyone." Angrily, he looked around him. "Remember what the English priest John Ball said over a hundred years ago? 'When Adam delved and Eve span, Who was then the gentleman?' We ought not to put up with it any longer."

Sperlin the apothecary cleared his throat and adjusted the pince-nez on his nose. "You may be right, Jockel. But what are we to do about it? Fight?" He shook his head morosely. "Those great men have money and weapons at their disposal. That's the way it has always been and the way it always will be."

"The way it always will be because we accept it as meekly as my sheep would," hissed Jockel. "If we all rise up together, no duke or bishop can withstand us."

"Do you mean we should really rebel and fight?" groaned Markschild, the woolens weaver. "But that would be against the divine order of things. I was thinking that if only we had a word with the mayor, then—"

"We're not the only ones rising up against tyranny," Jockel interrupted. "In the Allgäu, on the Upper Rhine, in Franconia—there's seething unrest everywhere. The church itself is divided. Luther is one of us. He's declared war on the depraved state of affairs in Rome."

"Luther only wants to breathe new life into the church," murmured the apothecary with his head bent. "He says nothing about any new order in the villages, towns, and cities of the realm."

"You cowards!" spat Jockel, bringing his hand down furiously on the tabletop. "You want changes, but nothing to disturb your peace of a Sunday. You want to eat roast meat, but feed honey to the great men of the empire at the same time. It can't be done. You're either in favor of fighting or against it; there's nothing between the two."

"Hold your tongue, Jockel. You forget who you're talking to." Old Nepomuk Kistler the tanner straightened up in his chair and bent a menacing gaze on the shepherd. With his snow-white hair and deeply lined face, he emanated the authority of an experienced councilor who had already seen many wars. Trembling, but with his head held high, he turned to the men at the table. "Trust me, I was there in my youth when the peasants rose to rebel over thirty years ago, under the banner of the Bundschuh movement." He was speaking of the laced peasant shoe that the rebels had taken as their symbol. "And what good did it do anyone then? It brought in its wake only death, suffering, and even more famine. Rebellion leads only to the gallows, or even death by fire at the stake. That's no way to prevail upon us citizens of Annweiler."

"A wise decision. It will be quite enough for one of you to burn."

Startled, Mathis looked at the open doorway from which that quiet voice had come. In the heated exchange, no one had noticed that the mayor of Annweiler had been standing there for some time. As on the day of the execution, Bernwart Gessler wore a black un-

belted coat trimmed with fur and a velvet cap, also black, surmount-
ing his thin face and bushy eyebrows. Behind Gessler, Mathis saw
three or four of the town's bailiffs, armed with halberds and crossbows, waiting, stone-faced, for orders. Someone must have told the
mayor about the secret meeting.

"Your rabble-rousing speeches have been a thorn in my flesh for a
long time, shepherd," Gessler said now, scrutinizing Jockel with a
mixture of distaste and interest. "Now I've had a chance to hear one
for myself. Extremely . . . entertaining, I must say." He gave a thin-
lipped smile and then turned to the citizens and tradesmen of
Annweiler, sitting on their chairs as if they'd been turned to stone.
"Did you think your little gatherings were any secret from me?" He
picked up a bag of money hanging from his belt and made it clink.
"There's always someone who'll talk. You fellows should know that
better than anyone."

"Your Excellency, we beg you to forgive us. Heaven knows this
meeting isn't what it looks like." It was the woolens weaver Markschild
who dared to speak up first. He trembled as he nervously passed a
hand over his pale forehead.

"Ah, and what does it look like?" Bernwart Gessler hissed in a
voice accustomed to command. "A comfortable morning drink with
your good fellow citizens? Or is it, rather, a conspiracy with the aim
of ousting me, the mayor of Annweiler, appointed by the duke, from
my position? Speak up, Markschild! And think carefully about exactly
what you say. It could be the last I ever hear from you before I hand
you over to the authorities in Zweibrücken."

As the weaver struggled for words, Mathis watched the mayor,
who now, with an expression of revulsion on his face, entered the
stuffy backroom with its strong smell of beer and male sweat.
Bernwart Gessler was a quiet but determined man who always seemed
to be surrounded by an aura of power. Only a few years ago the citizens of Annweiler had protested against the duke's harsh demands for
tribute. His Highness Duke Ludwig II had immediately sent in

troops and installed Gessler as the new mayor. Since then, as Ludwig's right-hand man, the mayor had ruled the town with a rod of iron. Taxes and dues were arbitrarily set. Expensive tanned calfskin vellum was confiscated as what was called war tribute. Whole families were ruined.

"We . . . we only wanted to ask Your Excellency to discuss the matter in the town council," stammered Markschild, nervously kneading his hands. "On account of the high taxes."

"So to do that you have to meet secretly in backrooms and listen to the wild talk of a heretic?" snapped Gessler.

"If you heard us correctly, Master Mayor, then you know that we were not planning any uprising." That was old Nepomuk Kistler, speaking in a soothing tone. "But the taxes really are too high. We are afraid . . ."

"I don't enter into discussion with conspirators. This will have consequences, Kistler, I can promise you that. Now seize that filthy shepherd. He can tell us all about it on the rack."

Those last words were spoken to the bailiffs. Halberds raised, they made for Jockel, who was pale as a corpse. The shepherd had said not a word all this time. His lips were pressed together, his eyes glittered with cold fury. Now he suddenly jumped up and scurried, like a frightened spider, along the wall and away from the bailiffs. The other men, who had been listening to him so raptly earlier, were hunched on their chairs in silence, keeping their eyes down.

"Is that all the thanks I get?" Jockel asked, and then spat contemptuously. "Is that my reward for opening your eyes? You cursed and complained, and now that the mayor of this town crooks his little finger you knuckle under like mongrel puppies. Cowards! Is there no one in this room with the courage to defy Gessler and his henchmen? Not one of you?"

But the men remained silent. Suddenly they all seemed to Mathis very vulnerable and weak, even the sturdy landlord Diethelm Seebach stooped like an old woman. Mathis remembered how excited he had

been before coming to the meeting. He had felt he was joining a
sworn company who opposed the injustice of the world. Now nothing but unspeakable revulsion filled him. These men were like his
father—weaklings who did nothing but complain instead of really
wanting to change things.

Without further thought, he leapt to his feet, seized the heavy oak
table with both hands, and overturned it. It was easier than he had
expected. Wine glasses and beer tankards broke as they crashed to the
floor. Everyone present began shouting and falling over in the general chaos. The bailiffs, who were only a few steps away from
Shepherd Jockel by now, found themselves stumbling over chairs,
cursing. Jockel looked around briefly and then, surprisingly fleet-
footed in spite of his hump, he ran for the doorway where Bernwart
Gessler still stood.

"Stop him!" cried the mayor. "Damn it all, stop that man!"

Gessler himself made a half-hearted attempt to grab Jockel by his
shirt collar, but the shepherd eluded him and gave the slightly built
mayor a push that sent him splashing into a pool of beer and wine.
When Gessler had struggled to his feet, his cap hung askew over his
face and his expensive fur-trimmed coat was smeared with dirt.

"You'll burn for this, heretic," he snarled after the fleeing figure of
Jockel. "You and your damned accomplices will burn for it, by God!"

The mayor's furious gaze wandered around the room and suddenly fixed on Mathis, who had flinched back in horror. "It was you!"
Gessler cried. "You helped him. Seize that lad!"

Once again Mathis reacted without stopping to think. He ducked
down under the arm of one of the bailiffs reaching for him, jumped
over the wailing apothecary Sperlin, who was searching desperately
for his pince-nez, and raced to the doorway that was blocked by
Bernwart Gessler. The mayor's hand shot out to grab him, but Mathis
moved faster. Sidestepping to avoid Gessler, he ran through the front
room of the inn, where several of the old men stared as he passed,
startled, and then he was out in the street and making for the millstream while the mayor shouted angrily.

"Get hold of that fellow! He and Jockel mustn't escape, or I'll lock you all in the Hunger Tower with my own hands!"

His heart thudding frantically, Mathis looked for a place to hide. He ducked into a nearby doorway for a moment to get his breath back, and then, behind a cart loaded with dung, he saw Shepherd Jockel crouching. The man who had always seemed so sure of himself was trembling. Like an animal brought to bay, he peered out anxiously from behind the stinking cart. When the shepherd recognized Mathis he breathed out, visibly relieved.

"You must distract them, boy," he whispered. "Go on, run!"

"But then they'll catch *me*," Mathis replied uncertainly.

"What d'you think will happen to you? A snotty boy with only the beginnings of a beard. At the most they'll give you a thrashing, believe me." Again, Jockel's voice sounded as gentle and persuasive as Mathis had so often heard it. "But as for me, they'll burn me at the stake, you heard it yourself. Will you do it, my boy? Tell me, will you do it?"

Mathis nodded his head.

"Then do as I told you and run, damn it. I'll pay you back someday."

Briefly, Mathis hesitated, but when he saw the shepherd's pleading eyes, he did run.

"There he goes! There's the boy! Stop him!"

Mathis couldn't believe his ears. It was Shepherd Jockel calling for the bailiffs at the top of his lungs. Was it only a trick to distract them from Jockel himself? Or had his hero shamefully betrayed him? Mathis had no time to wonder; he already heard footsteps coming after him. Without looking around, he turned into another alley, knocking over a couple of frames with leather hung out to dry on them as he did so. At last he saw the millstream ahead, but to his horror, two bailiffs were converging on him from the left, and another two from the right. In panic, Mathis looked around. Should he venture to jump over the broad millstream? If he missed the opposite bank by even a hair's breadth, he was done for.

He thought frantically, and then he noticed one of the millwheels nearby slowly churning through water clouded by garbage and excrement. Plucking up all his courage, Mathis flung himself on the slimy waterweed-covered wheel, clutched one of its struts, and let it lift him up. Ice-cold water ran over his face and hair. Once he reached the top of the wheel, he cautiously straightened up. For a moment, he had a view of the whole town from his unsteady vantage point, and then, with a mighty effort, he leapt to the opposite bank. The bailiffs, baffled, were left behind. Two of them adjusted their crossbows, but Mathis had already disappeared down a small side street.

Passing several more startled townsfolk, he hurried along by the wall, down narrow, twisting paths, until at last, in a blind alley, a narrow opening overhung by ivy appeared ahead of him. He had often made his way out of Annweiler through that opening, when the gates were closed at six for curfew. Today it probably saved him from a dungeon, or worse.

Mathis brushed the ivy aside and wriggled through the narrow gap until he somersaulted into the dried-up side of the moat. He made a soft landing in a heap of stinking refuse. Without caring what he looked like, he struggled up, climbed the side of the dry moat, and hurried toward the nearby wood of oak trees.

Only when he could no longer see the town's rooftops between the branches of the oaks did Mathis feel safe. But he knew that his sense of security was misleading and would not last long. Never mind what might yet happen, after today his life would never be the same.

Mathis had become a wanted rebel.

"And the houses there are as high as the tallest trees. You simply can't imagine it. Elisabeth thinks that people in Cologne all eat with silver spoons. She was at a banquet like that herself, well, only as a servant, of course, but she really saw those spoons, she can swear to it. And the dishes and pans are all made of gold, she says . . ."

Agnes closed her eyes as this torrent of words from her lady's maid, Margarethe, went relentlessly on. They were in her bower, where the dim morning sunlight came in through the windows. Now and then the castellan's daughter nodded, simulating interest, but mostly she kept silent as she let Margarethe strip the wine-red linen gown with its velvet-trimmed sleeves off her. It was the only expensive dress that she possessed. Philipp von Erfenstein had bought it from a Flemish merchant traveling through the countryside, and the merchant had asked a fortune for it. Purely to please her father, Agnes always wore it for the divine service held for a small congregation in the castle chapel every Sunday.

Since the castle chaplain, Father Tristan, her confessor, had been away at Eusserthal monastery for some weeks, his place was taken by a young monk who always fell into a fit of nervous stammering at the sight of Agnes. She had stoically allowed the service, like Margarethe's flood of gossip, to wash over her while her thoughts kept circling around her strange dream of three nights ago. The precious red gown had reminded her of it. The magnificently clad guests in the Knights' House at Trifels, the songs that had been sung, indeed the whole dream had been so uncannily realistic. In particular, Agnes couldn't get the young man in the chainmail shirt, the hauberk, out of her head.

Under the linden tree, on the moorland, there we made a bed for two . . .

"Elisabeth says Cologne is the biggest city in the world. However far you walk, there are houses everywhere. You can get lost there as you might in a forest. They say people have died of hunger and thirst because they couldn't find their way home again . . ."

As Margarethe poured out her never-ending cascade of words, she carefully undid the polished horn and silver buttons. Ever since her cousin Elisabeth, who worked as a maidservant for a trading company based in Worms, had told her about the distant city of Cologne, Margarethe could talk of nothing else. She had been lady's maid to Agnes for many years now. As she was only a little older than her mistress, they had sometimes played with dolls together in the past. But even then, Margarethe had been too frivolous and talkative to be a real companion to Agnes. As the daughter of a weaver of woolen cloth in Annweiler, she dreamed of a faithful and, above all, rich husband who could offer her something better than life as a servant in a drafty castle.

"And the privies they have in Cologne are nothing like the stinking cesspits we use here in the Wasgau hills," she continued. "In this castle we can think ourselves lucky if we don't fall into the sewage below, along with the plank of rotten wood we were sitting on." She winked at her mistress. "But I hear that things will soon be changing for you."

Agnes was immediately alert again. She turned to Margarethe and stared.

"What are you talking about?"

"Well . . . your father has let slip this and that . . ."

"Have you been listening at doors again, Margarethe?"

Under the stern gaze of Agnes, Margarethe seemed to shrink visibly. "I was just standing close to the doorway when your father and his steward were talking. I mean, Master von Heidelsheim isn't a bad match . . ."

Agnes took Margarethe's arm in a firm grip. "Are you saying that my father is really marrying me off to Heidelsheim?"

"Not marrying you off, no. They were discussing your future, that's all. And Master Heidelsheim wouldn't even expect a dowry." Suddenly a touch of mockery came into Margarethe's eyes, and her lips curled. "I think you should be glad the steward is making such a handsome offer. In your place—"

"I am not going to marry Heidelsheim. A pale-faced clerk who smells of onions—never! If there has to be a wedding, then let my father look around for a knight, or the son of a lord of his own rank." Agnes turned brusquely away from her maid. "Now bring me my doublet and hose for riding. I'm in urgent need of some fresh air."

Margarethe gasped a few times, like a fish on dry land, and then nodded coolly. "Doublet and hose for riding. Just as my lady wants," she murmured in a deliberately formal tone, but shook her head.

"If you have anything to say, then say it," Agnes commanded.

"Well . . ." Margarethe was struggling with herself, but then she did speak her mind. "A woman in doublet and hose . . . that's not right and fitting. And that falcon of yours. All that is man's business." She lowered her voice to a confidential tone. "It may interest you to know, mistress, that tongues are already wagging about you in Annweiler."

"I imagine your own tongue has played a not inconsiderable part in that." Agnes pulled the unbuttoned gown off over her shoulders, so that she was standing in the drafty bower in nothing but her thin shift. For a moment she thought of reproving Margarethe for her boldness, but then she brushed the idea aside. They had known each other too long, and furthermore she couldn't risk Margarethe telling her father about her occasional secret rides. Theirs was a tacit understanding, and Margarethe's reward was that from time to time she could speak disrespectfully to her mistress.

"Now, bring me those garments," said Agnes roughly. "And for heaven's sake make sure that no one sees you."

"As you please, my lady."

Without another word, Margarethe turned away and left the room, slamming the door behind her.

Shivering, Agnes sank on her bed, the blood pulsing in her temples. So it was true, and Heidelsheim had not been making it all up. Her father did indeed want to marry her to his steward. The mere idea filled her with revulsion. She wound her arms around her torso and drew up her knees, curling into a ball as if that would make her as small as a chick in an egg, protected by the eggshell from the outside world. Why couldn't everything stay the way it used to be, when she had her falcon, her father's fast horse, the forest, and a castle full of stories? That was enough for her. But of course she knew that marriage was inevitable. Without a husband beside her, she could never keep Trifels Castle.

Briefly, she saw Mathis in her mind's eye, but thinking about him was painful. He was the only man she really liked to be with. It had been like that in their childhood, when they used to play at being prince and princess in the castle cellars, with a mossy rock as the bridal altar and a bunch of wild roses in front of it. But even then they had known that a real marriage between them was out of the question. Agnes was the castellan's daughter, while Mathis was only the son of the castle smith.

The squeal of the door roused Agnes from her thoughts. She sat up and nodded to Margarethe as the maid came in, handing her the doublet and hose without a word, still obviously cross with her mistress.

"Thank you, Margarethe," Agnes muttered. "And I'm sorry for the way I spoke just now. Things have been difficult for me recently."

Margarethe gave her a thin smile. She was never angry with Agnes for long, but all the same she couldn't refrain from making a cutting remark. "No need to apologize. Not to a stupid maidservant." She bowed deeply. "Behave yourself, my lady."

She quietly closed the door, as Agnes hastily began putting on the doublet and hose. She had made the hose, a pair of leather leggings, for herself last winter. They fitted like a second skin and were much more practical for riding than a woman's long, flowing skirts. Thus clad, she hurried down the spiral staircase to the castle courtyard, where Parcival's aviary stood beside the dog kennel.

She would have loved to take Parcival with her, but after his long flight a few days ago the little falcon was still too weak. In the meantime Agnes had mended his tail feathers and was spoiling him by feeding him raw blackbirds' livers, but now, when she went into the aviary, she sensed at once that it would take Parcival a little longer to recover. In addition, he had begun his annual molt, and some of his smaller feathers had already fallen out. He fluttered for a moment and uttered a soft cry, but then he sat still on his perch. Agnes had picked up a few pieces of meat for him in the kitchen, and now the little falcon ate them greedily.

"Where in the world did you go, Parcival?" she murmured thoughtfully as she fed him the raw, bloody strips of meat. "What happened to you out there?" She shook her head. "What a pity you can't talk. I'm sure you would have an interesting story to tell. *Al reveire!*"

Whispering this Occitanian farewell to him, she closed the grating of his aviary and ran over to the stables. She must get out. Out into the woods, alone on a fast horse, even though the memory of her encounter with the robber knight Hans von Wertingen still sent a shudder down her spine. All the same, she felt that the castle walls would slowly press her to death if she spent as much as a moment longer in Trifels.

The stables were right beside the former Knights' House at the back of the castle courtyard. Agnes opened the grating over the doorway and, closing her eyes, breathed in the smell of straw, wood, and dung. Once a dozen fine horses must have been stabled here, but now there were only three, one of them lame and another so old that the knacker would soon have to be sent for. The big chestnut munching his oats happily in the right-hand box belonged to Agnes's father. He had allowed her to take him out now and then, but he had no idea how often she really went riding on the animal. At the moment Philipp von Erfenstein had ridden out on the old gray horse to Neukastell to ask the ducal steward there for a reduction in his dues. The knight had sensibly left his own horse at Trifels Castle. The value represented by the chestnut might give the steward the wrong idea.

"It's all right, Taramis," Agnes soothed the tall chestnut, who began to whinny with pleasure at the sight of her. "We're going for a little ride, what do you say?"

She put a slice of dried apple that she had taken from the kitchen in the horse's mouth. When she heard footsteps behind her she turned, expecting to see the old groom, Radolph. But it was Martin von Heidelsheim approaching.

Before Agnes could react, the steward was inside the stable, closing the door behind him. Dim daylight filtered in through the rotting boards and cast a shadow on his face. Agnes felt a lump in her throat.

"Margarethe told me you would be here," he began with a smile. "She sends her greetings." On seeing Agnes's indignant expression he raised his hands in apology. "Don't be cross with her. She only wants the best for you."

"Apparently everyone at Trifels Castle only wants the best for me." Agnes defiantly folded her arms and scrutinized Heidelsheim as she leaned against one of the crossbeams. She was trying to fight down her fear, but her voice trembled slightly. "Well, what now? Are you going to assault me again? If you so much as touch my little finger, I shall scream so loud that my father will break all your bones."

"But unfortunately your father is in Neukastell just now, and he'll have difficulty in hearing you." Heidelsheim grinned. "Don't worry. No harm will come to you."

He pointed invitingly to a bale of straw in a corner nearby. When Agnes made no move, he sat down on it himself, sighing.

"I'm sincerely sorry for what happened the other day," he began gently. "It . . . was a mistake, believe me. I am a man of honor." He struck himself on the chest. "All the same, my offer was honestly meant."

Agnes stared straight ahead, her arms still crossed. She was feverishly wondering how she could crush Heidelsheim's expectations once and for all.

"Forget it. I . . . I am already promised to another," she suddenly said. At the same time she knew how ridiculous that was. A word to her father, and Heidelsheim would know that she had lied to him. But the steward stopped short. He seemed to be struggling with himself, and then his mouth suddenly twisted in an unpleasant smile.

"Indeed? And to whom are you promised?" he asked in a deliberately light tone. "To the noble Sir Lancelot, or maybe King Arthur himself? No, wait! Surely not that dirty son of the smith, the lad you like to go around with?" His grin abruptly disappeared, and a serious, urgent undertone came into his voice. "Agnes, understand this. I am the best you can get. Not everyone is willing to marry the daydreaming daughter of a castellan, and what's more, one who has nothing to bring to her marriage but a falcon and a few gowns that not even a girl herding goats would want to wear." He looked with contempt at the stained hose that Agnes wore. "Think it over. I won't ask again."

"I'm glad to hear it." Agnes took Taramis by his reins and led him to the stable door, which was standing just ajar. "I won't be saying yes to you, Heidelsheim, even if you've wrapped my father around your little finger. I'd rather escape into the forest. Now, please excuse me."

She was about to mount the horse when she felt Heidelsheim's hand on her shoulder. His thin fingers dug into her skin and forced her to the floor.

"Not so arrogant, *contessa!*" he hissed. "You've no right to put on such airs, spoiled brat that you are—and a brat without a dowry at that. And if you think you can go on flirting with that . . . that grubby journeyman smith, then let me tell you that he won't be working at this castle much longer."

Agnes froze. Then she slowly turned to Heidelsheim. "What do you mean?"

"What do I mean?" Heidelsheim smiled slyly when he saw the anxiety in her eyes. "Well, the master gunner and I inspected the armory before mass today. And what do you think we found? One of our arquebuses is missing. Maybe your young friend the smith knows where it is? After all, he's known to take an interest in such things."

Agnes narrowed her eyes to slits, but she answered with great composure, "Mathis has nothing to do with it."

"Oh, and what was that mighty noise in the forest a few days ago? By the way, Sebastian, the man-at-arms, swears blind he saw Mathis disappearing with a large piece of cloth over his shoulder that very day. A *very* large piece of cloth that was obviously wrapped around something large." Heidelsheim's pale face was so close to hers now that yet again Agnes could smell the unpleasant mixture of onions and schnapps on his breath. "What do you think your father will say to all this?" he asked softly, stroking her cheek with his cold hand.

Suddenly there was an ingratiating, flattering note in his voice again. "I'll make you a suggestion, Agnes. I'll keep my mouth shut, so that young Mathis can go on forging nails and horseshoes here, and you will agree to marry me. Believe me, that will be best for all of us." Heidelsheim gave a twisted smile, at the same time running one finger from her chin down to the neckline of her doublet. "For you, for me, *and* for Mathis. Well, what do you say?"

Suddenly he opened his mouth and groaned softly. Agnes had rammed her knee right between his legs.

"You . . . you'll pay for that, you whore," Heidelsheim moaned as he bent double with pain. "You and your precious Mathis."

"Be quiet! You're pitiful, Heidelsheim. The mere sight of you makes me sick to my stomach." Agnes had straightened up to her full height and looked down at the writhing steward like a queen. "How dare you threaten me? Me, the *mistress of Trifels Castle.*"

"Mistress of Trifels Castle, ha!" Martin von Heidelsheim pressed his hands to his crotch, his face distorted with pain. "The cheap, stuck-up daughter of a castellan, that's all you are. And once your father is dead you won't even be that. You'll be only a nobody without land or possessions."

"And you're nothing but a pompous clerk stinking of onions."

Without deigning to look at Heidelsheim again, Agnes swung herself up on the horse and spurred Taramis on. His face filled with hatred, Martin von Heidelsheim reached for the reins, but the chestnut reared up, whinnying, as he did so.

Only at the last moment did Heidelsheim throw himself aside. Taramis raced forward, sweeping out of the unlocked doorway. Agnes galloped out into the castle courtyard, bending low over the horse's neck.

"A nobody!" she heard Martin von Heidelsheim shout after her, beside himself. "Mark that, a nobody!"

But Agnes had already reached the ramp down to the outer bailey. The horse's hooves hammered on the cobblestones, and she raced through the open castle gateway, making for the forest.

. . .

For some minutes, Agnes was unable to form a single sensible thought. The world around her was a tunnel of green and brown as Taramis galloped down the slope and along the castle acres as if the devil were after him. Martin von Heidelsheim's voice still rang in her ears.

Branches and twigs reached for her like greedy fingers as the horse plunged into the forest. Agnes, bending low over Taramis, breathed in the sharp sweat of his coat. It was the smell that gradually calmed her down. She went along with the horse's regular movements, letting him carry her on. They rode along the narrow crest of the hills with Trifels Castle standing at their northernmost point, past the ancient ruins of Anebos Castle—only a few remnants of the walls still stood—along towering sandstone cliffs, and finally over to Scharfenberg Castle, another abandoned fortress no more than a few bowshots away from Trifels. Only here did Agnes slow her pace, for the path was steep and slippery, and she did not want to endanger Taramis unnecessarily.

She looked up at Scharfenberg Castle, which was even more dilapidated than Trifels. Like many other fortresses in the area, it had once been built to protect Trifels, but its last castellan had died several years ago and the duke had not appointed a successor. Since then the castle had been steadily deteriorating, peasants had already begun using parts of the outer walls as a stone quarry, and the empty windows stared, black and hollow, down on the valley. Did Trifels Castle face the same fate? Suddenly her own proud boast of being mistress of Trifels struck Agnes as ridiculous. If anything, she was mistress of a domain that had long since ceased to exist.

Mistress of Trifels . . . mistress of a few starvelings and a ruin, no more.

Agnes abruptly pulled on her horse's reins and rode back again until she reached the fork in the path leading down to the valley. When she had finally reached the marshy meadows on the other side of the Sonnenberg, she was breathing fairly steadily again. On the muddy road that led over several cleared hills down to Rinnthal, she let Taramis fall into a leisurely trot. Now and then carts or other riders came to meet them, but she hardly noticed them. Lips firmly compressed, she was trying to assess her present situation. Heidelsheim had threatened to give Mathis's theft away to her father, and after all that had passed between her and the steward, Agnes felt sure that he would put his threat into practice. Was she to come to terms with Heidelsheim, apologize to him, just to postpone the inevitable for a little longer? Few things were certain in her life, but this was: she would never marry him. She would rather go away with Mathis and live with the vagabonds in the forest.

Agnes took a deep breath and let Taramis trot slowly along as the first peasants' houses outside the town appeared behind a rise. At such moments she wished with all her heart that she still had a mother. Katharina von Erfenstein had died of a severe fever when Agnes was only six years old. Her memories of her mother were so blurred that, in her dreams, she often saw only a bright face without any detail, bending over her and talking in a quiet, soothing voice. It was only melodies and certain aromas that still linked Katharina to her. The sweet flavor of milk with honey in it, a delicate violet perfume, an old Occitanian lullaby . . .

Coindeta su, si cum n'ai greu cossire, quar pauca son, iuvenete e tosa . . .

Agnes couldn't explain to herself why her mother had sung her a song in the Occitanian language. Although she had asked her father several times, he couldn't provide an explanation either. Later, Agnes had found the song again among several old ballads in the castle library. It was both beautiful and sad, and her father said that was just the way her mother had been, too, in the past, sad and beautiful. As she turned off down a narrow path over the fields with Taramis, Agnes was humming its antiquated tune.

I am pretty yet in great grief, because I am small, a young thing and a girl . . .

By now Agnes was in the forest again and on her way back to the castle. She was perspiring, her breath came fast, and her limbs ached from riding, but at least she felt a little better. The low branches stroked her hair gently, as if to comfort her. She was about to spur Taramis on to a last gallop when a quiet, barely audible sound suddenly made her stop.

It came again, this time distinctly, from the treetops directly overhead.

"Pssst!"

Agnes looked up and saw someone on one of the lower branches waving to her furtively. It was Mathis.

Pleased, she was about to call his name when she noticed how exhausted and worn out he looked. The sleeves of his shirt were torn, his hose stained with dirt. Even his hair was stiff with mud, and there was a large scratch across his forehead.

"My God, Mathis! What happened to you?" Agnes cried, swiftly dismounting. "Do you need help?"

Instead of answering, Mathis put a finger to his lips.

"Are you alone?" he whispered. When she hesitantly nodded, he let himself slide off the branch. With Agnes leading the horse by his reins, they walked a little way off the path and into the forest together.

Mathis sank onto a fallen tree trunk and ran his hands through his sandy hair. "I'm in serious trouble," he said, still keeping his voice low. "The mayor of Annweiler is looking for me."

Agnes smiled soothingly. "What for? Were you trying to get back through the town gate under cover of darkness?"

"If only that was all. It's much worse, Agnes. I helped Shepherd Jockel to get away, and now I'm wanted as a rabble-rouser myself."

Hesitantly, Mathis told her about the secret meeting at the Green Tree, the appearance of the mayor, his own flight and Jockel's. When he had finished he looked despairingly at Agnes. "I've been wandering in the forest for hours," he said. "Agnes, I really don't know what to do. One thing's certain: I can't go back to my parents. If the bailiffs find me they'll hang me from the tallest tree around. And if the mayor is having a bad day, my whole family will be strung up beside me."

"Aren't you exaggerating a bit?" asked Agnes, stroking his shoulder. Doing so sent a slight, pleasant thrill through her.

"It was just a silly prank," she went on. "At the worst you may have to spend a day standing in the pillory in the marketplace. You'll survive that."

"Agnes, you didn't see the look in the mayor's eyes. I made him look foolish in front of half the Annweiler town council. He'll never forgive me for that." Mathis hunched his shoulders and hid his face in his strong hands. "Think of the boy they hanged a few days ago in Queichhambach. He did nothing worse than stalking deer in the woods with bow and arrows." He uttered a hollow laugh. "And you think the mayor would let me off with a day in the pillory? This world is all askew. The great ones feast and celebrate, small folk go hungry and get hanged. How can God allow such things? I just wish I knew what bastard gave our meeting away to Gessler. Then, then . . ." He pressed his lips together, but all the same he couldn't keep the tears from running down his cheeks. Agnes didn't know if they were tears of fury or fear.

For a while there was no sound but the occasional snorting of the horse. At last Agnes plucked up her courage.

"We must go and see my father," she said briefly.

"Your father?" Mathis wiped his tears away and looked at her in horror. "He'll hand me over to the mayor, if he doesn't string me up himself."

"That's nonsense, Mathis. That conceited mayor of Annweiler has been a thorn in his flesh for a long time. And I can't imagine that Gessler is going to start a feud over a journeyman." She stopped for a moment. "But there's one thing we must do first."

"And what's that?"

"We must tell my father about the stolen arquebus. If we don't, someone else will."

Wearily, Agnes sat down on the tree trunk beside Mathis and told him about Heidelsheim and his plans. Mathis listened in silence, stoically, merely cracking his knuckles now and then. Finally he jumped up and kicked a rotting birch so hard that it keeled over to one side with a creaking sound.

"That lecherous bastard," he said furiously. "I'll murder him. I always knew Heidelsheim had his eye on you. Even when you were little, he looked at you with a greedy expression. I'll tan his hide if he ever crosses my path again. I'll—"

"Mathis! Mathis, stop it!" Agnes tried to get her angry friend to listen to her, first pleading gently, then speaking louder and louder. She burst into tears. "Don't you understand? Heidelsheim is going to marry me. He and my father have agreed on it. Even if you save your neck from the noose, and my father doesn't hand you over to the mayor of Annweiler, nothing will be the same. Heidelsheim will make me his wife. And then take me off to Worms, where I'll spend my time in some little house doing embroidery and scrubbing floors and crying my eyes out. You'll never see me again. That's the way of the world, and even God can't change it."

Her voice echoed through the forest so loudly that they both fell silent for a moment in alarm. Had anyone heard her? Maybe the mayor's bailiffs? But nothing happened.

"Let's go," Mathis said at last.

Agnes dried her tears and looked at him with red-rimmed eyes. "Go where?"

"Where do you think, silly? To see your father, of course. It looks like there's something we have to discuss with him."

"But . . ."

With a fluid movement, Mathis mounted Taramis, got into the saddle, and reached his hand down to Agnes. "Come on. Tears won't get us anywhere now. If your father is going to explode, we'd better get it over and done with. And who knows, when his anger has blown over, it may be possible to talk to him about Heidelsheim. He can't want his daughter to marry a brute like that."

Agnes got up on the horse behind him, and together they rode Taramis through the forest. Heart beating fast, she held on to Mathis as he made for the castle, his face pale and grim.

Eyes full of hatred glared at them from behind a thicket not far away. Only when the sound of galloping hooves had died away did Martin von Heidelsheim come out, spitting contemptuously. Then he marched up the muddy path toward the castle, with the blood still surging wildly in his head.

That whore. That damned little whore.

When Agnes had ridden out of the stable earlier, Heidelsheim had felt so angry that he thought he would explode. How could he ever have fallen in love with that spoiled brat? Let her molder away behind the walls of Trifels; he would surely find someone better. A faithful wife who didn't put on such airs, someone young and willing who opened her mouth only when he wanted, and who knew how to value marriage to a prosperous steward from a good family.

In his blind fury, Martin von Heidelsheim had followed the tracks of the horse's hooves over the fields. And if he had caught up with Agnes, he couldn't have said for sure what he would have done. But he soon lost the trail, and his anger cooled as he walked through the forest.

Finally, chance had come to his aid. He had heard voices and crept closer to the couple.

As he eavesdropped on Agnes and Mathis from his hiding place, his anger returned. Cold anger, corroding him inside. He had always disliked young Mathis. The fellow was all defiance and wild talk. No wonder the mayor of Annweiler wanted to hang him. And hang he would. Those two turtle doves were going to tell Philipp von Erfenstein the truth? Very well, then he would also tell the truth. The whole truth. Everything he knew.

Heidelsheim smiled unpleasantly, and then he made a plan.

With a soundless tune on his lips, he went on through the forest, which was now bathed by the afternoon sun in a dim, unreal light.

Yes, he would put his plan into action tomorrow. Everyone would know. It didn't matter to Heidelsheim that he would risk his position at the castle. Clever, skillful stewards like him could always find employment. And weren't the Scharfenecks looking for a new steward as administrator of their castle at this moment?

Heidelsheim had taken a shortcut known only to him, one that would lead him along the narrow, barely visible tracks used by game animals to the eastern flank of the Trifels. He had spent far too long at that tumbledown place anyway; it was high time he looked for something else.

When he had gone about half the way, Heidelsheim made a curious discovery. Taken aback, he stopped and examined the place more closely. The tracks were fresh, and in addition he was sure that he had never seen anything of the kind here before.

"What the devil . . ." he murmured, bending down. He felt the soft earth with his fingers.

At that moment he heard rustling footsteps on the forest floor, which was covered with a thick layer of dry beech leaves. Heidelsheim looked up, and his face twisted into a mask of boundless astonishment.

"You? Here?" he stammered. "But why . . . ?"

There was a click, followed by a piercing pain that spread from Heidelsheim's belly through his whole body. When the steward, open-mouthed, looked down at himself, he saw a feathered crossbow bolt sticking in his doublet.

"But . . . but . . ." he croaked. A second bolt plunged into his throat. Heidelsheim fell to the ground and saw his blood spurting over the beech leaves and trickling away into the forest floor where the frost had dried it out.

The last thing that his failing eyes saw was a pair of leather boots, polished to a high shine, standing directly in front of him.

The boots moved away, and soon there was nothing to be heard but the peaceful call of a cuckoo.

• • •

That afternoon, Philipp von Erfenstein, castellan of Trifels Castle, was approaching Neukastell Castle after an hour's ride on his decrepit old nag. The ducal seat of administration was a massive fortress, towering above the little town of Leinsweiler, and in part hewn straight out of the rock. Beyond it, the land fell steeply away, giving a view of the plain of the Rhine reaching all the way to the milky horizon.

Exhausted by the stress of the ride, the castellan looked up at the ducal fortress. A broad paved ramp led up to its main gateway. Neukastell itself had seen better times, but the castle still had a formidable look. It had once served Trifels Castle as a defensive fort, but now it was the seat of administration, enabling the duke of Zweibrücken to collect his outstanding taxes.

Taxes that Erfenstein could no longer afford to pay.

The castellan of Trifels took a deep breath and then forced his mount into a trot for the last few yards. No one must say that he had become a feeble old man. The guards nodded to him as he rode through the wide gateway. Erfenstein was well known in the countryside here.

The knight was surprised to see several other horses being watered at troughs in the castle courtyard already. Their coats were black and gleaming, and a groom was just rubbing them down.

"Does the duke's steward have visitors?" Erfenstein barked.

The groom nodded. "Young Count Friedrich von Löwenstein-Scharfeneck has just arrived. He's paying His Excellency Castellan Rupprecht von Lohingen the honor of a short visit."

"That's all I need," Erfenstein said under his breath. He dismounted and scrutinized the other magnificent steeds with an expert eye.

"I suppose the count didn't come alone?" he asked out loud.

"No, sir. Brought his squires and a few men-at-arms." The groom grinned. "They're eating and drinking at our castellan's expense over in the annex at this moment."

Erfenstein's lips narrowed. The idea of Scharfeneck's men making merry here while he had to deprive his own peasants of the last few grains of their harvest turned his stomach. As so often when he was displeased, the empty socket under his eye patch began to itch. In silence, he climbed the stone steps to the tower where the castle's dwelling quarters were located and entered the main hall through a double doorway.

The hall was adorned with carpets, furs, and tapestries, some of them hanging in multiple layers on the walls. Rushes and sweet-smelling herbs lay on the floor, and a huge fire burned on a hearth almost three yards wide. The sudden warmth almost made Erfenstein retreat into the cool air outdoors.

"Ah, Philipp! They told me you were on your way. I hope you bring good news." The duke's steward rose from a long table set with wineglasses, silver platters piled with steaming meat, and bread baskets. Rupprecht von Lohingen was an elderly, battle-hardened knight whose girth had increased in recent years as a result of his consumption of wine and good food. His hair was sparse, and like Erfenstein he had a bushy beard in the old fashion. The two knights had known one another for a long time and had both been faithful companions of Emperor Maximilian in the old days. But unlike the castellan of Trifels, Lohingen had won the favor of the duke of Zweibrücken by means of soft words and gifts, and had been installed as his steward here several years ago.

"As I can hear, I come at the wrong time," Erfenstein said. "You already have a guest."

Lohingen smiled. "Those who bring me money never come at the wrong time. I hope you do have the outstanding rents with you?"

Philipp von Erfenstein cleared his throat to say something, but the steward interrupted him.

"How discourteous of me," said Lohingen, shaking his head. "We should satisfy the rules of courtesy first, don't you agree? So please pay young Count von Löwenstein-Scharfeneck the honor due to him."

Only now did the castellan of Trifels notice another figure sitting at the far end of the table, partly hidden by the smoke from the fire.

The young man was clad in black and in the Spanish fashion, with a high white collar showing above his close-fitting doublet. A neatly trimmed beard adorned a handsome if rather pale face with two mocking eyes sparkling in it. He might have been in his early twenties.

"Your Excellency." Erfenstein bowed his head briefly. "I didn't see you—I beg your pardon."

"Granted." Friedrich von Löwenstein-Scharfeneck waved the apology away. "Sit down and join us, Erfenstein. You must be hungry after your strenuous ride."

The castellan nodded hesitantly but sat down at the richly laid table. He did not touch any of the aromatic dishes. Only when a cupbearer came over and poured wine for him did he drink deeply and in long drafts. Young Löwenstein-Scharfeneck scrutinized him attentively.

"The duke's steward here has just told me that you're behind with the payments?" he said, his eyebrows raised. "Obviously you aren't taking enough from your peasants."

"Where there's nothing to be had, it can't be taken." The castellan of Trifels wiped his beard, wet as it was from the red wine, and suppressed a curse. All he needed was for this young upstart to criticize him. The Löwenstein-Scharfenecks were the richest landlords in the district. Their fiefs bordered on the duchy of Zweibrücken, and also on Erfenstein land. It was said that Friedrich's father, Ludwig von Löwenstein-Scharfeneck, knew no mercy and would squeeze the last drop of blood out of his peasants. "Last winter was the hardest for a long time," Erfenstein went on. "The peasants are starving. And you know as well as I do that my fief is much smaller than your father's. As for the toll from the Bindersbach Pass . . ."

"Excuses." Lohingen interrupted him brusquely. "The young count is right, Philipp, you're too soft. If your fief is small then you must raise the rents to make up for it." He leaned over the table, lowering his voice. "The emperor is fighting those damned French down in Italy again, as I'm sure you know. Francis I may have lost the election to be king of Germany, but he still thinks he'd make a better ruler of Europe. And Charles isn't so firmly settled in the saddle as one might think. The German princes will always come down on the side of whoever can be most useful to them. So we all have to do our part, however insignificant it may be." Lohingen pointed to the count. "His Excellency has just placed a company of landsknechts at the duke's disposal."

"I have no landsknechts, Rupprecht," Erfenstein said. "I have three men-at-arms and a drunken master gunner, that's all."

"Is the master gunner any good at his trade?" asked Lohingen curiously. "Maybe . . ."

"I can count myself lucky if he doesn't blow himself sky-high."

The steward sighed. "Then you're bound to make payments, one way or the other." He leaned forward in a comradely manner. "Philipp, think about it. Major tithes, minor tithes, socage, tallage—there must be something to be had by imposing those. I'm open to all suggestions, for the sake of our long friendship. Raise the toll for using the pass, why don't you?"

"First we'd have to get the better of that robber knight," replied Erfenstein, picking up his wineglass again. "As long as Hans von Wertingen is out and about on the Bindersbach Pass, the merchants will take a long detour around it. That dog almost abducted my daughter recently."

"I've heard of your daughter," remarked Count Löwenstein-Scharfeneck, gnawing a pheasant leg with relish. "She's said to be a real beauty, if also . . ." He smiled broadly, and wiped his mouth. "If also, well, a little strange."

"She takes after me. We Erfensteins have always gone our own way." Philipp von Erfenstein tried to appear calm, although inwardly he was furious. What business had this young fop to talk like that about his daughter? Although he had to admit that Agnes really did behave strangely in many respects. He ought at least to forbid her to wear those leather hose.

"As for Black Hans the robber knight," said Rupprecht von

Lohingen, pouring more wine for himself and the count, "smoke the brute out, Philipp. It can't be so difficult. I hear that his castle's in a pitiful condition, and he has only a few scoundrels to stand beside him."

"Damn it all, Rupprecht!" Philipp von Erfenstein set his glass down so hard that the wine in it slopped out over the table. "You've besieged castles yourself. How am I to do that with exactly four men? You've just heard that I can't afford any landsknechts. And since the emperor did away with feudal law, I'm not allowed to pick a quarrel anyway."

"Unless you get the duke's permission," Lohingen pointed out. He shook his head. "Although I doubt that His Highness will put men at your disposal if you can't even afford to pay your own dues."

"Then you can borrow mine."

Scharfeneck's voice had been so quiet that it took the castellan of Trifels some time to understand his offer.

"I can *what?*"

The young count nodded. "You heard me, Erfenstein. You can make use of my men. As soon as permission comes from the duke, they will fight for you. I have three dozen battle-hardened lands-knechts—that should be enough to deal with those louts."

Erfenstein grunted derisively. "If Wertingen digs himself in up there in the Ramburg, even an army won't get him out. It's a hard place to crack. Old Hans von Ramburg sold it to the Dalbergs a few years ago, but they posted only a single guard, and Wertingen took the castle." He sipped his wine again. "Black Hans may be a bastard, but he knows how to fight."

Friedrich von Löwenstein-Scharfeneck frowned. "Are you by any chance refusing my offer?"

"I'd call the count's suggestion very generous, Philipp," Rupprecht von Lohingen put in. "Think: if you defeat Wertingen, the pass will be safe again. And you'll take loot, so you can pay your debts right away."

"And the ducal permission?"

The steward shrugged his shoulders. "I'll see to that." He gave a knowing smile. "And in return I get some of the loot—agreed?"

With his one remaining eye, Erfenstein cast a suspicious glance at the young count as he sat waiting for an answer, with his arms folded and a slightly mocking expression on his face. Friedrich von Löwenstein-Scharfeneck came from an influential family; his father was an illegitimate son of the former elector of the Palatinate. Erfenstein had met Friedrich only a few times, at court occasions. He was the youngest of ten children and regarded as a daydreaming ne'er-do-well. Hitherto the youth, who always seemed to be cool and composed, had been in his father's shadow, and his suddenly forthright stance surprised the castellan.

"And?" asked Erfenstein, hesitantly. "What do you want from me in return?"

"Why would I want anything much?" Löwenstein-Scharfeneck shrugged his shoulders. "After all, it's in my own interests for that wretched cur to stop making trouble. His castle is a disgrace, and it also lies close to one of our own seats of government. He's already laid waste several of our villages and has even attacked a monastery. It's high time we sent him packing." He leaned forward, smiling. "So I get half the loot—that's only fair."

"Is that all?"

Scharfeneck shook his head as he rinsed his greasy fingers in a bowl of water. "Well, it's possible that I shall be asking you for a small favor in the near future."

Erfenstein frowned. "Out with it."

"You'll know what it is when the time comes. Well, how about it? Do you agree?"

Friedrich von Löwenstein-Scharfeneck offered his now clean hand, and after a brief moment of hesitation Erfenstein took it. The young man's fingers felt cold and surprisingly hard. Erfenstein wondered whether the count was really as soft and foppish as everyone thought.

"Then that's all settled," said Scharfeneck. "Now, please forgive me." He rose and smoothed any creases out of his doublet that came from sitting so long. "I promised to visit my landsknechts over in your annex. They're to receive their monthly pay. It seems that we'll soon be needing their swords and their daggers." Smiling, he looked at the steward. "I'm sure you will do all you can to get the necessary permission from the duke?"

Erfenstein and the ducal steward stood up and bowed formally.

"It has been an honor, Excellency," said Rupprecht von Lohingen. Then he turned discreetly to Erfenstein. "You heard the count, Philipp. I will ask the duke to put off the due date for the payments you owe, although only for a year, and only part of them. This is your last chance. I very much hope that you will soon get permission to drive that bastard Wertingen away for good." He winked. "Just like the old days, eh, Philipp?"

The knight nodded as bile rose in his throat. *Just like the old days*, he thought. *You sit here in comfort while I do the dirty work.*

He closed his eyes and took a deep breath. He should really be pleased; he had gained at least half of what he wanted. Yet, strange to say, that did not give him satisfaction. Lost in thought, Erfenstein looked at his hand. It still hurt after the count's firm grasp of it.

It felt like it had been burned.

Agnes and Mathis waited, on tenterhooks, for Philipp von Erfenstein to return. At last, early in the evening, they found the castellan in the upper bailey, where he had just unsaddled his horse and was throwing some large pieces of meat to a pack of hounds. He spoke to the dogs quietly and affectionately, as if they were his children.

Agnes smiled involuntarily. At such moments her father was calm and composed. He visibly blossomed when he went hunting, and it had been the same at tournaments in the old days. That was the life he knew and loved. The life of a knight, not of an impoverished, drunken castellan who had to wring taxes out of starving peasants and lived only on his memories.

When Philipp von Erfenstein turned around to them, Agnes could see that his conversation with the duke's steward had not gone well. For some years now, the lines had been digging ever deeper into his face, bloated as it was by alcohol, and today it seemed to have some new ones.

"Ah, Agnes," he muttered. "Good news. Rupprecht von Lohingen listened to me. He'll defer part of the payments. So we're snatched from the jaws of death this time."

"I'm glad." Agnes frowned. "But there's something wrong, Father, isn't there? Or you wouldn't be looking like that."

"I . . . I'll tell you about that some other time."

Erfenstein stared gloomily into space. He didn't even seem to have noticed Mathis, standing right beside Agnes. After a while the castellan turned his eyes on his daughter and scrutinized her with displeasure.

"I've told you hundreds of times that I don't approve of women wearing doublet and hose like a man," he snapped suddenly. "It's not right for ladies of high rank." He frowned. "Have you been out riding like that? What are people going to think when they see you?"

"Father," began Agnes, hesitantly. "Mathis and I have something to confess to you."

"Aha." Philipp von Erfenstein smiled wearily. Only now did he seem to notice the journeyman smith who was still standing beside his daughter in silence. "I suppose the pair of you have been out in the woods with Taramis. Just as well you told me. I'd have found out anyway."

Agnes shook her head. "That's not it, Father. But maybe we should go over to the Knights' House." She looked around the castle courtyard, where Margarethe and Hedwig were feeding the geese and looking at them curiously. "It's not something that everyone has to know," she added quietly.

Philipp von Erfenstein clucked and went on throwing meat to his barking hounds. "There are no secrets on the Trifels, mark that. Or at least none that a daughter can't tell her father out loud. Who do you think you are? The emperor's wife? Go on then, talk or let it drop."

"Very well." Agnes took Mathis's hand and held it tightly. "Mathis . . . Mathis took an arquebus out of your armory, and now he's wanted by the mayor of Annweiler as a rabble-rouser as well."

The dish containing the meat slipped out of Erfenstein's hands and dropped to the ground, where the hounds immediately fell on it. The castellan stared at Mathis, wide-eyed. "He's *what?*"

"It was a mistake," Mathis began formally. "Not about the arquebus, I mean, but about Shepherd Jockel. I was just so . . . so angry with all those councilors sitting on their broad bums, and I suddenly lost it . . ."

Agnes sighed and trod on her friend's toes. If Mathis went on like that he really would be talking his neck into a noose.

"Maybe it would be better for me to tell him," she said quietly.

Philipp von Erfenstein's eyes went back and forth, between anger and bafflement. The hounds jumped up at him, but he pushed them aside impatiently.

"Yes, maybe that would be better," he said curtly. "Before I set my hounds on this bastard. But hurry up, because they're hungry."

Agnes closed her eyes for a moment and said a silent prayer. Then she began telling her father the story, from the arquebus that Mathis had pilfered to his flight from Annweiler. She left out only her encounters with Martin von Heidelsheim. This was certainly not the right moment to speak to her father about his plan to marry her to the chamberlain.

When she had finished, there was absolute silence for a while. Only the geese cackled, while Margarethe peered inquisitively across the courtyard. But her lady's maid was too far off to be able to hear anything. Her heart beating fast, Agnes watched her father, who was clearly agitated. You could never tell how Philipp von Erfenstein would react. Since he had taken to drinking more and more, his fits of rage had been increasingly violent. Sometimes, however, he merely brooded in silence instead.

Thoughtfully, the castellan rubbed his unshaven chin.

"The arquebus . . . that was bad," he began quietly. "Even if it was old and rusty, you stole from me, Mathis. I can't tolerate that. Thieves have no business at Trifels Castle. What's more, presumably the fire-arm is now in the hands of my worst enemy. So one way or another I must banish you from my castle."

Agnes felt something break inside her. Mathis, too, was white as a sheet, but he stood erect and looked the castellan in the face.

"As you command, sir," he managed to say.

"On the other hand . . ." Philipp von Erfenstein went on. "On the other hand you killed a scoundrel with that arquebus, and you res-cued my daughter. And I can't have the mayor of Annweiler doing as he likes with one of my vassals without so much as a by-your-leave. If I throw you out, Bernwart Gessler will be sure to take you prisoner and put you on trial. What times are these, when the word of a wind-bag of a mayor counts for more than anything the lord of Trifels can say? What in God's name are we coming to?"

Philipp von Erfenstein was talking himself into a rage now. His face was red. "Don't those newly rich fine folk know that I was a friend of Emperor Maximilian himself? We rode together in many tournaments in our young days, we fought together at Guinegate against the damned French. I lost my eye protecting him. I come of a highly regarded family—my great-grandfather served the emperor of his time as a knight. And now some patrician is going to tell me what I can and can't do? Never!"

He snorted and then pointed to Mathis. "I can't banish you; I'm not about to do the mayor that favor. But I can't let you off scot-free either, or I'll be the laughingstock of my own household. So I am go-ing to lock you up in the dungeon here until I know what I'm going to do with you." His eyes narrowed. "And maybe you'll wish yet that I *had* banished you, Mathis."

After the gamut of emotions she had been exposed to in the last few minutes, Agnes didn't know whether to laugh or cry. Mathis was not to be banished; he was staying near her in the castle. But her father was throwing him into the dungeon, and presumably worse would soon threaten him.

"But, Father," she implored, "Mathis took the arquebus only to help you. He wanted to repair the firearms, he wanted—"

"Save your breath," Philipp von Erfenstein replied brusquely. "I've told the lad often enough to leave gunpowder alone. I never could abide it—diabolical stuff. He ought to be forging swords like his good father. Instead, he steals from me and goes around with a pack of rebels. But those who won't listen must be made to feel. Ulrich! Damn it, where are you? *Ulrich!*"

Erfenstein shouted across the courtyard, and soon the old master gunner emerged from the Knights' House. The gray-haired former landsknecht walked with a stoop, and his scarred face was also marked by brandy.

"Your Excellency?" he mumbled, wiping barley broth out of his beard.

Erfenstein pointed to Mathis. "This lad has stolen one of my arquebuses out of the armory. I've a good mind to lock you up along with him, you drunken sot. Left the key lying around somewhere again, did you?"

Guiltily, Ulrich Reichhart looked at the ground. "It's a mystery to me how he ever—"

"Forget it." Erfenstein silenced the master gunner with an abrupt gesture. "We'll talk about it later. Now, take the boy to the dungeon. I have yet to think what I'll do with him. But until then I don't want to see his rebellious face here."

Reichhart nodded and turned to Mathis. "You heard it yourself," he grunted, almost as if placating him. "That was a stupid thing to do."

For a moment Agnes thought that Mathis was going to run for it.

But when he looked at her, all the fire seemed to go out of his eyes. He let himself be led away.

"Mathis! For heaven's sake, Mathis!" Agnes cried after him. "Hold out, I will—" But her father seized her by the shoulder.

"I always knew that boy was good for nothing," he said angrily. "His father, now, he's a capable, good man. But the son was always contrary." He shook his head. "Keeping company with the likes of Shepherd Jockel. You'll see, creatures like that hunchback will bring death and destruction to our country yet."

Agnes wasn't looking at him. Instead, she was watching Mathis, who disappeared into the castle, walking with his head held high. It looked like he was leading the master gunner away, instead of the other way around.

"And put that boy out of your mind," her father said, more sympathetically. "He's not fit company for the daughter of a castellan, a girl who lives in this proud castle." He tried to summon up a smile. "I wanted to talk to you about this anyway, Agnes. I've discussed it with Martin von Heidelsheim. He's a decent man, and above all a man of means. I know I always promised you a knight, but the situation has changed. I don't have the money to provide you with a dowry, and Heidelsheim can envisage taking you even—"

"I'll never marry Heidelsheim, not after all that's happened. It . . . it would be the death of me." Agnes tore herself away from her father, fighting back her tears, her face a stony mask.

Philipp von Erfenstein looked at her in surprise. "How do you know . . ." he began. But then he straightened his shoulders. "Pull yourself together, child. I'll forgive you—you're not mistress of your own feelings. Obviously that lad Mathis has turned your head." He wagged a threatening finger at her. "I am the lord of Trifels Castle, and I'll decide who you marry. And I can tell you one thing: from now on there'll be an end to all your whims and fancies. Wearing doublet and hose like a man, flying a falcon, your head always in a book—bah! I've put up with it far too long." Beseechingly, he took Agnes by the shoulders. "Don't you understand that we can save Trifels only if you marry a man of property? It's about the fate of the castle, not you. Get that into your head. Heidelsheim will take you as his wife, and that's that."

Agnes turned around, weeping, and set off for the living quarters in the tower. Out of the corner of her eye, she saw Margarethe watching her with a mixture of curiosity and mockery, and then turning to the cook, Hedwig, who stood beside her. Clearly the two servants had heard the end of the conversation. Now it would soon be all over the castle, and in a week at the latest the whole countryside would know. Agnes dried her face and walked past them with her head held high.

"Stupid child," Margarethe whispered to fat Hedwig. "I don't know why she's carrying on like that. Master Heidelsheim is a good match, and that Mathis is no great loss."

Agnes spun around, her hand raised to strike the maid. But at the last moment she thought better of it. "Be quiet," she said coldly. "Mathis is worth more than all of you put together."

With that she hurried up to her bedchamber. She felt as though an icy fist were slowly squeezing her heart.

· 4 ·

MORE THAN A WEEK PASSED, and Agnes was not allowed to see Mathis. Her father had had the young journeyman smith locked up in the dungeon in the former keep and forbade her from communicating with him in any way. Philipp von Erfenstein did not say what he was going to do with Mathis, and Agnes suspected that he didn't know himself. His anxiety about the rents and the new demands that the duke's steward kept making occupied his mind entirely, and, as usual, Philipp von Erfenstein drowned his troubles in brandy. Whenever Agnes mentioned Mathis to him, he either replied evasively or growled at her to put the young man out of her head.

"As I guessed," was all he would mutter, "you've fallen in love with him. I can't let him out until you're cured of that, anyway."

Agnes protested vociferously, but later, in her bedchamber, she threw herself on her bed in tears. She felt her inevitable fate approaching, and it was like a rock slowly pressing the life out of her. There was no doubt of it: she must bury all hope of Mathis forever. Sometimes, when she thought angrily that he had only himself to blame for his predicament, she didn't understand what she really saw in him. He could be wild and headstrong—but he had brains in his head, and she loved the way he was equally passionate in his enthusiasm for better methods of harvesting, the rights of poor peasants, and new developments in firearms. And it broke her heart to know he was still down there in the dungeon.

From time to time, Agnes had tried talking to Mathis through a narrow crack in the masonry going down from the castle courtyard to the dungeon, but after only a few words she had always been discovered by the guards, who had her father's orders to send her away.

Now she stood at the top of the Trifels rock formation and looked out over the countryside. Although it had been a long winter, the cold weather was slowly but steadily coming to an end. There were still persistent patches of snow in a few deep, shadowy valleys, but otherwise the warm sun shone over the vineyards of the Wasgau, and the fresh green buds of oak and beech leaves swayed in the wind. Agnes breathed deeply. Then her thoughts returned to Mathis, and her face darkened.

It's still dark and cold for Mathis down there.

The mayor of Annweiler had arrived the very day after Mathis's spectacular flight to Trifels Castle to take the journeyman smith away. But Philipp von Erfenstein had made it very clear to the mayor that he had no intention of handing Mathis over. Nonetheless, Agnes had a sinking feeling that they had not by any means heard the last of that business.

Another of her anxieties, however, had unexpectedly disappeared, dissolving into thin air. Martin von Heidelsheim, the steward, had apparently turned his back on the castle. At least, there had been no sign of him since his angry outburst in the stables, and Agnes suspected that he had accepted a position somewhere else out of a sense of injured pride—something that had Philipp von Erfenstein drinking more heavily than ever. After all, he now had to deal with all the tiresome paperwork on his own.

"I suppose I could understand that you didn't want to marry Heidelsheim," he complained to Agnes now and then, in his cups, "but damned if I can forgive you for scaring my chamberlain away. As if I didn't have enough on my mind as it is. But don't entertain any false hopes—I'll see you married this year yet. Even if I have to marry you off to that mayor of Annweiler. Curse it all, I need the money."

A sudden gust of wind tugged at the dress Agnes was wearing, and she stepped back from the edge of the cliff for fear of stumbling and falling into the depths below. She was about to go back to the out-buildings of the castle when she noticed a small black dot down there on the castle acres. Agnes peered at it. Her heart leapt up as the dot came closer and turned out to be a stooped figure in a monastic habit. She had been expecting him all morning, and now here he came. Her tutor, the castle chaplain, Father Tristan, was on his way back to Trifels after almost five months.

Soon Agnes could see his frail figure clearly as he came over the fields. Like all Cistercian monks, Father Tristan wore a black robe, the scapular, over his white tunic, which was now stained and splashed with mud after his long walk. But when he saw Agnes up on the rocks he gave her a friendly wave.

"Father Tristan! Father Tristan!" she called, although she knew that he couldn't hear her down there.

With her heart racing, Agnes ran across the castle courtyard, through the gate, and out into the narrow road until she met her tutor on the other side of the well tower. She embraced him tightly. Besides her father, the frail old man was the only person who sometimes made her feel like a little girl again. After a while Father Tristan, laughing, pushed her away and struggled for breath.

"My word, Agnes, you'll smother me. I've been on pilgrimage to Eusserthal, not Rome!"

But when he saw her sad face, his own expression grew darker. "Child, what's happened?" he asked anxiously. "You look so pale, like you've been in mourning and haven't eaten for days."

Father Tristan was nearly eighty years old, and his face was covered with lines and wrinkles. Yet his clever, friendly, watchful eyes shone. For as long as Agnes could remember, the monk had been her teacher and spiritual guide. When he went to Eusserthal monastery for several months every year, she always longed for the day of his return. And now she needed his help more than ever before.

"Some bad things have happened while you were away, Father," said Agnes gloomily. "I've been waiting for you so long."

Father Tristan smiled mildly. "You know the cold, damp winters up in this castle don't agree with me. The heating is better in the monastery, and Abbot Weigand needs me to check our accounts. The new bell may sound beautiful, but it was far from cheap. However, here I am now." He put his pilgrim's staff aside and took Agnes by the shoulders. Then he looked at her gravely. "So, tell me what has happened."

Agnes fought back her tears. "My . . . my father has thrown Mathis into the dungeon for stealing an arquebus," she began quietly. "And he's wanted by the mayor of Annweiler as a rabble-rouser too. And I'm supposed to marry Heidelsheim, but he isn't here anymore . . ." Her voice faltered.

"I can see that your story will take some time." Father Tristan picked up his pilgrim's staff and led her across the courtyard. "Why don't we go up to the library and talk about it there at our leisure?" he suggested. "I could drink a glass of hot spiced wine there, too— now that I'm an old man, the cold lingers in my bones, even though winter is behind us." He shook his head in annoyance. "This windy weather has played the devil with me."

Relieved, Agnes nodded, and together they climbed the steps to the living quarters in the tower.

The library was on the fourth floor of Trifels Castle, just above the chapel. A grate the size of a cart wheel gave a view of the chapel below. Once, persons of high rank could attend mass from this exalted viewpoint and did not have to mix with commoners. It was said that kings and emperors had been among them. But these days the grate covered only a drafty shaft. Agnes knew that her father had been talking of walling it up for some time, but so far he had not put the plan into practice.

Rapt in thought, Agnes looked around the large square room with a tiled stove rumbling away in the left-hand corner. The walls were lined with shelves of all kinds on which a number of parchment scrolls, dusty books, and leather-bound tomes lay. The main archive of the dukes of Zweibrücken was still kept here at the Trifels, and Father Tristan was its official curator. His was a task as interesting as it was unrewarding, for many of the volumes were nothing but old inventories and balance sheets that had to be numbered properly. Other documents were stored in moldering chests down in the castle cellars, where they were slowly falling to pieces. But from time to time, as he sorted through the records and lists, Father Tristan came upon genuine treasures: magnificently illuminated volumes, old collections of ballads, and treatises by ancient Greek philosophers like Aristotle and Plato. Agnes had spent half her childhood up here among the books.

"Ah, I see that good Hedwig has already been kind enough to light a fire for us," said Father Tristan, approaching the tiled stove with his hands outstretched. "This accursed gout, dear child! Be glad you're still young." With his teeth chattering, he picked up a jug standing in a niche beside the stove and poured himself a goblet of steaming spiced wine. Agnes herself felt cold. Particularly in spring, the castle was like a cave in the ice. The mild sunbeams were not enough to bring any real warmth to its ancient walls.

"Now, tell me all about it," Father Tristan told her, sipping the hot drink. He settled comfortably on the warm bench beside the stove, and Agnes sat down on a stool in front of him. "And don't leave anything out," the old monk added, raising a finger in playful warning. "After all, I am still your confessor."

Agnes took a deep breath and then told Father Tristan about all the recent events at Trifels, including her father's marriage plans for her, and the strange ring tied to Parcival's leg. Father Tristan listened in silence, only drinking a little spiced wine from time to time.

"And Heidelsheim has simply disappeared, leaving no trace at all?" he finally asked. "He took nothing with him and left no farewell message?"

When Agnes assented, the monk shook his head skeptically. "I can't believe that. You know that I never thought very much of the man, Agnes, but all the same, he was a clever and reliable steward. That just isn't like him. He's not one to walk out in a temper, leaving all his worldly goods behind. I begin to fear that some accident may have happened to him."

Agnes sighed. "I suppose we'll never know. At least, my father hasn't had a search mounted for him. He just sits brooding to himself. Now that he can't count the rents anymore he is drinking harder than ever. It was only when he was showing the mayor of Annweiler the door that he was his old self again." She smiled, but she was serious again the next moment. "Father still hasn't said what he is going to do with Mathis. And I'm not allowed to visit him either."

Father Tristan nodded his head thoughtfully. "The mayor won't have liked being dismissed so unceremoniously by Erfenstein," he murmured. "Gessler has right on his side. If I know him, he'll have sent a messenger straight to the electoral court in Heidelberg. This may not turn out well for your father."

"And it may not turn out well for Mathis, either," Agnes added gloomily.

Father Tristan nodded, and then looked hard at Agnes. "That ring you mentioned. May I see it?"

"Of course." Agnes took the ring, which until now she had worn only at night or when she was unobserved, off her finger and, with some hesitation, offered it to the monk.

Father Tristan rubbed the gem in his gnarled fingers, held it up to his eyes, and looked at the engraving. Then Agnes heard his sharp intake of breath.

"Do you know the ring?" she asked hopefully.

The old monk hesitated. He seemed to be about to say something, but then he only shook his head. "No," he said briefly. "But I know the seal. To say any more would be mere supposition."

"So? What kind of seal is it?"

"Well, as I'm sure you have noticed, it shows the head of a bearded man," began Father Tristan quietly, giving the ring back to Agnes. "There are many men who wear beards, but only one was ever so powerful that the beard became, so to speak, a symbol of the man himself and served him as a seal."

Agnes felt her heart beat faster. "And who was that?"

"Barbarossa."

The name seemed to hang in the air while Agnes leaned back thoughtfully. Emperor Barbarossa featured in many of the stories she had devoured up here in the library of Trifels Castle. He had been the first of the famous emperors from the Hohenstaufen family who had ruled the German Empire for several generations about four hundred years ago. Barbarossa had been tall and strong, and his red beard was legendary. At a great old age he was drowned in the Saleph River while on Crusade, but there was a story that he was still sleeping under the Trifels. It was a legend that had probably arisen because, after the Hohenstaufens, there had been a time without an emperor when lawlessness prevailed.

"Does that mean this ring belonged to Emperor Barbarossa himself?" Agnes asked at last, amazed.

"No, certainly not!" Father Tristan laughed and leaned comfortably back against the warm side of the stove. "There were many such rings at the time, you see. Each of the ministerial officials of the empire, the authorized representatives of the emperor, had one so that he could seal important documents in His Imperial Majesty's name. But I have no idea how that ring came to be on your falcon's leg. Perhaps . . ." He hesitated, and Agnes looked at him expectantly.

"Perhaps what?"

Father Tristan shook his head. "No, nonsense. I must be getting old and strange." He smiled. "Well, at least that links the two of us.

You were always, well, an odd child. Too many dreams can turn one's head."

"I did have another dream recently, Father," Agnes said softly. "Like my old dreams, only this time it was more vivid than ever before. And I had it for the first time on the night when I found the ring. I've had it half a dozen times since."

"Tell me about it."

So Agnes told him about the dream that had made as strong an impression on her as if it were reality. It had been even more graphic the last few times, and it had always ended with the young man in the hauberk looking at her like he wanted to tell her something.

"It was the Knights' House here at Trifels Castle, looking as it once did in the past," she said. "I'm sure it was. I could recognize it all. The niches with people sitting in them, the great hearth, even the paneling on the ceiling was the same."

The monk said nothing for a moment, then, laboriously, he got to his feet and turned to the shelves. "Wait a moment, my child," he said. "I want to show you something."

Murmuring quietly to himself, he searched among the bound volumes for a little while, and then pulled out a thick book with irregularly cut parchment pages, some of them charred here and there. Lettering in gold leaf stood out on them. Father Tristan carefully laid the book on the table in the middle of the room and began looking through it.

"Here," he said at last. "Is that the hall that you saw in your dream?"

Agnes bent over the open book and froze. She was looking at a magnificently illustrated page, already yellowing, with intertwining letters at the top. The picture showed a high-ceilinged hall in which a banquet was being held. Men and women in flowing, colorful robes sat at long tables, servants were carrying in delicious-looking dishes, a juggler was throwing balls in the air. It was the very same hall that she had seen in her dream.

"My God!" she breathed.

"It is indeed the Knights' House here at Trifels Castle," the monk replied quietly. "This picture is many hundreds of years old. It dates from the time when the Trifels was still an imperial castle."

"It's all just as it was in my dream," whispered Agnes. "The guests, the musicians . . ." Her voice faltered. With a trembling finger, she pointed to a figure at the side of the hall that she had only just seen. It was a young man in a hauberk, with his head bent, kneeling before an older man, a knight. Her breathing sped up.

"That . . . that young man," she asked. "Who is he?"

Father Tristan bent over the book and looked more closely at the picture. "My eyes aren't what they used to be," he complained, "but unless I'm much mistaken, it shows the scene of an accolade. A young man is being dubbed a knight." He hesitated, and then shook his head vigorously, as if to dispel dark thoughts. "But for the life of me I can't tell you who he is. It was far too long ago. The young man will have fallen to dust and ashes by now."

"Not in my dream," Agnes murmured.

Father Tristan slammed the book shut. "One shouldn't look too far back in the past," he said rather too quickly. "That leads to no good." He looked at her sternly. "And as for this ring, Agnes, let me implore you. Don't wear it on your finger, and don't show it to any stranger. Will you promise me that?"

"But why?" asked Agnes, taken aback. "Is it so valuable that someone would want to steal it from me?"

"Its value is of a different kind. Just promise me. Maybe I can tell you more about it another time. All right?"

In silence, Agnes nodded, and the monk smiled and stood up. He slowly made his way to the door of the library, and then turned around to Agnes, a twinkle in his eyes. "Come along, we both ought to eat something. And after that maybe I'll think of a way to help your friend Mathis out of his fix. The living should always be closer to us than the dead, especially when the dead died so long ago. Come with me, then." He reached for his pilgrim's staff and climbed downstairs to the kitchen. "You know stout Hedwig doesn't like her food to get cold."

With some hesitation, Agnes followed him. She cast one last glance at the book, now lying closed on the table, before she left the library. What other secrets might be concealed within?

Mathis's stomach grumbled, as if the guards had locked a bear in the dungeon with him. Although it was already afternoon, he had had nothing today but some thin soup and a crust of moldy bread. He stared at the dirty wall as though his eyes could burn a hole in it. He had made a mark on the stone with a piece of charred wood for every day that he spent down here. There were ten marks now, ten days and nights in almost complete darkness. Today he would be adding an eleventh.

The castle dungeon was directly under the Trifels storeroom in the cellars. His prison was a shaft cut deeper into the rock, and the bottom of it could be reached only by means of a rope. Stinking straw covered the floor, with stones, rotten planks, and pieces of wood that someone or other had thrown in at some time. By night rats squealed and scurried from one hole in the walls to another. There were two slits at a height of a good twelve feet up the walls, allowing a little daylight in, but otherwise darkness reigned. The men-at-arms let water, soup, and bread down to Mathis twice a day, and took away the bucket in which he had relieved himself. Ulrich, Gunther, and the other guards obviously did not like to think of the young man they had known since his childhood being shut up down there. But the castellan was not to be moved. They were not even allowed to talk to the prisoner. So Mathis stared gloomily at nothing, day in, day out. Now and then, to keep himself reasonably fit, he paced up and down the dungeon, which was just fifteen feet square, or lifted weights in the form of several chunks of stone that had fallen out of the wall.

Agnes had once told him that great noblemen and bishops used to be imprisoned in the imperial fortress of Trifels. Even Richard the Lionheart, the famous king of England, had languished here at one time. With the ransom money that Barbarossa's son Henry VI got for the Lionheart, the German emperor later conquered Sicily and came back with a great treasure. Not that Mathis could imagine King Richard having to fight rats for his food down here. Presumably the ruler of England had been accommodated in one of the upper rooms, as befitted his rank, until the ransom finally arrived. Apparently His Majesty had even written several poems when he was in captivity at Trifels.

Mathis laughed bitterly at the idea of writing love poetry with quill and parchment here among the rats. Who would he write them to? Agnes? His feelings for her had cooled off a good deal these last few days. Why had he listened to her instead of running away into the forest as he had planned? People said that more and more malcontents were gathering in the deep, green valleys of the Wasgau, indeed of the whole Upper Rhine area, to organize uprisings against the injustice of the princes, counts, and dukes. Very likely Shepherd Jockel had joined them after fleeing from Annweiler. Mathis cursed quietly. The whole empire was seething in ferment—and here he lay, rotting in the dungeon of Trifels Castle.

Agnes had kept trying to talk to him through the slit in the wall that admitted light, but only until the guards sent her away. To tell the truth, however, Mathis didn't want to talk to her. She was the daughter of the castellan who was responsible for this situation in the first place—a nobleman's daughter. And what had Philipp von Erfenstein ever done to improve life for his peasants? Nothing. Agnes would say that her father hadn't made the laws, as if laws couldn't be changed. Maybe Jockel was right when he lumped all the powerful men together. Mathis thought of what his father had said. Since he had been locked up here, he couldn't get it out of his head.

Agnes is the daughter of the lord of Trifels Castle, and Mathis is only a journeyman smith. Where is that going to lead?

A scraping sound roused Mathis from his thoughts. When he

looked up, he saw that the stone slab in the roof above was being pushed aside. The face of Ulrich Reichhart, the master gunner, appeared in the opening. Mathis's heart began to beat wildly. Was the mayor of Annweiler here to take him away to stand trial? Or had Philipp von Erfenstein relented and was setting him free?

"Got a visitor for you," old Ulrich growled. "The castellan said your mother could see you."

Next moment, the face of Martha Wielenbach appeared above him. Although it was a good fifteen feet up to the ceiling, and there was hardly any light, Mathis could see at first glance how sad his mother looked. Her once black hair had much more gray in it than when he'd last seen her.

"Mathis!" she called down, "Mathis! My God, how are you?"

"As anyone might expect, after spending so long in this hole," replied Mathis, trying to sound as calm as possible. "Fighting the rats for every bit of bread." He felt how rough and dry his throat was, and a bitter fluid rose in it. In spite of the grief that suddenly overcame him, he was determined that his mother wouldn't see him in tears.

"I brought you something to eat," said Martha Wielenbach, her voice faltering. "Ulrich is going to be kind enough to let me down to you."

"Believe me, Mathis," the old master gunner assured him, "if it was up to me you'd have been free long ago. But the castellan can be as stubborn as a donkey. At least he isn't handing you over to Gessler. That's something."

The men-at-arms Gunther and Sebastian lent Ulrich a hand, and between them they let Martha Wielenbach down in a loop of rope. With her free hand, the smith's wife clutched a basket in which Mathis could see new bread, still steaming from the oven, and cheese as yellow as honey. His stomach rumbled again.

Down in the cell, Martha Wielenbach quickly climbed out of the loop and hugged her son. "Mathis, dear Mathis!" she whispered. "At least you seem to be in good health." She shed a few tears. "Oh, why did it have to come to this?"

Mathis gently pushed her away. "It's all right, Mother," he said. "I don't mind atoning for the theft. But I'm not sorry for the rest of it."

His mother wiped away her tears, and looked at him questioningly. "You mean helping Shepherd Jockel to get away?"

Mathis nodded. "It had to be done. If the citizens of Annweiler are going to knuckle under, then it's for us ordinary folk to show the powerful that things can't go on like this. We're not criminals and cutthroats, we only want justice. God made all men equal."

His mother shook her head sadly. "Oh, Mathis, what kind of talk is that?" she said. "Who gave you these notions? Shepherd Jockel? Don't let your father hear them—he's in a bad enough way as it is."

"What's the matter with him?"

She sighed. "When he heard about you, he didn't speak to anyone for three days, not even me. Since then his cough has been worse and worse, and at the end of last week he had to take to his bed. He won't let me mention you—he's beside himself if I do."

Mathis felt all the anger suddenly go out of him. As a child, he had almost taken his father for God. Hans Wielenbach had been a tall, strong, traveling craftsman when the castellan took him into his service ten years ago, along with his family. There had been five of them then, but little Peter had soon died while still at his mother's breast, and their big sister had been carried off by severe whooping cough five years ago. Mathis, the middle child, had always had ideas of his own, and over time he had quarreled more and more often with his father. Suddenly Mathis felt dreadfully afraid that Hans Wielenbach might die before he could ask his forgiveness.

"Give Father my love," he murmured in a faltering voice. "Tell him I'm . . . I'm very sorry I've dragged you both into this situation."

Martha Wielenbach stroked her son's dirty cheek. "I'll tell him. You're a good boy after all. It will be all right again, you wait and see. Now, have something to eat."

She gave him bread and cheese from her basket, and Mathis began to eat greedily. Over the last few minutes he had quite forgotten how hungry he was.

"And your little sister sends you love," said Martha Wielenbach, smiling, as she watched her son eat. "You're a hero to her. At least, the children of the peasants down on the castle acres told her you were, and of course she believes it. Oh, and I'm to give you this from Agnes." She handed him a folded piece of parchment.

"What am I supposed to do with it?" he asked, more roughly than he had intended.

"She'll have written you a few lines, I expect. I was always so proud that Agnes taught you to read." Martha Wielenbach took her son by the shoulders. "Mathis, you shouldn't be so hard on her. How can she help it that her father has locked you up here? I know very well that she keeps pleading with him for you."

"Ha! She's already shown how much influence she has on her father. None at all."

But in spite of his annoyance, Mathis took the parchment. Surreptitiously, he stroked the carefully folded note. Up above, the scraping sound of the stone slab came again. Martha Wielenbach looked at the ceiling, sighing.

"I must go," she said. She hugged her son one last time, so hard that it almost hurt him. "If you want to soften the castellan's heart, then stop all your seditious talk," she warned. "Be penitent, and it will all turn out well yet."

"I'll think about it, Mother," Mathis replied.

Martha Wielenbach planted a kiss on his forehead and then took hold of the rope loop that the men-at-arms had let back down.

"Don't forget, you will always be my boy, whatever happens," she said as tears ran down her face. Then her swaying figure was drawn up through the twilight in the shaft. Next moment the stone slab slid back into place, and Mathis was left alone with his thoughts.

He held the folded note up to his face and smelled it. It carried the odor of spring and sunlight.

And Agnes.

Slowly, Mathis unfolded the parchment and stared at it. Agnes had not written a letter; she had painted him a picture. A picture in shining colors, showing the two of them in a forest clearing. It was bright in the darkness of the dungeon, like someone had suddenly lit a torch.

Mathis stroked the note once more and then sat down in a corner with it and looked at the picture again and again.

And once again that bitter flavor rose in his throat.

Early next morning, Agnes found another opportunity to speak to Father Tristan. She met the monk in the kitchen, where he was pounding some dried herbs in a mortar. The smoke of the fire on the hearth drifted through the room, and so it took the old man a little while to see her.

"Ah, Agnes," he said, pleased, rubbing his red-rimmed eyes. "Well, did you dream of Trifels Castle again last night?"

Agnes shook her head. "Not this time. At least, I don't remember doing so." She took a piece of bread and dipped it in a beaker of goat's milk that Hedwig had left ready for her. "Were you able to speak to my father about Mathis?" she hesitantly asked. "His mother came to see him yesterday and brought him greetings from me. She says he's not in a good frame of mind."

"No, I fear I haven't spoken to your father. He was out hunting all day yesterday, and early this morning he was . . . let's say, not very well." Father Tristan shrugged his shoulders, smiling. "I've already given him a decoction of herbs for his headache, and I expect I'll be able to talk to him sometime soon. Until then, maybe it would be better for you not to go anywhere near Mathis. Or your father will simply lose his temper again and be as stubborn as ever. Will you take my advice?"

Agnes hesitantly nodded. "All right. If it's any help to Mathis."

She munched the hard slice of bread without much of an appetite and finally put it down, pointing with interest to the mortar. "What exactly are you doing there?"

"Pounding arnica, comfrey, and angelica together. Mixed with bear's fat they make an excellent ointment." Father Tristan stopped using the pestle and looked at Agnes with a grave expression. "Down in Hahnenbach yesterday I examined a little boy whose leg had been run over by a cart. I told his parents I'd see what I could do." He tipped the herbal mixture into a pan and stirred it into the softened fat. "I wonder, would you perhaps come with me?"

Agnes was happy to agree. She had often visited the sick with Father Tristan in the past and had picked up a few of the principles of medicine. However, that was some time ago, and so she was particularly glad of his invitation now. Anything to take her mind off Mathis and his unfortunate situation was welcome to her.

When Father Tristan had strapped up his satchel, they went down over the castle acres together to Hahnenbach, a hamlet not far from Annweiler. The old man strode ahead at a good pace. In spite of his great age, he could walk well enough with the help of his staff. It was a warm day, the birds were twittering, and the willows by the roadside were already bearing their soft, fluffy catkins. Not far away the river Queich flowed by, and there was a slight smell of rotting in the air from all the garbage left by the tanners for the river to carry down into the Rhine valley.

Taking the monk's advice to heart, Agnes had taken the ring off her finger the previous evening. She was wearing it on a thin chain over her heart now, concealed from view. She said nothing for some time that morning, but then she couldn't restrain herself. She had been brooding all night over what Father Tristan had said about Emperor Barbarossa and her dream.

"Tell me, Father—that young man in the picture," she tentatively began. "Why did you—" But Father Tristan testily waved her question away.

"I told you I don't want to talk about it. You think about the past far too much anyway."

Agnes sighed. "Very well. Then at least take my mind off it by telling me something about the Norman treasure. I was reading about it again in the library only the other day. But I have only fragments of its history. And I love those old tales so much."

"And I told you about it a dozen times when you were a child," grumbled Father Tristan, but with a smile playing around his lips. "Oh, very well." He stopped for a moment to get his breath back, and then he pointed up to the Sonnenberg with the Trifels crowning it. "Up there, on the site of the castle acres of today, there used to be a great tournament ground. The jousts held there were famous throughout the whole country. And it was the place where Emperor Henry VI, Barbarossa's son, assembled a mighty army over three hundred years ago, to go to fight the Normans in Sicily. His wife was a Sicilian princess, so Henry thought he could seize the throne there for himself. At the time, warriors from the entire empire came to the Trifels—there must have been thousands of them. Knights on horseback, men-at-arms, foot soldiers with bows and spears . . ." Father Tristan spread his arms wide, and Agnes recognized him as the old storyteller she had loved so much as a child.

"Henry rode out, won the victory, and took a terrible revenge on his enemies," the monk went on. "He had a red-hot crown nailed to the head of the leader of a conspiracy while the man was still alive. When the emperor returned, he possessed the greatest treasure ever seen in Christendom. It's said the Norman treasure was so enormous that a hundred and fifty donkeys were needed to carry it up to Trifels Castle. There was a magnificent coronation robe in it, but above all there were huge amounts of gold, silver, and jewels."

"And where's the treasure today?" asked Agnes, curious to know. "Obviously not at Trifels, or my father would have nothing to worry about."

Father Tristan laughed. "You're right there. No, it's said that Henry's son Frederick II, known to this day as *Stupor Mundi*, the Wonder of the World, had it taken later to Apulia, where his faithful Saracens guarded it. And the imperial jewels are no longer here either."

"Imperial jewels?" Agnes frowned. "You mean the insignia used in the coronation of the German king?" She knew that, as far back as anyone could remember, the king was crowned in an established ceremony, usually held in the imperial city of Aachen. The insignia played an important part in the coronation, but it was news to her that those sacred objects had once been kept at Trifels Castle. "I thought the imperial insignia had been kept in a church in Nuremberg." she said.

Father Tristan shook his head. "Once, at the time of the Hohenstaufens, the imperial jewels were here in Trifels Castle. The Cistercians of Eusserthal took care of them. They are the holiest objects in the empire. The sword of Charlemagne, the imperial orb, and the scepter, crown, and coronation robe. And of course the Holy Lance that once pierced the side of Our Lord at Golgotha . . ." The old monk stopped to draw breath again. Groaning, he stretched his back. "Whenever a new king is crowned, they are part of the ceremony. They give the ruler his power. Without the insignia, there can be no coronation to this day." He sighed. "But the jewels are no longer here. No one cares about Trifels these days, reluctant as your father may be to admit it."

"But in my dream—" Agnes began. However, the monk interrupted her.

"Forget your dreams, Agnes," he said brusquely. "You're living here and now. And look, we've nearly arrived."

Soon they had reached the village. Mud-stained children were playing with pebbles in the only road, where slurry stood in puddles. The children were barefoot and wore only rags tacked together; they were all shockingly thin, their bellies swollen with hunger. They looked at the new arrivals out of eyes sunk deep in their faces, and only when they recognized the monk did they break into muted rejoicings.

"Father Tristan, Father Tristan!" they shouted as they danced around the old man. "Have you brought us a treat?"

"Maybe," said Father Tristan, smiling. "But please make sure that everyone gets a fair share, you scamps."

He took a few wrinkled dried plums from last fall's harvest out of his satchel and divided them among the shouting children, who greedily stuffed the sweet fruits into their mouths at once. When there was nothing left, Father Tristan turned left, with Agnes, to where a small, crooked cottage stood a little way back from the road.

"Here we are," he said, knocking softly on the door. "Let's hope the child is no worse."

A careworn old woman let them in. She smiled wearily on seeing Father Tristan, and Agnes was shocked to see that she had lost nearly all her teeth. Her hair was gray, her skin lined.

"Where's your son, goodwife?" asked Father Tristan. Only his words told Agnes that the woman was not the child's grandmother but his mother.

"God bless you, Father," replied the woman in relief, beckoning him in. "The boy's lying on the floor back there. He has a high fever." She glanced suspiciously at Agnes. "But that is . . ."

"The castellan's daughter," said Father Tristan. "I know. She wants to make herself useful."

"Make herself useful?" The woman laughed. There was contempt in her voice as she said, "How can a girl like that be any use?"

Agnes suddenly suspected, uneasily, that Father Tristan had not brought her with him just to tell her more about Trifels Castle. She stared at the dark interior of the cottage, which was built of willow branches daubed with dried mud. A fire burned in the middle of the room, its smoke escaping in thick clouds through a hole in the roof. In a corner at the back lay a boy of about six on a bed of leaves and twigs. His right leg was wrapped in blood-stained rags, and the foot seemed to have swollen to twice its proper size.

Father Tristan knelt down and put his hand on the boy's forehead, which was wet with sweat. "Yes, the fever is very high," he murmured. "We must try to lower it a little." Putting his hand in his satchel, he took out a little leather bag and gave it to Agnes. "Here, make us a decoction of these dried linden flowers."

Soon Father Tristan had cleaned the dirt and dried blood from the boy's swollen foot. "Is that decoction ready?" he asked Agnes.

She nodded and handed him the pan.

"I am going to clean the wound with the decoction now," said Father Tristan. "It must be boiled first, that's important, remember."

He bent over the boy, washed the injury with a clean rag, and rubbed some of the ointment he had brought into the injured leg. Meanwhile, Agnes poured what was left of the hot liquid into an earthenware beaker and got the boy to drink a little of it. He moaned, but he did as she wanted.

Father Tristan's small eyes, surrounded with little lines, twinkled at her. "You're doing well, Agnes."

"Maybe I should do such things more often," replied Agnes quietly, but with a grin. "If you will let me, even though I'm a fine gentleman's daughter."

◆ ◆ ◆

A mild wind caresses her face. Agnes opens her eyes and sees that she is on the battlements of Trifels Castle, at the very top, above the staterooms and living quarters. It is a warm afternoon in fall, with the leaves of the trees around the castle changing color, their branches swaying slightly in the breeze. Agnes turns her head and sees Scharfenberg Castle on the neighboring hill, distempered red and white, a fortress rising proudly above the woods. Halfway between Trifels and Scharfenberg stands Anebos Castle, not quite as large as its sister, but equally stately. Not a ruin as Agnes knows it in her waking life, but a sturdy tower built on sandstone rock and surrounded by houses, cottages, and walls. She can see men on horseback holding brightly colored banners and standards. Farther away, other sandstone rocks with platforms and watchtowers on them rise like spikes on a dragon's back. The whole Sonnenberg is a single huge fortress, from Trifels to Scharfenberg Castle.

Agnes looks down at the courtyard. Where she sees only piles of rubble and empty spaces when she is awake, there are stables, sheds, whole buildings. The Knights' House, in her own day so dilapidated, is attractively covered with red tiles, and black smoke curls up from its chimney. There is busy coming and going everywhere. Huntsmen clad in green hold back a pack of yap-

ping hounds; washerwomen with buckets hurry down to the cisterns in the outer bailey, laughing. A group of mounted men gallops through the open gateway, with pheasants and partridges hanging from their saddles. Grooms, chattering noisily, carry a dead bear slung over a tree trunk into the courtyard. A horn blows somewhere, to be answered by another, and then a third horn calls.

Suddenly Agnes senses a slight draft on the back of her neck. When she turns around, she sees the young man from her first dream. He looks more mature this time. His hair is as thick and black as before, but his features are more marked and less soft. The stubble of a beard makes him look older, more virile. Once again he is wearing his shining hauberk, but she sees the shape of broad shoulders under it. Pine needles cling to his muddy cloak, and his right hand wears a leather glove on which a gray-blue sparrowhawk perches. Now the young man hands the falcon over to a groom and approaches Agnes smiling, with his arms spread wide.

Her heart leaps. She loves this man as she has never loved anyone before. And she knows that her love is returned. She was never happier than at this moment. When he embraces her, she smells his sharp sweat mingling with the resinous aroma of the pine needles. She wishes he would never let her go. She thinks of the song she heard when she last saw him.

Under the linden tree, on the moorland, there we made a bed for two . . .

When he moves back from her, he suddenly takes her hand and speaks to her imploringly. The expression in his eyes is very serious now, and his lips move, but Agnes cannot hear what he is saying. All that comes to her ears is the sound of the wind. Yet she knows that he is saying something of great importance, a matter of life and death.

The young man takes her hand and holds it even more tightly. It hurts. Something is cutting into her finger. When she looks down she sees that it is a ring causing the pain, a ring like an iron band getting tighter all the time.

It is the ring with the seal showing a bearded man.

Barbarossa's ring.

She looks into the young man's face again. His lips are forming sounds that she can't hear. "Take the ring off! Take the ring off!" he seems to be calling to her.

Agnes cries out soundlessly herself. She tries to remove the ring, but it digs its way deeper and deeper into her flesh. She feels it slowly come to rest around her finger bone. Like a necklace cutting off air from her throat.

The ring becomes one with her.

When she looks up again, the young man has disappeared. The castle courtyard is empty, and she is all alone.

✦ ✦ ✦

Gasping, trembling all over, Agnes awoke with the moon shining brightly into her room. She jumped out of bed, panic-stricken, and ran to the open window.

Where am I?

But she saw only the courtyard of Trifels below, just as she had known it since her childhood. From up here, she could see the outlines of the kennels and the aviary, the tumbledown walls and the Knights' House leaning to one side, not as she had just seen it in her dream, a fine sight with its red tiles. Her hand went to her throat, and she pulled out the chain with the ring on it from under her nightgown. White moonlight lay on the engraving. The ring looked just the same as in her dream, and although it had been next to her heart all night, it felt cold as ice.

What on earth does it mean? What is this ring doing to me?

Agnes took a few deep breaths and finally managed to put her thoughts in order. Things from real life kept slipping into her dreams. That was nothing unusual; the same happened to other people. The only unusual part of it was the way her dream, and so the ring too, had seemed so real. As before, she had felt and heard everything—the mild wind on her skin, the resinous aroma of the pine needles, the sharp sweat of the man she loved . . . What was it about that young man whom she obviously desired so much? Who was he? Now that she was awake, she felt nothing for him, almost as if she had been someone entirely different in her dream. Agnes frowned. The young man had warned her against the ring. Did it represent a danger for her? Father Tristan had suggested as much.

She instinctively put her hand to the cool metal and shook her head. Very likely Father Tristan's warning had simply influenced her dream. That was all. She was beginning to see ghosts.

You should work in the garden more often, then you wouldn't have time for such fancies.

Only now did Agnes notice how cold she felt in her thin night-gown. She went back to bed, shivering, and slipped under the covers. She thought of taking off the ring but decided to go on wearing it over her heart. Without it, she felt strangely naked.

Not until the first rays of the sun fell on her face and a rooster crowed in the distance did she fall into a brief, feverish sleep.

· 5 ·

Annweiler, near Trifels Castle, 8 April, Anno Domini 1524

ONLY A FEW DAYS LATER, three men on tall horses reached Annweiler early in the morning.

The few tanners standing by the town's millstream, washing animal skins still matted with blood and the remnants of flesh that clung to them, looked up for a moment, no more, as the trio rode by. Then they quickly ducked their heads. The strangers' clothing was unusual. They wore the costume of landsknechts, but the fabric looked expensive and was of colors not generally seen in this part of the country. In the normal way, it boded no good for strange folk to visit a place. They were often messengers from the duke, coming to collect dues and taxes, or heralds announcing new electoral edicts—edicts that demanded yet more dues. Taxes had been raised five times in the last twelve years, and as many activities had been banned in the same time. Not just hunting, but fishing, and even chopping wood were now forbidden. The rulers were squeezing more and more out of the peasants and other ordinary folk; it was as if they were in a grape press, but no juice came out—only blood.

The tanners saw at first glance that the leader of the three men, riding a fine steed, was a great gentleman. He wore slashed blood-red hose, a doublet of black velvet, and a fur-trimmed coat over these garments that was also black as night. The cap pulled well down over his face was adorned, in the military fashion, with several colored feathers. A certain indefinable aura of menace surrounded the stranger, like a disturbance in the air suggesting a coming thunderstorm.

"Hey there!" he called in the tone of a man accustomed to giving orders, to one of the tanners by the millstream, an emaciated elderly man. His voice had a curious foreign accent. "Where will I find your mayor?"

"He'll probably be over at the town hall, sir," the old man muttered without looking up. "Just ride along the street here to the marketplace, and then you're outside it."

Without a word of thanks, the well-dressed stranger spurred on his horse, and the other two men, muscular fellows with shaggy beards and long hair, followed him. The hooves of the three horses clattered down the dirty street. Somewhere a rooster crowed, a few pigs squealed, and morning mists drifted slowly through the town.

The leader dismounted in the empty marketplace and tied up his horse to a trough. He gave his companions a curt order in a foreign language. They nodded and then let their eyes wander without interest over the square. A young maidservant had just been opening the shutters to hang out some washing, but at the sight of the horsemen she slammed the window shut in alarm.

"Boo!" said one of the two men. They laughed quietly as their horses, which were sweating heavily, drank water from the trough.

Meanwhile, the leader went into Annweiler Town Hall. It was a half-timbered house, painted red and white, and its size and grandeur recalled the heyday of this former imperial city. It looked curiously out of place amidst the other low-ceilinged, crooked buildings. The man's boots echoed on the steps up to the town hall, which were stained oxblood red.

Up in his study, Bernwart Gessler was brooding over some files. The mayor of Annweiler was busy completing the lists of the dues and taxes that had already been collected. All the villages and hamlets had now paid up. There was to be a meeting of the newly elected council in an hour's time to discuss measures that might be taken to counter the increasingly subversive activities of the so-called Lutherans. These days more and more monks and peripatetic priests were emerging and preaching against papal decrees. After what had happened at the Green Tree Inn recently, Gessler had insisted on a quick reelection of the council. Opponents were removed, supporters and the undecided left in office. The mayor was sure that he was now more or less back in control of the town.

When there was a knock on the door, the mayor didn't even look up.

"Oh, for God's sake, not now!" he snarled. But the door opened anyway.

The man who entered the study looked both dangerous and distinguished. As a result, Gessler bit back the curse already on the tip of his tongue and looked expectantly at his visitor.

"Yes?" he asked cautiously.

The stranger pulled up a stool, sat on it, and crossed his legs. His cap was still pulled well down over his face. "I am visiting this little town of yours in search of something," he began in a curious, soft accent. "Maybe you can help me."

The mayor gave a thin-lipped smile. "Maybe. You'd better come back tomorrow. Around noon. Then I can . . ."

"I do not have time for that," the man interrupted him. "I come from far away." He pushed his cap back, and now Gessler saw that the stranger's face was as black as night. White eyes shone in it like cold, sparkling diamonds. "From very far away."

Suddenly he reached into his full slashed upper hose and brought out a bag of clinking coins. With a quick movement, he pushed the purse over the table so that it stopped right in front of the mayor. "A payment for granting my modest wish. And there will be as much again if your help turns out useful."

In surprise, Bernwart Gessler opened the bag, which contained golden coins in some foreign currency, so many that it had to be worth more than Gessler had made all last year. His heart was in his throat, but he kept his composure.

"And what is this wish?" he asked in as neutral a tone as possible, while the little bag disappeared into a drawer in his desk.

The stranger told him.

Bernwart Gessler listened with close attention. The request was rather strange, like the man himself. For such a large sum, he could have commanded Gessler to poison the millstream or have all the houses in Annweiler painted blue. Gessler thought for a moment before finally, and hesitantly, he answered.

"Yes, in a case like that the church registers would indeed help you. But, sad to say, they were all destroyed in a fire three years ago. What a pity . . ." He paused, and he smiled when he saw the other man frown. "But as this matter is obviously very important, I might know someone who can help you further. There could be papers, or at least something similar. Although I can't promise anything."

"And who would that someone be?" asked the stranger.

Gessler told him.

With a supple movement, the man rose and sketched a bow. Only now did Gessler notice the curved sword hanging from the man's waist. Its sheath, hand guard, and hilt were scratched, with deep notches in them, and rusty red patches disfigured the otherwise excellent workmanship. The saber looked as if it had seen a great deal of use.

"It has been a pleasure to do business with you," said the stranger. He spoke fluently, if with an accent that Gessler had never heard before. "If your suggestion leads to the desired result, I will be back. If not . . ." He paused for a moment. "Well, I will be back anyway. I am sure I need not emphasize the importance of keeping this conversation of ours confidential. A word to anyone else, and . . ." He let his unfinished sentence die away.

"Are you by any chance threatening me?" the mayor replied coldly.

"Think of the other bag. It could soon be yours."

The stranger turned away, without a word of farewell, and disappeared through the open doorway. For a while Gessler could hear his boots going down the steps, and then there was silence. Shivering, the mayor drew his warm woolen coat around his shoulders. It was as if a cold wind had blown through the study.

Bernwart Gessler opened the drawer, and weighed the heavy bag of coins in his hand again.

Oddly enough, it gave him no real pleasure.

In the dungeon of Trifels Castle, Mathis had made five more marks on the stone wall since his mother's visit. Every day he expected the castellan to hand him over to the mayor of Annweiler, or his mother to bring him news of his sick father's death.

The endless hours passed monotonously, interrupted only when Ulrich Reichhart or one of the other guards brought him something to eat. Then the trapdoor would open, and light would fall on Mathis's pale face. Now and then Ulrich said a cheering word, otherwise Mathis was alone with his thoughts.

To occupy his mind, he had begun recalling the forbidden writings that Shepherd Jockel had once given him to read. When he closed his eyes, he could see the letters clearly before his mind's eye, and so in his thoughts he reread the peasants' demands, repeating in a whisper the lines telling the tale of a better world—a world without princes, counts, and clerics. But another image kept coming in front of those lines, distracting his attention.

The face of Agnes.

For perhaps the thirtieth time that day he took out the piece of parchment on which Agnes had painted herself and him in the forest. By now it was stained, torn, and the bright colors were fading, but Mathis still thought he caught a faint perfume that reminded him of Agnes. She had not been near him for days. At first he had told himself that was for the best, but then he felt how much he missed her. Why did she have to be the daughter of that damn pig-headed castellan?

Mathis was on the point of crumpling up the picture in anger, but then he thought better of it, folded the parchment carefully, and put it under his doublet. He rose and began pacing from wall to wall of the dungeon. Fifteen feet one way, fifteen feet back, fifteen feet one way . . .

Several mice kept him company on his short walk. Mathis had fed them a few crumbs of bread, and in time they had become used to him. Now they would run up and down in front of his feet, squeaking, hoping for food. Mathis was particularly fond of one of them, a little larger and bolder than the others. It had a few black and white spots on its gray coat. As a joke, Mathis had called it Jockel, and he sometimes threw it a particularly large crumb. Jockel had just scurried over the laced leather shoe on Mathis's right foot, disappearing into a corner of the dungeon where there was a heap of dirty straw. Mathis knelt down and made a few enticing sounds, but the mouse did not come out.

"Come on, Jockel, where are you? Out you come, stupid."

Mathis cautiously approached the heap of straw and swept it aside with his foot.

"Got you!"

But Jockel wasn't there.

How was that possible? He hadn't trodden the mouse underfoot, had he? Baffled, Mathis leaned down, and that was when he saw the hole in the corner, just where the stone blocks of the wall met the floor. Curious, he put his finger into it . . . and froze.

The block was not very thick, and there was obviously a hollow space beyond it. Paying close attention, Mathis knocked at the area around the hole through which the mouse had slipped. Sure enough, the stone block, which came up to around his waist, was thinner than the others in the walls. He had not found that place before because of the straw and other debris in front of it.

Mathis frowned thoughtfully. What did it mean? He knew that when an enemy stormed a castle, the keep was often the last refuge. The walls there were usually many feet thick, and the entrance to the keep could be reached only by a ladder. But sometimes there were secret passages offering a way of escape. Where the keep of Trifels Castle had once been, there was now the dungeon, the cellar storerooms, and up above those the kitchen and the living quarters. But if the castle was really as old as Agnes always said, it was perfectly possible that there could still be hidden passages.

Passages leading to the outside world.

His heart beat frantically. He looked up the shaft in which the dungeon stood and tried to get his bearings. The block was on the side of his cell facing the castle courtyard. From there it would be only about twenty yards to the other side of the western wall of the castle. Could he really have found a way of escape?

He examined the block more closely. It was solid rock, and apart from the tiny hole in the corner it was just the same as the other massive stones beside it. There were remnants of gray mortar where their edges met. Mathis scratched it, but it was hard as rock too. A tiny, now almost illegible inscription was engraved in one corner.

ALBERTUS FACIEBAT LEONES EXPULSOS ESSE . . .

Mathis frowned. He had consulted some books in Latin in the library of Trifels Castle, and translated the passages that mattered to him, but he did not know much Latin vocabulary. Had a prisoner left his mark here in the past? But never mind what the inscription meant, time was short. He had to find out what was behind the block.

Mathis looked around, desperate to find something that would serve as a tool to scrape away the mortar. Finally he picked up a flat pebble and began working away at the edges of the stone block. It took him some time, but after an hour or more he had removed enough mortar to reveal a crack no wider than a finger. Experimentally, Mathis pushed the block, but nothing happened. He threw his full weight against it, cursing, but it was set in place as firmly as a tree trunk.

After working at it for several more minutes, Mathis had to accept that the block really was set in the ground. He had no idea how deep down it went, and he would have to dig to find out. But what with? He had no knife or spoon. And even if he did, how long would it take him to break the block out of position? Weeks? Months? By that time Philipp von Erfenstein would have handed him over to the mayor of Annweiler or thought of some other fate for him.

Bitterly disappointed, Mathis sat hunched in a corner and buried his dirty face in his hands. His original delight turned to despair. He wouldn't last much longer down here. He had to get out before the darkness, the cramped space, and his isolation drove him crazy. He couldn't wait another month, not even another week. Every single day here was too much.

Once again he tapped the stone block. It seemed to him much thicker and set more firmly in place than before. An insuperable obstacle weighing a ton. How was such a hunk of stone ever to be moved out of position? Unless . . .

Mathis suddenly stopped short in the middle of his train of thought. A slight smile spread over his face. Why, of course there was a way to do it. It was unusual and risky, in fact almost deranged. And it would mean burning all his bridges behind him. But wasn't that what he wanted to do anyway?

Once again Mathis began pacing up and down, but this time driven not by despair. Instead, he was thinking hard.

A plan was forming in his mind.

Walking fast, Agnes climbed the steep path from the valley up to the Trifels. She had been down in Annweiler and had bought a little fresh salt for Hedwig and a small bale of fabric for herself, though not of the best quality. She had been meaning to make Father Tristan a new habit. His old one was so threadbare that he must be cold in it. He would never have thought of a new garment himself. Over the last few days, Agnes had not had much time to think of Mathis. Since she had gone to Hahnenbach with Father Tristan, the old monk had been to visit the sick near the castle four more times. Each time Agnes had gone with him, giving him what help she could. She had splinted the broken arm of an old man who had fallen at work in the fields; she had spooned blueberry juice, as a cure for diarrhea, into a hollow-cheeked girl suffering from hunger and a fever; she had boiled up honey and sage to help with a dry cough. And she had watched Father Tristan administer extreme unction to a wrinkled old woman. Later,

Agnes discovered that the woman had been just forty years old and was the mother of eight children. She had been suckling the youngest at her breast only a few days before she died. In the last three days, Agnes had learned more than in the previous three years.

Above all, she had seen the suffering of the peasants. They lived on rotting turnips and hard bread made from acorn flour and beech-nuts. They worked from sunrise to sunset to cultivate their poor fields and meager kitchen gardens. They bent their backs to dig, while their babies rocked in the wind, hanging wrapped in cloth from trees at the sides of the field, crying their lungs out with hunger.

This life had nothing in common with the stories and pictures that Agnes knew from the castle library. She felt like she had spent all her time until now in a small room full of books, and someone had suddenly opened the window to let real life in.

And real life stank. It was wretched, ugly, and its injustice cried out to heaven. Agnes often wondered how God could allow such things.

Breathing heavily from the steep climb, she looked up after a while and saw Margarethe coming from the opposite direction. The maid walked with a spring in her step, her hair was prettily combed, and she had a glittering ornament around her neck. As she came closer, it proved to be made of cheap polished copper with a few glass stones in it. All the same, Margarethe wore it as if she were a great lady. When they were level with each other, the maid bobbed a curtsy, but Agnes saw that the meeting made her feel uncomfortable.

"All in your Sunday best?" asked Agnes with a smile. "You don't look like you're on your way down to wash clothes in the river."

"I've done all my work, my lady," replied Margarethe uncertainly. "I've been on my feet since sunrise, helping Hedwig in the kitchen. Now she's said I can have the rest of the day off until evening. Unless my lady needs me . . ." She paused, and looked pleadingly at Agnes. But Agnes only waved the idea away.

"You've earned a little free time." Agnes's eyes twinkled as she spoke to her lady's maid. "That is, if you'll tell me who gave you that pretty necklace."

"Oh, that." Margarethe pretended that she had only just noticed it. "It comes from Annweiler." She put her hand to it, and a smile played around her roughened lips. "It's lovely, isn't it? A merchant's journeyman from Speyer gave it to me. He comes to these parts quite often and I think he likes me."

"I expect he's in Annweiler again today?" suggested Agnes.

Margarethe nodded, and Agnes felt a small pang. If her lady's maid had really found a prosperous suitor, she was to be congratulated. All the same, she felt something like jealousy. No doubt Margarethe would marry the man she wanted eventually, but what about Agnes herself? By now she could only hope that the next bridegroom her father presented to her would at least be better than Heidelsheim. She supposed that Mathis would never be more than the man of her dreams.

And after a while, dreams fade away, she thought sadly.

"I wish you well, Margarethe," Agnes said. She pulled herself together. "Now, off you go before your friend from Speyer gives up and goes away."

"Thank you, my lady."

Relieved, Margarethe curtsyed again and hurried downhill. Soon she had disappeared around the next bend in the path.

Agnes turned and walked slowly on, passing the high wall of the castle and the well tower. She couldn't keep her thoughts from dwelling on Mathis, and she felt another pang. Taking Father Tristan's advice, she had not tried to visit him again. Unfortunately, however, the monk had not yet been able to soften her father's heart. Since his first visit to the ducal steward in Neukastell, Philipp von Erfenstein had been there again twice, and each time had come home even more withdrawn and morose than usual. What could have happened? She often saw her father brooding as he paced up and down the Knights' House, and several times he had asked Ulrich Reichhart to go to the armory with him. After that he had looked even gloomier.

What also weighed on Agnes's mind was her latest dream of

Trifels. It took clearer shape in her mind with every passing day. By now she could see every single scene vividly before her: the young man in his hauberk on the battlements, his soundless words, the ring on her finger. She had read the plea from his lips.

Take the ring off! Take the ring off!

Agnes took out the strange signet ring that was still hanging around her neck on its chain. Was it really a danger to her? Were those dreams warnings from the past? Shaking her head, she put the ring back under her bodice. Maybe they were simply the result of the strange few weeks that had just passed. For some reason, Father Tristan had warned her against the ring, and now his warnings tormented her like nightmares.

At the gateway, Agnes nodded to the man-at-arms on guard, Gunther. He muttered something incomprehensible into his beard, but she did not stop. Instead, she hurried up the ramp to the lower bailey, where the aviary, which was as tall as a man, stood in a corner. Parcival beat his wings happily at the sight of her. He was better now, and Agnes had been out into the woods with him again. He was molting too much to go hunting, but since that encounter with Hans von Wertingen and his companions, Agnes had felt less like hunting in any case. She kept thinking a figure might leap out from behind the nearest tree.

"I haven't taken you out much recently, have I, little one?" she said consolingly to Parcival. "I promise we'll soon go for a good long expedition together."

Only now did she notice a strange horse standing at the back of the courtyard by the stables. He was a fiery mount with a freshly combed mane and a well-brushed coat, and at present he had his head in a bucket of oats. The other two men-at-arms, Eberhart and Sebastian, sat on the steps leading to the upper bailey, playing dice. They had an almost empty jug of wine in front of them. When they caught sight of Agnes, they rose to their feet, swaying slightly.

"God be with you, mistress," Sebastian said, slurring his words. "I hope you had a pleasant day."

"Not as pleasant as yours, I suspect." Agnes pointed to the strange horse. "I see we have a visitor."

"Very dis . . . distinguished visitor," Eberhart babbled. "Brought a cask of French wine as a present to the castellan. Three cheers for the count!"

"The count?" Surprised, Agnes looked at the two guards. But as they said no more, she went on to the upper bailey. She quickly looked in at the kitchen with her bag of salt, and put the bale of cloth away before climbing the stairs to the Knights' House, curious to meet the visitor.

When Agnes entered the great hall, she saw her father sitting on a stool in front of the cold hearth. Beside him sat a pale young man dressed in fine fabric. He wore a black cap, a black doublet, and close-fitting silken hose, with a gold chain hung around his neck. In the dim light of the hall, he looked like a messenger from another, richer world. The two men were obviously deep in serious conversation. Two chipped glass goblets, filled with wine, stood on a small table. Agnes knew that her father brought out his precious glasses only when an important guest visited. When Philipp von Erfenstein saw his daughter, he interrupted the conversation.

"I thought you were still down in Annweiler?" he muttered, perhaps displeased, and then pointed to the stranger. "Well, be that as it may, we have a guest. This is young Friedrich von Löwenstein-Scharfeneck. I've told you about his family. Show the count the honor he deserves, please."

Agnes bent her knee. Her father had in fact mentioned the Löwenstein-Scharfenecks now and then—or rather, he had abused them roundly. To the castellan of Trifels Castle, the Scharfenecks were one of those noble families who were more notable for their descent than their deeds. Their castle was only a few miles from Annweiler, and not far from the stronghold of the robber knight Hans von Wertingen. The links between the Scharfenecks and Frederick, the former elector of the Palatinate, had made the family rich and powerful. Their estate was the finest in all the countryside.

"You really are as pretty as I was told," said Friedrich von Löwenstein-Scharfeneck, smiling, as he sipped from his goblet. "Your mother must have been a great beauty."

Agnes looked up and examined the count more closely. He leaned back in the wooden armchair in jovial mood, his legs crossed. His neatly trimmed black beard made him look older than he really was. He was a handsome, well-made man, even if Agnes suspected that he was very much aware of the fact. The young nobleman's entire bearing was that of a man who always got whatever he wanted. A curious aura surrounded him, and at first Agnes didn't know whether it repelled or attracted her.

"Thank you, my lord," she replied. "I'm afraid my mother has been dead for many years, so I can't remember what she looked like."

Laughing, the castellan intervened. "Well, luckily she doesn't take after me," he said, reaching for his goblet. From his heavy voice, Agnes could tell that he had drunk several glasses of wine already.

"Maybe she does, if she likes to get her own way." Scharfeneck winked at his host. "People say all kinds of things about your daughter, Erfenstein. A young woman who can read, likes the stories of the Round Table, and goes hunting with her falcon—in doublet and hose like a man, no less." He laughed quietly and scrutinized Agnes with obvious approval. Today she was wearing a plain linen skirt and a close-fitting bodice. "I for one prefer you in skirts."

"I'm glad to hear it, Excellency," said Agnes coolly, casting a quizzical glance at the count's own fashionable clothes. "But your hose would be too tight for me. I imagine they would be rather a hindrance in a fight between men."

"Agnes!" said her father reprovingly. "Are you out of your mind, speaking to the count like—" But Scharfeneck raised a hand to silence him.

"Let her speak, castellan," he ordered. "I like women with something to say for themselves." His eyes twinkled as he looked at her. "They're said to be particularly passionate in bed. What about you,

Agnes? What lucky man will soon be able to slip between the sheets with you?"

Erfenstein cleared his throat. "I was going to betroth her to my steward, Martin von Heidelsheim," he murmured. "But, unfortunately, he's run off."

"What, leaving such a beauty behind him?" Friedrich von Löwenstein-Scharfeneck raised his eyebrows. "Then either he's a fool, or your daughter is stranger than I thought. How old is she?"

"I am sixteen, Excellency," Agnes said, speaking for herself. "I'll be seventeen this summer."

"Nearly left on the shelf already." The count laughed softly, smiling with that twinkle in his eyes. "Well, for your father's sake I hope he soon finds another husband for you. On the other hand, this means that I'll have a chance to talk to you now and then in the future." He raised his glass. "I hope we shall be good neighbors, dear lady."

"Good . . . good neighbors?" Agnes looked in confusion from the count to her father. "I'm afraid I don't understand."

"Scharfenberg Castle has been transferred to the Löwenstein-Scharfenecks by the duke of Zweibrücken," Erfenstein murmured into his beard. He stared into space. "The young count here plans to put that fine building in order again and move into it in the summer."

"*Move into* Scharfenberg?" Agnes laughed out loud, a strange sound in these bleak surroundings. "Into that ruin? But why, Excellency? You already have a magnificent castle, one of the finest in the whole Wasgau district. So why would—"

"Agnes, how often do I have to tell you to keep your mouth shut unless someone asks you a question?" Erfenstein growled.

Count Scharfeneck gave a thin-lipped smile and looked Agnes up and down with curiosity. "It's a justified question, and shows that your daughter has an astonishingly acute mind, for a woman. You ought to have her at your side more often, Sir Castellan." The smile disappeared, and Agnes thought she saw an expression of cold hatred in Scharfeneck's eyes. "As you very well know, Neuscharfeneck is my beloved father's castle. And as the good man, God willing, has many more years to live, I need a property of my own. Old documents show that Scharfenberg Castle used to belong to us Scharfenecks in the old days. So I am going to restore it to the glory it deserves. I like this part of the country, too, full of history as it is. It conceals, let's say . . ." he smiled mischievously at Agnes, "many interesting secrets. Don't you agree, Agnes? I'm told you have a weakness for such things."

"The duke has decreed that Trifels Castle and Scharfenberg Castle will raise the toll for the Bindersbach Pass together," Philipp von Erfenstein said through narrowed lips. He had obviously reconciled himself to his daughter's presence. "The count has just shown me the edict. His Grace wants us to be good neighbors."

"The toll? Together?" Agnes felt her mouth drop open. "But I thought that the income from the toll . . ."

"Will be shared," said Scharfeneck, getting his word in first. "But as we are raising the toll, your good father will not lose much by it. I have just been discussing the matter with him." He leaned forward, smiling. "Furthermore, I am going halfway to meet the castellan of Trifels in another respect."

"What is it?" asked Agnes, skeptically.

"I don't think that is anything to do with my impertinent daughter," Erfenstein said, staring into his glass.

The count dismissed this objection. "Ah, well, she's going to hear about it sooner or later anyway." He turned to Agnes. "I am making the services of my landsknechts available to your father in order to drive that bastard Wertingen out for good. If we storm his castle together, we'll both gain by it. Wertingen still has several villages as his fief, and they will then come into our possession. Not to mention the loot we take. So it's a fair bargain. We are waiting only for the duke's permission, but that is a mere formality."

Agnes looked in silence at the two dissimilar men—the well-dressed young count, and her wheezing old father with his eye patch. He poured himself another glass of wine. She guessed that the bargain would take her family closer to ruin.

"It has been a real pleasure to make the acquaintance of you both." Friedrich von Löwenstein-Scharfeneck rose, and made Agnes a slight bow. "I am sure we'll have many more delightful meetings." His eyes wandered over her tight bodice. "But you'd better leave the doublet and hose to us men. It would be a shame if no one could see your pretty ankles."

The castellan rose as well, swaying slightly, but Scharfeneck waved away his offer to show him out. "I can find my way by myself, Erfenstein. These rooms are not so full of elegant furnishings as to confuse me." He smiled again, then turned and disappeared toward the staircase. Soon shouting and finally the clatter of a horse's hooves could be heard outside.

"That . . . that puffed-up popinjay!" Erfenstein roared when he could be sure that the young count was out of earshot. "Who does he think he is? Under Emperor Maximilian—"

"Yes, yes, I know, no such thing would have happened," Agnes interrupted him, with a weary smile. "But, sad to say, your old friend Emperor Maximilian is dead. So like it or not, you'll have to go along with that conceited fellow."

Erfenstein sighed. "I know that." He slapped his broad thigh. "Damn it, I knew at once that he had a plan of some kind at Neukastell, when he suggested letting me use his landsknechts. Now he'll make double the money. From the pass and from storming Wertingen's castle. And we still don't know how to pay next year's rents."

Agnes nodded. Now she, too, realized why her father had been looking so grim these last few weeks.

"How can you be so sure that the two of you will defeat Hans von Wertingen?" she asked. "He's a dangerous man. I know that from my own experience."

"Damn it all, Agnes, I *must* defeat him. Don't you understand?" Erfenstein jumped up, his hand sweeping one of the two glass goblets to the floor, where it broke with a crash. "And I know that it will hardly be possible even with Scharfeneck's landsknechts, if the dog creeps into Ramburg Castle. It's an impregnable stone fortress. But there's no going back now. If I don't defeat Wertingen, I can't pay the duke, and he will take Trifels away from me." His eyes were clouded, and he was shaking slightly. "Do you see? And then I myself would soon be a dishonored knight," he murmured. "A murderous rogue, earning a crust of bread from highway robbery, or else going to the dogs."

The castellan of Trifels dropped back onto his stool and reached for the other and still intact glass goblet.

"Leave me alone now," he said quietly. "I want to be alone, for God's sake."

At first Agnes was going to say something, but she refrained. She looked at her father for a while longer as his glazed eyes stared at the cold ashes on the hearth. Finally she could bear it no longer.

"I love you, Father," she whispered, "no matter what happens."

With those words she turned and ran down the staircase to get away from that cold, dark place. In the upper bailey, she almost collided with Ulrich Reichhart.

"I was looking for you, Agnes," said the master gunner. He leaned closer to her with a conspiratorial air, and she could smell the brandy on his breath. "Mathis wants to see you," he whispered. "I'll let you down to him. Only for God's sake don't let your father know."

Agnes smiled despairingly. "Believe me, Ulrich, he has other things on his mind at this moment."

Her mood swung between gloom and sudden joy. Mathis wanted to see her. Had he forgiven her? Or maybe he was sick? Quivering with anticipation, she went down to the keep with Ulrich.

They let Agnes down into the dungeon with the rope. Although it was midday, only a little light fell through the window slits, so it was some time before she could finally make out Mathis in a corner of his cell, wrapped in a blanket that the sympathetic Ulrich had probably thrown down to him. Agnes was shocked when she saw him. Imprisonment had changed the smith's previously strong son. Lack of food, grief, and rage had made him visibly thinner. His dirty face was emaciated, his shoulder blades stood out, angular under his pale skin. Apart from his hose, encrusted with dirt, he wore only a ragged shirt. He looked small and bowed. But his eyes burned like fire.

"Agnes!" he cried, as she slowly hovered down to him on the rope. He sounded more surprised than pleased.

When her feet touched the dirty stone floor, Agnes stumbled slightly and then stood upright in front of him. The rope disappeared into the darkness above them again. Neither of them spoke for some time, but finally Agnes took his hands and held them firmly.

"Mathis," she whispered. "I . . . I'm so sorry."

Mathis let go of her hands. There was an angry glint in his eyes. "Your father obviously isn't," he replied icily. "He's probably going to leave me here forever and a day—if I haven't starved or frozen to death before then."

"Mathis, I can't help it if my father—"

"Mathis, I can't help it . . ." he imitated her in a high-pitched voice. Angrily, he kicked a heap of straw aside, and several mice ran away, squeaking. "Damn it, why did I listen to you? Why didn't I run straight into the forest? Why did I trust you?"

Agnes swallowed painfully. Mathis had never spoken to her like that before. "I asked Father Tristan to speak to my father," she said quietly. "I'm sure he won't leave you here forever. We'll find a solution."

Mathis turned away with a contemptuous snort. He went back to his corner and let himself slide down with his back to the rough stone wall. He stayed there, sitting cross-legged, with his arms folded.

For a while there was silence. Finally Agnes spoke. "Did you get my picture?" she asked in a faltering voice.

Mathis nodded. "It . . . it's beautiful," he murmured. Suddenly he grinned. "Even if you've made my ears rather large."

"But you do have large ears."

"So do you. Only you have longer hair to cover them up."

Agnes couldn't help smiling. At least Mathis hadn't lost his quarrelsome nature or his sense of humor in the dungeon.

"We'll find a solution," she repeated it as if it were a mantra. "You wait and see—you'll be out of here by Ascension Day at the latest."

Mathis laughed dryly. "Do you really think I'll let myself be cooped up as long as that? My father is mortally sick, the peasants are starving under Mayor Gessler's tyranny, and I'm rotting away here. No, I must get out, and you'll help me."

"What are you planning to do?" Agnes didn't like the look of Mathis at all; she would have taken him for a man possessed.

Suddenly he stood up and went over to her. "I've found a secret escape route," he whispered almost inaudibly. "But I'll need your help to get away."

In an undertone, he told Agnes about the stone block that had been mortared into place, and his plan.

Agnes flinched as though a stone had hit her. "You're going to *blow up* the wall?" she cried, louder than she had intended.

"*Sh!*" Mathis glanced up for a moment, but there was no one to be seen at the square opening.

"It's not as violent as it may sound," he went on quietly. "I only need a little gunpowder; a couple of ounces should be enough. I'll build myself a small barrier from the rubble and stones down here so that I can take shelter behind it. By the time the guards up there have slept off their hangover, I'll be over the hills and far away."

"But Mathis." Agnes shook her head, unable to grasp the plan. "That's lunacy! Even if you manage to blow the block out of the wall, you have no idea where the passage leads. Perhaps there isn't a passage there at all. It could have fallen in, or maybe there's only a hollow space on the other side of the wall." She seized his hands. "Think what my father will do to you if you try running away from here and he catches you. Can you imagine that?"

"Can *you* imagine what will happen if I have to spend even a few days longer here?" hissed Mathis. "Can you even begin to think what it's like to have rats scurrying over your face at night, being eaten alive by fleas, stifled by your own stink? Can you think what it's like to stare at nothing but a wall for weeks on end? No, you can't—after all, you're a castellan's daughter."

He tore himself away and began pacing, gesticulating wildly. "I'm already hearing voices at night. I have confused dreams about Richard the Lionheart, who may once have been locked up here. Don't you understand, Agnes? If I don't get out soon, your father will find only an idiot babbling to himself in this dungeon."

"Maybe the king of England really did escape along a passage, and they walled it up later," Agnes said distractedly. Suddenly a shadow seemed to fall on her mind, and she had to prop herself against the wall to keep on her feet.

"What's the matter?" asked Mathis, taken aback.

"It's nothing." Agnes shook herself like a wet dog, and the feeling went away as quickly as it had come over her. All the same, she felt strangely faint, just like she had awoken from a feverish nightmare.

"I was wondering only now whether Richard the Lionheart really did escape from this dungeon," she went on at last. "They say his faithful minstrel, Blondel, went from castle to castle, singing Richard's favorite song, until at last Richard replied to him from his dungeon in Trifels Castle. Maybe Blondel and his companions really did dig a tunnel so that King Richard could escape through it."

Mathis came over to her. "Yes, that's what I'm saying. There's a way out. Agnes, please. You must help me." begged Mathis. "Bring me the gunpowder. It's under a slab in the pigpens beside our house. I knew I might yet need it." He looked pleadingly at her. "If you really like me as much as you always say you do, then bring it to me."

Agnes bit her lip. "There must be some other way," she said. "If I bring you the gunpowder then that's the end of it. One way or another."

"Agnes, trust me. I know how to handle that stuff." Mathis clenched his fists. "Damn it all!" he cried. "If only your father would have let me show what I can do, I wouldn't have stolen the accursed arquebus, and none of this would have happened."

Agnes suddenly froze. An idea came into her head, rooted itself there, and slowly took shape.

If only your father would have let me show what I can do . . .

She seized Mathis by his arms. "Give me until this evening to find another solution, Mathis," she whispered. "If I haven't succeeded by then, I'll get you your gunpowder. I promise."

Mathis looked at her suspiciously. "What are you planning?"

"Just leave it to me. You'll get your damn gunpowder. But let me try it my way first. Please."

For a while there was only the soft scurrying and squeaking of the mice. Mathis seemed to be wrestling with himself. "All right," he said at last. "I don't have a choice, anyway." Suddenly he hugged her, holding her so close that she could feel his heartbeat. "I do trust you, Agnes," he whispered. "I trust you because . . . because I . . ."

Agnes held her breath. "Because you what?"

He shook his head and pushed her away from him as suddenly as if he had been burned. "Forget it. Such things happen only in your stories, Agnes. Real life is different. Hey there, Ulrich!" Those last words were for the old master gunner up in the storeroom in the cellars. "We've finished. Take the lady back to her father." He turned away and crouched in a corner, where the darkness swallowed up his figure.

Soon the rope was hauling Agnes back up into the daylight. Her heart pounded, and not only because of the last words Mathis had spoken. For the first time in a long while, she felt a little hope again.

But first she must have important conversations with a few people.

"You want me to do *what?*"

The axe fell from the castellan's hand, and he stared at his daughter with his one eye open wide.

"Appoint Mathis assistant gunner," Agnes calmly repeated. "If you want to get Wertingen out of his castle, you'll need firearms. Otherwise it won't work, you said so yourself. And Ulrich isn't going to be very much use."

Agnes had thought hard about the best time to take her father by surprise with her idea. Several hours had passed since the count's visit, and she had used them to make preparations. Philipp von Erfenstein seemed reasonably sober again, having done some work up by the well tower. The castellan had carried several new lengths of wood over from the courtyard himself, and had sent the men-at-arms, Gunther, Sebastian, and Eberhart, into the forest for more timber. So Agnes could be sure of speaking to her father alone for a while. However, when she saw his angry face now, she feared that she hadn't thought her idea over well enough.

"You want me to make a boy who's only just getting a beard my gunner?" Philipp von Erfenstein asked, bending to pick the axe up again. "A sly fox who stole one of my arquebuses, and who's wanted as an insurgent by the mayor of Annweiler? Are you out of your mind?"

"Father, Mathis has been in that dungeon long enough. Is he to rot away down there?"

"It's all the same to me." Stoically, Philipp von Erfenstein chopped a length of timber to size with his axe. Finger-length splinters of wood flew in all directions.

Angrily, Agnes watched her father at work for a while. She finally decided to stake everything on a single card. "You said you were going to think what to do with Mathis." The words burst out of her. "But you haven't done anything. Anything at all except to brood over your worries and get drunk. So do something now, Father. Hand Mathis over to Gessler, banish him, even chop his hand off—anything, just don't leave him wasting away in the keep." She took a deep breath before she went on. "But I'll tell you one thing: you're making a great mistake. Mathis is the only person here who really understands anything about firearms. He can cast the guns you need for a siege, and he knows how to fire them, too. If you want to lose Trifels Castle, hand Mathis over to the mayor of Annweiler. But if you want to defeat Wertingen, let Mathis do what he can do best, forging firearms."

Agnes had never spoken to her father in such a tone before. The old knight stood motionless for some time, his mouth open like the mouth of a stranded fish, the axe in his limp hand. All at once he raised the heavy tool, and Agnes feared that he might strike her down. But he simply brought it down on the handrail of the bridge, where it stuck fast.

Suddenly Philipp von Erfenstein began laughing heartily. His powerful chest rose and fell, tears of laughter ran down his cheeks.

"Damn it all!" he finally gasped. "My own daughter reading me a lecture. Just as my Katharina used to, God rest her soul. You women-folk use tongues the way we men use our swords." He wiped the tears from his face. "Only a woman could suggest something like that." All at once he was serious again. "Even if I set Mathis free and let him cast the guns, where will I get the bronze for them, eh?" Erfenstein pointed to the ramshackle well tower, where one of the merlons was missing. "Have you forgotten that we don't even have the money to carry out emergency repairs on this castle? It's falling apart under us."

"Melt the old weapons down," replied Agnes coolly.

"What?" Her father looked at her, taken aback.

"Melt down the weapons in the armory," she repeated. "I was discussing it with Ulrich just now. They're old and rusty, good for nothing anymore. Melt them down and let Mathis forge new firearms. They cast a new bell over in Eusserthal monastery only last year. They still have furnaces for both melting and casting metal there. Father Tristan will ask the abbot to let us use them."

Agnes sounded as matter-of-fact as she could. She had worked it all out in advance, taking both Ulrich and Father Tristan into her confidence. But she knew that her father could be as stubborn as an ox, particularly when he thought he was being driven into a corner.

"Oho, so that's it." The castellan crossed his muscular arms over his chest. "So you've talked it over with everyone except your own father. Who else knows about your crazy plan? Come on, tell me. Who else?"

Agnes sighed. "No one else, Father. But Ulrich also thinks that Mathis—"

"I couldn't care less what that drunken sot thinks," Erfenstein snapped. "I hate those stinking guns, anyway. Shooting a brave man from a hundred paces away—what kind of a chivalrous fight is that? In the old days, these things were settled with swords, man to man."

He fell silent for a moment, and then nodded his head thoughtfully. "But you're right. Much as I abhor them—without something like that to breach the walls we'll never take Wertingen's castle. What can we summon up on the Trifels?" Sighing, Erfenstein counted on his fingers. "A few dozen hackbuts, maybe, three rusty falconets, and a handful of mortars dating from your great-grandfather's time." He laughed bitterly. "Most of them are good as pots and pans for Hedwig's kitchen at the best, but they're probably too full of holes even for that."

Smiling, Agnes took a step toward her father; she felt that the ice was slowly breaking. "There, you see," she said gently. "Let Mathis melt down the whole lot. I promise he'll forge you something to breach castle walls instead, a gun such as we've never seen here. And we'll break into Wertingen's castle with it. Mathis has assured me that it's possible."

The old knight frowned. "How would he know? He's never made one. Yes, maybe he can mix gunpowder. But casting cannon like that is another trade. Particularly if it's to be a really good one. You need years of training for that."

"He's read all about it, Father."

Philipp von Erfenstein looked at her suspiciously. "Read about it? The lad can read?"

"I taught him. There are several books about firearms in the library here. He knows them all. And he kept thinking of new techniques and drawing guns in secret." Agnes reached for her father's hand as he stood there on the bridge, still undecided. "At least let him try," she begged. "If he fails, you can always send him back to the dungeon or hand him over to the mayor of Annweiler. What do you have to lose?"

Erfenstein's mind was visibly working. His glance went out over the countryside, over to the hills beyond which Wertingen's castle stood. He tugged thoughtfully at his eye patch.

"Very well," he growled at last. "I'll give the boy a chance. If he can make a gun big enough for Ulrich to use in the fight, he can go free as far as I'm concerned. But on one condition." He looked sternly at his daughter.

"Anything, Father, anything," Agnes sighed in relief.

"If I catch you just once in the hay or anywhere else with that lad, if my men tell me the least little thing about you two turtle doves, I'll send Mathis back to his cell and let him rot there. Is that clear?"

"But Father—"

"Quiet!" he interrupted her brusquely. "Do you think I can't see what's going on? I can see the two of you flirting. There must be an end to that. Mathis isn't fit for you. Even if that fool Heidelsheim has made off, God alone knows why, keep away from Mathis, understand?"

Agnes flinched as if at the touch of a whip.

"Very well," she finally murmured. "I'd do anything to get him out of there."

"Right." Her father walked over the swaying bridge, smiling, and toward the upper bailey. "Then let's get the little bird out of his cage before he breaks his wings."

Down in the valley, the old midwife Elsbeth Rechsteiner lay behind a bramble bush in the Annweiler woods, trying as hard as she could not to breathe too loud.

Not ten yards away, a man dismounted from his horse in the light of the setting sun. Behind him, half hidden in the shadow cast by the midwife's little house, two more men, wild-looking characters, sat waiting on their own mounts.

As the stranger slowly turned and looked in her direction, Elsbeth put her hand over her mouth to keep herself from screaming. The man was clad in expensive black fabric and wore a black cap, but the skin of his face under the cap was almost as black, and so was his throat, as were his hands with their long, fine fingers. Elsbeth had never seen such a man before. There were tales of dark-skinned people who lived far in the south, where there were also cannibals and two-headed lions. So the black man must come from very far away. He and his companions had certainly not come to pay her a harmless visit, or to buy some kind of herbal remedy for a cough or cold. The midwife shivered. What she had feared for so many years, what the Brotherhood had warned her against only two weeks ago, had actually happened.

The enemies had come back.

Elsbeth had been in her little garden in front of the house when she heard the hoof-beats and whinnying of horses. Her hut might be in the middle of the forest, and it was protected by a dense thicket of hawthorn and bramble bushes, but the road to Waldrohrbach was not far away, and there was a trodden footpath from the road to her house. Her visitors were usually simple folk—tanners, linen weavers, or peasants who couldn't afford the expensive medicines sold by the apothecary in Annweiler. Certainly none of her patients had such a magnificent horse, and so a healthy distrust had made Elsbeth duck down behind the bushes.

That and a certain presentiment.

From the ground, the midwife stared at the stranger in the black cap. The other two horsemen had dismounted now and were letting their horses graze on the tiny cabbage leaves in Elsbeth's small kitchen garden. A curved sword dangled from the dark-skinned man's saddle, and the fluid movements with which he approached her hut betrayed a military training. For the last time, his eyes passed over the garden, and then he knocked on the crooked door of the little house.

"Hello. Is anybody there?" His loud voice, accustomed to giving orders, had a curious accent.

When no one opened the door, the man finally kicked it, cursing.

The two rotten halves of it swung open with a *creak*, and the stranger entered the low-ceilinged cottage. The other two men followed him. Elsbeth couldn't see what was going on inside, but she heard them walking around. Dishes and plates clattered, then her bed and her chest were pushed aside. The men were looking for something, and Elsbeth could already guess what it was. Someone must have told them where the ring could be found. But who? Only the members of the Brotherhood knew that she was the guardian of the ring. So was there a traitor among them? Or had the men already tortured the others and made them tell the secret? Elsbeth Rechsteiner made the sign of the cross and said a silent prayer of thanks that the ring was no longer in her keeping.

Dear Lord in Heaven, you have assuredly led me all this long way. Do not leave me now.

After a while, the men came out of the little house again. Elsbeth hoped they would mount their horses and ride away, but then the dark-skinned leader suddenly turned his head and looked up at the roof of the cottage. The midwife groaned quietly.

White smoke was curling out of the small, brick-built chimney.

No sensible person left a fire unattended for long, as Elsbeth knew, and so did the stranger. It must have been clear to him, at that moment, that she couldn't be far away. Once again his gaze wandered over her recently sown garden with its trellises and beds, and finally he walked right across the raked black soil. He carelessly trod down the little seedlings and plants, until he was right beside the thicket of thorns. The man was now so close that Elsbeth could hear him breathing.

"*Onde está a velha bruxa?*" he hissed quietly through his teeth.

The midwife pressed herself far down into the moss, as if to merge with the forest, which was now lying in darkness. Not far away, she heard a couple of branches crack, and then the footsteps went away. When she dared to look up at last, she saw the man going back toward the hut. With a broken branch, he carefully brushed away the marks of his footsteps on the garden beds, and then he quietly said something to his two companions. Finally they all three led their horses back into the woods.

For some time, there was no sound but the twittering of the birds.

Elsbeth was about to heave a sigh of relief when the dark-skinned stranger suddenly came back without his horse. Once again he entered the hut, but this time he carefully closed the door behind him. Elsbeth felt a cold shudder run down her back.

He's waiting for me to come back. And the other two are lurking in the forest.

Elsbeth waited for what seemed a small eternity, and then slowly straightened up. Her joints ached from lying in the moss so long, her back throbbed, but she made no sound. Like a deer scenting the air, she stood perfectly still for a moment behind the bushes. Then she cautiously turned and went on into the forest, step by step, doing all she could not to tread on a dry branch or twig. After endless minutes, she had finally reached the almost invisible trodden footpath that led, by a long way around, to the road. Only now was she far enough from her hut to venture to run. Gasping for breath, she hurried along the narrow path. She must get away from the black man waiting in her hut for her return, waiting to kill her. She must get away from his companions lying in ambush in the forest. Bending low, with her heart beating wildly, the old woman hobbled past green ferns and birch trees putting out new leaves, until at last she reached the open road.

A cart belonging to a peasant from Annweiler, drawn by two oxen, was coming toward her. She hailed it, and the kindly driver took her up and drove her toward Waldrohrbach, where a niece of hers lived. She would have to go into hiding there for the next few weeks, maybe even months. And she must warn the circle of initiates as soon as possible! There were important decisions for them all to make. The midwife knew one thing for certain: the men who had traveled so far to come here to the Wasgau were not going to give up in a hurry.

Once again, Elsbeth's eyes went back to the apparently tranquil part of the forest where death still lay in wait for her.

It felt like his breath had touched her already.

· 6 ·

Eusserthal Monastery, April, Anno Domini 1524

O N   T H E   F I R S T   M O R N I N G   A F T E R he was set free, Mathis inspected the armory in the Knights' House with Ulrich Reichhart. It
was better stocked than he had expected. The room contained more
than a dozen arquebuses, stored in chests and troughs or wrapped in
oily cloth; seven double hackbuts; and twenty small, old-fashioned
handguns. With its three falconets, Trifels Castle also had several
larger guns suitable for storming an enemy castle. There were two
casks of gunpowder, a number of heavy stone cannonballs weighing
two pounds each, and four bronze mortars, but three of them had so
many holes that Mathis immediately decided to melt them down.

Meanwhile, Father Tristan was as good as his word, and he spoke
to Abbot Weigand on behalf of Mathis. As a result, Mathis was able
to use the two furnaces that stood not far from Eusserthal monastery,
on the bank of a stream diverted from its original course. He, Ulrich,
Gunther, and the other men-at-arms from Trifels carried out some
improvements, brought along new bricks, and built a workshop for
the rest of what had to be done in a shed near the monastery wall.
Finally they began modeling a core for the mold from mud, linen,
and hemp.

Now and then Erfenstein came over to Eusserthal from the castle and examined the progress of the work in silence. "All I see is dirt," he growled. "How that's ever to become a bronze gun is a mystery to me."

"It's basically the same as casting a bell," Mathis tried to explain. Producing some crumpled sheets of parchment, he pointed to a few hastily executed sketches. "You cover the core with a layer of clay—it's called the false bell—and then with a second layer on top of the first. You fire the whole thing in the furnace, then you carefully remove the outer layer and break the false bell." Mathis carefully put the sheets of parchment away again, and wiped the dirt from his forehead. "Then, when you put the core and the outer layer together again, you have a hollow space between them; that's the mold, and you fill it with molten bronze. I helped the master bell-founder last year, and so did some of the monks. So with God's help it ought to work."

"Like a bell, eh?" The castellan grinned. "Don't let the priest in Annweiler hear you say that. One is Christian work, the other's the work of the devil."

Mathis waved that away. "I'm having no more to do with priests and monks anyway, never mind how long that man Luther preaches against the pope."

In three weeks' time, the mold for the gun was ready at last. Now it was time to cast the barrel.

With that in mind, Mathis had divided all the weapons in the armory into those that could still be used and those that could not. Old and damaged rifles and mortars went into the smelting furnace, along with several pounds of bronze and tin that Mathis had gained by melting down beakers, goblets, and broken or useless old tools. Ulrich and the other men-at-arms searched every nook and cranny of the castle for material to use. Even some of Hedwig's old pots and pans had to be sacrificed, and so did the cracked bell in the castle chapel. Finally they had enough metal to be melted down.

"Damn it all, letting you out of that cell was the best decision the castellan ever made," Ulrich Reichhart said. He stood on a ladder propped against the six-foot-high furnace in the shed, and tossed another tin beaker into the smoking opening. The monastery church, built of red sandstone and richly ornamented, was only a stone's throw away, but Mathis, Ulrich, and the other men-at-arms were living in their own little world, full of smoke and poisonous vapors.

"We'll show that bastard Wertingen," swore Ulrich Reichhart, deep in thought as he looked at the bubbling, red-hot mass beneath him. The old master gunner had stopped drinking quite so heavily since they began work on the gun. It was as if he had been infected by Mathis's own enthusiasm for the mighty weapon.

"We'll shoot his castle from under his fat ass," he cheerfully went on. "You wait and see, we won't even need the landsknechts of that young count." He laughed, and even Mathis couldn't restrain a grin. But his smile faded suddenly when he thought of his father's reproachful face. *Why can't he understand that times have changed?* thought Mathis. *Why must he be so angry with me all the time?*

The bronze melted down for half a day, until at last it was as red and fluid as lava. Finally Mathis opened the taphole and poured the steaming mass through clay pipes into the mold prepared and set in a pit underneath it. After the casting had spent two days cooling, the crucial moment came when the outer casing was struck away. A huge gun barrel six feet long was revealed, with a muzzle as large as a child's head. It was solid, without any cracks, and cast in a single piece.

Mathis had made his journeyman's masterpiece.

He smiled happily: the gun looked exactly as he had always imagined it in his dreams. Mighty and massive—a deadly weapon in the hands of a man who knew how to use it. And by God, he was going to show everyone—including his pig-headed father—that he did know how.

Mathis was kneeling in front of the muzzle a day or so later, filing away the last uneven places from the gun barrel, when he suddenly noticed that someone was looking over his shoulder. He turned around and saw Agnes standing behind him, looking down with a teasing smile. Had she walked all the way to the monastery, a journey of several hours, just to pay him a surprise visit?

"Anyone might think you had nothing in your head but that gun barrel these days," she teased. "If things go on like this, you'll be taking it to bed with you at night."

Mathis shrugged apologetically. It was true that over the last couple of weeks he had devoted far more thought to the gun than to Agnes. On the other hand, it had been her idea to get him out of prison to act as her father's new gunner.

"The tough part of the work's behind us now," he said, straightening up. His face and hands were blackened from heavy labor. "It's mainly a matter of filing and polishing now. And of course we have to build a gun carriage. That's why Ulrich and the others have just gone off to where the charcoal burners work, looking around for suitable tree trunks."

"Gun carriage?" Agnes looked at him, her expression blank.

Mathis proudly paced the full length of the bronze gun barrel. "Well, it used to be very hard work moving the heavy cannon, let alone aiming them properly," he began, with the enthusiasm of a small boy describing a toy. "The recoil was very strong, and it was still difficult to hit the target. So gunners went over to mounting their gun barrels on movable frames, the gun carriages. They make it possible to move the gun around by turning a crank and taking aim."

"I see." Agnes did not sound particularly interested. She sat on the gun barrel, legs apart, and looked at Mathis thoughtfully.

"I've been back to the library a couple of times myself recently," she said at last. "I thought I could find out more about my dreams in Father Tristan's book. But the book . . ." She hesitated.

Mathis nodded absent-mindedly and pushed his sandy hair back from his dirty face. Agnes had told him, more than once, about her recurring dreams of Trifels Castle as it had been in the distant past. Agnes had also told him how Father Tristan had shown her a book with a picture of the young man in it.

"What about it?" Mathis finally asked.

Agnes shrugged her shoulders. "Well, it's gone. I've looked for it everywhere. I almost think that, for some reason, Father Tristan may have hidden it from me on purpose." She angrily struck the bronze gun barrel with her hand, making it boom softly. "And I want to ask him about it, but whenever I mention the book or the ring, he avoids answering me properly."

"He probably wants you to think more about the present and less about the past." Mathis smiled. "I've heard that many of the peasants think very highly of you these days. They say you're a great help to Father Tristan when he goes visiting the sick."

"Maybe. But death is often stronger than anything we can do." Agnes shook her head sadly. "Yesterday we had to close the eyes of a little girl who was only four. She'd been worn away by fever and the flux until nothing was left of her but an empty husk. Sometimes I don't understand why God sends us into the world if he's going to make us suffer so much." She looked at Mathis with concern. "How is your father now? It's a long time since I've seen him."

"He's a tough man," replied Mathis . "But I think the smoke from the forge has eaten his lungs away. He's getting weaker daily. Although he still feels strong enough to tell me off."

Agnes moved closer to him along the bronze gun barrel. "You mustn't hold it against him," she said gently. "You took advantage of his trust in you, and it will take him a while to get that back." She leaned down to him and touched his cheek. "Mathis . . . about the two of us . . ." she hesitantly began. "Sometimes I think . . ." But Mathis turned away.

"You know what your father said," he muttered awkwardly. "He doesn't want to see us together, or I'll have to go back to the dungeon."

Agnes rolled her eyes. "I suppose we can talk, all the same. Anyway, my father is a long way off, over at Trifels. So what are you afraid of?"

Without looking at her, Mathis picked up his file and set to work on the muzzle of the gun. "All I know is that I have to finish smoothing any roughness away from this gun, so that when we start working on the gun carriage tomorrow—"

"Oh, do stop talking about that gun carriage," she snapped. "This is about us, Mathis. If we . . ." But Agnes stopped when, out of the corner of her eye, she saw Ulrich Reichhart waving in agitation as he ran down the winding path that crossed the fields. Gasping for breath, the master gunner came to a halt in front of them.

"My God, what's happened?" Mathis asked. "Did someone have an accident? Are Gunther and the others all right?"

Reichhart nodded his head. It was some time before he had enough breath to speak again. "They . . . they've found a dead body over where the charcoal burners work," he finally managed to say. "It's horribly disfigured now, but by God, I swear it's the steward Martin von Heidelsheim."

Thick black smoke filled the air above the place where the body had been found, so that it was difficult for Mathis to make out anything at first.

A few weeks ago, Ulrich Reichhart and the other men-at-arms had built up two charcoal kilns in a small spruce wood close to Trifels Castle. One of them was still smoking heavily. In digging the site to build a third kiln, they had come upon the decomposing corpse.

Mathis knelt down on the edge of the pit they had been digging and rubbed his eyes, which were reddened by the smoke. What lay down there had obviously been a human being once, but no one could say at first glance whether it was Martin von Heidelsheim. Buried in the ground, the corpse had been safe from wild animals, but all the same decomposition had made its mark. Only the clothes were still reasonably well preserved; the dead man was wearing close-fitting hose, a now ragged shirt, and a simple doublet smeared with dried blood. Retching, Agnes put a hand to her mouth. She had to turn away. But finally, standing a little way from the pit, she nodded to Mathis.

"That . . . yes, that's Heidelsheim," she said faintly. "No doubt of it. That's the doublet he had on the day I last saw him in the castle stables."

The other men were standing at the side of the pit in silence, their arms folded, staring down at the human remains.

Finally, Mathis and Ulrich Reichhart climbed down into the pit. Holding their breath, they lifted the body onto an improvised stretcher made of saplings and fir twigs and brought it up to ground level, where they put it down some way from the smoking charcoal kiln.

By now Agnes had overcome her urge to vomit. She chewed a piece of resin to drown out the sweetish smell of decay and knelt down beside the dead body of Heidelsheim. Her eyes passed over the doublet, now encrusted with blood and smeared with earth.

"That's a crossbow bolt," she said at last, pointing to a feathered shaft that stuck out of the ragged garment. "And look, there's another."

"That bastard Wertingen." Ulrich Reichhart spat on the woodland floor. "I expect he lay in wait for him here in the wood and simply shot him down."

"And then buried him as carefully as a dog burying its bone?" Mathis shook his head. "Why would Hans von Wertingen go to all that trouble? It would have been more like him to leave Heidelsheim's body at the castle gate. What's more . . ." He stood up, and pointed to the feathers on the shaft. "Those are eagle feathers, and the arrow is well made. I don't think Wertingen or any of the other bandits hereabouts has bolts as good as that."

"True," Gunther said. "Only great gentlemen have such expensive bolts. They take them when they go out hunting deer." He turned to Agnes. "I think your father has arrows just like those."

"And there's another odd thing," Mathis added. "The bolt went right into his flesh up to the feathers. Which means the archer must have been very close to his victim."

"You think Heidelsheim knew his murderer?" Agnes asked.

Mathis shrugged. "Possibly. Or else the assassin hid his weapon and brought it out only at the last moment." He cast a pitying glance at the remains of the steward. "One way or another, the man deserves decent burial. Let's take him up to the castle chapel."

The men nodded, and they carried the stretcher up the narrow path to the castle, only half an hour's walk away. Meanwhile Agnes and Mathis went a little way off on their own. Agnes looked troubled and seemed to be leaving something unsaid.

"What's the matter?" asked Mathis, confused. "I can see that there's something on your mind."

Agnes stopped and waited until the other men had disappeared beyond a group of beech trees. "Mathis," she began, hesitantly. "Listen, did you by any chance . . . I have to know . . ."

"Know what?"

She pulled herself together before going on. "When I told you that Heidelsheim wanted to marry me, and my father had agreed, you . . . you were so angry, you raged and shouted. Tell me honestly: was it . . . do you have Heidelsheim on your conscience? Did you kill him?"

For a moment, Mathis's mouth dropped open in sheer surprise. "Did I . . . ? How . . . how on earth can you think such a thing?"

"Well, you knew that he was going to tell my father about the stolen arquebus. You could have taken one of the crossbows from the castle and—"

"Agnes, for goodness' sake, think!" Mathis took her firmly by the shoulders. "After you told me about Heidelsheim, your father put me in the dungeon. So how could I have killed him?" His face suddenly darkened. "If you're going to express suspicions, then why not think of your father himself?"

"My father?"

Mathis defiantly crossed his arms. "Well, after all, your father has exactly the same crossbow bolts. Suppose Heidelsheim turned you down because he didn't want to marry you anymore, and that infuriated your father?"

Agnes narrowed her eyes to slits. "And why would Heidelsheim have wanted to turn *me* down?"

"Maybe he decided you were a little stranger than he'd thought at first. People talk about you. And since Parcival brought you that ring, you've behaved even more strangely."

"How can you . . . ?" Agnes flinched and raised her hand to hit him, but then lowered it again. "You . . . you're . . ." she stammered. Tears of anger ran down her face. "And I always thought you were fond of me."

Without another word, she turned and ran into the forest.

"Agnes!" Mathis called after her. "I'm sorry. I didn't mean it like that!"

But Agnes did not come back. For a little while he could still hear her footsteps, and then the trees swallowed them up.

Cursing, Mathis kicked a rock standing on its own among the trees. Why did women always have to be so complicated? That girl could always make him furious, yet all the same he couldn't get her out of his mind.

Finally, brooding gloomily, he went after the other men, who had disappeared around a bend in the path.

A pair of watchful eyes followed him for some time. When Mathis's footsteps had died away, a figure stepped out of the shade of the bushes and disappeared into the forest without a sound. Thoughtfully, head concealed by a scarf, the eavesdropper hurried down into the valley, murmuring almost inaudibly and making the sign of the cross.

The watcher in the bushes had wanted to find something out, and he had done so.

They buried Martin von Heidelsheim the next morning, in the castle graveyard, not far from the well tower. The tombstones there stood askew, most of them so covered with moss and ivy that little of the inscriptions chiseled into them could still be read. A number of castellans and their families lay buried here. The slabs on their graves showed stone knights with mighty swords and long-forgotten coats of arms. Farther away were the graves of the simpler folk, including stewards and clerks, as well as captains of the guard, chaplains, and even a smith.

Behind and a little way from the few other mourners, Agnes saw Mathis, who had come to the funeral with his mother and his little sister, Marie. The thought of what she had said to Mathis yesterday made her close her eyes in shame. What could have come over her? Today her suspicion seemed ridiculous. Had it been because recently Mathis had taken an interest only in his work, and not her? Even if Mathis had killed the steward in the course of a quarrel, he would have told her about it—she thought that after all these years, she knew him well enough to be sure of that. But who *had* killed Heidelsheim with a crossbow?

"*Requiem aeternam dona eis, Domine, et lux perpetua luceat eis . . .* Amen.*" After Father Tristan's last words, the inhabitants of the castle went their separate ways, murmuring and hastily making the sign of the cross. Mathis left as well, without looking up. Agnes sighed softly. He obviously hadn't forgiven her yet.

On impulse, she decided to go up to the library. That was the place where, ever since her childhood, she had been able to pursue her own thoughts best.

As she entered the library on the fourth floor of the castle tower, she was met by the odor of dust, old parchments, and wood smoke, so familiar to her from her childhood. It was the beginning of May, but Father Tristan liked to keep warm, so the stove on the hearth was burning. However, the old monk himself was not here, and Agnes was both relieved and disappointed. She would have liked to ask Father Tristan more questions about her dreams. On the other hand, she liked being alone. Besides, the chaplain was very reluctant to say much about her dreams and the old stories.

Agnes thought about that. Why didn't he want to talk about them? Why had the old book with the picture of the Knights' House disappeared? And why had Father Tristan asked her not to wear Barbarossa's ring publicly on her finger?

Lost in thought, she walked past the bookshelves. She ran her fingers over the volumes, hoping to come upon that strange book again, but in vain. Agnes vividly remembered the leather binding and the gold lettering on it. The book was large and thick, not something to be easily hidden. Did the chaplain have it down in the cellar, where many documents and rolls of parchment were still stored in chests?

Agnes was about to give up the search when, at the end of one shelf at chest height, she noticed the spine of a remarkable book. As she ran her finger over that one, she noticed that the binding was very hard, made not of leather but of wood. She tapped it, put her head to one side, and was able to make out a Latin title.

Divina Commedia. Decimus circulus inferni . . . Dante's *Divine Comedy*, the Tenth Circle of Hell.

Agnes stopped. She had in fact read Dante's account of hell three times already. She loved his graphic descriptions, and they sent an enjoyable shiver down her back, especially at night. But she had never heard of a *tenth* circle.

Curious to find out more, she tried pulling out the book, but it seemed to be stuck. She pulled harder. There was a sudden click, and part of the shelf swung open like a door, though just a crack. Cautiously, Agnes opened the space as far as it would go, and then stood there amazed.

What in the world . . .

There was a stone niche behind the shelf, just large enough to fit a small child. Several books and scrolls lay inside it. Agnes reached for them and realized that many of them were not handwritten, but printed. They seemed to be recent works by German scholars. The names on them were those of Philipp Melanchthon and Johann von Staupitz, and the name of Martin Luther also appeared several times. Agnes was about to look at the scrolls as well when her glance fell on a book behind them.

It was the book that Father Tristan had hidden from her. The title made her heart beat faster.

Magna Historia de Castro Trifels . . . The Great History of Trifels Castle.

She hastily leafed through it. Written in Latin, with many magnificent illustrations, illuminated initials, and colored lettering, the work described the beginnings of Trifels as an imperial castle. A drawing showed the three castles of Trifels, Scharfenberg, and Anebos, with the guards' sandstone outposts between them, just as Agnes had seen it all in her dream. The book told the tale of Trifels in the twelfth century, when it had been the center of the German Empire, and how kings and princes used to meet here. It described the imprisonment of Richard the Lionheart in 1193, and the campaign in Sicily against the Normans only a year later. One picture showed the legendary Norman treasure being brought to the castle by Emperor Henry VI, with what looked like an endless line of beasts of burden crossing the chain of hills, with knights in shining armor among them. So the treasure was real.

Still turning the pages, Agnes finally came to the page with the picture of the Knights' House at Trifels. Once again she recognized the many guests at the banquet in her dream, including the black-haired young man in his hauberk, kneeling in front of an older man. Turning a page back again, she came upon the title of the chapter. It was written in simple Latin, and she was able to translate it quickly.

The Accolade of the Guelph Johann of Brunswick, Anno Domini 1293 . . .

Her heart skipped a beat. Now, at last, she knew the name of the strange young man in her dream. The Guelphs had once been a powerful family, enemies of the house of Hohenstaufen at the time of Barbarossa. They, too, had once appointed a German emperor. The center of their power, as in the old days, was still in Brunswick, although they did not exert anything like the influence they had in the past.

Agnes looked more closely at the text. The picture of the young man was on one of the last pages of the book, and the chapter to which it belonged had to do with the gradual deterioration of the castle, parallel to the decline of the house of Hohenstaufen.

Just as Agnes was about to read on, she heard footsteps on the stairs. They were slow and measured, with the tapping of a stick in between them. Father Tristan was on his way to the library.

Agnes thought for a moment, and then decided to put the book back and close the niche again. She was sure that the monk wouldn't be happy that she had found the secret compartment. And if he knew, she ran the risk of his hiding the book somewhere else. Then she would never be able to look at it again.

The door in the bookshelf was just clicking shut when Father Tristan entered the library. Agnes turned to him, an innocent expression on her face.

"I was waiting for you, Father," she said calmly. "For one thing to thank you for the funeral eulogy. It was beautiful, and very sensitive. It was really more than Heidelsheim deserved."

"Thank you," said Father Tristan, smiling. "Although I don't suppose that is the only reason you're here." For the fraction of a second, his eyes lingered on the secret door, but his face showed nothing.

Agnes sighed and sat down on the bench by the stove. "As usual, you are right, Father. I wanted to be alone for a little while. Heidelsheim's death touched me more than I would have expected. After all, he was murdered, and no one knows who killed him."

"Much in life remains inexplicable," the old monk said. "Only God knows everything."

"Do you think my dreams are among the puzzles that will never be explained?" Agnes asked.

Father Tristan smiled, and then sat down, with a groan, on the stool at the desk "I knew you wouldn't give up so easily," he murmured. "But I must disappoint you. Even I can't interpret the meaning of your dreams."

"Here, the ring." Agnes took the ring on its chain out from under her bodice "I saw it clearly in my dream. Couldn't it have been here in Trifels Castle at that time? Like the young man I saw?"

Father Tristan slowly nodded. "Maybe. But even so . . ." He struck the floor with his staff, and then shook his head fiercely, as though he had just come to a decision. "You are living here and now, Agnes, not three hundred years ago. So put the accursed thing away. It would have been better for you to throw it in Mathis's furnace to be melted down with the rest of that stuff." In a gentler voice, he went on, "I've been very glad to have your company visiting the sick. You have it in you to become a good healer, and you also show people that fine ladies and gentlemen don't always have to be trampling the peasants' freshly sown fields underfoot. You are doing good, Agnes. And now, in our own time. That's worth more than all your dreams put together."

Sighing, Agnes tucked the ring into her bodice again. "And yet my dreams are a part of me. I can't simply get rid of them." She looked pleadingly at him. "At least tell me more about Barbarossa and the house of Hohenstaufen. They were such a powerful family. Why did they simply disappear?"

"Those who have power make enemies," Father Tristan replied thoughtfully. "In the end, the Staufer dynasty had too many. France, the pope, the German princes—they all distrusted the family. But in the end it was their own weakness that destroyed them. When such a mighty empire rests on the shoulders of a single man, a few blows of fate are enough to bring it down. And finally such misfortune struck the Staufers that you might have thought God himself was conspiring against them."

"What happened?" asked Agnes curiously.

Father Tristan rolled his eyes and, groaning, went over to one of the bookshelves and took out a heavy volume. "You don't give me any peace, do you?" he grumbled. "Right, listen to this." He opened the leather-bound tome to one of its early pages and pointed to the picture of a strong man with a long red beard, holding a golden orb in his left hand. "This is Emperor Barbarossa, whose portrait is on your ring," he began. "I've already told you about him: he was the first great member of the house of Hohenstaufen. Once a minor family from Swabia with the title of count, they had come a long way by dint of skill and cunning, and finally they produced a line of kings and emperors. When Barbarossa drowned on crusade to Jerusalem in 1190, he was succeeded by his son Henry VI."

"The emperor who brought the Norman treasure to Trifels," Agnes put in.

"Yes, that was Henry." Father Tristan nodded and turned to the next page, showing a stern man with a crown seated on a throne. Several men knelt in front of him with their heads bowed. "Henry VI was a capable ruler, but also very cruel," the monk continued. "Like his father before him, he had first to contend with the strongest opponents of the Staufers, the princely family of the Guelphs. Henry would stop at nothing to achieve his aims. He laid waste to half of Italy, took King Richard the Lionheart of England prisoner, and with Richard's ransom he finally conquered Sicily, the country of his wife, Constance. When the Norman noblemen of Sicily rebelled against him, he imprisoned the conspirators at Trifels Castle and had them all blinded except the bishop of Salerno. He had a red-hot crown nailed to their leader's head back in Sicily, and other conspirators were impaled or thrown into a vat of boiling pitch." Father Tristan shrugged his shoulders. "Yes, you are right. Henry did bring a vast treasure home with him—but at what price."

Shivering, Agnes thought of the cellar in the keep where Mathis had been imprisoned. What terrible scenes might have been enacted down in that dungeon? She almost thought she could hear the screams of the Norman conspirators. It was as though Trifels Castle lived and breathed like a mighty animal.

She shook herself and went on listening to the monk, who had just turned another page in the chronicle of the Staufer dynasty. It showed the picture of a knight bringing his raised sword down on the head of a man wearing a crown. A pool of red blood lay on the floor of a large hall.

"Henry VI died of a fever in his early thirties," Father Tristan said quietly. "Or maybe he was poisoned by his wife. Others claimed that God himself had punished Henry for his wicked deeds. No one knows for certain. Regardless, his son Frederick II was still too young to be crowned as the German king. So a majority of the electors chose Frederick's uncle, Philip of Swabia, also of the house of Hohenstaufen, much to the displeasure of the Guelphs, who were gaining more and more influence at this time and were at odds with the Staufers for power. For several terrible years there were two kings in the realm, Otto the Guelph and Philip." Father Tristan sighed. "Finally, King Philip was assassinated at the wedding of his daughter Beatrix, just before the pope could crown him Holy Roman Emperor. To this day, no one is sure whether or not the Guelphs were responsible for his murder."

Agnes felt that her head was buzzing with all these names. But she now knew that the young man in her dream had been a Guelph. What was he doing in a castle that had been the center of the Hohenstaufen realm? Had the Guelphs taken over Trifels at a later date?

"You say that Frederick II, Barbarossa's grandson, was still too young to ascend the throne," she said. "But after his uncle Philip's death, he was the rightful heir, wasn't he?"

Father Tristan nodded. "Yes, that is right. Frederick II came to the throne when he was sixteen. He put an end to confrontations with the Guelphs, who even let him have the imperial insignia—the crown, the imperial sword, and the scepter. He was crowned Holy Roman Emperor by the pope in 1220 and is still regarded as the greatest ruler the empire has ever known." The monk turned another page, and Agnes saw an emperor in a blue cloak seated on a throne. A speckled brown falcon sat on a perch beside him.

"Oh, I know that picture," she cried happily. "It's in my book of falconry."

"Yes, the famous *De arti venandi cum avibus*." The old monk smiled. "*The Art of Hunting with Birds*. Frederick II wrote that book himself, but he was a great scholar in many other fields as well. He grew up in Sicily, where the Arab and Greek sciences were studied. Frederick spoke several languages fluently. He had many interests, and he managed to conquer Jerusalem without even fighting for it. So his contemporaries called him *Stupor Mundi*, the Wonder of the World. The pope, however, ended up regarding him as the Antichrist made flesh."

Father Tristan sighed again, looking thoughtfully at the picture of the tall man on the throne. An almost imperceptible smile played on his lips.

"Frederick II died in 1250," he went on at last. "His reign, which lasted nearly forty years, was the best that the German Empire ever knew. It welcomed strangers and was open to new ideas, yet it preserved its unity both at home and abroad. None of Frederick's four sons managed to follow in his footsteps. The eldest, Henry VII, rebelled against his father and was deposed as the German king. In despair, he threw himself off his horse and broke his neck." With a gloomy expression, Father Tristan went on, counting the sons off on his fingers. "The second son, Conrad, died of a fever while fighting in Italy. Manfred, the third son, fell in the famous battle of Benevento, trying to defend Sicily against Charles of Anjou, brother of the French king. Finally, Frederick's favorite but illegitimate son, Enzio, was held prisoner in Bologna for over two decades; he died there alone and forsaken by all his friends."

"And was that the end of the Staufer dynasty?" asked Agnes.

Father Tristan turned to the last page of the chronicle, where a black-clad executioner was shown in front of a large crowd of onlookers, cutting off the head of a young, fair-haired man with his sword. "Frederick's second son, Conrad, had a son known as Conradin," said the chaplain sadly. "Little Conrad. A good-looking boy. Everyone liked him, and he might perhaps have been able to take on his great inheritance. But Charles of Anjou captured Conradin and had his head cut off in Naples when he was only just sixteen. France had won." With a bang, Father Tristan closed the book. "And that really was the end of the house of Hohenstaufen. Then there was a terrible time without any emperor. Fear, chaos, and lawlessness reigned in the German Empire. Not until a whole generation later did peace finally return, with the accession of King Rudolf von Habsburg."

Agnes frowned. Names of emperors and dynasties were swirling around in her mind like a swarm of buzzing bees, and her limbs were stiff from sitting on the bench beside the stove for so long. All the same, she concentrated on what Father Tristan had been saying. "Are those the same Habsburgs as the family of the present emperor?" she asked.

"Yes, indeed, like his grandfather Emperor Maximilian before him, and Maximilian's father, Emperor Frederick III. The Habsburgs have ruled the German Empire for a long time now, almost uninterruptedly." The old monk rose with another groan and put the heavy book back on the shelf. "But people still look back to the Staufers nostalgically. They sing songs about them, they tell stories about their return. And in these times, when many simple folk are weighed down by the burden of poverty, and schism threatens the church, the legendary reputation of that family of rulers is particularly enticing." He chuckled. "Even though their line died out almost three hundred years ago. Yet we could certainly do with such a capable ruler as Frederick II these days. All the injustice that we see getting worse from year to year . . . I don't know where it will all lead."

All of a sudden, Agnes found her mind going instinctively to the books she had seen in the secret compartment. Works by Martin Luther, that critic of the church, had been among them. Why was Father Tristan keeping such books, and in secret too? Could he be on the side of the agitators himself?

"Mathis thinks the church wants to gut poor people the way you'd pluck and draw a Christmas goose," she cautiously ventured. "Priests selling indulgences travel around promising eternal life if you give the pope money for his palaces. The local peasants talk about Martin Luther more and more, too. Is that what you mean when you mention schism in the church and injustice?"

It was some time before the priest replied. Only after a while did he say, in a soft voice, "The Church of Rome is old, ancient. We try to bear witness to the word of Jesus, but much has been forgotten, and much else may have been distorted in the course of time. Who knows the truth? However, the message itself has never changed: Jesus preached love, not hate. We must never forget that."

He went over to the window and looked out for a long time. Peasants were treading the castle acres with their plows, always following the same tracks. Twittering swallows flew to their nests under the castle rooftops, announcing the arrival of summer.

"I can sense a storm coming," said the old man at last. "I feel it in my bones, every one of them. It will blow away much that still stands like dry straw. May God protect us."

Suddenly a smile played around his almost toothless mouth. "But what am I saying, Agnes?" he said firmly. "The weather is much too fine for such sad thoughts." He made for the door at last with his staff in his hand, his footsteps slow. "Let's go to the forest together instead and gather bogbean and shepherd's purse. Then we will visit one or other of our sick patients this afternoon. That is a more rewarding occupation than brooding and lamenting."

On the fifth day after Agnes and Mathis had quarreled, after she had thoughtlessly accused him of murder, she found him alone at last in the shabby little workshop beside his parents' house, where he was finishing forging a few horseshoes. After work on the guns for the coming siege, Mathis was often occupied for many hours on other jobs in the castle smithy. It was weeks since his father had been able to stand at his forge. Mathis brought his hammer down powerfully on the red-hot iron. He didn't seem to hear Agnes as she hesitantly approached him.

"Mathis, I . . . I'm sorry," she began quietly.

Mathis stopped hammering for a moment, but he did not turn to her. "What for?" he asked stonily.

"Well, for suspecting you of Heidelsheim's murder. Will you forgive me?"

Once again Mathis hammered away at the horseshoe, making a noise that almost drowned out his words. "If you can really imagine a thing like that, you don't have to apologize for it. You obviously think I'm a murderer and a cutthroat. Why not? I'm only a coarse, uneducated smith."

"Oh, Mathis, do stop it!" She seized him by the shoulder so hard that he almost fell over backward. "I know I made a mistake, and I've said I'm sorry. That ought to be enough," she went on angrily. "You weren't exactly nice to me, either."

For the first time Mathis did look at her, grinning broadly. All at once his annoyance was gone. "I almost got the impression you thought I was jealous," he said, with a twinkle in his eye. "You'd like that, wouldn't you?"

"You brute!" Agnes gave him another push, and this time he did end up sitting on the floor. "Just forget it, can't you?" she hissed. "Why am I fighting my father over you when you're not worth it?"

Mathis raised his hands apologetically, but he was still smiling mockingly. "If your father sees us here, we'll be in for it. Although I'm the one he'll thrash soundly, not you. I'm obviously not the sort of company you ought to keep." He stood up and wiped the oil and ashes off his hands on his leather apron. "Suppose we go over to Anebos, like we did so often in the past? We won't be disturbed there, and you can lecture me in peace." He glanced up at the sky, which was now red with the light of the setting sun. "It will soon be too dark to work, anyway."

Agnes smiled. "That's the best idea you've had in a long time," she replied in relief. And they set off along the path to the nearby wooded hill.

As they walked along the narrow, trodden path, Agnes thought how often, as a child, she had been to Anebos with Mathis. In that picture in the chronicle of Trifels she had seen the little castle that used to stand there, but by now its ruins looked more like a natural rock in the form of a gigantic anvil, the shape to which it owed its name.

When they reached the top of the slope, slightly out of breath, the sun had set behind the range of hills, and there was a sparkling starry sky overhead. The full moon, just rising, bathed the whole clearing in a pale, ghostly light. In the middle of the space, which was surrounded by tall beech trees, stood the tall pillar of rock, some thirty feet high, with other rocks scattered around it. In some places the outline of the foundation walls could still be seen, but otherwise nothing showed that a castle once used to stand here.

Just below the rocky pillar was a cave hollowed out by rain and wind, where they had liked to hide as children. Once again they sat in it together, looking at the sky above, where little shooting stars fell to earth from time to time. Agnes nestled close to Mathis, smelling the smoke of the smithy fire in his hair.

"How is your father?" she asked.

Mathis took a deep breath. "He's spitting blood more and more often," he replied hesitantly. "Father Tristan did give him some dried lungwort again today, but he doesn't think it will do much good. He says it comes from working such long hours at the forge. My mother is crying her eyes out."

"I tried to talk to you a couple of times recently," Agnes said softly. "About my own father, too. I have a sinking feeling that he's planning something again. But you were obviously too busy."

"You know I had to build a gun carriage," Mathis replied a little roughly. "Don't forget, your father can lock me up again any time if he isn't satisfied with me. And you've been out and about with Father Tristan all the time yourself."

Agnes leaned her head against his shoulder, just as she used to when they were playing in the hay as children. "You're right," she said, sighing. "It's the fever that's going around. People need help, and now, of all times, Elsbeth Rechsteiner the midwife has gone missing. It's as if she'd disappeared from the face of the earth. No one knows where she could be."

Mathis frowned. "Maybe Hans von Wertingen has her on his conscience. That devil is venturing farther and farther into our forests. I wouldn't even put it past him to cut an old woman's throat just for a few chickens and goats."

"Possibly. But no body has been found." Agnes hesitated for a moment, as a slight shudder ran down her back. "It's the same as with Martin von Heidelsheim," she went on at last. "Maybe it's just a co-incidence, but something is going on out there."

For some time they just looked up at the starry sky while Mathis held Agnes's hand. An owl hooted somewhere close.

"And by the way, I found the book that Father Tristan was hiding from me," Agnes suddenly said. "It's in a kind of secret compartment in the library."

Mathis rolled his eyes, and pushed her hand away. "I thought you wanted to talk about the two of us, and now you're starting on about those strange stories again. I curse the day when Parcival brought you that wretched ring. You're obsessed with all that stuff."

Agnes reached for the ring, hanging around her neck on its chain. She was so used to wearing it now that she sometimes forgot about it for days on end. At the moment it seemed to be heavier than usual. She sat up in their little cavern in the rock. "Don't you understand, Mathis? I can't get that ring, and above all the dreams, out of my mind. They seem so . . . so real. And now I know that someone who appears in them really existed."

She told him hastily about the young knight Johann of Brunswick, and the other information that she had found in the chronicle of Trifels.

"That knight, Johann, was a Guelph," she offered. "He was here in the castle almost a hundred years after the death of Barbarossa. In my dreams, he wants to tell me something about the signet ring. He seems to be giving me a warning."

"Agnes," Mathis tried to calm her down, "those are dreams, that's all. The ring is on your mind, yes, but that's not surprising, consider-ing how you came by it. And you know about this knight Johann from the book. You're simply dreaming of things you know about from waking life. That's normal."

"You're forgetting that I dreamed of Johann before I saw him in that picture. Would you call that normal, too?"

Mathis shrugged his shoulders. "Maybe you did see the book before, but you forgot about it. After all, you spent half your childhood in that dusty old library."

"Oh, damn it all, Mathis!" Agnes sprang to her feet, bumping her head on the low, rocky roof. Tears of pain and rage ran down her face. "Just because I like to read books, it doesn't mean I'm crazy." she said crossly, rubbing the sore place. "Even if everyone says so, including you. I dreamed of that knight Johann *before* I saw him in the book, I swear by God I did. And I know that the ring didn't come to me by chance. It was fixed to Parcival's leg by someone who wanted me to have it."

Mathis sighed. "And I really thought we were going to talk about us."

"I want to do that too, but—"

Agnes suddenly stopped, and Mathis looked at her, intrigued. "What's the matter?" he asked.

She pointed down the hill, to the south. "See for yourself."

Mathis crawled out of the cavern, and together they stared at about a dozen little lights moving up and down in a dip in the ground between Anebos and Scharfenberg Castle.

"Torches," said Mathis in surprise. "What's anyone doing up here in the middle of the night?"

Suddenly Agnes thought of the dwarfs in the old story. Didn't they watch over Barbarossa's sleep in Trifels Castle? But she took care not to say anything like that to Mathis. He thought she was a crazy dreamer anyway.

"Didn't you say young Count Scharfeneck was going to move into the castle at Scharfenberg?" Mathis asked, still looking at the lights. "Maybe his men are here already."

"Dragging new furniture uphill by night?" Agnes shook her head. "That's nonsense."

"Then in God's name let's go and see who's down there," replied Mathis, turning to move away.

"Mathis, wait!" Agnes whispered. "You can't . . ." But he was already on the narrow path leading to the ridge down below.

Cursing quietly, Agnes followed him. Her back tingled. She remembered the night, almost two months ago, when they had found Parcival in the forest and had seen those strangers just after that. The men had nothing good in mind. Could they have come back again?

Soon they were standing on the broad hilltop ridge that linked the three castles like an axis. Several natural rocky towers stood among the beech, chestnut, and oak trees, places where guards had once been posted. The path wound its way past them, dividing now and then and following narrow tracks up into the rocks.

They cautiously made their way in the moonlight toward Scharfenberg Castle, which stood on the farthest height of the Sonnenberg. Briefly they lost sight of the lights, although they soon saw them again in the dip just below the castle. The torches, or whatever was burning, now looked very close together. Apart from the faint rushing of the wind, there was not a sound to be heard. All of a sudden the lights formed a regular line, began moving . . .

And disappeared.

Mathis, behind a rock and on his way down into the dip, stopped, taken aback.

"What in the world . . . where did they go?" he whispered. "Did they put the torches out?"

"All at the same time, and so quickly? How could they?" Agnes frowned, but she couldn't think of an explanation either.

"They can hardly have dropped into a crack in the ground that suddenly opened up," Mathis snapped.

Agnes did not reply. Once again she was thinking of the legend of Barbarossa and the dwarfs. The little people of folktales were famous for suddenly disappearing into holes in the ground. Could this be the place where the old emperor slept until the world needed him again?

And suppose that time is about to come?

She felt a little dizzy. It was like the feeling she had had not long ago in the dungeon in the keep. What was the matter with her? Was she beginning to believe in the old wives' tales told to small children at the fireside?

"Whatever it was," said Mathis, interrupting her train of thought, "it's gone. And in the dark we'll only break our bones down in that dip in the ground." Shrugging, he turned away. "Let's turn back and have another look tomorrow in daylight. I promised my mother not to be home too late. She has enough to worry about already."

They walked back to Trifels Castle in silence, following the line of the hilltop ridge. As they passed the rise on which Anebos stood, Agnes thought she saw another light moving up on the rocks. She closed her eyes for a moment, and when she opened them again, the light had gone. With difficulty, she kept control of her breathing.

Sometimes she thought that people were right when they said she was rather strange.

✦ ✦ ✦

A long passage with a door at the end of it. Agnes knows who is on the other side of that door. The three men arrived early today, wearing fine fur-trimmed cloaks under which shirts of mail clinked. They rode into the castle at dawn, mounted on noble warhorses, each of them worth the price of three farms. Agnes felt their eyes on her when the castellan introduced them, and at the same moment she understood that these men wished her ill.

Their ill will was unbounded.

Agnes goes on along the passage. She is carrying a carafe of wine that she is supposed to take to the hall. But when she approaches the door, which stands ajar, she suddenly stops. Through the crack in the doorway, she can see the men. They wait for the castellan by the open hearth, and they are deep in conversation. They speak quietly, but a few words reach her ears, like the echoes of evil spells. Words of death and destruction.

The men are discussing her death. Hers and Johann's.

What they speak of is so incredible that, for a moment, Agnes thinks she can't have heard it correctly. Her breath falters, her hands tremble. The whole of Trifels is in danger. She must warn the castellan at once. But above all, she must warn Johann, and tonight the two of them must . . .

At that moment the carafe slips out of her fingers, now moist and slippery with the sweat of fear. It falls to the floor, where it breaks with a crash like a mountain exploding. The wine flows into a puddle on the stone floor, and for a fraction of a second Agnes see her own distorted face reflected in it. But it is not her face. Or is it? She is older, there is a metal circlet adorned with flowers on her fair hair, the first lines show on her skin, her face is a terrified mask.

The men in the hall fall silent, and their eyes go to the doorway where Agnes is still standing.

She runs back down the passage as angry cries ring out behind her, quickly coming closer. She hears doors slamming, hauberks clinking, the sound of a sword being drawn from its sheath.

The men have come to kill them.

✦ ✦ ✦

Agnes woke with a hoarse cry and looked around her bower, trying to get her bearings. She almost expected the door to be kicked in at any moment, and then she would see the men storming into her room with their swords drawn. But all was quiet. Outside, the first birds were singing to greet the new day.

The dream had gone, broken like a soap bubble, but for some time afterward Agnes could still see her reflection, distorted by fear, in the puddle of wine.

Only when the sun rose above the treetops in the east did that image, too, fade away.

Deep down in the damp, cool crypt of the church of St. Fortunatus in Annweiler, a small group of people stood around a stone altar that early morning, holding hands. They were humming an old Latin hymn in chorus, as they did at all their rare meetings. Few knew about this gathering, not even the priest of the town of Annweiler. In the old days, whoever was priest of the congregation had been an important member of their sworn fellowship. But the present priest, Johannes Lebner, was a fat, greedy drunkard who pocketed part of the money from the sale of indulgences himself, and who was hand in glove with the mayor of the town. He was a scholar from Cologne, far away, washed up by chance in this place, and he knew nothing about the old customs.

Particularly not this one.

There were twelve of them, the same number as the Apostles, simple citizens of Annweiler whose families had made up the members of the order for over two hundred years. Only when one of them died was a new member brought into their circle. They called themselves the Brotherhood of the Ring, and since those dark days of its founding, they had been keeping a secret on which the fate of the empire might depend. Once, and not too long ago, that secret had almost come to light, but they had managed to preserve it just in time.

Now danger threatened again, even if none of them guessed how close they really stood to the edge of the abyss.

The last notes of the hymn died away within the weathered stone walls that were adorned with symbols and coats of arms. Then the head of the Brotherhood spoke. He was well past seventy years old, his face was as wrinkled as dry leather, his hair was white as snow. In a different life he was an ordinary tanner, a good, hard-working man with eight grown children and a countless number of grandchildren and great-grandchildren, but down here he was surrounded by the magical, commanding aura of an ancient priest. As a sign of his office, he wore a plain cloak that had once been white, but had become gray and threadbare with the passage of the centuries. The back of it bore the image of three lions rampant.

"Good brothers and sisters," the old man began in a loud voice that echoed through the vault. "As you know, our enemies are now on the point of discovering the secret, for the second time. I must inform you that they have already been in these parts, reaching out their hands for it." An anxious murmur arose, and the speaker raised his arms to calm the others down. Then he turned to the midwife Elsbeth Rechsteiner, who had stayed in the shadows until now.

"Some time ago we warned Elsbeth, as keeper of the ring, of the coming of the enemy," said the old man. "All the same, she was found and has had to keep out of the way for the last few weeks. Many of you thought that she was dead. It is good reason for rejoicing that she is back among us again." He paused for a moment before going on. "I very much hope that Elsbeth can give us more grounds for rejoicing, particularly in all that concerns the safety of the ring . . ." His voice held a note of menace, as all eyes were turned to the midwife.

Elsbeth Rechsteiner straightened up. She had spent the last few weeks with her niece Sophia in Waldrohrbach, in constant fear of discovery. That and lack of sleep had dug deep lines into her already careworn face. At last she plucked up her courage and turned to the members of the order.

"The men of whom our brother and leader spoke," she began hesitantly, "did indeed come to my house. They turned it upside down to find the ring. But they did not succeed."

The head of the order nodded in relief. "Then you hid it well."

"I didn't hide it. I gave it away."

For a while there was absolute silence in the crypt. Then they all began talking in agitation at the same time, until the old man angrily clapped his hands.

"Quiet! Quiet!" he cried. "If you go on like that, you'll certainly be heard in the church above us. Morning mass is about to begin." When the members of the order had calmed down at last, he turned to Elsbeth, his face red with anger. "You did *what* with it?"

"I placed the ring in the hand of God, for that is where it belongs." Her voice faltered, but she chose her words with care as she told the Brotherhood what had happened.

"I am sure those men were sent to finish the work begun so long ago," she concluded. "That black-skinned man is clever and cunning, and he comes from very far away. Someone extremely powerful must have sent him. I asked people I knew. He also visited other midwives in this area, and he asked them all the same question. And he went to inns and taverns, he visited graveyards, he looked at church registers. He and his henchmen are not going to give up until they have found what they want. I had to do something."

"You . . . gave our ring to a falcon?" The old man shook his head, unable to believe it. "That should never have happened. Didn't I tell you how important your task is? Who knows what will happen to the ring now? It is no longer in our power."

Elsbeth straightened her back. "It is not *our* ring. If I had kept it, it would now be in the hands of the enemy. Would that have been better? When the bird perched on my window sill, I had a strange premonition . . ."

"Devil take it!" A sturdy man in a leather apron of the kind worn by carters in the Palatinate raised his voice angrily. It was Diethelm Seebach, the landlord of the Green Tree Inn. "Are you saying you gave the ring away because of a *premonition*? You were its keeper, Elsbeth. The order entrusted the ring to you. What came over you?"

"The . . . the bird . . . it was like a sign," the midwife replied uncertainly. "Like a messenger from another time." She thrust out her chin. "And wasn't I right? What would have happened if those men had found the ring in my home? Don't forget, the secret that we keep can change the whole empire, the whole of Europe. Do you think such men would have asked politely where the ring came from, and then they would have gone away again?" She laughed despairingly. "No, they would have tortured me until I told them our secret."

"Then why didn't you simply hide the ring somewhere?" asked another member of the Brotherhood. The ropemaker Martin Lebrecht had been a member of the order for many years, and his word carried weight among its members. "You could have buried it in the forest, or given it to one of us for safekeeping. We would all have understood."

"Do you suppose I didn't think of that, Martin?" The midwife's laughter had no mirth in it. "The men would have looked for me, found me, and tortured me just the same until I told them the secret."

"Those are excuses, Elsbeth," snapped Diethelm Seebach. "You were afraid. And because of your fear the fate of the whole empire may be at stake."

"You are right, Diethelm. I was afraid. I don't think I could have withstood such pain. The fire, the blows, wrenching my sinews apart, breaking my bones. Could you have held out, Diethelm? Tell me, aren't you afraid?"

Diethelm Seebach hesitated, then he crossed his arms over his broad chest defiantly and said nothing.

"There remains the question of how the men knew that Elsbeth had the ring," said the head of the order thoughtfully, looking closely at each and every one of them. "Only the Brotherhood knows that Elsbeth is the keeper of the ring. That means one of us must have talked."

Elsbeth Rechsteiner slowly shook her head. "I thought of that myself. Maybe that's so, or maybe the men just came to ask me questions. As I said, they visited other local midwives." She had formed her own opinion, but she was not going to express it openly here.

Who can I trust? If one of us is a traitor, he should know as little as possible.

"All the same, we must be on our guard." The head of the order straightened his shoulders. "A traitor in our ranks would be the end of us." Suddenly the church bells up above began to ring. The head of the Brotherhood took off his cloak, and once again he was only an old man with a wrinkled face. "We had better go up before divine service begins," he said wearily. "Otherwise the priest will suspect something. We must not take any more risks." Once again, he shook his head. "A falcon bearing the ring," he murmured. "May the Lord guide it to safe pastures."

Then they all went up, with heads bent, good brothers and sisters on the way to Sunday mass.

To their ears, the ringing of the church bells sounded like a death knell.

· *7* ·

*The Rhine Plain between Trifels and Neukastell,
16 May, Anno Domini 1524, morning*

A CART DRAWN BY TWO OLD nags jolted along the outskirts of
the Rhine plain on its way to Neukastell. Gunther and Sebastian, two
of the men-at-arms from Trifels Castle, sat on the driver's seat.
Although this was the end of May, it was uncomfortably chilly so
early in the day, and thin wisps of mist hung in the dark fir trees that
grew to right and left of the road. The two men had decided to take
the longer way, which led below the line of hills. It had more traffic
on it and therefore seemed safer to them. All the same, Sebastian kept
looking to all sides and was unusually quiet.

"Anyone might think you were watching out for ghosts," muttered
Gunther, sitting beside his friend and colleague. He had the reins in
his hands and was chewing a piece of straw.

"Not ghosts, you fool," replied Sebastian, scrutinizing the firs
again. "I'm looking out for robbers and suchlike rabble. There's all
sorts of shady folk out and about in these woods."

"You mean like Shepherd Jockel, gathering all the malcontents
and runaway gallows birds around him over in Eusserthal?"

Sebastian shook his head. "If only that was all. Haven't you heard about the old midwife Elsbeth Rechsteiner? Vanished without a trace, like it was magic, and folk talk about a black man haunting these parts."

"Black man—ha!" retorted Gunther. "You superstitious idiot. I told you three times already, it's that bastard Hans von Wertingen. Not a black man, it's Black Hans they mean. See what happens when folk get to gossiping and telling tall tales?" He looked grimly at the surrounding woods. One of the many castles in this area stood on top of a hill not far away and, looking through the trees, Gunther saw rows of vines growing on the lower slopes. The cart was rolling along easily now.

"It may be dangerous these days on the way to Eusserthal and on toward Speyer," said Gunther. "But not here on the road to Neukastell. Not before the very eyes of the duke's steward." The man-at-arms laughed, although it sounded forced. "Not even Black Hans would venture that. What's more . . ." and he lowered his voice to a con-spiratorial tone, "what's more, who's to know that we're on our way with the dues for the duke? Looking like we do, we could be carting a load of firewood through the forest."

Sure enough, the two men-at-arms wore shabby peasant smocks over their hauberks, and their iron helmets were hidden under simple hoods. Formerly peasants themselves, they had been working as guards at Trifels for the last ten years, and so far it had been a calm and peaceful life, on the whole. They kept their weapons in reason-ably good shape, they mended a breach in the walls now and then, or helped to bring in the harvest from the castle acres. Now, for a change, they felt genuine fear. As well as Martin von Heidelsheim and the midwife Elsbeth Rechsteiner, other local people had fallen victim lately to robbers and murderers. So the castellan Philipp von Erfenstein had decided to have the dues taken secretly to Neukastell. Hidden under threadbare blankets, the cart carried six sacks of grain, a few pounds of precious salt, two barrels of pickled fish, some smoked hams, and a cage full of cackling geese. In addition, Sebastian had thirty newly minted Rhenish golden guilders in a purse under his jerkin, and several pieces of jewelry, with which Erfenstein had parted with a heavy heart.

"How much longer before we get to Neukastell?" Sebastian asked anxiously, feeling the full purse.

Gunther shrugged. "Maybe an hour? Once we get this damn deep lane behind us, the road goes steeply up the mountain. Then we'll be able to see the castle."

"Hell, it's time we polished off Black Hans," Sebastian cursed. "In my grandfather's time, these parts were as safe as a kitchen garden. But since the knights began going into decline, there's been a starveling cutthroat in every other castle. And the emperor buys himself foreign landsknechts the way the likes of us would buy a tankard of beer. What sort of a world are we living in?"

Gunther sucked his straw thoughtfully. "You wait and see, old Erfenstein will have to join the robber knights soon. Another couple of bad harvests, and that'll be the end of chivalry, tournaments, and minstrelsy. And we can go lie in wait for travelers crossing the Bindersbach Pass, like Wertingen's men."

"Before I cut the throats of children and old women up there," Sebastian said, "I'd sooner be a landsknecht and go to war with the French."

"Where you'd be cutting the throats of children and old women anyway." Gunther laughed and spat the straw out. "Me, I'd sooner do anything than toil in the fields. What . . . ?"

He stopped as a crow flew up into the cloudy sky not far from them. Several others followed it, rising from a nearby thicket.

"I don't like the look of that," Gunther said under his breath.

"It was probably an animal scared them," said Sebastian, trying to reassure Gunther and himself. "A fox or something."

"By God . . . that's no fox." His face white as a sheet, Gunther pointed ahead to where the road went around a bend. Several felled fir trees lay there, piled up on each other like a green wall. The carthorses trotted to the barrier and stopped, snorting and pawing the ground with their hooves.

Gunther's eyes wandered around in panic. Then he reached for the loaded crossbow lying under the driver's seat.

"Those swine," he groaned.

At the same time, there was a quick hum, and a feathered arrow buried itself in Sebastian's thigh.

"Jesus and Mary!" cried the man-at-arms. "God punish you!" More arrows rained down on the cart. Gunther tried to find a target at which he could aim the crossbow, an enemy that he could kill, but all he saw were the dark fir trees on the other side of the deep-set lane. An arrow hit him in the right hand, another whistled just past his throat. Cursing, he dropped the crossbow, plucked the arrow out of the burning wound, and flung himself off the cart. While more arrows fell around him like hailstones, he climbed the steep slope, bending low as he stumbled toward the nearby wood. Just before he reached the safety of its thickets, another arrow hit his lower leg. Screaming in pain, he fell into a bush and lay there, breathing heavily.

Meanwhile, Sebastian had drawn his rusty short sword and stood swaying beside the driver's seat in the cart. Like Gunther, he wore an old hauberk with holes in it, but by now there were three arrows in his legs, and a crossbow bolt had made its way through the metal rings of the shirt. Sebastian was still on his feet, but Gunther knew from experience that most times arrows did not kill at once; instead, the victim bled to death slowly and painfully. Just then another bolt went through the thin hauberk. Sebastian staggered for a moment and then fell off the cart headfirst. He crawled a little way toward the slope and finally lay there, moaning.

Only now did four men appear on the outskirts of the wood, coming slowly down to the road. The tallest of them held a huge black mastiff on a leash. The dog followed the trail of blood left by Sebastian and licked up a large puddle of it beside the fallen man-at-arms. Gunther recognized the black-haired giant at once.

Hans von Wertingen.

The robber knight looked around attentively. He wore a breast-plate and a round helmet. His broadsword was so long that it almost dragged over the ground. The other three men were more shabbily dressed. Two of them held longbows, the third was aiming a freshly loaded crossbow at the groaning Sebastian.

"Leave the poor devil where he is," Wertingen ordered. "He's no danger to us now. Anyway, I need him alive a little longer to tell us all he knows. Where's the other fellow?"

"Ran into the wood over there," replied one of his men, pointing to the other side of the road. "But I think we winged him."

Wertingen grinned. Then he began undoing the leash from around the dog's neck. "He won't get far. My Saskia will soon find him, won't you, Saskia? Good girl."

The enormous mastiff tugged at the leash, growling, and Wertingen had difficulty letting her off it. "Damn it—hold still, will you?" he cursed.

In the cover of the bush, Gunther froze. It was pointless to try running away with the arrow in his leg. Furthermore, the mastiff would soon catch up. He thought for a moment, then said a silent prayer and reached for the wound in his leg, which was already bleeding profusely. Gritting his teeth, he passed his hand through the blood and then raked it over his face until it was smeared red all over. Then he lay back as if he were dead.

Only a moment later, the mastiff appeared behind the bush.

She barked and bared her long, sharp fangs. But since the prey in front of her did not move, she only lowered her head slowly and sniffed at the motionless body. Gunther felt damp nostrils on his leg, and then a tongue stinking of carrion passed over his cheeks, soiled as they were with blood, dirt, and fir needles. He almost screamed.

He heard the crunch of footsteps. His eyes were wide open, and he stared blankly at the milky white sky like a corpse.

Is that the last thing I'll ever see, he wondered, *a bit of cloudy sky?*

"This one's dead as mutton!" someone called.

"Are you sure?" Wertingen called back.

"If not he soon will be."

Gunther heard a blade being drawn from its sheath as someone bent over him.

Oh God, don't let me die, please don't let me die . . .

"If he's not dead, I'll eat my hat," muttered the man above him. "But very well, I'll help him on his way . . ."

Gunther was about to jump up to defend his life as long as possible, but the mastiff suddenly began barking wildly and raced into the wood.

"What's going on over there?" Hans von Wertingen shouted.

"It's Saskia. She must have scented something. She ran after it."

"Then go after her, damn it all. Do you know what that animal cost me? If she doesn't come back, I'll feed you to her brothers."

Cursing to himself, the man moved away. Gunther was still lying on the forest floor. He had already prepared for death, and now God was giving him a second chance. But he wasn't safe yet. The robber would soon come back, and Gunther dared not slink away. Black Hans and the other two men would be sure to hear him. So he stayed where he was. But he turned his head slightly, so that if he looked through the bushes he could see Wertingen and the severely wounded Sebastian. The robber knight was kneeling beside the guard, feeling under his hauberk with a practiced hand. Triumphantly, he pulled out the purse containing the guilders and the jewelry.

"There we are," he announced. "Along with the cart and its load, this will make it a convivial year for us. We'll have wine, women, and feasting until we're brimming over." The other two men laughed, and Wertingen probed the wound in Sebastian's thigh with the arrow that was sticking in it, making the man-at-arms scream in pain.

"You can have a quick death or a slow, painful one, my friend," said Black Hans in a surprisingly kindly voice. "But you're going to die. You've lost too much blood already, as you must know for yourself. So tell me, when does old Erfenstein plan to attack my castle?"

Gunther suppressed a cry of alarm. So Hans von Wertingen knew about the planned attack. Yet the castellan had imposed strict silence on everyone. Either scouts had found the charcoal kilns in the forest and the metal-casting workshop at Eusserthal and had put two and two together, or . . .

Or someone at Trifels Castle had been talking.

"By God, I don't know when the castellan means to attack you," Sebastian wailed. "Truly I don't. Sometime in the summer, when the . . . the weapons are ready."

Hans von Wertingen drew his long sword and looked coolly down at the gasping figure of Sebastian. "I promised you a quick death, and as a knight I keep my promises. So go to hell, and give the devil my regards."

He raised the sword in both hands and brought it down on the writhing, screaming man-at-arms.

Gunther turned away as Sebastian's screams were abruptly silenced. He had seen enough. Tears ran down his face, mingling with the blood on it. He had known Sebastian for many years. When the other man talked big, it sometimes got on his nerves, but they had been almost as close as brothers. Now he couldn't even bury his body. He would probably molder away beside Sebastian here in the forest.

The barking of the mastiff could be heard again in the distance, but coming closer.

"Sounds like Manfred has found my Saskia at last," commented Wertingen. "Let's get out of here before those fat guards from Neukastell turn up."

His two followers climbed up on the cart behind him, and it began to move away, jolting. A little later the fourth man emerged from the forest, now leading the mastiff on a long leash.

"Hey, wait for me!" he shouted. "How can I help it if this bitch wants to chase hares?" Then he ran after the cart with the dog, cursing.

They've forgotten about me, thought Gunther. *God heard my prayer. They've really and truly forgotten about me.*

For a while the squealing of the cart wheels and the sound of the barking dog could still be heard, and then the peaceful silence of the forest reigned again.

Gunther lay behind the bush, his face smeared with blood, shedding soundless tears.

Philipp von Erfenstein picked up the glass goblet and flung it against the wall of the Knights' House at Trifels, where it shattered into a thousand pieces. It was followed by another glass, two copper plates, a roast pheasant, and finally the entire table, carafe of wine and all. The wooden table splintered, and the wine left red channels like blood on the stones of the floor.

"That bastard!" the castellan bellowed. "That godforsaken bastard! I'll have his guts, I'll stick every one of his limbs on the battlements of this castle, I'll throw his head into the deepest well!" He picked up a stool and was about to throw that at the wall as well, but Agnes intervened.

"If you carry on like that, we'll soon have to eat off the bare stone floor." She cautiously forced her father's arm down. "Better save your strength for Wertingen's castle."

Erfenstein hesitated for a moment, and then nodded. Breathing heavily, he put the stool back in its place beside the hearth. "You're right, girl," he wheezed. "A waste of good wine. But I don't know whether we'll be able to storm the Ramburg, now that Black Hans knows our plans."

He sat down on the stool again, rubbing his angry face, already bloated with alcohol. His eyes were tired and glazed, and he was still shaking all over. Father Tristan had just brought the injured man-at-arms, Gunther, over to the Knights' House, where the monk was tending his wounds. In spite of the arrow that had hit him, Gunther had managed to drag himself all the long, sometimes steep way from Neukastell back to Trifels Castle. At first he could hardly speak after his exertions, but finally he told them what had happened to him and Sebastian. The castellan had been perfectly quiet at first. Agnes, who knew her father, recognized that as the calm before the storm. Sure enough, his outburst came some minutes later, when they were both alone in the Knights' House, and it was all the more violent for that.

"How did that cowardly dog know about Mathis and the gun, eh?" said Erfenstein so menacingly that his two hounds cringed away into a corner, whimpering. "And he also knew my two men-at-arms were secretly on their way to Neukastell, and he knew about the money. Someone must have given us away."

"He may have known about the gun anyway," Agnes replied reassuringly. "The smoke from the furnace could be seen for miles around. But it's certainly odd that Wertingen knew the exact time the cart would be passing, and what the men had with them." She frowned, but however hard she tried, she could think of no possible betrayer.

"Curse it, how am I to pay what I owe the duke now?" the castellan complained, his shoulders drooping. All the anger seemed to have drained away from him, like air from a pig's bladder. "I've squeezed all I can out of my peasants. They have nothing left to give. And the ducal steward couldn't care less. Rupprecht and I were friends once, but he doesn't let that trouble him when there's money at stake." The castellan ran his hand through his hair. "This is the end, Agnes. They'll finally take Trifels away from me now."

"No one will take Trifels away from you, Father," Agnes said. She went to sit beside him, and took his shaking hand. "Not yet. I've looked in the accounts. We still have a little saved up. If we sell Mother's jewelry, Lohingen may be content with that as an installment."

"Oh, Agnes, your mother's jewelry was already in the stolen purse with the money. And twice its worth wouldn't have been enough." Erfenstein shook his head, sighing. "What's more, we need money not just for Lohingen but for Mathis too, so that he can finish making that damn gun. We can melt down all the metal we can find, but sulfur still costs money, and there are other costs as well. Now the lad needs lead, and twenty feet of rope for fuses from the ropemaker in

Annweiler." He laughed mirthlessly. "It's enough to drive me crazy, Agnes. Either I admit defeat to the duke's steward and lose the castle, or I can't arm us well enough, I lose the battle against Hans von Wertingen, and I lose Trifels all the same. I have no other choice."

Agnes thought for a while. "Then borrow the money," she said at last.

Erfenstein's large figure seemed to shrink as he sat on his stool. "Who from? The other knights in these parts aren't much better off themselves, and I'm not bowing and scraping to that young upstart Scharfeneck anymore, by God. I'd sooner go around in sackcloth and ashes."

"You know some merchants in Speyer. They have plenty of money." Agnes shrugged. "I'm sure they'd lend you something. If necessary, you can pay them back a little more than you borrowed."

"A *little* more?" Erfenstein sighed. "The interest they charge is outrageous. It was better to borrow from the Jews before those poor fellows were driven out. And you yourself don't believe the merchants of Speyer will lend me money at no interest, out of love of their neighbor, just to help me out of trouble. Why would they? They'd get nothing out of the deal, unless . . ." Suddenly the castellan stopped. Deep lines showed on his forehead as he scrutinized his daughter thoughtfully. "Well, why not?" Erfenstein murmured at last. "It might work."

"What do you mean?" asked Agnes.

Philipp von Erfenstein rubbed his beard, which was wet with wine. "Last time I went to Speyer, the cloth merchant Jakob Gutknecht dropped a few words about his son. He's twenty years old now, and still something of a rascal." The castellan grinned, as if he had suddenly cast off his anxieties. "Gives his father all the trouble he can. That's why Gutknecht wants to see him in safe harbor as soon as possible."

Agnes felt her heart beating faster. "You don't mean . . ."

"Agnes," her father said brusquely. "You're not going to get a noble knight for a husband, can't you understand that? We knights have come down in the world. Although I'm sorry to say so, the future belongs to the merchant class. I know those fops. They look down on us, but at heart they all look enviously at our titles. Any patrician would be happy to show off a pretty baroness or a castellan's daughter as his wife." He clapped his hands. "Yes, it might just work."

Agnes said nothing, but her expression darkened. *A jewel for a patrician to wear. So that's all I mean to him . . .*

"We should visit Speyer soon," said Erfenstein, his cheeks glowing with wine and enthusiasm. "In fact the sooner the better. Now that Black Hans knows our plans, we must attack before he makes his castle impregnable. Every day counts." He looked sharply at Agnes. "And don't you think you can go there in doublet and hose. Your best gown will be only just good enough. We want to bargain for a good price, and . . ." Only now did he seem to interpret his daughter's expression correctly. "Not sulking, are you?" he asked suspiciously. "How much longer are you going to hide yourself here? I've always told you this day would come. And there are worse things than marrying the son of a rich merchant."

Yes, for instance, not marrying anyone, was the thought that shot through Agnes's mind. *A woman without a husband, unprotected, and without a castle . . .*

She said nothing for a while. At last the words came hesitantly out. "I . . . I'll do what I can. If we can save Trifels Castle that way."

Erfenstein smiled. "That's my girl. And it may not come to that. It could be enough to hint at something. Hold out the prospect of a marriage, and get credit from Gutknecht at no interest." Swaying, he rose to his feet and went looking for two intact glasses for new wine. "Ah, now we can blow up Black Hans's castle right under his fat ass," he said triumphantly. He held out a glass to Agnes. "We should drink to that."

Agnes took the goblet and sipped from it. Then she put it down on the dirty floor.

"We'll need a new table," she said quietly. "At least we can still afford that." She turned to the door. "I'll go and see the head groom and tell him to look for suitable timber in the woodshed."

Without another word, Agnes left the Knights' House, while her father tipsily hummed an old war song. His words still gnawed away at her.

Any patrician would be happy to show off a pretty baroness or a castellan's daughter . . .

Was that to be her future task? Playing the part of a piece of cheap jewelry, just to save Trifels Castle? She sighed deeply. It really did look like she must soon resign herself to her fate. And any husband would be better than Martin von Heidelsheim, even if she would never have wished the steward of Trifels to meet with such a terrible end.

As Agnes stepped out into the bright light of the midday sun in the castle courtyard, she saw Mathis standing down by the cisterns. She quickly dismissed her gloomy thoughts and went toward him.

"I've heard about Sebastian. I came straight here," he said sadly as they met near the stables. "He was a decent man. Talked rather too much, maybe, but good at heart. And I'll miss him at the furnace, too. There's so much to be done at the moment that I hardly know whether I'm coming or going."

"We'll have to be finished sooner than expected, all the same, now that Black Hans knows the plan. As soon as possible, in fact. Father and I are going to Speyer to borrow money there." Agnes told Mathis about her father's plans, leaving out the fact that she was supposed to act like a pretty decoy. She did not want to hurt Mathis unnecessarily, and she felt ashamed of the plan as well.

"I can't be through with it before June," he replied at last. "We'll need at least a week for the fine adjustments to the gun. And I have yet to make the gunpowder. Besides sulfur, which is expensive, and charcoal, I'll need saltpeter, which we can scrape out of the privies. Maybe, if we all work together—"

"It must be fast," Agnes interrupted him. "The longer we wait, the more time Black Hans will have to prepare for Father's attack. He'll fortify his castle—and do it with the money he stole from us."

"I'll do my best, all right? I can't promise any more than that." Mathis took a deep breath and then went on, more calmly, "I actually came to tell you that your comical count really is moving into the ruins of Scharfenberg. I saw a crowd of soldiers and carters down on the pass with heavily laden carts. Furniture, chests, armor, spears, crossbows . . ." He grinned at her. "Why don't we go and look at it from close quarters? That may take your mind off Black Hans."

When they reached Scharfenberg, the huge baggage train had already drawn up outside the castle gates. Agnes counted over a dozen heavily laden carts. Their way had taken them along the dip in the ground where, a week ago, she and Mathis had seen the strange lights that disappeared so suddenly. When they happened to pass the same place the next morning, they had noticed nothing out of the ordinary.

Now, hearing the carters shouting, the horses whinnying, and the servants cursing as they unloaded the heavy crates one by one, Agnes felt like that nocturnal incident had been unreal. In bright sunlight, the castle and its surroundings seemed almost homely.

Knights of the Neipperg family had lived in Scharfenberg Castle until a few decades ago. But when the last of that old family died, the ducal steward had not bestowed the fief on anyone else. Stormy winds, rain, and snow had knocked out the once magnificent thickly glazed windows in the lord's apartments. Tiles had blown off the roof, and some of the merlons on the battlements had fallen into disrepair. But otherwise Scharfenberg was still in reasonably good condition. The small company of guards left to protect it had ensured that potential looters were at least kept away from the inner ring of walls. Agnes knew other castles that had deteriorated within a few years and became stone quarries for peasants, who used what material came to hand for their own houses. Again and again, you found stones in peasant cottages with inscriptions indicating an earlier noble owner.

Scharfenberg Castle, like Trifels, lay on the Sonnenberg, on a south-facing plateau of rock, but it was much smaller. Its most striking feature was the tall keep standing in the upper bailey, close to the castellan's apartments. Lower down there were sheds, stables, and dwelling quarters, surrounded by a circular wall. A deep moat lay on three sides of the buildings, and on the western side a drawbridge led to the first castle gate, through which some of the carts now leisurely rolled. Workmen had put up scaffolding against the outer walls and were beginning to render them with new mortar, while other men retiled rooftops. A group of colorfully clad landsknechts sat on a mossy rock in the sun. They were playing dice, laughing, and singing so loudly that Agnes had heard them from a long way off.

Agnes and Mathis stood at some remove, watching all this activity. The castellan's daughter was trying to work out how much money Count Friedrich von Löwenstein-Scharfeneck would be paying to restore this castle. It must amount to thousands of guilders, such a sum as her father had never even seen in his entire life.

"Father Tristan told me that Scharfenberg was once a prison," she told Mathis, as they watched a couple of glaziers at work. The workmen were just putting in new stained-glass windows on the first floor of the castellan's dwelling. "When they've finished, this will look as grand as the elector's palace in Heidelberg."

"And down in Leinsweiler and the other villages, the peasants are starving." Mathis shook his head. "It's shameful. This castle is being renovated with human blood."

"You're forgetting that the count will help the local workers to earn a good living," replied Agnes. "They have to earn their bread one way or another."

"It may help these glaziers—they're craftsmen—but it won't do anything for the peasants. And as for the money our fine count uses to pay the craftsmen, he took it out of their pockets first as taxes. It's high time things changed in the empire. Well, look!" Mathis nodded his head to the left. "Speak of the devil . . ."

Sure enough, there was a horseman on the road from the pass to Scharfenberg, riding a tall steed whose harness sparkled in the sun.

Agnes, too, now recognized Friedrich von Löwenstein-Scharfeneck. The young count wore a flowing woolen cloak, clasped at the neck with a golden brooch. The cap tipped jauntily over his forehead was made of the finest Flanders cloth, and he wore close-fitting silken hose.

When the count saw Agnes, he rode over to her and took off his cap. She noticed, for the first time, that the black hair under it was already thinning slightly.

"God be with you, noble lady," he said, smiling. "Didn't I say we'd be meeting again soon?"

Agnes made a dutiful little curtsy. "You do me honor, Excellency." She indicated Mathis, who was standing beside her with his eyes lowered and his arms crossed. "May I introduce Mathis Wielenbach, who is the son of the smith at Trifels Castle? It's Mathis who has been casting the heavy gun with which my father plans to take Wertingen's castle."

The count nodded pleasantly. "I've heard of you already, boy. Indeed, they say amazing things about you. Although I still cannot believe that a young, simple armorer is capable of such things. Who taught you? Your father?"

"I found the art of it in books, Excellency," Mathis replied coolly.

"In books?" Scharfeneck grinned. "You don't mean to say that you can read, fellow? Or rather, did you just look at pictures?"

"With respect, the fact that my father is a smith makes me no more stupid than any fine gentleman."

"Indeed?" The count raised his right eyebrow, offended. "I suppose you are one of those who consider all men equal. Then what else I am told about you must be correct? They say that the mayor of Annweiler wants to arrest you for sedition."

"By my honor, I have done nothing to shame me before God."

"Mathis is under my father's protection," said Agnes, trying to make peace between them. "He may sometimes be a little outspoken, but . . . but he knows his place."

"So I should hope." Friedrich von Löwenstein-Scharfeneck leaned down to her on his prancing horse. "But if I may offer you my advice, young lady, be careful of the company you keep. Only last week, I hear, a countess on her travels had her throat cut in Worms by a gang of savage peasants. These are dangerous times for those of noble birth. Rabble like that are getting bolder every day."

"Mathis would never hurt me. He is my friend, he—" Agnes began, indignantly, but the count waved her protest away.

"Some are servants and some are masters, castellan's daughter. God has given every living creature a place in the established order. A fish does not want to fly, an eagle does not dig damp burrows in the ground. Why should it be different for human beings?" Friedrich von Löwenstein-Scharfeneck sat up very straight in the saddle, turning his eyes sternly on the silent Mathis. "Those who try meddling with the divine order of things offend against God. Remember that, peasant."

"I am a smith, for heaven's sake," Mathis hissed through gritted teeth. But the count was not listening to him.

"I must go and see how the workmen are doing," said Löwenstein-Scharfeneck, taking a firm grip of his horse's reins. "Scharfenberg Castle will shine with new radiance. A worthy home for our ancient family. I would be glad if I might welcome you to my hall in the near future, Lady Agnes. On your own," he added smugly. "Over a glass of wine and beside a warm fire burning on the hearth, those like you and me can enjoy ourselves very well speaking of old sagas and legends." With that, he spurred on his horse and rode away.

Agnes turned to Mathis, who stood beside her, white as a sheet. His nostrils flared slightly; that was the only movement she could see in him.

"Just forget what that idiot said, Mathis," she told him, laying her hand on his shoulder, but he shook it off.

"'He knows his place,' right?" he said, mimicking her voice. "That stupid smith."

Agnes sighed. "I only said that to—"

"I don't care why you said it. Those were the words that came out.

And maybe that self-satisfied popinjay is right: there are two kinds of people, and one kind should have nothing to do with the other."

Mathis abruptly turned away and hurried along the path back to Trifels Castle. After only a few steps, he had disappeared among the sandstone rocks.

"Mathis!" she called after him. "Mathis, wait for me! Damn it, don't be so pig-headed."

She stamped her foot angrily. This was their second quarrel within a few weeks. Why did he always have to be so stubborn?

She was going to hurry after him when she suddenly heard the soft sound of a lute coming from the castle. A pleasant tenor voice sang along to the lute and was very different from the earlier raucous bawling.

As Agnes turned to the castle again, she saw that another man had joined the group of landsknechts playing dice on top of the hill. Like the count, he wore close-fitting hose, but his doublet was brightly colored and slashed in the military manner. The cap on his head was adorned with bright purple feathers; Agnes could not have said what strange bird they came from. He wore a sword with a handguard by his side, a weapon also favored by the landsknechts. But he held a wooden lute in his hands and was just striking up another merry song on it. The crude text of the song tickled the soldiers' sense of humor.

"Come landlord, ere we die of thirst, bring in the wine, bring in the wine. Although your belly be fit to burst, bring us more wine, bring us more wine . . ."

Feeling curious, Agnes went closer. The minstrel was so delicately built that she took him for a youth at first, but now she saw that he was no longer young, perhaps in his mid-thirties. The hair under his cap was red, like parts of his colorful costume, and freckles were sprinkled over a face that sported a ridiculously small pointed beard. He was not exactly handsome, but he had a natural air of distinction that marked him off from the landsknechts surrounding him. When the minstrel noticed Agnes, he stopped singing abruptly and made her a slight bow.

"Forgive my coarse words, noble maiden," he said in a rather affected and old-fashioned tone of voice that made Agnes instinctively smile. "Had I known that such a lovely young lady was listening to my risqué rhymes, I'd have chosen a courtly love song instead."

"Oh, but I liked it," replied Agnes. "It sounded old, like a song from another time."

"You heard it correctly. It was—"

"Hey, none of your blarney, minstrel," called one of the landsknechts. "Go on playing. And the girl can dance to it—and maybe drop her skirt."

The others laughed and roared, and the red-haired man cast them an indignant glance. "Fool that you are, don't you recognize when you have a genuine lady before you?" he roughly asked the spokesman, who was still grinning suggestively. "Apologize to her at once."

"It really doesn't . . ." Agnes began, but the minstrel interrupted.

"I must insist, fair maiden. I cannot tolerate such manners. Well, how about it? Where's your apology?"

The last words were directed once again at the landsknecht who had insulted Agnes. The man had a wild growth of untrimmed beard, and wore wide, colored hose, with a sword as long as an arm dangling from his belt. His grin disappeared, and he straightened up, growling.

"Listen to me, you joker," he began, grasping the pommel of his sword. "You may have a fine, high singing voice, but I can make sure it's soon higher yet, if you take my meaning."

"I take your meaning perfectly," the little minstrel replied coolly. He carefully laid his lute down on the moss-grown rock and put his hand to his own sword. "Never mind that, you will now apologize to the lady at once."

The landsknecht laughed, then suddenly drew his sword. With a loud cry he made for the delicately built minstrel, who was a full head shorter than he was.

"You windbag of a—"

But he got no farther, for the minstrel had stepped aside with surprising speed. As the soldier ran past, he put out a leg and tripped the man up, so that he slipped on the moss and fell to the ground, cursing.

"Let that be a warning to you," said the minstrel. "Now, get on with that apology, and we'll let the matter rest."

But the landsknecht had no intention of apologizing. He stood up and flung himself at his opponent, shouting and raising his blade. The minstrel stoically stood his ground and raised his own sword only at the last moment, thrust under the other man's blade with it, and immediately stepped to one side. Baffled, the landsknecht stood there staggering for a second time, but now he was quicker, and did not fall but swung around with a cry of triumph—only to feel the tip of the minstrel's sword at his throat. He stared in horror as the steel tip just pierced his skin, so that a few drops of blood ran down his neck.

"The apology," whispered the minstrel. His voice was as soft as it was determined. "I'm waiting."

"I . . . I apologize," the other man muttered.

"Louder. I don't think the lady heard you stammering like that."

"I apologize."

"You must say: I apologize, fair maid."

The landsknecht rolled his eyes. His comrades stayed where they were on the rock, their own weapons half drawn. No one dared to move, including Agnes.

At last, after what felt like an eternity, the soldier murmured the right words.

"I apologize, fair maid."

His sword still stretched out in his hand, the delicately built man turned to Agnes. "Will you accept his apology?"

When Agnes nodded, a boyish smile spread over his face. Slowly, he lowered his sword. "There, that wasn't so bad," he said in the general direction of the landsknecht, who still stood in front of him, sweating profusely. His comrades were about to draw their own swords fully, but the minstrel raised a hand in the manner of one used to command.

"That's enough. No one has lost face. This man has apologized, and just as well." There was suddenly a note of menace in his voice, something that did not quite suit the smile on his face. "Or were you thinking of attacking a nobly born knight, when you'd all end up on the gallows? And a knight who, in the bargain, is under the personal protection of the count? Do you want to be dangling from the oak trees over there this evening, with your blue tongues hanging out while you piss in your slashed hose? Tell me, is it really worth it?"

On getting no answer, he put his sword back in its sheath and picked up the ivory-inlaid lute that was still lying on the rock. Gallantly, he offered Agnes his other arm. "I think these gentlemen have had enough music for now. Let us leave this place, my lady. I will happily sing you a courtly love song somewhere else."

Agnes smiled and did not object when he led her away. The whole situation had been as unreal as one of her dreams. Only now did she feel able to say anything.

"That was very dangerous," she pointed out as they walked over to the castle gateway together. "One wrong word, and those men would have struck you down."

The minstrel smiled. "Well, you see, that's it. You have only to choose your words well enough to avoid unnecessary conflict. Words and songs are the strongest weapons of all." He stopped, and struck his forehead. "But how uncivil of me. What with all of that, I quite forgot to introduce myself." Taking off his cap, he bowed so low that his red hair fell over his brow. "Allow me to do so now. Melchior von Tanningen, by my condition knight of the Tanningen family in fair Franconia, and at present a traveling minstrel."

Agnes could not suppress a smile. The little man was as amusing as he was touching. However, he had been a dangerous opponent in a quarrel.

"I didn't know that there were still any minstrels," she replied. "I thought they'd all died out long ago."

Melchior von Tanningen shook his head indignantly. "By God, no! Has love died out? And music? And great deeds? So long as all those exist there will be minstrels, too. We report what goes on in these turbulent times. And we are often there to provide consolation when mourning clouds the mind." He took his lute and played a chord that sounded both cheerful and melancholy, and to the melody that followed he sang a short verse of lamentation.

"D'amor m'estera ben e gent, s'eu ma dona vis plus sovent . . ."

"That was in Occitanian," Agnes marveled.

Melchior von Tanningen looked surprised. "You know the old language of singers and minstrels?"

"Well, only a little. I have read about it, but I've never heard it sung so beautifully before."

A blissful smile spread over Tanningen's lips. "Then you are indeed a lady. Would it be appropriate to ask your name?"

"I am Agnes von Erfenstein, daughter of the castellan of Trifels Castle."

The minstrel seemed taken aback for a moment, but then he beamed at her. "Trifels Castle! The residence of Barbarossa, Richard the Lionheart's prison, the stronghold of the legendary imperial insignia. What finer place could a minstrel celebrate? To see Trifels was one of the reasons that brought me here to the Palatinate." He bowed deeply. "Lady Agnes, it is an honor to make your acquaintance."

Once again Agnes could not help smiling. No man had ever talked to her like that before.

"You say you are a knight," she replied at last. "Then why are you not living in your castle?"

Melchior von Tanningen straightened up again, looking slightly embarrassed. "Well, to my deep regret I share it with two of my brothers. An unedifying tale of a quarrel over our inheritance. I did not care for that, so I went out into the world. I have traveled through Flanders, Saxony, and Sweden. I have been to Venice, to distant Aragon, and to Castile, where the sun burns down like fire from the sky. I go wherever great lords need a minstrel."

"And now Count Friedrich von Löwenstein-Scharfeneck is your master?"

Melchior von Tanningen nodded. "The very same. After troubled times, most recently where they are fighting in Italy, I thought it better to make the sleepy German Empire my base for the time being. The count kindly allows me to roam around these parts if, in return, I entertain him in the evening with songs about the quiet forest."

"If only it really was quiet," Agnes sighed.

"What do you mean by that? Are there adventures and quests here as well?"

"None worth celebrating in song. They're too disreputable and probably too ordinary for that." Laughing, Agnes tossed her hair back and scrutinized her chivalrous companion. He must be over ten years older than Mathis, yet in a certain way he reminded her of her friend. He had the same restless nature, the same youthful curiosity. But in addition this Melchior seemed to come from a different world. A world known to Agnes only from her books and her dreams, and one that she had often longed for. Now that world stood before her in the shape of a delicately built, entertaining man.

They reached the castle gateway. Carters were still unloading heavy chests and crates, and the carts rumbled past the two of them.

"I was about to pay the count a visit," Melchior said, letting two men with a heavy chest pass as they carried it into the castle. "I am sure he would be delighted to meet you. Well? Will you come with me?"

"I know the count already," Agnes replied. "Another time, maybe. But now I must go home before my father begins to worry about me."

Melchior nodded eagerly. "I understand. Then let me at least escort you to your castle. So that those coarse fellows don't trouble you again."

"Thank you, but that won't be necessary. I can look after myself. And I am sure the count will be expecting you." Agnes bobbed a curtsy. "So fare you well."

Good heavens, I'm beginning to talk in the same old-fashioned way myself.

Melchior von Tanningen bowed politely. "As you wish. All the same, I hope to see you again soon."

"That . . . I'm sure that can be arranged."

With a twinkle in her eyes, Agnes turned away and passed the noisy carters, glaziers, and carpenters on her way back to the narrow path leading to Trifels Castle. She smiled to herself, and her heart felt lighter. All the anxieties of the last few weeks—her strange dreams, the robbers' attack on the Trifels men-at-arms, her father's wedding plans—all that had made life seem gray and dismal to her on many days. Melchior von Tanningen was the first person to have made her smile in a long time.

She was still smiling as she passed the tall sandstone rocks, while the noise of the workmen slowly died away behind her. At least life would not be so boring with her new neighbor and his minstrel.

Deep in the cellars of Annweiler Town Hall, the mayor, Bernwart Gessler, was poring over a stack of yellowed parchments. The records were old and stained; many of them could have been hundreds of years old. They all told the story of Annweiler, which had once risen to power and riches with Trifels Castle, and like the castle was now slowly falling into decay.

He hoped that his research would get him on the track of what was obviously an extremely valuable secret.

The visit of the black-skinned man a few weeks ago had left the mayor both anxious and curious. His curiosity had been increased by the visit of another stranger asking the same questions in the last few days. He, too, had given Gessler a heavy bag of coins. He should have been glad, for that money, along with all the other sums that he had put aside for himself over the course of time, was easily enough to allow him to turn his back on this filthy hole in the near future. Gessler hoped that the duke of Zweibrücken would give him a profitable fief, not one of these half-ruined castles but a fine residence, or perhaps an abbey. Anyway, a place where a gentleman could live well, and where the peasants knew who their master was.

Since the early hours of the morning Gessler had been reading records and church registers going far back into the history of Annweiler. It was like digging away layers of damp, dark earth to get to a buried treasure. So far he had brought nothing of interest to light, but Gessler knew that if two such strangers asked the same questions, then there must be something very important behind it all. The instinct that had brought him, the son of a simple councilor's assistant in Speyer, to the position of mayor in this town had also advised him to keep the documents in the cellar of the town hall a secret from both men.

First he must find out what they were really worth.

The mayor was just pulling another mountain of files across the table toward him when a slight sound attracted his attention. It made no more noise than a draft of air. Before Gessler could turn around, he felt a hand on his shoulder. A cry of alarm—almost a squeak of alarm—escaped him, and next moment he regretted it. Never mind who was standing behind him, whether it was a murderer, a thief, or simply a curious councilor—the mayor of a town should never show fear. It detracted from any kind of authority.

Bernwart Gessler forced himself to keep calm. He slowly pushed the stack of documents away again.

"Whoever you are, you have no right to make your way in here," he said.

"Forgive the intrusion. The guards upstairs told me this was where I would find you."

The hand moved away from his shoulder. Only now did Gessler slowly turn his head. The black-skinned stranger stood by the shelves behind him, leafing through some of the files stored there.

"You have signed a great many death sentences over the last few years," the man said appreciatively. He indicated a sheet of paper in his hand. "People condemned to death by hanging, breaking on the wheel, drowning in the millstream—even a case of quartering, the criminal torn apart by horses. What a magnificent spectacle. You do not often get to see that in the empire."

"Michel Schultheiss. A wanted murderer, rabble-rouser, and arsonist," Gessler replied with as much composure as possible. "These are hard times. One has to make an example."

"Hard times, to be sure, to be sure. And not just here in the Wasgau. The whole empire seems to be aflame."

The man leafed through the documents in silence. After a while the mayor could stand it no longer. He cleared his throat.

"I'm sure you're not here to discuss the verdicts of trials with me. So tell me what you want, and then leave me to go on sorting out these old parchments. One of my young assistants got them all mixed up. It's going to take me some time to put everything back in order."

"You are right. My own time is severely limited." The stranger strolled over to him, casting a fleeting glance at the documents on the table. Gessler felt the blood shoot into his face. It wasn't going to take this man long to find out what he was looking for. With as much composure as he could muster, Gessler quickly moved a few harmless financial lists to the top of the older documents.

For a moment the stranger seemed to hesitate. Then he went on calmly, "The midwife Elsbeth Rechsteiner, of whom you told me, has disappeared without a trace. We kept her house under observation for several weeks, but she never turned up. Either she is dead, or someone has warned her against us." He leaned over so close to Gessler that the mayor caught the scent of an exotic perfume: carnations, aniseed, and spices unknown to him. The black-skinned man's voice was very low now. "Did *you* warn her?"

Gessler gave a thin-lipped smile. "Why would I do that?"

"Did anyone else inquire about her?" the stranger persisted.

In a fraction of a second, the mayor came to another decision. He made it as instinctively as his determination not to tell the black-skinned man about the documents. In a long life in politics, he had found that, as a rule, it was better to keep one trump card in your own hand. You never knew how the game would turn out.

"You are the only one to have asked me," he said firmly. "And why you take an interest in these old stories is a mystery to me. Not that I really want to know. It can be a bad thing to know too much."

The stranger smiled. "Very true." Suddenly he pulled up a stool standing by the shelves and sat down on it opposite the mayor. He took out a bag of coins from under his coat.

"When we met before, I promised you another sum of money if my search proved successful," he said quietly, putting the clinking purse down on the table. "Unfortunately that has not yet been the case. Unless you have more information for me. Do you?"

"I can look in the archives here," replied the mayor, lowering his eyes. "There may be more records where such things are written down. And maybe I'll find them yet. But I can't promise anything."

"Then go on looking, if you want this second purse." There was a short pause. Finally the man went on. "Aside from that, there is something I would like to show you." Feeling under his coat again, this time he produced two strange metal items, each about the size of a man's hand, and fitted at one end with a polished wooden grip inlaid with ivory. Curious gadgets were fitted to them: a trigger, little wheels, metal levers. Cautiously, almost devoutly, the man placed both handguns beside the purse of money on the table.

"I sent to Brunswick for these pretty things," he said after a while. "They are handguns with a wheel-lock mechanism. A wonderful invention. A gun that will fire itself by means of clockwork fitted to it. You have only to squeeze the trigger. In Constantinople, the sultan's bodyguard is armed with them. I am sure that this brilliant device will soon be adopted here as well."

The man turned the barrel of one of the handguns so that it was now pointing straight at Gessler, like the hand of a clock. "Its firepower is truly enormous. I myself have seen the head of a traitor disintegrate into blood, splintered bone, and white brains. One moment the head was there, next there was only the man's torso mounted on a horse and spouting blood. Impressive, do you not agree?"

"I think I take your point." Repelled, the mayor nudged the

weapon so that the barrel no longer pointed at him. "Please excuse me now. I still have a great deal to do."

"Of course." The stranger got to his feet and put away the bag of money and the two weapons again. "I have already taken up too much of your time. When do you think I may trouble you again?"

"Come back a week from now. No, let's say two weeks. This is an old town; there are many records to be examined. And as I said before, I can't promise you anything."

The man nodded briefly, and turned away without another word.

"One more thing," Gessler called after him. "I'm accustomed to know the name of a man with whom I do business. So what's yours?"

The stranger hesitated, and then he smiled, white teeth shining in his black face. "Call me Caspar," he said at last. "Like one of the three kings from the Orient. For I will tell you that a star has fallen to earth in these parts, and we must look for it. I wish you good day, Master Mayor."

Like a dark shadow, he disappeared through the open door. Soon his footsteps had died away on the cellar stairs.

· 8 ·

Trifels, 25 May, Anno Domini 1524

Days of summer came at last, like a much-missed guest. Grain crops grew in the fields. The white blossoms of fruit trees gave way to swelling apples, pears, and plums. In contrast to the last few years, everything seemed to promise a plentiful harvest. That lifted the mood in the villages around Trifels Castle, and there was a festival with music and dancing almost every day. It was like the people were banishing the long winter and the cold, wet spring with their songs. Even if work in the fields was as hard as ever, the peasants often had smiles on their perspiring faces.

Erfenstein had firmly made up his mind to take Agnes to Speyer in search of a rich bridegroom for her, but it was a little while before they actually set out. The castellan of Trifels wanted to wait for the next great market day in the city. In just under a week, that time came. Two horses were saddled, the castle gate opened, and the travelers rode out.

Philipp von Erfenstein was mounted on Taramis, while Agnes had to make do with the old gray, who stopped at every blade of grass and could often be induced to move on only by kind words. With every step that they rode away from Trifels, Agnes felt her heart grow heavier. Soon they had left the castle behind and trotted along the dusty road to Speyer, which was some two days' journey away.

So far as the reason for their expedition was concerned, her feelings were mixed. She had not been to the cathedral city since she was a little girl, and then she had been overcome by amazement at the sight of all the houses and the crowds of people surrounding her. So she looked forward to seeing the city again. But she also knew that she was to be offered for sale there like a cow in the cattle market.

She had not told Mathis anything about her father's intentions yet. Since making up from their last little quarrel at Scharfenberg Castle, they had secretly spent every spare moment together. They had grown closer to each other than they'd been since they were children romping innocently in the hay. For that very reason, Agnes did not want to let her friend in on the plans for her marriage. Nor did she mention her dreams to him again, now that she saw how brusquely he reacted to them. Those two things together would inevitably have spoiled their last summer of freedom. So Mathis thought that Agnes had gone to Speyer with her father only to buy cloth and wool at the market, and so Erfenstein might borrow money at a reasonable rate.

Philipp von Erfenstein sang cheerfully as they rode, now and then telling stories of the old days. Soon they left the tree-covered mountains of the Wasgau district behind. Beyond the last of the foothills, the land fell steeply away, the woods thinned out, and the Queich, a rushing river back where they had come from, flowed on at a more leisurely pace as it went to join the Rhine. They stayed the night at a village inn not far from the little town of Landau, sharing a large if flea-infested bed. Early next morning, after a meager breakfast of barley groats, hard bread, and cold pheasant, they were off again on the road to Speyer. Agnes was silent, although her father did not notice. Nor did her gloomy mood improve when it began to rain steadily, drenching them to the skin.

Early in the afternoon, the rain finally stopped, and the sun broke through the clouds. Ahead of them rose the rooftops of the city of

Speyer, its cathedral towers reaching to the sky. Below them the roofs of the many half-timbered houses surrounding the cathedral precincts, still wet with rain, shone like colorful mushrooms. The city seemed to have grown even larger since Agnes had last visited it. It was surrounded by a tall, recently plastered wall with several watchtowers, and in the background was the harbor, where the broad stream joined the river Rhine.

"You'll be amazed to see what goes on in the city on market day," said her father, smiling. "You've never seen so many people all at once."

Several gates were let into the wall, and the two travelers now rode toward the largest of them. It was surmounted by a tall tower and had a broad archway leading through it. The two iron-studded halves of the gate stood wide open, and Agnes and her father joined a line of other people waiting to get into the city. Agnes saw sleepy peasants with carts carrying crates full of radishes, spinach, and other early summer vegetables. An ox cart full of dripping wine casks drove along; there were whinnying horses and people shouting, laughing, and arguing. The air did not smell the same as in Annweiler, where it reeked mainly of rotting leather. Here the mingled smells of vegetables, wine, the river water of the harbor, rare spices, and human body odors were a beguiling mixture. Agnes and her father led their horses through the gateway by their reins, and Agnes felt her mouth open in amazement, as it had when she was a child.

Before her was a promenade as wide as a whole village, with a stream of water running down the middle of it. The magnificent houses of the patricians rose to right and left, and at the eastern end of the street stood the cathedral. Its towers were so tall that they cast long shadows over the forecourt. A colorful crowd was coming and going in the alleyways or strolling among the market stalls. At some of the stalls people were tasting the wares for sale, at others they were haggling, while all the different voices united to make a deafening noise.

"Well, what do you say?" cried her father, laughing. "What scolding and chattering. It makes me feel glad of the peace and quiet at home."

Agnes nodded absent-mindedly as she observed the crowd. Only at second glance did she notice that very few of them wore good cloth. Most were clad in the poor garments of peasants and the lower class of workmen; some looked emaciated and lingered around the stalls like hungry dogs while stout merchants' wives showed off their latest gowns and painted faces. The difference between rich and poor seemed far greater here in the city than in the country outside.

At least we are all poor in our neighborhood, thought Agnes. *Except for Count Scharfeneck and the Abbot of Eusserthal, of course.*

Philipp von Erfenstein pointed to a two-story stone building standing on its own in the middle of the broad promenade. Well-dressed patricians were going in and out of the shade of the arcades on the lower floor.

"The mint," Erfenstein explained. "The city's countinghouse, where the merchants do business, is there. Jakob Gutknecht has his establishment there as well. We'll soon be paying him a visit." He looked at his daughter, who was still bedraggled from that morning's rain. "But first let's take a room at an inn, and you can freshen up a little. You look like a horse-coper's daughter."

They turned into a side street where the houses were nothing like as grand as those in the wide main street, stabled their horses at a shabby tavern, and hired a room under its roof. As Erfenstein gave the bowing landlord a few coins, Agnes thought how much this journey had cost her father already. He had had a new dress made for her, and he now carefully unfolded it in their room and held it up to the light. It was of good Flanders cloth, dyed red and trimmed with lace and silver buttons, the kind of garment that might be worn only by the nobility and the families of great lords. Ordinary citizens' wives could find themselves in the pillory for wearing such a showy gown.

"Here, put that on and comb your hair," Erfenstein told her brusquely. "We'll show Gutknecht what a jewel he's getting in you."

Agnes swung around, her eyes flashing at her father. She had meant to keep silent, but she couldn't stand this any longer.

"I'm not a cheap brooch to be bought and sold just like that," she snapped. "I'm your daughter, have you forgotten? If I'm to marry the son of a cloth merchant, then you might at least treat me like a human being."

Erfenstein sighed. "Agnes, we've discussed this. There's nothing else for it. Think of Trifels Castle. And furthermore . . ." His eyes twinkled as he looked at her. "Don't pretend you don't like the dress. Put it on. You'll look like a queen."

"A sad queen," Agnes said defiantly. All the same, she slipped into the dress, taking care not to let her father see the ring that she wore around her neck. If he did, he might get the idea of selling the gem that she treasured so much to a goldsmith in Speyer.

The dress fit her perfectly. As she stroked its fabric, she felt how soft it was. It fell in gentle folds to her feet, showing off her breasts and hips to good advantage, and it was the most expensive garment she had ever worn.

"It . . . it's beautiful," she admitted at last, turning in a circle while the afternoon sunlight fell in through the narrow window.

"There, you see? What can be wrong with wearing it while we pay a visit to this family of moneybags? And, Agnes . . ." Her father raised a finger in warning. "Nothing presumptuous, no sharp remarks, understand?"

"I'll keep quiet like a good girl about to marry a patrician. Well, let's get it over and done with."

Agnes turned away and climbed down the steep stairs to the bar of the tavern, where the few guests looked at her enviously. Out in the street, too, she attracted many glances, particularly from the merchants' wives, who stared at her, whispering. Her father walked beside her, proud as a peacock. Once again Agnes noticed how clothes change you. She no longer felt like a young girl, but a lady born to high rank.

"These are the big farmers, the carriers, and the free craftsmen who bargain for their pay with the patricians," Erfenstein whispered to his daughter. "Prices have been falling for years, and the rich merchants on the town council can fix them just as they please." His face darkened. "We knights have no say in anything these days. Damn slave drivers. To think it should come to this—my own daughter, and I have to let them . . ." He broke off and shook his head. "But never mind that. After all, it's for the sake of Trifels Castle."

He asked the way to the cloth merchant Jakob Gutknecht, and then knocked vigorously at one of the doors. When there was no answer, Erfenstein simply walked in. It was not long before he came back to Agnes.

"What is it?" she asked in surprise. "Have we come to the wrong room?"

"We're to wait," Erfenstein said through gritted teeth. "Gutknecht is with some customers who obviously matter more than we do."

At last they were asked in. The merchant Jakob Gutknecht sat at a massive table covered with papers, parchment scrolls, and full coin purses. He was just dropping some guilders, with a clink, onto a pair of scales to check their weight, and had taken no notice of his visitors yet. Only when Erfenstein cleared his throat several times did the patrician look up, in pretended surprise.

"Ah, the castellan of Trifels Castle," he said in a bored voice. "I'd expected you earlier. Well, never mind that." Wrinkling his brow, he turned to Agnes. "And this is the feast for sore eyes whom you have praised to me so fulsomely in your letters."

Agnes managed to produce a thin smile and a curtsy. She could only hope that Gutknecht's son took after his mother. The merchant was fat and pale, his cap sitting on his head like a black pimple. Two small, red, piggy eyes with large bags under them examined her, moving back and forth all the time. Agnes felt like a beast in a pen at the market.

"How old are you, may I ask?" inquired Gutknecht, as he went on weighing his coins. He still had not invited his guests to sit down.

"She will be seventeen next month," her father replied for her, letting himself down on the small stool that stood in front of the merchant's table. "Agnes is a clever child. Quick-minded, well-read, she can calculate and write . . ."

The merchant waved that away. "If I'd wanted a clerk, I could have spared you your journey. My son and I read the balance sheets. Nothing else is necessary. It matters more to me for his wife to be demure, silent, and not as quarrelsome as my own spouse." He sighed. "Unfortunately I didn't pay enough attention to such matters at the time of my marriage." A touch of suspicion came into Gutknecht's eyes as he went on scrutinizing Agnes. "Why isn't she betrothed yet, eh? She is of noble blood, after all. I've made inquiries. The Erfensteins are an old family. A noble title like that would be good for us Gutknechts. So what's the snag? Is she sick? Does she limp? Out with it, Erfenstein, before I lose patience with you."

"The right man for me has not yet come along," Agnes replied coolly. "And it remains to be seen whether your son is the right man." She straightened her shoulders and looked challengingly at the merchant. "So it would be a good idea for me to meet him first. Or has he preferred the company of some other lady to mine today? One hears that he is not very choosy."

For a few moments no one said anything. Then the merchant began to bleat with laughter. "Now I know what's the matter with your daughter, Erfenstein!" he crowed. "A pert tongue, that's her trouble. No wonder her suitors have taken to their heels."

"It's not like that," the castellan muttered, casting his daughter a furious glance. "I'll admit that Agnes has a mind of her own, but—"

"Yes, yes, wears men's hose and goes hawking with a falcon, so folk say," Jakob Gutknecht interrupted him. He grinned when he saw Erfenstein's startled expression. "I've made inquiries of my own, of course, Sir Castellan. I don't buy a pig in a poke. And before asking my son, I'd prefer to get an idea of her for myself." Gutknecht raised his eyebrows. "I'm not sure whether I like what I've heard. But a title is a title . . ." The merchant paused thoughtfully and then turned to Philipp von Erfenstein as if Agnes was not even in the room. "May I make a suggestion, Castellan?" he asked, although it sounded more like a command. "Let us discuss this on our own for a start. There is a good deal to talk about, particularly from the financial point of view. If we should agree there, I may want to take another look at your daughter. But until then, this is man's business."

He jerked his head toward the door. Understanding his gesture, Agnes made a small bow and took her leave.

"I'll wait for you downstairs, all right?" she whispered to her father, but the castellan did not reply. He sat like a rock on the tiny stool, avoiding her eyes. Finally she turned away and hurried through the door into the open air. Running down the steps, she passed many startled patricians and was finally out in the lively, crowded street. Only here did she stop to take a deep breath.

How could she have made such a spectacle of herself? It had all been too much for her, and now maybe she had wrecked her father's last chance of keeping Trifels Castle. He would never forgive her.

Her dress suddenly felt unseemly, almost indecent. Agnes blushed for the way she looked in it and buttoned up the bodice right to the top. On the spur of the moment, she decided to go into the market, to distract her mind. Her father would surely be some time yet. Judging by his face when he looked at her, it would be better to keep out of his way for a while. Instinctively, Agnes found her footsteps taking her over to the cathedral that she had admired so much as a small child. She stood in silence before the tall porch, looking up at the four towers that rose to the sky. The imperial family of the Salians had built the cathedral as a monument to themselves half a millennium ago. Since then it had been renovated again and again, bearing witness in stone to human capabilities.

There was also constant coming and going on the cathedral forecourt, and in the precincts of the bishop's palace next door to it. Beggars leaned against the pillars of the entrance, holding out their hands; murmuring pilgrims passed with bowed heads. Agnes saw the great stone bowl, known as the cathedral font, which for hundreds of years had marked the border between the imperial city and the diocese of Speyer. Criminals who took refuge beyond the font were in sanctuary, under the bishop's protection, and civic bailiffs could not seize them. Agnes wondered briefly what would happen if Mathis fled to Speyer. Would he be safe from the mayor of Annweiler here?

And then what? she asked herself. *Would he spend the rest of his life behind the cathedral walls? Not much of a solution.*

She put the idea out of her mind and entered the great basilica. Immediately the world was bathed in muted colors. Rays of light fell through the stained-glass windows like gigantic spears. The crowd that had looked so large milling around the forecourt was lost inside the huge building. The voices of worshippers sounded soft and echoed in the basilica. Peace such as she had not known for some time spread through Agnes; sorrow and despair left her as she knelt before the altar in one of the many side chapels and made the sign of the cross.

Dear God, let my father find the right husband for me. If I can't have Mathis, then at least let him be a kind and modest man . . .

After praying silently for a while she went on to the apse, where a monument as tall as a man stood in front of the choir screen. It resembled a huge stone cube, surmounted by a kind of canopy, and with a gilded inscription on the front. From her earlier visit with her father, Agnes knew that it contained the tombs of no less than eight German rulers, together with several of their wives. The people therefore reverently called this monument the Imperial Vault. Two stone reliefs on the sides of the cube showed all the kings who had been laid to rest here long ago, including many Salians as well as Philipp of Swabia, Barbarossa's son, and Rudolf von Habsburg. For a long time, a tomb had been kept ready for Barbarossa himself. After his death, his flesh had been boiled and removed from his bones to be buried in the distant city of Antioch, but to this day no one knew where his bones lay.

While Agnes admired the weathered stone reliefs, something odd suddenly happened. A strange shudder ran from the nape of her neck down her spine, and then back up again to her scalp. At the same time she thought she heard a voice calling to her quietly from somewhere distant. It was only just audible.

"*Agnesss*," the voice seemed to breathe, again and again. "*Agnesss, Agnesss, Agnesss . . .*"

Agnes swung around, startled. She remembered the rustling leaves outside her bedchamber window at Trifels Castle, on the night when she had been plagued by the worst of her dreams by far. She had hardly had time yet to think properly about the dreadful images and sounds that it showed: the puddle of wine reflecting the face of a strange woman who nonetheless resembled her, and the conversation between men planning her death. With the faint voice, it all came back to her.

"*Agnesss . . . Agnesss . . . Agnesss . . .*"

What in heaven's name is that?

She strained her ears to hear the voice. It was so low that she couldn't be sure whether she might not be simply imagining it. She felt that the sound did not come from the main nave of the cathedral, but from below. A slight fit of dizziness overcame her. Without more thought, she went down the steps leading from the right-hand aisle down to the cathedral crypt. The dimly lit vaulted ceiling of this cross-shaped hall rested on a row of columns rising like stone trees into the darkness, where they were lost from view. Only when Agnes was down in the crypt did it occur to her that, if anyone had evil designs on her, she was in far more danger here than up above. In contrast to the nave and aisles, there was not a human soul in the crypt. Two torches at its entrance cast a little light on at least that part of it, but between the columns at the back all was as dark as a moonless night. She held her breath as she concentrated on her surroundings.

"*Agnesss, Agnesss, Agnesss . . .*" The whisper seemed to come from somewhere else again. This time the voice was above her once more. Or was it on one side of her?

What in the world is going on?

Agnes closed her eyes for a moment and mopped her forehead. Did she have a fever? Had a journey of two days in wet weather exhausted her so much that she was imagining things? She could vaguely make out some altars at the far end of the crypt. Only now did she see a monk kneeling in front of a candle on the extreme left, with his head bent. Her heart was beating as fast as if she had run here all the way from the market. What was the matter with her?

"*Agnessss, Agnesss, Agnessss . . .*" whispered the voice.

Could the monk have been calling to her? She was about to address the kneeling figure, but suddenly held back.

Suppose it wasn't a monk at all?

The kneeling man abruptly stood up and came toward her, walking fast. Agnes opened her mouth to scream, but no sound came out. She suddenly felt like the sheer weight of stone and rock overhead were crushing her. The monk in front of her had been wearing the hood of his cowl well down over his face, but now he put it back, and his face shone as bright as daylight in the darkness of the crypt.

It was an old face, and very kindly.

"What's the matter, child?" asked the monk, looking at her in surprise. "Are you feeling unwell?"

"It . . . it's nothing," Agnes gasped. By now she had recovered her voice. "I must be seeing ghosts."

She stared into the darkness, one last time, then finally tore herself away and raced up the steps. At the top she stumbled, fell full length, and scrambled up again. With the last of her strength, she ran along the central nave and out into the open air. At once the sense of oppression went away. Pilgrims passing nearby looked at her curiously.

Agnes looked down at herself. Her dress was dirty, and there was a tear in one place. Pale and trembling, she was a sorry sight. She leaned against the cathedral font, exhausted, and waited for her breathing to calm down. Could someone really have been watching her? Could that someone have called her name? Cautiously, she looked around, but apart from a couple of old women and some beggars, there was no one close to her. In retrospect, the whispering seemed to her strangely unreal.

Agnes shook her head and tried to dismiss the entire incident as one of her bad dreams. Maybe she really was a little feverish. And heaven knew she had enough difficulties already. All at once it occurred to her that her father would surely be waiting for her by now. She straightened up and hurried back through the market to the mint, which already looked less crowded than before. Only a few merchants still stood around the building, while the stream of water in the middle of the street carried away the stinking refuse of a long day.

Agnes was about to go up to the second floor when she saw her father. He was sitting on a stone bench under the arcades. At first she hardly recognized him. He was sitting hunched up, like a lonely old man, staring straight ahead as he ran his fingers through his hair and his beard. He looked worn out. Agnes cautiously approached him.

"Did Jakob Gutknecht . . ." she began quietly, but her father just shook his head.

"The deal is off."

Agnes felt weak at the knees. She sat down beside her father, not sure whether to shed tears or feel glad.

"Father . . ." she stammered. "I . . . I'm so sorry. I never ought to have . . ."

Erfenstein dismissed that. "It wasn't your outspoken remarks. Or at least, they didn't decide it. It was the money. Gutknecht wouldn't have insisted on a dowry, but when he heard how little we own, when I showed him the papers, the meager yield of our fief, then . . . then . . ." The castellan's voice failed him. "Then he laughed," he said at last. "That bastard laughed at me—a knight! If I'd brought my sword, I'd have struck him down like a rabid dog." He shook his head, and Agnes thought she saw new gray hairs in his once thick black mane. "What have we come to, Agnes?" he asked wearily. "What have we come to, for a merchant to laugh at a knight?"

"Times have changed, Father." Agnes took his hand and held it tightly. "So what now?" she asked, after a few minutes of silence.

"What do you think?" The castellan stood up, groaning. "We'll go and borrow money from the wool merchants. One of them promised me credit not long ago. At an exorbitant rate of interest. And unless a miracle happens, I won't be able to pay my debts next year, and I'll be leaving Trifels Castle. But at least I still have you." He turned to Agnes, and gave her a long, loving look. "How could I ever have thought of selling my little bird to a moneybags like that?" he said quietly. "I'd sooner jump from the tallest tower of Trifels than let one of those upstart Speyer patricians have you."

In silence, he walked away over the marketplace. Agnes hurried after him. At that moment, she wasn't sure how seriously her father had meant that last remark.

The journey back to Trifels the next day was a silent one. Philipp von Erfenstein brooded, while Agnes alternated between anxiety and relief. She wasn't going to marry a merchant in Speyer. At least for the moment, she could give herself up to the illusion that everything was the same as before. But she knew the day would soon come when her father looked for another husband for her. And it wouldn't be Mathis.

For a while Agnes occupied her mind by wondering who could have been lying in wait for her in the cathedral crypt. But then she decided that she had merely imagined her pursuer, and above all that voice. So she thought it better to keep her father's spirits up by asking him about old battles, and the tournaments in which he had once fought. That at least cheered Erfenstein a little.

They were going to ride back by way of Eusserthal, because the castellan had fallen out with the monastery some time ago over a small wood to which both parties laid claim. It was time to settle the quarrel in a conversation with the abbot, although Agnes feared that her father was not in the mood for a constructive discussion.

As the two of them approached the monastery at last, they could smell coal and slag from some way off, and a thin black thread of smoke was rising to the cloudless sky from the metal-casting workshop. Since the beginning of May, and with the help of the castle's men-at-arms, Mathis had put the weapons of the Trifels arsenal into good order and had even made some new ones. But his most impressive work was the mighty cannon that, at over a ton in weight, would be too heavy to be moved except on the gun carriage that would be specially made for it. Next to the workshop containing the furnaces the men had put up a wooden storage shed, where Mathis was filing rust away from the old arquebuses, while Reichhart stood beside him.

When the two of them saw Agnes and the castellan coming, they bowed deeply.

"Good to see you back, sir," Ulrich Reichhart excitedly greeted his master. Since he had been working with Mathis, he seemed years younger and much livelier than before. "The great gun to breach Wertingen's walls is taking shape," he went on. "We're even making some smaller firearms. It's all going according to plan. We'll soon be able to attack his castle. All we really need to do now is—"

"Tell me about it this evening, Ulrich," the castellan interrupted him. "I'm too tired now. And I have to talk to the abbot. Let's hope the monks here at least have a decent drop of wine."

Without another word, he turned his horse and trotted toward the entrance of the monastery. Ulrich Reichhart's jaw dropped.

"What's the matter with the old man?" he said at last. "He watches every little thing we do for weeks on end, and suddenly he's not interested in the work anymore."

"He's worried," replied Agnes gently. "It's because of money. All we managed to do in Speyer was borrow at too high a rate of interest. And now he's afraid the duke's steward will take Trifels Castle from him."

"Then we'd better get on with attacking Wertingen," Reichhart rubbed his hands. "My fingers are already itching to smoke out that bastard. What's more, we'll soon be ready, and—"

"Nothing's ready!" Mathis interrupted roughly. So far he had gone on with his work in silence, and without so much as a glance for Agnes. When he looked up, she could tell that he had been sleeping poorly. His face was pale, and he had dark rings around his eyes. "I'm still finishing the gun carriage for the big cannon," he said. "And we don't have nearly enough saltpeter for the gunpowder, although we've cleared out all the local privies."

"Gunther and Eberhart are on their way to Dahn," Reichhart said soothingly. "There's said to be plenty still there. I'm sure we'll have enough saltpeter next week." He grinned and nudged Mathis in the ribs. "I know what it is—you're never satisfied anyway. If you had your way, we'd still be filing the muzzles of the guns next winter."

"Nonsense!" Mathis snorted.

Turning away, he went over to the furnace and began stirring it up, scraping sticky remnants of slag out of the great melting pot. Agnes watched him thoughtfully. He seemed to have something on his mind.

A movement of her head told the master gunner to leave them. She did not speak directly to Mathis until Ulrich Reichhart had disappeared behind the newly built storage shed. Then she asked, "What's the matter with you? It's not the work making you so tired and quiet, is it, but something else?"

Mathis put another log on the fire in the furnace. Then he straightened up and nodded. "It's my father," he began unsteadily. "I . . . I don't think he can live much longer. His cough gets worse every day, he's always bringing up blood . . ." His voice died away.

Agnes took his callused hand, which was black with ashes and slag. "You must talk to him," she said softly. "End your quarrel. Right away, before it's too late."

Mathis laughed bitterly. "How can I? He's so obstinate he won't even look at me. As he sees it, what I'm doing here is a betrayal of our whole profession. But who needs swords and spear points now that there are guns? However, he thinks I've sold my soul to the devil. Sometimes I almost believe it myself." His face darkened. "Do you remember how the arquebus blew the body of Wertingen's vassal to bits? Maybe God doesn't want us playing with this kind of fire."

Agnes sighed. "I'm afraid it's too late for such doubts now. If we don't conquer Wertingen's castle, my father will certainly lose Trifels, and then there are his debts. And you will lose your job here. Maybe you ought to tell your father *that*."

"I'll try." Mathis was looking into space. Only after a while did he glance at Agnes again. "Old Ulrich Reichhart is right," he said at last, hesitantly. "The longer we wait, the greater the danger of Black Hans arming his men against us. He probably knows just what we plan to do. Gunther has mentioned a great many tracks left around here. They were probably made by Wertingen's men."

All at once Agnes remembered the lights below Scharfenberg Castle that they had seen a few weeks ago. Could they have been left by Wertingen's spies? And could it have been one of his men in Speyer Cathedral, trying to find out what she and her father were doing?

"What's more, it will soon be summer," Mathis went on in a firmer voice, bringing her back from her thoughts. "At that season, Wertingen can't count on his peasants. They're fully occupied working in the fields; even the offer of money won't induce them to help him defend the castle." He nodded. "We really ought to attack, if possible, in the next few days . . . Damn it! Why did that poor devil Sebastian have to give away our plan, on top of everything else? Well, we'll have to make do with less saltpeter. And my father . . ." He did not finish his sentence. Lost in thought, he wiped his hands on his apron and then strode over to the storage shed beside the workshop.

"I'll begin mixing the gunpowder today," he called back to Agnes. "Tell your father we can make our move in three days' time. That's if I don't blow myself to kingdom come first." It was meant as a joke, but Agnes detected a touch of fear in Mathis's voice.

She wearily closed her eyes. When she opened them again, the sky overhead was still as clear and blue as before, but suddenly there seemed to be something menacing in the shimmering heat. Like the kind of thunderstorm that can be felt long before it finally breaks.

War was coming.

Not far from the little hamlet of Ranschbach, a small stream ran through a woodland clearing, flowed over a rocky projection, and cascaded down into a pool that reflected the rising moon. The splashing sound was monotonous and peaceful, and for a while at least it drowned out the crunch of footsteps coming closer, along a hidden game trail.

The old man led the way. In accordance with the order's ancient laws, he wore the graying cloak with the coat of arms showing three lions rampant. Groaning, he sat down on a rock and waited for the others. He had meant to hand off his post as leader to someone younger by now, but then the first rumors of the enemy began to circulate, and he had decided to stay on. There was one last task for him, and he hoped that he could still perform it.

And what happens after that, God alone knows.

There were more footsteps. They were those of Diethelm Seebach, arriving from Annweiler with the ropemaker Martin Lebrecht. The old man surreptitiously scrutinized them both. Since the strangers had found the keeper of the ring, suspicion had been smoldering in him like the embers of a fire that never really went out. Could it really be true that one of their order had given them away? There were twelve of them, just as there had been twelve Apostles, and one of the Apostles had also been a traitor.

Who is the Judas among us, or did those men really come upon Elsbeth entirely by chance?

In silence, the head of the order nodded to the two new arrivals, and they waited together for the remaining nine. The midwife Elsbeth Rechsteiner was the last to appear. She carried her satchel, in which she had already stowed several herbs that she had picked. The moon was in a favorable phase. Smiling, the old man glanced at her. Elsbeth had always been especially dear to him among the members of their order; they had known one another for so many years. Indeed, years ago they had even been lovers. The old man remembered many delightful dances at festivals commemorating the consecration of the church—and many nights in the hay. Now Elsbeth's back was bent, and her legs seemed to be giving her pain again. Over the last few weeks, her hair had become as white as snow. The old man sadly shook his head. He too had aged even more in all the anxiety of recent months.

How could you have done such a thing to us, Elsbeth? A bird as keeper of the ring . . . It is high time to act.

The head of their little order looked intently at each individual member in turn, and then he began to speak.

"I am sorry I had to ask you to come here at this late hour," he said quietly, "but the church is no longer safe enough. We know from a reliable source that the enemy has been questioning the mayor of Annweiler, and who knows how much our pastor knows of what's afoot? We can trust no one now, not even each other." He paused, and looked at the brothers and sisters again. They all wore dark cloaks and hoods so that they would not attract attention at night on the road or in the forest. He hoped none of them had been followed.

But he could not be sure that an enemy was not already here among them.

"The ring is gone. There's no help for that now," he went on. "But we still have the deed. You know that, as our senior member, I keep it in a safe place. Today I have brought it here to show you."

Putting his hand under his doublet, he brought out a crumpled scroll of parchment. The scratched seal on it showed the portrait of a bearded man. The parchment itself was stained, and torn at the edges. It looked old, very old. When the head of the order held it up, a murmur ran around the forest clearing. Some of the members knelt down and made the sign of the cross.

The leader carefully put the parchment back under his doublet, and then he cleared his throat.

"I have decided to take the deed away," he said. "Tomorrow. It is no longer safe here."

There was anxious whispering, and some of the members shook their heads.

"But then there is no more point in our order," Martin Lebrecht said at last. "It has been our task to protect the deed. Have you forgotten that? The deed and the ring. If you give them away, then that's the end of the Brotherhood. You said so yourself." And he repeated the prayerlike prophesy that they had been passing down for centuries. "When ravens no longer circle above the castle, and the empire is in danger, when the eagle drives all evil things away and the dwarfs speak his name—"

"And suppose that day has now come?" Elsbeth Rechsteiner suddenly interrupted him. Several members of the order looked at her in alarm.

"What do you mean?" asked their leader.

"Danger threatens the German Empire from all quarters. It's said that the French could invade at any time, even here in the Palatinate, and there's war in all the Italian cities already. The peasants are suffering starvation and they rebel against all the many injustices, and not a few regard Martin Luther as a new savior." Her voice became steadier, and she straightened her shoulders. "Maybe this is the time of which our founding fathers spoke. The end of the world as we know it. Knights are disappearing, fire and the sword lay waste their castles. Perhaps it is time for the secret to be made known at last." The old midwife looked around at her fellow members of the order. "Isn't that our task? To keep it until the time is ripe? I tell you, the time is ripe now—indeed, more than ripe. And if we do not act, our enemies will do so ahead of us."

Once again a murmur went around the clearing. Many of those present were talking quietly, others were praying aloud.

"Silence, brothers and sisters! Silence!" Their old leader raised his hand and waited until all was quiet again at last. Somewhere, a nightingale trilled.

"Elsbeth may be right," he finally said in a measured tone. "The founders of this order, long ago, did not tell us how to know when the time had really come. The signs and omens are . . . well, extremely vague. It is for us to interpret them. But even if the right time has not come yet, I can no longer guarantee the safety of the deed." He paused and looked gravely at each member in turn. Only then did he go on. "I therefore suggest that we take the deed to a place that is truly secure. And I know of such a place. The monks there have been guarding the knowledge of the empire for nearly a thousand years. Our secret will be safe with them."

"And suppose the document goes on gathering dust there for another thousand years?" Diethelm Seebach inquired skeptically. "How are those monks to know when the time has come if even we don't?"

"For God's sake, you've heard how close on our heels these men are," the head of the order argued. "And you know the diabolical skill they bring to their work. We are simple craftsmen and peasants, Diethelm. Not knights in shining armor who could take on such a pack in battle." He shook his head. "Our founders never foresaw this. We must get the deed to safety, and as soon as possible."

"So where are you going to take it?" Martin Lebrecht asked.

The old man's face was hard as stone. "Only I and Elsbeth, as the former keeper of the ring, should know. For the time being, that is the safest way," he said firmly. "I can't vouch that we don't have a traitor in our ranks. Can you, Martin?" When there was no answer, the old man turned to those standing around him. "Those who agree with me, raise their hands."

At first there was silence, a silence in which only the chirping of crickets and the nightingale's song could be heard. Then, very slowly, trembling and pale-faced, the first of the members raised their hands. One after another, each of them said yes.

In the end, only Elsbeth Rechsteiner, Diethelm Seebach, and Martin Lebrecht had not yet raised their hands. Of those three, the midwife was the first to do so, if with some delay.

"I would have chosen another path," she said. "I would have acted to get the thing out of circulation once and for all. But like this at least we can make sure that the deed does not fall into the wrong hands. The rest may yet happen later." She shrugged her shoulders. "A few months more or less will not make much difference."

"How about you two?" the leader asked the two still left to vote.

"Damn it, what else can we do?" Seebach spat noisily on the ground, and then he raised his hand as well.

"What do you say, Martin?" asked the head of the order.

The ropemaker hesitated. Only after what felt like an eternity did he too slowly raise his hand.

"It's probably the best protection we can provide for the secret now to get the deed away from here," he said quietly. "I just hope it's really God and not cowardice guiding what we do."

"Then it's decided." The head of the order nodded. He looked at Elsbeth Rechsteiner and thought that in the moonlight he saw a slight smile on her lips. Once again, for a brief moment, she was the young girl he had asked to dance long ago.

The pressure has simply been too great. This is best for us, and for our common cause. Let others decide when the time has come.

The old man took a deep breath and then asked them all to kneel. "Let us pray together now."

"Sanctus Fridericus, libera me, libera me, libera me . . ."

While they all spoke the ancient words that had been handed down in Annweiler from generation to generation, every one of them was aware that this meeting would be their last.

The order had ceased to exist.

On the afternoon of the following day, Mathis finally summoned up the courage to speak to his father. Time was pressing, for Castellan Philipp von Erfenstein wanted his new gun maker to let him know what artillery they now had available and how Mathis proposed to use it. Meanwhile, the duke of Zweibrücken himself had sent a letter empowering Erfenstein to go into the field against the robber knight Hans von Wertingen. They were to set out in two days' time.

If the situation had not been so serious, Mathis would have laughed out loud. A few weeks ago he had been a young journeyman smith imprisoned for theft, now the coming campaign had made him assistant gunner of legendary Trifels Castle. But Mathis had no illusions. If the campaign against Wertingen failed, that would be the end of his new career manufacturing artillery. And probably the end of his work at Trifels. Erfenstein would turn him out, if only to save face.

Over the last few days, Mathis had kept refining his recipe for gunpowder. In the end he had decided on five parts sulfur, seven parts saltpeter, and five parts charcoal. In his many experiments, the trunks of young hazel trees had made the best charcoal, although not many of them were available, as few hazels grew in the dry sandy soil of this part of the country. All the ingredients had to be ground fine and then mixed carefully in the powder mill in the shed. To get larger grains that would explode faster, Mathis had then mixed the powder with vinegar and urine and let the liquid evaporate from the mixture.

He had spent a good two hours turning the sharp-smelling mass again and again in a long, shallow trough. As he worked, he was aware that every spark or violent movement could set off an explosion, leaving nothing of himself and the shed but a large hole.

When Mathis had finally finished his work, he carefully laid the wooden scraper aside and set off on the path to Trifels. It was a good two hours' walk. He had not been home for days. Little Marie was all the happier to see him, and she stood in the doorway rejoicing.

"Mathis, how lovely to see you back!" she cried excitedly. "Can I go to the forest with you again when you make a big bang? Please, please?"

Mathis smiled wearily. "Not today, Marie. Maybe some other time." He glanced around the little room, where his mother sat on the bench beside the stove, looking careworn as she picked over an earthenware dish of berries gathered from the forest. He was struck, even more forcefully than usual, by the cramped conditions in which they lived.

Unrest in the German lands had been steadily increasing over the last few weeks. Mathis was suddenly reminded of his gunpowder. He wondered when some spark would make the empire itself explode.

"How is my father?" he asked his mother quietly, gesturing toward the bedroom, from which a metallic wheezing emanated.

Martha Wielenbach rubbed her tired eyes, leaving red juice from the berries on her forehead, where it looked like blood. "It . . . will soon be over for him. Father Tristan has been to see him twice and says that all he can do now is pray for him. At least he feels no pain when he is asleep." She compressed her lips and went on picking over the berries in the dish. Marie sat down beside her mother on the bench and laid her little head in her lap. Mathis was shocked to see how thin his sister had grown.

At last he plucked up his courage. "Do you think I can speak to him?" he asked his mother.

Martha Wielenbach looked up from her work, smiling, and for a moment her face showed the laughter lines that Mathis had always loved so much. "Of course," she replied. "He's awake. I looked in on him just now." Her eyes twinkled as she looked at Mathis. "And think nothing of it if he scolds you. It's his way of showing that he loves you."

"I know," Mathis murmured. "It's just hard to understand that sometimes."

He cautiously went over to the bedroom door and opened it. Hans Wielenbach was lying on a bed with a straw mattress in the tiny, box-like room. Mathis involuntarily flinched at the sight of the frail bundle of bones that had once been his strong father. Under the thin blanket, he looked like one of those shrunken figures made of dried plums that Mathis had seen at fairs. The face of the once vigorous smith was emaciated, his eyes and mouth much too large for it, his few remaining brownish teeth showing. Then he was shaken by a fit of coughing that seemed to go on forever. Hans Wielenbach spat out red mucus into a bowl beside his bed. Only then did he notice his visitor.

"What do you want?" he asked roughly. His voice was surprisingly firm and loud.

"I'm going up to see the castellan today," said Mathis. "We're to discuss the campaign against Wertingen. You must have heard about it." He cleared his throat. "The firearms are cast and forged, and we'll probably set out the day after tomorrow. We just have to tell Count Scharfeneck, so that he can send us his landsknechts as he promised."

"And what's that to do with me?"

"Can't you think?" Mathis asked quietly.

For some time neither of them said anything; nothing was to be heard but Wielenbach's rattling breath. At last he spoke. His voice sounded strangely dreamy.

"When I was a child, my parents took me out and about in the countryside," he began, staring up at the low ceiling. "My father was a traveling smith, a poor tinker who mended pots and pans, straightened horseshoes, and sometimes pulled out teeth with his big pincers." A smile spread over Wielenbach's face. "One day we were in a little place on the other bank of the Rhine when we heard a noise like thunder. I looked up at the sky, but it wasn't the sky—it was the earth thundering. Half a dozen knights on their horses were coming along the high road. They wore magnificent armor, shining swords hung at their sides, and their stallions had thin visors of the finest iron. The knights carried brightly colored standards showing their noble origin. They were announcing the emperor's arrival in a nearby town. The old emperor . . ." Hans Wielenbach closed his eyes, conjuring up that image again.

"They were like a vision, Mathis, like archangels come down to earth to fight all evil. Before long they had disappeared into the forest again. But I swear, on that day I knew that I would be a smith who made weapons." He coughed again. "It was Sir Philipp von Erfenstein who finally employed me."

"And God knows he can be proud of you," Mathis said quietly.

There was another moment of silence.

"Why has all that gone?" said Hans Wielenbach, more to himself than to Mathis. "Where are all the knights with their swords who protect the weak? Where is the wise emperor who can hold back all today's wild unrest?"

"Times change, Father," replied Mathis. "New times are coming, but they don't have to be worse times. On the contrary: maybe we can make a better world."

Hans Wielenbach laughed, but his laughter soon gave way to another coughing fit. "With those stinking guns, eh?" His voice was more of a croak now. "Once upon a time the strongest knight won, the knight who had learned how to fight longest and best. The fight was dirty and bloody, but not many lost their lives in it. And now? The powerful buy hundreds of landsknechts and set them firing guns at each other. And whoever spends more money will always win the war." He shook his head. "The old castellan and I don't belong in this time. We should leave it to younger men." Groaning, he sat up in bed and took his son's hand. Talking had become difficult for him. "Your . . . your mother says the castellan is very pleased with you. You're a good craftsman and a born leader, she says. She is very proud of you. And I . . . damn it, so am I. Even if I can't say I like what you're doing." He let himself fall back and closed his eyes. "Go now," he said, so quietly that Mathis could hardly make it out. "I wish you well, my son. You and these new times. May God be with you. And make sure that your damn gunpowder at least hits the right targets."

"I . . . I promise I will."

Mathis waited a little longer, but his father seemed to have fallen asleep. The young man stood by the bed in silence, looking at the tiny, shrunken figure from whom a rattling breath escaped at regular intervals. A single tear ran down Mathis's cheek.

He wiped it away and turned his back on the cramped room.

· 9 ·

Trifels, 31 May, Anno Domini 1524, early morning

WHILE THIN WISPS OF MORNING mist drifted toward the valley, the men-at-arms of Trifels gathered on the castle acres before setting off to do battle with the robber knight Hans von Wertingen.

The feud letter, as such a challenge was called, had been taken to the enemy by a messenger the day before, and, as expected, Black Hans had not complied with its demand for him to submit himself and his men to the duke's authority. On the contrary, the ducal messenger had been met with insults and crossbow bolts; he'd managed to save his own life only by headlong flight. That satisfied all the official specifications, and now, at last, the attack could begin.

But when Mathis surveyed the small troop of men who had gathered around him, he was suddenly no longer sure that their venture would really be crowned by success. Philipp von Erfenstein sat his nervously prancing chestnut horse Taramis in old-fashioned ceremonial armor, with his sword, mace, and dagger at his belt. A polished bascinet of the kind worn at tournaments in the old days hung beside him; it tapered to a pointed visor in front and was adorned with a plume of feathers. Surrounded by the castle guards, who carried only the necessary minimum of weapons, the castellan looked not like a radiant hero but a sad old man on his last journey. Ulrich, Gunther, and Eberhart wore rusty hauberks and dented helmets. The old head groom, Radolph, had buckled on a breastplate that had probably once belonged to his grandfather. In addition there were about a dozen young local peasants, recruited by Erfenstein with stirring words and the prospect of loot and adventure, although the actual wages he offered were low. They were armed mainly with scythes and threshing flails, though two of them had brought battered short swords. Mathis suspected that the peasants would run screaming at the first real clash with the enemy.

But really the peasants were there for only one purpose: to help in transporting the heavy guns from Eusserthal Monastery to the Ramburg, just under four miles away.

Mathis glanced over toward Trifels Castle and recognized Agnes and Father Tristan on Dancing Floor Rock, waving to him. The old monk would be meeting them in a few days' time, when it was to be assumed that there would be wounded men in need of care—or the first dying men to be given their last rites. At first Agnes had wanted to come with him, but her father had strictly forbidden that idea.

When Mathis saw her looking so small up there, his heart sank. They had talked for a long time yesterday evening, and he had tried not to show any fear, although he knew that the campaign was extremely dangerous—for him as the new gunner, as well as others. He would not be the first practitioner of his craft to risk blowing himself up along with his gun. There was an added danger in the fact that lack of time had made it impossible to test most of the newly cast firearms or those that had been repaired. The thought had hardly allowed Mathis to sleep at all last night.

"Let's just hope our fine Count Scharfeneck doesn't back out now," growled Philipp von Erfenstein from up on his horse. "It was agreed that he'd set off at dawn, and the sun is already high above the woods."

"I wouldn't put it past that dandy," muttered Ulrich Reichhart, fidgeting nervously with the catch of his battered helmet. "Talking big and then making off. Well, too bad. We'll just snuff the living daylights out of Black Hans on our own."

Mathis didn't like to think what would happen if Count Friedrich von Löwenstein-Scharfeneck really did let them down. With their own tiny troop, they wouldn't even be able to get the guns up to the Ramburg, let alone give battle. But at that very moment a horn signal sounded from the neighboring castle, and he heard the clatter of horses' hooves. Soon a colorfully clad troop of landsknechts emerged from the woods on the mountain: three dozen men, about twelve of them mounted. They all carried light swords, halberds, and spears. A cart drawn by two donkeys had also been loaded up with winches, boards, and the tools for building barriers. The young count himself trotted at the head of his noisily bawling troop, on a horse with sparkling silver on its bridle and reins. Friedrich von Löwenstein-Scharfeneck was the only one of his men to wear a light breastplate, greaves, and gauntlets. He looked much more mobile than the castellan in his heavy ceremonial armor.

"I thought you were never going to arrive," Erfenstein called brusquely.

The count calmly smiled and let his eyes sweep over the tiny group of peasants and men-at-arms from Trifels. "You could have gone on ahead," he replied. "I'm sure it wouldn't have been long before we overtook you." Then his glance fell on Mathis. "Ah, the young master gunner. Now we'll find out what your big gun is good for in the heat of battle. If need be we can always use its metal to cast a bell, ring it, and pray for Wertingen's soul."

The mercenaries laughed, and Mathis felt the blood shoot into his face.

I'm more likely to cast a bell from it to ring your own death knell, you arrogant upstart, he thought.

Among Scharfeneck's men, he now saw the slight figure of the minstrel whom Agnes had described to him. He was as colorfully clad as the landsknechts, with red feathers on his cap that fluttered in the wind, and he carried his lute buckled on over his shoulder. Mathis could not refrain from smiling. It was hard to imagine the little man overcoming one of the sturdy mercenaries in single combat.

The count shouted several orders, and the landsknechts got into position around the baggage train. Philipp von Erfenstein was just about to give the signal for them to set out when someone came hurrying toward them over the recently mown castle acres. From the figure's flowing hair, Mathis soon realized that it was Agnes.

"Didn't I tell you to stay up there?" the castellan snapped at her.

"Surely I can wish your men well for the battle," she replied breathlessly when she had reached them. Going over to Mathis, she pressed his hand, and he felt a tiny object passing to it from hers.

"It's nothing much," she said softly. "Only a medallion that I carved from walnut wood. It's supposed to bring you good luck."

He nodded, slipping the little thing into his pocket unseen.

"It's always good to see a beautiful woman before fighting," the count called, "but I agree with your father, lady. These men are not the kind of company you should keep."

"Don't worry, I am used to keeping exactly such company at home in our castle," retorted Agnes, laughing. "And your own landsknechts already know that there's someone in their ranks who will defend me if necessary."

Baffled, Mathis frowned. Who did Agnes mean? Himself? But there was no time to think more about that. The castellan's daughter gave him one last, grave glance, and then went over to her father and dropped a kiss on the old man's hand. Finally she turned away in silence. Erfenstein bellowed an order, and at last the baggage train set off.

It was still quite early morning when they reached Eusserthal and began the tedious work of loading up. First they had to get the two larger of the light cannons known as falcons onto the gun carriages built for them. The men also packed half a dozen arquebuses into an ox cart, along with a handful of the artillery pieces called falconets: small cannons with muzzles the diameter of a finger's length.

But the showpiece of the baggage train was the great cannon, six feet long, that only yesterday Ulrich Reichhart had affectionately christened Fat Hedwig, because its girth reminded him of the stout cook at Trifels Castle. Unlike the cook, however, this Hedwig weighed over two thousand pounds, and it had to be lifted cautiously by means of a pulley onto the two-wheeled gun carriage, laboriously built for it by Mathis, where it was fixed in place with iron clamps. By the time the men had finished the job, they were bathed in sweat, and it was nearly midday.

Now the most difficult part of their journey began. The four vehicles rolled along at walking pace, while the mounted men and foot soldiers went along leisurely beside them. The men had to keep stopping when the heavy bronze gun threatened to shift position on its carriage. The landsknechts and peasants sweated and swore, while more and more curious onlookers accompanied them on their way. Ragged, laughing children ran after them, and some of the older peasants and women wished them luck and handed them bread and water from the roadside.

After a short rest, the company went on along the banks of a stream winding its way through a marshy valley. Only yesterday there had been a violent thunderstorm, so the oxen had to be taken out of the shafts of the cart again and again, and boards were then placed under its wheels to keep the heavy vehicle from sticking fast in the glutinous mud.

At last, late in the evening, they reached the little village of Ramberg, ready to spend the night on its outskirts. The landsknechts brought the vehicles to a halt and wasted no time in setting up a small encampment. Campfires were lit, and soon a fragrantly aromatic stew was simmering in a pot hanging from a tripod, while some of the men sang hearty war songs. Later, when the castellan left the tent that had been put up for him and the count, he looked well satisfied. He was swaying slightly and humming one of his old tournament songs.

"Well, master gunner?" Erfenstein called to Mathis, who was sitting beside one of the fires. "How does war feel to you? We went on many such feuds in my youth. Those were the days! Doesn't this rejuvenate a man?"

Mathis forced a smile. "I hope to live to be old enough to tell you."

"I hope so too. If not, we still have the count's minstrel. I trust he'll write us a long and warlike ode." Erfenstein laughed, belched heartily, then turned to Ulrich Reichhart and got him to pour him another beaker of wine.

The moon rose beyond the hills, and the landsknechts' songs became louder and coarser. They frequently referred to priests and monks. All the men knew stories of fat clerics who stuffed their bellies while everyone else went short of food. The peasants, too, had tales to tell.

"How about burning down the monastery on our way back from the Ramburg?" one of the Trifels peasants murmured so quietly that only Mathis and a few bystanders could hear it. "They're robber knights there as well, and as bad as Black Hans, except that they go raiding with the cross, not the sword."

Some of the other peasants nodded agreement. "They're all the same," replied one. "We ought to do as the likes of us did down on the plain of the Rhine, where they set fire to a couple of monasteries, and—"

"And ended on the gallows for their pains, with their bellies slit open," interrupted a landsknecht who was the worse for drink. "Forget it and don't talk so big. Things will stay the way they always were. Peasants bend their backs to toil, landsknechts fight, and meanwhile the abbots, counts, and dukes eat their fill."

"But maybe not for much longer," said another peasant. "That Martin Luther is giving the pope his marching orders and no mistake. He's the right kind of monk for me. You wait and see . . ."

"*Psst!*" the landsknecht silenced him, pointing to the minstrel, who was just approaching their fire. "Here comes distinguished company."

The men bent back over their plates of stew. Melchior von

Tanningen did not seem to have overheard what they were saying. He turned to Mathis, who was still sitting by the fire, and made him a slight bow, raising his cap.

"My respects, Master Wielenbach," he began. "Such, I believe, is your esteemed name?"

Mathis nodded, unable to keep back a smile. No wonder Agnes liked this fellow. He sounded just like a herald from a bygone age. "Just call me Mathis, that's fine," he replied, gesturing to the minstrel to sit down on the ground beside him. The other men moved away, so that they were soon alone.

"I have the utmost admiration for your handiwork," said Melchior. "It is truly amazing to think what a man can do." A frown spread over his freckled brow. "Even if what you do is not quite what I understand as the honorable way of fighting. But at least I suppose that makes it successful. I am correct there, am I not?" Melchior looked inquiringly at the young smith.

Mathis felt himself going red in the face again, like the minstrel had seen through him. Damn it, why hadn't he tested Fat Hedwig thoroughly at least once in advance? The stone cannonballs seemed to fit, but if just one of them stuck in the barrel of the gun, the whole thing would blow up.

But at least then I won't live to feel ashamed of myself . . .

"Well . . . I'm assuming that the . . . the battle will turn out well," he replied at last. "We shall have to wait until tomorrow to see."

Melchior von Tanningen nodded, and twirled the end of his little pointed beard. "Yes, the battle begins tomorrow. It will be noisy, dirty, and vicious. Not the kind of battle worth immortalizing in song. But the fact is, there are no such battles today. Maybe there never were." He smiled dreamily and then pointed to something shining in the forest at the foot of the mountain opposite. "Do you see those lights? I'll be bound those are Wertingen's spies. By now he knows all about our weapons. Let's hope that he doesn't have a master gunner of his own. But if he does, I'm sure the gunner will not be half as good as you."

Mathis jumped. Sure enough, there was something shining on the slope. It seemed to be moving away from them, up the mountain and toward the castle, which was hidden from view by trees. If he narrowed his eyes and looked hard, he thought he could make out flickering lights.

Black Hans was expecting them.

When the sun set over Trifels Castle, Agnes lay awake in her bed for a long time, thinking of Mathis. How was he feeling at this moment? Would he come back to her safe and sound? She felt fear spreading through her, some of it for her father as well. In spite of his armor, he had looked so vulnerable beside the young count, so old and stooped. Philipp von Erfenstein might once have been a fine warrior. But the miracle of Guinegate was many decades in the past; times and weapons had changed since then, and she was afraid that her father was overestimating his abilities in battle. He was no longer a steely warrior, but an old man of almost sixty, even if he refused to believe that himself. In addition, he had only one eye, and God alone knew whether that would be good enough for ferocious hand-to-hand combat.

She had not been dreaming so often in the last few weeks, probably in part because, after visiting the sick with Father Tristan, she slept very soundly. All the same, she kept seeing images from her dreams before her mind's eye—the Guelph, Johann of Brunswick, a man to whom she felt strangely drawn, warning her against the ring; the words of the men planning to kill her and Johann; the reflection in the puddle of wine. She had seen a strange but yet familiar face there. Who in God's name was she in the dream? If not herself, then who?

Who are you?

She slipped slowly into sleep as her fears changed into visions of violence. She saw Mathis standing beside the big gun, and suddenly the bronze broke into thousands of splinters, piercing his rib cage like spears. She saw her father riding over the battlefield headless, yet swinging his sword. Then these dreadful images died down, giving way to other and more real visions.

◆ ◆ ◆

As she runs, Agnes catches a glimpse of Johann. Even in the darkness, it is easy to see his tense expression. Beads of sweat run down his forehead, his breath comes by fits and starts, he looks back at her again and again, signaling to her to run faster. Agnes remembers the men talking in the Knights' House. They want to kill them. Her and Johann and the child.

The child as well.

At last they have reached the steep rocks at the far end of the castle. The rock wall falls sheer to the depths below here; it must be a drop of a hundred and twenty feet. There is nothing to be seen but the wavering darkness underneath.

Only now does Agnes notice a leather bag on Johann's back. It is open at the top, and moving slightly. Suddenly a shock of fair hair emerges from the opening, a small head turns her way, and two large, tearful eyes stare at her.

There is a little boy about four years old in the rucksack, trembling with fear.

Without knowing why, she puts a finger to her lips. The little boy, who had been about to start crying again, keeps his tears back. Meanwhile, Johann takes a rope out of another bag slung around him and ties it to a projecting carpenter's nail. It drops into the depths without a sound.

Now Agnes realizes that she, too, is carrying a bag. It is not particularly heavy. When she puts her hand inside it, she feels something about the length of a man's forearm, wrapped in cloth. It is hard and angular. Looking at Johann again, she sees that he is already letting himself down the rock wall on the rope. Only the child's hair is still in sight. There is a leaden, expectant silence in the air.

She suddenly hears an ugly sound from down below. Stones fall, the child disappears from her field of vision, a suppressed cry of pain from Johann follows. He has obviously slipped on the smooth rock.

And then the child does begin to cry.

He wails and screams, howling in extreme fear, and the sound goes right through Agnes. It seems to climb the rocky walls, crawling up and over the castle walls, seeping in through the windows. Only a little later the alarm is raised. Footsteps fast approach.

Agnes shoulders her bag, hurries to the rope, and lets herself down on it. Her hands burn like fire; it hurts so much that she almost lets go. The rock scrapes her shoulder and tears her dress. Farther down, she can make out a swaying black shape; Johann with the boy. He, too, seems to be falling rather than climbing down the rope. The forest floor can't be far away.

As Agnes tries to feel a glimmer of hope, something hisses only just past her face. A crossbow bolt. A second sticks in her full skirt. Then the rope begins to vibrate. Suddenly there is a jolt, and she falls several feet down. The swaying is stronger now.

The rope, they are cutting through the rope!

Shouts can now be heard up above. Another crossbow bolt only just misses her. How much farther to the ground? About forty feet? Too far to jump, anyway.

At this moment there is another jolt, and then Agnes is falling fast. The ground comes closer and closer, like an open mouth, like a toothless, gigantic pair of jaws.

And swallows her up.

❖ ❖ ❖

When Agnes awoke in the middle of the night this time, she knew at once where she was and what had happened. Breathing heavily, she closed her eyes and tried to imprint everything she had seen on her memory. She didn't want to forget any of it by tomorrow morning. Johann had obviously been fleeing, and he had had a fair-haired little boy with him. When the boy cried out in terror, Agnes had felt for a moment as if he were her own child. Could she be the mother of that boy in the dream? Was Johann his father? And why did they all have to escape from Trifels anyway?

Agnes thought of the men in the Knights' House talking in her dream from a few weeks ago. Instinctively, she flinched. The warning against the ring, the overheard conversation, the flight . . . The separate dreams seemed to fit together. They told a longer story, although she could not work out what it was. So far she had merely found out who the man she loved so much in her dream was.

Agnes gave a start. Suddenly she knew where she could find an explanation of all these visions. The chronicle! She had put it back in the secret compartment in the library. Since then she had thought, several times, of taking it out again, but something had always prevented her: her father's plans for her marriage, all her visits to the sick, and most of all the time she had spent with Mathis—all that had driven the chronicle from her thoughts.

Excitedly, she got out of bed and blew on the still-hot embers in the warming pan that stood in a corner of her bower. Soon little flames were licking up from them. She lit a candle and left the room. It was much cooler out in the passage, even though it was nearly June. Agnes threw a woolen shawl around her shoulders and set off, holding the candle, for the library.

Bur first she climbed down a narrow spiral staircase to the Knights' House. The moon shone through the pointed arches of the windows, and outside, above the treetops, soft gray light showed. Agnes guessed that it was about four in the morning. The hall itself was still in total darkness. Empty and abandoned like this, it was even uncannier than in daylight. The stuffed boars' heads mounted on the walls seemed to be looking angrily at her; the threadbare tapestries moved in a draft; and only a faint glow was left of the fire on the hearth.

Barefoot, her toes cold, Agnes hurried through the hall and to another spiral staircase, this one leading up to the castle tower. Suddenly she stopped in alarm.

There seemed to be a faint whimpering coming from somewhere.

Agnes felt her heart miss a beat. The whimpering was almost like the crying of the child in her dream. But as she listened more closely, the sound changed. It was deeper now, like a woman weeping.

And it came from somewhere below her, followed by a monotonous knocking.

Knock, knock, knock . . .

Agnes was in the grip of almost animal terror. She stumbled up the worn steps until at last she came to the fourth-floor landing. Running to the library door, she pressed the handle.

It was locked.

Knock, knock, knock . . .

Desperately, she shook it, cursing her own stupidity. Of course Father Tristan had locked the library. How could she have expected it to be open in the middle of the night? All of a sudden she remembered that the old monk often left the key in an empty wine pitcher on a ledge in the anteroom. Searching the pitcher, sure enough, her fingers found it. She put the long, rusty key into the lock, opened the door, and entered the library.

The familiar smell of the parchments immediately had a soothing effect on Agnes. Her fear went away, and immediately her sense of something uncanny seemed ridiculous. When she lit the wax-encrusted candleholder on the table, and warm light filled the library, she could almost laugh. How could she have let herself get into such a state? Surely the whimpering had been only the sound of the wind whistling through cracks in the stone, and there would be a natural explanation for the knocking as well.

She still had no idea of the identity of the woman whose eyes she saw through in her dreams. Or of the men who clearly had designs on her life. It was all still a mystery. At least she thought she now knew that Johann and that woman had a child together, a boy of about four. Or wasn't the little boy her son?

Purposefully, Agnes went straight to the shelf with the false spine of Dante's *Inferno* on it. She pulled it out, and the little secret door opened. Everything behind it was in the dark, but she managed to fish out the *Historia Trifels* from among the other books.

She sat down at the old table, which was covered with parchments,

and began leafing through the pages of the chronicle until she came
to the chapter in which Johann was dubbed a knight. She skimmed
the pages she had read last time again, looked at the faded picture of
the Knights' House once more, then turned the page—and stopped
short.

The following pages had been torn out.

Agnes felt the irregular, ragged edges. There was no doubt of it:
three pages were missing. The chapter began with the accolade of
Johann of Brunswick in the late thirteenth century, and it was directly
followed by the section on the fifteenth century.

It was as if an entire century had been extinguished.

Agnes frowned. Obviously, someone didn't want her to know any
more about Johann of Brunswick and the rest of his story at Trifels.

But who?

She was about to close the book and put it back again when a
sound made her jump once more. It was the faint squeal of the door
now being opened, as though by a ghostly hand. A bowed figure stood
in the doorway.

Father Tristan.

For a moment it seemed to Agnes like the old monk was looking
at her like someone unknown to him. But then his gaze cleared.

"I had no idea that anyone else in this castle was up and about so
early," he began, smiling. "Are you anxious about Mathis? You'll see,
the lad will soon be back and . . ." His glance fell on the book on the
table, and his expression darkened.

"I see," he said quietly.

"I . . . I . . ." Agnes stammered. Then, shrugging, she gave up. "Very
well, you've caught me. But I assure you, it was pure chance that I
found that secret door. And why did you hide the book from me, anyway?"

"Because it touches on matters that are better left alone." The old
monk went over to the table and drew the book toward him. "Enough
blood has been shed already over the centuries."

"Did you tear out the pages?" asked Agnes.

Father Tristan shook his head. "It was done long before my time. I expect someone wanted that dark chapter to be forgotten forever. Not a bad idea, either."

"What happened?"

Groaning, the old man sat down on a stool beside her. He seemed to be wrestling with himself, and finally he raised his hands in a gesture of resignation. "Oh, very well, before you get everything here muddled up. You don't give me any peace! In return, I expect you not to say a word to anyone about it, nor about the other books in this secret compartment. Understand?"

Agnes nodded in silence. The old monk sighed, and then he began telling the tale in a low voice. As he spoke, he looked thoughtfully at the book as it still lay open, showing the picture of the accolade of young Johann of Brunswick.

"Johann of Brunswick's father, Bernwart, was a powerful man in the empire, descended from the only Guelph emperor, Otto IV. Bernwart of Brunswick sent his son to be a squire in this castle and to win his spurs here. But obviously, after becoming a knight, Johann made plans of his own."

"What kind of plans?" Agnes asked curiously.

"Well . . . nothing was ever proved. But it's said that Johann of Brunswick wanted to be the German king. As you know, the Guelphs had once been the most powerful family in the empire, along with the Staufers. After the terrible time when there was no emperor, however, not the Guelphs but the Habsburgs came to the throne. Johann is said to have plotted against the German king of the time, King Albrecht, who was unpopular. The young Guelph had already won the support of the very influential burgrave Reinhard von Hoheneck, castellan of Trifels at the time, and several princely houses. But the plot was discovered at the very last minute . . ." Father Tristan paused, and Agnes looked at him intently.

"What happened then, Father? Tell me."

The old monk sighed deeply. "The Habsburgs made short work of the matter. They had the entire garrison of Trifels Castle imprisoned. Reinhard von Hoheneck and some of the leaders were tortured, then gutted like animals and quartered in the castle courtyard. Their heads were displayed on pikes on the battlements of Trifels as a warning." Father Tristan sadly shook his head. "At first young Johann of Brunswick escaped, but his murderers caught up with him at last in Speyer Cathedral. He fell fighting before the real part he had played in the conspiracy could be discovered. Soon after that, King Albrecht withdrew all privileges from Trifels and made a man subservient to him its castellan. The famous imperial insignia were taken to Kyburg Castle, far away in Switzerland." Father Tristan sadly shrugged his shoulders. "That was the end of Trifels Castle as a center of the empire, and from then on the castle increasingly fell into disrepair. Today only ballads and stories speak of its former glory."

Agnes leaned forward. The weathered old chronicle still lay on the table between them. She drew the book toward her again, and pointed to the young knight. "Father, I have had another dream of Johann," she began in a low voice. "I think I was dreaming of his flight from here. There was a woman with him, a woman and a child. Do you happen to know who—"

"Agnes, please stop it!" Angrily, the monk struck the table with his wrinkled hand. "Believe me, you're making all this up. Dreams of past times, what balderdash!" He took hold of the sleeve of her nightgown. "I'll tell you what has happened. You had a dream about a noble knight, yes, very well. That may happen to many young women. But when you saw Johann's picture in the chronicle, you simply *imagined* that he was the knight in your dream. And now you're making up more stories. I am sure that any tale I could tell you would suit one of your dreams. Your imagination is playing tricks on you, Agnes, that's all there is to it."

"But there was the woman, and the child. I was the woman myself, I saw her face. And I dreamed of several men who were planning to kill them." Agnes defiantly pursed her lips. After a moment of hesitation, she went on. "I . . . I think I heard her just now, crying; it somehow seemed to come out of the castle walls. And there was a knocking sound as well . . ."

Father Tristan laughed in relief. "There, you see, now I can prove that it's all your imagination. I was knocking myself. I was out in the courtyard gathering healing herbs in the garden. As you know, their effect is at its strongest when the moon is full. Hedwig locked the door behind me, silly woman, and I had to knock for quite a long time to get her to let me in again. That's all it was." He rose to his feet with a groan. "I should never have told you those old stories. Even as a child, you had so much nonsense in your head that you couldn't sleep. Let's go to bed at last, before it's full dawn outside. And promise me that from now on you'll keep your hands off this book and the secret compartment." His eyes twinkled as he looked at her. "I hope you don't want to see your father confessor in the pillory in his old age for harboring seditious writings."

"No, no, of course I don't." With some hesitation, Agnes too rose. Meanwhile, Father Tristan took the disfigured book and put it on one of the top shelves. Feeling weary and confused, Agnes went out into the anteroom of the library. Was the old castle chaplain right, and she was running after something only imagined in her dreams? Was it all just the fantasies of a young woman with her head in the clouds, longing for past times? Pining for a knight in bright armor on a tall, white horse?

All the same, it had seemed that her confessor was keeping something from her. As they talked, Father Tristan had trembled more than usual, and his eyes had looked nervously back and forth.

He may not be lying, but he knows more than he wants to admit.

On the way to the stairs, her eyes looked once more through one of the narrow castle windows. The wan light of the moon—a slender crescent, no more than a thin, bright ribbon—shone through the opening. It took Agnes some time to understand what that meant. Baffled, she looked at Father Tristan as he climbed down the worn steps in front of her. What exactly had he just told her?

I was out in the courtyard gathering healing herbs in the garden. As you know, their effect is at its strongest when the moon is full . . .

Humming quietly to himself, the old monk walked on. Agnes stayed where she was, thinking. Father Tristan had lied to her. But why? And anyway, what had he come up to the library for? Wouldn't he have wanted to take his herbs to the kitchen, if anywhere?

On the bottom step, Father Tristan stopped and looked up at her. "There's something else," he said quietly. "That ring. I have noticed that you still wear it around your neck. Promise me solemnly that you will not show it to anyone." His usually mild eyes suddenly looked sterner than Agnes had ever known him to appear before. "Show it to no one. Do you understand? And keep your dreams to yourself."

With some hesitation, Agnes nodded. "I . . . I promise. But why . . ."

"Now, get some rest." All at once Father Tristan was smiling in the kindly way that she had known since her childhood. "Go riding tomorrow, or fly Parcival, and try not to brood. I'll soon be following your father to the Ramburg to tend the wounded in this accursed feud. So I can give you the week off with an easy mind." He traced the sign of the cross in the air. "May the Lord bless you and protect you."

His back bent, Father Tristan limped off to his bedchamber beside the kitchen. Agnes stood there for some time, watching him go, as her hand felt the ring under her nightgown. Then, with her heart beating fast, she returned to her own bed.

But, weary as she was, she could not fall asleep.

· 10 ·

Outside Ramburg Castle, 1 June, Anno Domini 1524

MATHIS MOPPED THE PERSPIRATION FROM his brow and looked up at the robber knight's castle rising on the hill ahead of them. They had set out before dawn, and his shirt and doublet were already drenched in sweat. The peasants and landsknechts had pushed the carts and gun carriages, yard by yard, up the castle mound along a narrow, muddy pathway. Now, at nearly noon, their target lay before them. Ramburg Castle had certainly seen better days, and much of it was overgrown by moss. Time had done its work on the battlements. But the walls of the main building seemed to have been repaired only recently, showing fresh mortar and new masonry in many places.

"That fat badger has done his spring cleaning and crawled away into his sett," growled the old master gunner Ulrich Reichhart. "Winkling him out of there is going to be tricky."

Mathis and the other soldiers scrutinized the terrain suspiciously. The castle was built on a spur of rock that fell away steeply on three sides. To the northwest, it was linked to the neighboring hill by a shallow saddle of rock, and the mightiest defensive wall that the young smith had ever seen rose in front of it. A stone's throw away, another wall enclosed the outer bailey, while a steep ramp to the west led up to the castle gate.

Before him, Mathis saw a bleak surface with smoking heaps of ash here and there on it. Hans von Wertingen had devastated the entire hilltop, so as not to offer his enemies any chance of approaching under cover of shrubs or groups of trees. Some of his men-at-arms now appeared on the battlements of the defensive wall. They made obscene gestures directed at the besiegers; one man turned his bare buttocks to them.

"They won't be laughing much longer," swore Philipp von Erfenstein, who had just joined Mathis and Ulrich Reichhart. In spite of the increasing midday heat, the knight wore his heavy armor, and broad streams of sweat ran down his face.

"Hey, Wertingen!" he called up to the defensive wall. "Come on out, you cowardly carrion, and fight like a man!"

But apart from some scornful cries, there was no reply.

"How high do you think that wall is?" Reichhart asked skeptically. "Fifty feet? Sixty?"

Philipp von Erfenstein shrugged his shoulders. "I have no idea, but it's the highest defensive wall I've ever seen. If Trifels had a wall like that, I'd turn my bare ass to invaders myself."

"Ah, but we have our master gunner with us, don't we?" It was the cutting voice of Friedrich von Löwenstein-Scharfeneck, who now appeared among his landsknechts, his breastplate shining. "What do you think, boy?" he asked with a smile, turning to Mathis. "How long do you expect that gun of yours will need to breach the wall?"

"That . . . depends entirely on the wall's thickness," replied Mathis uncertainly. He glanced with some doubt at Fat Hedwig, resting on her gun carriage.

"Oh, I'll be happy to answer that question." Friedrich von Löwenstein-Scharfeneck drew his sword from its sheath, and tested the edge of it with a bored expression. "The defensive wall of the Ramburg is exactly nine feet thick and almost sixty feet high. It's the tallest and thickest in the whole Palatinate."

"And why, damn it, do we learn that only now?" Erfenstein interrupted. "If you know the castle so well, Your Excellency, it would have been helpful of you to share your knowledge with us earlier."

"What difference would that have made?" Scharfeneck thrust the sword firmly back into its sheath. "Would our boy genius here have built a bigger gun? Believe me, Erfenstein, that carrion Wertingen has been leading us Scharfenecks a merry dance for a long time." He pointed to the neighboring hills, where the blurred turrets of Neuscharfeneck Castle could just be made out. "Do you think we didn't consider taking this den of robbers several times before? Do you think I'd have asked for your help if I could have done it by myself? What I said holds good: raze that castle for me, and I'll make sure that you enjoy your rightful position and regard as castellan of Trifels again. If you fail, you can crawl back into the dirt you came from. And in that case I'd also withdraw my other offer. Have I expressed myself clearly enough?"

"You . . . you arrogant . . ."

Under his helmet, Erfenstein's face colored red, and his hand twitched. For a moment he seemed tempted to give the young count a resounding slap in the face. Then the old castellan took a deep breath and thought better of it. Meanwhile, Mathis was wondering what Scharfeneck had meant by his other offer. Were there to be more feuds?

"It may be the tallest and thickest wall in the whole Palatinate," Erfenstein said. "But wait until you see my gunner blow Black Hans away, castle and all."

The young smith gulped. Once again he was aware that all expectations of this campaign rested on his shoulders. A wall nine feet thick. If Scharfeneck was right, even Fat Hedwig would hardly be able to breach the defensive wall. Narrowing his lips, Mathis scrutinized the fortifications again.

"I see that the wall is lower at the sides," he said quietly, trying not to sound uncertain. "Is there any particular place where it isn't quite so thick?"

"Yes, there is." That was Ulrich Reichhart. "My scouts have taken a good look at the terrain there. But it turns steeply downhill, and we can't set up large artillery pieces on that spot. The angle is too sharp."

"And out here we'll be shot down like rabbits, damn it all!" Erfenstein spat. "This place is as bare as a whore's cunt. We might just as well shoot ourselves."

"Not if we make large wooden shields and hide behind them," Mathis said thoughtfully. He had recovered his confidence, and his brain was hard at work. "We can keep carrying out mock attacks elsewhere with the smaller firearms, while I adjust Fat Hedwig. And we can set traps on the south side."

"Traps?" Friedrich von Löwenstein-Scharfeneck raised his eyebrows skeptically. "You expect Wertingen to fall for that? Ridiculous."

"I read about it in a book," Mathis replied coolly. "Konrad Kyeser's *Bellifortis*, if you've heard of it. We can use sturdy birch trees. From a distance, the silver color of their bark will look almost like iron. If we add some of our old guns to the display, and leave cannonballs and ropes lying about, they'll look like the real thing. Wertingen won't know that we can't fire at him from that sloping terrain."

Or I hope not, anyway, he thought, *but I'm damned if I'm going to say so out loud here.*

"Kyeser's *Bellifortis*? Forgive me, I quite forgot that you can read." Scharfeneck grinned. "Well, if that's the only way, let's try it. But I'm not sending my men into a useless skirmish just because our master gunner is too craven to fight."

"You're welcome to stand beside me when I fire Fat Hedwig," replied Mathis, his face expressionless.

The count was about to make some retort, but Erfenstein intervened. "That's enough," he snapped. "Deeds, not words, decide the outcome of war. We'll do as Mathis says. I have every confidence in this young man. So let's start making preparations."

He glanced at Mathis. There was hope in the castellan's eyes, but also a touch of threat.

Erfenstein shouted orders, and soon the landsknechts and peasants were going off to find and fell trees and unload the materiel from the baggage train. Mathis stood in the middle of the turmoil, looking thoughtfully at the high defensive wall. How many feet of stone would Fat Hedwig be able to penetrate? Mathis hoped that the wall was more vulnerable in parts than it looked; in building castles, solid stone was often used only on the inside and outside of defensive works, while the space in between was filled with rubble.

"Afraid?"

Mathis turned and saw Melchior von Tanningen, standing right behind him and smiling. The minstrel had come up without a sound.

"Would that be so bad?" asked Mathis after a moment's pause.

Tanningen shook his head. "Oh no, far from it. Only fools are never afraid. Fear keeps us from doing stupid things." He pointed to the heavy gun being unloaded from its carriage by a dozen landsknechts. "What do you think? Will that monster be able to breach the wall?"

Mathis sighed. "To be honest, I don't know. Not at the first shot, that's for sure, but maybe at the fifth or sixth. Or maybe the gun will explode first and blow me up too. Then you'll need a new master gunner."

"What you said just now was very impressive," said Tanningen, without going any farther into Mathis's uncertainty. "You made the right decision very quickly."

"We have yet to see whether it really was right."

Melchior von Tanningen shrugged his shoulders. "There's justification for doubts. The songs always speak of the doubts of great generals."

"Great generals!" Mathis laughed. "Don't forget, until very recently I was only the dirty son of the Trifels weaponsmith. We produce great wines in this part of the country, not great generals."

"That can soon be altered. Don't you sense something in the air?" Melchior von Tanningen had come very close to Mathis. "More and more complaints from the peasants, that monk from Wittenberg with his seditious talk, the calls for change . . . a day may come when great generals are needed again. Even in the Palatinate. Good luck, Master Wielenbach."

Without another word, Tanningen turned away and walked toward the woods. Mathis shook himself. That minstrel really was a strange fellow. When he talked, you might really think you were standing in the midst of one of those old battles, with knights and archers. Well, as a master gunner he had something more important to do.

He hurried toward the landsknechts and helped them get the heavy gun off its carriage, with the aid of ropes and winches. Now they must dig out a level position, build protective shields, determine the angle of inclination, and re-mix the gunpowder. Mathis nodded grimly. Fat Hedwig was his only hope, and he would do all he could to help her make her entrance to good effect.

When Agnes woke, late in the morning, she heard a slight noise out in the corridor. "Who's there?" she murmured sleepily.

"It's only me, Margarethe," replied her lady's maid. "May I come in?"

Without waiting for an answer, Margarethe entered the room. She was wearing a fine white linen gown with fur. She looked expectantly at her mistress.

"What is it?" asked Agnes.

"I only wanted to know if you'll be needing me today." Margarethe curtsyed. "If not I'd like to go down to Annweiler."

"And meet someone there?" asked Agnes, smiling. She sat up in bed, rubbing her eyes.

Margarethe looked defiant. "It's market day. I have to run some errands."

"Run some errands. Well, well . . ."

Agnes stretched, and then asked Margarethe to give her a shirt and the hose in which she went riding from her clothes chest. She was still feeling haunted by her dream and that late-night conversation with

Father Tristan. She had lain awake until long after sunrise, trying to think why he had lied to her.

Why was he out and about at night?

Agnes thought of the seditious writings in the secret compartment in the library. Maybe, in secret, Father Tristan met the rebels who gathered in the forest. Shepherd Jockel, for instance? Or was it something to do with her father's campaign? The thought of him and Mathis made her uneasy. That was one reason why she had decided to take the monk's advice and go hawking in the woods with Parcival. It would take her mind off her anxieties.

The pleading tone in her maid's voice brought her back from these thoughts. Margarethe was impatiently holding out her leather shoes. Agnes shook herself and then looked indulgently at her maid's fine dress.

"He must be a rich suitor if he can buy you a gown as beautiful as that," she said, amused. "Is he the same one who gave you that pretty piece of jewelry after Easter?" When Margarethe did not reply, she dismissed the subject. "Well, never mind. It's not suitable for a hawking expedition anyway."

"A noble maiden does not go hawking," Margarethe replied coolly. "She sews and does embroidery. And waits for a lover to come along."

Looking at her maid, Agnes thought, once again, of Margarethe's appearance. She was a thin woman with a rickety look, and there were deep lines at the corners of her mouth that gave it a rather bitter expression.

Like an old maid, thought Agnes. *It's certainly time she found a husband, and I ought not to stand in her way.*

Suddenly she gave a start.

What in God's name . . .

Agnes felt her heart miss a beat. The silver clasp in Margarethe's hair seemed to her strangely familiar.

"Where did you get that?" she asked sharply, pointing to the ornament.

In alarm, Margarethe took a step back. "It . . . it was a present."

"A present from your suitor?"

Margarethe nodded defiantly. Small red patches showed on her thin throat.

"What did you give him for it?" Agnes persisted.

The lady's maid frowned, but Agnes could tell that Margarethe was only pretending to be puzzled. "What do you mean?" she asked. "I'm afraid I don't understand . . ."

"You understand me very well." Agnes was on her feet now. She had always been a little taller than Margarethe, and now she looked angrily at her maid, who seemed to writhe like a worm in front of her. "I'll tell you what happened," she went on, with a cutting edge to her voice. "There was a man who made eyes at you. He invited you to drink wine with him, he gave you money for that dress. But he wanted something in return, didn't he?" Her forefinger was boring into Margarethe's bodice. "You told him when Gunther and Sebastian would be going to Neukastell with the tithes. And later you told the same man what firearms Mathis was forging."

"How dare you suspect me of such things!" Margarethe retreated to the wall, her arms crossed defiantly over her breast. "You ought to be ashamed of yourself."

"It's you who ought to be ashamed." Agnes came over to her and snatched the silver clasp from her hair. "Silver, like Judas's reward, and it's given you away. Do you even know what it is? This clasp used to be my mother's. A few weeks ago, my father added it to the coins that the castellan of Neukastell was to receive. Because he didn't want to squeeze our peasants for more money." There was incredulous horror in Margarethe's eyes now. She started shaking all over, and her formerly crossed arms fell to her sides.

"You can't have known that, because you've never seen the clasp before," Agnes went on, scarlet with rage. "But I've known it since my childhood. Your suitor gave it to you after the tithes were stolen, presumably to get more details out of you. Isn't that so? You . . . you snake in the grass!"

By now Margarethe had slipped down to the floor, with her back to the wall, and had her hands in front of her face to ward off blows.

"Please, please don't tell your father!" she begged. "It wasn't what you think. I didn't know that man was one of Wertingen's people. He was well dressed, like a good craftsman. And he gave me wine—a lot of wine. After that, I swear, I don't know just what I told him."

"But all the same you went on meeting him and told him even more," snapped Agnes. "You ought to have been suspicious when Wertingen's men knew about the money being delivered and killed Sebastian."

Margarethe sat hunched up, her voice a mere whimper. "I didn't want to believe it," she said. "I thought here at last was the man to take me away from this place. I thought I could sit beside a fire in a nice house with him, have a couple of children in my arms . . ."

Agnes left Margarethe to her tears, coolly examining her.

"I could almost believe you were that stupid," she said at last. "I'd *like* to believe it, if only for the sake of our old friendship. But I can't. I think, deep down inside, you knew what you were doing. But you thought only of yourself."

"So suppose I did?" Margarethe had suddenly stopped crying. Defiantly, she dried her tears and straightened up. "How would you know what it's like, waiting here for years for a man to come along? Getting older and fearing the time when it will be too late? Fearing the castellan will kick you out into the forest to die when you're old? What do you know about real life, castellan's daughter? What Shepherd Jockel says is true: When Adam delved and Eve span, who was then the gentleman?"

Margarethe had uttered those last words like a curse. Now she gathered up the skirts of the dress for which she had paid such a high price and ran out without another word. For a moment Agnes could have taken her not for a maidservant but a mistress. Then the door slammed, and she was alone.

Still trembling with anger, Agnes sat on her bed and tried to calm down. Margarethe had the death of Sebastian on her conscience, and perhaps, soon, the deaths of many others—now that Black Hans presumably knew all about the firearms Mathis had been making. But had she really acted intentionally? Could Agnes tell her father how Margarethe had betrayed them? The penalty for treachery was death in its worst form: traitors were quartered, impaled, or boiled in hot oil. What would her father do? Agnes thought of Margarethe's last words, and all the poor peasants struggling out there, year after year, against starvation, cold, and all the injustice of the powerful.

What do you know about real life, castellan's daughter?

Maybe Margarethe was right, and she was only a spoiled brat who went hawking with her falcon and dreamed of the tales of knights in bygone days. Suddenly she no longer felt like taking Parcival out into the forest. Brooding, she stared up at the ceiling, where a couple of bees, buzzing angrily, were desperately searching for a hole to slip out through.

It was evening of the next day by the time the landsknechts and peasants had unloaded all their equipment on the plateau in front of the robber knight's castle and set it up. The longest job was building the large wooden shields behind which Fat Hedwig and some of the other firearms were to be concealed. What made it more difficult was that Wertingen's men had dug pits all over the empty terrain and had set some wolf traps. The day before, a peasant from Trifels had walked into one of the large metal devices, whetted until it was sharp as a knife, and now he was lying on a bed of branches in the forest, his screams reminding his companions that war was a dirty, cruel trade.

When Mathis looked over at the newly rendered masonry of the Ramburg, he realized once again that Hans von Wertingen had prepared well for this attack. He must have been warned. Beside him, Philipp von Erfenstein was offering, for about the dozenth time, a reward for whoever told him the name of the traitor. Again and again, the old castellan inspected the progress being made on the entrenchments, while Friedrich von Löwenstein-Scharfeneck spent most of the time in the shade of his tent.

As the sun sank behind the trees again, Hans von Wertingen appeared on the battlements of his castle for the first time.

"Hey there, Erfenstein!" he bellowed down from the tall defensive wall. "What a wretched little company you've scraped together. Do you really think you can take my castle with those men?"

"The number doesn't matter so much as whether they're really men," Philipp von Erfenstein retorted. "All I see up there with you is a passel of rogues." His voice echoed over the ravaged terrain.

"And what do you have? Lily-livered peasants and paid mercenaries. Ha! I shit on them!" Wertingen's vassals laughed. Mathis saw half a dozen of them up on the battlements with him, armed with crossbows and longbows. Metal muzzles also protruded from some of the embrasures. So Wertingen obviously had a few firearms as well.

"And if you think you can intimidate me with your magic fire, then let me tell you," Hans von Wertingen went on grandiloquently, "the walls here are so thick that even your one-ton gun won't make any impression on them, let alone your pathetic arquebuses."

Mathis cursed quietly. Wertingen was well informed about their artillery. That meant they must depend all the more on the surprise factor. As ordered, the landsknechts had built up several tree trunks on the steep south side of the terrain to look like traps, including one huge trunk of about the same circumference as Fat Hedwig. Along with cannonballs, two falconets, and a little other materiel, it really did look like they planned to launch their main attack from that spot. On the more level northwestern side, however, only some tall wooden shields faced the defensive wall, giving the impression that only a few archers armed with crossbows sheltered behind them. Black Hans couldn't possibly guess that this was where Fat Hedwig was waiting to be fired.

Count Friedrich von Löwenstein-Scharfeneck had come out of his tent. He curiously scrutinized the defenders.

"In the old days we'd simply have starved the bastards out," he said moodily to Erfenstein. "But I don't have time for that. When do we mount the attack?"

The castellan looked at Mathis, who felt his heart beat faster. It was clearly up to him to give the orders.

"Work on the entrenchments is nearly finished," he calmly replied at last. "We'd better wait overnight and attack at sunrise. Then I'll have enough light." He turned to Scharfeneck. "I suggest a few of your men stay with the peasants by the traps, putting on a fireworks display. Meanwhile Ulrich Reichhart and I will see to Fat Hedwig. The rest of the landsknechts should divert Wertingen's attention by attacking the castle gate from the west."

"A mock attack?" Scharfeneck frowned. "With my well-trained men?"

"They must believe we're really storming the gate," replied Mathis. "That's why the landsknechts should try a genuine attack."

"Erfenstein's peasants can do that just as well." The young count shook his head. "I'm not risking my expensive mercenaries on an attack that's only meant to be a sideshow."

"But the peasants will be defenseless against their weapons," said Mathis angrily. "That's plain murder. They have no experience of warfare."

Scharfeneck shrugged. "That's why they're dispensable. I've said all I have to say. The peasants can attack the gate, my men will remain in the background."

"But . . ." Mathis began again. However, a strong hand coming down on his shoulder stopped him.

"I'll lead the peasants," said the old castellan firmly. "I brought them here, so I will ensure that they go home to their families safe and sound." He paused, thoughtfully. "Most of them, at least."

Then he turned away and went over to the tent. "And now to oil my armor for the last time," he murmured, more to himself than anyone else. "It's been a few years since Guinegate."

Tired and hungry, the midwife Elsbeth Rechsteiner crouched on a jetty, looking out over the cloudy waters of the Rhine. To the west, the sun was just setting behind the mountains, and evening brought cool weather that made Elsbeth shiver. She pulled her threadbare shawl around her shoulders and then looked back at the wooded hills rising beyond the plain of the river from which she had fled like a hunted beast two days ago. But here, on the bank of the Rhine, her journey had been forcibly interrupted, for the last ferry to the opposite bank had left several hours earlier. The local peasants had told her that the next boat would not cross the river until dawn. She must wait until then.

Wait in fear, wondering if the pursuer was already on her heels.

Elsbeth Rechsteiner shivered under her thin woolen shawl. She had suffered severe pangs of conscience since the Brotherhood's last meeting in the forest clearing. Had it really been right to place the fate of the empire in the hands of unknown monks of some kind? Who knew whether they might not use the document for purposes of their own? If the order was dissolved, not a soul would know where the parchment deed was. So Elsbeth had decided to share the secret with one other person, an old and wise friend. Let him decide when the time to reveal it was ripe. After that, Elsbeth had felt easier in her mind at last.

But then something terrible happened: as she was going to slip back into her niece's house in Waldrohrbach that night, someone had already been there asking about her—that black-skinned stranger who had already lain in wait for her once before. Elsbeth could not say whether he had found his way to her by himself or with the aid of a treacherous member of the Brotherhood. Ultimately, it made no difference.

Since then, the midwife had been on the run.

Exhausted and hungry, the old woman rubbed her sore toes while the evening mist slowly closed in. Broad rafts and barges lying deep in the water passed her. She heard soft music coming from one of the boats. The air smelled of waterweeds, fish, and peat fires. The other bank was only about fifty yards away, but in the gathering dusk, all that Elsbeth could see of it was a black strip of land. About a quarter of a mile farther on, she saw the soft lights of a village: Dettenheim, where her cousin lived. There would be a warm place for her to sleep and a steaming bowl of stew waiting for her there. Once over the river she would soon make it there.

Elsbeth was about to dip her sore feet in the cool water of the Rhine when she heard the crunch of footsteps on the path behind her. Turning around, she saw a single black-clad figure coming down the broad access path to the river. It might be only another traveler who, like Elsbeth, had missed the last ferry of the day, but something made the midwife hold her breath. Only after a while did she know why the hairs on the back of her neck were standing on end.

Not only was the man's cloak black, so was his face.

With a cry of terror, Elsbeth jumped up and ran off the jetty, into the reeds. The stranger hesitated for a moment and then quickened his pace. The midwife ran along the bank, where a narrow towpath followed the river. The reeds here were as tall as a man, and soon she could not see whether the pursuer was still following her. He was indeed the black devil who had been after her for weeks to get the secret of the order out of her.

Elsbeth Rechsteiner stood where she was for a moment, gasping for air, and listening. Not far away, she heard the reeds rustling, and the sound of muted footsteps on the marshy ground.

The stranger was following her.

She went on along the towpath, praying soundlessly to all the saints. Had the black man's henchmen tracked down the other members of the order as well? Then it occurred to Elsbeth that, besides her, only the head of their order knew about the monastery to which, she supposed, he was on his way at this moment.

And then of course there is a third person who knows, she suddenly thought. *By Our Lady, I never ought to have passed the information on. They will torture us and find out the hiding place. More than two hundred years of silence, over so many generations, and now it's all over.*

Gasping, she ran through the reeds, while their rustling could still be heard behind her. That sound came closer. Suddenly the path ahead of her branched into two even narrower paths. She decided to take the right-hand path and stumbled on, until all at once she was on the edge of a crumbling dock. Ahead of her lay the broad black ribbon of the Rhine, behind her the reeds swayed in the last faint light of the evening sun. Elsbeth Rechsteiner gritted her teeth to keep from screaming.

She had run into a dead end.

Only a little later, the reeds parted, and the black man stepped out of them. In the dark, he looked even more surreal than when she had seen him outside her hut. When the stranger saw her, he raised his hands in a reassuring gesture and smiled.

"What a delightful surprise," he said slowly. His voice was hoarse from chasing her, and he had a strange accent. "So what your pretty niece in Waldrohrbach told me in exchange for a bag of coins was true."

Elsbeth closed her eyes, whimpering quietly. Could Sophia really have given her away? Her husband, a carpenter and a drunk, had an injured leg and hadn't been able to work for weeks. Their children were going hungry. But would she have gone so far as to hand her own aunt over to this devil?

"You must not be angry," said the black man, as if he could read her thoughts. "She could not pay the rent, those brats of hers were wailing most pitifully. And I promised her I would not hurt you. At least, not if it could be avoided." He shrugged with an air of boredom. "All I want is for us to talk a little. Is that so difficult?"

The midwife looked at him with a stony expression, although her breath was still coming fast after the chase. She had been running away from this stranger for weeks. She had given the ring away, she had warned the order, the deed had been taken to a safe place—but none of it had done any good.

He knows, she thought. *He knows what happened in the past. Someone must have given the secret away to him. What a mercy that I didn't tell the Brotherhood everything . . .*

Elsbeth Rechsteiner made her decision. She closed her eyes and murmured a last prayer.

"Sanctus Fridericus, libera me, libera me. Vade satanas . . ."

Then she jumped.

"Maldito, estupida gallina!"

The stranger swore out loud in a foreign language and then strode to the end of the landing stage. Looking up through the surface of the water, Elsbeth saw his face blurred, distorted like a diabolical mask, dissolving into oily streaks. Finally it was gone, and the midwife felt herself drifting almost weightlessly down the river. Like a bird, like the falcon to which she had entrusted the ring, she was flying away. She opened her mouth for a final prayer, and water streamed into her lungs. Briefly, a terrible pain overcame Elsbeth, but it soon gave way to deep contentment.

She had not told the secret.

The attack on Ramburg Castle began shortly before sunrise.

The woods at the foot of the hill were still deep in darkness, with the first faint touch of red in the sky showing only above the tops of some tall beech trees. It was the time when the birds began singing their dawn chorus. Then the first shot rang out over the terrain around the castle. Another followed, then another, and the peasants, who had been hiding behind trees until now, ran toward the castle gate, shouting. Philipp von Erfenstein strode ahead of them, bellowing orders. The surprise tactic seemed to be working; at least, so far no guards had appeared on top of the walls.

Mathis watched the attack from his hiding place behind one of the wooden shields. Beside him, Ulrich Reichhart was calmly and carefully charging Fat Hedwig with granular gunpowder, tamping it down with a wooden rammer.

"Now we'll see if this gun is really worth something," he said. "And if so, Mathis, when all this is over, Erfenstein will make you an iron throne." His voice was almost drowned out by the screaming and the sound of shots all around them.

"Or a cage, to put me in it and drown me," Mathis muttered, hardly paying attention.

He was breathing heavily as he pushed a stone cannonball weighing almost thirty pounds through the mouth of the gun into the barrel, ramming it in with a staff wrapped in fabric. One last time, he checked for small cracks. Even a crack as fine as a hair could cause the bronze to explode.

At least if it does, I won't get to hear whatever little rhyme Melchior von Tanningen composes about my inglorious end, he thought.

After making sure the ball was well down in the body of the gun, Mathis began adjusting the barrel's angle with a large crank fitted to its side.

"Curse it, why is this taking so long?" complained Reichhart, looking at the peasants, who were now climbing ladders that they had put up against the castle gate. The young men were using sickles, short spears, and axes as weapons. "If we don't hurry up, the castellan won't be taking a single one of these young hotheads back to his parents," the old master gunner went on gloomily. "At least not all in one piece."

"I must get the angle just right," Mathis replied curtly. "It won't help our peasants if we're firing cannonballs at the moon."

As he turned the crank, Mathis looked through a slit between the shields and saw one of the peasants fall off a ladder, screaming, the shaft of a spear stuck in his chest. The only armor that Philipp von Erfenstein now wore was a helmet and a hauberk, so that he could be more mobile as he fought at the head of his troops. He was tackling three men at once with a short sword as they tried to get him down on the ground. Another of the peasants, arms flailing, fell directly in front of the castle gate and lay there, writhing in pain. Occasional shots could be heard now from the other side of the castle, but so far there was no sign of Scharfeneck's landsknechts. Erfenstein did indeed seem to be confining the effort to the mock attack on the southern side.

Where it's safest, thought Mathis. *And our peasants have to bleed.*

At last he had the angle of the barrel adjusted to his satisfaction. He got Ulrich Reichhart to hand him the burning stick with the fuse at the end of it, and through the touchhole he set fire to the charge, which began burning calmly and regularly. The crackling noise of it sounded to Mathis like a hissing snake. He signaled to Reichhart, and they both covered their ears.

The ensuing blast was so powerful that the two gunners fell to the ground. In spite of her weight, Fat Hedwig had rolled several feet back from where she was suspended, until she came up against an earthwork piled up for that purpose. Thick smoke rose before Mathis, cutting off his view. His eyes streamed, and there was a roaring and rushing in his ears. He knelt down and tried to see through the clouds of smoke as they slowly dissipated. The tall wooden shield that had been standing in front of the muzzle of the gun had disappeared entirely, leaving only a few charred splinters of wood scattered on the ground. A ghostly silence suddenly reigned over the charred terrain. It was as if all the attackers and all the defenders, too, were staring at the mighty monster that had made that infernal clamor. Only after some time could Mathis see the defensive wall of the castle through the smoke from the gunpowder.

A narrow, egg-shaped hole gaped open in the middle of that wall, about thirty feet up.

"Damn it, we aimed too high," Ulrich Reichhart cursed. "Our men will never get through as far up as that."

Mathis bit his lip. The moment of surprise had come and gone. And no one knew how much more often Fat Hedwig could be fired without exploding. Mathis put his hand on the barrel, and snatched it away in surprise. The bronze felt red-hot.

"We can't venture on more than one or at the most two more balls!" he shouted through the din of battle that was swelling again now. "Then we'll have to stop for a break, or Hedwig will explode all around us."

"Stop for a break?" Reichhart looked at him blankly. "We're much too close to the wall for that. They'll pick us off like rabbits. And we can't leave the big gun standing here unprotected for too long, or they'll smash our prime artillery piece."

Mathis ducked as the ball of an arquebus whistled over their heads. Sure enough, the defenders had the two gunners under fire now.

If anyone hits the gunpowder, at least it won't hurt for long . . .

Wondering what to do, Mathis looked at the peasants, who were still trying in vain to get up the ramp and storm the castle gate. Four of them already lay on the ground, dead or wounded. Only Philipp von Erfenstein had almost succeeded in reaching the breastwork of the fortifications by ladder. But by now his sword arm looked tired as he brought it down on the defenders, and his movements were slower.

"Someone must tell Scharfeneck's landsknechts to come and help the peasants," Mathis said. The noise was so loud that he had to shout to make himself heard. "If the soldiers don't distract Wertingen's men, I won't be able to readjust the barrel."

Ulrich Reichhart hesitated briefly, and then nodded. "You go to the count. I'll deal with Hedwig."

He gave Mathis a comradely clap on the shoulder, but the young man disagreed. "I have to stay here," he said firmly. "If anyone knows how much powder the barrel will stand now, I do. It'll be all right."

Reichhart looked at him for a moment and finally grinned. "You're a good lad," he grunted. "Your father can be proud of you."

With these words, he turned and hurried toward Sharfeneck, giving the castle a wide berth. Two or three arrows were fired at him, but he was out of range of the archers.

Meanwhile, Mathis turned back to the gun and readjusted the angle of the barrel. Finally he took a deep breath. Now he must expose himself to the greatest danger yet.

Charging the gun with powder and shot.

Since the wooden shield was destroyed, the muzzle of the cannon was now exposed, unprotected. Mathis estimated that it would take him a minute to charge the gun—a minute during which Wertingen's men could pick him off like a fat capon. He closed his eyes and decided to think of something good. It might be the last thought of his life.

He thought of Agnes. Instinctively, he put his hand in his pocket and felt the wooden amulet she had given him when they said good-bye. It was warm in his hand.

Then he took hold of one of the heavy stone balls, picked it up with a groan of effort, and ran to the mouth of the gun with it. As he pushed the ball into the barrel, he heard a sudden hissing behind him. He ducked, and a crossbow bolt flew past just above his shoulder. He counted seconds in his mind.

Twenty-eight, twenty-nine, thirty . . .

There was another crash beside him, and a second wooden shield splintered, but Mathis did not allow it to distract him. He now had the ball almost at the back of the barrel, where the force of the explosion would be strongest.

Forty, forty-one, forty-two . . .

The next crossbow bolt hit Mathis in the thigh.

He cried out, but he did not run away. One last time he pushed the stick so deep into the opening that it almost disappeared. Only then did he let himself fall behind the last remaining wooden screen. He picked up the fuse stuck into the ground beside him, and, breathing heavily, he lit the charge.

Fifty-nine, sixty.

Once again, there was such a mighty crash that for a moment the world seemed to stand still. Mathis curled up like a baby, the broken shaft of the bolt sticking out of his right leg. He felt the ground shake beneath him, and shouts came to his ears, but their sound was muted.

They were shouts of joy.

This time he had hit the foot of the tall defensive wall. A hole almost the height of a man could be seen in it behind the drifting smoke. Stones fell from the battlements, clattering, and two of Wertingen's vassals lay on the ground with their limbs strangely distorted.

Mathis felt his heart leap up. He had actually done it. He had breached the wall. Only then did he see that the hole did not go quite all the way through. It was more of a deep dent that Fat Hedwig had left, and there was still solid stone behind it.

One more shot, he thought. *One more shot and we'll be through!*

But would the gun fire another ball without exploding? How much more heat could Fat Hedwig stand?

Suddenly Mathis heard more shouting, and shots as well this time. Scharfeneck's landsknechts had actually come to the aid of the few peasants still fighting. Melchior von Tanningen was also among the attackers. Together they were climbing the siege ladders or firing their arquebuses, from a safe distance, at the defenders on the battlements, who were now running back and forth frantically. Philipp von Erfenstein had made it to the breastwork, where he was fighting two of Wertingen's men like a berserker. Melchior stood on a ladder level with the battlements, circling his sword in the air. Screaming, another defender fell off the wall.

His hands shaking, Mathis turned back to Fat Hedwig. It was a good moment. Wertingen's men had been distracted; no one seemed interested in him and the gun. He began frantically cleaning the inside of the barrel of most of the remaining powder and cooling its exterior with wet rags. The bronze was so hot that a hissing cloud of vapor instantly rose in the air. Mathis poured powder into the mouth of the gun, picked up another cannonball, put it into the still-hot barrel, and rammed it down with the stick.

It's going to explode. I'm sure it's going to explode.

The air was still full of stinking smoke from the last explosion. Mathis coughed and sweated, and at last the ball was in the right position. He ran back again and lit the charge from there.

As the powder ate its way, hissing, through the touchhole, the young smith looked for cover behind some splintered casks. Then he looked ahead of him at the dent in the wall. Yes, they were nearly through it.

But something seemed to be digging or burrowing in the indentation. Soon after that, he heard a deep, angry barking that seemed to come straight from hell.

Mathis thought his heart was about to stop when a large, black shadow suddenly leapt out of the hole. It was the mastiff, Saskia, racing toward him, growling and baring her fangs. He had never seen any animal run so fast. The dog, who was the size of a calf, was already crouching to spring.

At that moment Fat Hedwig blew up.

The world in front of Mathis dissolved into blood and smoke. The explosion tore him off his feet. Something large shot just past his ear and crashed into a group of trees a good fifty yards away. The ground beneath him was wet and warm. Only after some time did he notice that he was lying in a pool of blood, probably his own. When he managed to look up, Mathis saw that the huge gun was lying on its side, torn open like a length of fabric, with black smoke pouring out of it.

There was no sign of the mastiff. Only a piece of smoking fur stuck to the muzzle of the gun.

More cries of joy rose, as far away as if they came from another world. Swaying, Mathis got to his knees and stared into the smoke ahead of him. At last he had dragged himself far enough to be able to see the castle wall.

A hole the size of a wide doorway gaped in it, and beyond that the castle courtyard lay open.

With a last sigh, Mathis fell forward and lay in his own blood, as the peasants and landsknechts stormed toward the breach in the wall, yelling with delight. His hands clasped the wooden amulet that Agnes had given him an eternity ago, or so it seemed.

Then he lost consciousness.

· 11 ·

MATHIS WOKE WHEN SOMEONE THREW a torrent of water in his face. He opened his eyes and saw the grinning Ulrich Reichhart above him, holding a dripping-wet wooden bucket.

"I think you've been asleep long enough," said Reichhart, his eyes twinkling. "You ought not to miss the celebrations, that's what the castellan says. And Father Tristan has already tended your injuries. He came over from Trifels at midday. So you have no excuse to laze around any longer."

"Celebrations . . . Father Tristan . . . ? I don't understand." Mathis rubbed his eyes wearily. All at once his memory came back. They were outside Ramburg Castle. He had breached the wall, the battle was won. Yes, Fat Hedwig had exploded, but at least she had served her purpose with the last shot that she fired. All the same, Mathis felt sorry, after all the work he had put into her. The big gun had been his masterpiece.

Shakily, he got up from the bed of straw and twigs where he was lying, and saw that he was in the middle of the temporary field camp on the saddle in the hills, not far from the robber knight's castle.

Night had fallen. Several campfires crackled, and the landsknechts sat beside them, drinking and bawling out songs. A few of the soldiers were so drunk that they lay asleep in their own vomit. Two peasants were performing a folk dance beside one of the fires, while a third played his fiddle.

"Have I been asleep all day?" Mathis asked Ulrich Reichhart, who had been drawing himself a tankard of beer from a large cask. The old master gunner laughed out loud.

"All day? Devil take it, you've been asleep for two whole days. We're going back to Trifels tomorrow."

"But . . . what have you been doing here all this time?" Mathis asked in surprise.

Reichhart took a long draft. He wiped the foam off his lips before replying. "What people do in war. We've been looting. First the castle, then the whole district. After all, the Ramberg peasants supported that bastard."

"Only because they had to."

"Huh, who cares about that?" Reichhart shrugged. "Don't be so soft-hearted, Mathis. We got good loot, and the district's secure again. That's all that counts. That minstrel, Melchior, is on the way to tell the other feudal lords about it." He grinned. "Fought like a demon, that frail little fellow. If you ask me, he's better with a sword than a lute."

Mathis was going to say something, but at that moment Father Tristan approached, leaning on his staff. The old monk raised a threatening forefinger.

"Good God in heaven, Reichhart! Didn't I expressly say the boy wasn't to get up?" he scolded. "He's lost a great deal of blood. It'll be your fault if he dies on me."

Reichhart grinned guiltily. "He's not going to die anytime soon, Father. A man who stands beside Fat Hedwig when she blows up isn't going to be killed so easily."

Laughing, Reichhart clapped Mathis on the shoulder and went

away to get himself another tankard of beer. Only now did the young smith realize how tired he still was. He had fresh bandages on his leg, neck, and shoulders; his whole body felt as if it were wrapped in damp leaves. He felt slightly dizzy and had to sit down again.

"There, just as I said. Well, it looks like nothing will get you down."

Father Tristan looked hard at Mathis and then sat down beside him on an upturned cart wheel. "There aren't many I can help," he said sadly. "So it would distress me a great deal if I'd been working on you in vain as well."

Mathis glanced at the outskirts of the forest, where the bodies of at least half a dozen men hung from the branches of a large beech tree. They swayed gently in the evening wind, and several crows had already come down to feast on them. The outlines of Ramburg Castle stood out against the darkening sky. Thin threads of black smoke rose from it in several places, and some of the sheds and stables were still burning in the outer bailey.

"How many men died?" asked Mathis.

Father Tristan frowned. "I haven't been counting, but just about all Wertingen's men-at-arms, and a good many of the peasants who were helping him. Not so many on our side, but five of those young peasants are among them. And an arquebus exploded in the hand of one of Scharfeneck's landsknechts. Even the Lord God will have difficulty recognizing the man when he comes before him." He made the sign of the cross, and glanced at the makeshift gallows. "And any help is too late for the men over there."

"How about Black Hans?"

"Count Scharfeneck is keeping him for a public trial," replied the monk wearily, cracking his gouty knuckles. "The idea is to have him hung, drawn, and quartered in Speyer, but Philipp von Erfenstein doesn't go along with that idea. He and the count are discussing it in Scharfeneck's tent right now."

Mathis suddenly felt queasy and propped himself on Father

Tristan's shoulder to keep from falling over. The monk took out a little bottle and handed it to him.

"Drink that. It's a mixture made of tormentil and arnica to strengthen you. Agnes made it especially for you just before I set out."

Gratefully, Mathis took a good draft of the aromatic medicament. It tasted sweet, and the fluid seemed warm as it lay in his stomach. He immediately felt a little better.

"How is Agnes?" Mathis asked hesitantly.

"How do you think? Worried to death about you, you idiot! When the first messengers came yesterday with the news that Erfenstein had won, her thoughts were all for you." There was a twinkle in Father Tristan's eyes. "She'd like to be here, but I said her father would murder her if she came, so she decided to wait for you at Trifels."

Suddenly they heard loud voices from the camp. When Mathis turned around, all that he saw at first was a large black shadow being pushed into the large tent by several landsknechts. Only after a while did he see that it was a man wrapped in chains from head to foot. He stumbled several times but remained upright. When he stepped into the light of the largest fire, Mathis recognized who it was at last.

Hans von Wertingen.

He stood there, his face sooty and covered with dried blood, one eye swollen, his breastplate dented, glaring angrily at the mercenaries who surrounded him, laughing and grinning. Black Hans had fought like a lion in yesterday's battle for the castle, splitting the skulls of two of his adversaries before five men finally overpowered him and put him in chains. Now one of the soldiers picked up a hard clod of soil from the ground and threw it at the knight. Wertingen ducked, but the clod caught the side of his forehead and fresh blood ran down his cheek.

"You cowardly swine!" he bellowed, shaking himself so that the chains rattled. "Oh yes, like a crowd of washerwomen, you can throw dirt at a man in fetters."

"Who's the swine here, us or you?" crowed one of the bystanders.

"Just look at the sow. Someone stick him with a boar spear in his fat belly to make him hold his tongue."

The others laughed, and the first stones began flying through the air, although most of them bounced off the prisoner's chains. One, however, hit Wertingen hard on the shoulder, and he staggered. For a moment it seemed that he might fall into the fire, but then he straightened up again. Mathis remembered how terrifying the robber knight had been when he and Agnes met him in the forest. Now he almost felt sorry for the man.

"Stop that! Stop that at once, I say!"

The order had come from the large tent. Erfenstein and young Count Scharfeneck were just emerging from it. The castellan of Trifels was looking to all sides, with his one good eye flashing angrily. "No one touches my prisoner, no one!" he cried. "Or I'll string up the guilty man with my own hands from the battlements of the castle ruins."

Friedrich von Löwenstein-Scharfeneck smiled, amused, as he watched Wertingen struggling for breath. "Well, I suppose my men may be allowed a little fun with this brute," he said, making a casual gesture to keep his landsknechts within bounds. "But you're right, Erfenstein, it would be a pity to extinguish the spark of life in Black Hans here before he makes his big entrance in Speyer, to deter other robber knights. There are still too many gallows birds like him in the Palatinate, calling themselves noblemen but worth no more than mangy dogs."

"I am of a great house," Wertingen managed to say, with his chains clinking as he braced himself. "My forebears were imperial ministers. You have no right to treat me like a common thief."

"Yet that's what you are," Erfenstein growled. "There may have been times when you were still rightly called a knight and a baron. Now you are nothing but a marauder and highwayman, and death awaits you."

Wertingen thrust out his blood-stained chin, threw back his long, matted hair, and stared at his archenemy. "And you've become this fellow's henchman, Philipp. Tell us how long you'll be able to hold Trifels Castle before His Excellency the count here drives you out of it like a dog."

"We have an agreement," said the castellan tonelessly. "The house of Erfenstein will not perish like yours, Wertingen. It . . . it will live on . . ." His voice died away, and from where Mathis was sitting, he could hardly make out the words.

Finally the count, still standing beside the castellan, spoke up.

"You can come to terms with power, or you can fight it and lose forever," said Scharfeneck quietly, looking at the sorry state the robber knight was in. "Believe me, Wertingen, I'll make sure that your name is erased from your family's records forever, as if it had never been."

"It will be your name that—"

"Quiet, Hans!" Philipp von Erfenstein straightened up to his full height of six feet and looked sternly at his old adversary of past tournaments. "I've had you brought here before us to tell you your fate. As you know, the count wanted to have you executed in Speyer, in atonement for your crimes and as a lesson to others. But I thought differently." He paused. When he went on, his voice was firm and menacing. "Listen, Wertingen. You have plundered my peasants, killed my men, and threatened my daughter. But you were once a knight, so you should die like a knight, even if you don't deserve it. At sunrise tomorrow morning you and I will fight in single combat, with swords and our fists, until one of us lies dead. That is my verdict."

A murmur passed through the crowd. Some of the landsknechts shook their heads incredulously. Even Father Tristan frowned. "I'd never have expected young Scharfeneck to allow this," he muttered. "The count could have made a name for himself in these parts by executing Wertingen in Speyer. In fact I thought that was what he wanted all along, not what little loot he could take here."

"And why is Erfenstein letting himself in for such a fight?" asked Mathis, surprised. "Why risk his life when the outcome of the feud is decided?"

Father Tristan sighed. "I'm afraid you don't understand, Mathis. Philipp von Erfenstein comes from another age. He must see this fight as a tribute to the battle of Guinegate. He wants to be a proud knight, not an impoverished castellan submitting himself to the mon-eyed aristocracy. If he wins he'll feel that his honor is restored."

"And suppose he loses?"

Father Tristan shrugged. "He won't lose, believe me. Wertingen is injured, and despite his height, he's not as strong as Erfenstein, who to the best of my knowledge always used to defeat him in tourna-ments."

Hans von Wertingen had listened to the verdict with his head held high. Now he lowered it, almost humbly.

"Thank you, Philipp," he said, and his voice broke slightly. "I will not disappoint you. It will be a good fight." A smile crossed his face. "What if I win?"

"Then the duke will declare you an outlaw," replied the castellan coolly. "I'll make sure you get half a day's start before the hunt for you begins." He turned to the landsknechts standing around them. "Now get him out of my sight before I think better of my offer."

As the guards took the prisoner away, Mathis again felt queasy. He sank back on his bed of twigs and closed his eyes. He was asleep within a few minutes. But the loud laughter and the singing of the landsknechts accompanied him into his dreams.

Agnes jumped as the first lightning bolt flashed across the heavens, soon followed by a crash of thunder.

Alarmed, she looked up at the evening sky, but the storm was still a little way off and would probably move eastward before it reached Trifels Castle. With a little hesitation, she continued going along the track into the forest. She thought that the clouds might be shedding rain over the Ramburg at this moment. How were Mathis and her father? She had been told that Mathis was alive, but wounded. Agnes had wanted badly to go to the scene of the battle with Father Tristan, but the old monk had made it clear that her father did not on any account want to see her there. So she had stayed at home, still brooding on what Father Tristan had been keeping from her in the library a few days ago. By this time she was firmly convinced that he had met with someone outside the castle early that morning.

Only who? And why? And what brought him up to the library?

To take her mind off the riddle, Agnes had spent the last few days making medicines. The old monk had the use not only of the castle kitchen but also of a tiny room where he kept ointments, tinctures, and medical instruments. Over the last few months Agnes had learned a great deal about the art of healing from him. She had studied the *Macer Floridus* of the Benedictine monk Odo Magdunensis, admiring its beautiful drawings of healing herbs. She could now recognize the symptoms of several dozen diseases and knew when to pick which plants.

Today, the day of St. Alexius, the country calendar advised you to pick cuckoo flower and, in particular, ground ivy. The moon was waxing, and that intensified the healing power of its blue flowers. So Agnes had put her leather satchel over her shoulder and gone out into the Trifels woods. She knew where to find ground ivy, that inconspicuous little plant that grew best in marshy clearings surrounded by birch trees farther down in the water meadows of the Queich.

As she climbed down the steep, narrow path from the castle to the valley and listened to the thunder in the distance, she thought again of Margarethe and what the lady's maid had done. Agnes still was not sure whether her treachery had been unintentional or deliberate. Not that it really made much difference now. Since the incident of the silver clasp, Margarethe had not been seen at the castle. Agnes suspected that her maid had fled from the castellan's wrath and was now trying to make a new beginning somewhere else in the Palatinate. Maybe she was even on her way to the distant, rich city of Cologne, where her cousin lived. She had spoken of it so enthusiastically a few months ago.

Agnes had been sad about Margarethe's disappearance for a little while for, after all, she had known her maid since childhood. But at heart she had never been especially fond of the simple-minded and talkative young woman, while Margarethe had always been envious of her mistress. Still, Agnes hoped that she would find the rich husband of her dreams at last.

By now she had reached the marshy water meadows of the Queich. The storm had moved away. Agnes saw the blue flowers of ground ivy among the trunks of birch trees. She bent down and began cutting the plants singly from their rootstock with a knife, putting them into her satchel.

A strange noise made her spin around. She realized it was the sound of a lute being plucked, and it was followed by another note, and then another, building up at last into a little melody that seemed to come from the river. Curiously, Agnes shouldered her leather satchel and set off to discover the source of the music. After only a few minutes, she reached a mossy curve on the riverbank where a single weeping willow dipped its branches low into the water.

Under the willow tree sat Melchior von Tanningen, playing his lute.

The minstrel was performing a tune that sounded old and made Agnes feel both sad and happy.

Agnes's face brightened. She fervently hoped that the minstrel could tell her more about Mathis and his injuries. In addition, a chance meeting with him was always a welcome diversion.

For a while she listened in silence, and she came out from the trees only when the song had died away. When Tanningen heard footsteps, he got to his feet, put the lute aside in a single fluent movement, and drew his sword, but on seeing Agnes, his face relaxed.

"Noble lady," he said, smiling, and put the weapon back in its sheath. "What a delightful surprise. But shouldn't you be in bed at this time of night?"

"And shouldn't you be with Count Scharfeneck over at the Ramburg?" Agnes replied.

"My presence was no longer necessary. I was sent to give Scharfeneck's father and the neighboring feudal lords news of the outcome of the battle." The minstrel picked up his lute again and plucked several strings. They mingled with the sound of the little river flowing by, making an almost ghostly melody. "I fear that feud was too small and dirty for a heroic epic, anyway. Although your friend Mathis acquitted himself well in it."

"How is he?" asked Agnes anxiously.

Melchior von Tanningen's eyes twinkled as he looked at her. "Well, he has a couple of wounds, but he'll survive them. There's no doubt that Mathis has the makings of a leader of men. But you'd better keep your fingers off him, all the same."

"How dare you . . ." Agnes began, but the minstrel played a soft chord, and she reined in her temper. "What . . . what makes you think there could be anything between me and Mathis, anyway?"

"God gave me eyes to see with, and a heart to feel with as well. Anyway, didn't you give him something before the battle?" Melchior smiled. "Furthermore, don't forget that I'm a minstrel. Yours wouldn't be the first sad love story I've had to sing."

"Then sing about doomed princes and princesses or something, and leave me and Mathis out of it."

For a moment Melchior von Tanningen looked as if he was about to reply, but then he just looked sympathetically at Agnes. "I'd like to spare you disappointment, that's all." He put his head to one side. "And what do you think of my present feudal lord?"

"Friedrich von Löwenstein-Scharfeneck? Are you by any chance recommending the count as a husband?" She uttered a little laugh that dismissed the subject. "Too kind of you. But the daughter of an impoverished castellan is certainly no fit match for such a man. In addition, between ourselves, that fine count thinks far too well of himself for my liking."

"Yet you share the same passion."

Agnes wrinkled her brow. "Indeed? And that would be . . . ?"

"The count loves old stories. Friedrich von Löwenstein-Scharfeneck reads, indeed devours, everything to do with Trifels Castle. Did you know that? In particular, he's obsessed with the

Norman treasure said to have been kept at Trifels once." Melchior sighed. "I have orders to write His Excellency a powerful ode about it. I'd rather write about the legend of Barbarossa." He cleared his throat and began to sing.

> *There was an emperor wore a beard as red as any fire*
> *He slept for centuries, I've heard, a loss to our empire.*
> *If he should ever rise again, our countries to unite,*
> *All other princes' power will wane before his royal might . . .*

When he had finished, Agnes, pleasantly surprised, looked at him. "That was lovely," she said. "Did you write it yourself?"

Melchior nodded and stroked his little beard as if embarrassed. "But it's only the opening. There's to be a minstrels' contest at the famous Wartburg next year, and I'd like to take part in it. I'm still looking for the right ode, but Barbarossa's slumber under Trifels Castle strikes me as a good subject."

"The Wartburg?" Agnes wrinkled her brow. "Isn't that the castle where Luther translated the New Testament into German a few years ago? Father Tristan once showed me a copy of it."

"To be sure, it is a castle with a long history. Almost as long and important as the history of Trifels." Melchior cast up his eyes. "But the count wants his ballad about the Norman treasure, so old Emperor Barbarossa will have to wait. If Scharfeneck goes on like this, I'll be writing an ode to his receding hair soon enough."

Agnes chuckled. The entertaining minstrel could always make her laugh.

"I'm sorry I spoke roughly to you just now," she said at last. "But these days I sometimes can't stand even my own company. There are things in my life that are simply too . . . too strange."

"Strange?"

For a moment Agnes considered telling Melchior about her dreams and the ring, but then she remembered her promise to Father Tristan some days ago.

*Promise me not to show it to anyone. And keep your dreams to yourself,
too.*

"I suppose everything is rather too much at the moment," she
hesitantly replied. "My father's debts; the feud with Black Hans; your
master, Count Scharfeneck, as our new neighbor; and then of course
the situation with Mathis. You are right, he . . ." Her voice faltered,
and Melchior von Tanningen leaned down to take her hand.

"There are matters that one doesn't understand until one is older,"
he said quietly after a while. "They may appear cruel, but they serve
a higher purpose."

Agnes was about to ask what he meant by this puzzling remark,
but suddenly the minstrel bowed courteously to her.

"I'm sure we'll have time some other day to talk about Barbarossa."
He smiled. "Barbarossa and, for all I care, the Norman treasure as
well. It seems that such old tales warm your heart, and who can de-
scribe the past better than a minstrel?" He gestured invitingly toward
the castle. "Have you ever heard the ballad of Sir Gawain and his
fight with the Green Knight?"

They walked up the path to the castle together, and the exciting
story made Agnes forget her sad thoughts, at least for a while.

Next morning, the wind drove rain over Ramburg Castle. The last of
the fires in the stables and sheds were extinguished, the castle itself
was a burned-out ruin, the holes where its windows had been now
stared into the distance like blind eyes.

Although it was nearly summer, it was unseasonably cool. The
storm shook the tents of the field camp as if to awaken their occu-
pants. Father Tristan had had another tent put up for the wounded
men, made of several lengths of cloth from the loot that had been
taken, and at least Mathis was dry. He had slept badly that night, with
his right leg throbbing and painful where the crossbow bolt had hit
it. Some pieces of shrapnel had also penetrated his face and his shoulder area; yesterday Father Tristan had removed them with a pair of
pincers. Mathis would be left with an ugly scar on his right cheek, but

it was a miracle that he was alive at all. When a large cannon exploded, all that was usually left of the gunner manning it was bloody scraps of flesh.

Day was slowly dawning outside the tent, and the voices of the landsknechts and the whinnying of horses came more and more insistently to Mathis's ears. He stood up with some difficulty, limped past the other injured men, made his way to the tent flaps, and folded them back.

Outside, a storm raged. The many landsknechts who had not found a place in the tents sat in what shelter the carts and gun carriages could offer, cursing and with hats drawn well down over their faces. They were all staring intently at a circle of spears thrust into the ground not far from the largest of the campfires. The circle was about twenty feet in diameter, the ground was soft and muddy. Someone had placed the head of a dead man-at-arms on one of the spears, and it now seemed to be gazing at Mathis with a frozen, blood-stained rictus of a grin.

When the young weaponsmith turned his eyes away, he saw that Philipp von Erfenstein was standing outside the large tent to his right. The castellan was wearing full armor, the visor of his helmet was up, his hands rested on a mighty two-handed sword with its point stuck in the mud in front of him. Lost in thought, Erfenstein was looking up at the clouded sky, where the sun was showing for the first time today as a wan disk behind the clouds. Soon the rain settled into a steady drizzle.

"Like Guinegate," Philipp von Erfenstein said. "It was so wet there that our horses and the baggage train got stuck in the mud. And it was a devilishly bloody battle."

At this moment the sun came out from the clouds, shining on Erfenstein's face. To his surprise, Mathis saw that the castellan was beaming.

He's about to fight in single combat to the death, and he's happy about it, Mathis thought. *I'll never understand these knights.*

And now, with the *clink* of metal, Hans von Wertingen, flanked by four guards, approached the circle marked out by the spears. The landsknechts had removed his chains and given him back his dented breastplate and round helmet. He carried the mighty broadsword that Mathis had noticed on their first meeting in the forest. The robber knight looked around almost reverently, noticing, with obvious satisfaction, the many spectators who had begun taking their places around the improvised arena.

"Weather worthy of this encounter, don't you agree?" Hans von Wertingen said to his adversary, grinning.

In silence, Philipp von Erfenstein strode toward the circle, his armor clinking slightly with every step he took. It was well oiled, and so highly polished that it flashed in the sun. Looking at the castellan, no one could have known that he had been drinking well into the night and had snatched at most a couple of hours of sleep. Among the hung-over landsknechts with their colorful costumes, wild beards, and rusty pikes and arquebuses, Philipp von Erfenstein looked like an envoy from another world. The soldiers watched him in a mood somewhere between admiration and mockery. Many of them were no older than Mathis and knew fully armed knights and tournaments only from the tales told by their fathers and grandfathers. None of them had ever seen two knights in chivalrous single combat.

When the castellan of Trifels finally reached the circle, he bowed slightly to Wertingen, who returned the gesture. It was as if the two of them were conversing in a silent language that only they understood. There was a tense silence in the air.

Suddenly, slow hand-clapping began. Mathis glanced toward the count's tent. Friedrich von Löwenstein-Scharfeneck emerged from it, applauding the two adversaries mockingly. Then he sat down on a folding stool.

"An impressive sight, to be sure. Two knights showing courtesy to one another," he observed in a self-confident voice. "You surprise me, Erfenstein. What makes you bow to a brute like that?"

"There are certain conventions to be observed," the castellan replied haughtily. "But you'll be too young to understand them."

"Maybe. Too young and too impatient. Now let's have an end to this mummery and get on with it." The count incredulously shook his head. "A song of farewell to the old days. What a pity our minstrel isn't here to see it. Very well." He clapped his hands once more. "What is it that they say? May the best man win."

The two knights raised their swords and began circling one another. Only after several minutes did Wertingen begin the fight by storming forward, sweeping his two-handed sword through the air, and bringing it down toward Erfenstein. The castellan parried the stroke, and for a while the two of them stood head to head. There were beads of sweat on both their faces, and their muscular arms trembled. Then they moved apart again, and a murmur of disappointment went through the crowd. Anyone who had expected a short, bloody battle was going to learn better.

Mathis observed the two knights closely. Now they circled again, like two hungry lions, exchanging blows in turn, each sword stroke from one parried by the other. Since they were fighting without shields, each stroke had to be fended off by the sword-arm alone—a very strenuous and painful procedure that quickly tired the combatants. In addition, the mud made every step twice as laborious to take.

The fight went this way and that, all in silence; only the sound of the two men's swords and their heavy breathing was to be heard. The landsknechts standing around the circle had been betting on the outcome, and they shouted encouragement to whichever of the two they had backed. Only the count still looked bored. Mathis saw that he was sitting on his stool, showing no emotion except for an expression of satisfaction that came into his face when the blows fell faster.

By this time Philipp von Erfenstein had driven Wertingen, step by step, to the outer limit of the circle. The robber knight kept retreating and did not notice that one of the spears driven into the ground was right behind him. Coming up against it, he stumbled, flailed his arms in the air, and finally fell into the mud, cursing. Only at the last minute did he raise his sword to parry his adversary's stroke.

All of a sudden Wertingen threw himself to one side, sweeping his own blade over the ground like a sickle. The crowd cried out when the broadsword struck the castellan's leg with a clang. Philipp von Erfenstein staggered, and then he, too, fell.

Horrified, Mathis held his breath. A knight in full armor who took such a fall was virtually finished. He could seldom get to his feet again unaided because of the sheer weight of his armor, so lay on his back like a turtle, where he could easily be stabbed by his opponent.

Wertingen, with his light breastplate, found it easier to rise. He struggled to his feet, groaning, and immediately struck the knight still lying on the ground with his sword. The blade caught Philipp von Erfenstein on the inside of his elbow. The spectators cheered or cried out in dismay, depending which man they were supporting.

Black Hans took a step back and looked down, with satisfaction, at the castellan writhing at his feet. Blood ran from Erfenstein's arm. Hans von Wertingen smiled, and for a moment he looked up at the heavens as if in prayer. Then he prepared to deal the death blow.

"Give the Devil my regards," hissed the robber knight.

As the blade came down, Philipp von Erfenstein did something strange: without trying to avoid it, he stretched out his hand. He reached for the sharp broadsword with his armored gauntlet, and the blow that had so much strength behind it was abruptly halted. Wertingen uttered a cry of surprise. The castellan of Trifels tugged sharply at the sword blade, so that Wertingen lost his balance and fell directly on top of his adversary. He cried out in pain, and then, groaning, turned on his side.

Erfenstein had rammed his hunting knife into the other man's belly.

A loud cry passed through the crowd, some of the landsknechts applauded, and even the young count had jumped up from his stool.

"Bravo!" he cried, clapping his hands. "What a magnificent spectacle, Erfenstein!"

The two men lay side by side, on their backs. Blood flowed from the wound in Wertingen's stomach, his face was so muddy that it could hardly be recognized, but he was still moving. He ran his sword into the moist ground, from which vapor rose in the morning mist, and tried to stand by leaning on it. But Erfenstein, too, was moving. The old castellan rolled over and seized one of the spears driven into the ground. Bellowing with rage and pain, he hauled himself upright with its aid and stood there, swaying, but on his own two feet. With a single swift movement he pulled the spear out of the ground, and strode over to Wertingen, who was still kneeling in the middle of the arena, breathing heavily and with his head lowered. Both men had exhausted their strength.

Raising the spear, Erfenstein uttered a loud cry and brought it down in Wertingen's shoulder. The blow was so heavy that the weapon broke apart into splinters. Blood shot from the wound in a jet and seeped into the damp earth, while the robber knight, still kneeling, stared incredulously at the shaft of the spear, its point still in him.

Erfenstein looked around for his sword, which was lying on the ground a little way off. Groaning, he picked it up, took the hilt in both hands, and went over to Wertingen.

"Hans von Wertingen," he gasped, "I sentence you to death for all the evil deeds you have done in the forests of the Palatinate. For your robberies and rapes. For the murders of my man-at-arms, Sebastian, and my steward, Martin von Heidelsheim. For all these I—"

Black Hans looked up in surprise. "I have robbed, whored, and killed," he wheezed, "but I don't have your steward on my conscience, Philipp. I swear it by all that's holy to me."

Confused, Philipp von Erfenstein held back, but the count cried harshly, "What are you waiting for, Erfenstein? Get it over and done with, or I'll have the bastard gutted after all."

"By God, I swear . . ." Black Hans repeated.

"I said kill him!" Count Scharfeneck's face was white as marble. "Let's have an end to this farce."

Grimly, Erfenstein nodded. Then his sword came down, severing

Wertingen's head cleanly from his body. The head rolled a few paces and then stopped, mouth open, eyes staring, right in front of the count's stool.

Mathis turned away. He staggered several steps away from the crowd and vomited, groaning, while the men nearby broke into loud rejoicing.

· 12 ·

The village of Ramberg, 5 June, Anno Domini 1524

THEY BURIED THE DEAD DOWN in the village on the morning of the next day.

More than twenty men had lost their lives in the attack on Ramburg Castle, as well as three old women who had worked there as maids and strumpets and had been slaughtered like animals in the murderous frenzy. But those worst affected of all were the Ramberg peasants. Most of their houses had been burned down, and their fields laid waste. When Mathis stood beside the fresh graves that the landsknechts had dug in the valley near the village graveyard, women and children stared at him with tearful, red-rimmed eyes. Many families had lost their fathers and breadwinners, and this year's harvest was destroyed. By next winter at the latest, the weakest villagers would be dead of starvation. A small, grubby baby wrapped in a bundle of rags and tied to its mother's back was howling at the top of its voice, and Mathis felt the sound go to his heart.

"What crime did these people commit for us to punish them so severely?" he asked quietly, more to himself than anyone else. He was standing a little way from the graves, watching the peasants' families saying a last prayer together for their dead.

Beside him, Ulrich Reichhart shrugged indifferently. "They chose the wrong feudal lord."

"But they had no choice in the matter at all." Mathis shook his head without taking his eyes off the ragged figures at the gravesides. Several of them glared angrily back. "They can't leave their own fields, that's the law. Even if they want to marry someone from another village, they need their lord's permission. They're bound to him forever, until they die."

"All the same, they're better off than those fellows," Reichhart said, nodding his head in the direction of the robber knight's burned-out castle. The heads of Wertingen and his robber knights were stuck on the battlements, painted with tar, so that they would stay there as a deterrent until the crows had pecked away the last of the flesh from the skulls.

"That's the way of the world," Reichhart went on. "Peasants work, the clergy see to the salvation of our souls, and knights go to war. And that's how it's always been."

"It doesn't have to stay that way. Peasants can go to war as well."

The old master gunner laughed. "Don't let your father hear you say that. To him, knights are still messengers from heaven. Well, maybe he'll soon be finding out for himself . . ." He stopped short when he saw the stony expression on Mathis's face. "I'm sorry," he said, clearing his throat. "I didn't mean to . . ."

"That's all right. Hey, stop! Not so fast!"

Abruptly, Mathis turned away to help the soldiers now loading up carts and preparing to leave. His bandaged leg still hurt, but he ignored it. Grimly, he pulled one of the ropes now hauling up the wreck of Fat Hedwig. Once melted down, his masterpiece would be worth a good sum of money.

Mathis tried to give the work all his attention. He hadn't thought of his sick father for days. Now he was suddenly overcome by frantic anxiety that the old man might be dead by now, and he, Mathis, had not even said goodbye to him. Would he soon be standing by his grave, like these peasants, stammering words that the dead could no longer hear? The hard work of pushing and shoving the stubborn oxen helped to distract his mind a little.

"Stubborn beast! As pig-headed as my daughter."

That was the angry voice of Philipp von Erfenstein as he grabbed the horns of a nervous ox between the shafts of the cart in front. His sword-arm was bandaged, and he limped a little, but he could not be kept from taking part in the work—in spite of the disapproval of Father Tristan, who had last examined him only a few hours ago. The monk came over to Mathis, shaking his head.

"That wound could get inflamed anytime, and he's lost a lot of blood," said Father Tristan brusquely. "It won't be for want of care on my part if the castellan dies of gangrene."

"If he does, at least he'll be complaining at the top of his voice."

Mathis smiled. In fact it was hard to believe that Philipp von Erfenstein had fought in single combat to the death only yesterday morning. The old knight was in high spirits, and in spite of his injuries the duel seemed to have breathed new life into him. He seemed unmoved by all the dead around them. Mathis suspected that the castellan had seen far more carnage than this in his past battles.

It was another two hours before all the guns and the loot were loaded and tied down with ropes. The soldiers had commandeered two more carts from the village, which were now heavily laden with chests, bales of cloth, sheaves of grain, and pieces of furniture. Finally Mathis got up on the driver's seat of the cart at the back, while the count and Erfenstein led the procession on their horses. An order was called, and then at last the baggage train set off with all the booty and the war materiel.

When the young weaponsmith raised his head, he noticed that a number of the landsknechts and the surviving peasants from Trifels were looking at him with respect. Since Mathis had breached the defensive wall of Ramburg Castle with Fat Hedwig, many of the men now regarded him as a kind of sergeant. They obeyed his orders, and no one laughed at his abilities as a gunner anymore.

When they were over the marshiest places in the valley, and the oxen were drawing the carts along the grass-grown road at a comfortable pace, Mathis wearily mopped the sweat from his brow. It was already getting late in the afternoon when they approached the first hamlets outside Annweiler.

"We worked hard back there," said the man-at-arms Gunther from Trifels, sitting down for a brief rest. "All that shooting, stabbing, and swinging axes. I reckon we've earned a drink or two. You most of all, Mathis." He winked. "Well, how about it? Coming with us?"

Baffled, Mathis looked at him. "Coming where?"

"We're going to Annweiler this evening." Gunther grinned. "The count has given most of his men the night off so that they can squander their loot. Ulrich, Eberhard, and I thought we'd spend a few kreuzers ourselves. The Annweiler innkeepers are donating a big cask of wine in honor of the day, the curfew is lifted, and there's to be whores as well. How about it?"

Mathis smiled, and made an apologetic gesture. "You're forgetting that the mayor of Annweiler is still after me. And what's more, Agnes—"

"Oh yes, Agnes," Gunther replied roughly. "Forget Agnes for once and think of yourself. Look around you." He pointed to the landsknechts and peasants pitching camp beside them and beginning to chant a rough-and-ready war song about Black Hans and his end. The name of Mathis also came into it.

"You're kind of a hero to the men," said Gunther enthusiastically. "Why not celebrate for once? You can go back to your sooty smithy later and welcome, until the guns you make explode around your ears. But the way you always look as grim as the devil, I reckon a bit of fun would do you good."

Mathis laughed. "You may be right. But that doesn't change the fact that the mayor won't want to see me amusing myself in Annweiler."

"Seriously? You think Gessler would dare to arrest the hero of the battle of Ramburg?" Gunther produced a small silver flask, probably looted from the robber knight's castle, and drank deeply from it. "The men here would snatch you from hell and beat up Old Nick himself if need be," he went on. "Anyway, no one will know you in all the turmoil there." He encouragingly held the silver flask under Mathis's nose; a strong smell of spirits rose from it. "So are you coming?"

"Well . . . all right," said Mathis at last, although he still had his doubts. "Yes, I'll join you. But no whores," he added, making a dismissive gesture. "That's my condition."

Gunther grinned and pressed the little flask into Mathis's hand. "No whores, then. Agreed. If you drink this you won't be able to get your prick up anyway. We'll be off in an hour's time."

Mathis drank deeply, and the fiery spirits spread through him. He immediately felt a little better. He was a hero, at least for a couple of days.

And heroes certainly had earned a little fun.

Agnes stood on the battlements of Trifels Castle, watching from a distance as the baggage train approached over the fields below the castle. She had been waiting all day, and now, early in the evening, here they came. Six carts crammed with all they could carry were jolting up the steep path to the castle at snail's pace. Agnes could hear shouted orders and loud laughter from where she stood above the living quarters. She picked up the skirts of her gown and ran down the stairs toward the soldiers. When she finally reached the castle acres below, they were just beginning to unload the loot. From horseback, Count Scharfeneck was directing several peasants taking chests and crates over to his own castle. Frowning, he turned to Agnes, who was sweating and breathless after running so fast.

"I hope your unladylike conduct is solely due to your delight in seeing us back safe and sound," he said, at the same time counting the separate crates again. "As I'm sure you have seen, we were very successful. That cunning dog Wertingen had hoarded all kinds of things in his castle, although I'm afraid the pickings were poor from his peasants' houses." The count sighed as he let another crate pass. "Well, never mind. Even subtracting what I must pay my landsknechts, there's still a good sum of money left for me." He hesitated before going on, with a smile. "And for your father too. But first, of course, he must pay what he owes the duke out of it."

"A profitable business for everyone, then," said Agnes coolly. "Especially you and the duke." She looked around inquiringly and at last saw her father among the men. The old castellan was laboriously dismounting from his horse. Beads of sweat stood out on his pale face, and he was shaking.

"Father! Are you all right?" Agnes ran to give him her hand. "I didn't know that you were wounded . . ." she began, but Erfenstein morosely pushed her aside.

"I'm well enough," he muttered in a slurred voice. "I need no help."

"Your father cut off Hans von Wertingen's head after a single combat worthy of a knight," said the count. "You can be proud of him."

"Proud of him for putting himself in unnecessary danger?" Concerned, Agnes looked at her father, whom Father Tristan was now leading up to the castle. Erfenstein was swaying and seemed to find every step hard to take.

"I thought the battle was long over," Agnes said.

"It was. But yesterday morning your father decided to bring the campaign to a . . . well, a chivalrous conclusion." Scharfeneck sighed, and watched the progress of the last crate as his men took it up to the castle. "I warned him, but he's a stubborn man. Wertingen is dead now, yes, but your father injured one arm and a foot in the fight. He obviously has gangrene."

"Gangrene?" Agnes frowned. "After less than two days? That's hardly possible. How badly is he wounded?"

"You'll have to ask your old monk that question. Maybe the wound became inflamed while he was dressing it."

"Nonsense!" Agnes said indignantly. "Father Tristan would never—"

"Now listen, Lady Agnes," the count interrupted, his voice suddenly unusually mild. "I don't want to quarrel with you. Far from it.

Over the last few days your father and I have had many opportunities for conversation." In spite of his youth, Friedrich von Löwenstein-Scharfeneck looked down at Agnes from his horse with an almost paternal expression. "You are a beautiful child, and I—"

"Forgive me, Excellency, but I'm afraid your compliments will have to wait," Agnes said as she scanned the peasants and landsknechts on the castle acres. "First I'd like to know where Mathis is. I don't see him anywhere."

"Ah, the playmate you miss so much." Friedrich von Löwenstein-Scharfeneck said nothing for a moment, and then he added, with a sour smile, "I must disappoint you, lady, but the young smith would rather drink cheap brandy in the town with fellows like himself than come to see you. When I last saw him, he was on the way to Annweiler with a crowd of my landsknechts. As I heard it, they were looking for willing whores."

For a moment Agnes was incapable of speech. Scharfeneck used the pause to continue.

"You must forgive him," he said indulgently. "He's a young man from a simple family. The kind of man whose idea of amusement is wine, women, and song. The whores will take off his bandages and . . . treat his injuries in their own way."

Almost fainting with fury, Agnes turned and marched up to the castle. As if through a wall, she heard the count's angry voice behind her.

"Devil take it, didn't your father teach you any manners?" he shouted. "How dare you simply walk away? You won't go until I, Count Friedrich von Löwenstein-Scharfeneck, tell you to go, understand? Well, we'll soon see an end to this kind of thing, I promise you. I'm tired of your whims and fancies, castellan's daughter."

The count's voice faded as Agnes climbed the flight of steps to the castle. Her own rage made her blind and deaf. She had been so worried about Mathis, indeed terrified when she heard of his wounds. When she had given him the carved wooden amulet before he left, she had been convinced that he did feel something for her in return.

And now he had nothing better to do than make merry with whores and drunks in Annweiler. Men were all the same. It was best not to get involved with any of them.

In her fury, she made her way up the steep path to the Dancing Floor Rock, the southernmost point of the Trifels. She was so lost in thought that she didn't even notice someone coming quietly up behind her. Only when a wrinkled hand was laid on her shoulder did she start, uttering a slight cry. It was Father Tristan, his face gray with sorrow.

"I've been looking for you everywhere, Agnes," he said, and she could feel his hand shaking slightly. "It's your father."

Agnes put her hand to her brow. Even infuriated as she was by Mathis, how could she have forgotten her father? She turned anxiously to Father Tristan.

"His injuries?" she asked quietly. "Are they serious?"

Father Tristan sighed. "I must admit that I hardly know what to say. I cleaned and bound up his wounds only this morning. They are not particularly deep, and I thought they were going to heal well. But now . . ."

"Then Count Scharfeneck was right, and gangrene has set in?" Agnes asked. But the monk shook his head.

"I've just removed the bandages and looked at the wounds. They are clean. But I will readily say that your father gives the *impression* of suffering from gangrene."

"Impression?" Agnes frowned. "What do you expect me to make of that?"

Father Tristan looked cautiously around them, and then lowered his voice. "What I say now must remain between us," he whispered. "Do you understand? If not, it could cost me my life."

When Agnes nodded, he went on, quietly, "Your father is feverish and has shivering fits. His heart is racing, there seems to be some paralysis on his right side. And he speaks of tingling sensations on his lips and tongue. All those are symptoms for which, to be honest, I know of only one cause."

"And that is . . . ?" Agnes asked hesitantly.

"Monkshood."

"*Monkshood?*" Agnes clapped her hand to her mouth so as not to shriek out loud. The blue flowers of monkshood were the strongest poison known to Christendom. As few as five petals, or an extract made from them, could lead to death. And the plant grew in this part of the countryside. Father Tristan had warned Agnes against it when she was little.

"You think that my father has been poisoned? But why? And by whom?"

Father Tristan leaned very close to her. The rocky abyss yawned below them. "When we left today, he was still doing well," he whispered. "But we stopped to rest just before the baggage train reached Annweiler. I saw your father drinking wine with Count Scharfeneck. They seemed to be celebrating something with a toast." There was a wealth of meaning in the pause that followed.

"You think that Count Scharfeneck poisoned my father?" Agnes stared at the chaplain in horror. "Oh God! But . . . but why?"

Father Tristan shrugged his shoulders. "I can't tell you why. All I know is that this strange fever set in only after we had rested on the way, and since then it has been worse with every passing hour."

The news was so terrible that Agnes could not even shed tears. She just stared into the void. If her father was really suffering from monkshood poisoning, there was no hope. The poison would gradually paralyze him, until at last he stopped breathing. She held Father Tristan's cold hands tightly. Her face was white as a sheet.

"Please, Father," she sobbed at last. "This can't be God's will. Why would he allow such a thing?"

"God allows many terrible things to happen, and we can never understand him. But maybe I am wrong, and your father is feverish only because his wounds are inflamed."

Agnes looked at him hopefully, but when she saw his expressionless eyes she knew that Father Tristan was trying to comfort her, nothing more.

He gently stroked the unruly hair back from her face. "He has been asking for you," he said gently. "You ought to go to him now."

Narrowing her lips, Agnes nodded. Then she straightened her back and, holding her head high, walked to the living quarters of the castle and her sick father's room.

While the returning fighters loudly celebrated throughout Annweiler, Mayor Bernwart Gessler sat in his study in the town hall, trying to concentrate on his calculations in spite of the noise.

He rubbed his temples as music and laughter came to his sorely tried ears through the closed window shutters. The municipal balance sheet was as full of holes as a threadbare rug, and some of the citizens seemed to believe that the new, higher rate of taxation did not apply to them. The duke's courier would be here next week, and he must have all the accounts drawn up and proof against any queries by then. And those stupid fools out there could think of nothing better to do than drink and make merry.

However, it was not just the noise that prevented Gessler from going through the accounts once more. It was also the memory of the stranger who had been there again, only yesterday, asking for more information. A letter that he brought had vouched for him as the representative of a ruling house that must be unconditionally obeyed. The man had been there three times in all, like the black-skinned devil who called himself Caspar. Gessler had been able to put them both off on every occasion, and so far neither knew about the other. But the mayor guessed that a time would come when he took the game too far. It seemed that the patience of that man Caspar, in particular, was running out. The mayor smiled to himself as he thought of what, last week, he had finally dug out of the depths of the Annweiler archives. He loved to gamble; the higher the stakes, the higher the ultimate profit.

But then again, the higher was his own risk.

Gessler shivered as he thought of the curious little handgun that the man Caspar had shown him last time he was there. What was it the black man had said to him then?

I myself have seen the head of a traitor disintegrate into blood, splintered bone, and white brains . . .

Well, Gessler was going to make one more move on the chessboard before bringing the game to an end. For there was a third party who might be interested in his find. Tomorrow he would seek that man out, and then he would see which of the three was ready to pay the most.

Sighing, the mayor of Annweiler pushed his balance sheets and calculations aside and went over to the wall of pine veneer paneling that had a secret niche behind it. When he pressed part of a carved vine, a flap swung open, and the mayor felt around inside the little compartment until he finally had the well-worn document in his hands. Gessler felt a slight tingling as his eyes rested for about the twelfth time on the scrawled lines of writing. The document was dated 28 June in the year of Our Lord 1513, and it described an event in the countryside near Annweiler. Gessler's predecessor, old Helmbrecht von Mühlheim, had included it in a list of unsolved robberies. One of many cases—the forests of the Wasgau were dangerous, and it wasn't the first time that a young family had fallen victim to marauders and highwaymen. The incident many years ago was not really very remarkable—or not until two men, obviously sent here by powerful ruling houses, took an interest in it at the same time. Along with the second find, he thought, the information was worth a lot of money.

Bernwart Gessler smiled and put the piece of paper carefully back in the niche. As he had told his two strange visitors of these last few weeks, playing for time, he had gone in search of it himself. He had asked in the right quarters and leafed through the right books. Both of those strangers were fools if they thought he was going to act as their henchman. By now Gessler was more or less sure who they were after, even if he didn't know why.

He closed the secret door with a click. The mayor of Annweiler went back to his desk and resumed his work, humming quietly. Arithmetic was easy now that he knew he would soon have enough money to turn his back on this filthy dump forever.

After a while he heard a knock on the door. Looking up in annoyance, he put his quill pen down.

"Yes?"

The door opened, and the apothecary Konrad Sperlin came in. He had been Gessler's secret informer for years. Only a few months ago, he had told the mayor about the meeting with Shepherd Jockel at the Green Tree Inn.

The little man nervously twisted his shabby cap in his hands and bowed low. "Your Grace," he hesitantly began, "you were right. That boy Mathis has indeed come back to Annweiler. He's in the Green Tree at this very moment."

"Aha, in the Green Tree." Gessler smiled. He blew sand over the parchments to blot his writing, and watched the little crystalline grains trickle to the floor. "He does seem to like that tavern. Thank you, Sperlin, that's all."

Bernwart Gessler tossed his messenger a coin, which, for all his apparent clumsiness, Sperlin caught skillfully. With another bow, the apothecary went away before anyone in the town hall could see him.

Quickly stowing away his papers, Gessler put on his coat and his velvet cap and climbed down the broad staircase of the town hall building with a smile. When he gave orders for the gates to be opened for the landsknechts, he had hoped the impudent young smith from Trifels Castle would be one of those coming to celebrate here. And obviously he had been fool enough to do so. The lad must think himself safe, but Gessler would show him who was really master of Annweiler.

On the first floor of the town hall, the mayor turned to the guardroom on his left, where three men were on duty day in, day out.

"Follow me. We're going to—"

Gessler stopped short, and the smile vanished from his face. The guards had gone, the room was empty, except for a few dice and two empty tankards standing on the table.

Cursing, the mayor kicked the table leg with the toe of his boot, and the dice clattered to the floor. Those layabouts had actually ventured to leave their posts and go to join the celebrations. Well, he would set them straight and no mistake. Presumably they were down in the guardhouse by the lower gate, drinking with their comrades. Gessler decided to look in there, and then go on to the Green Tree with a couple of chastened guards in order to take that young rabble-rouser into custody at last. If the count's landsknechts got in his way, a sharp command would bring them to see reason. After all, the duke himself had appointed him mayor of this town, thus giving him authority over His Excellency the count as well.

Leaving the town hall behind, Bernwart Gessler hurried over the empty square, past the pillory, which was daubed with excrement, and on in the direction of Mühlbach, where the noise was coming from. The guardhouse lay at the end of Market Alley, not far from one of the town gates. Gessler swiftly approached the channel in which the squealing millwheels turned. Several leather skins, covered with greenish mold, were fastened to poles in the water to the right and left of a little bridge, left to soak there overnight. Even at this hour there was a smell of decay in the tanners' quarter. Nauseated, the mayor spat into the murky water. How he loathed this town. High time to shake the dust of it off his feet.

The door of one of the sheds on his left was wide open, and Gessler could see the pits inside, filled with tanbark fluid, or lye. The skins lay for up to three years in these stone basins, soaking in the acrid brown liquid until they were soft and supple at last. The stink of the liquid and the decomposing skins was so penetrating that the mayor had to hold his hand in front of his face.

Gessler was going to hurry on when, near the bridge, he noticed a row of wooden posts with skins hanging from them to dry. From a distance, these frames looked like mangy scarecrows who seemed to be waving their arms. Fat bluebottles flew around them, buzzing, and the leather flapped in the wind. Surprised, the mayor stopped short.

What wind?

All of a sudden, one of the skins seemed to ruffle up, the leather was moved aside like a curtain, and a black figure emerged from behind it.

"Forgive me for troubling you so late, Master Gessler," said Caspar, "but I can reassure you, this is the last visit I will be paying you."

In his right hand, the black-skinned man was holding the remarkable little gun he had shown the mayor before. The muzzle pointed directly at Gessler.

"I am afraid I am losing patience with you, Master Mayor," Caspar went on. "The fact is, I cannot stand being taken for a fool. And my hearing is acute, very acute. Did I not tell you not to talk about my business to anyone else?"

"I . . . I really don't know what you mean," Gessler stammered. At the same moment he felt angry with himself for sounding so anxious and uncertain. Fear was the death of any negotiation.

"You cut a pitiful figure, Mayor. Annweiler really deserves a better man in charge of it."

For the first time in his life, Bernwart Gessler felt that he had taken a game too far. He looked around in panic, but there was no one in sight who might help him. He heard the sound of music and laughter in the distance.

"I . . . I have good news for you," he croaked, slowly taking several steps backward. "I have found something in the archives."

"And how much did the other side pay you for that information?" asked Caspar, as he took out a little key and used it to slowly wind the weapon's clockwork.

Gessler flinched. "I swear by all the saints I haven't told a soul about it," he protested. "You're the first, believe me. I . . . I have found the person you are looking for. Truly!" He retreated a little farther, until he suddenly felt resistance behind him. He had come up against more posts with leather skins hanging from them. The leather was smeared and slimy, and it clung to his expensive coat.

Caspar put the key away again and pushed the trigger over the flash pan. The weapon was now loaded.

"I tracked down Elsbeth Rechsteiner, the woman whom you mentioned to me," he said in a dangerous voice. "Your advice was very sensible: as a midwife, she could indeed have known the name. But for some reason the good old soul jumped into the Rhine rather than have a harmless conversation with me." He looked sharply at the mayor. "Tell me, why did she do that? What in the name of three devils did she know to make her prefer death to answering my questions?" Caspar took another step toward Gessler. "What is going on in this filthy little place of yours, Master Mayor?"

"I swear I don't know! But that's not important now." Gessler tried to smile. The stranger's hesitation told him that he was back in the game again. "What matters is that I have the very information you asked me to find. So put that devilish device of yours down, give me my money, and I'll tell you what I know."

Grimly, Caspar shook his head. "I'm afraid the nature of your reward has just changed. Spit out the name, and I'll let you have your life." He paused. "Maybe."

Gessler bit his lip. It really did look like he must divulge his valuable knowledge for nothing. Well, there was still the other man, and that knowledge was worth gold to him. Now, however, the first thing was to save his own life.

"Very well," he hesitantly began. "The person you are looking for is . . ."

At that moment, singing and laughter arose from the other side of the bridge. A group of drunken landsknechts approached from the guardhouse. A spark of hope came into Gessler's eyes. Maybe he might yet win the game. He turned, supple as a cat, and slipped through the leather skins toward the safety of the bridge. Moldering leather touched his face like the fingers of a corpse, but he hardly noticed.

"Help!" he called. "An attack! I'm—"

The sound of the shot drowned out his screams. The leaden bullet penetrated the skins and smashed the back of Gessler's head like a mealy apple. Blood and brain matter spurted out on the tanned leather, and the mayor fell forward, bringing one of the frames down with him. He ended up buried under a mountain of calfskins streaked with green mold.

A last twitch ran through his body, and then Bernwart Gessler really had made his last move.

· 13 ·

Trifels Castle, 5 June, Anno Domini 1524, at night

AGNES HOVERED OUTSIDE HER WOUNDED father's room, not daring to go in. She trembled slightly when she thought of what Father Tristan had told her about Erfenstein's sickness.

Could Count Scharfeneck really have poisoned her father? But why?

She had already been in the castellan's room twice since early evening. But he had been fast asleep, his face waxen and wet with sweat, his breathing hoarse and irregular. It was late at night now.

Feeling a terrible presentiment, Agnes listened at the heavy oak door and was relieved to hear a stertorous, gasping sound; it meant that her father was still alive. She knocked, and without waiting for an answer, she entered the room.

The once proud castellan, Philipp von Erfenstein, lay shivering under a heap of blankets and bearskins that almost concealed his massive body. Only his bearded face was showing, and it looked positively tiny. His hair stuck to his forehead, his eyes wandered like those of a cornered animal. Only when he saw Agnes did Erfenstein become a little calmer.

"Ah, daughter," he said in a failing voice, turning his head to her with a groan. He obviously found talking difficult; he kept having to swallow, as if something were stuck in his throat. "I . . . I've been waiting for you. Come . . . closer, before it is too late."

"Father, what are you talking about?" Agnes began, going over to him with a wan smile. Out of the corner of her eye she saw, on a table beside him, a bowl of water and an untouched pitcher of spiced wine mixed with St. John's wort and extract of willow bark, prepared for him by Father Tristan only a few hours ago. "You must rest for a while now."

Philipp von Erfenstein seized her hand and drew her so close to him that Agnes could smell his sick breath. Her father gave off a musty, bitter odor of old sweat, pus, and dried blood.

The breath of death, thought Agnes.

"I didn't ask to see you to hear sweet nothings, child," he growled. For a moment he had his old voice back. "I know the state I'm in. This gangrene is consuming me from the inside. I wouldn't have thought it would be so quick."

In silence, Agnes nodded, as tears rolled down her cheeks and fell on her father's pale face. Obviously Father Tristan had not told the castellan of Trifels what he suspected. No doubt he did not want to distress Erfenstein farther, and in any case it would have made no difference to his condition.

The old knight closed his eyes, summoning up new strength. Only then did he go on, wearily. "Damn Wertingen! Not such a poor fighter as I thought. Well, I have lived like a warrior, and now I will die like a warrior. That's no cause for grief."

"Father, you're not going to—"

"Be quiet and listen to me, you impertinent girl," he interrupted her harshly. "There's something I have to discuss with you. I really wanted to tell you the news down in the Knights' House, over a goblet of good wine, with music and candlelight, but now it must be like this." He paused for a moment. "The . . . the count and you are going to be married."

For a moment Agnes thought she must have misheard. Or maybe her father was raving in delirium? She let go of his shaking hand and stared at him.

"What did you just say?"

"The two of you are going to marry. Is that so hard to understand?" Erfenstein stretched, forcing his heavy body up among the blankets and furs, and looked straight at her for the first time. "I've been looking for a suitable husband for you for a long time. It's God's providence that the count has asked for your hand. The Löwenstein-Scharfeneck family is one of the most powerful in the Palatinate, related to the elector himself. The house of Erfenstein will not die out, it will merge with a flourishing dynasty, it will—"

"Father, I *can't* marry the count!" cried Agnes. "The count has . . . has . . ."

"You'll do as I say," Erfenstein snorted, his face now dark red. "Are you going to deny your father his last wish? Is that what you want? Believe me, you'll understand my decision later. A castellan's daughter rising to become a countess. You'll dress in silk and velvet, all those accursed stewards, mayors, and clerks will have to bow to you. Our family will finally take the place that it deserves in the history books."

Agnes decided not to further agitate her father. His arms were already cold as ice. For a while she said nothing, and the only sound in the room was Erfenstein's hoarse breathing. The world seemed to stand still.

"Why would Friedrich von Löwenstein-Scharfeneck want to marry me?" she asked at last, breaking the silence. "He is vain, ambitious, and he doesn't love me. None of this makes any sense."

Her father had calmed down a bit. A thin-lipped smile spread over his face. "Do you think that didn't occur to me? I know he's a vain popinjay. It's not you that the count wants, it's Trifels. He's besotted with this castle. I think that is why he moved into Scharfenberg. He wants to find out all about the secrets of this part of the country, and if he marries you, then all doors here will be open to him."

"What secrets?" asked Agnes, surprised. She felt a slight shudder run down her spine. Suddenly she thought of her last conversation with Melchior von Tanningen. He, too, had said that the count was crazy about Trifels Castle. Trifels Castle and, above all, its past.

"As you know, the Emperor Maximilian gave me Trifels as my fief, for my services to him in war," Erfenstein began, hesitantly this time. "A good piece of land. But your mother and I were never much interested in the old stories that haunt this castle like ghosts. In contrast to you." He laughed a little. "You . . . you were always different from us. All that reading, your thirst for the stories and legends of the old days . . . I'm sure you yourself know what secrets the castle holds by now. Secrets with their origins back in the distant past."

Agnes felt her heart beat faster. Did her father know more about the subject of her strange dreams? Did he know about Johann of Brunswick's alleged conspiracy, and his flight from Trifels?

"Do these secrets by any chance have something to do with a certain Guelph called Johann and a woman?" she asked in a faltering voice.

The old castellan looked at her in surprise. "Guelph? A woman?" He shook his head, exhausted. "I know nothing about that. You disappoint me, Agnes. I thought all that reading would at least mean you could help the count in his search. No, as always it's about gold. A great deal of gold."

"*Gold?* Here? But . . ."

Agnes stopped short in surprise, and then, suddenly, a vague idea came to her. She thought of the men in the forest when she had found the ring, the lights at night, the legend of Emperor Barbarossa sleeping somewhere in Trifels Castle. She remembered all the old tales that Father Tristan had told her in the past.

"It's about gold and the power that it gives," Erfenstein went on, gasping for breath. "Young Scharfeneck has only dropped hints so far, but I'm no fool. I know what the count has in mind. It's a case of . . ." Suddenly he reared up, his whole body shaking, before collapsing like an empty sack. For a moment Agnes thought that her father had died before her eyes, but then she realized that he was still breathing faintly.

"You needn't say any more," she whispered quietly and pressed his hand. "I think that now I, too, know what the count has in mind."

And why he wants you out of the way, she thought, as an invisible hand seemed to close around her heart.

She stayed at her father's bedside for what seemed an eternity. He breathed more weakly every second. Thoughts raced through her head.

I can't marry him. He murdered my father!

But could she really be sure it was the count who had poisoned him? Couldn't she comply with her father's last wish? And what would happen if she refused? Agnes had never really considered the situation if her father died and left her behind in the castle, a woman still unmarried. Trifels would pass into the hands of another family, one entirely loyal to the duke. And she herself? She had no family, not a single relation to whom she could go. Her mother had died long ago, her father had never mentioned any other members of his family. Would she be turned out of the castle like a mangy dog, the fate that her maid Margarethe had always feared for herself?

Suddenly Agnes felt that she could never give up this castle. An unexpected sense of strength rose in her. Trifels was her family, her all, the center of her world. She was, and would remain, mistress of Trifels.

Mistress of Trifels . . .

She had called herself that once already, when the steward Martin von Heidelsheim was about to molest her in the stables. That was only a few months ago, but to Agnes it felt like years. She had grown older now, older and more mature—and she would not let herself be driven away from this castle.

My castle.

Distractedly, she dipped a strip of fabric into the bowl of water beside the bed and wiped the sweat from her father's pale brow. Philipp von Erfenstein shuddered all over, and his heart raced. His mind seemed to be caught up in confused dreams now.

"Guinegate," he whispered again and again. "Guinegate . . ."

Suddenly the castellan sat up again. His numb lips tried to form words. "Agnes . . ." he managed to say, gasping. "Something else you ought to know. I . . . I've always loved you, even . . ." He fell back, and his words turned into a gurgling sound that soon ebbed away to silence.

Sadly, but with her head held high, Agnes sat at her dying father's bedside, singing him an old Occitanian lullaby as his body slowly stiffened.

The first thing Mathis felt the next morning was a stabbing pain that filled his whole head. He briefly opened his eyes, and bright rays of light dug holes in his brain. Next time he blinked more carefully, and the pain was not quite as bad. He also heard voices. Peering through the eyes he had opened just a slit, he saw branches covered with green leaves above him. It took him a moment to realize that he was looking at the old linden tree around which people danced outside the Green Tree Inn. Curious faces appeared in his field of vision, forming a circle around him. Someone nudged him with a foot.

"I think he's coming back to his senses," said a deep voice.

"Go carefully, for heaven's sake. Who knows what he may be capable of yet." replied a second voice, obviously that of an anxious woman.

Mathis groaned, and then gradually worked himself up against the trunk of the tree until he was sitting upright. He felt queasy, like he might vomit. With one hand he shielded his face from the bright sunlight, and then, frowning, he looked around. He was surrounded by about two dozen of the citizens of Annweiler, most of them gawping at him with a mixture of curiosity, fear, and revulsion. Mathis also saw several of the town guards. It seemed to be early morning.

What in God's name happened? he wondered. His head was still ringing like the bell in a church tower.

Then he remembered the spirits he had drunk yesterday evening, the wine, the beer . . . he had danced with a great many girls, particularly that redhead who had kept reaching between his legs. He remembered standing on the table and singing at the top of his voice, while people slapped him on the back and drank to him. At some point he felt unwell, and he couldn't remember what happened next.

"Hey!" One of the town guards was shaking him violently, and Mathis felt queasy again. "Wake up, young fellow. We want a word with you."

He swallowed down his urge to retch, and wiped his mouth. "What about?" he asked faintly.

The guard laughed unpleasantly. "What about? Well, about what you did to the mayor, you cowardly murderer."

"*Murderer . . . ?*"

At once Mathis was wide awake. He pulled himself together and, still leaning against the linden tree, stared at the crowd standing around and gawping at him. Now he recognized some of the Annweiler town councilors. The woolens weaver Peter Markschild was among them, the ropemaker Martin Lebrecht, and also the apothecary Konrad Sperlin, who seemed to be bending a particularly hostile gaze on him. Finally, the parish priest of Annweiler, Father Johannes, stepped forward and spoke to him.

"Mathis Wielenbach," he said firmly while his small, fat fingers fidgeted with a wooden crucifix, "you are accused of the cowardly murder last night of the town mayor, Bernwart Gessler, by means of your ungodly firearms. Do you confess your guilt?"

"But . . . but that's nonsense," Mathis replied, wiping the cold sweat from his brow. "Why on earth would I have done a thing like that?" In spite of his splitting headache, he tried to think as clearly as possible.

"Why?" Sperlin snapped. "You know why only too well. Because

Gessler wanted to see you in prison for insurgency." He looked around a little uncertainly before going on. "I . . . er, I myself saw the mayor yesterday evening setting off for the Green Tree to call you to account. And this morning we find his body bestially disfigured. The connection is obvious."

"Bestially disfigured?" Mathis looked around, at a loss.

"We'd better take him to where we found the mayor," suggested Markschild the weaver, looking at the other members of the town council. "Maybe the terrible sight will bring him to confess his crime."

Father Johannes nodded, and two of the guards immediately took Mathis by the shoulders and pushed him ahead of them along the narrow alleys. The crowd followed like a large, hissing animal, with shouting children and yapping dogs running on ahead. Mathis desperately looked for his friends, but he could see them nowhere amidst the turmoil.

At last they reached the bridge near the town mill, where two more guards stood grimly outside a closed shed. Father Johannes gave them a sign, whereupon the guards pushed open the wide door of the shed and stepped aside. At once the caustic smell of the corrosive tanning fluid met Mathis's nostrils, although another strong smell almost overwhelmed it.

It was the smell of blood, a great deal of blood. The shed stank like a slaughterhouse.

On the ground near the entrance lay the corpse of the mayor—or rather, what was left of it. Bernwart Gessler could be recognized only by his clothing, for half his face and the back of his head had been ripped away, as if by a demon's claw. His costly woolen coat, his doublet, and also his bare arms, throat, and legs were dyed dark brown like a gnarled root. Cracks and fissures reminiscent of the weathered bark of a tree showed on his hands. Mathis had to swallow to keep himself from vomiting.

Bernwart Gessler, mayor of Annweiler, had been tanned overnight in corrosive lye, like a piece of leather.

Nepomuk Kistler stepped out of the crowd. His face was ashen, and the old tanner could barely keep his voice steady.

"When I came home yesterday from a journey of some length to see my sick sister, I checked the shed, and then I must have left the door open," he said quietly. "I went back this morning to close it, and I saw the mayor in one of the tanning pits, with his head down and only his feet sticking out." He suddenly looked sharply at Mathis. "Tell me, young man, was it you? Are you capable of such a deed?"

Mathis, horrified, said nothing. He gaped at the tanned body of Gessler, with corrosive acid dripping from his garments. White brain matter shone through the splintered bone of his skull.

"When we took him out and saw his wounds, we thought of a wild beast at first," the parish priest said. "But then our apothecary here found certain proof that our mayor was killed by one of those new-fangled firearms."

Sperlin nodded eagerly and brought out a leaden bullet. "Here's the *corpus delicti*," he said triumphantly. "The diabolical thing was still in his head. Well, Mathis, does this ball look familiar to you?"

"It . . . it's a bullet for an arquebus, but a very small one," replied Mathis hesitantly. "However, that doesn't mean I fired it. Any of the other landsknechts—"

"The landsknechts left the town two hours ago. None of them had arquebuses with them inside the town walls," Father Johannes put in. "All weapons were locked in the guardhouse yesterday. Swords, spears, those new firearms, and, above all, gunpowder. It was strictly forbidden to bring that devilish stuff into the town." With relish, the priest crossed his arms over his greasy cassock and looked challengingly at Mathis. "I searched your pack while you were sleeping off your hangover just now. And what do you think I found?" Reaching under the cassock, he brought out a little bag, presenting it with a smile. He cautiously sprinkled some of its contents on the palm of his hand, and wrinkled his nose with distaste.

"This is gunpowder, am I right? You're the only one here who knows how to handle it. The only one who could have committed such a murder last night. And you have a strong motive. So go on, confess!"

Mathis groaned quietly. He had completely forgotten the little bag.

"Aha, he feels guilty!" cried Sperlin the apothecary. "See, he's giving way. His crime has caught up with him."

Desperately, Mathis shook his head. He felt the noose tightening around his neck. "I may have been in possession of this powder, but I had no gun." he protested. "And where would I have gotten one? What's more, my companions can bear witness that—"

"Your companions were so dead drunk that they couldn't even have said whether there were stars in the sky last night," the woolens weaver Peter Markschild interrupted. "We've locked them in the guardhouse for safekeeping. One of them, that man Reichhart, hit out wildly when he was arrested, and we had to make him see reason. Who knows, maybe he's hand in glove with you. Isn't he a master gunner himself?" Thrusting out his chest, the weaver turned to the gawpers and council members standing around. "As head of the town council, I am taking over authority in this town until the duke sends us a new mayor. If this young man won't talk, then the executioner in Queichhambach and his red-hot pincers will teach him how. Do you all agree?"

The men nodded, all but white-haired Nepomuk Kistler, who looked skeptical. "I still can't believe that the boy really did such a thing," he said. "From all we hear of him, he's a right-minded young man. On the other hand . . ." He hesitated, and his lined face went a little paler. "If he didn't do it, who did?"

"The fellow will have an opportunity to prove himself innocent," Markschild said in a placatory tone. "But first we must keep him in custody. Take him away."

"But none of this is true!" Mathis cried as two of the guards seized him and dragged him out into the alley. He looked around for help. One of those now standing beside the millstream was Diethelm

Seebach, landlord of the Green Tree, looking at him with a shame-faced expression.

"Diethelm!" cried Mathis. "You know me. I would never . . ."

But Seebach turned away. His face disappeared in the noisy crowd, which now began throwing dirt, stones, and rotten vegetables at Mathis.

"You brute," Konrad Sperlin snapped at him. "You've killed like an animal, you will die like an animal." He threw a handful of sheep dung, and Mathis only just avoided it. The next missile hit him in the middle of his face. Mathis thought about how he had been celebrating with many of these people only last night; a few months ago he had even been sitting with some of them while they all cursed the mayor to the devil. And now they were pelting Mathis with stones and spitting at him.

As the guards dragged him on, Mathis glanced around once more, looking into all the angry faces of the shouting inhabitants of Annweiler. They belonged to tanners, joiners, shopkeepers, linen weavers, maidservants, grooms, and peasants—all of them simple folk for whose rights Mathis had always wished to fight. And now they wanted to see him dead.

Then a stone hit his forehead, and he staggered on with blood running down his face.

Agnes had spent all night sitting beside her father's deathbed, holding his hand as his breath grew weaker and weaker. Father Tristan had joined them a couple of times, but when the monk saw that there was nothing more he could do, he had given the castellan of Trifels the rite of extreme unction and then left father and daughter together. By the end, Erfenstein's body was as hard as a rock. He reminded Agnes of the stone knights on tombs, watching over the dead until the day of judgment.

When the first rays of the sun came through the window and the birds began to sing, the castellan finally drew his last breath. Near the end only his eyes still moved in his rigid body, looking almost pleadingly at Agnes to the last. By then his voice had long since fallen silent. Just before the end, Philipp von Erfenstein had obviously wanted to say something else to her, but only stertorous, incomprehensible sounds had come out of his mouth.

After the longest night of her life, Agnes closed her father's eyelids and wept without a sound. Philipp von Erfenstein had been rough in his ways, but he had loved Agnes in his own fashion, even when he had probably wished for a different kind of daughter. A more feminine, charming young lady who did embroidery, sang, and chattered to other girls, instead of one who hunted crows with her falcon. Now her father had left her, and she was alone. The only friends she still had were Father Tristan and Mathis—though he apparently preferred to amuse himself with whores down in Annweiler.

Minutes dragged on and felt like hours. At last Agnes pressed a final kiss on her dead father's brow and decided to go in search of the monk. She had a great deal to discuss, and she had never needed his advice so much. She thought she now knew why her father had been doomed to die, but she had no idea what use that knowledge was to her. So she was far from being able to call the murderer to account. Furthermore, her knowledge was presumably more of a threat to her than a blessing.

Agnes quietly closed the door and went over to the chapel in the old tower of the castle. Failing to find Father Tristan, however, she climbed the steep stairs to the library. Maybe he was there, going through the lists of the castellan's few personal possessions, which would now belong to Agnes.

She was relieved to hear the rustle of pages on the other side of the library door. Agnes turned the handle, but flinched back when she saw who was sitting in the chair behind the broad desk.

It was Count Scharfeneck, reading several old parchment scrolls and books. He looked up with interest. Agnes immediately felt her heart turn to stone, and an invisible hand seemed to clutch her throat.

Murderer . . .

"Ah, how delightful to see your face," said the count, smiling and pointing to the documents in front of him. He did not seem to feel at all like he had been caught doing something wrong. "I've been told that you like to read. You have a really interesting collection of old books."

"What are you doing here?" Agnes asked, her breath coming short.

Friedrich von Löwenstein-Scharfeneck raised his hands in an apologetic gesture. "Forgive me for not saying so before, but while we were still in Ramberg, your father gave me permission to explore his library, and I thought it better not to disturb him." He played with the golden chain that hung around his neck. "However, we can ask him now. How is he feeling?"

"He's dead," Agnes said tonelessly. Her lips were narrowed, and she had to be careful not to let her voice break. "Philipp von Erfenstein, castellan of Trifels, died within this very hour. Was that what you wanted?"

The count leaned back in silence, drumming his fingers on the desk. For a while neither of them said anything.

"I am sorry your father is dead," he said at last. "But forgive me if I do not burst into tears. He did not have to challenge Wertingen to single combat."

"It wasn't the fight that killed him."

Scharfeneck's head darted forward like the head of a snake. There was a menacing spark in his eyes. "Oh, so what did kill him, then?"

"It was poison. Presumably monkshood. And you gave it to him. *You!*" Agnes had not intended to say those last few words, but when she saw the count sitting there looking so pleased with himself, they had suddenly burst out of her.

Friedrich von Löwenstein-Scharfeneck looked at her for a long time. There was no sound but the crackling of the logs burning in the hearth. Finally he laughed quietly, with a sound like the sweet ringing of a bell. "I suppose that old monk told you so, did he? And you believe him."

"I know quite enough about herbs myself to be sure of it," replied

Agnes coolly. She remembered that Father Tristan had told her to keep quiet. And in no circumstances must suspicion fall on him. If it did, the count would surely find a way to get rid of her tutor.

"Shivering, a racing heart, hesitant breathing, and progressive stiffening of the body," she said, enumerating the symptoms. "That was not gangrene, it was cold-blooded murder."

With a violent movement, Friedrich von Löwenstein-Scharfeneck swept the books and scrolls of parchment off the desk, and rose from his chair, a threatening figure. In his close-fitting Spanish doublet with its high collar, with his thinning hair and pale face, he resembled an evil angel. It was as though an icy wind were suddenly blowing through the library.

"I don't mind what nonsense you talk within these four walls," he hissed, "but if you were to tell the outside world that I had your father on my conscience, then I swear by God and all the saints—my family has a long arm, Lady Agnes, and you would wish you had never been born."

Agnes flinched back in shock. It was a fact that she had no concrete evidence against the count, and even if she had, to what court could she go with it? For some years now there had been the imperial supreme court in Nuremberg, set up by Emperor Maximilian for just such cases, but the trials there often went on for many years. And you needed money, a great deal of money, something that Agnes did not have.

Neither evidence nor money, she thought. *And he knows it.*

"Where is Father Tristan?" she asked suddenly, to change the subject.

"That old fool?" Friedrich von Löwenstein-Scharfeneck sat down again, with a smile. All at once the cutting edge had left his voice. "I told him to go and tend some of my wounded landsknechts. A far-sighted decision, I now see. As a doddering old man, but with some knowledge of medicine, he's more use to the living than the dead."

And you can snoop around here to your heart's content, thought Agnes. *As soon as the stag is dead, ravens come down on the carcass, croaking.*

"Before he died, my father told me about the . . . agreement between the two of you," she said quietly.

"Did he? Oh, I'm glad." The count clapped his hands. "I would have liked to tell you myself, but I fear that recently you have been a little gruff with me." Reaching inside his velvet doublet, he brought out a sealed paper. "To be on the safe side, your father confirmed it in writing just before his fight. What a fortunate circumstance, now that he is dead and, unfortunately, can say no more about our happiness, don't you agree?"

The count waved the paper in the air, eyes twinkling, and gave Agnes a smile that almost provoked her into striking him in the face. She took a deep breath to help herself calm down. Then she took a stool from beside the fire and sat down directly opposite her future bridegroom. She stared at him with hostility as, unmoved, he put the document back inside his doublet.

"Why this marriage?" she asked at last. "My father is dead. You could simply turn me out of the castle and ask the duke to let you have Trifels. You have enough influence."

Friedrich von Löwenstein-Scharfeneck shrugged. "The duke is a fickle man. No one knows how he would make up his mind, and there are other powerful families for him to cultivate. So I asked his permission to request your hand in marriage. It was safer. In addition . . ." He leaned forward and, in a playful gesture, placed the fingertips of his hands together. "You may not believe me, Lady Agnes, but I am genuinely disposed to like you. I even think that we share more than you know. A passion for old stories, for dreaming, our love of these ancient walls . . ." He heaved a theatrical sigh. "In addition, I have a fancy for self-willed women. What am I to do?"

Agnes made a face. "Then set your mind at rest," she replied bitterly. "That's the only kind of wife you'll get."

"So I may hope?"

Defiantly, Agnes folded her arms. Through all the hours that she had spent beside her father's deathbed, holding his hand, she had been wrestling with herself. She owed the decision that she had finally made entirely to her uncertain future, and her father's last wish.

The house of Erfenstein will not die out, it will merge with a flourishing dynasty . . .

She breathed deeply before forcing herself to answer. "Let's not beat about the bush," she said coolly. "You know as well as I do that I don't have many options open to me. So very well, I agree to the marriage. But only on three conditions." She raised a finger. "First, you will let me lead my life as I have always led it before. Second, Father Tristan and Mathis will stay at the castle as my friends. And third— don't think that I am letting you into my bed. You would be unpleasantly surprised."

Friedrich von Löwenstein-Scharfeneck fiddled thoughtfully with the pointed end of his neatly trimmed black beard, while he inspected Agnes like something laid out for sale on a market stall. Once again, she noticed his thinning hair. Young as he was, he would probably have a bald patch within a few years. Apart from that, and despite his pallor, he was an attractive man—and above all, very prosperous. Agnes could not help thinking how many women would envy her this match.

"The devil only knows why I let you speak to me like that," Friedrich von Löwenstein-Scharfeneck finally replied. "But very well, you have my word. The old man and that young fool won't bother me. And as for your last point, there are other beautiful women who will warm my bed." He smiled suggestively. "What's more, I am convinced that time heals all wounds."

"In your dreams, maybe. And now to the reason why you are so keen to possess Trifels Castle. May I?" Agnes rose abruptly to her feet and went over to one of the bookshelves. She took a large tome off it, and put it down on the desk in front of the count. "This is what you were looking for just now, isn't it?"

Surprised, Count Scharfeneck looked at the well-worn book in front of him. It was the *Magna Historia de Castro Trifels*, the book that Agnes herself had read in secret again and again during the last few months. Last time, Father Tristan had simply put it back on the shelf and then had obviously forgotten about it. But Agnes had always known where to find the volume.

The count began turning the pages with trembling fingers. His eyes shone like a child's. "The old chronicle of the castle," he said. "On the finest vellum, illustrated, and with initial letters in gold leaf. I've heard a great deal about it, and now I actually have it in my hands. What a precious jewel. How did you . . . ?"

"What you want is roughly in the middle of the book," Agnes said. "The chapter about the time of the house of Hohenstaufen. I'm afraid that a few pages have been torn out, but it's a different part that interests you anyway." She looked out of the window, where the morning sun was shining brightly now, and quoted from memory the section about the Norman treasure.

"The crown of all treasures," Count Scharfeneck said reverently. "I have dreamed of it since I was a child." He looked up and scrutinized Agnes with a smile. "You are a clever girl, Lady Agnes. I couldn't wish for a better bride. How did you know that was why I wanted Trifels Castle?"

"My father indicated as much. He said you were concerned with gold, a great deal of gold. And then there were . . . certain hints." Agnes almost told the count about her conversation with Melchior, but at the last moment decided to keep the minstrel out of this. She turned back to Scharfeneck, shrugging her shoulders. "Your enthusiasm for Trifels and everything to do with it gave you away. Father Tristan claims that Emperor Frederick II had the treasure taken to Apulia later, but I can see that you don't share his opinion. You suspect it's still somewhere in this area, don't you? Perhaps even here on the castle rock itself."

The count laughed softly. "Emperor Frederick II was a great teller of romantic tales when it came to his money. He would never have parted from such a huge fortune. I have sent messengers to Lucera in

Apulia, to research that theory. It is said that Frederick stationed the Saracens whom he had pacified to guard the treasure there, but that was a lie told by the Staufers." Quivering with excitement, he pointed to a picture on the page in front of him, showing several donkeys loaded up with chests. Armed warriors rode tall steeds and carried blood-red standards. "The treasure is still at Trifels. They hid it here," he went on, with conviction. "There are ancient sources proving it. Even as a little boy I dreamed of finding it. And a quarter of a year ago, we began the search at last."

Agnes wrinkled her brow. *A quarter of a year ago?*

All at once, she remembered the men in the forest, the men she and Mathis had met just after they had found her falcon. Both of them had suspected Wertingen's henchmen, but it had been the count with his landsknechts, searching for the treasure. Suddenly it all made sense.

"So that's why you bought Scharfenberg, isn't it?" she asked quietly. "Not because you were intent on moving into your ancestors' castle, but because you needed a base in these parts. You were digging here. Mathis and I saw lights in the woods. We were thinking about the old legend of Barbarossa, but it was you."

Scharfeneck shrugged. "The tale of Barbarossa certainly came in handy. It kept the superstitious peasantry away from us. All the same, I fear that something always gets out. There was a little . . ." Here he hesitated. "Well, let's call it an incident. That was when I knew I must buy Scharfenberg Castle, if only to keep other curious and interfering folk away from me." He smiled at her. "Unfortunately I had no prospect of acquiring Trifels at that time."

Repelled, Agnes turned her eyes away and once again looked through the window at the view of the lower bailey, the stables and sheds, the herb garden, the graveyard, and the well tower. Soon it would all belong to the count, and she would be nothing but a pretty ornament for him to wear. But what choice did she have?

Suddenly her eye was caught by a detail outside. The tombstones in the castle graveyard. One of them still shone new and white in the morning sun, with only a few red poppies flowering on the mound of soil heaped over the grave itself. It was the tombstone of Martin von Heidelsheim, the former steward of Trifels. Two bedraggled crows perched on the murdered man's grave.

Agnes remembered the gruesome find of his body, and the way in which Heidelsheim had been killed. The expensive crossbow bolts, fletched with eagles' feathers, had gone so far into the steward's body that his murderer must have been standing directly in front of him. So Heidelsheim had known the man—either that, or he had assumed that he represented no danger.

Agnes looked into a void. What had the count just said about his excavations?

There was a little . . . well, let's call it an incident.

Cawing, the two crows rose from the tombstone.

"How fortunate that my father did not marry me off to Martin von Heidelsheim," said Agnes calmly, still looking out through the window. "Or you'd have gone away empty-handed. I'm sure you remember Heidelsheim?"

"What, the faithless fellow who left without a word?"

"That's not entirely true. He was found in the end, buried in a makeshift grave, with a crossbow bolt in his throat."

Agnes turned to the count, whose face now assumed a sympathetic smile. "How terrible," he sighed. "But this part of the country is simply not safe. One can easily fall victim to highwaymen and murderers. Many a man goes too far into the forest and then can't find his way out." Scharfeneck's voice was very low now, but it cut through the air like a sharp knife. "If I were you, Lady Agnes, I'd take care not to venture very deeply into the forest. It would be a shame for any harm to come to that beautiful face." Count Friedrich von Löwenstein-Scharfeneck looked at her for a long time, his smile frozen like ice. Finally he laughed, and the threatening atmosphere relaxed.

"But why are we talking about the dead?" he went on affably. "Let's speak of the living." He rose to his feet and went over to the bookshelves, where a carafe of wine and two glasses stood ready.

Humming a tune, he poured the wine and handed Agnes one of the sparkling crystal goblets.

"You are a clever child, Agnes. Clever and endowed with an inquiring mind," he said in a confidential tone. "A miracle, really, with such a stupid clod for a father. You ought to be proud that you will soon be able to call yourself a Scharfeneck."

Agnes felt her hand tighten around the glass so firmly that she thought it would break. "I'll never be a Scharfeneck," she replied coldly. "I remain the mistress of Trifels."

Surprised, the count raised his eyebrows. "The mistress of Trifels? A worthy title, to be sure. It seems to me that you are growing up at last." Smiling, he raised his glass. "Here's to the mistress of Trifels, then. And to the Norman treasure that we'll soon find here."

Agnes did not touch her goblet to his, but put it to her lips and drank the heavy red wine down in a single draft.

It tasted like blood.

With weary eyes, Mathis watched the fat bluebottle flying in wide circles around the cell. The heat of the summer day seemed to have made the insect as dizzy as he felt himself. Buzzing angrily, the fly collided with the wall several times before finally coming to rest on the floor, which was covered with dirty straw. A large spider shot out of a crack in the woodwork and disappeared into a dark corner with its prey.

Leaning against the wall of his cell, Mathis closed his eyes, but it was impossible to sleep. He had been crouching here all day, in the heavy heat of the top floor of the guardhouse. Much of the time he had been able to see the glaring sun through a barred window, but it had now disappeared behind the town walls. Evening was approaching, and Mathis thought how, only a few months ago, he had been locked up in the keep of Trifels Castle. He had spent many days and nights there, yet he hadn't felt as lonely as he did now, in Annweiler.

They had put him in the notorious "drying-out cell," a room reinforced with iron that sat above the guardhouse, by the lower gate. In winter, a prisoner's saliva froze to lumps of ice in his mouth here; in summer it was as hot as hell under the metal ceiling. The cell could bring any troublemaker, however rowdy, to see reason.

In spite of the heat in the stuffy room, Mathis was shivering—from fear. This time there really did not seem to be any way out. His sentence had been as good as passed already: he had allegedly murdered the mayor of Annweiler, and if he didn't confess, the executioner in nearby Queichhambach would presumably leave him dangling from the ceiling of the torture chamber, with stones hanging from his feet, until his bones were dislocated from their joints. Mathis had once seen Master Jakob dragging a stubborn thief, convicted of stealing from the offertory box, to the gallows. The man could no longer walk by himself, his limbs as slack as those of a puppet with its strings cut. How long would Mathis be able to endure torture? Or was it better to confess at once in order to buy a quick, clean death?

Mathis groaned and licked his cracked lips. He was thirstier than he had ever been in his life. Last night's hangover had not entirely worn off yet, and the heat left him feeling like a dried apple. Presumably the town councilors of Annweiler were hoping to get a faster confession by these means.

They need me, thought Mathis. *Only if I confess will no suspicion fall on the municipal dignitaries, and the duke will be placated.*

For the hundredth time, Mathis went over to the barred window on the eastern side of his cell and looked out over the rooftops of the town to the Sonnenberg, on which Trifels Castle stood enthroned. Inaccessibly far away. Why had he let himself be persuaded to visit Annweiler? Up there Agnes was waiting for him, and so were his mother, his little sister, his father . . .

Father.

Mathis felt a stabbing pain in his chest when he thought of his father, lying mortally sick in bed. Was he still alive? Hans Wielenbach would surely have been proud of his son. Mathis gritted his teeth.

Now, at the most, his family would only be able to wave goodbye to him while he was choking on the gallows.

Footsteps on the creaking stairs made him spin around. Now clattering and shouting could also be heard. Obviously another prisoner was being brought up to the drying-out cell.

"Unhand me, you filth!" cried a deep voice. "I can walk on my own."

Mathis jumped when he recognized that voice. It belonged to the old master gunner, Ulrich Reichhart.

Only a few moments later, the cell door opened and the guards pushed the recalcitrant Trifels man-at-arms in. He fell to the floor, cursing, while the bolt of the door was shot with a loud *creak* behind him. For a moment Reichhart stayed on the floor, then he scrambled up and looked at Mathis.

The old gunner was grinning hugely.

"Done it," he growled, knocking dust off his shabby hose. "Wasn't so easy to get taken up here. You have to really rile the guards if you want to be brought up from the cellar to the drying-out cell. However, no one likes to be called the stinking son of an idiot knacker." He winked at his young friend.

Mathis smiled wearily. "I'm glad to have your company, Ulrich, but I must warn you, the heat here is downright unbearable."

"Then it's a good thing we won't be hanging around for long." Reichhart grinned again, and Mathis stared at him, taken aback.

"What do you mean?"

"You don't think I want to dry out in this dump like a toad, do you? There's no way of escape down in the cellar, but the prospects look different up here." Reichhart rose and crossed the small square cell, knocking cautiously at the iron-clad ceiling as he did so. There was a place in the far corner where it suddenly sounded hollow.

"Aha." Satisfied, Reichhart nodded. "That's the spot they meant."

"Who?" asked Mathis, confused. "What spot?"

"Mathis, Mathis." Ulrich Reichhart shook his head impatiently.

"You may not have noticed, but you've set an example to a lot of the poor folk hereabouts, and not only since the storming of the Ramburg. They still tell the tale of how you helped Shepherd Jockel to escape and fooled the mayor of Annweiler. Then you defeated the terrifying Black Hans. And now they love you for sending that miserable bloodsucker Gessler to fry in hell. You're a hero, Mathis, can't you see that?"

"But I didn't—"

"You don't have to pretend to me." Reichhart shook his head impatiently. "That scoundrel fully deserved to have his head blown off." He lowered his voice to a conspiratorial note. "But when we're out of here, you must tell me over a glass of wine or two sometime how on earth you smuggled the arquebus into the town. Can't have been easy, I bet."

Sighing, Mathis gave up. It was hopeless. To the people here, he was the mayor's murderer and nothing was going to change that.

"You were suggesting that someone's prepared a way of escape for us?" he asked.

Reichhart nodded. "They often shut peasants with rebellious notions up in here to get them to see reason. Last time, three weeks ago, the town council was holding a few men from Waldrohrbach in the drying-out cell. Their getaway was carefully planned, but at the last moment the men from Waldrohrbach were taken to Speyer and strung up there, as a deterrent to the locals." He grinned and pointed to the ceiling. "Too bad for them, good luck for us. There's only a thin sheet of metal between us and the sky. We're expecting a visitor tonight."

Mathis was so astonished that he could hardly believe his good fortune. "Is . . . is that really true?" he managed to say. "You mean we can soon get back to the castle and . . ." Then it occurred to him that from now on he was wanted not just for sedition, but murder, and his expression darkened. "Well, this time I suppose the castellan of Trifels won't be taking me back into his good graces, what do you think?"

Ulrich Reichhart cleared his throat. "I . . . I overheard a conversation just now," he hesitantly began. "There's bad news from Trifels, Mathis. The castellan is . . . he's dead."

"Dead?" Mathis shook his head incredulously. "But how can he be dead?" he finally asked. "I mean, he wasn't severely wounded."

"It was apparently worse than any of us thought, and gangrene set in. He died in the early hours of the morning. His daughter was with him the whole time."

And I wasn't there to comfort her, thought Mathis.

Beside him, Ulrich Reichhart bit his lip. He seemed to be wrestling with himself.

"I guess that's not your only piece of bad news, is it?" Mathis asked tonelessly.

Reichhart nodded. "You're right. The conversation I overheard was between one of the guards and . . . and . . ." He sighed deeply. "And your mother. The guards wouldn't let her see you, by order of the town council. Even though she wept and begged them, with your little sister holding her hand. Bloody pen pushers!" He spat on the floor, and then he looked seriously at the young weaponsmith. Mathis knew what was coming.

"And your father died last night as well. They say he asked for you."

"Oh, God." Feeling empty and burned-out, Mathis slid down the wall of the cell to sit on the floor, among the rubbish, mouse droppings, and dry wheat straw scattered over it. He drew up his knees and, in the last of the sunlight, stared at the ceiling and the dust drifting in the air below it.

Why wasn't I there? Why?

"Your father was old and sick, Mathis," Reichhart tried to console him. "If he hadn't left us yesterday, it would probably have been tomorrow or the day after. The time for every one of us comes someday."

Mathis thought what his father had been like when Mathis was still a child. Hans Wielenbach had been a tall strong man, invincible, a giant at the anvil. The castellan of Trifels had also been invincible —a noble knight and his loyal weaponsmith. And now they were both dead.

"My father and the castellan," he began quietly, with his eyes closed. "They came from another time. I thought the new time was better, but by God, I don't know. I really don't know."

He fell into a brooding silence, and Reichhart left him alone. Soon the sun sank entirely, and the room became dark and pleasantly cool. Mathis still had his eyes closed, but he was not asleep.

Why wasn't I there?

About two hours before midnight, faint sounds could be heard on the roof, like the paws of little mice scurrying up and down. Rafters and tiles were removed from the roof above the prisoners, and then Mathis heard the cautious boring of a drill. Looking up, he suddenly saw a tiny hole in the ceiling, with stars shining through it.

"Ah, there they are," Reichhart said, rubbing his tired eyes. "I was beginning to think they'd forgotten us."

The hole grew larger. Finally, someone pushed a sheet of metal aside, and in the light of a torch, a bearded face surrounded by unruly hair looked down at them.

It was Shepherd Jockel.

"Good evening, Mathis," he said, grinning. "Didn't I promise to pay you back someday? This time it's *your* pretty face I'm saving; next time it'll be your turn again." He chuckled, like he had cracked a good joke. Quiet whispering could be heard behind him, and then a rope was let down to the prisoners.

"Come along," Jockel whispered. "The two guards down at the gate are on our side, but I can't speak for the men in the guardhouse. Fat Markschild and the other town councilors will kick the shit out of the guards when they find that you've given them the slip."

By now Jockel's assistants had enlarged the hole until one man at a time could get through it. Mathis took hold of the rope and hauled himself up on it. A sharp metal edge at the top of the hole cut painfully into his left side, then he was out on the roof. Breathing heavily, Ulrich Reichhart followed him.

Hunchbacked Shepherd Jockel stood in the moonlight with two peasants from the neighborhood whom Mathis knew by sight. One of them owned fields where the young crops had recently been trampled down by Scharfeneck's mounted landsknechts, the other was the father of the boy who had been hanged in spring, on Bernwart Gessler's orders. With his sparse gray hair, and his few remaining stumps of teeth, he looked old before his time. Trembling, the frail man took Mathis by the hand, and shook it.

"All of us peasants hereabouts are glad you finished off that bloodsucker," he whispered. "You're welcome to our company, weaponsmith."

Mathis said nothing . He glanced at Shepherd Jockel, who smiled as he pointed over the rooftops to where the black ribbon of the forest stretched away beyond the town walls.

"There are more and more joining us every day, Mathis," said Jockel, with a sparkle in his eyes. "Peasants and laborers, but also tanners, weavers, shepherds, knackers, runaway monks. The whole empire is a keg of gunpowder with the fuse burning. We live in the woods, waiting for the day when we can strike at last. It won't be much longer, you wait and see. The era of the knights, the clergy, the princes and dukes is finally coming to an end." He lowered his voice and looked around as if he were facing a large audience. "For a long time I thought we'd have the help of townsfolk as well. But you've seen where that leads. Now we simple folk must take our destiny into our own hands."

"When Adam delved and Eve span, who was then the gentleman?" the two peasants whispered in chorus. It sounded like a prayer, and the old master gunner Ulrich Reichhart nodded agreement, too.

"You were right, Mathis, when you said the old times were over," Reichhart said, clapping Mathis on the shoulder paternally. "New times are coming, and there'll be plenty for a couple of gunners like us to do. The castellan of Trifels was a good master, but there aren't enough of those. So let's make sure that we can be our own masters."

Once again, Mathis found his eyes straying to the forest. How many might be waiting there, armed with scythes, boar spears, and threshing flails? A hundred? Two hundred? Maybe even more? It was what he had always wanted, and yet his heart felt strangely heavy. It was as though he had only just realized that they must fight for their rights, with sweat, tears, and blood. A great deal of blood. He thought of the first shot he had fired in the forest from the stolen arquebus, the shot like thunder that had turned the man before him into a shattered heap of flesh.

New times are coming.

Shepherd Jockel and the two peasants were looking expectantly at him.

"What are you waiting for?" Jockel asked suspiciously. "You don't want to go back into the drying-out cell and let those fat moneybags hang you tomorrow, do you?"

Mathis shook his head. *Do I have any alternative?* he thought. Then he hurried after the other four men as they jumped from roof to roof over the narrow alleys of Annweiler, on their way to the town wall.

The forest awaited them, its trees like a rank of fierce soldiers, ready for anything.

Book Two

THE STORM

APRIL TO JUNE 1525

· 14 ·

Tʜᴇʀᴇ ᴡᴀs ᴀɴ ᴇᴇʀɪᴇ sɪʟᴇɴᴄᴇ in the Knights' House of Scharfenberg Castle. Only the logs on the hearth crackled, and the solitary guest sitting at the table smacked his lips loudly.

From one of the window niches, Agnes watched old Count Ludwig von Löwenstein-Scharfeneck eat his supper. Bending low over the table, her father-in-law did battle with a well-seasoned haunch of venison. Ludwig's shaven chin shone greasily in the light of the torches, bones crunched, and his knife cut through the roast meat and grated on his silver plate. Finally the imperial count wiped his mouth, belched with satisfaction, and reached for his goblet of wine, only to push it aside with an expression of distaste.

"This wine tastes like horse piss. Don't you have anything better?"

The old man drew down the corners of his mouth and then tipped what was left of the red wine in his goblet onto the rushes on the floor under the table. Like all the Scharfenecks, he had thin hair and a penetrating glance, which he now bent on his son Friedrich, who sat in an armchair beside the large fire. For a moment Friedrich seemed about to utter a retort, but then, looking bored, he simply snapped his fingers. A young servant appeared from behind a column and bowed low to him.

"Fetch our guest some of the new Rhine wine that was delivered only yesterday," Friedrich ordered tonelessly. "Maybe a cool white will be more to my father's liking than this heavy Palatinate red, although considering his rheumatic limbs I doubt it. However, he's old enough to know his own mind." With a tilt of his head, he indicated the door. "The wine is down in the kitchen, so off you go—or do I have to make you get a move on?"

The boy nodded and hurried away. Silence fell in the great hall again, a silence that made Agnes shiver even more than the unseasonably cold weather outside. Although it was April, winter had returned, as if refusing to accept its dismissal this year. Agnes had been sitting at the window for almost an hour, looking out at the dense and driving snow, and leafing now and then through the printed pages of *Parcival*, the epic poem by Wolfram von Eschenbach. She had paid good money to have it sent from Worms. All this time the old imperial count had hardly exchanged a word with her or his son. Instead, he had set to work on steaming game pies, capons, quails' eggs, and cakes fragrant with honey—a feast interrupted only by the brief orders he barked out as he waited for the next course to be brought in.

Friedrich's relationship with his father had been at rock bottom for months. The old man had not forgiven his son for marrying a mere castellan's daughter and moving into this drafty ruin of a castle. It was true that Scharfenberg Castle had changed considerably over those months—walls had been repaired, damp patches plastered, and rotting wood replaced by new oak rafters—but in spite of everything, the old imperial castle must still seem not much more than a hovel to Ludwig I von Löwenstein-Scharfeneck, who, after all was a son, if an illegitimate one, of the former elector of the Palatinate. He had let Friedrich, the youngest of his five living children, have his way for a long time, hoping that one of these days he would finish sowing his wild oats. But now the old man's patience seemed to be running out at last.

Agnes looked around the renovated Knights' House and tried to take her mind back to the days when her father still lived in nearby Trifels Castle. It seemed an eternity ago now, yet it was less than a year since Erfenstein's mysterious death. Even though in that time Friedrich had excavated half the surrounding area, he still had not found the legendary Norman treasure. The constant hoping and waiting had taken their toll on his temper, which was not improved by a sudden visit from his father.

"At home in Löwenstein we drink Tokay and Burgundy," announced Ludwig von Löwenstein-Scharfeneck, picking scraps of meat out of his teeth with his fingers. "Bright red Burgundy at thirty guilders the cask. The ducal court honors us with a visit almost every week. And what does my son do? Buries himself here in the dark forest, looking for *treasure*, like a little boy. This has been going on for years. How much longer am I expected to put up with your daydreams?" He spat on the rushes. "Bah! Tongues are wagging about you at court in Heidelberg."

"Is that why you came?" retorted Friedrich. "To give me that information? A messenger would have sufficed."

"I'm here to get you to see reason. Your mother is crying her eyes out because her youngest child has obviously lost his mind." Ludwig sighed and looked piercingly at his son with watery eyes. "I've spoken to the duke, Friedrich. We can get this tiresome marriage annulled at any time. Keep the woman as a concubine if you like."

"Excuse me, Your Grace, but since you are speaking of me, the *concubine* . . ." Agnes said. She had listened for some time, but now her patience was at an end. Angrily, she closed her book and sat up very straight. "Your son married not just me, but Trifels Castle. And I don't think he can take the castle to your court with him, can he, honored *father-in-law?*"

The old count spared her only a sidelong glance and then turned back to his son. "Friedrich, tell your woman to keep her mouth shut until she's asked to open it. In your place I'd have forbidden her to read books long ago. Books only make women pert and disobedient."

"And above all, books make them clever," Agnes replied. "So I also know that your son will never give up Trifels. Not until he has found out all its secrets."

"Hold your tongue," Friedrich snapped. "Or I'll have you locked in your bedchamber again."

"Better that than lying in the bed of a tyrant." Agnes defiantly crossed her arms.

The young count had indeed tried to approach her at night a couple of times, but she had reminded him forcefully of their original agreement. Agnes knew that she would never in her life share a bed with the man who had murdered her father. Soon after that, Scharfeneck had given up and had contented himself with choosing a playmate now and then from among the maids.

"You let her speak to you like that?" said Ludwig scornfully. "I'd have tanned her hide long ago."

The young count was about to reply, but a clinking sound and then a crash came from the doorway leading from the staircase. The young servant had slipped on the smooth top step and fallen, tray and all. The goblet, set with semi-precious gemstones, rolled before Friedrich's feet, and a pool of pale wine spread on the floor. The count's lips narrowed, and he spoke in the quiet, cutting tone that showed he was particularly angry.

"You clumsy oaf," he hissed. "I'll set the dogs on you for this, I'll have you flayed. You'll wish you'd never been—"

"I will go and get more wine for our guest," Agnes interrupted him. "That will be the quickest way." She rose from her place in the window niche, picked up the goblet from the floor, and swiftly pushed the trembling servant out of the room. "I am sure the gentlemen can do without my company."

Before her husband could say anything, she had disappeared into the stairway tower, along with the servant.

"Thank you. Thank you, my lady," the young servant whispered. He couldn't be more than thirteen years old. "How can I . . ."

"Go out into the courtyard and feed my falcon," Agnes replied, smiling. "But mind you don't drop the food dish, or Parcival will peck your fingers off. He can be just as short-tempered as my husband."

She watched the relieved boy hurry to the door, and then she set off down to the kitchen herself.

As Agnes walked along the low-ceilinged passages, their walls hung with thick tapestries, she thought how her life had changed in the last few months. The wedding had been held in July, in the chapel of Trifels Castle, and had been a very modest occasion. Only about fifty guests had been invited, among them many of the lower nobility who owed allegiance to the count. They had looked at the damp, moldering rooms with scorn, and since then Agnes had seldom visited Trifels herself.

Friedrich had built her a golden cage at Scharfenberg Castle. He had bought her many books and had her bower furnished with silk and damask. Agnes wore the finest clothes and precious jewelry; meals were served on silver platters by an army of servants. She was no longer a simple castellan's daughter but a real countess. Margarethe would have been green with envy. Yet Agnes sometimes felt like a fly caught in a piece of amber, and the days passed as if in a mist. Her heart still mourned for her father.

Her dreams, too, had ceased. All she had left was the mysterious signet ring, which she kept hidden in a little box under her bed, taking it out only occasionally.

Feeling despondent, Agnes entered the large kitchen on the first floor of the castle complex. Old Hedwig stood beside the smoking fireplace, above which a huge, sooty flue protruded into the room. She was just putting a steaming copper pan on a tripod. The cook's was the only familiar face from the past that Agnes saw here. The men-at-arms Gunther and Eberhart still served at Trifels Castle, the old master gunner Reichhart had gone away to join the rebels, and Abbot Weigand had summoned Father Tristan back to Eusserthal weeks ago to help him with the laborious work of keeping the abbey's records straight.

Agnes felt a pang go to her heart as she thought of the one who had been closest of all to her and yet was the farthest away.

Mathis . . .

Agnes had not seen her childhood friend since before his escape from prison in Annweiler. It was said that, like Reichhart, he had joined the rebels, and she had heard rumors that the peasants now regarded the young weaponsmith as one of their leaders. Her silly, stubborn little Mathis. How long ago was it that they had played in the forest together? How long . . .

"What's the matter, my child?"

Hedwig's voice brought her back from her gloomy thoughts. Glancing up, Agnes saw the stout old cook looking at her with concern. Hedwig sighed.

"You look paler every day. You must eat more, and then everything will be all right, just wait and see. The good Lord means well by us, to be sure." Nodding, Hedwig stirred the stew over the fire as she went on muttering, half to herself. "Out there, peasants are freezing and hungry, there's murder and violence everywhere, terrible times these are, terrible times. We can be thankful to sit by a warm fire here and have enough to eat, indeed we can."

"It might be better to freeze and die fighting than to lie in a warm bed with those who exploit the peasants," said Agnes sadly.

"Now, now, don't let His Grace the count hear that." Hedwig shook her head. "You're a countess now, Agnes, and don't you forget it. You have nothing more to do with us common folk."

"Oh, Hedwig," sighed Agnes, "I still remember so well how you used to break into a freshly baked loaf, all warm and steaming, and spread honey on it for me." She smiled. "And how you scolded me when I brought dirt into the kitchen on my shoes. Am I suddenly supposed to act like a countess? I'm afraid I'll never in my life learn how to do that."

"There are many other things that you must still learn, my lady."

Agnes glanced at the low doorway from which the new voice had come. The minstrel Melchior von Tanningen stood there with her falcon, Parcival, perched on his leather gauntlet. The bird had his hood on and was as calm as if Agnes herself were carrying him.

"Outside I met a kitchen boy who said the countess was going to carry wine up to the hall herself," said Melchior, smiling. "You'll be asking the son of the Annweiler goatherd whether you can polish his shoes next."

"The servant spilled the wine by accident," replied Agnes. "You know my husband. I thought it best to keep the boy out of his way." She looked at the minstrel suspiciously. "And what are you doing with my falcon?"

"He was calling. Probably because he missed you. And he'll soon be molting again. See for yourself." Melchior pointed to several ragged feathers. "While he's still fit to be seen, we ought to fly him a few times out in these wintry clouds. What do you think?" The minstrel sketched a bow. "I would consider myself fortunate if I might accompany her ladyship the countess hawking tomorrow. It would surely cheer her."

Agnes could not help smiling. In fact her rides with Melchior were among the few pleasant experiences of her present life. On their expeditions, when she rode her father's horse, Taramis, Melchior would tell her tales from the time of the Nibelungs, or sing her the sad ballads that he was practicing for the singers' contest at the Wartburg next fall. Although she had known Melchior for only a few months, he had become a faithful friend. His old-fashioned appearance and manner of speech could always bring a smile to her lips. Even now she actually laughed.

"Well, her ladyship the countess would think herself equally fortunate to ride out hawking with you," she replied, imitating his formal invitation. Suddenly she put her hand to her mouth. "My God, the wine! I quite forgot. I imagine my father-in-law will be cursing and spitting fire by now."

"Let me do it for you." Melchior carefully put the falcon down to sit on the rim of a pan. Then he took a recently washed goblet and filled it with some Rhine wine from a small cask. "It's a minstrel's fate to be cursed and spat at. After a while one no longer minds." His eyes twinkled. He turned to the stairs leading up to the great hall.

"A good man," murmured Hedwig, when he was out of sight. "So courteous and clever with words. Just a little short of stature, if you ask me, my lady."

Agnes laughed. "Short, to be sure, but he has a great heart."

The savory aroma of the stew over the fire rose to her nostrils. Only now did she realize that she was indeed hungry. She sat down at the well-scoured kitchen table with a steaming bowl taken from the pan and began spooning it up.

It tasted a thousand times better than anything the imperial count had been stuffing into himself upstairs.

Snowflakes fell lazily on the forest clearing, turning the many tents and lopsided huts into regular white hillocks. Mathis stood at a rusty anvil, hammering away at a rusty arquebus. The steady sound of his hammer blows rang out over the clearing like a church bell tolling for a funeral. Although he was close to the fire, his fingers would not warm up, nor was the firearm hot enough for him to bend it into shape. Finally he gave up and threw the piece of iron to the ground, where it disappeared, hissing and steaming, in the knee-deep snow.

"This is all a waste of time," he said angrily. "Without a proper furnace, I'll never get enough heat going. We might as well use the arquebuses as clubs to beat the duke's landsknechts with. That would be more useful."

"You must be patient, Mathis," Ulrich Reichhart told him. He was standing beside the younger man, blowing up the fire with a bellows. "The heat was nearly high enough. We can't offer you a real smithy out here in the forest, as you know yourself. Now we'll have to begin again." Cursing, he pulled the firearm out of the snow and put it back over the fire. "What's the matter with you, Mathis? For days you've been looking like a sinister forest spirit. The men are beginning to duck their heads when they pass you."

"Let them," growled Mathis, stirring up the embers with the poker. "I don't feel like conversation anyway. And nor do most of the rest of us here."

Morosely, he let his eyes scan the clearing, where just under a hundred rebels had assembled. They had pitched camp in an isolated valley near the little village of Dimbach, just a few miles from Annweiler. The men sat hunched around small, smoking campfires, wrapped in furs and ragged blankets. They sharpened their scythes and boar spears, they drank watery acorn soup and talked in muted voices. Someone was playing a fiddle somewhere, but no one felt like singing or dancing to it. The mood of elation that had reigned only a few weeks ago had given way to leaden apathy. Cold settled in the men's limbs, making them feel more and more doubtful.

In the fall, it had looked as if it were only a matter of time before the peasants throughout the empire rose up and confronted their oppressors. In the Hegau and the Allgäu districts, in the Black Forest, in Franconia, Alsace, and Thuringia, they had come together to defend themselves against the burden of taxation, the ban on hunting, the death tax, and other kinds of harassment by the great lords. The whole countryside around Lake Constance was in an uproar. It was said that thousands of peasants had joined together to fight under the banner of liberty. But there had been no new reports for some months, and the wave of rebellion had clearly not rolled on as far as the Palatinate. So they waited here day in, day out, while their ears, noses, and fingers slowly froze. It seemed that winter would never end, and some men had already returned to their villages. Those who stayed fed on acorns, beechnuts, and now and then a skinny hare or squirrel.

"We can't hold out here much longer," Mathis quietly said, almost to himself. "We promised the peasants a life of freedom, but it's far worse here than the life they knew before."

"Jockel says that men minded like us have already burned a few castles and monasteries," replied Reichhart. "He says it can't be long now."

"Jockel says a great many things. Many fine, roundabout words, but whether they're true is another matter."

Mathis spat into the fire and then resumed hammering the iron arquebus. The steady rhythm at least helped to calm him down a little. The fact was that their joint struggle against the nobility and the church seemed to him increasingly futile. In addition, he kept thinking of Agnes these days. It was almost a year since they had last seen each other. Only now and then did he hear, from peddlers or runaway servants, what was going on at Trifels and Scharfenberg Castle. Agnes was married, a countess living in luxury, and she seemed to like it. Did she ever think at all of him, the former smith at Trifels Castle, now an outlaw? Mathis seethed with anger, anger mixed with another emotion that he could name only after a little thought.

Love.

The two feelings were very, very similar.

Suddenly loud voices were heard shouting. Grateful for anything to distract his mind, Mathis looked up and saw a group crossing the clearing toward him. When they came closer, he saw that one of them was Shepherd Jockel, accompanied by some men whom he had never seen before. The new arrivals kept a little distance between themselves and the hunchbacked shepherd, whether out of dislike or respect it was hard to say.

Biding his time, Mathis watched the leader of their small, freezing band. Jockel had exchanged his old ragged clothing for a blood-red doublet and slashed hose such as the landsknechts wore. On his head he wore a shabby velvet cap with roosters' feathers in it as if it were a crown. Jannsen and Paulus, two former vagabonds from Baden who liked to call themselves his bodyguards, were with him.

"Make way for the leader!" they shouted, pushing aside a few peasants who were wearily sitting together in a hollow in the snow. "Make way, will you?" With spears and rusty helmets that they had stolen somewhere, the two bodyguards looked like a travesty of brave paladins.

"Ah, here's my loyal weaponsmith," said Jockel at last, turning with a smile to the strangers and, with a lordly gesture, indicating Mathis. "Take my word for it, Mathis is the best master gunner from here to Lake Constance. With him at our side, we'll chase the knights and clerics out of their castles and abbeys like vermin."

"A master gunner without any guns, I see," remarked one of the newcomers ironically. He was a broad-built man getting on in years, with a watchful look, and dressed like a respectable craftsman. Mathis thought he was probably mayor of his village. The man pointed to the bent gun barrel lying on the embers in front of him. "You'll never make a decent arquebus of that again. I'm a smith myself; I know what I'm talking about."

"We have a whole arsenal of firearms," replied Jockel coolly. "This is just a looted weapon that we're trying to make serviceable again, isn't that so, Mathis?"

It was such an audacious lie that Mathis almost laughed. In reality, they had three arquebuses and one rusty culverin. Calling that collection an arsenal verged on megalomania. Mathis frowned. Over the last few months his admiration for the leader of the Wasgau peasants had turned increasingly into distrust. Jockel, who wanted to see all kings overthrown, was acting like one himself.

"You're welcome to stand here instead of me, blowing up the fire, Master *Smith*," Ulrich Reichhart growled at the village mayor before him. "Then we'll see if you can do better. Or I could always reshape your nose."

Shepherd Jockel raised his hands in a mollifying gesture. "No quarreling here. These men bring good news." He paused for dramatic effect before going on in a loud voice. "The peasants of Dahn and Wilgartswiesen have risen at last. They are on their way here to join our band. And there's unrest down in Landau as well. The fight can begin at last."

Mathis looked up in surprise. This was indeed good news. "How many of you are there?" he asked the village mayor.

"A hundred, maybe a dozen more," replied the man solemnly. "And new recruits are arriving every day. The harsh winter and famine have done their work. The peasants are determined not to put up with the injustices of the gentry any longer."

Beside Mathis, Shepherd Jockel rubbed his hands together with satisfaction. "The time has come at last," he cried. "Aha, Mathis, and you doubted it. Isn't that so? I could see that you doubted. Well, who's right now?"

"Nonsense," growled Mathis. He pushed his hair back from his forehead, which bore a scar as long as a finger; it was all that was left of his injuries from the battle for the Ramburg, and it made him look fiercer than before. He did not like it when Jockel spoke to him in that tone. He was coming to feel that the hunchbacked shepherd regarded him as a rival. His own reputation in the camp had grown during the last few months, and there was now a self-confidence about him that could often silence even men older than he was.

"When can your people be here?" Mathis asked the envoy from Dahn.

"In about a week's time. We're just waiting for the anxious and undecided to join us. Messengers are going from hamlet to hamlet, and meanwhile we are hiding in the forest." The village mayor smiled. "The duke has set a price on my head—but so have we set a price on his."

"We'll need a new camp," Mathis pointed out. "This clearing is too small. We'll have to build more huts and chop down trees for firewood, or half the men will be frozen before we even go into battle."

The village mayor looked thoughtful. "Well, it may not come to that at all," he began, with some hesitation.

"What do you mean?" Jockel demanded. "Speak up."

"They say that in Memmingen, in Swabia, the peasants and the nobility have been talking together. The Baltringen Band, the Allgäu Band, and the Lake Constance Band were all represented by their leaders. The noblemen will go along with our demands." The man handed Jockel a crumpled sheet of printed paper. "Here, this is being distributed all over the empire. It talks sense. Tithes will be abolished, we'll be able to choose our own parish priests, and hunting will be allowed again."

Jockel took the paper; frowning, he examined the lines of small print. He had taught himself to read during the long days and nights herding his flock of sheep, but it was obviously still difficult for him. However, woe betide anyone who made fun of him for that. As Jockel read, moving his lips, silence reigned. Finally he looked up. His fingers moving fast, he tore the document to pieces that fell slowly to the ground, mingling with the snowflakes.

"Nothing but empty promises," he replied defiantly. "They butter us up and send us back to our hovels, only to fleece us even more thoroughly later." He turned to the bystanders, among whom his two bodyguards nodded more vigorously than anyone. "They're scared. *That's* what this talk of negotiations tells us. Those fine gentlemen are shitting their hose—the abbots, the knights, the counts, all of them. Now, of all times, we mustn't give way by as much as an inch."

"But suppose they really do want to negotiate?" Mathis asked.

Jockel looked at him sardonically. "Is that what you believe? Do you believe they'd voluntarily give up their sinecures and their tithes?"

"Not all of them, for sure. But we ought to at least listen to what they have to say."

"Ho, of course!" Jockel laughed contemptuously. "Go to Memmingen in Swabia and listen. Let them lull you into a sense of security while they assemble their landsknechts." He lowered his voice to a confidential tone. "They need time, Mathis, don't you understand that? Too many of the imperial soldiers are still fighting in Italy. The nobility negotiate while they're already planning our downfall behind our backs. But we're not taking any of that. We're not silly, innocent little lambs to be led to the slaughter. We're fighting men, and we will win!"

More and more peasants had come over to them from the campfires, curious to know what was going on. The bodyguards pushed a few who were coming too close to their leader away. Here and there someone cheered.

"We must send out a signal," Jockel cried, turning to the crowd. "We must show those moneybags, those dukes and abbots, that we're not being taken in. Let's show the allies who will soon be here what we're made of. Are you ready for that?"

The men shouted approval, first hesitantly, then louder and louder, and Jockel, his eyes burning, went on, "Then let's burn down Eusserthal monastery! The fat clerics there have been a thorn in our side for too long. This part of the country needs just one spark to light the fire, and Eusserthal will be that spark. We'll prepare a fitting welcome for our friends. A monastery as the headquarters of a band of peasants. The church can be our stable, and the abbot's wine cellar our tavern. How do you like the sound of that?"

The crowd laughed and hooted. Many men held up their spears and scythes, making a field of spikes that waved in the wind and filled the whole forest clearing.

"Three cheers for Shepherd Jockel! Three cheers!" they cried, and their leader, satisfied, nodded. Then he glanced at Mathis, and a slight smile flitted over his face.

"That's what you wanted, Mathis, didn't you?" he said, speaking more calmly now. "A sheltered place for our future army. Thank you for giving me the idea. If you go on like that, I'll make you my deputy yet."

Briefly, Mathis closed his eyes. There was no point in turning to the crowd again now. Even the initially skeptical envoys from Dahn and Wilgartswiesen had joined in the general rejoicing. By getting his word in first, Jockel had quickly regained the leadership that, for a moment, had threatened to slip from his grasp.

Eusserthal monastery, unlike the castles in its neighborhood, would be easy both to capture and to defend. It would offer them shelter, and its conquest would be a clear signal to the country round about that battle had begun. And wasn't that, after all, what Mathis wanted?

But then Mathis thought of all the monks there. Abbot Weigand might be a swine, but what about kindly Brother Jörg in the gatehouse? In the old days, Mathis had often brought him new horseshoes for the monastery's two horses. What about the many young novices? At least Father Tristan would be safe at Trifels Castle, thought Mathis, and gave a sudden start.

Or will we soon be attacking Trifels, too? And then, what about Agnes?

"Death to the prelates, down with the palaces!" The clearing echoed to the shouting of the crowd. Even old Ulrich Reichhart had joined in. Only Mathis remained silent.

He brought his hammer down on the iron of the gun, which at last was red-hot, while Shepherd Jockel scrutinized him distrustfully.

The next day, Friedrich von Löwenstein-Scharfeneck stood on the edge of the well in the Trifels well tower, looking down at the dark hole before his feet. Deep below him there was a bubbling, rushing sound, a distant cry, and then two guards turned a squealing winch. After a while a man appeared out of the darkness of the well shaft, tied to a long rope and wearing nothing but a loincloth. He was shivering hard, coughing, and spitting out mucus and water.

"Well?" Scharfeneck asked impatiently. "Find anything?"

The man shook his head, spraying water in all directions, like a wet dog. "Nothing, Your Grace. I searched the whole of the bottom of the well with my hands, there's stones there, old pieces of wood, a few rusty kreuzers, but that's all, I swear, God be my witness."

"Then keep searching, damn it all! There must be something down there. All the written records suggest it."

"Please, my lord," croaked the man, one of Friedrich's close circle of soldiers. He was still shivering with cold. "I'm frozen to the marrow. And it's dark as hell down there. The Devil only know what monsters may be . . ."

His voice died away as his two comrades went back to work, winding the winch the other way, and the soldier, gesticulating wildly, slowly disappeared into the depths. It was obvious that the two guards wouldn't have changed places with their friend even for a year's wages.

"Does he have to do this?" asked Agnes, who was leaning against the wall of the little shelter above the well with her arms crossed, watching as the outline of the poor guard grew smaller and smaller as he went down. "He's already been searching the well for ages. This is the fourth time you've sent him down. It must be well over two hundred feet down to the groundwater. Much more of this, and he'll freeze to death on you." She pointed to the dripping icicles hanging from the winch. A thaw had begun to set in during the last couple of days, but nonetheless it was still bitterly cold, even at midday and in bright sunlight.

"How often do I have to tell you not to interfere in my business?" Friedrich snapped. "And what do you know about it, anyway? I've been studying this castle for years. The well tower is one of the oldest buildings at Trifels. It was erected just after Emperor Henry VI brought the Norman treasure here. There couldn't be a better hiding place."

"If the treasure really is hidden somewhere here," Agnes said sharply. "But I for one am more and more inclined to believe it's just a legend, like so much about Trifels."

"Believe what you like, but spare me your chatter, woman." The count turned to the two smirking guards, who had not refrained from listening to this marital disagreement. "And as for you two, I'll soon wipe that stupid grin off your faces," Friedrich threatened. "If your friend comes back up again without good news next time, then we'll bale out the well. That'll give you something else to think about."

One of the guards answered, horrified. "But Your Grace, no one knows how much water there is down there. It could take weeks."

"We'll do it even if it takes an eternity!" the count shouted. "That accursed treasure must be somewhere."

Sighing, Agnes left her husband alone in the tower and crossed the ramshackle bridge to the castle courtyard. From the battlements, she looked at her new home, nearby Scharfenberg Castle, now attractively plastered in red and white. There was a kind of armistice between the young count and his wife. When they were alone, Friedrich was quite likely to accept the suggestions that Agnes made. In that way, she had made sure that not just Scharfenberg but Trifels, too, profited from the renovations. Now and then the count could even be good company. He sent to Speyer for books for her, and he did not forbid her either to go hawking or to wear the hose in which she felt comfortable when riding.

Yet Agnes never forgot that it had been Friedrich von Löwenstein-Scharfeneck who had callously murdered her father. He was unscrupulous in his pursuit of power and fanatical on some subjects, notably the legendary Norman treasure. Sometimes it seemed to her that Friedrich's obsession was tipping over into madness. It was a long while since that she, too, had believed that Emperor Henry had hidden part of the loot from his wars somewhere here. Presumably the money had simply been squandered in the course of time.

On the spur of the moment, she decided to pay a visit to the guards Gunther and Eberhart. She had not been to Trifels for some time. As usual, the two men-at-arms, wrapped in their threadbare woolen coats, were sitting on the stairs to the upper bailey. When they saw Agnes, they jumped to their feet and stood at attention.

"Welcome . . . welcome, my lady," stammered Gunther, bowing low. "It's good to see you."

Agnes smiled. She remembered how these same men used to tell her off not so many years ago.

"That's all right, Gunther," she replied. "Don't bow too low—it won't do your old bones any good. Tell me how things are here at the castle instead."

"The bones of Trifels are considerably older than mine," the guard replied, grinning. "But it's good for the castle that someone's taking a little care of it." Suddenly, however, his expression grew more serious. "All the same, it's not like the old days, when your worthy father was alive."

Agnes nodded. To these men, Philipp von Erfenstein had died of gangrene. Only she and Father Tristan knew what had really happened, and she felt hatred of her husband rise in her again.

I ought to poison him as he poisoned my father, she thought. *I just don't have the courage to do it.*

The two men-at-arms were looking at her, baffled, and Agnes realized that it was some time since she had said anything. "I'll go and make sure that all is well indoors," she finally said, hesitantly, so as not to confuse the men any more. "I think I feel a little homesick."

"Of course, my lady. You still know your way around, don't you?"

"Better than I know my own heart," she said sadly.

Bowing again, the guards stepped aside, and Agnes climbed the steps to the upper bailey. Once there, she entered the tower. As if some inner urge were guiding her, her steps led her to the library door on the fourth floor. It was weeks since she had last been here. When she pressed the handle of the door, it swung open without a sound. The smell of old parchment, dust, and yellowing paper received her like an old friend. Her glance moved over the many rows of books and scrolls in the shelves along the walls. Dreamily, she closed her eyes. How often she had sat by the stove here, reading, and forgetting the world around her. She thought of Father Tristan, and a sharp pang of nostalgia rose in her. She hadn't seen her father confessor for weeks.

Aimlessly, Agnes went over to one of the shelves and stroked the spines of individual books. Friedrich had taken the chronicle of Trifels to Scharfenberg Castle with him, as well as several other works that he thought would tell him more about the Norman treasure. All the same, there was still enough here for anyone to read on many long winter nights. She wondered whether to take a few of the books back to Scharfenberg herself.

Suddenly Agnes remembered the banned books of Martin Luther and Philipp Melanchthon, and the secret compartment where Father Tristan used to keep them. Had her husband discovered it yet? She looked for the secret wooden spine, pulled it out, and the little hidden flap opened to show the space behind it.

The niche was empty.

Agnes frowned. If Friedrich had found those forbidden books, he would surely have welcomed that as a reason to get rid of the old monk—and she would have heard about it. So it was more likely that Father Tristan himself had destroyed the books or maybe taken them to Eusserthal with him. She leaned to look farther into the space, felt its dusty base again, and suddenly her fingers touched a scrap of parchment. When she took it out into the light, she saw that it was of the same consistency as the parchment pages that had been removed from the chronicle of Trifels. As Agnes recollected, several pages had been torn out. Could this be a piece of one of them?

The scrap was not much larger than her thumb, and charred at the edges. Only a few words could still be made out on it. Agnes held it close to her eyes so that she could read them better in the dim light of the library.

Ioannes et Constanza fugae se mandabant . . .

"Johann and Constanza took flight," she quietly murmured.

Agnes felt her heart beat faster. Johann was clearly Johann of Brunswick, who had featured so often in her dreams. And Constanza? Agnes thought of her own feelings during the dreams, of the love she had felt for Johann. They had not been her own emotions, but those of a woman through whose eyes Agnes experienced her dreams.

Constanza . . .

At last she knew her name. Breathing hard, Agnes closed her eyes and tried to remember everything that she had dreamed since finding the ring. The woman called Constanza had obviously met Johann of Brunswick when he was dubbed a knight at Trifels Castle. According to the chronicle of the castle, that had been in 1293. The two of them became lovers and had a child, but something stood between them.

Something that, in some way, had to do with the ring that Constanza carried with her. Had Johann really been plotting against the Habsburg king Albrecht, or had that just been an excuse to get rid of him and Constanza? When the little family fled from Trifels, Constanza had been carrying something wrapped in a cloth. What, for heaven's sake, had happened then?

Agnes remembered what Father Tristan had told her about the missing pages.

Someone probably wanted that dark chapter to be forgotten forever . . .

The monk had thought at the time that the Guelph, Johann of Brunswick, had been captured and killed in Speyer during his attempt to escape. But that was not the whole truth. Johann and Constanza had fled from Trifels together.

Lost in thought, Agnes felt the crumpled scrap of parchment. What had happened to that woman? And why did she keep thinking of her? Why had the pages been torn out of the book? Why . . .

Realization hit her like a blow.

Father Tristan had claimed that the pages had been torn out long ago. But the forgotten scrap in the secret compartment suggested a very different interpretation: he himself had removed the missing chapter.

Agnes closed her hand around the little piece of parchment. Getting to her feet, she went to the library door, her thoughts still hard at work. Father Tristan had lied to her, probably several times. Just before her father's death, for instance . . .

Pursing her lips, Agnes hurried down the steps of the tower and out into the yard, where the surprised guards hastily rose and bowed again. But the new Countess von Löwenstein-Scharfeneck, mistress of Trifels Castle and daughter of the knight Philipp von Erfenstein, took no notice of them.

Agnes had to talk to Father Tristan, and soon.

· 15 ·

Eusserthal Monastery, 8 April, Anno Domini 1525

DAWN WAS BREAKING WHEN THE peasants attacked Eusserthal monastery, just before Lauds, the first divine office of the day.

The sun was still hidden behind the treetops of the forest, announcing its imminent rise with a tinge of reddish light on the horizon. It lent a glow to the sandstone of the monastery building—it reminded Mathis of blood.

All the blood that will soon be shed here, he thought. *And not the Savior's blood transformed into wine, but real, spurting blood.*

In the faint light of dawn, the usually beautiful valley that lay hidden between two chains of hills suddenly seemed strange and uncanny, like a pit full of murderers. There were about a hundred men lurking behind low brushwood and hawthorn hedges, listening for their leader's command. Shepherd Jockel had not waited for the band from the country around Dahn and Wilgartswiesen to join them. Mathis suspected that he wanted to present the others with a situation showing who, in the band they were forming together, had the last word. A leader who could offer his allies a camp in a monastery with cellars full of provisions could be sure of many supporters.

Mathis looked to right and left, seeing the determined faces of peasants and laborers, sooty charcoal burners, ragged shepherds, cowherds, knackers, and journeymen millers; there were even a few Annweiler citizens among the insurgents. As weapons, they carried scythes, threshing flails, spears, sickles, and rusty daggers. Many of them did not even possess shoes but had only rags to wrap around the chilblains on their feet. Their leather hose were torn, their bearded faces gaunt with hunger and want. Mathis had no illusions: as soon as these men met the fat monks, with their full larders and richly adorned altars, greed would carry them away like a raging torrent. It was true that Mathis himself, Ulrich Reichhart, even Shepherd Jockel had warned the peasants against unbridled excess—after all, they wanted to be able to use the monastery as an army camp once they had taken it—but he had only to look into their eyes to know there was no prospect of their paying any attention to that warning.

They had the eyes of hungry wolves.

At a whistle from Jockel, a vanguard party of about a dozen men ran, bending low, to the gatehouse with its two massive oak doors. The monastery lay in a large clearing, near several peasants' cottages whose inhabitants had joined the revolt, whether they had wanted to or not. The monastery buildings themselves were surrounded by a wall nine feet high with a gatehouse on the western side. A small stream had been diverted to flow directly into the monastery, at a point roughly where the flat roof of the metal-casting workshop showed behind the wall. Once again, Mathis felt his conscience prick him. The monks had let him cast the heavy cannon within their precincts, they had put their furnaces at his disposal, and they had been as helpful and obliging as on the earlier occasion when he had watched the bell being cast. On the other hand, Mathis had seen their lavish way of life, while peasant children were starving only a stone's throw away.

It is as it is, he thought gloomily, *and I can't change it now. I can only try to prevent more people from dying than is absolutely necessary.*

In the light of dawn, Mathis now saw a peasant directly below the wall throwing a hook through the air on the end of a rope. The hook caught in the wall, and four of the men climbed the rope in silence. They made their way along the wall to the battlements above the gatehouse. Mathis heard several dull sounds and muted screams, and then a lifeless body fell from the wall to lie before the entrance. Soon after that, both halves of the heavy door swung open, and the peasants, who had been waiting anxiously in the undergrowth, ran across freshly sown vegetable beds and fallow fields to the monastery.

At that moment the high sound of a bell came from the gatehouse. It rang several times before abruptly falling silent.

"Damn it!" swore Shepherd Jockel, still waiting behind the hawthorn hedge with Mathis. His two bodyguards, Paulus and Jannsen, and the old master gunner, Reichhart, were lurking there beside them. "The second gatekeeper has managed to raise the alarm. I told the fools a hundred times to cut both men's throats at once. Now half the monastery will be roused."

And indeed, another bell soon rang, while loud shouting and the noise of fighting came from behind the wall. Mathis ran to it without paying any attention to the others. He had meant to hold back from the looting of the monastery, but now it was a case of preventing the worst of it. As he ran, he looked back for Shepherd Jockel, who was still watching from behind the hedge. After some hesitation, he too began to run, shouting as he drew the shining sword that he had taken from a marauding landsknecht. His two bodyguards stormed forward with their spears, and finally they were followed by Ulrich Reichhart.

"Down with the clerics and their ilk!" cried Jockel. "Kill them all!"

Mathis cursed quietly. This went against their agreement to conduct the attack with as little bloodshed as possible, if only to avoid infuriating the duke of Zweibrücken unnecessarily, bringing an early intervention by his landsknechts down on them. Now he got the impression that Jockel was positively anxious for a bloodbath.

When Mathis raced through the open gate toward the monastery, the fighting was in full swing. Several lifeless monastery servants and two monks were lying bent double on the ground outside the church, and there were also some peasants among the dead. A tall, broad-shouldered giant in the white habit of the Cistercians was fighting with a broken-off spit against three of the insurgents at once. He was bleeding from several wounds, reciting an Ave Maria at the top of his lungs in the morning light as he ran the spit into the side of one of the peasants. Horrified, Mathis recognized the usually kindly Brother Jörg, who had helped him to cast the cannon last year. Mathis stepped into a warm pool of blood. Looking straight ahead, he ran on to the dormitorium, where the monks had their cells. Maybe he could save at least a few lives.

There was already fighting outside the dormitorium, a large red sandstone building next to the church. Three men on an upturned cart were fighting with swords against the attacking peasants. In the last few decades, the monastery had been raided again and again, and the Cistercians had employed a series of men-at-arms—men such as these, now desperately opposing the attackers. But it was only a question of time before they were all massacred.

Mathis ran past two men fighting each other with daggers on a dunghill steaming in the cold, ducked away from a stone thrown from the shadows, and entered the building that he knew from previous visits. A few cheering peasants came toward him, heavily laden with candlesticks and all kinds of glittering loot. From somewhere, Mathis smelled smoke.

When he turned the corner, he finally found himself in the passage leading to the separate cells where the monks slept. Most of them were open. Monks passed him, wailing. Some of them were kneeling to pray, others already lay lifeless and bleeding among their brothers.

"Never fear!" Mathis called loudly, realizing at the same moment how ridiculous those words must sound, in view of the surrounding horror. Nonetheless, he went on. "If you do as I say, no harm will come to you."

Briefly, the monks stopped lamenting and stared at him anxiously.

"I know you, don't I?" said one of them at last, a particularly cor-pulent Father whose voluminous white habit was stretched taut over his belly. "You're the son of the smith at Trifels Castle." His face distorted into a mask of hatred. "God curse you. You and your murderous band."

"God will judge me later," retorted Mathis. "Maybe he won't be so hard on me if I save the lives of some of his servants first. Follow me. Anyone who stays here is a dead man."

For a few instants the monks stayed where they were, undecided, muttering and praying. But Mathis had already hurried on. Finally, they ran after him, some of them helping their injured brothers, dragging them along the corridor, where the smell of burning was getting stronger. The first sheds and stables were on fire, and smoke billowed up from the metal-casting workshop as well.

If those fools out there carry on like this, we soon won't have a camp for our band at all, thought Mathis.

He turned left and had soon reached the portal leading to the cloisters. The square courtyard, surrounded by columns, linked the main building to the church. Mathis stepped into the secluded square. A marble fountain burbled in the middle of it, and stone benches between the columns invited one to sit down. For a brief moment the fighting and killing seemed to be very far away, but then a long, drawn-out scream was heard coming from somewhere, and the monks cried out and again fell to their knees.

"Get to the church," Mathis ordered. "They won't dare touch you there. And then you can go on praying, for all I care, but hurry up."

He ran across the square of the cloisters to a low door, opened it, and shooed the terrified Cistercians into the church. It had a nave, two aisles, and glazed windows through which red light now came. It took Mathis a moment to realize that it was not the light of sunrise, but of fires. The peasants had indeed set fire to the surrounding outbuildings of the monastery, the granaries, storehouses, and barns. Shouts of jubilation could be heard in the distance.

They're burning their new home. And when the fires have gone out tomorrow, we'll be cold and hungry again.

When Mathis turned his head to the altar, he suddenly saw the fat abbot of Eusserthal standing there. Weigand Handt was regarded as a poor administrator who owed his position solely to his noble birth. He was the third son of a count from the Baden area, and he exploited the resources of the monastery to enrich himself. Only Father Tristan's expert bookkeeping had kept the abbot from disgrace. At this moment, Father Weigand was throwing assorted silver candlesticks, golden goblets, and brocade-and-gem-covered jewelry boxes into a sack.

"Drop that sack if you value your life," Mathis snapped.

The big-bellied abbot jumped. When he saw who it was addressing him, his mouth twisted into an ingratiating smile.

"Ah, the young master gunner," he croaked. "I didn't expect to see you here, after all we've done for you." He ducked his head, like an animal at bay. "But I'm sure you'll see that they let me go, won't you?"

"If you leave that sack here, I'll put in a good word for you," Mathis said reluctantly.

The abbot looked at him in alarm. "But . . . but these are the holiest of relics," he stammered, running his tongue nervously over his fleshy lips. "They must be saved from the flames. Would you go against the will of God?"

Mathis gave him a thin-lipped smile. "I had no idea that silver candlesticks were holy relics. And what about the coins there in your sack? Did St. Peter himself give them to the monastery?" He indicated the brimming purse from which recently minted golden guilders clinked as they fell to the floor.

"Those . . . those are donations made by God-fearing folk," stuttered the abbot. "I—"

"Then they should be used for the good of other God-fearing folk. Put the sack down."

Abbot Weigand's shoulders drooped. For a moment it seemed like he was going to do as Mathis said, but then he suddenly shouldered the heavy sack and ran to a door beside the altar. Mathis hesitated. Ought he to go after the abbot and leave the monks to their fate? As he was still thinking it over, whimpering came from the other side of the small door, and then, finally, a shrill scream that stopped abruptly.

The door flew open, and in came Shepherd Jockel and his two bodyguards. The shirts of the two former vagabonds were wet with sweat and blood, and their faces blackened with soot, so that they looked like the devil himself. Jannsen wiped his long dagger on his coat, while Paulus flung the abbot's sack over his own shoulder. Shepherd Jockel stood between them with his arms folded, grinning at Mathis.

"Well, fancy that! Here's Mathis in the church," he said in a voice that echoed through the large building, so that even the monks farther away would be bound to hear it. "You must have a good nose for the whereabouts of a fat rat like the abbot. My compliments." He winked at Mathis. "Although you almost let him get away. It's a good thing we picked him up out there. The swine actually begged for mercy before he died. But he couldn't expect any pity from us." Shepherd Jockel spat on the consecrated ground. "Did he ever have mercy on the poor himself? A few crusts of moldy bread for the poor, and gold for the clergy. But that's all over now."

He held out his hand to Paulus for the heavy sack and greedily searched its contents. "What do you think, Mathis?" he chuckled. "How many arquebuses can be bought with this? How much gunpowder? We'll be able to blow Speyer cathedral sky-high if we want, won't we?"

"I hope that won't be necessary," replied Mathis curtly.

Now the great west door opened as well, and the peasants entered the church in silence. Mathis noticed some of them taking off their caps. Others surreptitiously made the sign of the cross.

They'll never dare to kill the monks in here, he thought. *Not beside the font where their own children were baptized.*

The monks, still uninjured, about ten or them, were now kneeling at a side altar in front of the statue of the Blessed Virgin Mary, peering in trepidation at the peasants. There was a pregnant silence in which only the sound of the flames from the nearby outbuildings could be heard.

Jockel strode firmly toward the stone pulpit that stood several feet high beside the chancel. He climbed the marble steps, placed his hands on the parapet, and looked down on his dirty troop of peasants like the proud commander of an army.

"Friends, brothers, we have won a victory," he announced, his voice ringing through the large church. "But it is only the first of our victories. Many others will follow. The power of the nobility and the church is over at last."

The men shouted and cheered, and only now did many of them seem to cast off their awe of the consecrated building entirely. They stamped their feet, raising their sickles and scythes into the air.

Now Shepherd Jockel pointed to the band of monks crouching in front of the altar to the Virgin like frightened lambs. "These clerics drank your wine, they ate your bread, they slaughtered your calves," he cried. "You obediently paid your tithes to the church year in, year out, yet your children went hungry while these fat monks in their white robes lived like lords." All of a sudden he tipped the contents of the sack over the parapet of the pulpit, sending the silver candlesticks, goblets, and coins crashing to the floor. "They stole all this from you," he shouted. "And now they must have their due punishment. So I say, hang them! Hang them high from the windows of their church, so that their fellow brothers in other monasteries can see what happens to those who have stolen from us for so long."

Once again the men cheered him, but not so wholeheartedly this time. Mathis saw a number of them glancing around anxiously. Ulrich Reichhart, standing at the back of the crowd, shook his head and made a disapproving sound. The wailing and praying of the monks rose to a single litany of lamentation.

"Be quiet, all of you. Be quiet, I say!"

Mathis had raised his voice without actually intending to. Now all the men were looking expectantly at him.

They want me to tell them what to do and what not to do. Damn it, why didn't I keep my mouth shut?

"We have done all that we intended," he went on, feeling his way. "We have captured the monastery, the larders and cellars are ours and the church treasures too, and the abbot has met with his just fate. Now let's show these bloodsuckers how true Christian folk behave. They show mercy."

A murmur went through the body of the church.

"Our enemy is not God," Mathis went on, in a stronger voice. "It is the Roman church that oppresses us. The pope and his cardinals and bishops. As Martin Luther has said—"

"Luther's no better than the rest of the clergy," Shepherd Jockel roughly interrupted him. Speaking from the pulpit above them, his voice was much louder and more audible than the voice of Mathis. "Oh yes, he promises you the kingdom of heaven, but only if you've been meek and mild here on earth. The man Luther is hand in glove with the elector of Saxony; he's not one of us, he's one of the oppressors."

"And so are we, if we act as they do," Mathis protested, turning almost pleadingly to the peasants standing around. "I tell you, if we hang these monks we're not a whit better than that accursed Mayor Gessler, who's burning in hell now for his evil deeds."

That last remark aroused more discussion among the men. Mathis saw them nodding, and angling their heads together. Jockel's fingers clutched the parapet of the pulpit. His eyes roamed uneasily over his followers down below. He clearly felt his control over them slipping slowly away.

"If we let these monks go, they'll run to their bishop and tell him we are craven, a soft touch," he tried again, this time in a milder tone. "Friends, we can't show any mercy or we have no prospect of victory. We must—"

"I've killed three men in the last hour," Ulrich Reichhart interrupted him. "That's enough for me. I want no more blood on my hands."

"Not all those monks were bad," said another man, an old man, trembling as he leaned on his scythe. "Think of Father Tristan. He cured so many of us with his medicines."

"Brother Emanuel always had a bit of bread for our children," pointed out a younger peasant. "And now he's lying out there in his own blood. That can't be right."

Shepherd Jockel rolled his eyes. "You'll always find some little monk ready to give a poor peasant a crumb of bread," he replied. "But they keep the meat for themselves. The good meat and the gold. They soothe you, they sing you to sleep, and after that . . ."

"I've made my choice," Ulrich Reichhart announced firmly. "I'm not killing any more monks. Let's go and put those fires out instead, or we won't have a roof left over our heads anymore."

Without another word, he turned and went out. Two or three other men followed him. The others went on whispering for a while, and finally they, too, left the church singly or in groups. In the end the only insurgents left were Mathis and Shepherd Jockel, while the Cistercians quietly began singing a hymn in front of the altar to the Virgin. Many of them were shivering and weeping, or had thrown themselves down on the cold flagstones of the church floor with their arms outspread, like living crosses.

"I'll never forgive you for this, Mathis, never," Jockel hissed from the pulpit. With his hunched back, missing fingers, and piercing gaze, he made Mathis think of one of the gargoyles looking down on them both from the roof of the church. "Undermining me like that. I still have authority over you, and don't you forget it."

Mathis shrugged. "I thought the whole point of our insurgency was to cast off the authorities," he replied coolly. Then he turned and, with his head held high, he left the church by the great west door. Outside, buildings burned in the early morning air.

But sensing the hostile glance of Jockel behind him, he guessed that he had made a powerful enemy.

. . .

A good two hours later, Mathis was trudging through the last of the snowdrifts lying in the grounds of the monastery, helping to clear up. There were fires to be extinguished, doors to be nailed back in place, the injured to be tended, and dead men to be carried away.

The peasants had laid all the bodies out neatly, side by side, near the graveyard. Rigid and pale, monks and monastery servants lay beside the insurgents, united in death. Under the watchful eyes of the bodyguards Jannsen and Paulus, the looted treasures were stacked up in a heap outside the church. Greedy eyes kept going to the many silver candlesticks, the chests and caskets, gilded crosses, and figures of saints. But Jockel had made it clear that any theft would be harshly punished. Mathis gave his own support to that threat. After all, the money was to be used to buy weapons, yes, but above all it would be spent for the common good. In that way, everyone would benefit.

Jockel sat cross-legged beside the glittering pile, drawing up a list of the looted items in a well-worn notebook with a quill pen. He did not deign to give Mathis a glance when the younger man passed him. But some of the peasants clapped the young weaponsmith encouragingly on the shoulder, clearly glad that Mathis had managed to put an end to the bloodbath.

The peasants had locked the surviving monks of Eusserthal in one of the cellars used for storage. They were to stay there as hostages until the monastery was ready to be defended against attack, and reinforcements from Dahn and Wilgartswiesen had arrived. Mathis labored under no illusions: they wouldn't be able to hold out for a single day against a well-equipped army of landsknechts, even behind the high monastery walls. By attacking Eusserthal, the peasants of the Annweiler area had declared war on the bishop of Speyer, the duke of Zweibrücken, indeed the entire Palatinate. An answer would soon follow, and before then they must have gathered as many men as possible around them. That was their only chance.

There was no going back now.

Mathis decided to take another look at the monastery dormitorium, in search of a suitable place for a future arsenal that could be kept under lock and key. He turned right, crossed the chapter where, until yesterday evening, the monks had met for daily readings and sermons, and cast a brief glance at the refectorium. The peasants had done a great deal of damage to the monks' dining room. Chairs and tables had been overturned, shards of broken plates and dishes lay all over the floor, and one of the insurgents had left a stinking pile of shit on the cushioned chair where the abbot used to sit enthroned. Wrinkling his nose, Mathis climbed the stairs to the floor above. There was less destruction here, as many of the peasants had never found their way to the upper floor. On the left there were several rooms, but one in particular interested Mathis, since it had a large lock on the door. That might be a good place to keep the firearms they would have in future. A notice on the door itself told him what the room was currently: SCRIPTORIUM.

When Mathis tried the handle, he found that the door was already slightly ajar. It swung open, revealing a row of desks with an inkwell and a stack of parchment pages cut to size on each of them. A white-robed figure lay over the desk at the back, his head down on the top of it, his fingers convulsively clutching a quill pen. Looking more closely, Mathis saw blood dripping steadily, like thick ink, to the floor. A moment later, Mathis froze, rigid with shock.

The lifeless man at the desk was Father Tristan.

"Oh, my God!" Mathis ran to the old man and cautiously raised him. Father Tristan was still alive, but his breathing was stertorous and irregular. A deep wound gaped open on his neck, and the right side of his white habit was wet with blood.

"Father!" Mathis cried. "I . . . I am so sorry. By all the saints, I didn't want anything like this."

He had assumed that Father Tristan was still at Trifels Castle, and it almost broke his heart to find him here so badly injured. He had known the old monk since he was a little boy. Father Tristan had helped him when he was learning to read and had always had a kind word for him or some little snack for him to nibble. When Mathis had been closer to death than life at the age of nine, feverish and coughing, the old man had cured him after watching over him during long nights. Suddenly the whole of his short life seemed to Mathis pointless. All he had ever done was quarrel, fight, and make things that killed other people. How could he have abandoned himself to such madness?

"Who did this?" he asked, although he knew that the answer was irrelevant. Some peasant, spurred on by his anger, had stabbed the old man like he might slaughter a pig. Mathis saw a large pool of blood in one corner of the scriptorium. Presumably the old monk had fled there before the spear or knife caught him. A red smear of blood formed a trail to the desk, on which a sheet of parchment lay, drenched with blood, but partly covered with writing. Had Father Tristan been trying to write a farewell letter?

"Mathis, my dear Mathis . . ."

Mathis gave a start at the sudden sound of the old man's hoarse voice. Father Tristan had opened his eyes and was looking at him with a smile. His skin was pale, and as wrinkled as a dried apple, his face seemed to consist entirely of lines, and his aquiline nose stood out from it.

"I knew that God would hear me," he murmured. "You . . . you were sent here by heaven."

"Hell, more likely," Mathis said sadly. He felt for Father Tristan's heart. It beat weakly and unsteadily. "Father, I'm going to get help," he went on. "We'll move you down to the infirmary of the monastery, and then—"

Father Tristan held Mathis's hand so tightly that he stopped talking in alarm.

"No time . . ." the monk gasped. "The letter . . . Agnes . . ."

Confused, Mathis looked at him, and then at the sheet of parchment lying on the desk.

"What about the letter?" he asked. But Father Tristan had already closed his eyes again, and only the faint rattle of his breathing was to be heard.

"Curse it!" Cautiously, Mathis laid the injured monk down on the cold floor of the scriptorium and glanced at the desk. The letter had been written in a hurry and was stained with blood. Father Tristan had managed to complete only a few lines. Leaning over the letter, Mathis began to read it, murmuring to himself.

Dear Agnes, when you read these lines I shall probably be with my God. Do not grieve; I am an old man, and have been granted more years than most others. What I feared has happened: the peasants have confused anger with justice and are storming the monastery. I hope that in his boundless kindness, the Lord will allow one of the monastery servants to escape and bring you this letter.

You have often asked me what your dreams mean, and I told you they were only figments of your imagination. I was lying. It is the ring that awakened something in you, something that had been hidden for a long time. I thought it best to tell you no more. But now I believe you have a right to learn about your past. There is an ancient monastery near Bingen, on the river Rhine. Its name is St. Goar. The canons there have guarded the knowledge of the empire for hundreds of years, and they also know that

The letter ended abruptly, with one more stroke of the pen running right across the parchment. Mathis suspected that was when the peasants had stormed the scriptorium. He hastily hid the letter under his coat. He would think about it later. But for now he must make sure that Father Tristan survived, at least for the next few hours. Maybe there was still hope.

Carefully, he lifted the old man's astonishingly light body and put him over his shoulder as he might carry a small child. Then he staggered out into the corridor and went downstairs to the first floor.

Tears were running down his face. He would tell the peasants they were from the smoke of fires not yet extinguished. They would believe him, because they considered him one of their leaders.

But he could not lie to himself.

. . .

Agnes saw the smoking fires from one of the hills crossed by the narrow track as it wound its way down into the valley. She might still be a good mile away from the monastery, but it was already easy to see the separate buildings. It looked like the whole of Eusserthal had fallen victim to the flames.

It was now two days since she had found the scrap of parchment bearing the names of Johann and Constanza in the secret compartment in the library. Since then Agnes had been waiting for a chance to leave the castle in secret. On no account must Friedrich have any idea that she wanted to see her old father confessor. The count knew that Father Tristan suspected him of murdering Philipp von Erfenstein with poison, and he did not trust the old monk an inch. But today her husband was out in the forest around Trifels Castle and would be supervising several excavations there until evening. So it was a good opportunity. Late in the morning, dressed inconspicuously as a pilgrim, she had set out on the narrow donkey track through the woods and over the hills to the monastery, a walk of just under three hours.

Holding her breath, Agnes stared at the large clearing, over which a pall of gray vapors hung. The fires in the monastery and the church had seemingly been put out already, but thin threads of smoke still rose, and red tongues of flame still licked at many of the sheds and surrounding buildings. Up here on the hill she caught the acrid smell of smoke. What in God's name had happened down there? There had been no thunderstorm recently, and the fire had been too large to be the result of a minor accident in the bakehouse. Had the monastery come under attack? By whom?

Dear God, don't let anything have happened to Father Tristan, Agnes thought. *Let all this be just a bad dream.*

She began to run, but after only a few steps she hesitated. If there really had been an attack down there, brigands could still be roaming nearby. On the other hand, she really must find out about Father Tristan.

The steep, winding track turned to a broader one that could take a cart; it was set between high banks. The first of the monastery's fields and meadows came into view. Agnes took a deep breath and then decided to make straight for the monastery itself.

After only a few moments, she knew it had been the wrong decision.

Mathis stared at the three figures approaching the forecourt of the monastery, unable to believe his eyes.

But the girl between the two men who had been on guard really was Agnes. Mathis had just carried Father Tristan down to the infirmary, where one of the monastery's terrified maidservants would tend him along with a few injured peasants. Mathis had felt for the strange letter under his coat several times, always thinking of Agnes—and now here she was, staggering toward the monastery gate with her hands tied and her forehead bleeding. She wore her old leather hose and a thin, torn shirt; her hair was dirty and untidy; and she was trembling all over. Nonetheless, Agnes still looked as lovely as he remembered her from their last meeting, just before the siege of Ramburg Castle.

By now a whole group had gathered around the captive. The men laughed and cheered like the guards had shot a royal stag. One of them pulled Agnes's hair, another tugged at her shirt so that it tore even more over the shoulder, exposing her breasts. Agnes covered them with her bound hands, ducking and turning while more and more hands reached out for her hair, her face, her bosom. In spite of her unfortunate situation, she still had the aura of pride that Mathis had always admired.

"Stop that at once!" Mathis stormed toward the group, pulling a couple of the men aside, and pushing one of them away so hard that he fell on the seat of his hose, dazed. He hit another in the face.

"What's the big idea?" the man demanded, a hand to his split lip. Blood dripped on the ground. "You get to the back of the line if you want your share of the fun."

"You're no better than animals," Mathis swore at him. "Stinking, rutting animals." The other men stepped aside, looking at him suspiciously.

Agnes still had her bound hands raised, this time to protect her face. She slowly lowered them, and her eyes widened. Only now did she seem to realize who had come to her aid.

"Mathis!" she cried, looking at him in horror. "You, here? But . . . but . . ."

"I see those two know each other already."

It was the voice of Shepherd Jockel, who had heard the uproar and was now approaching the group. His eyes went slowly from Mathis to Agnes and back again. An expression of mock surprise came over Jockel's face.

"Why, of course, the daughter of the castellan at Trifels and her former weaponsmith. What a delightful reunion." He looked distrustfully at Mathis. "I might almost think you had some special interest in the girl, from the way you were acting."

"I don't like to see men behaving like animals, that's all." Mathis looked down awkwardly. None of the peasants knew how close Agnes really was to him. To them, he was only the former smith at Trifels Castle, and she his former mistress, now Countess von Löwenstein-Scharfeneck. His conduct must surprise the men, who would probably think him more likely to spit in her face.

"No woman deserves to be treated like that," he said brusquely.

There was an unpleasant spark in Jockel's eyes. Suddenly, in a feminine gesture, he put a finger to his lips.

"Oh, Mathis! You, here? But . . . but . . ." he said, imitating Agnes in a shrill, piping voice. The men roared with laughter.

"If I didn't know that you're my best man, and hate the nobility like the devil himself, I might think there was something between the two of you," said Jockel at last. "Tell me, Mathis, is there? Come on, speak up! Have you been rolling in the hay with the pretty countess here?"

"Nonsense," Mathis replied, doing his best not to look either Jockel or Agnes in the eye. "We're acquainted with each other, that's all."

The men were perfectly quiet now, expectantly watching the quarrel between their two leaders.

Finally Jockel gave an understanding nod. "If you say so. Then you won't object if we lock up Her Excellency the countess now. The peasants' council can decide this evening what we do with her." He turned to the bystanders, speaking loudly, and pointing with visible disgust to Agnes. "Look at this woman, men. She may appear innocent now, but her husband is one of the greatest scoundrels in the Palatinate. His landsknechts have devastated our fields, his stewards squeeze the last kreuzer out of us peasants. And with that money he buys his wife the finest clothes while our children go in rags. Now she'll bleed for what he's done to us!"

The peasants cheered. Greedy eyes wandered over Agnes in her torn shirt.

"It's not the countess who did you wrong," protested Mathis. "Don't forget, it was the count. Let me—"

"You won't cheat us of our reward this time," Jockel said to him in a dangerous whisper. "The monks can go free for all I care, they're harmless old fellows. But not the countess. She is ours. God himself has brought her to us."

Mathis's attempts to reply were drowned out by the shouting men. They roared, bellowed, bawled. Only when Agnes herself raised her voice did it become quieter. She had raised her head proudly, and no one but Mathis noticed the slight tremor spreading from her hands over her whole body. At that moment, Agnes did indeed look like a great lady born.

"Where is Father Tristan?" she asked in a firm voice.

Jockel scrutinized her with hate-filled eyes. "Who, castellan's daughter?"

"My father confessor. I came to visit him. If I am to die, I want to see him one last time, at least." Agnes hesitated. "Or is he dead?"

"How would I know? We slit the fat bellies of a few of those clerics. Could be that your father confessor was among them." Shrugging his shoulders, Jockel looked around at the peasants. It was Mathis who finally replied.

"Father Tristan is lying in the infirmary, gravely injured," he said quietly, still not looking at Agnes. "His breathing is faint, but he is still alive."

Jockel laughed. "Then take her to him, and look sharp about it. Before it's too late. For both of them," he added after a pause, with a malicious smile. "We'll decide what's to be done with the woman this evening. The Wasgau needs a clear signal that our patience is at an end." Casually, Jockel nodded to his two bodyguards. "Jannsen, Paulus, take her ladyship to the old fool. Mathis can show you where the infirmary is. If the priest's still alive, he can hear her confession, whether in a shed or the latrine, I don't mind."

"It'll be better if I go too," Ulrich Reichhart said, suddenly speaking up as he stepped out of the crowd. "I've known Mathis a long time. He fancies the woman, believe me. Devil only knows what he might be persuaded to do."

Shocked, Mathis looked at the old master gunner from Trifels Castle. When Reichhart merely raised his eyebrows in a warning gesture, he said nothing.

Jockel frowned suspiciously, but at last he nodded. "You're right, better safe than sorry." He gave a lordly wave of his three-fingered hand. "Now, off with you, before I regret my good deed."

With arms outspread, he turned to his supporters. "The clergy promised us the kingdom of heaven on Earth!" he shouted. "And nothing came of it. So now we'll make hell hot for them. A cleansing fire to sweep all rulers from the face of the earth. Are you ready to tread that path with me?"

The men roared like a single great animal.

While the peasants rejoiced, Agnes walked over to the big monastery building with Mathis, Ulrich Reichhart, and the two guards. She stared straight ahead, her lips set in a frown. She would never let the men see her shed tears.

She did not know which horrified her more: the fact that Father Tristan was dying or Mathis's betrayal. She had known that he had joined the insurgents, but she would never have expected to find him here among murderers and hell-raisers. Yes, he had often talked about injustice and the imminent likelihood of the peasants rising, but it had always sounded so harmless. Now she saw what it really meant —murder, robbery, and the devastation of the countryside. Could she have been so mistaken about him?

But then it occurred to her that soon none of her doubts would make any difference. The peasants would kill her to revenge themselves on her husband. Slowly, she fell victim to mortal fear. When she entered the cold, drafty corridors of the monastery, everything went dark before her eyes for a brief moment. She swayed on her feet, and Mathis caught her.

"Are you—" he began, but Agnes pushed him away.

"Leave me alone!" she snapped. "And don't you ever touch me again."

Startled, Mathis stepped aside, and the two guards grinned.

"Look at that, then—the little turtle dove pecks," said Jannsen, nudging his friend in the ribs. "Well, we'll soon teach her better."

Paulus uttered a coarse laugh, gave Agnes a push, and she made her way on, swaying down the monastery corridors, past the ruins of the refectory and several of the monks' cells. Her shoulder was still throbbing from her fall, the wound on her forehead wouldn't stop bleeding, but one thought kept her going: if she was to die soon, she at least wanted to know, first, what her dreams meant, and who Constanza was. Deep inside, she sensed that Constanza's fate and her own were connected in some strange way.

They finally reached the door of the infirmary. Paulus kicked it, and it swung open, creaking. A strong smell of incense, herbs, and excrement rose to Agnes's nostrils. The room had been burned out, and in the smoky air it was difficult to see the rickety beds. A couple of the injured peasants looked up in alarm.

"Where's the monk?" asked Jannsen.

Hesitantly, one of the monastery's maidservants pointed to a corner where a single bed stood in the lingering smoke. The figure on it was as frail and withered as a scarecrow.

"Father Tristan!" Agnes cried, starting toward the bed before Jannsen seized her shoulder.

"Not so fast, little turtle dove," he growled. "We want to be there when you pour out your heart."

"This is a confession, you blockhead. Have you forgotten?" Ulrich Reichhart propelled the startled guard toward the door. "If there's still a spark of Christian charity in you, let's go out and wait."

The four men did indeed go to wait outside the door, and Agnes approached the bed in the corner on her own. She knelt down, her heart beating fast, and took Father Tristan's wrinkled hand. It was as cold as death. Drifting smoke from the incense enveloped them both, leaving the rest of the infirmary in twilight.

"Father," Agnes whispered. "Can you hear me?"

Father Tristan had closed his eyes, but now he opened them, and looked at Agnes with a smile. A sigh of relief escaped his roughened lips.

"I knew that God would hear my prayer," he murmured. "Tell me, dear girl, do you have my letter?"

Agnes frowned. "What letter, Father?"

A coughing fit shook the old man. He brought up blood that dripped on the white sheet.

"I . . . I wrote you a letter," he gasped at last. "In the scriptorium. It is very important. I waited far too long to tell you everything. I wanted to . . . shield you. But it's useless. The midwife Elsbeth Rechsteiner told me that they were after you. You must get away, Agnes. Leave the castle as soon as you can."

"Midwife?" Agnes shook her head. "Get away? I don't understand . . ." Thoughts fluttered around in her mind like butterflies. She had wanted to know so much from Father Tristan, and now she heard only new puzzles.

"I found a scrap of parchment from the old chronicle," she began, faltering. "There were two names on it. Johann and Constanza. They ran away from the castle together. Father, who is Constanza? I have to know."

Father Tristan tried to smile. "She is closer to you than you may guess. Ask the canons of St. Goar, they can help you. You should find out at last who you really are. The . . . the document . . . it's in their hands. The Brotherhood gave it to them . . . the Brotherhood . . ."

His voice was failing. Agnes took his thin, wrinkled hand and held it fast.

"Father!" she cried, in such an urgent voice that the other patients in the infirmary looked at them in alarm. "Father, you can't leave me. Not now. Oh, God!"

Tears poured down her face as the old man's hand suddenly went limp. She heard a long, deep breath, and then his head fell to one side. An expression of ineffable peace spread over Father Tristan's face.

The other patients were silent, too, when they realized that the old man had left them. Even their coughing died down for a while. One of the monastery maidservants murmured a quiet prayer and dried the tears in her eyes.

"*Coindeta sui, si cum n'ai greu cossire, quar pauca son, iuvenete e tosa . . .*"

Without knowing why, Agnes found herself singing the old Occitanian lullaby that she had learned from her mother. She was still holding Father Tristan's hand and caressing it gently. It was all over. He had not answered any of her many questions, but that hardly mattered. She would soon be seeing Father Tristan in Paradise, as well as her long-dead mother, her father . . . She smiled sadly. This was where it all ended.

At that moment there was a mighty noise outside the infirmary, as if the devil himself were demanding entrance.

Next moment, the door flew open.

Mathis, waiting outside the infirmary, cursed Shepherd Jockel, himself, and the world in general. All the life had gone out of him when Agnes looked at him with hatred in her eyes. As she saw it, he was nothing but a murderer and hell-raiser, and damn it, she was right. One glance from her had brought down his whole false edifice of a just world, free peasants, and a revolt carried out with God's blessing. As long as there were men like Jockel around, nothing would ever change. One commander would take over from the last—whether a bishop, a duke, or a beggar, men were all of them evil. Had he really thought that bloodshed and arson could usher in the kingdom of heaven on Earth? Now the woman he loved was about to be killed by men whose freedom he had once longed to see.

They're like animals, he thought. *We're none of us any better than animals* . . .

He was staring at the floor, downcast, when a gentle nudge in the ribs brought him back from his thoughts. Ulrich Reichhart was giving him a meaningful look. Reichhart's eyes then went to the door on the opposite side of the passage. It had a bolt, and it looked massive. Mathis was at a loss.

What in heaven's name is his idea?

"By my grandma's ass, if I'd known this confession was going to take so long, I'd have had something to eat first," said Reichhart in annoyance. "All that killing makes a man hungry." He lowered his voice to a conspiratorial tone. "I'll just go and get a nice fat sausage from the larder."

"Larder?" Jannsen looked at him suspiciously. "What larder?"

Ulrich Reichhart pointed to the door opposite. "Didn't Jockel tell you two? We put everything edible we could find in there." He grinned. "Smoked ham and sausages, candied plums, dried cod, mead, cold roast meats . . ."

Jannsen's eyes popped out of his head as he heard this list of delicacies. "You're joking, right?"

"God, no!" laughed Reichhart. "Go and look for yourself if you don't believe me."

"Damn right I will." Jannsen drew back the heavy bolt and opened the door. It was pitch dark on the other side, so that he had to go a step or so into the room to see anything.

"Trying to make fun of me, are you?" he said. "There's no sausages in here, this is only—"

"The lumber room. I know." Ulrich Reichhart gave the guard a kick on the buttocks that sent him falling forward with a cry. Flailing his arms, Jannsen landed among chests, ladders, shelves, and dusty pitchers that broke with a deafening crash.

By now Mathis had understood the old master gunner's plan. Swiftly drawing his dagger, he put it to the throat of the startled Paulus. "In there with you, and quick." he snapped. "Before I spill your blood all over this passage."

With his hands in the air, Paulus stepped backward into the lumber room. Then, suddenly, he opened his mouth to shout for help. At the same moment, Reichhart hit him on the head with the flat of his sword. The guard toppled over on his back, and Mathis shot the bolt of the door after him. Already the bodyguards were knocking angrily.

"We don't have much time," Reichhart said. "I was here earlier, during the looting. There's a little door at the end of this passage leading into the laundry. We can reach the other side of the monastery from there. Fetch Agnes, and hurry up."

In a daze, Mathis nodded. Then he hurried into the infirmary. Agnes was still kneeling in the corner at the back of the room, beside Father Tristan's bed. She turned in alarm and stared at him. The other patients and the two maidservants looked like they had been turned to stone. Open-mouthed, they gazed at the young man gasping for breath, and at the dagger in his hand.

"Come on, quickly, Agnes!" shouted Mathis. "Get out of here."

When she did not reply he ran to her, took hold of her collar, and dragged her to the door. Only now did she seem to have overcome her fright.

"What do you think you're doing?" she spat at him. "Leave me alone. I haven't finished my confession yet. You'll be killing me soon enough."

"No one's going to kill you if you just get a move on." Mathis pushed her along the passage toward the end of it, where Ulrich Reichhart was already waiting impatiently. Jannsen was still hammering against the bolted door of the lumber room.

"We're escaping," explained Mathis breathlessly. "You, me, and old Reichhart here, so run!"

They ran along the passage and slipped together through the low door leading into the laundry room.

Mathis looked around frantically as the noise behind them grew louder. The large room, damp with steam, contained several washtubs, monks' habits hung up to dry on several wooden poles, and in the corner a large fireplace where water could be heated in a vast cauldron. Only now did Mathis notice the steady, rushing sound that came from behind the habits drying on the wooden frames. Pushing the garments aside, he was surprised to see a narrow channel of water flowing right through the laundry, toward several wooden cubicles that could be easily recognized as latrines from the stink of them.

"Devil take it!" cried Ulrich Reichhart, who had now reached the far end of the room and was flinging himself desperately against the door there. "It's locked. We can't get any farther this way."

Rapid footsteps now came from the other side of the passage to the infirmary. Mathis slammed the door through which they had come, and barricaded it with one of the wooden poles, jamming it under the catch. Soon after that, there was angry knocking.

"Open up!" cried a furious Jannsen. "This minute, or we'll burn you all inside the laundry here."

The door shook, and cracks showed in its frame. Mathis knew that it wouldn't hold for long. He looked around in a panic.

Where can we go? Through what mouse hole can we escape?

His glance fell on the channel of water flowing by and passing under the latrines. Beside him, Ulrich Reichhart seemed to have had the same idea. He jumped in, and the water came up to his knees.

"We'll probably get stuck in petrified monastic shit," he growled. "But I don't see any other way out of here."

Agnes, who seemed to have calmed down a little by now, shook her head. "No one's getting me to climb into that," she said. "Who knows where this channel leads?"

"It leads out to freedom," Ulrich Reichhart said. "I've seen that for myself. They diverted the stream. It goes right under and through the monastery, coming out again on the other side. The monks use it for washing and relieving themselves."

"Suppose there's a grating across the channel somewhere?" Agnes insisted.

Something crashed into the door behind them. The blade of an axe came through the wood.

"And anyway, who says I want to go with you murdering—" Agnes was going on, but at that moment Mathis pushed her, and she fell into the water with a cry of surprise. Ulrich Reichhart had already disappeared under the latrines.

"Dive down!" Mathis called to Agnes. "Dive, or let Jockel burn you alive. Because that's the very least he'll do to us."

"Oh, Mathis, you . . . you . . ." Agnes's voice was somewhere between terror and anger. Finally she took a deep breath and vanished under the latrines herself. As Mathis dove down after her, he heard the door breaking behind him, and shouts of triumph. Then all around him was dark.

The water was so cold that his limbs hurt. Mathis pushed himself forward along the slippery sides of the channel, fearing all the time that he might suddenly come up against a weir or simply get stuck. But the current carried him on and on. Ahead of him he could faintly see the outline of a wriggling body, which he took to be Agnes. Air was running out; an invisible hand seemed to clutch his rib cage.

There was still no end to the underground watercourse in sight. Nothing but hard rock around and above him.

Just as the first stars started to dance in front of his eyes, it suddenly grew lighter again. Pushing off with his legs, Mathis came up above the surface of the water. Cold air streamed into his lungs, filling him with life. The bright sunlight shone on his face.

When he looked up, Mathis saw Ulrich Reichhart about thirty feet ahead of him, helping Agnes out of the flowing water of the stream. She was coughing and spitting water, but at least she was alive. Fields stretched to the right and left of them. The monastery wall was only a stone's throw away.

Paddling like a dog, Mathis let himself drift a little way farther. Then he, too, climbed out of the stream and hurried after the other two, who had already reached the outer wall of the monastery, where the metal-casting workshop also stood. Pale, and still fighting for breath, Agnes glared at him.

"I'll never forgive you for this, Mathis Wielenbach," she gasped. "First you join that band of murderers, then you almost drown me like a kitten."

"How about a little gratitude for a change?" retorted Mathis, equally breathless. "I just saved your life, but oh no, her ladyship the countess—"

"Maybe you two could put off your argument to some other time," Ulrich Reichhart interrupted, pointing to the wall. "We're not safe until we're on the other side of that. The forest begins then, and they won't find us there."

He began climbing the wall, which was about nine feet high, with some protruding stones offering handholds. After a little hesitation, Mathis and Agnes followed him, with the castellan's daughter casting Mathis furious glances. On the other side of the wall there was a muddy ditch, still full of lingering snow. They jumped down, made a soft landing in the slush, and crawled to the outskirts of the forest, where they hid behind a group of bramble bushes.

For a while all three lay there as though they were dead, but fighting for air. Mathis shivered. His wet shirt and hose clung to his skin. The others were no better off. Agnes was rubbing her icy arms and legs, and Mathis caught himself staring at her breasts. He could see the shape of them under her soaked doublet. Water dripped from her blonde hair to the ground, where it formed a puddle. At least the sun was shining now, and gave some warmth. But soon they heard the first shouts from the monastery.

"They're starting the chase," Mathis gloomily said, sitting up. "If we don't hurry, we'll have escaped for nothing. Jockel will flay us alive."

"At least they have no dogs," Ulrich Reichhart pointed out, frowning. "All the same, it would be good if we could go to ground somewhere for a while. There are a hell of a lot of them, and with all the snow still around we won't make fast progress in the forest. If there was some kind of hiding place . . ."

"I know one," said Agnes suddenly. She had risen to her feet and was wringing out her wet hair. "It may not be very comfortable, but at least we'll be safe there for the time being. Although the smell inside it leaves something to be desired." She looked fiercely at Mathis, but then, finally, she gave a deep sigh. "Mathis Wielenbach, you're as obstinate as a mule, you're a dangerous insurgent, and absolutely unbearable. But for some reason or other I like you all the same. So if you insist on staying around me, then come with us if you like."

Without another word, they disappeared among the trees of the forest.

· 16 ·

The forest outside Eusserthal Monastery, the same day

AFTER THEY'D TRAVELED A NUMBER of miles, Agnes, Mathis, and Ulrich Reichhart found themselves huddling together in the darkness of a cave, while the cries of their pursuers echoed far off in the forest and finally died away entirely.

Agnes had found this hiding place, halfway between Eusserthal and Trifels, years ago on a hawking expedition. It was a cave once inhabited by a bear, now deserted, at the foot of a sandstone massif, and she used it as an occasional shelter if a sudden storm arose. Last fall, she had taken the precaution of building up a barrier of rocks to keep wild beasts out. Inside, there were some dry furs, dried fruit, and even a fireplace with a natural flue in the roof above, but they were not using that for fear of discovery. There was ice on the walls; down here it was still as cold as winter. The cave had a musty smell of dead leaves, mold, and decay.

"I think they've given it up," said Mathis wearily, wrapping himself in a bedraggled wild boar skin. "One way or another, I can't hold out here any longer. I'm near freezing to death."

"I'd say we ought to wait another quarter of an hour before venturing out," suggested Ulrich Reichhart.

"And then where do we go?" Mathis laughed in desperation.

"We're outlaws, did you forget that, Ulrich? And now it's not just the duke's henchmen looking for us, but our own people too." He looked at Agnes with a mixture of mockery and melancholy in his eyes. "At least you have somewhere to go."

"And suppose I don't want to go there?"

Agnes shot daggers at Mathis. Until now, she had said little, keeping her thoughts to herself. Now they came bursting out of her. "Did you ever stop to think what it's like to be married to a tyrannical, cold-blooded murderer?" she cried. "A man who more than likely has my father on his conscience. Have you thought how it is for me, trapped in a cage, where I'll grow gray and embittered, condemned to a life of silent patience? Did you ever think of that?"

"At least you won't have to starve," retorted Mathis. "And there's always a hot fire burning at Scharfenberg Castle."

"A hot fire, yes. While my heart slowly grows cold."

Quietly, Agnes looked at the icicles hanging from the roof of the cave, just above the entrance. The grief she felt for her dead father confessor weighed on her like a heavy burden. It was like a sheet of ice covered her heart.

While they traveled, Mathis had given her the letter from Father Tristan. Though the water had damaged it greatly, it was still just legible. Blinking in the poor light, she skimmed the few lines.

Agnes leaned against the cold rock wall behind her. In the hour since their escape, a decision had been slowly forming in her mind. Her father confessor's letter had set off a train of thought that had long been slumbering within her. All at once she realized that in these last few weeks and months, she had been only a shadow of herself. She was living with a man who had driven her family to ruin, had presumably killed her father, and had robbed her of Trifels Castle. She had let him bribe her with expensive books, wine, and the prospect of a secure and comfortable life. How could she have sunk so low? This farce must end, even if it meant throwing her father's dying wish to the four winds.

Agnes nodded firmly. Father Tristan's letter, and his last words, gave her a purpose in life again, a task to carry out. What was it the old monk had said to her on his deathbed?

"You should find out at last who you really are."

After a long silence, she finally raised her head.

"I'm not going back to Scharfenberg Castle," she said resolutely.

"How . . . what . . . what do you mean?" Mathis stared at her, astonished. "Are you out of your mind? Unlike us, you have a life ahead of you—a future. That's not something to be lightly tossed away. And anyway, where would you go?"

"To St. Goar." Agnes pressed her lips firmly together. "I'm going to St. Goar. Father Tristan said I could find out more about my past there. Constanza, the ring . . . all of it is connected with me somehow or other. Oh, heavens!" She shook her head. "I don't know much myself. I only know that I can't go on living as I have been. Either I go away or I slowly turn to stone, if I don't throw myself off the castle keep first. And if Father Tristan was right, there are people in pursuit of me anyway, so I *have* to get away from here."

"In pursuit of you?" Ulrich Reichhart wrinkled his brow. "What people? What do you mean?"

"Father Tristan said the midwife Elsbeth Rechsteiner told him there was someone after me. He . . . he asked me to leave the castle and go to St. Goar. There's a document there to do with my past. A document that used to be in the hands of some kind of brotherhood." Agnes indicated the soaked and blood-stained letter in her hands. "This place St. Goar is a monastery on the Rhine, somewhere downstream near Bingen. He wrote about it."

The old master gunner laughed hoarsely. "Have you any idea how far from here Bingen is? Well over a hundred miles. And there's war there, Lady Agnes. The peasants are coming together in bands everywhere. A young girl like you will soon be caught between two fronts."

"I'll disguise myself as a man," replied Agnes coolly. "I'll hide my hair and wear doublet and hose. A traveling journeyman. That's nothing unusual, even in times of war."

"And you really think we'll let you go just like that?" Mathis shook his head. "Forget it."

"What are you going to do? Tie me up and leave me in this cave?" Agnes stuck her chin out. "I'm going wherever I please, understand?"

"Of course you are. But not on your own." Mathis had hesitated for only a moment. Now he grinned and winked at Ulrich Reichhart. "Because we're going with you. Aren't we, Ulrich?"

The old master gunner looked up in surprise, and then sighed deeply. "Devil take it, I'm afraid my days as a rebel have come to a sudden end. And war is the only trade I know. So I'll go on standing at the side of my lady the countess." He put his head to one side. "If she's agreeable to that."

"You . . . the two of you would go with me? You'd really do that?" Agnes felt her heart lift. All at once, her decision seemed less gloomy and hopeless than it had a few minutes ago.

"I'll go anywhere with you," Mathis replied, smiling. "Mind you, I'd prefer sunny Venice, or for all I care Cologne or Mainz. But if you're set on it, it'll have to be that dusty monastery of yours. Anything's better than living as an outlaw in the forests of the Wasgau, slowly starving to death." He got to his feet. "Or freezing to death. Let's get out of this icy cave at last."

Ulrich Reichhart rose, too, breathing heavily. Agnes hesitated for only a little while, then she stood up, smoothed down her shirt, which was still damp and clammy, and nodded decisively.

"Then we'll be off," she said, bending low as she went to the mouth of the cave. "But first, for better or worse, I must pay a visit to my worthy husband's castle." With a resolute expression, she clenched her fists. "There's something there that I don't on any account want to leave behind, even though it's only a little ring."

A good hour later, the three fugitives were climbing the steep, slippery slope that led to the Sonnenberg and its three castles. After some initial hesitation, Mathis and Ulrich Reichhart had agreed to follow

Agnes into the lion's den once more, although Reichhart in particular didn't see why they should expose themselves to the danger of discovery by the count's guards, just for the sake of a tiny trinket. But Agnes had insisted on taking the signet ring with her. She felt she could not possibly set out for St. Goar without it. Everything had begun with that ring, and she couldn't leave it behind. Furthermore, Father Tristan had written about it in his letter, so it must be important.

Since her marriage to Friedrich von Löwenstein-Scharfeneck, the ring had been kept safely in her bower, in a jewel box under her bed. That, and the prospect of dry clothes and a little money, induced Agnes to return to Scharfenberg Castle for the last time.

Brooding on her situation, she made her way through the dark forest, her clothes catching again and again on frozen twigs and branches. What had Father Tristan meant by his letter and his last words? What linked her to the ring, and to a woman called Constanza who had lived three hundred years before her own time? And what was hidden behind all the dreams that had tormented her for so long? The answer to all those questions seemed to lie in St. Goar. What would happen after she reached the monastery, Agnes could not begin to imagine. She knew only that she must clear up the mystery.

Evening twilight was falling. Snow persistently lingered in the shadow of the trees, and the ground was moist, so they made slow progress. Every step was an effort, but they wanted to avoid the known paths; there was too much danger of pursuers there. In some places they tried to obliterate their trail by wading through icy streams or dragging branches over the ground after them, but the result was far from satisfactory. More than once Agnes thought she heard Jockel and his band behind them, but it was only a startled deer or some other woodland creature.

At times, Agnes felt as though she was in a trance. Grief for her dead father confessor weighed heavily on her, and only the cold and the danger of discovery kept her from constantly bursting into tears.

Yet at the same time she sensed a new determination within her. It was as if she was drawing on her sorrow to give her fresh strength.

I suppose I am finally growing up, she thought wryly.

At last, between the tops of the trees, Trifels Castle loomed up in the evening light. It stood enthroned on the great plateau of rock, proud and impregnable. They made a long detour around it, and Agnes thought of all the dear memories that bound her to the castle. That dark building had been her home. Would she ever return to it?

"How are you going to get into the castle?" Mathis asked, interrupting her melancholy thoughts as they approached nearby Scharfenberg Castle along a narrow path. "You can't very well just knock at the front gate and ask your husband to bring you out the ring and a warm cloak." He pointed to her torn, damp shirt and the wound on her forehead that she had sustained when she fell into the trap at Eusserthal. "And if the count sees you like this, he'll ask questions. He may not be happy to let you go off again."

"I know this castle pretty well by now. There's a small concealed door, and I have the key to it." Agnes looked at him with a twinkle in her eyes. "After all, I'm not letting my dear husband tell me when I have to go to bed. It will be all right, wait and see."

The last quarter of a mile up to the castle was the most strenuous part of the climb. They made their way to the north side, where the land rose most steeply. There was no outer perimeter wall here, only a vertical rockface, ending deep down in a moat that ran in front of it. Once there may have been water in the moat, but now it was only a muddy ditch. Holding on to a root for support, Agnes let herself down into it and picked her way over to the other side, using some large rocks in the bed of the moat as steppingstones.

"Now you know why I prefer doublet and hose to a gown," she told the two men as they watched her from the side of the moat. "With fluttering skirts, I'd already have fallen flat on my face a dozen times." She signaled to them to stay where they were. "You wait, and I won't be long, I promise."

"What if Jockel and his men turn up?" asked Mathis.

"If the peasants had really followed us, they'd have struck long before now. Trust me."

Agnes climbed up the other side of the ditch and approached the rockface, which was densely overgrown with ivy. Pushing the woody stems of the plants aside, she revealed a small, rusty iron door. When Scharfenberg Castle was under siege, men-at-arms had once sallied out from here, but now this entrance to the castle was known only to a few. Friedrich had told her about it in one of his more agreeable moods, and then she had stolen the key and, later, asked the smith in Annweiler to make her a copy of it. So far her husband had noticed nothing.

The door squealed open, and damp, musty air streamed out. Agnes entered the dark passage beyond the door and groped her way forward. By now, she had gone along the tunnel carved into the rock here so often that she could have found her way with her eyes closed.

The tunnel ended after about sixty feet. There was a trapdoor in the roof above it. Agnes opened the trapdoor and braced herself to clamber through, first looking cautiously around. The trapdoor led to an inconspicuous corner of the lower part of the castle, right below the battlements. Now, just after sunset, the lower bailey lay dark and deserted in front of her. A few chickens were cackling as they pecked up grain, and she heard the laughter of several watchmen in the distance.

Agnes slipped through the narrow opening and hurried to the upper bailey, which was reached through another barred gate in the rock. A guard was doing his rounds there, looking bored. On recognizing Agnes, he stood at attention, seeming not to notice her torn, damp shirt in the dim light.

"My lady," he rasped. "What is your—"

Agnes waved his question away. "Is my husband back yet?" she asked.

The guard shook his head. "I'm afraid not, my lady, but we expect him anytime now. He meant to be back before nightfall."

"Ah, good. Don't tell him I'm here already." Agnes assumed her sweetest smile. "I want to surprise him in his bedchamber."

With a dutiful expression, the guard let her pass, and she ran up the stairs to the living quarters beside the tall keep. As she hurried along the drafty vaulted corridors, she once again saw, out of the corner of her eye, the costly tapestries, the mighty sets of antlers, and the gorgeous colorful paintings on the walls. Friedrich had built her a lovely cage. It was high time she broke out of it.

Reaching under her bed, Agnes pulled out the chest containing her personal possessions, including the valuable book about falconry by Emperor Frederick II that Father Tristan had once given her. She reverently stroked the finely tanned leather of its binding. She would have to leave the book behind, like many other treasures.

Like everything except the ring.

She took the little box in which it had been lying for months out of the chest. When she finally put it around her neck on a silver chain, it felt both hot and cold on her skin. A strange shudder ran down her spine. It was like a mosaic stone had been fitted back into its original place.

What is this ring doing to me?

She looked around her magnificently furnished room for the last time, then hurried along the corridor to her husband's chamber at the far end. As she had expected, its door was locked, but with provident foresight Agnes had had a second key made for this lock as well. She swiftly unlocked the door and went in.

Friedrich's bedchamber was the largest in the whole castle. Fragrant rushes were strewn on the floor, an earthenware pot full of glowing embers ensured that the room would be warm when he came home.

Agnes turned to the three chests standing by the window wall and took out several garments at random. Friedrich was not too much larger than she was, and a couple of fur coats would surely fit Mathis and Ulrich Reichhart. In addition, they could always sell the expensive furs at a good profit.

After making a bundle of the clothes and putting them in a sack, she finally turned to the drawer in the desk. She knew that her husband always kept at least a small sum of money there, and sure enough, she found a well-filled leather purse. When she opened it, dozens of gleaming golden guilders and ducats rolled toward her. She smiled and put the purse into the sack with the items of clothing. With as much money as that, they could even travel to distant Venice if need be.

"You're not leaving us for any length of time, are you? How regrettable."

The voice came from the unlocked door. Startled, Agnes dropped the sack and turned around. Melchior von Tanningen entered the room. With an expression of curiosity on his face, the minstrel scrutinized the open chests and the coats, shirts, and other garments spilling out of them. "Or are you tidying up after your husband? But there are servants for that." Smiling, Melchior said, "Although I remember you don't think yourself too fine to fetch wine from the kitchen."

"The fact is," Agnes hesitantly began. "The fact is, I was looking for a warm coat, and then I saw all this disorder and . . ." She fell silent, seeing Melchior's eyes dwelling on her torn shirt.

"Who did that to you?" he asked indignantly. "The count?"

Agnes shook her head. "No, no, I just took a harmless fall on the stairs."

"And that sack you have with you?"

"I . . . I . . ." Agnes realized that she was entangling herself ever deeper in her own lies. Melchior was watching her attentively. Finally she dropped onto the bed and raised her hands in a pleading gesture.

"If I tell you a secret, will you promise to keep it?"

The minstrel raised his right hand as if to swear a solemn oath and fell on his knees like a chivalrous knight of old. "By all that's holy to me, by heaven, earth, and the German Empire, I swear that—"

Agnes waved his oath away. "That's good enough for me." Briefly, she hesitated, and then went on quietly. "Dear Melchior, you have always been a good friend to me, but I must leave you now. I am turning my back on Scharfenberg Castle and my husband forever."

Astonished, Melchior looked at her. "You're going away? But where will you go?"

"I can't tell you that."

The minstrel bowed even more deeply, and stood with his head bent, as if in prayer. "I will accompany you, even to the mouth of hell."

"You can't do that," Agnes sighed. "It's too dangerous."

"That is exactly why I am going to accompany you. I would never allow a young woman to set off on a journey through the German Empire alone, not in times like these. Especially when she may possibly be pursued by her vengeful husband. In any case, I have been at this castle quite long enough. Minstrels must travel, or they have nothing to sing about." Melchior von Tanningen rose and put his hand to his breast. Every inch of his body, something over five feet tall, expressed pride. "I once took an oath to protect the weak. Allow me to be your paladin."

Agnes would have laughed if the situation had not been so serious. She was about to turn the idea down again, but then she hesitated. The minstrel could indeed be a useful companion. He had traveled widely and knew the world. Furthermore, he had already shown that, in spite of his apparent fragility, he was a good swordsman. They could certainly do with a man like that on their long journey through a country in turmoil. The only question was what Mathis would say if she let someone else into the secret of their plans.

Melchior was still standing in front of her with his hand on his breast, waiting. Finally, shrugging, Agnes gave in.

"Very well, then," she said. "You may come with me and my two friends on our travels, but you must swear not to tell a soul about it." Agnes thought, once again, of Father Tristan's last words.

The midwife Elsbeth Rechsteiner told me that they were after you . . .

"There may be someone following us," she went on quietly. "Although I don't know who, or why. So you must keep quiet."

Horrified, Melchior raised his eyebrows. "You are addressing a knight, my lady. I would not give the secret away, even under torture."

"Let us hope it doesn't come to that," she said gloomily. "Now, quick, before my husband comes back. If he finds us here, with all those clothes lying on the floor, he might draw the wrong conclusions, and I wouldn't like that."

Agnes threw the sack to the little minstrel and hurried to the door. In passing, Melchior picked up a winter coat trimmed with ermine and strode after her with his chest proudly thrust out, while the sword at his side clinked quietly in its sheath.

As they hurried over the castle courtyard in the evening twilight, Agnes stopped suddenly. "One moment," she said to Melchior. "I . . . there's someone I have to say goodbye to."

She left the surprised minstrel behind and went over to a corner of the courtyard where a small aviary stood in the shade. Her falcon, Parcival, was sitting on a perch, his head hidden by his leather hood. Carefully, she took it off, and the falcon fluttered excitedly up and down, making the little silver chain on his foot jingle. As the molting season began, his tail feathers were looking worn, getting ready to drop out.

"Parcival," Agnes whispered, stroking his head. "I'm afraid I must leave you. I am so sorry, but you can't come with me."

She had briefly considered taking the falcon and her horse, Taramis, but she would have been too conspicuous with the stately chestnut and trained falcon. So she had decided on another solution.

Hesitating for a moment, she undid the chain from the falcon's foot and opened the aviary door.

"Fly away, Parcival, fly away," she said softly. "There are mice and rabbits waiting for you out there, and I'm sure you'll find a pretty lady falcon as well. *Al reveire!*"

The bird tripped back and forth on his perch, and finally spread his wings and flew out into the courtyard. For a moment he settled on the battlements, then he rose high in the air with a shrill cry. He circled above the castle several times, almost as if he were saying his own goodbye, and finally flew away west, toward the setting sun.

Out in the forest, hidden behind a bramble bush, a crooked figure glowered, his eyes full of hatred for the two men who seemed to be waiting for something by the rockface below Scharfenberg Castle.

The hunchback cursed quietly. What, damn it all, were those two doing? Whatever it was, now was the time to close the trap, before he froze to death. Impatiently, Shepherd Jockel rubbed his cold hands and looked around for his men lurking in the brushwood behind him, awaiting his orders. That outspoken young smith would be sorry yet for making a fool of him in front of everyone. Oh yes, Mathis was going to be sorry—very, very sorry.

The peasants had followed the fugitives over the hills since midday. But at some point they had lost track of them in the forest. At first, Jockel had been furious, but then it struck him that he knew where at least one of the three must be going. Finally he had posted men outside Scharfenberg, although he assumed that the castellan's daughter would go straight to the main gate of the castle, rather than taking the steep approach along the northern flank. As a result, they had almost arrived too late.

But the peasants had been lucky; one of the men posted to keep watch had spotted the fugitives at the last minute. And now Mathis and that fool Reichhart were simply standing here in the snow, like a couple of stags flushed out of cover. But stupidly, they had let that spoiled girl slip through their fingers.

Jockel was about to give the order to attack, when suddenly two more figures appeared by the rockface. Where had they come from? Shepherd Jockel looked more closely. One was a small, delicately built man, dressed like a member of the minor aristocracy, with a sack slung over his shoulder, and the other . . .

The countess.

Jockel put his hand over his mouth to keep from laughing out loud. The stupid woman had actually left the shelter of her castle, thus showing him another way into it. There must be a hidden door in the rock. Now he had them all in his trap.

Curiously, Jockel scrutinized the man with the sack as he approached Mathis and old Reichhart. There were a couple of conversations conducted in an undertone, and finally the castellan's daughter took items of warm clothing out of the sack and gave them to the others in the party. Jockel grinned as he realized what was going on. Clearly the lady had tired of her castle, maybe the fop beside her was her lover, or maybe her husband had simply sent her packing—although with her tumbling blonde hair, her small, full breasts, and her well-formed figure, she really was a very attractive sight.

That gave Jockel an idea as wicked as it was brilliant. A thin, diabolical smile flitted over his lips. Sometimes his own intellect surprised him. Only Mathis could sometimes compete with him. The young man was cunning, and popular with the men. It would have been risky to strike him down in front of all eyes. But now he could dispose of the ambitious young fellow neatly, at the same time avenging himself on the young noblewoman—and in a way that would provide material for talk beside the insurgents' campfires for a long while to come.

No doubt about it; Jockel was a born leader.

"What now, sir?" asked Paulus impatiently. "Do we fall on them?"

The former vagrant had a bandage around his head where Reichhart had hit him with the flat of his sword blade. His eyes glittered with hatred and anger in the dim light. Jockel liked to hear Paulus calling him "sir," as though he were a knight or a count.

Shepherd Jockel shook his head. "I have a much better idea. You know the village of Rinnthal, not far from here?"

When Paulus nodded too slowly, Jockel went on, "There are a few shady characters there. Pimps and procurers they are, on their way to Strasbourg. They're looking out for pretty peasant girls eating their parents out of house and home in these hard times."

Paulus twisted his mouth into a grin as he finally understood. "You mean we can offer them something better than a peasant girl?"

"Oh yes, much better. A real countess." Jockel winked at him. "And in return they'll get rid of Mathis and the other two idiots for us. We won't even have to soil our hands." He nudged Paulus, who chuckled. "And now hurry up, before the golden goose flies away."

When the vagrant had disappeared, Jockel stared at Scharfenberg Castle thoughtfully for some time longer. It towered above him, and until now it had looked to him impregnable. The hunchbacked peasant leader grinned. The men from Dahn and Wilgartswiesen would soon be here. He would be able to offer them a monastery as an army camp, and a way into a fortress as well. Together they would storm Scharfenberg Castle. Trifels would follow, then Annweiler and the other towns and villages all the way down to the Rhine.

And there was no doubt who would be the leader of their large and ever-growing band.

Accompanied by the steady rushing sound of the river Queich, Agnes and the three men walked on toward the little village of Albersweiler, a few miles east of Annweiler. They had been on their way for over an hour now, and it was late at night, but the moon shone so brightly that they could easily see where they were going.

After some thought, they had decided to leave the part of the country that owed allegiance to the Löwenstein-Scharfenecks behind them as quickly as possible. Agnes was under no illusions. By now her husband would certainly be home. When he failed to find his wife and the minstrel at the castle, he would be suspicious, and the missing garments and stolen money would soon put him on the right track. So they must move quickly.

Mathis and Ulrich Reichhart went ahead on the towpath beside the river. The old master gunner kept his hand on the hilt of his sword and looked keenly around him as they walked on. Meanwhile, Mathis had cut himself a cudgel and was listlessly swinging it in the air as a little boy might. Agnes could not suppress a small smile. Since she had explained to Mathis that Melchior von Tanningen was going to be their companion, he had hardly said anything, apart from grumbling a few brief comments. It was almost as if he was jealous.

"And the dreams really began only once you had this ring?" the minstrel beside her asked. Agnes had decided to tell Melchior about her dreams, the ring, and the mysterious missing chapter torn out of the chronicle of Trifels. Since then he had been all enthusiasm. It was like he had finally found the dramatic tale that he had long been searching for. He had touched the ring on its chain around her neck, his eyes shining, and murmured something about a new Holy Grail.

"The dreams came only when I was at Trifels Castle," said Agnes. "Then they suddenly went away. Almost as though the castle itself were sending them to me." She shook her head. "But of course that's nonsense. It's probably just that Trifels sets my imagination working. That is what Father Tristan always used to say. All the same, it's strange. I saw in dreams everything that Johann and Constanza experienced at Trifels: their first meeting, when Johann was dubbed a knight; their wedding; their first concerns about the ring; the planned assassination; their flight with the child . . . I can't see what happened after that."

"The chronicle said that Johann of Brunswick, the Guelph, led a conspiracy against the Habsburgs, and died in flight when it failed," Melchior pointed out. "Maybe Constanza was also killed by the king's assassins."

Agnes shrugged. "We don't know what the chronicle said, because Father Tristan tore out those pages. But why? What did it say that no one was supposed to read?"

"A secret that we'll have to work out in that distant monastery on the Rhine. Ah, I love secrets! They are the bricks of every ballad." Melchior plucked his lute and struck a couple of chords. Then he sang a song in his soft tenor voice, hesitating briefly now and then as he tried to find the right words.

A noble maid, both proud and fine,
With friends went to the river Rhine.
They sought the canons who might know
What happened many years ago,
At Trifels. How it was a pair
Of lovers were united there,
Although in death. She had a ring
From fair Constanza, as I sing.
It sent her many a troubled dream . . .

Humming to himself, Melchior thought about the next line. Agnes looked at him in amazement.

"Did you make that up just now?"

The minstrel shrugged. "Well, it needs to be revised and polished, but it will do for a start . . ." He smiled. "Do you like it? I told you about the singers' contest at the Wartburg, and I think I now know what ballad I'd like to perform there." He plucked a couple of strings in a theatrical manner. "This song of mine will take the world by storm."

"But first and foremost it's likely to cost us our lives," Mathis interrupted. "If you carry on singing like that, we might as well ask out loud to be attacked. Maybe it's slipped your mind, Master Minstrel, but there are about a hundred peasants on our trail, as well as a very angry count."

"I'm sorry, you are right." Melchior shouldered his lute again, sighing deeply. "Where good stories are concerned, I can't restrain myself. Especially when the story is about love and death."

"You may soon be better acquainted with the latter than you like," remarked Mathis. "We must just hope that the count hasn't sent his mounted landsknechts in pursuit yet. They'll soon catch up with us on horseback."

"I think I have an idea," Ulrich Reichhart put in, turning to the others. "We're certainly going too slowly on Shanks's pony, but in a boat it would be different. Not far after Albersweiler the Queich flows fast, particularly at this time of year. Traveling by water, we'd reach the Rhine before we knew it."

"Oh, wonderful," Mathis said. "And where are we going to find a boat in the middle of the night?"

Reichhart grinned. "With enough money, you can even buy a galley in the Wasgau if you need one. There's a stone quarry just before we reach Albersweiler, and a tavern on the little river harbor. We'll roust the host out of bed and buy the fastest boat we can get." He looked up at the starry sky. "It's nearly full moon, so we can travel by night as well as day. What do you think?"

"A good notion." Agnes clapped her hands. "We could reach the Rhine by sunrise. And maybe the landlord could give us a sup of hot, spiced wine." Shivering, she pulled her husband's warm felt coat around her shoulders. In her hose, and a broad-brimmed slouch hat under which she had stuffed her unmanageable hair, she did indeed look like a young craftsman on his travels, although the coat seemed a little too expensive for that.

"Then let's get this part of the forest behind us," grunted Mathis. "Before the minstrel starts singing again."

Ulrich Reichhart's suggestion, and the prospect of some wine, made all four of them walk faster. The towpath continued along the bank of the river Queich. They soon passed a stone marking the border, telling them that they had finally left the county of the Löwenstein-Scharfenecks.

Agnes felt a curious relief, almost as if she had broken out of a magical charmed circle. She gave herself a little shake and then marched on. Once, she thought she saw a scurrying movement behind the branches of the trees, perhaps some large animal, but then deep silence fell again, broken only by Melchior's steady humming.

At last the pit of the Albersweiler stone quarry appeared on their left. A broad road led from it to the harbor, where stone was loaded into barges to go down to the plain of the Rhine. There were still lights on behind the thick glass windows of the harbor tavern, and smoke rose from its chimney, so obviously someone was still awake.

"Mmm, I smell roast wild boar, do you?" said Ulrich Reichhart. "Maybe we can take a few slices with us. And some good white bread, and a little cask of beer."

He opened the tavern door and raised his hand in greeting. Sure enough, late as it was there were still some guests at the inn. The landlord stood behind the counter, cleaning his fingernails with a dagger at his leisure. He looked up for a moment as the new arrivals entered the room.

"Still out and about so late?" the landlord asked, with a thin smile. "I'm afraid we have no beds left."

"Thanks, but we don't need a place to sleep," Mathis replied. "We're looking to buy a boat, that's all."

"And a mug of hot honey wine and a few slices of roast meat would go down well, too," Reichhart said, glancing hungrily at the table where the guests were sitting.

"A boat, eh?" The landlord drove his dagger into the table, where it stuck, quivering. "How much money do you have with you?"

"Enough for a ramshackle barge like yours out there," Agnes said. It occurred to her, too late, that her voice sounded far too high to be a man's. The landlord at the counter looked her suspiciously up and down.

"Boats are expensive hereabouts," he finally replied, pushing the hilt of his dagger so that it began to vibrate. "Especially for folk who arrive by night and are in a hurry."

Agnes looked more closely at the man. He had shaggy black hair, and an equally shaggy beard. His skin was dark brown, almost burned, like he spent a great deal of time out in the sun. Only now did it strike her that he spoke a strange dialect and did not seem to come from these parts.

The guests at the table also made a curious impression. There were four strong fellows, with slouch hats and scarred faces. With them sat a young girl, her eyes moving restlessly back and forth, terrified. A tense silence fell, almost physically present. Agnes felt the little hairs on the back of her neck slowly rising.

There's something wrong here . . .

The girl's eyes slowly moved to the counter. In the dim light, something could be seen sticking out from under it, on the right-hand side where a man would move to stand behind the bar.

Two feet, with a pool of bright blood around them.

At the same moment a shrill cry came from the counter. Turning her head, Agnes saw a monster that seemed to come straight out of her nightmares. A small, hairy demon perched on the bar, its mouth open and hissing. Sharp teeth stuck out of that mouth, and the monster had a face like a tiny copy of a wizened old man's. Red button eyes flashed angrily at Agnes, and then the demon gathered itself to spring.

"Damn you, Satan, stay here," the landlord scolded. He tugged at a thin chain, whereupon the demon, spitting, hopped up on his shoulder. Confused, Agnes looked from the little devil down to the pool of blood on the floor, and back again. When the landlord noticed her glance, he growled angrily, like a wolf.

"Kill those three fools, but leave the pretty countess to me."

For a moment time seemed to stand still. Then Agnes heard the sound of steel drawn from its sheath, and Melchior von Tanningen stormed toward the group at the table with his sword in hand. The men jumped to their feet. Roast meat, plates, and wineglasses crashed to the floor. The girl cried out and flinched aside as the strangers drew their own swords.

"Curse it, those are no guests! They're —" Ulrich Reichhart shouted.

The "landlord," clearly the band's leader, pulled his dagger out of the counter and threw it at the master gunner, whose cry stopped short. Incredulously, Ulrich Reichhart stared at the blade quivering between his ribs, and then slowly slipped down with his back to the wall until he lay on the floor.

For a moment Agnes stood still, frozen to the spot. Then she ran to the doorway, where Mathis was still standing. The young smith was about to rush into the fray when his eyes fell on Reichhart, now bleeding freely. Horrified, he lowered his cudgel again.

"My God, Ulrich!" he cried, running to his friend. "Those bastards, those damn bastards!"

"Get the womenfolk to the boat!" the leader bellowed, still standing behind the counter. The little demon sat on his shoulder, spitting and hopping up and down. "Kill the others, and then we'll clear out of here. Look sharp about it."

The slightly built minstrel now stood exactly in the middle of the room, fighting four men. The blade of his sword, gleaming silver, seemed to be in several places at once. It was like lightning striking the men. When they realized that, for all his small stature, their adversary's swordplay was far superior to theirs, two of the robbers suddenly turned away from him and ran for the door. They seized Agnes by the shoulder, her hat fell off, and her long hair tumbled out of it.

"Let me go, you murderers!" Agnes cried. "You . . . you—"

But she had no chance at all against the strong arms of her assailants. The men hauled her through the doorway by her hair. Someone hit her in the face, and the next moment she suffered another blow to her temple. It hurt so much that all went dark before her eyes for a moment. As if in a trance, she saw Mathis fall on one of the robbers, shouting and bring his cudgel down on the back of the man's head. That man let go of her, but the other went on dragging her through the dark. She felt dirt and slush underfoot, and the rushing of the river came closer and closer.

Mustn't . . . mustn't . . . faint . . . away . . .

Hands passed over her shirt and her coat, grabbed the fabric, and heaved her into a boat. She felt it rocking under her. Up and down, back and forth . . .

"Agnes! Agnes!"

It was Mathis calling to her. But he was not with her, he was far, far away. Mathis had gone away . . .

"Agnes! Agnes!" came the voice again, but higher this time, like a wicked witch screeching. "Agnes, Agnes, Agnes, Agnes . . ."

Then she sank into darkness blacker than the waters of the river Queich.

When Mathis saw the two men dragging Agnes toward the river, something inside him exploded. Rage and hatred ran through him, filling him entirely, displacing every other thought. Shouting, he made for one of the robbers and hit him over the head with his cudgel. There was a cracking sound, like a nut being broken open.

Mathis jumped over the dying robber and was about to hurry after Agnes when he suddenly felt a sharp pain in his thigh. An arrow had hit him, its feathered shaft buried a hand's length in his right leg. He threw himself to the ground, gasping, and in the light of the full moon saw two figures kneeling by the dock, firing arrows at the tavern. By now the second robber had reached the boat, with Agnes.

"Agnes! Agnes!"

Mathis straightened up, but at once another arrow struck the ground beside him. He instinctively dropped again and rolled a little way aside, where an empty cart gave him some protection. He wondered desperately how to help Agnes without getting into the two archers' line of fire himself.

Jockel must have sent them, he thought. *If we're out of luck, there'll be more of these bandits waiting out there.*

Screams and the crash of breaking crockery came from inside the tavern. Soon after that, the supposed landlord and another robber ran to the door. The leader held the young girl firmly, with a knife pressed to her throat. He looked cautiously to all sides. On his shoulder sat the small, hairy beast, a kind of animal that Mathis had never seen before.

The bearded man turned toward the tavern. Melchior von Tanningen appeared in the doorway, his sword ready for the next attack.

"Stay where you are," the leader hissed at him "Or this pretty chick will be bathing in her own blood."

While Melchior stayed in the door frame with his hands raised, Mathis crawled cautiously toward the dock. The darkness and a few casks and crates standing on the bank provided him with makeshift cover. The arrow in his thigh hurt like hell, and his hose were wet with blood. He clutched his cudgel convulsively as he made his way closer to the boat, where he thought Agnes would be.

"Stop hiding behind a girl; come out and fight like a man," Melchior called from the tavern. "I'm offering you single combat, man to man."

The robber chief roared with laughter. "What kind of a strange customer are you? Why would I fight you when I can have both girls anyway? Your massacre of my men in there is quite enough for me."

He drew the weeping girl very close to him, his knife directly above the artery in her throat. Slowly, he and his companion moved backward to the boat.

"Not a step closer," he warned Melchior, who was still hesitating in the doorway. "I've killed younger creatures than this."

"Would you really show violence to a weak woman?" asked the minstrel incredulously. "That is more than unchivalrous."

The bearded leader chuckled. "Who are you? A priest in disguise? Or a jester run away from your master? This stupid girl is nothing but an innkeeper's daughter, good enough for a rundown brothel on the Rhine. I slit her father's belly open in there before he could bat an eyelid. So why would I hesitate? This little thing won't make me much money anyway."

"Haven't you a spark of honor in your body?"

"Not a whit. Honor won't buy me anything. But selling a pretty countess will. Down on the Black Sea, the Turks will pay a good price for a white-skinned beauty of noble birth." The animal on his shoulder screeched agreement, just as if he could understand what his master said.

During this exchange, Mathis had been crawling closer and closer toward the boat. At first he had been staggered by the minstrel's astonishing naiveté, standing in the light in the doorway like a figure out of his own ballads, but then he had noticed the movement of Melchior's eyes. The minstrel was playing a trick on the robber with his old-fashioned show of chivalry. If Mathis could eliminate the archers down on the dock, Melchior might be able to free Agnes with a swift attack.

"That countess has a great secret," the minstrel said solemnly. "Let her go, and I'll tell you what it is."

"Well, well, a secret. When I'm alone with her she'll whisper all her secrets into my ear, large or small, take my word for it. Now, shoot that mad dog down."

The last words were for the archers. Two arrows whirred through the air, Melchior swerved back into the tavern, and the arrows fell somewhere behind the counter. Mathis knew that it would take the two men some time to bend their bows again. He straightened up and limped, shouting, toward the dock, where he fell on one of the two archers like a dark avenging angel. The man, who was not strongly built, dropped his bow and reached for his dagger, cursing, but Mathis was already on him. Flailing his arms, the robber fell into the river, screaming, and dragging Mathis down with him as he fell. The rushing waters of the Queich closed over them both.

Everything around Mathis turned black and cold. At last, after what felt like an eternity, he surfaced again. Out of the corner of his eye he saw his adversary thrashing about and heard him gurgling. Evidently he couldn't swim. The river swallowed up the struggling man and carried him downstream.

With a few strong strokes, Mathis swam back to the dock, but the boat had already cast off.

"No, no! Agnes! Agnes!"

In ultimate desperation, he clung to the handrail of the boat, but the bearded man kicked him in the face, so that he slipped down and sank for the second time. Muted by the water above him, he heard a shrill screeching, like a naughty child bawling.

"Rah for emp'or Charles . . . rah for emp'or Charles!"

The words made no sense, but Mathis had no time to wonder

what they meant. Water filled his mouth. He struck out frantically with his arms, but this time he couldn't make it up to the surface again.

Forgive me, Agnes . . . I wasn't able to help you . . .

Suddenly a hand grabbed Mathis by the collar and brought him out from under the dock. It was Melchior, who had leaned down to him and was now, with surprising strength, pulling him out of the river. Soon Mathis was lying on the planks like a stranded fish, spluttering and fighting for breath.

Together with the minstrel, he stared through the dark at a shadowy outline growing smaller and smaller. The screeching of the strange animal sounded one last time, like a contemptuous farewell.

Then the eerie sound and Agnes were both gone.

For some time there was nothing to be heard but the rushing of the river and Mathis's gasps. He was still too weak to get to his feet. Finally Melchior turned away from him and bent to pick up his sword, which was lying in front of him on the wet dock. With a soft *swish*, the weapon returned to its sheath.

"This is vexing," the minstrel murmured. "Extremely vexing."

"*Vexing?* Are you in your right—" Mathis was about to utter a curse, but the pain in his leg and the cold made him stop, groaning. "Agnes has been abducted," he finally went on, with difficulty. "Those devils will kill her."

Melchior silenced him with an impatient gesture. "They won't kill her. Didn't you hear what that oaf said? He's planning to sell her. Those scoundrels are obviously procurers, presumably put on our trail by the count or that rough-mannered peasant army. A countess will be far too valuable to such rascals for them to wring her neck the way they'd wring the neck of a goose. We only have to find Agnes, that's all."

Mathis uttered a despairing laugh. "And how are we to do that, for heaven's sake? Those fellows can put in anywhere with their boat, land on the riverbank, and continue their journey on foot. We'll never find her."

"Not if we go fluttering around in circles like headless chickens. We'll find Agnes again, trust me. You have my word of honor as a knight." Melchior placed his right hand on his heart and adopted a military stance, which with his slight figure and the cap askew on his head looked a little strange. "What's more, we ought to see to your injured friend now. If help of any kind is not too late for him already."

Mathis gave a start. He had entirely forgotten the master gunner in these last few minutes. Shivering all over, he limped after Melchior and was soon inside the tavern.

The room looked like two dozen inebriated landsknechts had been wrecking it. Chairs and tables lay broken on the floor, along with shattered tankards, dishes, and plates. Near the doorway they found the body of the robber whom Mathis had struck down with his cudgel. He lay in a puddle of blood, staring at the ceiling in death, his mouth twisted in incredulous astonishment. A second robber lay among the remains of a table. Melchior's blade had slit his throat. The body of the murdered landlord was still behind the counter.

Ulrich Reichhart was leaning against the wall under one of the windows, his head slumped forward, his limbs outstretched like those of a marionette with its strings cut.

Reichhart's eyes were half open, he was breathing heavily, and the robber chief's dagger was driven into his chest up to the hilt. Mathis could see at once that any help would indeed be too late.

"Ulrich, how are you doing?" Mathis gently approached his friend and comrade in arms. Reichhart had grown very close to his heart in the last year. "You . . . you'll be all right, believe me," he whispered. "I'll get us some shepherd's purse and birch bark, and then—"

Ulrich waved this away. "Young idiot. I know the state I'm in. Death is knocking at my door. Curse it!" He clutched his chest in great pain. "I . . . I always knew I'd end like this someday," he gasped. "I'm the son of a vivandière, born on the battlefield among dead bodies and corpse robbers. I know when it's over." He closed his eyes briefly, before going on. "Where's Agnes?"

"Those bastards have taken her." Mathis bit his lip. "But you can be sure we'll find her."

Reichhart nodded, and a slight smile played around his mouth. "You're a good lad, Mathis. Could have made it to sergeant in the army. You'll go far, with that head of yours." He laughed quietly, until he was suddenly spitting blood. "There I go, making clever firearms all my life, and a lousy dagger kills me. But dead is dead."

"Don't say that, Ulrich." Tears streamed down Mathis's cheeks. He felt like he had lost a father for the second time within a year.

"There . . . there's something else . . ." Reichhart managed to say. "It's to do with that ring, and the dreams tormenting Agnes. I ought . . . to have told you . . . much earlier. Now . . . now I guess it's too late . . . oh, curse it, this pain . . ."

Reichhart's fingers felt for the hilt of the dagger in his chest. Clutching it, he hesitated for a moment and then, with a swift movement, plucked the blade out of the wound. Blood poured from it, and Reichhart groaned. He fell to one side, and passed away.

"Oh God, no! It can't be like this!"

Mathis bent over Reichhart, but there was no life left in the old soldier. A peaceful expression had spread over his face, all the pain and sorrow gone. Trembling, Mathis closed the dead man's eyes.

"Out of the deep have I called unto thee, O Lord; Lord, hear my voice. O let thine ears consider well the voice of my complaint . . ."

When Mathis heard Melchior's soothing voice behind him, he joined in the ancient prayer. He had often spoken angrily to Agnes about the church and the pope, but now the solemn words gave him a strength that preserved him from despair.

"May he rest in peace. Amen."

When they had finished, Melchior bent over Mathis and felt the broken shaft of the arrow in his leg.

"It's not a deep wound, but it must be treated quickly or it will get inflamed. And you ought to take those wet clothes off at once."

Only now did Mathis feel the cold again. He had been swimming in icy water for the second time in a single day. Shivering, he stripped off his shirt, and Melchior handed him his own warm coat.

"I'll light a fire and see if I can find a few healing herbs in this place," the minstrel said, reassuringly. "But we ought to be out of here by daybreak, at the latest, before the first travelers arrive."

Mathis nodded in silence, feeling too weak to answer.

"What was it that Reichhart wanted to tell you just before he died?" Melchior asked thoughtfully. "Something to do with Agnes and her dreams."

"Whatever it was, he can tell it to God alone now," said Mathis, wrapping his trembling body in the coat. When he added no more, Melchior turned to the door.

"One more thing," Mathis called after him. "That creature on the robber leader's shoulder—what was it? It looked like a demon."

Melchior turned to him with a faint smile. "It can't breathe fire or work magic, if that's what you mean. It's a monkey. There are many of them in Sicily and the Spanish lands. They originally come from Africa. Mountebanks and quack doctors like to take them around the fairs."

"A . . . monkey." Mathis tried the sound of the strange word. Once again, he realized how remote from the world their life was here in the forests of the Wasgau. Beyond them, there were more things than he had ever dreamed of.

Exhausted, he watched Melchior take out the dead bodies and light a fire on the hearth. Until now, he had thought the minstrel merely amusing. However, now that he had seen him fighting, Mathis was beginning to develop something like respect for him. Melchior von Tanningen seemed to be a practiced swordsman, and experienced in other fields as well. He was probably the only one who could rescue Agnes now.

When the fire was burning, Melchior went out again. He came back only a little later, grinning, and carrying a bunch of dried herbs.

"I found this in the shed next to the tavern here: yarrow, plantain,

comfrey root. Hung up to dry, a farewell message from last summer."
He paused, his eyes twinkling as he looked at Mathis. "And I found
something else as well. Two horses. Not exactly noble steeds, but they
won't cost us anything. Mine host here won't be needing them again."
He smiled grimly and adjusted his sword belt. "Those fellows will yet
be sorry to have tangled with a minstrel knight from Franconia."

· 17 ·

Somewhere on the river Rhine, 22 April, Anno Domini 1525

THE BOAT MOVED STEADILY ALONG the sluggish waters of the Rhine. Vineyards, castles, and little villages passed Agnes like a toy landscape. A fishing boat went by only a stone's throw from her, closely followed by a raft laden with casks and timber, drawn along by two oxen on the bank. A few men were lashing the load down, so close to Agnes that they would surely hear if she shouted for help. But she knew it was a forlorn hope. And what could the fishermen do but wave to her?

Agnes sat in the bow of the boat, trailing her hands in the cool water. She would have liked to dangle her feet over the rail as well, but Marek and the man they called Snuffler were watching to make sure she didn't lean too far over. She had already tried jumping overboard once, on the day after her abduction. Thereupon Barnabas, the robber chief, had had her tied up. He no longer thought that necessary here, in the middle of the river, but all the same he had warned her.

"Next time you try getting away, I'll tie you up again," he had said. "And then I'll throw you over the rail with my own hands. I don't think you'd make it to the bank."

Agnes knew that he would carry out his threat. She was valuable goods, but the procurer with his wild black beard and shaggy hair suffered fits of rage, and in them he forgot any kind of reason. In addition, Barnabas had not forgiven Agnes for the fact that three of his men had lost their lives during her abduction.

"Death to the French! Death to the French!"

The shrill high screeching brought Agnes back from her thoughts. It came from a rusty cage standing on a traveling trunk in the middle of the boat. Two brightly colored birds with big hooked beaks sat on a perch in it, fluttering their wings in agitation. Agnes had been shocked when she first heard them speaking human language. By now, however, she realized that they were only imitating sounds. Barnabas called them *parrots*. He had bought them at a market in Naples, like the little monkey, Satan, who was on a leash, picking his way along the side of the boat as he stared at the bank. The monkey danced excitedly, like there were a wild lion lying in wait there, and the men laughed at the show he put on. Someone threw Satan a nut, which he caught skillfully and cracked with his sharp teeth.

Agnes hated Satan. It was true that she soon realized he was only an animal, not a demon, but all the same she sensed malice in the monkey. His little red eyes seemed to follow her all the time, he scratched and bit, and it was the noise he kicked up that had foiled her first attempt to escape. Sometimes she thought the animal had more brains than his master. He glared at her while he nibbled his nut.

"Hey, countess! Get your ass back into the boat before I make you move."

Barnabas stood in the stern and spat copiously into the water.

"I don't like the longing way you look at the other craft on the river," he went on. "You'll turn the fishermen's heads like a mermaid." He laughed and moved the rudder over to avoid a small whirlpool. The men had hoisted a sail, which made it possible for them to make slow progress upstream even without oars. A slight wind was blowing from the north, showing Agnes yet again that she was going farther and farther from her real destination.

She sighed quietly and slid down from the rail to sit on one of the front benches meant for oarsmen. They had been traveling for nearly ten days now. The fast-flowing river Queich had taken them to the Rhine, and since then their journey had been calm and monotonous. They were going upstream, which meant that the men sometimes had to row when the current was too strong. Now and then they put in at one of the harbors for ferries, to entertain the paying public with a genuine demon, two talking birds, and a few tricks. Barnabas held the attention of the audience with flamboyant speeches, while Marek and Snuffler picked pockets, and Samuel kept an eye on the two women.

Samuel was the worst of them. His malice was as great as the monkey's, and he was almost as hairy as the animal too. He was the brother of the man Mathis had killed at the Albersweiler tavern. Samuel's eyes often wandered like little spiders over Agnes and the innkeeper's daughter, Agathe, while he played with his knife and made suggestive remarks. He hadn't touched them yet, but that was only because Barnabas did not want his wares to be damaged. In addition, the pimp thought that little Agathe was still a virgin, which would put up her price. Barnabas had provided both girls with tight-fitting skirts and bodices such as the whores in the cities wore. When they put in at the little harbors, Agnes felt the men's eyes lingering on her like dirty fingers.

"Stop crying, little one. It will only make you tired and hungry." Agnes turned sympathetically to the innkeeper's daughter, who crouched in the bottom of the boat, her eyes red rimmed. She had wound her arms around her knees, as if that would keep anyone from touching her. Agathe was only thirteen years old, and she had lived alone with her father since her mother and little sister had died of consumption two years ago. Now her father was dead, too, and Agathe faced a short, unpleasant life as a cheap village whore or a landsknecht's wife.

"Would you like me to tell you another story about King Arthur and the Round Table?" asked Agnes, smiling as she bent down to the girl. When Agathe hesitantly nodded, Agnes drew close to her on the bench, and put an arm around her shoulders. Even if she was only a few years older, she felt almost like an anxious stepmother to the girl.

"The story of the Holy Grail," Agathe said, wiping her swollen eyes. "How Parcival found the castle of King Amfortas."

Agnes began telling the story in a steady voice. She knew the legend so well that it was easy for her to embellish it here and there, or make some slight changes. The girl listened, open-mouthed, forgetting her troubles at least for this short time. It was a mercy not granted to Agnes. She had never felt so alone. Tears rose to her eyes, and it was only Agathe's dreamy expression that kept her from flinging herself over the rail.

She needs me. She needs my stories.

Early in the evening, they put in at a place called Rotmühle. The town had a small ferry harbor, with a tollbooth and a long pier on which several bored quayside laborers were amusing themselves. When word got around that a boat from distant lands had arrived, with talking birds and a small hairy devil, the inhabitants of Rotmühle streamed down to the harbor. Barnabas and his men had made a kind of arena on the pier, with crates and bales of cloth. Inside the arena, the procurer stalked ostentatiously, announcing to the audience the sensational performance to come.

"The birds are from a country beyond the sea, where the dogs, the cats, even the much-feared lions can talk as well as we do," he told the gawping locals. "They are wiser than the pope, and more talkative than my revered mother-in-law."

The people laughed, while Agnes watched the show—which was always the same—from the rowing bench to which the men had tied her and Agathe. The rope chafed her wrists and, as always, Samuel kept a careful eye on her.

"You can be glad our master is spoiling you like this," the robber growled, cleaning his fingernails with the point of his knife. "If I had my way, you two would be feeding the fishes by now." He grinned.

"Of course not before I'd given you both a good seeing-to, by way of saying goodbye."

"You'd better hope I don't tell Barnabas you said that, blockhead," Agnes retorted. "We're valuable goods, and don't you forget it. No playing about with those."

She had found out, by now, that the procurer had been going up and down the Rhine and the Danube for several years, looking out for pretty girls he could buy from their destitute parents, selling them to brothels on the Black Sea as precious white-skinned ladies. It was a two-way trade, because he also brought Turkish slaves back to the German lands.

"Valuable goods, huh?" Samuel spat into the water. "Who says you're even a countess at all? Maybe those damn peasants lied to us. And if you are, what's the harm if we fuck you first?" He gave her a sly grin. "After all, we ought to try out our wares, eh?"

"Touch me and I'll scream so loud every soul in Rotmühle will hear it. And then we'll see what your master has to say."

Shrugging, Samuel turned away and went back to cleaning his fingernails with the knife. Meanwhile, Barnabas had taken the parrots out of their cage and had one perched on each arm.

"The pope is a glutton! The pope is a glutton!" one of the birds screeched. Barnabas had taught it that remark, because he had noticed that opinion in the German countries had turned against the Church of Rome, and this trick always got a good laugh. Then he pretended to be horrified and corrected the bird.

"Carry on like that, and you'll end up in the Inquisition's cooking pot," he threatened. "Follow your brother's example. He knows what's right." He pointed to the other parrot.

"Hurrah for Emperor Charles! Hurrah for Emperor Charles!" screeched the second bird. But this time the audience did not react.

"So where's the emperor when we need him, then?" someone shouted from the back rows. "The clergy, the dukes, the counts are taxing us out of house and home. But not for much longer. There's a storm brewing in the south fit to blow those fine gentlemen away."

Murmurs of agreement rose from the crowd.

"In Franconia the peasant bands have joined together into a large army," someone else called. "Even the knights are with them. And down by Lake Constance there's said to be thousands who forced the seneschal to sign a treaty. We ought to do that here."

"We don't need the emperor," several voices claimed. "We don't need Charles, nor his brother Ferdinand either. We'll take what's rightfully ours for ourselves."

Barnabas saw that the situation was getting out of hand. He raised both arms to appease his audience.

"Mercy, mercy! I promise you I'll pluck the bird this very day," he said, smiling, pulling a feather out of the screeching parrot's tail. "And then we'll see whether this stupid lickspittle goes on singing the emperor's praises."

A few of the spectators laughed, and Barnabas signed to Snuffler to hand him the monkey. It was time for the high point of the show.

"So never mind those two fawning courtiers the talking birds, we'll turn to a demon I caught in the jungle of West India with my own hands. That's where you'll find the entrance to hell, and I swear, this monster came crawling straight from the jaws of the inferno itself . . ."

Agnes turned away. She had heard the performance almost a dozen times now. Barnabas told his tall tales well, but she hated to see Marek and Snuffler secretly picking the pockets of the admiring crowd. She was about to turn back to little Agathe, when she saw something glinting on the bottom of the boat.

Samuel's knife.

The robber was now sitting in the middle of the boat, looking bored and throwing pebbles at the screaming seagulls. He had taken his eyes off the two prisoners, and the knife must have fallen out of his pocket.

Agnes reached her feet out, stretching as far as possible, but she could not get close enough to the knife. Finally she nudged Agathe, who was closer to it. The girl was about to protest, but then she saw what Agnes was looking at, and understood her meaningful gaze. Agathe nodded, and with her own feet pushed the knife within reaching distance of Agnes.

Both of them had their hands tied to the oarsmen's bench, but Agnes had no shoes on, so she could grasp the small knife with her toes. She slowly pulled it closer to her, until at last she felt the blade against her left calf.

"Curse it, when's the old fellow going to finish this performance? I want to go and get a drink before nightfall."

Samuel suddenly turned in their direction as he stared listlessly at the crowd of people on the quayside. Agnes gave a start, and the knife threatened to slip away from her toes. She felt sweat making her skin slippery. Beside her, Agathe let out a soft whimpering sound.

"What's the matter with you?" asked Samuel, looking suspiciously at the innkeeper's daughter.

"You want a drink, do you?" Agnes quickly put in. "There's a tavern over on the other side of the river. If you're lucky Barnabas may be going there later."

"Over where?" Samuel turned back to the river again. "Curses, I don't see anything."

"Over there, you slowworm. Near the three large linden trees where they're just unloading that raft."

While Samuel, baffled, gazed at the opposite bank, Agnes worked the knife far enough up the side of her leg to be able to take it in her fingers at last. Relieved, she hid it in the hollow of her hand.

"Oh, the light in the window has just gone out," she said with feigned surprise. "I'm afraid they must be closing."

"Stupid whore." Samuel threw a stone at her, but she ducked swiftly away. The knife in her hand felt cool and good. For a moment she considered cutting the rope at once, trying to overpower Samuel, and casting the boat off. But then she realized that Barnabas would soon be coming to the end of his performance, and there would be too much danger of his coming back before she had finished. So she thrust the knife up inside the sleeve of her dress. There would be a better opportunity soon.

Shortly the other men did indeed come back to the boat.

"Stingy Rhinelanders," Barnabas grumbled, while Satan hopped frantically up and down on his shoulder. "Devil take them all. Thinking twice about every coin they spend, and carrying on about rebellion until I thought the bailiffs would set the dogs on us." He grinned. "But all the same we relieved them of a few purses."

Marek spoke up thoughtfully. He was the most level-headed of the four men, and acted in a way as Barnabas's deputy. "Folk are saying there'll soon be war in Franconia, and Alsace too. It's all seething with unrest there. Peasants are gathering everywhere, setting castles and monasteries on fire. Maybe we'd do better to wait here."

"Nonsense," Barnabas said, heaving the cage with the squawking parrots on board. "The gentry have always cut the peasants down to size. Anyway, if it does come to war, we're no peasants, nor landsknechts neither. And whores are in even more demand when there's war than in peacetime." He laughed, and winked at the two young women.

"I'm sure we'll find a pimp ready to pay good money for you in Strasbourg, girlie, and as for the countess here . . ." His eyes went to Agnes, and he smiled broadly. "I've something special for you. One of the men from the raft told me just now that Khair Ad-Din's slave traders are out and about on the Black Sea."

Agnes frowned. "Khair who?"

"The lord of Algiers. A much-feared corsair and a mighty general, even if he's a godforsaken heathen. The man said he's looking for fairskinned noblemen's daughters for his harem. You'll fetch a good price for me, my little pigeon. A very good price."

The monkey on his shoulder bared its teeth and screeched. The sound was like mocking laughter.

• • •

With a loud cry of rage, Count Friedrich von Löwenstein-Scharfeneck smashed a goblet against the wall of his bedchamber and watched the wine drip to the floor, leaving blood-red streaks behind it. For a moment he was prey to the delusion that the wine really was blood, and the goblet a skull that he had beaten against the wall, again and again, with all his might.

Preferably the skull of that faithless bitch Agnes, he thought. *Or the skull of the minstrel who is probably fucking her somewhere . . .*

Friedrich sat down on the edge of the broad four-poster bed, closed his eyes, and tried to breathe calmly. These days he was overcome by fantasies of violence more and more frequently. Even as a small boy he had dreamed of battles in which he bathed in blood. But in the last few months such dreams had become increasingly graphic, and sometimes Friedrich wondered if it was these old walls slowly driving him mad.

These old walls, or Agnes . . .

A messenger had just arrived at Scharfenberg to tell him that the search for his wife had been fruitless. The landsknechts he sent out had not been able to find either Agnes or that damned minstrel. The trail petered out in nearby Albersweiler, and from there the two of them—seemingly accompanied by several others—had continued their flight by boat. Before that, their accomplices had killed an innkeeper and some of his guests. It was impossible to find out where they had gone. The German Empire was large, and Melchior von Tanningen was sure to know some castle or other where they could hide. For a moment the count had toyed with the notion of asking his influential father for help. But he would rather have cut off a finger than confess to the old man that he had been mistaken about Agnes.

Friedrich bit his lower lip so hard that he raised tiny drops of blood on it. Although he had been unwilling to admit it at first, he had really loved the girl. Even more, he had revered her as one of those old minnesingers might have revered the lady of whom he sang. Agnes was pretty, yes, but that wasn't it—a great many girls were pretty. Rather, it was her mixture of clever understanding and a passionately wild temper that had clouded his mind. Agnes was like a beast of prey that had to be tamed. In addition, she shared his passion for old times and the old stories. As a child, Friedrich had immersed himself in tales of knights and squires, and the bloodier the stories were, the better. He was crazy about legends of battles, treasures, and ancient mysteries. When, at the age of ten, he first heard of the Norman treasure, the greatest in Christendom, it was like he had been enchanted, and he had been under its spell ever since.

And now it seemed he had lost both Agnes and the treasure.

Friedrich rubbed his temples and tried to dispel the violent images that rose before his mind's eye.

I'll flay that minstrel, I'll flay him slowly. And I'll make Agnes watch.

Was the Norman treasure perhaps only a myth? All the sources he had studied indicated that some great secret lay buried at Trifels Castle. But what that secret was they did not say. Could those legends all be invented, like the tale of the sleeping Barbarossa? He had searched everywhere, in the castle itself, in the surrounding forest. He had even killed to eliminate anyone else who might know the secret.

Had all that been for nothing?

Friedrich was just about to go over to his large desk to study some old sheets of parchment when he heard a distant noise from the upper bailey.

Annoyed, he went to the window and was opening the heavy wooden shutters when an arrow flew past, only a hand's breadth away from him. It stuck in the tapestry on the other side of the room, its shaft quivering.

What the devil?

Alarmed, the count stood with his back against the wall, while the noise in the courtyard swelled. After some hesitation, he worked his way close enough to the window frame to venture a brief look outside.

It was sheer chaos in the courtyard.

Men-at-arms and landsknechts ran around, shouting. Some of the guards already lay twitching on the ground, while others had drawn their swords to fight. At first Friedrich thought that a few footpads had stormed the wall. But then he saw more and more men coming through an opening under the battlements. They were armed with boar spears, daggers, sickles, and small bows, and they were forcing the castle garrison farther and farther back under a hail of arrows. They came crawling out of the hole like a swarm of ants and flung themselves on the landsknechts, who had been taken by surprise. Only now did Friedrich realize who they were, and how they had made their way into the castle.

By God, the insurgent peasants. And they know about the sally port and the old secret tunnel.

Until now, the count had thought nothing of the warnings of other noblemen. He knew what had happened at Eusserthal, and he had also heard of other castles being captured over the last few weeks. However, Scharfenberg Castle was well fortified after last year's repairs, and Friedrich had far more men than most other feudal lords. But what use was that if the enemy could get into the castle along a secret passage?

It was Agnes. Agnes told them where they could come in.

Friedrich glanced down into the courtyard once again to get an impression of the situation. More arrows flew his way, but they bounced off the outer wall. A single man, a hunchback, stood on the steps up to the keep. The cripple was not fighting but watching the fray below him with an expression of satisfaction, like a general standing on a hill. He suddenly looked up at the window, and his face twisted in a grin.

"There's the count, men!" Shepherd Jockel shouted, pointing at Friedrich with his three-fingered hand. "Get him! We'll hang him from the highest pinnacle of his castle and watch him kick."

Count Friedrich von Löwenstein-Scharfeneck ran to his desk and snatched up the most important of the documents. Obliged to run away from a pack of peasants—how had it come to this? He must at least save the papers about the Norman treasure. Everything else would probably go up in smoke. Fear and fury swept over Friedrich at the same time, while the blood rushed to his head.

You'll pay for this, Agnes. Oh, you'll pay in full.

The count cast one last look at the courtyard. Then, in sudden panic, he looked for a possible route of escape. But wherever Friedrich turned his eyes, he could not see one anywhere.

Loud, heavy footsteps, like those of a large, angry animal, were hurrying up the steps to his chamber.

Mathis swayed in his sleep. He didn't know whether he was in a bed or on a horse. It was a steady up and down movement, accompanying him through his dreams. He was bathed in sweat. Yet he kept seeing Agnes with her hands stretched out to him, before she disappeared, screaming, drawn into a black whirlpool. The whirlpool was like a large ring, turning faster and faster. Mathis reached for her, but her hands slipped away from him, and she disappeared into the darkness.

"Agnes! The ring—the ring!"

Screaming, he opened his eyes and saw a termite-eaten wooden ceiling above him. A damp, moth-worried sheet covered his body like a shroud. Mathis threw it off, sat up, and realized that he had been lying in a bed. It stood in a low-ceilinged attic room with old, rotting rushes on the floor. The red globe of the sun setting in the west shone through the open window.

Where am I? How long have I been asleep?

He mopped cold sweat off his forehead, and memory slowly came back. Soon after they had set off from Albersweiler, he had fallen sick with fever, and they'd had to rest for a while. After that they had ridden for days, first along the Queich, then in the shallow valley of the Rhine, going upstream, because Melchior was convinced that the procurers would go south, toward the Danube and the Black Sea. They had asked in every tavern after a group of men with two women and a small, hairy monster, but no one could give them any information.

Meanwhile, the wound in Mathis's leg had become more and more inflamed. The healing herbs that Melchior had found in the Albersweiler tavern had failed to have the desired effect. Shaken by feverish fits, Mathis had ridden until he no longer knew if he was awake or dreaming. The swaying of the horse was his constant companion. The green landscape of willow, birches, and marshy water meadows blurred more and more indistinctly before his eyes into a thick mist that threatened to smother him. At some point he had simply fallen off the horse. From then on his memories consisted only of fragments in which Melchior spooned hot soup into him or changed his bandages.

Agnes. We must go on in search of Agnes. Or has that minstrel left me behind?

Mathis hastily stood up, but immediately felt dizzy. He staggered, and then fell full length on the wooden floorboards, knocking over a bowl of water that had been standing beside the bed. The crash of the breaking bowl echoed through the room.

Next moment he heard hasty footsteps on the stairs outside, and the door was flung open. Melchior von Tanningen stood in the doorway with a bowl of steaming soup in his hands.

"Who said you could get up?" asked the minstrel, wagging a mock-threatening finger at him. "You're far too weak still. Look what you've done."

He picked up the broken pieces of the bowl, helped Mathis back into bed, and then handed him the soup. "Here, eat this. A good meat broth, it'll help you to get your strength back."

Mathis pushed the bowl away. "We don't have time for that. We must—"

"What *you* must do is get better. A day more or less won't make any difference."

"How long have I been lying here?" Mathis asked.

"Three days."

"A whole *three days*?" Mathis sat up, horrified, but Melchior laid his hand on his shoulder.

"You can be thankful you're still alive. Another day on horseback and you'd have died of gangrene. I had to carry you the last few miles to this inn like a sack of flour." The minstrel smiled reassuringly and put a spoonful of soup in Mathis's mouth. "Anyway, we're no worse off for the delay. If I'm right, and those louts are going on upstream in their boat, they'll have to get it hauled along the towpath, or row it, or put up a sail. All that takes time. We'll be faster with the horses."

"Suppose they're going downstream?" asked Mathis.

"I don't think they are." Melchior's eyes twinkled. "I have good news, Master Wielenbach. While you were lying here sick, I've been down to the river harbor talking to some travelers coming from the south. They remember a group of men with a monkey and two talking birds. And they think there were two women with them. So my assumption was right." Melchior dipped the spoon in the soup again, and ostentatiously blew on it to cool it. "Now, eat up. The sooner you're on your feet again, the sooner we can set off and catch up with Agnes. How does that sound?"

Sighing, Mathis gave in and ate his soup. It tasted surprisingly good, of meat, salt, and fat. Every spoonful seemed to give him new strength.

"You spoke of a ring several times in your dreams," Melchior said, watching Mathis eating. "Was that the ring that Agnes has with her? Do you know anything about it?"

Mathis shrugged his shoulders. "Only what Agnes has probably told you, too. She found it one day tied to her falcon's leg. The ring itself dates from the time of Barbarossa, and it's a signet ring."

"Did she ever see it earlier?" Melchior persisted. "Maybe when she was a child?"

"Not that I know of. Her dreams began when she had the ring with her, but that is all I know."

Feeling pleasantly well fed, Mathis spooned up the last of the soup. "How have you been paying for food and these beds?" he asked.

"You didn't sell your lute, did you? Not that I'd exactly burst into tears over that, but all the same . . ."

The minstrel smiled. "No, I would never do that. But I'm afraid we'll have to content ourselves with coats of much coarser cloth. The count's garments brought in some money—the silver clasp on the cloak you were wearing was worth a small fortune in itself. What we have now should pay for the rest of our journey."

"And where will that take us?" Mathis's face darkened. "Even if the men are going upstream, they could leave the river anywhere. We don't even know if Agnes is still alive."

"She's certainly alive. She's too valuable to them that way. And the leader of those scoundrels gave us a clue, remember? They're going to sell our fair maiden, as he put it, on the Black Sea, and what with the stuff they're taking around with them, they'll go there by water as far as possible." The minstrel got up from the side of the bed. "I served a count in the Black Forest a few years ago. He was a drunken old sot, but he paid well and let me go around the local villages, so I know my way about those parts."

Melchior picked up a rush from the floor and used it to draw some lines in the dust on the floor. "This is the Rhine," he explained. "Farther east is the Danube, and eventually the Danube leads to the Black Sea. Those two great rivers are the largest in the German Empire. To reach the Danube from the Rhine, travelers often use a small river called the Kinzig, which flows, *voilà* . . ." The minstrel drew another line from the Danube to a certain place on the Rhine, "into the beautiful city of Strasbourg."

He made an elegant bow and threw the rush out of the window. "I'd wager my lute that the villains will stop off there with Agnes. If we make haste, we'll get there in time to rescue her from those scoundrels. Wonderful material for a ballad. When I appear at the singers' contest in the Wartburg this coming fall, the audience will love it, *bien sûr*."

Melchior von Tanningen raised his pleasing tenor voice and sang ardently:

But in the forest, sad to say,
The lady fair is stolen away
On board a boat—who now can save
Her beauty from a watery grave?
Two warriors bold are on her track,
Hoping to win the lady back.
In Strasbourg town they come to battle . . .

Here the minstrel hesitated, and shook his head. "No, nothing much rhymes with *battle* . . . cattle, rattle? They won't do. I'm afraid I'll have to polish up those lines a bit more, but we have a long journey ahead of us, so I'll have plenty of time."

Groaning, Mathis lay back in the bed again, too tired and weak to protest.

Agnes lay in the bottom of the boat, trying to breathe very quietly. Agathe was beside her, sobbing now and then in her sleep and tossing and turning restlessly from side to side. Agnes fervently hoped that her sobs would not awaken Samuel, snoring on one of the oarsmen's benches as he leaned on the rail.

It was now five days since she had stolen his knife, and so far something had always happened to keep her from using it. The men had not been sleeping soundly enough, or the place where they had stopped was not a favorable choice, or they were anchored too far from the bank. But here, not far from Strasbourg, she thought the right time for her to escape had come. The robbers had chained her and Agathe to the benches, as they did every night, to keep them from running away. A rusty padlock was attached to the chain around her right ankle, cutting off the blood supply. She had already practiced forcing the lock with Samuel's stolen knife several times in secret.

With the tip of the knife, she felt her way through the keyhole to the springs inside the padlock. She had to start again a couple of times, but at last there was a slight *click*, and the lock sprang open. Agnes managed to catch hold of the chain at the last minute, before it crashed to the bottom of the boat. She carefully placed it beside a coil of rope and rubbed her foot. Blood pulsed painfully through her ankle.

Then she was free.

Hesitating, Agnes looked at little Agathe, who was still crying in her sleep. It would be so easy just to let herself slip over the rail of the boat. A few strokes, and she could swim to the bank and safety. But she had made up her mind to take the girl with her. And besides that, she wanted to get hold of something first.

The ring.

Barnabas was keeping it in the seaman's chest built into the bottom of the boat, near the bow. Agnes knew that she was endangering her escape, if not making it impossible, but she couldn't go without Barbarossa's ring. It was almost as if it were calling to her. Everything had begun with that ring, and everything would probably end with it as well.

One way or another.

Moving at snail's pace, she straightened up and peered over the side of the boat. The moon was shining brightly above the Rhine, casting its pale light on the rooftops of the little town of Kehl that lay on the eastern side of the broad river. This was where they had anchored. A wide wooden bridge standing on piers led across the Rhine to Strasbourg. She could see a red glow of light in the city, and the tower of the famous minster pointed to the sky like a warning finger.

Over the last few days, Barnabas had been constantly boasting of the high price he would ask the Turkish slave traders for Agnes. He planned to make for the Danube by way of the Black Forest, and then they could reach the Black Sea within two or three months. However, he had looked increasingly concerned the closer they came to Strasbourg, for there were more and more signs of war on both banks of the Rhine, the Palatinate side and the Alsatian side. As the boat went along, Agnes saw churches, abbeys, and castles burning almost every day, and often hamlets and peasant villages were also engulfed in flames. The baggage trains of troops of landsknechts were seen on the great trading routes on the banks of the river more and more often, strung out like long snakes winding their way over the water meadows, with drums and pipes playing as they marched toward the peasants. The few times the robbers stopped to come on land and stock up on their provisions, they heard horror stories of burned fields, mass rapes, murdered peasant children, and landsknechts drinking blood. Yet it did indeed seem that the peasants were on their way to victory. In a small town called Weinsberg in Swabia a genuine count—the son-in-law of Emperor Maximilian, no less—had been made to run the gauntlet. The great city of Stuttgart had been conquered already, and more districts were falling into the hands of the peasants all the time. Agnes kept thinking of Mathis, who had always told her that the time of rule by the nobility would soon be over. Was that reversal of fortune really imminent?

She carefully took one step at a time, to avoid making the planks of the boat creak. Marek, Snuffler, and Barnabas slept beside the boat on the pier by the bank, wrapped in threadbare blankets. Agnes could see the procurer's hairy chest as he snored like a dozen woodcutters at once. Only Samuel had been left in the boat as a guard, but his head had slumped forward, and a thin trickle of saliva ran from the corner of his mouth. He did not look like he represented any danger.

Satan might, though.

The monkey was crouching on one of the front oarsmen's benches. In the dark, Agnes could not see whether his malicious little red eyes were open or closed. Presumably she wouldn't find out until he began chattering angrily. But she had to take the risk.

By now she had reached the monkey and was only a few steps away from the bow. She said a silent prayer, and then prowled past Satan like a cat.

One of the planks creaked.

Agnes stood as still as a pillar of salt, but the monkey had already heard her. Hissing quietly, it straightened up and tried to jump onto her shoulder, but the leash around its neck pulled it back. The steady scratch of its claws on the planks sounded as loud as thunder.

Swiftly, she reached under her skirt and brought out a few nuts that she had been secretly collecting for the last few days. She put them in front of Satan's nose, whereupon he first looked at her suspiciously, but then began nibbling with relish. Agnes heaved a sigh of relief. She would have at least a moment's peace.

She quickly went the rest of the way to the bow and slid back the bolt on the seaman's chest. She had to search about, but at last, among a few discolored coins and all kinds of cheap trinkets, she found her ring. Picking it up, she was about to hurry back to Agathe and set her free when there was a deafening sound.

It was a shrill horn signal.

Agnes had to control herself to keep from bursting into tears. It had taken her so much trouble to open the lock, pacify the monkey, and go on to the bow of the boat undiscovered, and now the horn signal had wrecked it all.

Barnabas and the others turned restlessly in their sleep, the parrots began to screech in their cage, and Samuel rubbed his eyes, muttering. The large quantity of brandy that he had consumed only a few hours earlier kept him from becoming fully alert yet. Agnes hesitated for a moment, and then put the ring back in the chest. If Barnabas found that it was missing before she made her escape, he would certainly suspect her before anyone else. The ring must wait.

She closed the chest, hurried back, and lay down beside Agathe, who was just opening her eyes. The padlock clicked shut again.

"What—" Agathe began, surprised, but Agnes put her hand over the girl's mouth.

"*Sh!*"

It was not a second too soon. Samuel was already making his way over the benches to them. He looked relieved to see both girls still lying at the bottom of the boat.

"Thought you two pretty birds had flown," he said. "What's that damned racket?"

Sure enough, more horns were blowing now, and they were joined by the clatter of horses' hooves, the sound of drums, and of soldiers' songs in the distance. Barnabas had risen to his feet on the pier, and now he stared at the bridge. A great troop of soldiers was crossing from Strasbourg and making for the town of Kehl. It stretched so far back that Agnes couldn't see the end of it.

"Curse it, what are those landsknechts doing in the middle of the night?" Barnabas growled angrily. "Can't they let decent citizens get a good night's rest?"

By this time the first soldiers had reached the bridgehead, only a few feet away from where the boat was anchored. Barnabas raised his arm and hailed the nearest landsknecht.

"Hey, what brings you here at this time of night?"

The soldier had a drum buckled in front of his stomach and was beating out a dark, monotonous rhythm on it. He looked at Barnabas without interest.

"Going north. The peasants are outside Speyer, and even the bishop there is shit-scared," he finally replied. "Didn't you hear of it? All Swabia, Franconia, and the Palatinate are in turmoil. Those stupid millet-eaters are a real plague. High time we tanned their hides."

Agnes pricked up her ears. If Speyer fell, Annweiler was not far away. Had the peasants already captured Trifels Castle?

"To be sure, you're doing God's work." Barnabas nodded earnestly, as he shifted from foot to foot. Agnes could almost see his mind busy at work. "Tell us, what's it like in the Black Forest? Has the war reached there, too? We were planning to go along the Kinzig and then . . ."

The landsknecht roared with laughter. "Not a good notion to travel in times like these, not a good notion at all. Didn't I just tell you? The land's laid waste, villages are burning. Only a fool would travel now—there's nothing but death waiting on the road."

At that moment one of the parrots screeched. "The pope is a glutton! The pope is a glutton!" The other bird joined in. "Hurrah for Emperor Charles! Hurrah for Emperor Charles!"

The astonished soldier looked suspiciously at Barnabas. "What in heaven's name is that?"

"Only my talking birds." Barnabas managed to smile at him. "We're a company of traveling entertainers. I have a monkey as well."

"Entertainers, with a monkey?" The landsknecht, enthusiastic now, looked at his comrades, who were about to move on. "Did you hear that? We could use them in the baggage train, right? The men like something to laugh at, after all the killing. And I see you have women too. Pretty women, at that."

His lascivious eyes lingered on Agnes, who was still beside the rail of the boat, observing the conversation. Meanwhile, Barnabas seemed to be thinking.

"Thanks," he finally called to the soldiers. "I'll think over your proposition."

"Do that. And remember, where we go there's loot. And women, wine, and gold. We thrash the whereabouts of those saucy peasants' money out of them and then hang them from the nearest tree."

Laughing, he beat his drum again and moved away with the procession as it rolled over the bridge like an army of ants. Barnabas stayed where he was for some time. Finally he turned to his men and the two captives, and twirled his black beard.

"You heard what he said," he announced in the tone of one used to giving orders. "The journey through the Black Forest is too dangerous. I'm not risking my life for a couple of savages hoping for an intact delivery. Particularly not when there's a better opportunity." He rubbed his hands together with satisfaction. "We'll go north with this baggage train. When the unrest dies down we can always go along the Danube and do business there. Until then, let's go where fate casts us up." Barnabas raised his head, sniffing the air like a dog. It smelled of burning torches, gunpowder, and horse dung. "I smell money, plenty of money. Unpack the crates, men, and let's steal a cart. We'll go along with the war."

When Mathis and Melchior reached the gates of Strasbourg, the city was pure pandemonium. The streets were crowded with fugitives who seemed to come from all over Alsace. There were many monks and Catholic priests among them, but also prosperous citizens with all their worldly goods in rucksacks or on handcarts. Babies were crying, small children whining for their parents, barkers and peddlers taking advantage of the crowds to offer their wares at greatly inflated prices.

During the last few days, the two men had ridden so fast that their horses were going lame. They had finally sold the animals to hungry landsknechts and came the last twenty miles on foot. The countryside through which they traveled was in turmoil. At first only the peasants of Upper Alsace and the Sundgau had risen, but soon the whole western side of the Rhine was on fire. The simple folk were now taking up arms in neighboring Lorraine as well. Their joint leader was a man called Erasmus Gerber, a craftsman who had unified the separate and sometimes conflicting bands and had many supporters in Strasbourg itself.

Melchior was just back from one of the many harbor taverns that lay on the Ill, a tributary of the Rhine. The minstrel, looking discouraged, shook his head. They had already tried a dozen inns, asking in vain if anyone had seen a group of entertainers with a monkey on their way to the Black Forest. They had also questioned beggars and pickpockets in the streets and had visited raftsmen, brothel keepers, and ferrymen, but so far with no success at all.

"I think we'd better try Kehl, on the other bank of the river," said Melchior, as they walked through Strasbourg's stinking tanners' quarter. "Maybe the fellows set off from there just before we arrived, leaving Strasbourg behind."

"If they ever came to Strasbourg at all," said Mathis, gloomily. His leg had healed up well in the last few days, leaving him with only a slight limp. But doubts still tormented him. Had Agnes and her companions really gone upstream along the Rhine?

They crossed the forecourt of the minster, which marked the center of the city. The cathedral was so enormous that for a moment Mathis forgot his troubles and looked up, marveling at the towers, the crooked rooftops, the figures of saints, and above all the gargoyles who seemed to mock him with their grimaces. He had heard that the minster now belonged to the Lutherans, who had established themselves in Strasbourg very early. The city was one of the spiritual centers of the German Empire; maybe the revolution would spread from here all over the country. But when Mathis saw all the weeping, wailing fugitives streaming toward the city gates, he doubted whether the peasants were going about it the right way.

Good never comes of evil, he thought.

They left Strasbourg and went toward the Rhine down a broad road that was spanned by a mighty bridge at this point. Handcarts and horse-drawn wagons came to meet them, and more and more often they saw people who wore bandages drenched with blood, or who had to be carried on stretchers. One-legged soldiers and beggars with horribly scarred faces held out their hands to Mathis and Melchior.

The scene was far pleasanter in Kehl. The gentle foothills of the Black Forest reached far to the east; barges and rafts rocked in the water by the bank, ready to go on along the little river Kinzig. There were a couple of taverns but, here again, no one had heard of a troupe of entertainers.

Discouraged, the two men sat down at last on a dock and dangled their bare feet in the cool water that washed away the dirt of the last few days and soothed the cracked skin and blisters that had developed as they walked the final miles.

"It's just as I said," Mathis sighed. "We've finally lost the trail."

Melchior von Tanningen said nothing, but Mathis could tell that his mind was hard at work. Empty-eyed, the minstrel gazed at the water as he bit his lower lip. Melchior had proved a valuable traveling companion. Not only was he an outstanding swordsman, his reason was almost as sharp as the blade of his Toledo steel sword. Until now, he had come up with a solution to all their problems, but this time even his store of knowledge seemed to be exhausted.

"I was so sure," he said, shaking his head wearily. "So damned sure."

They both fell silent. Finally Melchior stood up and put on his dusty boots again. Reaching for his lute, he strummed a few notes. "Well, we can always go on to St. Goar," he suggested.

"That monastery downstream along the Rhine?" Mathis looked at him blankly. "What would we do there?"

"Find out more about the secret Agnes dreamed about. My ballad can't end unfulfilled. What's more—if Agnes does manage to escape, she will surely set off for St. Goar herself. Maybe we'll meet again there."

"In a ballad, maybe, but not in real life."

A hoarse cry interrupted Mathis. It came from a small tavern at the far end of the harbor that they had not yet visited. Now a shrill voice could be heard, like someone calling out in mortal fear.

"Hurrah for Emperor Charles! Hurrah for Emperor Charles!"

Melchior von Tanningen gave a wry smile. "Sounds as if respect for Charles V still survives, even in these bad times. Rather dangerous but very praiseworthy, if you ask me."

"It sounds more like a child, or . . ."

Suddenly Mathis remembered the night of the abduction, the rocking boat, and the strange voice that he had heard. This voice sounded just the same, hardly human, more of an animal screech, almost as if it came from . . .

Mathis put a hand to his brow. Then he jumped up, pulling Melchior with him as he began to run.

"Come on, quick!" he cried. "Maybe we're still on the trail after all."

Together, they ran to the crooked little tavern that nestled against one of the warehouses along the harbor. Mathis pushed the door open and blinked at the dimly lit room inside. There was not a single guest to be seen, but a cage stood on one of the scratched tables, and there was a brightly colored bird inside the cage. It flapped and screeched at the top of its voice.

"Hurrah for Emperor Charles! Hurrah for Emperor Charles!"

Breathing heavily, Melchior stopped in the doorway. "By my faith, a parrot," he said at last, laughing. "Presumably one of the parrots those fellows had with them."

Mathis nodded. "I heard that cry once before, when they were taking Agnes away on their boat," he explained. "I couldn't understand the words, but I do remember that sound." He went up to the cage and looked at the strange bird. When he put his finger on the perch in the cage, the creature pecked at it with its large beak.

"Do you two want to buy it?" asked a deep voice. The bald-headed landlord had come up the steps from the cellar, puffing and blowing. He had a cask of wine in his broad, hairy arms, which he now put down carefully. "You can have it. That bird is getting on my nerves."

"Where did you get it?" asked Mathis.

"From a couple of loud-mouthed entertainers that wanted to be rid of it. I guess it was too risky for them, traveling through the German lands these days with a bird that loves the emperor." The landlord let out a bark of laughter. "Those louts said it could talk like any book, but that's all I've heard it say."

"Hurrah for Emperor Charles! Hurrah for Emperor Charles!" the parrot repeated.

"Well, how about it?" asked the man. "You want to buy it or not?"

"These entertainers," said Melchior von Tanningen. "Did they by any chance have a monkey and two women with them? I mean, one young girl, one slightly older girl with freckles and wild fair hair?"

The bald-headed man stared at him in surprise. "That's right. They were here at my place. Drank a mug of spiced wine apiece before going on their way again."

"Going up the Kinzig into the Black Forest, I expect?" the minstrel inquired.

"Oh God, no! Far too dangerous these days. Those oafs went off with the landsknechts from Lorraine. Bound north for Swabia. Hoping for good loot, I guess." Suddenly a calculating look came into the landlord's eyes. "You know them, do you?" he asked sharply.

Mathis dismissed this. "Er, no. We . . . we met them once, but . . ."

"Because they stole my handcart and left this lousy bird here in return. So I suggest you take it away with you and give me the money for a new cart." The landlord squared up to them menacingly. "How about it, then?"

"One more question before we talk business," Melchior persisted. "How long have you been in possession of this delightful little creature?"

"Three days. It was three days ago those scoundrels absconded." The landlord stretched his lips in a bitter smile. "Three long days and nights I've had to put up with this shrieking."

"Hurrah for Emperor Charles! Hurrah for Emperor Charles!"

The parrot beat its wings frantically, and Melchior made a little bow.

"Pleased to have made your acquaintance. Unfortunately we have no use for the bird. But I know that there are some exquisite recipes at the French court in which parrots play a leading role. Maybe you could offer your guests a truly exotic dish one of these days."

Without another word, they went out to the harbor, leaving the landlord hurling abuse after them. For a long time they could still hear the call of the parrot, risking life and limb as it went on praising His Majesty emperor Charles V to the skies.

"Hurrah for Emperor Charles! Hurrah for Emperor Charles! Hurrah for Emperor Charles . . ."

· 18 ·

Höchberg in Franconia, 4 May, Anno Domini 1525

Evening twilight was falling, a few days later and many miles farther away, as Mathis and Melchior walked through a devastated landscape.

Once the bald-headed landlord had told them which way the robbers had gone, the two set off immediately. Just beyond Kehl, Melchior managed to steal two old nags from a stable. But the horses had begun to go lame three days later, so they were back to traveling on foot. In spite of the pace they set for themselves, they had not yet caught up with the baggage train of the landsknechts from Lorraine. Or had they perhaps left it behind long ago? It was as if the war had swallowed up the soldiers lock, stock, and barrel.

By now, in conversation with some of the fugitives they met, Mathis had discovered that the landsknechts with whom the procurers were traveling were probably off to join the Swabian League. It was only for show that the commander of the league, Seneschal Georg von Waldburg-Zeil, had negotiated with the peasants near Lake Constance, and he was now preparing to strike a blow to utterly destroy them. Some ten thousand mercenaries were marching from the south, including over a thousand armored cavalry, murdering and burning all the country on the right-hand bank of the Rhine in an unparalleled campaign of vengeance. No one seemed to know just where those landsknechts were now, but Mathis suspected that he and Melchior, setting off in such haste, had gone much too far north.

"We're looking for the proverbial needle in a haystack," he murmured as they passed half a dozen burned-out cottages. "This war is everywhere, and Agnes is in the middle of it, unprotected, alone with those animals. She may not even still be alive."

The corpses of several peasants swung from the branches of two charred elms in the wind. There were women and children among them.

"You lack confidence, Master Wielenbach," said Melchior von Tanningen. Despite the gloomy atmosphere, he strummed a few chords on his lute. The wind carried the thin sound of the music away. "As long as Agnes is still with the robbers there's hope. A parrot and a monkey. Sooner or later someone is going to remember such strange creatures. And then we'll know we're on the right track again."

"Suppose Agnes has been sold to someone else?"

"Then we'll find the scoundrel who bought her." Melchior smiled confidently. "Don't forget, this ballad of mine is going to win the prize at the Wartburg. And the ballads that I compose always end happily."

He plucked a few strings again, and Mathis rolled his eyes.

"You'd be doing me a real favor if you'd only—" he began. But Melchior von Tanningen had already stopped playing and slung the lute over his shoulder. His hand went to the hilt of his sword.

"What is it?" Mathis asked cautiously.

They were just crossing a field of wheat, with its stalks rustling in the wind. Gray swathes of smoke drifted toward the two travelers. Melchior waved his hand in front of his face to disperse the smoke. He peered ahead, with some difficulty, for visibility was getting worse all the time, and in addition the sun was going down behind the trees.

"There's someone here," the minstrel finally said. "In this field. See for yourself." He pointed to some stalks of wheat bending away from the direction of the wind. "It's too late to run for it, so let's at least hope there are not too many of them."

And indeed, several figures now emerged from the smoke. There were about a dozen men, all of them shabbily dressed peasants, armed with scythes and flails. They had been hiding among the ears of the tall wheat and now slowly approached the travelers with their weapons raised.

"God be with you," Melchior called to them, with a friendly smile. "We are simple folk on our travels, and mean no one any harm." He raised his hands, whispering to Mathis, "If they attack us, we fight back until we've created enough confusion to let us run over to the outskirts of those woods, understand?"

Mathis nodded hesitantly and clutched his cudgel. The way the usually amusing minstrel could suddenly become a dangerous fighting man never ceased to surprise him.

The peasants reached them. They all looked exhausted, and many had blood-stained bandages on their heads, legs, or arms. The expression in their eyes was like that of hunted animals. Mathis suspected that they were the survivors of a major battle.

"Who are you, and what are you doing in these parts?" shouted a tall man with the mark of a recent wound on his face, running from his right ear to his lip. He was brandishing a scythe, ready to strike with it at any provocation.

"We are ordinary pilgrims on the way to Rome," Melchior said as calmly as possible. "We ask for free passage, as the old law prescribes."

"What old law?" The giant glared at him blankly. Mathis realized that he was not especially bright, but all the same, he seemed to be the leader of the band. "You're dressed too fine for a pilgrim," he grunted at last, and then pointed to Melchior's lute. "What would you want with that thing in Rome?"

"I am going to sing a song at the porch of St. Peter's Basilica about the sad plight of peasants in the German Empire, and pray to God to be with them."

There was a general murmuring. Obviously these men could not agree on what to do next.

"Curse Rome and curse the clergy!" one of them suddenly shouted. "That monk Luther is our new pope now. And the sale of indulgences is forbidden on pain of death."

"The sale of indulgences, maybe, but not pilgrimage," Melchior objected. "Didn't the venerable Master Luther himself go on pilgrimage to Rome?"

That left the peasants baffled, and they began whispering together again. Finally it was the tallest man who spoke up once more.

"One way or another, you're neither of you simple folk like us," he spat, looking Melchior von Tanningen up and down. "Particularly not you. You're a merchant or a baron or some such thing. Maybe there's even a ransom for the likes of you two. The knight can decide what we do with you, so come along with us."

Taking Mathis and Melchior into their midst, the men drove them on with kicks and blows into the shady beech wood that began at the far end of the field. Before long, the trees thinned out, and a wide plain with campfires burning all over it stretched out before their eyes. Now, as evening came on, it was as if the starry sky had come down to earth.

The smoke, thought Mathis. *And I thought it was hay burning. This is the largest camp I ever set eyes on.*

Almost all the men sitting beside the many fires in the twilight wore the simple, gray-brown clothing of serfs. Banners waved in the wind, most of them with the image of the tied shoe typically worn by peasants that had long ago become a symbol of the wars of liberation. Here and there, someone was playing a fiddle or performing a melancholy tune on a willow whistle, but many of the men had a weary, grim look, and a good number wore bandages stiff with dirt. As

Mathis and Melchior were led through the camp, they both drew hostile glances.

"Hang 'em from the nearest tree," someone called after them. "They're gentry, anyone can see that."

"Hold your tongue, you drunken sot, the knight will decide what to do with them," the tall leader retorted. "You know he wants all prisoners brought to him."

While Mathis was still trying to work out who this strange knight might be, they approached a plain black tent in the middle of the camp. Two elderly peasants with stooped shoulders stood on guard outside it, holding boar spears.

The giant cleared his throat and stepped nervously from foot to foot. "Here's two prisoners that might earn us a ransom," he said humbly, bowing his head. "Could be the commander ought to see them."

"We'll take them to him. You wait outside."

The guards pushed the two captives into the tent, which was illuminated by a large fire in a brazier. Beyond it, in the dimmer light, was a large table with many maps lying on it. A figure bent over them. With a grunt of dissatisfaction, the man rolled up one of the sheets of parchment again and turned to Mathis and the minstrel. Only now could they see him properly. Mathis noticed that Melchior von Tanningen gave a brief start, as if he recognized him.

The man whom the peasants called "the knight" was broadly built, and at first sight looked fat, but his sturdy arms and bull-like neck suggested that most of his bulk consisted of muscle. A scratched breastplate glinted in the firelight.

"Well, well, two prisoners," he growled. "So what were you doing so close to my camp? Spying? Come on, we'll find out anyway. Or do you want me to hit you with *this*, eh?"

The knight menacingly raised his hand, and Mathis instinctively flinched back. The man's entire right forearm was made of iron. The stiff fingers gleaming in the firelight were curled into a fist, with which he now struck the table so forcefully that some of the parchment scrolls fell to the ground.

"Speak up, or I'll have your tongues cut out."

"We are simple pilgrims on our way to Rome." Melchior began, but the knight swept a pitcher of wine off the table with his iron hand, silencing the minstrel.

"That story may satisfy my credulous peasants, but it's not good enough for me. You're clearly going in the wrong direction for Rome."

"We lost our way," Melchior replied.

The knight was about to make some reply, but then he suddenly narrowed his eyes and looked closely at the minstrel. "Wait a moment, I know you from somewhere," he murmured. "You're from Franconia, like me, right? I've seen you before."

"You must be confusing me with someone else. I'm just an ordinary minstrel in the service of a count in the Palatinate."

The knight came over to them with a threatening look. "Oh yes, just an ordinary minstrel, are you?" he boomed. "And I suppose the fellow with you is his lordship the count in person?"

"I'm a common craftsman," Mathis said. "We met on our pilgrimage only a few weeks ago."

"Ho, and what sort of craft is yours, then?"

"I'm a master gunner."

Mathis had spoken without much thought. Now that a sudden silence descended in the tent, and he saw the two guards as well as the knight scrutinizing him curiously, he realized that he might have made a mistake.

"A master gunner?" the knight finally inquired in a quiet voice. "Really? Then you're certainly serving in some army or other in times like these. Who knows, you may even be with the Swabian League?"

Mathis earnestly shook his head. "No, no. I learned my father's trade at the count's castle. I've never been beyond the Wasgau in my life. I would never—"

The knight's iron hand shot out and seized Mathis by the throat so firmly that he retched. Colored circles appeared before his eyes, while he struggled like a fish on the hook.

"You lie the moment you open your mouth," the commander snapped. "But you're in luck. As chance would have it, we need a trained gunner above all, now that we're facing Würzburg. I couldn't care less what you did before, so long as you fight on our side now." He let go of Mathis, who sank to the floor, gasping.

"The peasants are brave, but they don't understand either tactics or firearms," the knight went on more calmly. "I'll forget all your barefaced lies if you're telling the truth in this one point, and you really are a master gunner. If not, I'll have the pair of you shot from here to Würzburg by our falconet. Guards!"

He turned to the two grinning guards and gave them a signal. "Take these two over to our arsenal. There's an old cannon there that can't be charged properly. Let this lad show us what he can do. And if he fails, you know what *you* have to do."

As the two captives were taken away through the dark camp by a detachment of peasants, Melchior von Tanningen turned to Mathis at a moment when they were unobserved.

"Why the devil did you have to say you were a master gunner?" he whispered. "Now we'll either fly sky-high with their old cannon, or we'll be cannon fodder ourselves. We'd nearly caught up with the landsknecht army, and now our young lady is right out of our reach again."

"Oh, and why did you have to say we were pilgrims on the way to Rome?" retorted Mathis. "This is a peasant army. The pope is the antichrist to these people."

"The peasants are still devout believers. And I wasn't to know that they'd chosen one-armed Götz as their leader."

Mathis looked at him, taken aback. "You know the man?"

"Götz von Berlichingen is a Franconian robber knight with a thirst for blood. He's of good family and was brought up at the court of Ansbach, but at some point his true character emerged. He's been involved in over a dozen feuds in Franconia, some against members of my own family." Melchior von Tanningen nodded grimly. "It's just like him to join the peasants. Whenever there's robbery, loot, or plunder in the offing, Götz will be there."

"And that . . . iron hand?" Mathis asked hesitantly. "I never saw anything like it before."

"A stray bullet shattered his right hand at the siege of Landshut. Our bad luck that he didn't die of gangrene. Anyway, he had two artificial hands made. One for ceremonial occasions, one for fighting —that's the one you just met. They say that Götz can even wield a sword with it, and not badly either."

By now they had reached a part of the camp that was particularly heavily guarded. Tents and campfires stood in a circle around a dozen or so dirty artillery pieces, some of them bent out of shape, standing on gun carriages or horse-drawn carts. Casks that Mathis assumed held gunpowder stood on other carts.

"It's the cannon back there," said one of the peasants, pointing to a bronze artillery piece encrusted with dirt, and with a green tinge to it. "We took it at Weinsberg. Our smith, Michel Roider, says it's too dangerous to fire the thing." He grinned. "But you and your fine friend are welcome to try."

Mathis went over to the old gun and gave it a cursory inspection. It was of the kind known as a culverin, strapped to a gun carriage, and would fire cannonballs weighing some ten pounds. The muzzle and touchhole were badly encrusted, and the rotting wheels of the gun carriage would have to be replaced, but all the same Mathis could see no obvious cracks in the bronze of the barrel.

"I need spatulas and scrapers," he said, turning to the guards, who were gawping at him. "And a small barrel of coarse-grained powder to charge it, a dry fuse, and a ten-pound . . ." He hesitated. "No, an eight-pound cannonball. Can you get me those?"

The guard nodded, and went off to the carts of gunpowder with a couple of his comrades.

"Well?" Melchior whispered. "Will you be able to repair this gun?"

Mathis sighed. "With God's help, and yours, maybe. It's at least fifty years old. We'll have to clean it very thoroughly."

Having brought Mathis what he asked for, the guards retreated to a prudent distance and watched him and Melchior as they began freeing the culverin of verdigris and the remains of old powder. As they worked, Mathis kept checking all parts of the barrel for any cracks, cleaned the touchhole, and filed the muzzle like a man possessed. It took them until the early hours of the morning, but at last Melchior von Tanningen began charging the barrel with gunpowder.

One of the guards rose wearily from his station, rubbing his eyes. "Don't you dare fire it into our ranks," he threatened. "Or I promise you a slow death."

Mathis shook his head in silence, while the red glow of morning began to dawn. He was tense and excited. As usual, work on the cannon had put him into a kind of trance that was now slowly wearing off. Beside him, Melchior von Tanningen could hardly stay on his feet. His expensive garments were black with soot and gunpowder, his face pale and tired.

"It's going to be a fine day," said the minstrel, smiling wearily. "Time for a demonstration of your arts. My life is entirely in your hands. Who'd have thought it a few months ago?"

"And *my* life is also in *your* hands," replied Mathis quietly. "If you haven't cleaned the barrel properly, a bright flash of fire is the last thing either of us will see on this Earth."

He looked around and then pointed to a shed standing to one side in the middle of the trampled field. The derelict hut was about three hundred yards away from them.

"Is there anyone in there?" Mathis asked the peasants who were hurrying up from all directions. The sun was now above the horizon, and word had gone around that an alleged master gunner was about to put his skill to the test.

"The shed's empty," replied one of the guards, from where he had taken cover behind a large cart. "We searched it yesterday evening. Nothing but rats and mice."

"Then let's give those vermin a rousing morning greeting."

Mathis released a lever on the gun carriage and tilted the barrel until it was slanting up toward the sky. When he was satisfied with the angle of inclination, he pushed the cannonball into the muzzle, tamping it well down. Then he picked up the burning fuse and, with a shaking hand, held it to the touchhole.

"Holy St. Hubert, patron saint of metalworkers," he murmured, "carry this ball to its mark. Not for me but for Agnes, who may still need our help."

With his hands covering his ears, Mathis waited. For what felt like an eternity, the only sound was the hissing of the powder in the touchhole. Just as he was thinking that the powder must be damp, there was a sudden sound like thunder. The shock wave sent him falling backward on the soft ground. Mud spurted up into his eyes, and he could see nothing for a while.

Am I dead? Did the barrel explode?

When he sat up again, and looked at the place where the shed had been, he saw only a smoking ruin. Splinters of wood were scattered far and wide over the field.

There was an almost eerie silence in the peasants' camp, but then cries of jubilation were heard, first only sporadically, then more of them, in louder voices. Several of the peasants threw their hats into the air. They did not know what the shot meant, but it seemed to them a suitable demonstration of their own power. Very few of them had any idea how firearms worked, so their enthusiasm for a thunderous crash and a flash like lightning was all the greater. The guards cautiously approached, none of them threatening Mathis with their weapons. On the contrary, some nodded at him encouragingly.

"Hey, the knight will be glad we have such a damn good gunner in our own ranks," said one of the older peasants, laughing as he turned to his comrades. "You wait and see, next time this fellow will be shooting the mitre off the bishop of Würzburg's head."

Melchior von Tanningen took off his sooty hat and bowed low to Mathis. "My respects, Master Wielenbach. It looks to me that this band has found a new gunner, along with his humble assistant." He sighed. "I fear my ballad is going to be considerably longer than I first thought."

The Annweiler tanner Nepomuk Kistler raised the heavy wooden slab from the lye pit, trying not to breathe too deeply. The first moments when the accumulated vapors of the last few months spread through his workshop were always the worst. The corrosive smell of the lye made from oak bark and the stink of rotting flesh made tanning one of the least sought-after trades. The skins lying in the pit in front of Kistler had been washed and scraped, but tiny scraps of flesh still clung to them, and stank to high heaven.

Nepomuk Kistler ran his fingers, roughened from the chalk he used, experimentally over the cowhide. It was of good quality and would make a sturdy saddle. Much more valuable, however, was the calfskin on the shelves at the back, from which he would make parchment in the winter months. The white-haired old tanner smiled to think that the sublime knowledge of mankind was written down, for the most part, on the backs of thick-witted cattle.

Including that precious deed, he thought.

Kistler's expression immediately darkened. He hadn't thought of it for a long time. Too many things had happened. Annweiler had been in turmoil for weeks. After the peasants of Landau had risen up to attack the Palatinate, and were even now besieging Speyer, the citizens of Annweiler had decided to open their gates to the insurgents. There had been sheer chaos in the town ever since. Johannes Lebner the priest had fled, and so had several prosperous members of the town council, fearing for their money. And since the terrible murder of Bernwart Gessler, no new mayor had been appointed.

The older citizens in particular stayed in their houses, while outdoors the peasants and the younger people of Annweiler, who had joined the revolt, patrolled the streets. Meanwhile the wildest of stories were told in the taverns—tales of slaughter, of abbots crucified alive, of knights and their ladies hanged from the battlements of their castles like game animals caught in the hunt. The peasants had taken Trifels, and neighboring Scharfenberg Castle, too. There was no trace of Count Scharfeneck or of his young wife.

Nepomuk Kistler thought of what the midwife had said at their last meeting in the forest: *Maybe this is the time of which our founding fathers spoke. The end of the world as we know it. Perhaps it is time for the secret to be made known at last . . .*

Was the end of the world really coming? Many prophets had foretold that the present epoch would be a turning point. At least Kistler had done well to get the deed away last year.

Breathing heavily, Kistler took the stinking skins out of the lye pit and plunged them into a tub of fresh water as he pursued his own thoughts. His heart was troubling him more and more now that he was nearly seventy. He had not stood for election to the leadership of the Brotherhood but had inherited it many years ago from his father, who in his own turn had inherited it from his father before him. Ever since the days of Emperor Frederick II, Barbarossa's grandson who had granted the town of Annweiler its charter, the Brotherhood had held masses for the souls of the Staufers. But their true task was a different one, and as leaders of the Brotherhood the Kistlers had kept that immensely important document, the deed, safe over all those years. The ring had come into the order's possession only a few years ago.

They had been waiting ever since for the evil to return.

Last summer, when Nepomuk Kistler had discovered the mayor's dead body in the lye tub, he had been the only one who did not believe that Mathis was guilty of the murder. Secretly, he had believed that someone else was striking terror into the town of Annweiler. A monster sent by dark powers to do a deed that had been planned hundreds of years ago.

Maybe it was the sound of the dragging footsteps, or simply the strange, unusual smell that hung in the air of the room—something had attracted Kistler's attention all of a sudden. The hairs on the back of his neck stood on end. He slowly turned, and in the dim light saw a man in a plain but well-made black coat. Only his teeth gleamed white in his dark face.

"God be with you, Master Kistler," said the stranger. "It has taken me a long time to find you at last."

Trying not to tremble, the old tanner slowly retreated until he stood on the edge of the lye pit. In the taverns of Annweiler, they had been saying for some time that there was a black devil at large in the area. Now the devil seemed to be here. Nepomuk Kistler hastily made the sign of the cross. The old midwife had been right: this really was the end of the world, and their enemies were more terrible and powerful than he had ever guessed.

"*Vade . . . Satanas!*" he managed to say, with difficulty.

The black man sighed, sounding bored. "Let us not go through this pathetic routine. The midwife tried that, and I did not dissolve into smoke, leaving a smell of sulfur behind." He slowly came toward Kistler. "Just give me what I want before I really do turn into a devil. *Imediatamente, miúdo!*"

The strange sounds transfixed Nepomuk Kistler with shock. He had always been a deeply superstitious man. Now fear for his life, and the man's uncanny outer appearance, turned his presentiment to certainty. This really was the devil himself, and he was speaking the language of hell.

"Your pitiful Brotherhood is mentioned in the old charter of Annweiler," the devil hissed. "So do not play the ignorant fool. Unfortunately most of the documents have been destroyed or are up at Trifels, where the peasants are in charge now, and I have no access to them. It has taken me a whole week to find what I wanted in the ducal archives at Zweibrücken. A week to find out that the Kistlers have always been at the head of a mysterious order. This is enough. Tell me the name I want, or you shall suffer the same fate as your obstinate mayor."

The devil took out a strange instrument from under his coat, a thing that looked like a tiny cannon, with a handle and a fuse, and held it to Kistler's forehead.

He's stealing my soul. It was a terrible thought. *This black Satan is stealing my soul, just as he did to Bernwart Gessler.*

It was too much for the old man. His heart suddenly seemed to explode. He clutched his chest, breathing laboriously, and then collapsed and lay in the stinking pool of lye. Cursing, the devil bent over him.

"Here, what are you doing?" he said angrily. "If this is some kind of game, I can only advise you to think better of it. And now talk, you obstinate fool."

Kistler rolled his eyes as the devil tugged at him, preparing to drag him away to hell. He would have borne any torture, but the prospect of losing his soul made him weak. In the extremity of despair, he seized the devil's collar and pulled him down to his own face. "St. . . . Goar . . ." he stammered. "St. . . . Goar . . . And now . . . let me . . . depart in peace . . ."

Kistler's heart twitched once or twice more, and then at last it stopped. As the old man moved toward a point at the end of a tunnel, a point growing brighter and brighter all the time, he was filled by the happy thought that he had escaped from Satan just in time. If at the price of the secret he had kept safe for so long.

Then there was nothing but warmth and light, and a figure raising a hand in kindly greeting where the tunnel ended.

It had a red beard and wore a golden crown on its head.

Agnes held the hand of a dying peasant as a pulsating flow of blood streamed from his ruined throat. The man murmured a few indistinct words, twitched once more, and then his gaze went empty. A deep gray sky hung overhead, with flocks of crows cawing as they flew by. Agnes thought of her falcon, Parcival, and how she had taken him out hunting crows last year. That seemed a century ago, in another time, in another world.

She gently closed the dead man's eyes and looked at the battlefield. Dusk was already falling. Recently Agnes had seen many such scenes, but this was the most horrible so far. The golden rows of wheat that had reached to the outskirts of the forest yesterday were all trampled underfoot. The dead, the dying, and the wounded lay among them, like huge molehills. They wailed, screamed, and lowed like cattle, while the black birds circled above them, seeming to mock them with their croaking cries. Now and then the crows came down to settle on a corpse, pecking at it voraciously.

For two weeks now Agnes, Agathe, and the robbers had been traveling with the landsknechts of the notorious Swabian League. The mercenaries they had met in Kehl had been sent to fight the league by the duke of Lorraine. Together, they were expected to defeat the peasants of Württemberg, who were on the march through the countryside, looting and burning. There had finally been a decisive battle here near Böblingen. At first the insurgents had taken shelter within a barricade of carts, but the landsknechts turned their firearms on them from a neighboring hill. Thousands of peasants had been killed as they tried to escape. The soldiers shot down those who took refuge in the tops of trees like birds.

"Don't stand there dreaming. If Barnabas sees you, you'll get a beating again."

Agnes turned to the gray-haired woman who was limping toward her. Despite her fifty years, and her slightly stooped gait, Mother Barbara still cut an impressive figure. Her eyes were as bright as those of a girl of twenty, and she combed her ample, shoulder-length hair every morning. She had once been the most beautiful whore in the baggage train, but then an intoxicated landsknecht had broken both her legs in a fight, and now she earned her living as a vivandière. Barbara sold the mercenaries provisions and all kinds of trinkets, and she was also regarded as an experienced healer. She bound up wounds, removed crossbow bolts and leaden bullets, and had even been known to amputate legs with a bone saw. But most help of that kind came too late for the men on this battlefield.

"Look at this." Grinning, Mother Barbara held up a knife almost as long as a forearm, with traces of blood still on it. "Almost new, with a fine horn handle. I'll get at least half a guilder for it. Now, hurry up. If you go on staring into space like that, half the battlefield will be plundered already."

Agnes nodded without a word, and went over the trampled blades of wheat to the next stiff body. As often happened these days, she and little Agathe had been sent to plunder bodies after the battle. Most of the dead were poor peasants, so there was not much to be found. But at least many of them wore good leather boots that had presumably already been stolen from a dead landsknecht. In addition, she might find scythe blades, sickles, copper shirt buttons, colored feathers from hats, sometimes silver rings or knives such as the one that Mother Barbara had just found.

Agnes cast an anxious glance at her bag, still all but empty. If she didn't soon find something valuable, Barnabas would fall into one of his fits of rage. Now that he wouldn't be selling her, he had begun to fall on her like a predator. She had borne it in silence, lying unmoving as a pebble on the bed of a river with the water flowing over it. She had closed her eyes and tried to think of nothing but endless forests. At least it was soon over, and after it she had always washed herself very thoroughly. In return for her silence, Barnabas saw to it that the other men left her alone. But if she didn't bring back enough loot, that could easily change. Fortunately, she knew herbs that prevented pregnancy.

There were moments when Agnes imagined cutting Barnabas's throat in his sleep. But so far her fear had been stronger than her hatred.

The cart in which Barnabas and the others were traveling was not far from the large tent belonging to the master of the baggage train, who was responsible for keeping it in order. Agnes was still surprised by the speed with which Barnabas had adjusted to the new state of affairs. With Marek, Snuffler, and Samuel he gave a well-attended show almost every evening, featuring the monkey and the talking parrot. They had left the other bird with a tavern keeper in Kehl, taking a rickety cart and a lame old horse in exchange.

Barnabas had joined forces with Mother Barbara. The vivandière knew what the landsknechts needed, and Barnabas's men took it from battlefields and the surrounding countryside. Then she sold the stock from their two carts to the soldiers, at greatly inflated prices.

The procurer had just thrown the chattering monkey a few dried plums when Agnes and Mother Barbara approached.

"I send you off to get some plunder, and what do you come back with? Nothing!" he thundered. "What am I to do with you?"

"I . . . I found a silver crucifix. Isn't that something?" Agnes said.

"Show it here."

She offered the crucifix to the procurer, and he examined it. "Hmm, not bad," growled Barnabas at last. "It'll be worth something at least. But don't start thinking you can sell anything yourself and run away. I'll find you if I have to search all of Swabia for you, and then you'll wish I'd sold you to the Turks."

Agnes nodded in silence. She had in fact thought more than once of flight. In contrast to their time on the boat, Barnabas was not chaining her and Agathe up here, and Samuel and the other two oafs were very inattentive guards. But if she escaped, where could she go? The probability of being raped or killed out of hand by landsknechts prowling around was too great. Furthermore, Barnabas still had her ring, which he had taken to wearing on a chain around his neck. But so long as he, and the ring, kept going north, that hardly mattered.

Because northward, on the Rhine, was St. Goar.

Agnes gave a thin-lipped smile. Without the need for her to do anything about it herself, she was once again on her way to her real destination. Soon the day when she and Barnabas parted company would come.

Even if I have to cut your throat, you bastard.

She spent that night with Barnabas again, in the drafty cart with only canvas stretched over it, among casks of brandy, crockery, rusty weapons, and all kinds of junk. It smelled strongly of the old bales of leather that the procurer had stolen only today from a tannery that had burned down.

The smell reminded Agnes of Annweiler.

Little Satan stared malignantly down at her from a chest, while Barnabas snored beside her. At least his intoxication had sent him straight to sleep, so that he could not molest her. She gradually fell asleep only hours later. Suddenly the rasping breath of the man beside her sounded like an old oak tree creaking in the wind, and the cart in the baggage train seemed to carry her away.

The cart . . . she thought just before her eyes closed at last. *The leather . . .*

◆ ◆ ◆

A jolting cart, squealing and groaning. Agnes lies at the back among bundles of tanned leather tied up in bales. She knows the smell, a mixture of mold, acid, and the forest. She has encountered it often.

Agnes feels safe. She hums the Occitanian lullaby that her mother once taught her, and she is holding her little hand-carved doll. Finally she snuggles down into the leather and closes her eyes as the cart jolts on. Familiar voices up on the driver's seat soothe her. A hand caresses her hair and goes on singing the song. The voices are like a soft wave on which she is gliding away.

Coindeta sui, si cum n'ai greu cossire, quar pauca son, iuvenete e tosa . . .

But suddenly there is shouting, the cart stops, and Agnes wakes with a start. The clink of weapons and cries of pain are heard through the thin canvas cover over the cart. A shrill voice cuts through Agnes like a knife. She knows that voice, and a great lump comes into her throat. In fear, she crawls under all the leather skins. The smell is so strong now that she feels like a little animal, a calf being dragged to the slaughter. She hears someone tear the canvas over the cart into pieces. Muted sounds now come to her ear, someone is striking the bales with a sharp object, again and again, the sounds coming closer.

Suddenly there is another groan, a heavy body falls to the forest floor beside the cart, and a hand pulls the leather skins away from Agnes. She is very small now, very vulnerable, her eyes are closed, she doesn't want to see the monster that is going to eat her. But the monster doesn't eat her, it picks her up, jumps off the cart with her, and runs away. Blinking cautiously, Agnes sees the face of the kindly driver, Hieronymus. Behind her, she sees some shapes lying doubled up on the ground. Smoke rises to her nostrils, a fire crackles, but Hieronymus runs so fast that soon there is nothing but spruce and beech trees over her. Their branches stretch out long, scratchy tongues to stroke her. Blood drips from the driver's forehead onto her face and her little dress.

They are all dead, dead, dead . . .

Now she hears hoofbeats, coming closer fast. Hieronymus gasps, staggers, and finally he presses a kiss on Agnes's forehead and puts her inside the hollow trunk of an oak tree.

"For God's sake, keep quiet!" he whispers.

He hesitates for a moment, and then puts a chain with a small object hanging from it over her head.

"Your mother . . ." he begins, falteringly. "She wanted you to have this. You mustn't lose it, do you hear? Give it only to someone you trust, and let that person keep it for you."

Hieronymus kisses her on the cheek for the last time, and then the man runs on without her. Soon he has disappeared among the trees. Suddenly a hoarse scream echoes through the forest. After that there is silence.

She is alone.

Agnes feels spiderwebs on her face, beetles scrabbling over her, the crumbling dust of rotting wood running into her nose and ears. But she keeps quiet, just as Hieronymus told her. Even when the horses trot past her, and she hears voices calling out, she keeps quiet.

After a while it gets dark. Night is coming, the moon shines brightly in the sky, and Agnes cautiously comes out of her hiding place. She thinks of little Clara and how they always liked playing with their dolls together. One day Clara caught a bad cough, and then she was dead. She lay in a little casket, stiff and cold, and Agnes kept hoping Clara would stand up and get out of it. Just as she herself gets out of the hollow tree trunk now.

They are all dead, dead, dead . . .

Pale moonlight shines through the branches. She feels her way over damp moss, stumbles through brushwood, tears her lovely new dress on bramble bushes. And suddenly there is a woman in front of her, standing there like a wicked witch, with a stick in her hand and a basket on her stooped back. She bends down to Agnes, and her voice is very gentle, not like the voice of a wicked witch at all.

"What in heaven's name are you doing all alone here in the forest, my child?"

Only now does Agnes begin crying. It is a quiet whimpering, but the tears flow and flow. The woman looks at Agnes's torn dress and the blood on it, then she carefully looks around and makes the sign of the cross.

She lifts Agnes into the basket and carries her through the forest. The gentle rocking is almost as soothing as the jolting of the cart. And while Agnes sinks down into deep darkness, as if into a pond, words keep ringing through her head.

They are all dead, dead, dead, dead, dead, dead . . .

✦ ✦ ✦

Agnes woke with a cry and looked around frantically.

The forest, the witch. . . . Where am I?

Only after a while did she realize that she was in the cart with Barnabas. Beside her, the procurer grunted and opened an eye. His breath stank of vinegary wine, drowning out the smell of leather from the tanned skins around them.

"What is it?" he muttered drowsily. "Are the peasants attacking?"

Agnes shook her head. Her dress was damp with cold sweat. "I . . . I just had a bad dream."

"Then go back to sleep, or I'll give you something to have bad dreams about."

Trembling, Agnes lay back, her heart racing. The dream had been as real as the dreams at Trifels Castle. But this time she had not been Constanza, she had been herself, as a little girl of about four or five.

She could feel the roughly carved doll in her hand. And in her ears she still heard the Occitanian lullaby that her mother had sung to her.

Mother?

In the dream, she had not seen who was singing to her and stroking her hair. Had it been her mother? Katharina von Erfenstein had died when Agnes was about six years old. Could this have been a first, early memory? Agnes stared at the cover of the cart above her and brooded. Had the other people in the dream not been imaginary at all, but real? Then who was the woman she had taken for a witch, and who was the driver? Why had the cart been attacked?

Finally she shook her head and stretched her stiff limbs. It was much more likely that she had simply had a wild dream. No wonder, with all the killing around her, the cruelty that she saw every day. She must concentrate on the here and now. She must find a way to escape.

· 19 ·

THE MOON SHONE DOWN ON Würzburg, and Mathis was lining up the gun with the fortress of Marienberg yet again when, out of the corner of his eye, he noticed a flickering light. He turned and saw a peasant coming along the alleys close by, with a lighted torch raised aloft.

"Dear God in heaven, how often do I have to say I won't tolerate a naked flame anywhere near the guns!" Mathis said furiously. The peasant looked at him in alarm. The newly appointed chief master gunner of the Black Band pointed to several sacks of gunpowder, piled up on the ground. "A single spark, and there'll be a mere spoonful left of you and me."

The weedy man muttered an apology and set off quickly to join his comrades, though not without turning for another look at the young fellow who was soon going to turn the hated fortress of Würzburg into a burning heap of rubble.

Wearily, Mathis rubbed his eyes. With a detachment of peasants, he had been working since daybreak on the few rusty guns that the army took about with it, and he'd had only a few hours' sleep. Over the last ten days, they had been laying waste the countryside around Würzburg, always going farther north, storming castles, forts, and monasteries, while most of the villages and towns opened their own gates to the army. The reputation of Mathis as an experienced master gunner had grown with every new assault, and yet he felt no real pleasure in that. He and Melchior had asked those few landsknechts that the peasants took prisoner about a troupe of entertainers with a monkey and a parrot, but in vain. It was as if the war had swallowed up Agnes, and so the two of them had finally gone on to Würzburg with Götz von Berlichingen and his so-called Black Band.

The rich city, seat of a bishopric, had opened its gates to the peasants after some slight hesitation, and the citizens had come out to welcome them with enthusiasm. Only Marienberg, the archbishop's fortress, on a steep hill overlooking the river Main, was still in enemy hands. The hated Prince Bishop Konrad von Thüngen had fled to Heidelberg, and the provost of the cathedral was refusing to surrender the fortress. After heated discussion, the citizens of Würzburg and the peasants had finally decided jointly to attack Marienberg, and that meant they needed Mathis. But it was clear to him that he owed his elevated position mainly to one thing: trained master gunners were as rare in the insurgents' army as gold nuggets in a heap of Palatinate sand.

Mathis wiped the sweat, dirt, and powder dust from his forehead and hurried over to the next cannon. He must continue fighting for the peasants in this one battle before he could go on in search of Agnes. He had no other option: Götz von Berlichingen had described to him and Melchior, in the most graphic of terms, what happened to a gunner who deserted. Quartering was the very least of it.

He had had most of the artillery pieces set up near the Deutschlandhaus Church in the Main River quarter of the city, where he had the best angle of fire. The fortress of Marienberg towered above him, dark and defiant. Its towers had a solid look, and its walls were strong and firm. No enemy had ever taken it. Mathis had heard that the men under siege up there had a powder mill of their own, and newly cast guns, though he had to make do with what the peasants had captured on their campaigns: artillery often bent out of shape, some of it dating from the last century.

He was short of powder, cannonballs, and above all capable workers who could service the guns. Besides Mathis there was only a single
efficient gunner in Würzburg, along with a few smiths who had some
experience in forging weaponry and tools and understood a little
about firearms. Mathis counted himself lucky that Melchior von
Tanningen knew an astonishing amount about the art of war. After
only a few days of learning and experimenting with his new knowledge, the minstrel had been able to give the peasants the necessary
instructions. At the moment he was at the Nikolausberg fieldworks
with the master gunner of Würzburg, where several more artillery
pieces were in position.

The sound of swift footsteps made Mathis look up from his work.
For a moment he thought that another rash peasant was about to
endanger his own life and the lives of others, but it was a tall figure in
the garments of a nobleman.

"The moon is shining like a great lantern, Master Wielenbach,"
said the man, smiling and raising a hand in greeting. "Maybe we
should begin storming the fortress before daybreak. Then at least
we'd have it behind us."

Mathis bowed slightly as the dark-haired knight with his neatly
trimmed side whiskers came closer. He had met Florian Geyer three
or four times before, and had taken to him very much. Like Götz von
Berlichingen, Geyer was from an old Franconian family of knightly
rank living near Würzburg. As a young man, he had been sent to the
court of King Henry VIII as an envoy. He spoke fluent English, had
an easy command of courtly behavior, and was regarded as the great
hope of his family—but then he had suddenly thrown in his lot with
the peasants and their cause.

In his few conversations with Florian Geyer, the young weaponsmith had concluded that, like Mathis himself, he believed in justice
and the good in mankind. He was also a born leader. At his side,
Mathis had once again felt, for the first time in a long while, that the
peasants' struggle could be crowned by success.

"I need at least a little daylight to take aim," said Mathis, letting his gaze pass critically over the dark fortress. "After five in the morning it ought to be possible to fire the artillery. Although I don't believe it's really a good idea to attack this fortress," he added gloomily. "The men up there are extremely well equipped."

Geyer shrugged his shoulders. "And don't I know it. This siege is merely holding us up while the seneschal goes on arming his Swabian League. But for many of the peasants and citizens here, Marienberg is first and foremost the residence of their archenemy Prince Bishop Konrad. The fortress is a symbol, no more and no less."

"And we're going to beat our heads against it until they bleed, no more and no less," Mathis replied.

Geyer grinned. "Not if you aim the guns as well as you have so far. In addition we also have my lads—don't forget that."

"Certainly not." Mathis shook his head and began charging the next cannon. Since his baptism by fire, when he shot the empty shed to smithereens, he had made a name for himself among the peasants. In the field, he was now regarded as irreplaceable, despite his youth, and even Götz von Berlichingen had condescended to pay him a gruff compliment. But at least as valuable as the artillery were the men, some two hundred of them, whom Florian Geyer had trained himself, and who were under his direct command. They called themselves the Black Band, since they were clothed entirely in black. Unlike the peasants, many of them had fought in battles before, and in the field they were regarded as unscrupulous, quick, and invincible.

"A thousand men like yours and a hundred new guns, and this war would have been over long ago," said Mathis as he carefully charged the gun through its muzzle with the dark gray granular powder. "As it is, we're merely patching things up."

Geyer sighed. "I only wish it were. But the peasants are simply disunited. The Allgäu Band, the Lake Constance Band, the men from the Neckar valley, the Franconians, all the rest of them. There are too many different armies. What we need is a common flag, a symbol under which all would gather." He shrugged. "But that's not the reason I was looking for you." Suddenly the knight lowered his voice and looked around conspiratorially. "I'm setting out soon for Rothenburg ob der Tauber, to ask for guns and powder there. Just tell me what you need, and I'll try to make it possible."

Stunned, Mathis looked at the knight. "But the attack on the fortress . . ." he began. However, Geyer dismissed his objection.

"It can begin without me. And if Marienberg doesn't fall, that won't decide the war. However, if we go on fighting in so poorly armed and disorganized a fashion, our just war will soon be over. It can't go on like this, at least."

Mathis knew that Geyer was right. There were many peasants here, over twenty thousand encamped around Würzburg alone, but they had not the faintest notion of the way to wage war. Only Götz von Berlichingen and Florian Geyer seemed able to impose at least a little discipline on the various bands that were at odds with one another. Yet those two knights did not get on with each other at all. Geyer thought Berlichingen an unscrupulous careerist who would always veer with the prevailing wind, while Berlichingen called Geyer an obstinate dreamer—and Mathis thought they were both right.

"I need more granular gunpowder and bombards, if possible, and guns of medium size, and mortars," Mathis said, after some thought. "That's the only way we can breach those fortifications." He indicated the rusty gun in front of him. "What I have here is just about enough to blow a wooden wall down."

Florian Geyer nodded. "I'll see what can be done. Rothenburg is a rich city. If it can't help us, I'll try others." He hesitated, and then nodded his head. "And there's something else," he said at last, quietly. "You once told me about the girl you are looking for. The entertainers with the monkey and the talking bird . . ."

Mathis felt his heart leap up. He had indeed once told Geyer about Agnes over a goblet of wine, although without going into the details of her abduction. Could the knight really have found out anything?

"What about her?" he asked cautiously.

"Well, I know nothing for certain, but just outside Würzburg a couple of enemy scouts fell into our hands. We wanted them to tell us the size of the seneschal's army. Our captives said there was a large baggage train, with traveling brewers, booths selling brandy, smiths, whores, wandering preachers, and a group of entertainers with a monkey . . ." Geyer paused, while Mathis gazed at him expectantly. The knight finally sighed. "That's all I know, Mathis. It may be another monkey, but I think you deserve a little hope." He smiled. "Don't go running away just yet. We need you here. And we'll be meeting the Swabian League soon enough."

Mathis nodded. "I promise you I'll see this thing through. But after that—"

A loud explosion shook the ground around them. Several of the windows of the Deutschlandhaus Church broke with a crash, bringing Mathis back to the depressing present.

"Damn it, that was over on the Niklausberg," he shouted against the racket. "I told Melchior von Tanningen and the others there not to start firing before daybreak."

"It could have been the enemy," Florian Geyer pointed out. He looked up at the fortress, where red lights flared up. The crashing and the flashes of light went on. "I'm off now to Rothenburg. When I'm back, either the fortress will fall, or we'll move on."

And without a word of farewell, the knight disappeared into the turmoil.

"Wait!" Mathis shouted after him. "The Swabian League! Where can I find it?"

But Florian Geyer was already out of sight.

The noise and shouting were much louder now. Not far away, peasants armed with scythes and spears were running down the streets toward Marienberg. The bearded leader of one troop ran breathlessly up to Mathis with a hastily written scrap of paper in his hand.

"Orders from above to start the bombardment now," he managed to say, breathing heavily. "No time to be lost."

"But it isn't yet—" Mathis began to protest, but the broad-built man jabbed him angrily in the chest.

"Didn't you hear? That's what the leaders have decided, so get on with it."

Mathis shook his head. For a moment he thought of refusing, but then he called the peasants assigned to him to his aid. Together, they charged the guns and began firing into the darkness.

So pointless, he thought. *We're only wasting what little ammunition we have. It's time I got away from here.*

As he charged the barrels of the guns with acrid-smelling powder and listened to the familiar hissing in the touchholes, his thoughts kept returning to Agnes. He suppressed the fear that Florian Geyer had been talking about some other monkey. There was hope again, or at least a little hope.

That alone spurred him to do his work faster.

The bombardment went on until evening and continued the next day. But none of the sound and fury led to any result. The peasants' artillery struck the slope on which the fortress stood. A number of cannonballs stuck fast in the thick walls of the fortress. There was much crashing, and flashing lights, but Marienberg suffered no major damage. The attackers were beginning to grow impatient.

"Why are you firing at the slope?" the troop leader, now sweating profusely, snapped at Mathis. It was nearly midday, and he was running back and forth between the few heavy artillery pieces from which smoke was belching and giving orders to the overtaxed peasants. "You want to aim up there, where the castle stands, damn it."

"Do it yourself if you think you can aim better." Mathis had difficulty controlling himself. They gave him gunpowder of poor quality and falconets that were too short and misshapen, and they expected him to work miracles. "I couldn't hit the dome of St. Peter's even if I was standing right in front of it," he went on. "If Geyer doesn't get back soon with some larger artillery pieces, we might as well give up."

"Ho, you just can't aim right, that's all it is. Wait until Götz hears. There'll be trouble."

"Götz can go and . . ."

The curse on which Mathis was embarking was drowned out by a mighty crash, closely followed by screaming. When he looked to his right, he saw that one of the medium-size culverins had exploded. Its barrel lay in several pieces, as if a giant's fist had crushed it. Black smoke rose from the ground and hovered in the air. As the smoke died down, the bodies of several peasants, blown to bits, became visible. Mathis couldn't say how many of them there were. Limbs were lying everywhere, and blood spurted from a torso beside the gun. Farther away several men staggered along the streets like ghosts, hands to their ears, their faces black with soot from the explosion.

"You'll have to answer for that!" the troop leader shouted at Mathis, whose head was still echoing like the clapper in a bell. "We never ought to have let a young fellow like you fire the guns."

"And who else is going to do it? A few day laborers, or maybe your coppersmith? The last I saw of him, he was lying in the city moat, dead drunk."

"Quiet, damn it!" shouted a deep voice—a voice accustomed to giving orders. Götz von Berlichingen pushed his way through the crowd of injured men and curious bystanders. Muttering, the peasants stepped aside. The knight cast a brief glance at the wreck of the culverin, and then turned to Mathis.

"Charging the barrel with powder is the task of the master gunner alone," he said menacingly, pointing his iron hand at the groaning and screaming injured men. "It's your doing if we've lost a dozen men and a culverin."

Mathis went red in the face. "I did not charge the barrel myself— that was some of your peasants. If we're going to be firing artillery here all day long, one gunner is not enough. But you're welcome to light the fuses yourself, *sir knight*."

Götz von Berlichingen flinched slightly. He raised his iron hand as if to strike Mathis with it but then lowered it again. The knight knew that both he and Florian Geyer were regarded as suspect by many of the peasants, whose dislike of rich noblemen was too great to be overcome.

"I'll let it go at a warning today," Berlichingen growled at last. "Let's hope you'll take more care from now on." He turned to the peasants standing around. "The bombardment goes on until night-fall," he announced. "And then Geyer's notorious Black Band will storm this infernal fortress, come what may."

The men shouted jubilantly. Only Mathis stared at the knight in horror. "But that's a death sentence for the attackers," he burst out. "We'll never have breached the walls by then. Not unless Geyer gets back to us with larger cannon soon."

"Tauberbischofsheim isn't far away, and they're sending guns from there," replied Berlichingen coolly. "That will have to do."

"But they're not large enough. And Florian Geyer isn't here. Without him, how is his band to—"

"Not another word. I was always against storming Marienberg. But if it has to be done, it must at least be done quickly. This fortress has been holding us up far too long already."

Without any salutation, Götz von Berlichingen turned and marched away along the blood-smeared alley. Mathis could hardly refrain from shouting after the knight. Only yesterday he had ruled out any storming of the fortress, and now this. It looked like the one-armed knight was deliberately sacrificing Geyer's men. Did he mean to weaken his troublesome rival, now that he was not present, or was he really anxious to storm the fortress as soon as possible?

But there was no time for more thought. The peasants were be-ginning to charge several of the guns with powder again.

"Stop!" cried Mathis, running over to them. "Not like that. Do you want another bloodbath? And for God's sake take that torch away."

Soon the dead and injured had been removed, and the bombard-ment resumed. The attackers built rafts under the bridge over the Main so that they could cross the river more quickly. When a rainbow appeared in the sky early in the afternoon, the peasants saw it as a sign from God. Jubilation broke out, and they armed themselves for the evening's assault.

This is madness, thought Mathis. *Sheer madness. The ring of besiegers around the fortress isn't even closed. And there isn't a single breach to let Geyer's men through the walls.*

In fact it was mainly Geyer's Black Band, with a few other troops, who charged the Marienberg after nightfall. The fearless men tore down palisades and outworks in total darkness and made their way to the outer citadel. Finally they tried climbing the walls with the aid of ladders. Mathis heard their dying cries, he saw the muzzles of the defenders' guns flashing, and still he was desperately trying to breach the stone ramparts of Marienberg.

In vain.

When dawn came, hundreds of dead and dying men lay in the moat below Marienberg, many of them members of Geyer's Black Band. The peasants tried to retrieve their comrades, but they came under fire from the fortress and finally had to retreat. Mathis could still hear the cries and wails of the dying men until afternoon, and then, slowly, silence returned.

The assault was over.

Only a few days later, Agnes was standing on a hilltop, watching the flames licking up from the rooftops of Weinsberg like giant fingers. She heard cattle lowing in mortal terror in the burning sheds, the sound of houses collapsing in flames, and the strong wind roaring over the red-hot destruction of the town.

An old woman crouched on the ground beside her, crying out with the pain of her grief in the evening dusk. Her husband, a frail old man, had bent down and was trying to comfort her. A shabby little leather purse hung from his belt, all that the pair had been able to bring away from their house. They were not alone; the hills and high ground all around the town were covered with old people holding hands, weeping and wailing as they looked down at what had once been their homes. The younger citizens of Weinsberg had already taken their children and fled when news came, several days before, that the seneschal was on his way with his Swabian League. Only a month ago, the peasants here, led by Jäcklein Rohrbach, had made Count Ludwig von Helfenstein and his companions run the gauntlet and then murdered them, and this was the revenge exacted by Seneschal Georg von Waldburg-Zeil and the Swabian League. Not one stone was to be left on another in the town of Weinsberg and the surrounding villages. Those who did not get away fast enough were burned alive in their houses.

A groan passed through the people on the hills as a horse on fire galloped out of the open gates of the town. It whinnied shrilly, stumbled a little farther, and then collapsed and went on burning in silence. The man beside Agnes crossed himself.

"It's the wrath of God!" he wailed. "The wrath of God! We never should have risen against our masters."

"It's not the wrath of God, but the wrath of the nobility," Agnes murmured, so quietly that no one could hear her. "And I am one of them." Then she turned her face away, and climbed down the hill, deep in thought.

This will soon be over one way or the other. Not much longer now, and I can turn my back on all these horrors.

The last few days had shown her very clearly that this was not a just war. Wherever the landsknechts of the Swabian League went, with their baggage train after them, they killed the peasants like vermin. In Sindelfingen the seneschal's men had caught one of the peasant leaders responsible for the bloody murder of Helfenstein at Weinsberg. Now he was bound by a long chain to a tree surrounded by burning pyres. The poor fellow had run back and forth between the bonfires, screaming, until at last he was roasted alive.

"Hey, Agnes, come on! There are no pickings here."

That was Barnabas, standing beside his cart and waving to her impatiently. The procurer had expected good loot in Weinsberg, but now that the town was ablaze he wanted to get back to the baggage train as quickly as he could.

"We'd better be away before our landsknechts are called off," he growled as Agnes came slowly down the steep hill. "I've a notion the folk here won't have much good to say of us." He laughed. "Even the old can get nasty if you knock the gruel bowl out of their hands. When the seneschal does something, he does it thoroughly, you have to give him credit for that."

Squealing, the cart began to move, jolting away over burned and devastated terrain. From up on the driver's seat, Agnes stared into the twilight coming on. Not a shed or a stable still stood. The year's harvest was in ashes, and the people had fled.

Not much longer, she thought again. *I'll just wait for the right opportunity, and then I'll leave all this behind me.*

A few days ago she had been able to take a surreptitious look at a map offered to Barnabas by a wounded sergeant in lieu of payment. Their journey had already taken them over a hundred miles north, through Swabia and Franconia, but always going farther from the Rhine. If she really wanted to find out more about her dreams and the past, she must soon leave the baggage train and move west toward the river.

But not without the ring, and it was still around Barnabas's neck.

After a good hour, they had rejoined the baggage train, now encamped near a deserted village. As soon as the cart stopped, Agnes jumped down and hurried over to the campfire, where little Agathe and Mother Barbara were sitting. The old vivandière was holding a spit over the flames, roasting a skinned rabbit on it.

"You caught the smell of this all the way away in Weinsberg, did you?" she said, smiling.

Grumbling, Barnabas sat down beside the fire and poured himself a tankard of wine. Agnes sat as well, then she cut some meat off the roast rabbit and began eating, though without much appetite. She was shivering and wrapped herself in her woolen shawl. Although the end of May was approaching, the nights were still damp and chilly.

"Will you tell me a story about King Arthur again?" asked Agathe, who was muffled up in a rabbit-skin rug beside the fire. Agnes looked at her sadly. The girl had survived the horrors of the last few weeks remarkably well. Mother Barbara had taken a fancy to her, and soon Agnes would be able to leave her on her own. All the same, her conscience pricked her.

She'll be all right without me, Agnes thought hopefully. *I'm sure she will. I can't take her with me.*

"Want to hear a story, do you?" began Barnabas affably enough, after another good gulp of wine. "Ho, I know a good story, and it's true. They've caught that Thomas Müntzer in Thuringia now. You know, that crazy preacher, always carrying on about heaven on Earth." He spat into the fire. "Seems like Müntzer will get to know hell on earth first. They've been torturing him for a good week already."

Barnabas laughed uproariously, and Agnes, repelled, turned away. Suddenly she felt very tired.

"I'm afraid it's rather late for King Arthur and his knights today," she told Agathe, forcing herself to smile. "Maybe they'll ride again tomorrow, how about that?"

She gave the rest of her meat to the dogs, then climbed into the cart and slipped under the stinking, ragged sheet.

But sleep was impossible. From outside came the sound of men laughing and shouting, a pig was squealing pitifully somewhere, the smoke of the campfire drifted through the cart.

And in addition, her thoughts kept dwelling on Mathis. How was he now? She could only hope he was well. Very likely he had joined the insurgents as a master gunner, and Melchior von Tanningen would now be the guest of some nobleman who gave him a warm bed in return for music and singing. How was she herself? Agnes swallowed. The one thing keeping her alive was her determination to reach St. Goar.

What would happen after that, she had no idea.

Agnes thought of her latest dreams, so different from those she remembered at Trifels. She had now dreamed three times of that attack in the forest when she was a little girl, and how she escaped. Strangely enough, the dream came only when she was sleeping in the cart. By now she felt sure that it was a true memory from her early childhood, even if she could make no sense of it. The attack had probably actually happened. But why had her father never told her about it? In order to spare her feelings? Or was there something that he wanted to keep secret?

What happened after the attack?

Outside, beech logs spluttered on the campfire. Their wood was not dry, and the smoke drifting through the cart was black and dense. The smoke made Agnes cough. Finally, she turned on her side, the smell of it making her drowsy. Her eyes closed.

◆ ◆ ◆

A wrinkled hand clasps her own little fingers. She looks up—and sees the witch, who is not as old as Agnes had first thought. There are little laughter dimples to the left and right of her mouth, her bright eyes are wise and kindly.

"We're going to my house," says the witch. "You will be safe there for now."

Together, they go through the dark forest until they reach a crooked little house. Smoke rises from its chimney, and when they go in, the smoke is hovering over the table, two stools, a chest, and the bedstead. Open-mouthed, Agnes stares at the vials and jars on the shelves, full off dried snakes, frogs, newts, and other strange things. A human skull gapes at Agnes from the dresser above the open fireplace. The witch gives her a warm mug filled with steaming liquid.

"Drink that, child. You're cold, you need some sleep. We'll decide what happens next in the morning."

Agnes hesitates. Suppose the drink is poisoned? Suppose this is a wicked witch after all? But then she sees the smile on the woman's face, and she drinks the hot, sweet fluid.

"Where are your mother and father?" the witch asks.

Agnes says nothing.

"Did you lose them in the forest?" asks the witch, and suddenly there is great anxiety in her eyes. "By God, has something happened to them? Tell me!"

Agnes still says nothing.

Whenever she wants to answer, a lump forms in her throat. She sees those blurred shapes lying beside the cart in the forest like broken dolls, covered with shadows. As soon as Agnes opens her mouth the shadows will reveal their secret, so she prefers to keep quiet.

Instinctively, her hand goes to her breast and reaches under her torn dress. She brings out a small pendant hanging from a chain. It is the jewel that Hieronymus gave her before they ran away. Agnes thinks of his hastily whispered words.

"You mustn't lose it, do you hear? Give it only to someone you trust, and let that person keep it for you."

The witch's eyes fall on the jewel, and she leans down to Agnes to look more closely at the glittering thing. She starts instinctively, as though she had touched it and it was burning hot.

It is a ring. A signet ring with the portrait of a bearded man on it.

"Where did you get this?" asks the witch.

"From . . . from my mother," replies Agnes, croaking like a baby bird that has fallen out of the nest. "Where's my mother?"

They are the first words she has spoken since the attack.

✦ ✦ ✦

With a slight cry, Agnes awoke.

As usual, it took her a little while to realize where she was. When she heard the *clink* of tankards and men's laughter outside the cart, she dropped back, exhausted. But her breath came fast, and her eyes stung with the smoke from the burning beech logs.

She had seen the ring. The ring that Parcival had brought her so mysteriously last year, and that was now dangling around Barnabas's neck. She had owned it once before, as a child. Long ago, in the strange old woman's smoky cottage, it had been around her own neck.

A smoky cottage?

Agnes started. At last she could explain her wild dreams in recent nights. It wasn't magic, but merely the smoke reviving her memory, like a dragon that had lain slumbering for ages. And with those dreams earlier, it had been the cart and the freshly tanned leather skins in it. Those odors and sensations took her back to her childhood. That also explained why the dreams had begun at Trifels, just when she had been holding the ring in her hands. She had already known it from the past. The ring had brought memories to the surface that had been lying dormant somewhere in the depths of her mind. It was like walking into a dark room that had been locked for a long time.

All at once, Agnes remembered what Father Tristan had said to her.

And as for this ring, Agnes, let me implore you. Don't wear it on your finger, and don't show it to any stranger. Will you promise me that?

Agnes tightened her lips. What secret did the ring conceal? And what had happened to her mother, all those years ago? Philipp von Erfenstein had always said she had died of a fever. But obviously she had lost her life in an accident. And before that, she had made sure Agnes would be given the ring. Why . . .?

"Hey, Samuel!" boomed Barnabas in his deep voice, interrupting her train of thought. Obviously the men were still drinking heavily outside. "Wake that lazy slattern in the cart and tell her to give us some of that brandy she hoards, before she goes washing the master of the baggage train's arse with it."

The men roared with laughter, and Agnes got up before Samuel could come and give her a kick. As she climbed down from the cart, she looked in passing at the chain around Barnabas's neck, sparkling magically in the light from the campfire.

It was time to take the ring back.

And Agnes had a plan.

· 20 ·

Geyer's castle in the Lower Franconian village of Ingolstadt,
4 June, Anno Domini 1525

Mathis ducked when, with a mighty roar, another cannon-ball struck the ground only a few yards away from him. There were sounds of crashing and explosions all around him. Men shouted, horses whinnied in mortal fear, chunks of stone fell from the battlements. Gasping for breath, the young master gunner flung himself down behind the corpse of a thin horse and waited for the next thunderous salvo.

Out of the once proud Franconian peasants' army, only two hundred men of the Black Band were left. The few survivors had fled to one of Geyer's castles on the outskirts of the village of Ingolstadt. Here they were defending themselves doggedly against the inevitable end that probably faced them now, after a good three months of fighting, hunger, and torture.

Mathis flinched at the thought of the experiences of the last few days. At Königshofen the Swabian League had cut down thousands of peasants. Even those who pretended to be dead on the battlefield had been stuck like pigs, and the reports of horrors in nearby

Würzburg had at first been thought beyond belief. The hated fortress of Marienberg had still not been taken, but all the same the insurgents thought themselves safe. Not until Sunday did part of their army move, if hesitantly, against the enemy. After a little thought, Mathis and Melchior von Tanningen had joined the peasants in this venture. Mathis was still hoping that Florian Geyer had been right in his suppositions, and Agnes was somewhere to be found in the baggage train of the Swabian League.

It was here, in the small Lower Franconian village of Ingolstadt, about fifteen miles from Würzburg, that the final skirmish had come, and the peasants had fled from the storming cavalry. Only Geyer's Black Band had been able to reach nearby Giebelstadt Castle, and a life-and-death struggle had been going on ever since. Gunners of the Swabian League bombarded the old building on two sides. Mathis estimated that they had at least a dozen falconets and several larger artillery pieces. The seneschal clearly wanted to set an example. At present, all that remained of the main castle structure was ruins, although the thick walls, a good eighteen feet high, still stood.

"Attack on the south side! Attack on the south side!" one of the black-clad landsknechts shouted through the din of explosions. "All men to the ladders!"

From his cover, Mathis watched men hurrying to the southern wall with hastily cobbled together ladders, climbing them, and throwing back the many men already on the battlements. Once again, he admired the determination of Geyer's men as they faced the enemy. Even without their leader, who was still negotiating in Rothenburg, they were the hardened core of the peasant army. Mathis thought of his last words to Geyer: *A thousand men like yours and a hundred new guns, and this war would have been over long ago . . .*

But they didn't have enough guns or enough well-trained soldiers, so in the end the enemy would win. Probably also for want of real leaders—Geyer was wasting his time on negotiations when there was nothing left to be negotiated. And Götz von Berlichingen had long since made himself scarce. The one-armed knight knew when it was time to change sides. Mathis had not seen him since their headlong flight from the fields outside Ingolstadt.

Another salvo shook the walls of the castle. Not far from Mathis, a landsknecht fell from the battlements and was caught in the splintered remains of a cart. The bearded man's body twitched for a moment, then the life went out of his eyes. They stared at Mathis, almost reproachfully. Again the guns thundered. Mathis had once loved that sound, which seemed to promise a great future. Now he felt that the explosions came straight from hell. He cursed quietly, "The devil himself gave us the gift of this damned gunpowder."

A cannonball made short work of two soldiers who had flung themselves to the ground only a little way behind Mathis. Blood rained down on him. Where the men had been lying, a waist-deep hole now yawned, with a mangled torso and a single hand at the bottom of it. Shouting, Mathis got to his feet behind the dead horse and ran toward the walls. He must get away from here. It made no difference whether they stabbed him, throttled him, or shot him; he wanted an end to these raging sounds of crashing and explosions at last. He took hold of one of the ladders and began to climb.

"Damn it all, what are you doing?"

A hand on his shoulder held him back. When Mathis turned, he thought for a moment that he saw the dead master gunner Ulrich Reichhart before him, but it was only an old soldier with a badly scarred face, one of the Black Band. Mathis knew him from his few meetings with Florian Geyer. The man was an experienced landsknecht who had risen to be the knight's deputy over the last few months.

"Only death awaits you there!" the soldier shouted through the thunder of the guns, pulling Mathis off the ladder.

"And how about here?" Mathis snapped. "They'll shoot us to pieces. I'd at least like my corpse to be recognizable when this is over."

"If you climb up there I'll tear your arse open up to your ears so

as not even your own mother will recognize you," retorted the landsknecht. "Now, get a sword and go to defend the south side. We're
Geyer's Black Band, have you forgotten?"

"Curse it, I'm not one of you," Mathis said. "I'm a smith. I don't
belong here. I—"

The man pushed him, and Mathis staggered back. He fell over
another corpse and finally lay still. Breathing heavily, he closed his
eyes and tried to calm down.

This is the end, he thought sadly. *At least bear it like a man.*

At that moment he heard a whistle not far away—a whistle that
sounded familiar.

Mathis sat up with difficulty and saw a figure standing at the door
of the now ruined castle chapel, waving to him. It was hard to make
out more through the smoke of the powder, but eventually Mathis
saw the lute strapped to the man's back.

It was Melchior von Tanningen.

"How the devil . . ." Mathis muttered. But another cannonball
striking quite close interrupted his thoughts. Struggling to his feet
and bending low, he ran the short way to the chapel, which had already lost parts of its roof and the belfry.

"Time for us to get away from here, Master Wielenbach," said
Melchior, greeting him with a smile. "I fear this castle is past its
prime."

"How on earth did you get in here?" asked Mathis. "You weren't
with the men of the Black Band or I'd have seen you. And you can
hardly have climbed over the walls under this heavy fire."

Instead of replying, Melchior pointed to the interior of the chapel
and went in. Curious, Mathis followed him while the guns thundered
outside. The stained-glass windows were all broken, several rafters
had fallen from the roof to the floor and blocked the view of the apse.
The delicately built minstrel picked his way through the rafters where
they lay in a haphazard heap, and suddenly disappeared.

"Hey, wait!"

Mathis hurried after him and found himself standing in front of a small altar. On the floor there were several scratched slabs, tombstones bearing the coat of arms of the Geyer family. One of the slabs had been pushed aside. Hesitantly, Mathis went closer and stared into the dark hole, from which Melchior's voice suddenly echoed.

"Are you coming, or do you want to say a prayer first?"

Mathis gave a start. He blinked, and could then make out the muddy bottom of the hole, about six feet down. Plucking up his courage, he jumped into the darkness. Not a moment too soon, for immediately a sound like thunder shook the chapel above him. More rafters fell, blocking off the opening. Mathis ducked, avoiding several falling stones, and then hurried along the low, musty tunnel until he caught up with Melchior von Tanningen.

"You knew about this corridor?" he gasped.

The minstrel shrugged. "No, but it wasn't difficult to guess. Do you remember the escape tunnel from Scharfenberg Castle, the one that Agnes showed us? Many castles have a corridor like that, particularly when there's no well inside the walls. Without a hidden way out, those in the castle would die of thirst during a siege."

"But you've never been in this castle before," Mathis pointed out. "So how did you know . . ."

"That it has no well?" Melchior smiled. "I come from these parts, as you know. The rock of Franconia is often too hard to bore wells into, so I simply searched the surroundings of the castle to see if there was a hidden spring of water nearby. And *voilà* . . ."

The minstrel stopped and pushed a mat of hanging ivy aside, revealing a small pond surrounded by willows, with water lilies floating on it. The forest rose menacingly around the pond. They stepped out of the tunnel and found themselves outside the castle walls.

"When I lost sight of you at Ingolstadt, I thought at first you must be among the many thousand dead on the battlefield," said Melchior, stepping out into the fresh evening air. "But then one of our peasants told me you had gone with the Black Band. So I made my way here. And where do I find you but in the middle of the fray?" The minstrel shook his head. "You really ought to take better care of yourself."

Cautiously, Mathis too stepped into the open and looked around. The castle was barely visible behind the tall spruce and fir trees, but he still heard the rumble of the guns not far away, now mingled with the peaceful croaking of frogs. Mathis, who was still shaking, closed his eyes for a moment. He really had escaped death again.

"So now?" he asked faintly. "What do we do now?"

"What do you think?" Melchior smiled mischievously. "If what the revered knight Florian Geyer said is right, then Agnes is in the baggage train of the Swabian League. And as fate would have it, the League's landsknechts have pitched camp for the night only a few miles from here." He adjusted the sword at his side and began walking away. "It's about time we paid them and the noble lady a visit."

Agnes lay in the cart, stiff as a board, and listened to the procurer snoring beside her. It sounded calm and deep; Barnabas must be sleeping soundly. All the same, she waited another half an hour before finally, carefully, getting up.

The singing of drunken landsknechts outside came through the thin canvas cover of the cart, and the stink of gunpowder lingered in the air. The battles of Königshofen and Ingolstadt had been the dirtiest and cruelest of this war so far. Dead men lay all the way to the horizon, and as usual it had been the task of the women to collect the weapons, clothes, and jewelry from the bodies. A task that Agnes bore stoically on this occasion, particularly because she knew it would be the last time.

She had had to wait for a while before she could finally carry out her plan. Barnabas himself had given her the crucial idea a few days earlier, when he called for brandy. Now and then Agnes used the strong alcohol not just to wash wounds, but also to soothe her patients. It seemed an eternity ago that Father Tristan had told her what herbs, steeped in spirits, would induce sleep so sound that it was like a coma. Several more days had passed before she finally found the seed capsules of poppy in the fields and woods of Franconia, but together with wild hops and valerian, she had finally brewed her potion.

Tonight, at last, she had given it to Barnabas with his usual copious drafts of wine. Luckily the monkey was outside by the campfire, with Marek and Snuffler. Agnes took a deep breath. Now she would finally be able to leave the baggage train and go on alone to St. Goar. Once there she would learn more about the ring, her dreams, and her own past history, and she still hoped that she might come upon some sign of Mathis.

First, however, she must do one more thing.

By now Agnes was standing beside the snoring procurer, distrustfully examining his twitching features. Barnabas seemed to be dreaming. He smacked his lips in his sleep and muttered, then turned on his side, so that the chain he wore around his neck slipped into full view.

With her ring dangling from it.

Agnes had been waiting for this moment. Soundlessly, she brought out a small pair of pincers that she had found in Mother Barbara's chest of medicines and instruments, mainly used for pulling out teeth. Her hand approached the chain, she plucked up her courage to close the pincers, and the silver chain dropped silently into her fingers. They closed around the ring. She had it back at last. Now all she had to do was . . .

"Stop right there!"

Barnabas's hand shot out like a vicious snake. He grabbed her throat and forced her down beside him.

"Caught you at it, you witch," he hissed, glaring at her with eyes that were wide awake. "You thought I wouldn't notice you putting something in the wine. Ho, but Barbara saw you. First I didn't believe her, but then the wine had such an odd, sweet flavor that I spat it out. Planning to poison me and then run off, were you, sweetheart?"

"I only wanted—" Agnes croaked, but her abductor's hand was compressing her throat so hard that she could barely even breathe. Then Barnabas took it in his other hand too, strong fingers closing around it, slowly squeezing the life out of her.

"I never trusted you, you slut," Barnabas whispered. "Not from the first. Thought I could tame you, but you're still an arrogant, willful female. That sort's not worth anything on the market, so I'll have to throw you away like a bent piece of old iron. But first you're going to be at my service one more time . . ."

Barnabas chuckled. As he closed her mouth with one hand, the other wandered under her skirt like a spider, pushing it up. Agnes twisted and struggled, she tried to scream, but Barnabas was too strong. Forcing her down on her back, he pressed her thighs apart.

"I've always been nice to you before," he growled. "But that's all over now, you bitch. You'll never mix poison again."

Agnes could hardly draw a breath under his roughened hand. She smelled the cheap wine, his sweat, and the gunpowder clinging to his fingers. As the procurer, snorting, forced himself into her, she thought she would choke to death. Her hands hammered wildly on his back, but she might have been hitting a rock. Boundless fear and equally boundless hatred came together, so that she could hardly even think clearly.

Suddenly Agnes felt a small, cool object that had been under the tangled blankets. The pincers she had used to cut through the chain. Without another thought, she grasped the instrument and brought it down on the hand that was still over her face. When he still went on, she opened the pincers and pressed them together again.

With an ugly snapping sound, the jaws of the pincers closed, and Barnabas began to scream. He let go of her, sat up, and stared in astonishment at his right hand, which was covered with blood.

Its little finger was missing, and lay on the blanket in front of Agnes like a fat worm.

"You bitch!" shouted Barnabas. "You wait, I'll carve you up and throw you to the pigs for this!"

Bellowing, he flung himself on her, but at the last moment Agnes slipped aside. She had to get out of the cart, and quickly. It wouldn't be long before Marek, Snuffler, and the others would come to see what the matter was. Where was her ring? She couldn't leave without it. It had been in her hand just now, it must have fallen to the floor of the cart somewhere. But where? Everything was dark around her.

And now Barnabas fell on her again. Agnes picked up the blood-stained blanket and threw it at him, distracting his attention for a moment.

"Witch! Poisoner!" he bellowed. "Samuel, Marek, Snuffler, help me get this woman to the pyre."

At last she saw the ring.

It had rolled into a corner and was lying beside a heap of rusty swords. The moonlight was coming in through a rent in the canvas over the cart, making the gold glitter.

Agnes crawled over to the corner, snatched up the ring, and was about to escape out through the opening in the canvas when she felt Barnabas place his hand on her shoulder. He flung her, like a toy, to fall against one of the chests in the cart. His shirt and hose were smeared with blood. He stood above her like an angry, avenging god, and then threw himself on her once again. Agnes screamed as she had never screamed in her life.

"Get away, you devil!" she spat. "You've tormented me long enough. Leave me in peace, you evil spirit, you . . ."

But Barnabas was holding her throat as if it were in a vise, and her screaming died away.

"Look at me as you die, Agnes," the procurer rasped, licking his cracked lips. "My face will be the last thing you see in your—"

All at once he stopped short, and his eyes bulged out like two large glass marbles. Groaning, he opened his mouth to scream, but only a thin trickle of blood came out of it. His powerful body reared up, and then he tipped over to one side, lifeless.

Trembling, Agnes looked at the splintered sword that she was still clutching convulsively. It was red with her attacker's blood. When Barnabas rushed at her, she had instinctively picked up one of the weapons in the corner and rammed the blade into his belly.

She looked apprehensively at the limp, blood-stained body beside her, but there was not another sound out of Barnabas. His eyes stared blankly at the canvas over the cart.

Agnes felt remorse for no more than a split second. Father Tristan would certainly not have approved of what she had done. But then a sweet sense of satisfaction spread through her. It was as if another being who lived deep inside her had been longing for this moment.

I ought to have done it much earlier. For all the women on whom that brute forced himself . . .

Cries could be heard outside now, footsteps hurrying toward the cart. Agnes put the ring she had missed for so long on her finger and felt new strength flow into her. She cast one final glance at the dead procurer, then she cut a hole in the canvas at the back of the cart with the sword and slipped out into the darkness.

Outside, the war waited.

When Mathis and Melchior had at last reached the Swabian League's camp, after walking for a good two hours over trampled and burned fields, Mathis's heart was in his mouth. The army was so large that it seemed to stretch to the horizon in all directions. He had heard that the league had now joined the armies of the elector of the Palatinate and the bishop of Würzburg, and that their united forces consisted of almost ten thousand landsknechts and two thousand five hundred armored cavalry.

And Agnes may be somewhere in the middle of this, he thought, but with every step he took, his hope diminished.

It was dark, and the many campfires sparkled like fallen stars. Mathis was sure that someone would shout out at any moment, raising the alarm that would give them away, but nothing of the kind happened. The soldiers, some sleeping, others drunk and lying on the ground, ignored them. Now and then a few staggered past, singing at the top of their voices, but they were no danger either.

The most difficult moment had been getting past the guards posted on the outskirts of the camp. Melchior had told Mathis that a password was usually needed, and it changed from day to day. However, the guards were stationed so far apart that the two could easily slip past them under cover of bushes and thorny shrubs. Then, following a shallow, muddy ditch that was invisible at a distance, they finally reached the heart of the camp.

In battle, the landsknechts took their bearings from large flags representing the center of each unit, but here in the camp no one group could be distinguished from another. The many brightly clad soldiers in their slashed hose and padded doublets wore no identifying marks but a red and white armband or a ribbon in their hats. All the same, Mathis kept expecting some sergeant or lieutenant to accost and unmask them. It seemed to him that it took them hours to pass countless fires, gun carriages, carts, and tents.

"This is what I imagine walking through Rome or Constantinople must be like," Mathis groaned as he nervously looked around. "How can we ever find Agnes in such a crowd?"

"First we must locate the baggage train," said Melchior von Tanningen reassuringly. "That shouldn't be too difficult. Wait a minute."

Without any other explanation, he went over to a campfire and turned to the men singing and drinking around it. Mathis closed his eyes and murmured a quiet prayer, but the minstrel soon came back, smiling.

"I asked where to find whores cheap," Melchior explained. "All landsknechts know the way to the earthly paradise." He solicitously took Mathis by the arm and led him on. "Come along, Master Wielenbach. If you go on looking so anxious, someone really will get suspicious."

After another half an hour, the brightly colored tents of the camp at last thinned out. Instead, they saw more and more handcarts and carts covered with canvas, the latter drawn by broken-down nags or oxen. Pots, pans, and metal dishes hung from many of them. Now Mathis saw a number of women and even some grubby children kicking up a great racket as they ran about the camp. There was a smell of stew, fried onions, and gruel, and in spite of the day's dreadful experiences Mathis found that his mouth was watering. In contrast to the army camp itself, there was an almost peaceful atmosphere where the baggage train had come to a halt. Many of the landsknechts spent the night by warm fires with their families, who accompanied them right through the war, making sure there were regular meals, digging latrines, and plundering the abandoned battlefields. Mathis frowned. Looking at these people sitting together, eating, singing, and laughing, you would hardly believe that many of them had spent the day robbing, burning, and killing.

He just heard a fiddle pick up a tune when two women in red and yellow dresses, their faces garishly painted, came toward them, swaying their hips.

"Hello there, dearies," cooed one of them, who was not in her first youth. Mathis saw that most of her front teeth were missing. "Fancy a little fun in our cart? We could be on our own, just the four of us."

"By your leave, ladies, we're looking for a different kind of fun today," replied Melchior von Tanningen, raising his hat. "We hear there's a company of entertainers here with a monkey and a talking bird. Do you happen to know them, and where we can find them?"

"Oh, old Barnabas and his mangy creatures." The old whore made a scornful gesture. "No one wants to see his show anymore. Besides, he's sure to be sleeping off his drink now."

"The way you talk and the way you look, I'll bet it's not Barnabas you're after but his girl," intervened the second, younger whore, winking at Melchior. "She thinks herself something special, too. Forget it. She's Barnabas's sweetheart, and haughty as she is, the selfish old bastard keeps her on a tight leash, same as his monkey."

The two women laughed shrilly, while Mathis felt himself turning to stone.

"Is . . . is this sweetheart of his by any chance called Agnes?" he finally managed to say.

The younger whore, who wore an obvious and ill-fitting wig, looked at him suspiciously. "That's her name, yes. D'you know her?

I'd like to know where she comes from. Seems to be a good healer, so they say. Maybe she used to be a nun." She giggled. "That'll be why that wicked old goat Barnabas's mouth waters at the sight of her."

The other whore joined in her laughter, and together they pumped their hips provocatively. Mathis almost had to shout to get their attention again.

"Where do we find this Barnabas?" he asked desperately. "Tell me."

The older woman calmed down, with some difficulty, and gave Mathis a nasty look. "What'll you give me to tell you, eh?" she snapped. "That girl seems to be worth something to you. I'm beginning to think you're hiding something from us. Maybe we ought to tell the provost? So let's see the color of your money." Greedily, she stretched out the palm of her wrinkled hand. "Come along."

At that moment, not far away, there was a high, shrill scream, closely followed by a voice crying out in pain. Mathis knew that second voice at once. He would have known it among thousands.

It was Agnes, and she was crying out in mortal terror.

Agnes jumped down from the cart into the darkness and, to her horror, saw the sturdy figure of Marek already approaching, ready to fight. Here and now, trying to run away was too dangerous, so she crawled under the cart and kept as still as possible.

"The pope is a glutton! The pope is a glutton!" cackled the parrot suddenly in its cage, which hung from the driver's seat on the outside of the cart. All the ruckus must have woken the bird. Marek angrily hit the bars of the cage, whereupon the parrot squawked and fluttered frantically up and down.

"Damn you, keep quiet!"

Marek cautiously peered inside the cart, and then let out a soft, appreciative whistle.

"My God, someone did a thorough job," he said. "If it was really our willful Agnes, we've underestimated her—what a devilish woman."

He looked around for his companions. "Snuffler, Samuel, come here and look at this!" he called. "That girl stuck Barnabas like a pig."

Agnes heard more footsteps approaching, and then the three men's voices. Their muddy shoes were only a hand's breadth away from her.

"I always said the girl wasn't to be trusted," Snuffler said. "But Barnabas was crazy for her. And that's what he gets for it."

"Could as easily have been one of us," Marek pointed out. "So let's catch the bitch and cut her pretty tits off. Snuffler, you and me will search the baggage train. Samuel, you stay here. She can't have gone far."

The dirty shoes moved away, and Agnes breathed in deeply, only now noticing how long she had been holding her breath. She waited a little longer, then rolled cautiously out from under the cart and looked around. If she could manage to reach the carts and tents about thirty feet away, she would be safe for the time being. Or at least, her pursuers would have difficulty finding her in the labyrinth that opened up among the various tents and campsites. She only had to . . .

A shrill chattering sound struck up close to her ear. It was the monkey, Satan, who had jumped down from the cart and was hopping frantically up and down. His mouth was distorted in a wide grin.

"Go away! Go away, you little devil," Agnes whispered desperately. "Get off, hurry up."

But it was too late. She felt the heel of a boot grinding painfully down on her left hand. When she looked up, she saw Samuel leering maliciously down at her.

"Good boy." He threw Satan a nut and then seized Agnes by the shoulder, hauled her up, and held his knife to her throat.

"What you did to good old Barnabas wasn't nice, not nice at all." The robber shook his head disapprovingly. His knife toyed with Agnes's bodice, while the monkey went on chattering beside him. "Not that I got on too well with him, but he was the leader of our band. Who's going to fool the public with big talk now, eh?" He assumed an innocent expression. "Marek is going to cut your tits off for that. Dear me, what a waste."

He looked cautiously around, and then suddenly hauled Agnes over the short distance to Mother Barbara's cart, which stood a little way from the campfire.

"Get in there!" he hissed at her. Still with his knife to her throat, Samuel climbed the few steps up to it, and flung Agnes down inside the cart. Satan nimbly followed them, made his way along the poles holding up the canvas cover, and watched from that vantage point to see what would happen next.

"Old Barbara is dead drunk again," Samuel said, giggling so close to her ear that she could smell the sour wine on his breath. "Seen it myself. I'll be finished with you by the time the old hag is awake, and then Marek can carve you up any way he likes." The blade of his knife slit through Agnes's dress, slowly cutting it apart. "I guess I ought to thank you for dealing with Barnabas," he added. "Now I can do all the things to you I've only dreamed of."

Agnes lay there as if turned to stone. For the second time within a few minutes, she was threatened with rape. And this time there really did seem no way out. If she called for help, Marek and Snuffler would find her, if she kept quiet, Samuel would finish her off. Agnes had already seen for herself how quick he was with a knife; once, on meeting a drunken mercenary spoiling for a fight, Samuel had slit his nose and ears without another thought. This time it would be her turn.

The blade of the knife moved on through the fabric of her dress, and was level with her breasts, when a shadowy form suddenly emerged from the darkness at the back of the cart. There was a clattering sound, and Samuel collapsed, grunting. His knife fell to the floor of the cart with a *clink*, while the monkey hooted furiously.

"Now move yourshelf, girl—*hic!*—and get away from here fasht. If you really have Barnabash on your con . . . consciensh . . . then God forgive you."

It was Mother Barbara, swaying where she stood unsteadily in the back of the cart, with a heavy skillet in her hand.

"Shhh . . . Shamuel was right," she babbled. "I got quite tip . . . tipshy. But the fool never saw me come and lie down in my cart." She chuckled as she stared at the lifeless form of Samuel lying at her feet. Agnes thought she saw a puddle of blood beside him.

"Guessh why I got sho . . . sho tipshy, eh?" growled the old vivandière suddenly. "Becaushe I gave you away to Barnabash, that randy old goat. And then I feared for my immortal soul, that's why." Her foot nudged Samuel, and he rolled aside. "At least he won't hurt any more women. Bloody men!" Her glance suddenly darkened, then she looked gravely at Agnes, her eyes perfectly clear. It seemed that she was rapidly sobering up. With a sudden movement, she took off her threadbare woolen shawl and handed it to Agnes.

"Put this on, and be off," she said. "Limp a little, and they'll think it's me." She nudged Agnes and belched slightly. The sharp smell of brandy filled the interior of the cart. "I'll look after Agathe, I pr— promise. Now, off with you before I change my mind."

She spat copiously, and Agnes turned away. At the entrance to the cart, however, she turned around once more.

"Why?" she whispered.

Mother Barbara shrugged her shoulders. "How would I know? Because you're different? Because I can tell you don't belong here? Because I'm drunk, and I was once young myself? So be off. I'll count to twenty, then I'll scream and say you knocked Samuel out."

Agnes nodded a goodbye. At last she climbed down the steps of the cart, while Satan screeched and gibbered like a small, angry child behind her.

When Mathis and Melchior ran in the direction from which the scream had come, they saw, in the light shed by a campfire of some size, two men with long daggers hurrying toward them. Mathis thought they were being attacked, but the men took no notice of them and ran past. Putting out a foot, Melchior tripped one of them up, and the man fell to the ground, cursing.

"I do apologize," said the minstrel regretfully, "but we just heard a woman screaming. You were presumably hurrying to her aid. May I ask what has happened?"

"No, you damn well may not," swore the man, scrambling up. He was small, but sturdily built. Angrily, he brandished his dagger in front of Melchior's face. "Let me by, before I dig a hole in your fancy doublet."

"All we want is information," Melchior persisted. "There's no call to be offensive."

"Damn you, I said—" the man began, but his companion held him back by the shoulder.

"Let it be, Marek," he said soothingly. "We have more important business on hand. We'll catch up with these two later. For now let's get our hands on Agnes."

Melchior raised his eyebrows. "There now, that's the very girl we're looking for ourselves." Almost casually, the minstrel laid his hand on the hilt of his sword. "I'm afraid it's high time for you to tell us more."

At that moment, Mathis saw an old woman limping away from one of the carts that stood not far off. She walked with a stoop, and had a woolen shawl over her head, but something about her attracted Mathis's attention. He felt that he had seen this woman often before: her figure, the way she held the shawl wrapped around her, the tousled blonde hair coming out from under it . . .

"Agnes!" he yelled. "Agnes!"

Without stopping to think, Mathis ran to the woman, who stopped in amazement. At last she stood up straight and cautiously put back the shawl. Mathis laughed out loud. It really was Agnes. They had found her at last. He had followed her through all the horrors of this war, he had traveled hundreds of miles, and now she really stood in front of him, with her blonde hair, her freckles, her high, proud forehead. He could hardly believe his luck. With a cry of joy, he spread his arms wide.

"Agnes, my God!"

"Careful, Master Wielenbach!" Melchior screamed from behind him. Mathis turned in mid-movement to see one of the two men running toward him. The other was fighting fiercely with the minstrel, who had unsheathed his sword. Landsknechts were coming up from nearby fires.

"Hey, you there! Sheathe your weapons!" called one of them. "Or I'll tell the provost, and you'll be dangling from the gallows tonight."

But neither Melchior nor his opponent had any intention of breaking off their fight. The other man, too, had raised his dagger, and was about to rush at Mathis.

"Let me by!" he cried angrily. "That woman killed one of us. If you protect her, you're guilty as well."

Mathis stayed where he was. He raised his hands, smiling, and waited for the man to come up to him.

"There we are," the man said. "I knew you'd see sense. Now, you help me to—"

Without warning, Mathis kicked his adversary between the legs with all his might, so that he groaned and fell to the ground, like a dead branch falling from a tree. Then Mathis kicked him again.

"I don't know what you did to Agnes," he said through clenched jaws, "but judging by the look of you, it wasn't good. So just stay where you are if you want to keep your teeth."

Then he hurried over to Agnes, who was still beside the cart, motionless with shock. Now, at close quarters, she suddenly looked very small and vulnerable. It was less than two months since their last meeting, but she seemed to Mathis far older and more mature, although also sadder than before, like something in her had broken.

"Mathis . . ." she stammered. "You? Here? But, but . . ."

"I'll tell you all about it, Agnes," Mathis said, hugging her tightly for a brief moment. "All about it. But not now. We have to get away from here."

"My own opinion exactly." Melchior approached them, sheathed his blood-stained sword, and pointed behind him, to where an ever larger crowd was gathering in the light of the campfires. There were men, women, and children, but also several armed men with long spears who obviously worked for the provost, helping keep order within the ranks. They were shouting, and swarming in all directions, carrying burning torches and lanterns.

"Our opponents obviously have friends who are not especially well disposed to us," the minstrel went on. "How many landsknechts in this camp? Ten thousand? Yes, it's high time for us to say goodbye. *Allez!*"

Mathis took Agnes by the hand and the three of them ran past the tents, the carts, the crackling fires, and then on into the nearby wood, until at last the hue and cry behind them began to die down and finally fell entirely silent.

· 21 ·

Trifels Castle, 14 June, Anno Domini 1525

AT TRIFELS CASTLE, SHEPHERD JOCKEL sat on his throne, dispensing justice.

Two peasants knelt before him with their heads bowed, humbly waiting for his verdict. Crows flew past the empty windows, cawing as though they expected good pickings in the near future. Otherwise silence reigned, a silence that was almost tangible in the cold, sooty walls. Around the throne, which was made of woven willow, leather, and furs, stood about a dozen more men, waiting grimly with their arms crossed to hear what Jockel had to say. The peasants had introduced this sham court a few weeks ago, to show that they were their own masters. But, from the first, they had addressed no one but Shepherd Jockel as master.

He was toying with a silver goblet set with semiprecious stones, acting as though he was weighing up the case, but he had come to his decision long ago.

"You made off by night in secret, without permission of the Peasants' Council, even though we may be about to face the last battle, the one that will decide everything," he said in a low, firm voice, while he looked at the sparkling goblet in his hands. "What have you to say for yourselves?"

"Sir," began one of the two accused men submissively. He wore a torn, threadbare shirt over his thin chest and nervously kneaded his broad-brimmed hat. "I . . . I really don't know what battle you mean. But battle or no battle, we have to think of our fields at home. The wild boar have been rampaging all over them, trampling on everything, there was a terrible storm that blew down the barns, our wives and children just can't manage alone any longer."

"So you thought you'd leave your comrades in the lurch, and kill a few wild boar instead of the league's landsknechts?" Jockel asked with an innocent expression. Some of the men standing around laughed quietly. "You tell me what I'm to make of that."

"It would only have been for a few days," muttered the other peasant. He stared at the flagstones on the floor, which were covered with bones, animal droppings, and leaves, as if he could look straight through a hole there and see hell. "After that we'd have come back again for sure."

"And suppose the elector of the Palatinate and his men had turned up here first, eh? Did you stop to think of that, you two numbskulls? Did you think not of yourselves for once, but of our *common cause*, damn it?"

Jockel had risen to his feet. He threw the goblet straight at the crouching peasant with the broad-brimmed hat. It hit the man right on the forehead, and he collapsed, whimpering.

"We can't give in now!" Jockel shouted. "Not now! That's what they expect us to do—go back to our fields so they can slaughter us one by one. What you did was no less than cowardly desertion."

"In the town of Zabern in Alsace, they massacred thousands of us," ventured one of the dozen or so peasants in the great hall, doubtfully. "Don't get me wrong, Jockel, we have courage. But how about our wives and children?" When a couple of the other bystanders nodded, he went on more firmly. "They even killed the babies in Zabern. And the landsknechts took the women away as their whores. It doesn't look good for us here in the Palatinate, either. More and more towns and cities have been giving up, now that Würzburg's fallen into the hands of the enemy, and the elector here began sending his troops against us. In Speyer the bishop and the citizens have joined together, and over in the county of Neuscharfeneck the peasants live in fear of the old count sending a punishment battalion. Maybe this is the time to negotiate, before there's nothing left to negotiate about."

He paused for effect, and Jockel nodded mildly, like he took the man's point. He must go to work cautiously now.

"I see. Negotiate," he said at last, leaning back in his throne. "Not a bad idea. That's what the peasants did in Zabern, too. The duke of Lorraine promised them safe conduct. So they came to the city gates without weapons. And then what?" The men looked at him expectantly, and Jockel sighed. "Then the massacre began. Almost twenty thousand of us, slaughtered like cattle. Twenty thousand. Is that what we want? To *negotiate*?"

The peasants around the throne murmured quietly. Jockel could feel that he had them in the palm of his hand again. Recently he had found it harder and harder to keep his men under control, even though it had all begun so promisingly. After the discovery of the tunnel, storming Scharfenberg Castle had been child's play. Unfortunately Jockel had not been able to keep his men from burning and plundering the castle. With all the robbing, drinking, and eating, Count Scharfeneck had slipped through their fingers, and with him a good sum of ransom money. Jockel had been furious and ordered two of the worst drinkers to be whipped.

The peasants had not been so destructive the next day, when they took Trifels Castle, which was poorly guarded. Jockel had a suitable headquarters at last. Since then, he and his band had ruled over the entire Eusserthal area from the castle. The town of Annweiler had joined the rebellion, and paid tribute. The surrounding castles had been destroyed or were keeping quiet.

But for some weeks, things had seemed to be changing. Elector Ludwig of the Palatinate, after initially appearing willing to negotiate, had marched against the peasants with the archbishop of Trier, and town after town surrendered or was burned. The insurgents lacked a beacon, a signal that would unite them all again. Sometimes it seemed to Jockel that he was the only one who still knew what was to be expected from a leader.

He looked around the now filthy Knights' House and grinned at the thought that Emperor Barbarossa might once have dined here. Now he, Shepherd Jockel, was an emperor himself, lord of Eusserthal and Trifels, with the power of life or death. He clapped his hands in a lordly manner.

"Listen, my brothers," he proclaimed. "Nothing is lost yet. On the contrary, only yesterday I heard news that the peasants are rising in other countries as well. In England, in France, even far away in Spain —they're all on our side." That was a downright lie, but the members of his audience were glad to clutch at any straw. They looked up at him hopefully.

"But if we are going to win, we must be strong," he went on. "Strong and unyielding. And so my judgment is that the two accused be whipped, and then put in the pillory in Annweiler, as a warning to all. That is only just." He nodded graciously, and made a gesture that closed the matter. He had really wanted to have the two offenders hanged, but he felt that would have been going too far. However, the death sentence might be passed in the following weeks.

When they had finally won.

Because Jockel was still firmly convinced that the peasants would be victorious. Even if these meek lambs didn't share his opinion. What they needed, however, was something to believe in. A symbol, a beacon under which they would unite to sweep away the rulers of this world in a mighty storm of blood.

Jockel watched as the two sobbing offenders were dragged away by some of the other men, and then he snapped his fingers.

"Show in the next accused men," he ordered. "And bring me another goblet of Palatinate wine, quick as you can. Justice is a damn thirsty business."

A hundred miles away, a broad barge was making its way through the waters of the Rhine. It was a freighter, lying low in the water, loaded up with several dozen casks of wine and salt. The voyage was so slow that, out of sheer boredom, Agnes had taken to counting the sailboats, rowboats, and rafts coming toward them the other way. They had been obliged to put in, again and again, at the many little tollbooths erected on the riverbank by every county, every bishopric, every fief, however small. Mathis stood beside Agnes at the rail, yawning and stretching his limbs.

"I guess it would have been faster on foot," he sighed, turning to Melchior von Tanningen, who had also come forward to the bow. At least you could feel a little breeze blowing there. It was nearly midday, and the sun burned mercilessly down from the sky.

"Faster maybe, but not safer." Melchior von Tanningen pointed to the steep mountain slopes on the left bank, densely overgrown with trees and bushes. "There may be bands of plundering peasants here, too. How are you going to convince them that you're one of their men?"

"Am I?" retorted Mathis gloomily. "What with all this slaughter on both sides, I'm not so sure. And the outcome of the struggle was decided long ago. It's just that the local peasants don't yet know that."

"I don't think we, of all people, should tell them so," said Agnes. "The bearers of bad news are always the first to lose their heads."

Lost in thought, Agnes was looking at the wooded bank while at the same time she wondered what might be going on at home in Trifels Castle. Was her father's castle still standing? Had it been stormed, or even razed?

It was now ten days since they had set off together from the Franconian village of Ingolstadt, going west. So far they had covered almost a hundred and fifty miles, on foot and by water, through a countryside still in flames. Many of the local feudal lords had torched

their subjects' villages out of revenge. Captured insurgents were beheaded, burned at the stake, torn apart by horses, or blinded. Yet
there were still parts of the country where the peasants refused to
give up. Some bands were stubbornly holding out in the north of the
Palatinate, and near the Alps. Agnes was glad that they had reached
the Rhine without being ambushed or impeded in any other way.
Beyond Mainz, rumors of risings and punitive actions had gradually
petered out. Nonetheless, they were still on the alert.

To avoid unnecessary danger, Agnes had cut her hair short and
wore men's clothing. An extra coat—far too hot for the weather—hid
her figure. Melchior had also acquired a plainer doublet, so that now
all three of them looked like traveling journeymen or musicians. That
had also helped them to buy cheap passage on the freighter now taking them to the destination that Agnes had wished to reach for so
long: St. Goar.

This morning, Melchior had talked to the crew of the barge and
found out that they would reach the monastery in the afternoon.
Agnes still did not know what she hoped to find there. But she felt
that she must make this journey if she was ever to sleep easily again,
without those dreams—and she was glad to have the company of
Melchior and Mathis. Mathis in particular had been very solicitous
over these last few days. Agnes had not told him anything about those
dreadful nights with Barnabas, but he seemed to sense that something
deep within her had been injured and would only heal slowly. Since
their flight from the army camp, he had kissed and embraced her a
few times, but when he noticed that she froze in his arms, he quickly
ceased his gentle approaches. It would take much longer for her to
feel at ease with a man again, if she ever did. The memory of what
Barnabas had done to her was too horrible.

For that alone the bastard deserved to die, she thought grimly.

Gently, Agnes stroked the scratched engraving on the signet ring,
which she was now wearing on her finger again. For the hundredth
time, she traced the lines that made up the portrait of a bearded king.
So much blood had already been shed because of this ring. It was a

curse and a blessing at once. Agnes nodded firmly. It was high time
for her to find out more about its past.

About its past and mine, too . . .

Suddenly she heard the clear sound of a bell ringing three times
from the stern of the barge, and the boatmen fell on their knees and
began praying out loud. Agnes came back from her thoughts with a
start.

"What's the matter with the men?" she asked Melchior uncertainly. "Has there been an accident?"

"They're praying *not* to have one," the minstrel replied, pointing
to a tall slate crag rising high above the right-hand bank of the Rhine.
They were slowly approaching it. "The country people here call that
rock the Loreley. The river narrows here, and there are a number of
whirlpools and currents. The most dangerous spot is right ahead of
us. Many ferrymen and passengers have been dragged down to the
river bottom by the swirling water." With a slight movement of his
head, Melchior indicated the boatmen, who seemed to be looking
apprehensively at the three passengers even as they prayed. "They're
probably expecting us to pray as well, so let's do as they want."

"It can't hurt, anyway," said Agnes, kneeling down. After a moment's hesitation, Mathis and Melchior imitated her.

As the rock passed by, a mighty rushing sound was heard, seeming
to come from everywhere at once. Uncertainly, Mathis looked up at
the steep slopes, from which small stones tumbled.

"Never fear," Melchior reassured him. "What you can hear is only
the multiple echoes of the Galgenbach waterfall. But the locals think
it's the sound of dwarfs digging for gold in their caves." He sighed.
"I've been thinking for some time of writing a pretty ballad about this
part of the country. Maybe with a water spirit in it, or an enchantress
who lures men to their death . . ."

A shudder suddenly ran through the barge, and the three travelers,
taken by surprise, clung to the casks of wine that were strapped firmly
to the deck to keep from falling. The boatmen stopped praying,
shouted, and ran to the bows. Agnes saw a huge dead tree drifting in

the water directly next to the boat. It was an oak, over thirty feet long, with flotsam and jetsam caught in its crown. The tree trunk grated as it scraped along the port side of the barge, but the vessel held.

Looking down at the water again, Agnes saw two drowned men among the branches of the oak. A frayed rope floated after one of them. Both bodies were so bloated that they hardly resembled human beings but were more like swollen flour sacks. To judge by their ragged clothing, they were simple peasants.

"Poor devils," murmured Mathis. "I guess they were hanged very close to the Rhine as a warning to anyone coming up the river, and then a storm washed them into the water."

"Where they nearly dragged a few more mortals down into the abyss after them," said Agnes quietly. "God have mercy on their souls." She made the sign of the cross, while the oak with its terrible freight rocked in the water as it slowly moved out of their sight.

The rushing of the waterfall was not so loud now, but more and more whirlpools, crowned by white foam, showed on the surface of the Rhine, and a sandbar emerged from the water like the back of a gigantic fish. Sweat stood out on the brow of the boatman in the stern as he steered the barge now to the right, then to the left again, to escape the dangerous rapids and the sandbar. Agnes held her breath. The river, a swift torrent now, wound its way through the deep rocky fissures, and shadows on the banks reached out long fingers to the vessel as it bobbed like a nutshell through the many currents.

"Maybe I should have prayed louder," said Mathis, clinging to the rail convulsively. He looked pale, and the movement of the barge obviously did not agree with him. Trees and uprooted bushes floated past and disappeared in the seething whirlpools.

At last, after what felt like an age, they left the Loreley rock behind them, the sun came out, and the Rhine flowed on at its usual slow pace. Everything was suddenly so peaceful that the last few minutes seemed to Agnes unreal. Green vineyards stretched over the terraces of the river valley, and a pretty little town with a small castle towering above it came into view on the right-hand bank. There was another town on the left bank as well, with a red and white church. A strong castle, surrounded by fortified walls, stood above this town, with colorful banners fluttering from its freshly plastered battlements. It was the most beautiful castle that Agnes had ever seen; Trifels was like a rough-hewn rock by comparison.

"Ah, St. Goar!" said Melchior in relief. "So we have reached our destination."

Agnes looked at him in surprise. "You mean that castle is St. Goar?"

Melchior laughed. "No, no. That is Rheinfels Castle, the largest castle on the Rhine, owned by the landgrave of Hesse. I once spent several weeks here, entertaining the landgrave with my music. St. Goar is the town with the church at its center, over there."

"But I always thought we were looking for a monastery, not—"

Agnes stopped when she looked at the church in the middle of the town again. Only now did she notice other buildings annexed to its north and south sides, obviously part of a monastic complex of considerable size.

"You're looking at the famous monastery of Benedictine canons in St. Goar. It belongs to the powerful Benedictine abbey of Prüm," Melchior explained. "The landgrave of Hesse has always been much annoyed that the canons pay him no taxes. For centuries, the holy fathers have owed allegiance to the emperor alone, and they are very influential."

Agnes thoughtfully scrutinized the attractive church. After so many months of privations, she had finally reached the place where she hoped to find answers. But she did not feel the sense of real joy that she had expected.

"I don't know," she murmured. "I . . . I'd expected a lonely monastery, maybe on top of a mountain, or in a deep, shady valley. A mysterious building full of secrets, like Trifels Castle. But this is only a town church." She turned to Melchior. "Are you sure this is the right St. Goar? Maybe Father Tristan meant some other place."

The minstrel shrugged his shoulders. "It's the only St. Goar I know, anyway. And you're not doing the church justice. The bones of St. Goar himself are kept there, and pilgrims come from far and wide to touch his coffin."

"One way or another, we ought to see the church," said Mathis, who had a little color back in his face by now. "Seems like we'll have to stay here for a while." He pointed to the Rhine, which had a heavy chain stretched across it at this point, forcing the boatmen to steer the barge into the little river harbor below the castle. "And I didn't come hundreds of miles merely to turn around again. Particularly as I don't know where I'd go," he added quietly a moment later.

"You're both right." Agnes nodded, her mind made up. "I'm sorry. It's only that I'm a little confused. And I can't thank you enough for coming all this long way with me."

Creaking, the barge came in to the pier in the harbor, where the crew tied it up and began unloading casks of wine. The captain, with a grudging expression, paid the toll due here on every passing vessel. Only when that was done was the chain lowered into the river again. Agnes, Mathis, and Melchior took their leave of the boatmen and went along the pier, which led to one of the town gates.

Like many other towns in the Rhine valley, St. Goar was shaped like a narrow tunnel wedged between the river and the steep slopes above it. A high wall, with fortified towers along its length, protected the town from attack. Passing through the harbor gateway, the three travelers soon found themselves approaching the monastery complex in the middle of the town. Citizens clad in colorful fabrics strolled down the paved streets, laughing and talking. A small castle beyond the church was clearly the local mayor's residence. The attractive half-timbered houses, the plastered town wall, and the taverns doing a good trade all gave Agnes an impression of prosperity. Evidently the town did pretty well out of the income from the river toll. She suddenly thought of the shabby town of Annweiler at home.

Did our town once look like this? Back in the time of the Staufers?

"Black Hans may have been a robber knight," muttered Mathis, "but the men who run the river traffic here are no better. Squeezing the last of their money out of travelers, and dressing in velvet and good linen."

"I wouldn't mind a silk gown myself," Agnes retorted. She sighed, looking down at her plain coat. "Fine fabrics like that are much more comfortable to wear than these coarse, dusty men's clothes."

Mathis grinned. "Now you know what we poor men have to put up with every day."

Soon they reached the market square in front of the monastery church. On their right was the attractive town hall. A linden tree stood in the middle of the square, and there was an empty pillory smeared with dirt and rotten fruit beside it. Only now that they had reached the monastery complex did Agnes see how large it was. From the church itself, roofed cloisters stretched both left and right to the neighboring buildings, one of which she supposed housed the monks. Scaffolding stood along the facades of the buildings, showing that more construction work was in progress. Workmen stood on ladders, repainting walls, while farther off two monks were carrying a man on a stretcher into one of the buildings.

"The pilgrims' hospital at St. Goar is famous all along the Rhine," said Melchior, as his eyes moved appreciatively over the various buildings. "They're obviously still extending this place. At least, the nave of the church looks to be new. An interesting building, so tall and light. I know a church in Rome that—"

"That's nice for you," Mathis interrupted, "but we're not here to admire churches. We've come to track down a mystery. So let's go straight in and see if we can find someone to help us." He walked across the market square and opened the low church door, which swung inward, squealing.

Agnes shivered as she entered the church. After the heat of the day, it was surprisingly cool in here. Little light came in through the ornate stained-glass windows, so that the nave of the church was immersed in an almost eerie dusk. A freshly plastered gallery ran around it, about twelve feet above the floor, with its canopy supported on joists and skillfully ornamented with the likenesses of several saints.

From the apse at the east end, steps led down, and a steady brushing sound came from the bottom of them. When the three approached the steps, they saw a crypt borne up on columns, containing a sarcophagus on a plinth. An old monk in the plain habit of the Benedictines was sweeping the floor in front of it.

"The tomb of St. Goar," Melchior whispered. "A very holy place, and we should not omit to see it. Let us take a quick look." He signaled to the others to follow him. Then he climbed down the few steps and cleared his throat when he reached the monk.

"*Dominus vobiscum*," murmured the old man, still sweeping. His hood was drawn far down over his face.

"*Et cum spiritu tuo*," replied Melchior. "Good Father, forgive us for disturbing you. We have come on a long journey to visit this place."

For the first time, the monk stopped sweeping the floor and looked up. Two friendly, clever eyes shone under the hood, looking almost too young in his wrinkled face. His most striking features were his bushy eyebrows, which resembled two lively hairy caterpillars. He smiled mildly.

"Then you are in luck," the monk said. "The crypt is technically closed today, because we are preparing for the festivities on the day of St. Goar." He sighed. "But I suppose I forgot to lock the church door again, and, since you are here . . ." He made a gesture of welcome toward the tomb, crowned by a heavy stone slab. "By all means pay the saint your respects. I hope it will not take too long."

Agnes looked at the slab, on which the stone figure of a monk stood out in relief.

"Is that St. Goar?" she asked.

The old man nodded. "He came to these parts when the Romans were slowly retreating before the stormy advance of other peoples. He is believed to have saved many ships from being wrecked in the Rhine. In addition, the saint brought vines with him from his home of Aquitaine, to make wine in the Palatinate." He smiled mischievously. "Not the least of his good deeds, even if Goar himself was a hermit, and probably preferred the clear water of the Rhine. The crypt here stands on the site of his cave. When he died, his successors built a little church over it, then a larger one."

Mathis, standing beside Agnes, cleared his throat. "Forgive us, Father. This is all very interesting. But we are in search of someone who can help us in an extremely important matter."

"In fact, it would be helpful to speak to the head of this monastery," said Melchior. "Do you by any chance know where we can find the dean?"

"The dean?" The old monk raised his bushy eyebrows. "And why, may I ask, are you looking for him?"

"We have come a long way, Father," Agnes intervened. "My former father confessor told me that here, in St. Goar, I might find the answer to a question that has been weighing on my mind for a long time."

The monk laughed softly. "Many are seeking answers to their questions," he said at last, "yet the one true answer is always the same: God. There was no need for you to come to St. Goar for that."

Mathis shifted restlessly from one foot to the other. "Listen, Father, this lady is Countess von Löwenstein-Scharfeneck, and the two of us have been accompanying her on a long, laborious search that has brought us to St. Goar." He pointed to Melchior and himself. "Melchior von Tanningen is a traveling knight, and I am a simple weaponsmith. We have come together from Trifels Castle in the Palatinate, far to the south of this place, and . . ."

Suddenly the old man's eyes narrowed to slits. "Trifels?" he said suspiciously. "Did that strange man send you, I wonder? If so, your journey has been in vain. I have not changed my mind."

"What strange man?" asked Agnes. "Did he want to know something about Trifels too? Please tell me."

But the old man went on sweeping the floor around the altar in silence.

"Good Father," said Melchior, trying his luck. "This matter is really of the utmost importance . . ."

"Yes, that's what the man said as well. And I still say no."

"Oh, I've had enough of this," Mathis suddenly exclaimed, loud enough to make the walls of the deserted crypt echo. "We've withstood so many dangers, we've fought so many battles, we've come across devastated country and nearly lost our lives, just to reach this distant place. And there you stand, as silent as an ox. Tell us where the dean is. Then he can decide what may be said and what may not. So now talk, or else . . ."

He took a menacing step toward the monk, but Agnes held him back. "No, Mathis," she said. "You're committing a sin."

Without more thought, she fell on her knees before the old man, folding her hands as if in prayer.

"I beg you, Father," she pleaded. "I swear by all the saints that we come with good intentions. All we want is . . ."

Agnes stopped, seeing the old man's eyes suddenly fixed on her hands. A ray of sun had just found its way through one of the tiny windows in the vaulted roof above, lighting up the young mistress of Trifels Castle as though she were surrounded by a saint's aureole.

The ring glittered on her finger.

"Barbarossa's ring," the monk whispered. He put back his hood and bent to look at the jewel more closely. "Holy Mother of God. The prophesy was right. It really has returned to us. That changes everything."

All at once there was a strange silence in the old church, while the monk examined the ring. Finally, Mathis cleared his throat.

"You . . . you know this ring?" he asked.

The old man did not reply. Only after a while did he look at Mathis as though he had just awoken from a dream.

"Of course I know it," he replied. "It was described to me in detail not long ago." His glance moved down to Agnes, whom he studied thoughtfully. "The ring, but not its wearer. I would never have expected to see them both myself, and so soon. These must be terrible times indeed." Briefly, the old man looked at Mathis and Melchior, before he turned back to Agnes. "Are these your companions, and can you trust them?"

"If I can't trust them, I can trust no one," Agnes answered, confused. "But why . . ."

"Then they shall be told the secret as well. You will need all the protection you can get."

"Wonderful!" Melchior von Tanningen clapped. "Then this story will be cleared up at last, and my ballad can have an ending worthy of it." The minstrel looked searchingly around. "Forgive me, but could you please take us to your dean, and quickly."

The old man put his broom down in a corner and wiped his hands clean on his habit.

"I am the dean," he replied. "My name is Father Domenicus."

Then he shuffled over to the steps and climbed to the gallery, groaning with the effort.

"Please follow me. It is indeed time for you to know more about the ring and those who have worn it."

The man who had introduced himself as Father Domenicus went up the steps to the gallery without turning around to look at his three companions. They followed him, hesitantly. The canon led them to a narrow door to the right of the apse, which he unlocked with a rusty key from the bunch at his waist. Then he beckoned them in. The door opened into a small room with narrow windows, through which not much sunlight could fall. A few torches burned in their holders. Gravestones were set into the stone of the floor and the walls, memorials with reliefs showing the dead, who seemed to watch Agnes. There was a musty smell, and she felt a slight draft that she could not explain.

"This is the oldest part of the church," said the Father, and his hoarse voice echoed through the vault. "St. Goar's baptismal chapel. A series of great lords who had done good service to the monastery were laid to rest here." He pointed to one of the tombstones on the wall, showing an old man with a little lamb in his arms. "For instance Friedrich von Fels, abbot of Prüm at the time when the abbey became a principality under the Staufer emperors. Next to him is Abbot

Regino, who ruled the foundation during the bad times of the Norman occupation and was one of the greatest historians of his epoch. And Countess Adelheid von Katzenelnbogen . . ." With a shaking hand, Father Domenicus pointed to a gravestone let into the ground, showing an elegant lady in court dress with a veil. "She gave the monastery a large sum of money that enabled the library to be extended."

"Excuse me, Father," Mathis said. "But weren't you going to tell us about the ring that Agnes wears?"

"Quiet, boy!" Father Domenicus's eyes flashed at the young man. His bushy brows shook slightly in the torchlight. "Young people are always in such a hurry, they overlook what's really important. If you want to understand all this, then kindly listen." He took a deep breath and then went on.

"It is not by chance that so many abbots of Prüm lie here. That mighty Benedictine abbey has always watched over this foundation. It was no less than Frederick of the house of Hohenstaufen, Barbarossa's grandson, who made the abbey an independent principality a good three hundred years ago. However, the emperor had one stipulation . . ." Father Domenicus raised his voice, so that it filled the whole room. "Frederick was obsessed by knowledge. He was crazy about inventions, studies, written records, books, parchment scrolls—in fact everything that mankind has ever thought of. His clever mind was legendary. The scholars of that time called him the *Stupor Mundi*, the Wonder of the World. And he charged the abbey of Prüm with hoarding that knowledge. So the monks planned a huge library. It was to be in the middle of the German Empire, in a place that was easily accessible to travelers and could also be reached by water in troubled times. Their final choice was St. Goar."

"But I don't see any library here," Agnes objected. "I mean, if it was to be so large, where are all the rooms that would be needed, all the shelves? Not in this church, I suppose. Is it in the abbey nearby?"

Father Domenicus gave a small smile. "As I was saying, those who hurry ahead too fast miss seeing what is essential."

He went over to the last memorial stone on the wall. It showed an ecclesiastical figure with an abbot's crozier, holding a small box in his right hand. Only now did Agnes notice that the box was covered by a small plate also set into the stone. Father Domenicus pushed that aside to reveal a hollow space with a rusty handle in it. When the canon pulled the handle, there was a slight jolt, and the tombstone squealed outward. A spiral stone staircase came into view behind it, and a cold draft of wind met Agnes and the others.

"The library is down there," said Father Domenicus, as he took a torch from its holder on the wall. "The greatest collection of knowledge in the entire German Empire. Abbot Dieter von Katzenelnbogen had it built with his mother's money. Now his own memorial forms the door to it." Groaning, the old man climbed down the well-worn steps. "Come with me, and see the miracle of St. Goar."

Like the interior of a snail shell, the staircase wound its way deeper and deeper into the rock under the church. It finally ended at an arched gateway, with a door of solid wood reinforced with iron plates. Father Domenicus used his torch to light a sooty glass lantern hanging from a hook beside the arch. He carefully extinguished the torch, and only then did he take the large bunch of keys out from under his habit again and put one of the keys into the lock.

"Candles and torches are forbidden in here," he explained. "And the separate rooms through which we shall now be going are all secured with fireproof doors. If a conflagration were to break out, then at least we can confine it to a certain area. That has happened twice in the last three hundred years, and even so the loss was painful enough."

The door swung open. Agnes held her breath.

All she had known before was the little library at Trifels, and once she had been allowed to visit the library of Eusserthal monastery, but this was quite different. She saw a whole universe full of books spread out before her. Shelves full of large tomes, slim leaflets, documents, letters, and parchment scrolls towered many feet above her and went on back into the darkness, where she lost sight of them. Ladders and portable steps led to the upper rows, and there were small balconies around the walls. Agnes heard a rustling sound and saw a monk with an armful of books bending low to go along a passage to her left. He said not a word, but the sound of his footsteps rang through the vault, producing a strange echo that sounded like individual raindrops falling. There was also a slight fluttering noise, like they had scared an animal by intruding.

Meanwhile, Father Domenicus went ahead, holding up his lantern to show the full extent of the building, shelf by shelf. Agnes estimated that this hall must be over fifty yards long, and many corridors branched off among the shelves, leading to other doors. It all seemed to have been hewn out of the rock, a laborious task. Suddenly she was glad of her warm coat. It was cold as the grave down in this vault.

"Not exactly a comfortable situation for a library," remarked Melchior, shivering as he rubbed his hands and looked up at the high ceiling.

"But a safe one," retorted Father Domenicus. "The low temperature and dry air mean that the works do not go moldy. That is probably also to do with the salt that seeps out of the rock here, although we don't know for certain. However, there is no better place to store so many books."

"How many are there?" asked Agnes.

"We think about a hundred thousand. Most of them, however, are parchment scrolls and worn old records that need daily attention. Incidentally, the famous library at Alexandria had a stock five times as large. All the same, we think we can be proud of ours."

Father Domenicus went on past the tall shelves. Once again a single monk carrying books crossed their path, and he greeted the dean by bowing his head.

"How is it that no one knows about this library?" asked Melchior. "You said that travelers have access to it, so why have I never heard of it before?"

"Earlier, in the time of Frederick the Staufer, it was indeed open to all interested people. But then came the bad times when there was no emperor, and we thought it better to close our gates. These days, a few know about it again. We seek out such people, and there are more of them every year. Why not?" Father Domenicus sighed. "Since the invention of printing, books are not so special any longer. There are some in every city. That does make them less attractive to thieves, but their magic, sad to say, is also lost."

They had now turned off along a passage to the right and came to another door, which the dean opened with one of the keys from his bunch. The room beyond it was considerably smaller, but full to the roof with large volumes and parchment scrolls. Walls of books up to the ceiling divided the space into niches, corridors, and blind alleys, all in the dark. The center of the room, which was empty, contained a heavy round table, with a design of three black lions on a yellow field. Several rickety, ancient-looking folding stools were placed around it. Father Domenicus carefully put down the lantern on the table and lit a series of glass chandeliers hanging from the rock of the ceiling by chains. At last it was light enough for Agnes to stop feeling as if she'd been buried alive.

"This is the heart of the library," Father Domenicus began, as he walked along the bookshelves in search of something and disappeared behind a wall of shelves. "These are the books that Frederick the Staufer had read himself—or, in the case of some, had written in his own hand." He came back with a shabby book, its cover showing a crowned king beside a griffin.

"I know that book," Agnes cried in surprise. As if by magic, the room seemed to swallow her voice up. "I have it too. It is the—"

"*De arte venandi cum avibus*," the dean finished, smiling. "The art of hunting with birds. Emperor Frederick II wrote it himself. This is the original, which many think was destroyed in his own time at the siege of Parma." Lovingly, he stroked the leather spine of the book, and then put it back on a shelf and turned back to the three visitors. "But we are not here to discuss birds, but because of the ring you wear on your hand, are we not? May I examine it for a moment?"

Rather reluctantly, Agnes took the ring off her finger. Father Domenicus brought out a glass lens from under his habit and held it and the ring close to his face, so that a huge fish's eye seemed to be looking at Agnes. At last, satisfied, the dean nodded. "Barbarossa's signet ring, no doubt about it. There is only this one, which can be identified by the tiny initials hidden in the beard. To the untrained eye, they look like scratches."

"But I thought there were many such rings," Agnes said.

Father Domenicus laughed. "Whoever told you so either had no idea of the facts, or was trying to hide something from you. This one ring was handed on by the Staufers from generation to generation as a sign of their power. Frederick Barbarossa himself wore it first, then his son Henry VI, after him Frederick II, and then his sons Henry, Conrad, and Manfred. They all died, and so did Frederick's illegitimate sons, either in battle, by poison, or of sickness. When Conradin, Frederick's grandson, was killed by the French, the ring passed to the last male descendant of the Hohenstaufen line: his uncle Enzio, who was imprisoned in Bologna for twenty years, until his death."

Agnes nodded thoughtfully. "My father confessor at Trifels, Father Tristan, also told me about Frederick's descendants, although he didn't mention the ring in that connection. I'm more and more inclined to think that Father Tristan wanted to hide something from me. But why?"

In spite of her warm coat, she was suddenly overcome by a shivering fit. Mathis took her hand and gently pressed it.

"Agnes found the ring near Trifels Castle," he said, turning to the dean. "Or rather her falcon did. Have you any idea how it came to be there? Maybe it was all just coincidence."

"Coincidence? Oh no, I think not. Quite the opposite. But to understand that, you must first listen to a story of some length." With a wave of his hand, Father Domenicus indicated to his guests that they should sit at the table. Then he took another large book off the shelves and leafed through it. It contained a series of colored illustrations. When the dean had found what he wanted, he placed the book on the table in front of Agnes and pointed to a page showing a handsome young man with his hair cut in the bobbed style typical of the chivalric period.

"This is Enzio, Frederick's favorite son, even though he was born out of wedlock," he said mildly. "He is said to have been very like his father. Eager for knowledge, and inclined to poetry. But in his youth, he was taken prisoner at the battle of Fossalta and was kept captive in Bologna for the rest of his life. He was allowed to write letters and see visitors, but his guards took care that his meetings with those visitors never went unobserved. Except in one case . . ." Father Domenicus cleared his throat. "Well, there was a nun. Her name was Eleanor of Avignon, she was descended from the Norman nobility, and she must have been very beautiful. Enzio fell in love with her. And there was a child of their love, a daughter called Constanza."

"My God, Constanza!" Agnes said. She began trembling again. "The woman in my dreams."

"And a hitherto unknown descendant of the Hohenstaufen family." Melchior von Tanningen took his lute off his shoulder. "What a subject for a ballad. Listen to this . . ." He was about to play his lute, but a dark look from Mathis silenced him.

Father Domenicus looked at the minstrel with some annoyance, but finally he went on. "At the time of Constanza's birth, the Staufer dynasty had in practice died out. There were a few members of the family, but they had been scattered far and wide, and without the ring they lacked the necessary legitimacy. In addition, Frederick II had drawn up a deed to avoid quarrels over the succession. Only the ring and the deed made their possessor the one true heir of the Staufers, whether a man or a woman. Both were in the hands of Enzio, and he passed them on to his only child."

"Constanza," murmured Agnes. "Is that why she had to be eliminated?"

Father Domenicus nodded. "Enzio knew that his child's life was in danger. Charles of Anjou, the French king's brother, had already had the Staufer descendants Conradin and Manfred killed. He also had

Manfred's sons imprisoned in Castel del Monte, where two of the brothers were finally blinded and went mad. Only the third managed to escape, but he, too, died, in distant Egypt, his mind deranged. Charles of Anjou was not to know about Constanza." The dean leafed through the old book until he came to the drawing of a castle that was extremely familiar to Agnes. A shudder ran up her spine, and it was nothing to do with the temperature of the room.

"That was why Enzio secretly sent the child to Trifels, where she grew up in anonymity as a lady's maid," said Father Domenicus, reading on. "Constanza herself knew nothing of her high birth. Only Philipp von Falkenstein, then the castellan of Trifels Castle, was in on the secret. And it was he who kept the ring and the deed for Constanza. In the end, and while she was at the castle, Constanza met a handsome young squire about to receive the accolade of knighthood. His name was—"

"Johann," Agnes whispered. "Johann of Brunswick. My God—my dreams were all true!"

Father Domenicus looked at her in surprise. "Yes, Johann of Brunswick," he replied at last. "A Guelph, and thus a scion of the second most powerful dynasty after the Staufers. Only at their wedding did Constanza learn about her background from the castellan. Philipp von Falkenstein solemnly gave her the ring and the deed, and she let Johann into the secret."

Agnes now looked as if she were in a trance as she listened to the dean's words.

"Constanza bore Johann a son, and they called him Sigmund," Domenicus went on. "For a while they were happy. But then a terrible thing happened: the Habsburgs, now ruling the German Reich, heard about Constanza's true origins. And they also heard about the child . . ." Father Domenicus sighed deeply. "Imagine: a child descended in equal measure from the two most important dynasties in the empire—dynasties that had been at loggerheads with each other in the past. And his existence came to light in the difficult time when a power struggle for the German throne was in progress among the nobility. The princes would certainly have made little Sigmund their king. The Habsburgs could not tolerate that, so they sent their henchmen to murder the young family."

Lost in thought, Agnes nodded. She was glad she was sitting on the rickety stool, because her legs suddenly felt as soft as butter. Mathis was still holding her hand.

"But the three of them escaped," she murmured. "I saw that, too, in my dreams. What became of them?"

Once again, Father Domenicus sighed. "Johann was captured in Speyer and beheaded. Constanza also fell into the trap set by the Habsburgs' men. She was tortured, and then walled up alive in Trifels Castle. The Habsburgs were merciless."

"My God," breathed Agnes. "And the boy?"

"He had disappeared, and was never found. It was the same with the ring and the deed."

"Disappeared?" Mathis leaned over the table and looked keenly at the dean. "What do you mean, disappeared? I don't think you would have told us this whole story if that was the end of it."

Father Domenicus gave a small smile. "You may be right, my young friend. Very well, the boy had not really disappeared. At the last moment, Constanza managed to hide him with a family of tanners in Annweiler, and with him the ring and the deed. She told the family the secret of her origin, and asked them to protect her son. Sigmund grew up to be an ordinary tanner. Only when he was an adult did his foster parents tell him about his true descent. Sigmund told his own firstborn child later, and he in turn passed the information on in the same way. As time went on, these descendants of the Staufers took some other citizens of Annweiler into their confidence, relying on their help to keep their secret and protect them. This went on for many generations, and a myth grew up in the Wasgau around these last descendants of the first Staufer emperor." The dean rose to his feet and looked up at the rock of the ceiling, with his hands folded as if in prayer. "A myth that was preserved by a little order in Annweiler, a sworn brotherhood devoted to the protection of the heirs of the Staufers, who would pass on their knowledge from generation to generation until the day when darkness fell on the world once more, and a true emperor was needed again. Many think that day has now come . . ."

At last Father Domenicus fell silent, and only the echoing footsteps of other monks in the vast catacombs could be heard.

"How do you know all this?" Mathis asked at last.

"How do I know it? Well, there have long been rumors of a descendant of the Staufers called Constanza who had a baby at Trifels Castle. But we knew for certain only about a year ago. One of the legendary Annweiler Brotherhood came to see us, bringing bad news. He said that after so many centuries, the Habsburgs had learned of the secret that had been kept so long. They had already tried to kill Constanza's last descendants, several years ago, and now they were trying again."

Father Domenicus made his slow way to a shelf at the back of the room where a single scroll of parchment lay, tied with a leather thong. It bore a seal showing the head of a bearded man. The dean unrolled the parchment, carefully spreading it out on the table. It was written in Latin, the words slightly blurred but still legible, and standing out red as blood from the thin vellum of their background.

Nos Fridericus Dei gratia Sacri Romani Imperii possessorem huiusce diplomatis heredem singularem ducatus Sueviae declaramus . . .

When Agnes had deciphered the first line, she felt faint, and briefly all went black before her eyes.

We, Frederick, by the grace of God ruler of the Holy Roman Empire, hereby declare the possessor of this deed the sole heir of the Staufers. His sign will be the ring of this family, which he will always bear with him as the insignia of power . . .

"The messenger from Annweiler brought us the deed," Agnes heard the father go on, feeling like she were listening to him through a thick tapestry hanging on the wall. "Enzio himself had given it to little Constanza in the past, together with the ring, so that she could prove her birth. Later, the Brotherhood kept the document for whoever was then the bearer of the ring, to keep him or her from unnecessary danger. Ever since, the name of the next firstborn child has been added to the family tree. That identifies the mysterious descendant whom the Habsburgs are now, for the second time, trying to kill. The messenger told us the name, and said that we were to tell the whole secret if that person, or indeed one of that person's heirs, ever came to St. Goar bearing the sign of recognition, an object that, like the document, was handed down over the generations." Father Domenicus smiled, and at last gave the ring back to Agnes, who was sitting hunched on her stool, rigid and motionless. Then he knelt to her and bowed his head. Only now did Agnes see, as if through a veil, that other monks had come through the door, and they too went on their knees to her.

"Hail, Agnes von Erfenstein, baroness of the Staufer dynasty, last legitimate descendant of Barbarossa," said the dean in his hoarse voice. "I almost failed to recognize you in man's clothing, with your hair cut short. Now is the time when the German Empire needs your help."

Agnes sat on her stool, like she'd been turned to stone, while the dean's words echoed through her mind.

Hail, Agnes von Erfenstein . . . last legitimate descendant of Barbarossa . . .

About half a dozen monks knelt on the floor around her. Melchior and Mathis gaped at her, while she herself was incapable of any movement.

"But . . . but that can't be so," she finally managed to say. She tried to laugh, but it was a forced, difficult sound. "My parents were not from powerful families. My father was an ordinary knight, and he owed his post as castellan of Trifels to Emperor Maximilian, while my mother . . ."

"The mother you speak of was not your own," Father Domenicus gently interrupted her. "Agnes, it is time for you to know the truth. That messenger from Annweiler, an old tanner by the name of Nepomuk Kistler, told us all about it. Philipp von Erfenstein and his wife, Katharina, had no children of their own. Indeed, they couldn't have children at all. But one day they found a little girl of about five, weeping, a child with matted blonde hair, outside the gates of Trifels Castle. She had nothing with her but a crumpled piece of paper, saying that she was of high birth, and her real parents were dead. Your foster parents took this as divine providence and brought you up as their own child."

"My . . . my mother . . ." Agnes began again, with large tears rolling down her cheeks.

"Was not Katharina von Erfenstein, but Friderica of the house of Hohenstaufen. All the firstborn children of the secret line of Staufers after Sigmund were given the names Fridericus or Friderica, referring to their mighty ancestor. That was the decision of the Brotherhood at the time. The order also taught those firstborns the ancient language of minstrels, and their stories and songs from a time long past, so that the knowledge would never be lost." Father Domenicus smiled. "You are a Friderica yourself, Agnes. You were your mother's only child."

"And . . . and my father?" asked Agnes, with difficulty.

"He was a simple tanner of Annweiler, a member of the Brotherhood who knew the secret." The dean looked kindly at Agnes. "I wonder whether you still have any memories of your real parents? After all, you were already five when you came to the Erfensteins."

Agnes suddenly thought of the old Occitanian song that her mother always sang to her. She tasted the sweetness of milk with honey in it and smelled the distant perfume of violets . . .

Coindeta sui, si cum n'ai greu cossire, quar pauca son, iuvenete e tosa . . .

Could it be possible that those few memories were not of Katharina von Erfenstein at all, but of a strange woman called Friderica?

A strange woman who was her mother.

The monks were still kneeling before her on the stone floor as though they were waiting for something, for a sign, for an order. But Agnes had no idea what it could be. Mathis and Melchior were also staring at her as if, after the dean had made his declaration, she had become someone entirely different.

"A legitimate descendant of the Staufers and the Guelphs, hidden at Trifels," sighed Melchior, shaking his head incredulously. "If that's true, then I am definitely going to win the singers' contest at the Wartburg."

"I . . . I dreamed of my mother . . ." Agnes began, as if in a trance. Her fingers caressed the cool gold of the ring. "Only recently. It must have been the smell of freshly tanned leather in Barnabas's cart that took me back to the past. The leather, and the beechwood smoke . . ."

"Barnabas?" asked Father Domenicus, puzzled.

"My parents were tanners," Agnes went on as if she hadn't heard him. Her thoughts were far, far away, in a time many years ago. "We were out in our cart together. We . . . we were taking the tanned skins to market in Speyer as we always did. Father had treated the skins for three years, they were good calfskin, and among them was vellum for the parchment used in the bishop's archives. With some of the money they earned, they were going to buy me a new doll in Speyer. I'd wanted one so much . . ." Agnes was staring into space, her voice louder now. "But then we were attacked in the forest. I heard galloping horses, and screams, and gasping sounds . . . it was all so fast. Our servant, Hieronymus, he took me away. Oh God, my parents!" She stopped and stared at the dean. "What happened to them?"

Father Domenicus took a deep breath. "I am afraid the assassins of the Habsburgs killed them in the course of that attack. At that time the German king Maximilian, the grandfather of Charles, had already been crowned Holy Roman Emperor, but his throne was not secure. France was not satisfied with playing second fiddle in Europe. Maximilian feared anything that might reinforce the Staufer line. When news came of a hidden descendant in Annweiler, the Habsburgs acted ruthlessly. But you escaped the assassins at the last moment."

Agnes nodded. "An old woman saved me. She was in my dreams, too. She saw the ring that my mother gave me just before her death." Absent-mindedly, she took hold of Barbarossa's signet ring. It now felt as cold as ice around her finger. Suddenly it seemed tight, and much too heavy for her to wear for even one more day.

"You are right. It was probably a midwife of Annweiler who found you in the forest," the dean quietly replied. "Fortunately she was a member of the Brotherhood. Your meeting must have been God's own providence. She gave the ring to the order and took you to the gates of Trifels, the one place that she thought safe enough for you."

"But if the ring was back in the hands of the order," said Mathis, who, like Melchior von Tanningen, had been listening in astonishment until now, "then how did it return to Agnes?"

Father Domenicus sighed. "The messenger from Annweiler told us that, too. Last year, when the Habsburgs sent out their henchmen again, this midwife clearly felt very anxious. She wanted to be rid of the ring. When Agnes's falcon appeared at her house, she felt it was meant by fate—"

"And she fixed the ring to Parcival's leg," Mathis finished excitedly. He turned to Agnes, pressing her hand. "Now at least we know why those damned dreams came to you from then on. The ring reminded you of your early childhood. And your mother probably told you the story of Johann and Constanza back then."

Agnes said nothing. She suddenly remembered Melchior's ballad, the one he had composed when they set out from Trifels.

She had a ring, from fair Constanza, as I sing. It sent her many a troubled dream . . .

It was like those lines brought long-forgotten rhymes and stories back to her. Once more, her thoughts went back to a distant, misty land . . .

I am lying in my bed, the warm quilt pulled up to my chin, outside the wind is whistling around the houses of Annweiler. Tell me about Constanza, Mother. Tell me how she first saw handsome Johann in the Knights' House. Tell me about the ring. My mother sighs and casts up her eyes. Always that same, sad story, Agnes. Aren't you getting tired of it? Come along, I'll tell you the story of the Red Knight and . . . No! Constanza. I want to hear about Constanza and the ring. Please, please! I fidget and whine until my mother finally gives in . . .

"There must have been people who knew all along that Agnes wasn't the Erfensteins' own child," said Mathis, thinking out loud, bringing Agnes out of her reverie. "The old people at the castle, I suppose. Hedwig the cook, and good old Ulrich Reichhart. He said something suggesting it before his death."

Agnes still said nothing, caught up in her memories. But after a while she shook herself and glanced at the monks who, with Father Domenicus, were watching her expectantly. They still seemed to be waiting for something.

"Very well. So if all this is as you say," she said in a failing voice, turning to the dean, "if I really am descended from Barbarossa . . . what is that but a pretty story? Why are you so interested in it?"

The dean laughed quietly. "A pretty story, indeed. Do you know what power stories have, Agnes? Especially in times like these. Why do you think the Habsburgs are trying to find you again? Because people want to believe in stories. The empire burns from end to end. People need myths that will comfort them, they need someone who can stand for all their hopes and longings." He paused for a moment before he went on, smiling. "You are that someone, Agnes von Erfenstein, descendant of the house of Hohenstaufen. But only if you accept your inheritance. Its symbolic power can hardly be overestimated."

"What do you mean?" asked Agnes, frowning. "What inheritance?"

"Listen," replied Father Domenicus. "The story is not over yet. You must—"

At that moment the door opened with a crash. Agnes cried out in terror, seeing the devil himself walk into the underground room.

Immediately after that, all hell broke loose around them.

Mathis, too, swung around on hearing the crash. He was still utterly confused by all the strange news that the dean had told them. His confusion turned to horror when he saw the figure now standing in the room. He was a man with a face as black as night. His dusty coat was also black, but his hose were blood-red. The stranger had kicked the door open, and he held two handguns, both with their triggers cocked.

They're genuine wheel-lock pistols, thought Mathis. *He's no ordinary robber. Those weapons are worth a fortune.*

He stood as though turned to stone with fear and astonishment, staring at the two pistols. He had seen such things only in drawings. Now he was about to find out what they were like in reality.

Out of the corner of his eye, Mathis saw Melchior von Tanningen throw himself in front of Agnes. Then there was a deafening explosion, closely followed by a scream. The dean collapsed, groaning, beside Mathis, with blood spurting from his shoulder. One of the bullets must have hit him.

"The ring," moaned Father Domenicus, trying to stand up. "Save the ring and the deed. They must not . . . fall . . . into the wrong hands . . ."

The monks, screaming, rushed about like headless chickens, trying to get to safety in dark niches or behind the walls of books, where they flung themselves on the floor. One of them clung to the heavy framework of a shelf, which slowly tilted forward and fell to the floor with a crash. A shower of books, parchment scrolls, and loose pages fell on Mathis and Agnes. In the general chaos, Mathis crawled under the heavy oak table, closely followed by Agnes, who seemed to have recovered from her sudden faintness.

"Careful, the bastard's going to fire again!"

That was Melchior, suddenly appearing beside them. With a grunt of effort, he braced himself against the mighty table and pushed until it fell on its side and could act as a shield.

Another explosion shook the room. This time the bullet hit the tabletop. It splintered, and Mathis heard a hiss as the bullet emerged only a hand's breadth away from Melchior. It passed through his lute and stuck in the wall behind him. The minstrel took the instrument off his back and stared in disbelief at its shattered body and torn strings.

"He'll pay for this," he said angrily. "This Florentine model cost me two hundred guilders. With my initials on it in ivory." He gently stroked the neck of the lute one last time, and then threw the lute at the attacker like an ax, but it missed its mark.

Meanwhile, Agnes was crouching on the floor with her hands over her ears. "Who . . . who is that?" was all she could get out, gasping. Mathis could hardly hear her through all the wailing of the monks and the noise of falling bookshelves.

"I guess an assassin sent by the Habsburgs!" he shouted against the racket. "Stay where you are! Melchior and I will—"

He fell silent, as an almost inhuman cry met his ears. Cautiously looking up, he saw one of the canons, his habit blazing, stagger along the rows of bookshelves, screaming. During the fight, one of the chandeliers had evidently fallen to the floor, setting several loose pages alight. The fire had already spread to a pile of books, and red and blue flames licked at them.

Mathis ventured a glance over the tabletop and saw the burning monk move toward the stranger with his arms spread wide. With an incomprehensible curse on his lips, the black-skinned man swerved, and the canon went on into the great hall.

My God, the library, Mathis thought. *He's going to set the whole library on fire.*

The stranger had now cast aside his handguns and drawn his sword. Ready to fight, he approached the tabletop, while the other monks ran from the room behind him, screaming. Only Father Domenicus lay where he was on the floor, bleeding, with his eyes half closed.

By now there was so much smoke that Mathis could hardly see. Books and parchment scrolls burned everywhere, and several walls of shelves had fallen over, adding more fuel to the flames. Mathis could hear Melchior coughing beside him. The minstrel drew his sword. A slight smile was playing around his lips.

"I'm afraid I'll need your help again, Master Wielenbach," he said, with solemn formality. "That devil is after Agnes. I can deal with him, but you must get the noble lady to safety before this whole place goes up in flames."

"Never mind all that," Agnes snapped, rubbing her eyes, which were streaming from the smoke. "I can walk on my own two feet. But I swear to God I won't go a step from here if we don't help Father Domenicus too." She pointed to the dean, who lay behind a bonfire of books and had evidently regained consciousness. He was groaning. "I don't want him to die just because that lunatic hit an innocent man instead of me," Agnes went on, shaking with fury.

"Spoken like a true heroine," sighed Melchior. "Then take him out of here if you like, although I don't think that—"

At that moment, the stranger leapt over the tabletop and raised his sword to strike a mortal blow. Melchior lunged, thrusting with his own sword, but his adversary had foreseen the move and nimbly swerved. While their duel went on, Mathis and Agnes hurried over to Father Domenicus.

"We must get out of here, Father!" Mathis shouted against the crackling of the flames. "Are you able to walk?"

The dean did not utter a sound. His lips trembled, and a large pool of blood had already formed around him. Finally, Mathis took him under the armpits, and Father Domenicus cried out quietly.

"We must be careful lifting him," Agnes warned. "Any wrong movement could mean his death!"

"We don't have time. If we stay here any longer it'll mean the death of all of us." Mathis got the dean over his shoulder and staggered toward the door with him. In passing, he saw Melchior von Tanningen and the black-skinned stranger still fighting in front of the tabletop.

Then thick black smoke hid them from view.

With a hoarse cry, the assassin flung himself toward Melchior. The two wheel-lock pistols lay on the ground exactly between them. Reloading them would have cost too much time, and so now he and Melchior had to fight with their swords, putting them on a more even playing field.

For a while the sword fight went this way and that, and only the ringing of the two men's blades and the crackling of flames was heard. The brittle shelves, dry as dust, burned like tinder around them, their frameworks, breaking apart, crashed to the floor one by one, their contents feeding the flames as the fire grew and grew.

The smoke was so thick now that Melchior could sometimes see his opponent only in outline. Although his own cuts and thrusts were as precise as clockwork, somehow the assassin avoided them again and again. The man was obviously well trained.

The assassin raised his sword again, and the two blades met with an ugly scraping sound. The men's faces were now so close that they almost touched. The black man bared his teeth in a grin. The dark smoke and flying ash had made Melchior almost as dark. They stood opposite one another in the middle of the room, like two ebony chessmen.

"Drop your weapon before it's too late," the assassin cried. "You have my word as a man of honor that I'll let you go. It's not you I'm after."

Melchior only smiled as the sweat ran down from his forehead in channels, leaving white trails behind. "You destroyed my lute," the little man got out at last, panting. "I'm sorry, but for that alone I can't accept your offer."

"Bloody fool!"

With a last desperate show of force, the assassin threw the delicately built minstrel against one of the bookshelves. The shelf fell with a deafening noise, and both men landed in a sea of books. They both struck out like drowning men to free themselves from the tomes. Both got to their feet at about the same time, but Melchior no longer had his sword in his hand.

"Thinking of giving up yet?" the assassin growled, circling his sword in the air. "Too late for that now, I'm afraid."

But Melchior showed no fear. Instead, he linked his hands as if doing a conjuring trick, murmured a few words, and at last a bunch of keys appeared between his fingers, as though from nowhere. "Looking for something?" he asked with pretended guilelessness. "These must have fallen out of your pocket just now as you fell. I had to drop my own sword to feel for them, but I think it was worth it."

"What are you thinking?" the assassin said. "We can talk about—"

"I think it's time to say goodbye. As I told you, you shouldn't have destroyed my lute. I'd never forgive a thing like that. Never."

The little man kicked a pile of burning books into the assassin's face, and then ran swiftly to the door. Bellowing, the black man dropped his sword and shook some smoldering pages out of his matted black hair. Then he ran after his adversary.

The door slammed shut, and next moment the key was turned in the lock. The assassin shook the handle, flung himself against the iron-clad wood with all his might, but the door did not give way.

"Open this door! For heaven's sake open this door!" he kept shouting, although his pleas fell on deaf ears.

Breathlessly, Agnes ran after Mathis, who still carried the wounded dean over his shoulder. When they finally reached the great hall, they stopped in horror. It was considerably brighter than it had been an hour ago, when they came past the shelves with Father Domenicus. There seemed to be lanterns burning everywhere now. Next moment, Agnes saw where the brightness really came from.

My God, those aren't lanterns. The whole library is going up in flames.

In his flight, the burning canon had obviously set fire to books in several places. Separate fires had started everywhere, and the flames had spread to other areas. Wherever Agnes looked, books glowed like paper lanterns in the darkness of the cavernous hall. There was no sign of the other monks. Presumably they had already left the library through the entrance.

Agnes and Mathis wearily dragged themselves on, while around them the first of the balconies and their blazing contents crashed to the floor. A shower of embers and ashes fell on them both, and again Agnes found that her thick coat did good service, protecting her from flying sparks.

After what felt like an eternity, they reached the front door. Directly in front of it lay a charred bundle, still smoking. When Agnes was about to climb over it she cried out in horror. A tiny black face with its teeth bared grinned at her. For a split second Agnes thought it was the little monkey, Satan, but then she saw that it was the corpse of a monk, burned beyond all recognition.

"At least he's spared himself the fire of Purgatory," gasped Mathis, breathless from the weight of the dean. "I have a terrible presentiment."

Pushing past her, he tried the door handle, and swore.

"Locked. I was afraid of that." he said angrily. "These craven clerics! Locking us in here, because they thought the devil was on their heels. Now what?"

Agnes pointed to Father Domenicus, still hanging limp over Mathis's shoulders. "His bunch of keys," she shouted, against the crackling of the flames. "The dean still has it on him."

"Damn it, you're right." Groaning, Mathis carefully let the dean slip to the floor. Searching with quick fingers, he soon found the bunch of keys hanging from a cord around the waist of his habit. But as he was about to reach for it, the dean suddenly put out his hand, and clutched him by the shirt.

"Never fear, reverend Father," Mathis reassured him. "We're only taking the key to open the door. We'll get you out of here, and then everything will be—"

"Quiet, boy, and listen to me," Father Domenicus rasped. "There's something else that . . . you must know."

"Can't you tell us up above?" Agnes said, looking anxiously around. "If we stay here much longer, we may be buried by one of the burning shelves."

"It must . . . be now," the dean groaned. "I feel . . . my end approaching."

"Oh God, Father. You mustn't die now, you mustn't." Agnes bent down to Father Domenicus. Looking at his gaunt face, she thought of Father Tristan, who had died in an equally cruel way. The dean took her hand and held it with all his might.

"Agnes, remember what I said. I . . . I was speaking of your inheritance. Of the symbol that can unite this divided empire again. You . . . must look for it. That is your task."

"But what is it?" Mathis was leaning over the dean now, as well. Despite the heat, Father Domenicus was shivering all over. "Please tell us quickly, Father. There really isn't much time left."

Father Domenicus moaned. His voice was so low that they both had to bend down to hear it at all.

"On the day when . . . Constanza and Johann fled from Trifels with little Sigmund, they took something with them," he whispered. "It was to be security for them, their bargaining tool if anything happened. They were captured, but their bargaining tool . . . was never found."

The dean reached for Agnes's hand, and drew her so close to him that his lips almost touched her ear.

"That was why the Habsburgs tortured Constanza so cruelly," he said. "They . . . wanted her to tell them not just where the child was, but where she had hidden that inestimably precious thing. But she kept obstinately silent. Finally they walled Constanza up in Trifels Castle, leaving only a tiny gap open so that she could tell her tormentors the place. All they heard from her, however, was weeping and singing getting fainter and fainter until, at last, all was quiet. Constanza had taken her secret to the grave with her."

"But what was it?" asked Mathis, out of the corner of his eye seeing more shelves nearby fall to the floor in flames. A fierce firestorm was sweeping through the library now. "Tell us, Father. Before *all* of us here take Constanza's secret to our own graves with us."

"What had Constanza and Johann hidden?" Agnes added her pleading to his. "What is so valuable that anyone would let herself be walled up alive for it?"

Once again, a slight smile played around Father Domenicus's lips.

"Can't you guess, Agnes?" he whispered. "What is the most valuable thing that the empire possesses? What is the most important symbol of all German emperors and kings?" He briefly closed his eyes, before the answer left him, like a last sigh.

"It is . . . the Holy Lance."

At that moment, a huge explosion shook the library. Right above them, a burning balcony came away and fell down toward Agnes in a mighty shower of sparks.

The explosion shook the whole underground cavern like a huge earthquake.

At the last moment, Agnes managed to swerve aside as the balustrade of the balcony fell down toward her. The burning balcony buried the dean under it with a sound like thunder, while on the other side of it Mathis disappeared behind a wall of sparks and glowing embers.

"Mathis! Mathis!" she shouted. A few seconds that felt like an age to her passed, and then she heard a hoarse cough.

"I'm all right!" Mathis called. "Stay where you are. I'm coming."

At last the shower of sparks died down, and not far away Agnes saw Mathis rise from the smoking ruins. He was black as a raven in the face, his clothes had begun to singe in several places, but otherwise he seemed uninjured. Between them lay beams, glowing books, and the remains of the balcony, which until recently had been above the door. Nothing could be seen of Father Domenicus.

"Oh no—the dean . . ." Agnes said.

"He's with his God," Mathis said. Then he kicked some of the rubble aside. "And if we don't make haste, we'll soon be in paradise ourselves." Coughing, he held up Father Domenicus's bunch of keys, which he had managed to save from the falling ruins at the last moment. "This damned door opens inward, so we'll have to clear this . . ."

He broke off when a figure black with soot suddenly came tottering toward the two of them through the underground vault. The man was carrying such a high stack of books that his face was not in view. Only when he was within a few steps of them did Agnes see that it was Melchior von Tanningen.

"Thank God!" she cried. "I thought that devil had carried you down into the abyss with him."

"If I interpret that explosion correctly, he's just gone to hell himself," replied Melchior, who swayed slightly under the burden of the books he carried. "He shouldn't have destroyed my lute. I distinctly told him so."

"You're welcome to tell us the rest of it up above," Mathis said. "It would be kind of you to give us a hand clearing away this rubble first." Shaking his head, he looked at the books in the minstrel's hands. "What in heaven's name are you carrying about?"

"This one is Wolfram von Eschenbach's *Parcival* in a beautifully illustrated edition. Also a collection of the old minnesingers' works; Emperor Maximilian's book on tournaments, *Freydal*; and a few other books that deserve to be saved for posterity." Melchior sighed. "But you're right. It's time to get out of here." He carefully put the books on the floor and then helped Mathis and Agnes to push aside the burning beams near the doorway. Before long there was enough space clear for Mathis to approach the lock with the bunch of keys.

"Let's hope we can find the right one quickly, before the smoke dazes us," he choked. Then, disappointed, he took the first key out of the lock. "It's not this one."

"Hurry up!" Agnes was coughing. She stared, with watering eyes, at the pile of glowing beams beside her. The dean's body must be somewhere under it. "I don't know how long I can stand this smoke and heat."

"Not this one either," murmured Mathis. He frantically tried another key.

"I managed to get hold of a bunch of keys like that myself," remarked Melchior. "Maybe I might try . . ."

"Aha, this one fits!" Mathis cried in relief, as one of the keys turned, and the door opened, squealing. "Now let's get out. Before it all collapses on us."

Agnes and Mathis hurried up the steep spiral staircase together, while the smoke hovered behind them like a spirit. Meanwhile, Melchior had picked up his books again, and followed at a slight distance. With every step, the air became noticeably cooler and fresher. It was as if, like Orpheus, they were emerging from the underworld. Agnes heaved a sigh of relief when she saw the open doorway leading into the baptismal chapel above them. In their haste, the fleeing Benedictine canons had not closed the memorial stone of Diether von Katzenelnbogen after them.

"So much lost knowledge!" Melchior sighed. "A real shame. To the best of my knowledge, there's no such library any longer in the whole German Empire."

"At least you managed to save a few valuable works," said Mathis, who had now reached the way out.

Melchior grinned. "That I did. Not that I want to sell them, but every one of these books is worth as much as a dozen pure-bred horses."

Mathis looked at the minstrel in surprise. "Damn it all, don't say that again or I'll be going back down there to get some for myself."

Exhausted, trembling all over, Agnes climbed up through the

opening, through which thin wisps of smoke still crept. The dignitaries on the nearby gravestones seemed to be inspecting her and her two companions almost reproachfully. Their shirts and hose were torn and charred at the edges; their hands and faces were black with soot. Only the whites of their eyes showed. Agnes wiped the sweat from her brow and looked around her. The chapel was empty, and after the roar of the flames an almost unreal silence reigned.

Suddenly they heard the shrill sound of the church bells ringing nearby.

"It won't be long now before the monks reappear," said Mathis. "If we want to avoid trouble, we'd better leave this church as fast as we can."

"And what about all that we found out down there?" Agnes wearily rubbed her sooty eyes. She felt so weak that she had to lean against the wall to keep herself from fainting away. "It seems to me that this whole day was nothing but a nightmare, and I'm only just awakening from it."

"It may as well have been a dream," replied Mathis gloomily. "You a descendant of Barbarossa? Without Emperor Frederick II's deed, all that is just a pretty story. Yes, you have the ring, but that's not evidence that you're really descended from the Staufers, not by a long shot." He pointed to the smoking void behind them. "The proof of it lies in ashes down there."

"Maybe I don't want any proof. Maybe I'm glad I can simply be Agnes von Erfenstein, daughter of the castellan of Trifels Castle."

Mathis looked at her sternly. "So how about the Holy Lance? Father Domenicus said you had to carry out a task. Have you forgotten that?"

"For God's sake, why does everyone want to tell me what to do?" Agnes's eyes glittered in her black sooty face like well-cut gemstones. "Can't I make up my own mind anymore? I'll tell you something, Mathis Wielenbach. I'm glad that the wretched deed has been burned. At least that means the story comes to an end and we can go home."

"Maybe you can go home, my lady countess, but I'm a wanted insurgent. Have you by any chance forgotten *that*?"

"And I suppose *you* have forgotten that I ran away from my deranged, vengeful husband."

Beside them, Melchior von Tanningen cleared his throat. "I am very reluctant to interrupt your extremely interesting conversation," he said. "But as for the fate of that document, I fear I must disappoint my lady the countess." Smiling, he drew out a folded sheet of parchment, slightly charred at the edges, from under his stack of books. It was the deed that Father Domenicus had shown them down in the library. Agnes recognized the family tree that had been kept up to date, and the seal of the Staufer emperor below it.

"When chaos broke out down in that chamber, I thought it best to take care of the deed myself," the minstrel went on. "I think it is worth more than all the books I saved put together." He tucked the parchment away in his soot-smeared doublet, put his books under his arm, and with a delicate step made for the way out of the chapel. "And now let's get away fast, before we end up executed as arsonists who destroyed the greatest of all libraries in the German lands."

· 22 ·

Löwenstein Castle, near Heilbronn, 15 June, Anno Domini 1525

IN THE SKY NOT FAR from the family seat of the Löwenstein-Scharfenecks, a kestrel circled. In search of fat field mice, it flew over the fields where now, in mid-June, the ears of grain were turning gold as they ripened. It was nearly midday, and the sun beat down. There had been no rain for several days, and all who possibly could had taken refuge in the cool, shady rooms inside the castle, waiting for the worst of the heat to pass over.

Only one man stood on the battlements, watching the flight of the small red-brown bird. Count Friedrich von Löwenstein-Scharfeneck held his crossbow steady, not the slightest tremor passed through his body, he fixed his eyes on his target one last time, and then he shot.

As if drawn on the end of a string, the bolt flew toward the sun. It hit the kestrel right in the breast. The bird fluttered frantically, refusing to accept its death, beat its wings a couple of times, trying to rise, and then sank like a stone to the depths, where it finally vanished from sight among the ears of wheat and barley.

"Got you, my little friend," said the count, smiling.

Only now did he venture to exhale. Humming a tune, he unstrung the crossbow and put the string away with his remaining bolts and the hook used to string the bow, in a well-greased quiver. Before putting his yew-wood bow away, Friedrich von Löwenstein-Scharfeneck lovingly stroked the ivory intarsia work that adorned it. He had always loved shooting the crossbow: the *whirr* of the bolt, its silent flight, the deadly precision with which it finally found its mark. And he had always preferred it to those loud, stinking firearms that determined the course of battles everywhere these days. Any fool of a peasant could fire a gun at the enemy; for the crossbow you needed strength to string the bow, good eyes, and above all a great deal of practice.

These days he practiced almost daily.

His heart beat faster when he thought how he had shot down that inquisitive steward at Trifels like a deer last year. The act had given him a sense of absolute power that lasted for a long time. Not that the killing had been done for pure pleasure; it was a matter of necessity, or the man would have talked. The following murder of the drunken castellan, however, had given Friedrich no real satisfaction; the poison had taken effect slowly, with none of the thrill that you felt when your victim looked you in the eyes for the last time.

The crossbow was better for that.

"I might have known you'd be up here gazing into thin air, you ne'er-do-well."

His father's voice made Friedrich spin around. The old man was coming up the steps from the castle courtyard, breathing heavily and leaning on a stick. The mere sight of him was enough to turn the young count's stomach. It always reminded him of the abuse and vituperation so often inflicted on him by his father, ever since his earliest childhood.

"I'm thinking," replied Friedrich coolly. "You might try it yourself now and then."

"Ha! Thinking. You've done nothing but think for weeks. If only you'd at least go hunting like other useless young men of your age, but no, the young count builds castles in the air while a mob of idiot peasants loll at their ease in his castle."

Friedrich cast up his eyes. "Your own castle in the Palatinate was also burned, Father, don't forget that. You have Neuscharfeneck back only because the peasants there have now given up."

"Because they fear me. In your place, I'd at least have gathered a few men and won my property back."

"You know it's not as easy as that," Friedrich said, between his teeth. His hands unconsciously felt for the crossbow that was still with him on the battlements, and his fingers toyed with the trigger.

Just one bolt. Just a brief click . . .

"Those dogs have hidden away in Trifels, and that, as you know, is much more difficult to capture than the surrounding castles," Friedrich finally went on. "Do you want me to disgrace myself in public by standing outside my own property, a target for the peasants to shoot at?" His eyes flashed angrily at his father. "What's more, I have no money left to get myself landsknechts, with a miserly father cutting off my funds."

The old count frowned. "Take care how you speak to me, Friedrich. I'm still your father." He brandished his stick in the air. "And I'm not wasting my money on that old place. When I was your age, I could already call three castles my own, and they weren't decrepit ruins like Trifels. I never did understand what you saw in those old walls anyway. The Norman treasure—bah! Castles in the air . . ."

Friedrich von Löwenstein-Scharfeneck looked out over the fields, staring fixedly at them, while his father went on complaining. He'd have liked to throw the old man over the battlements, simply to put an end to his carping at long last. Almost two months had passed since Friedrich's headlong flight from Scharfenberg Castle. Long weeks that he had spent here at his father's ancestral seat, occupying himself with the study of old records and practicing the crossbow, all in the company of dull-witted brutes. At the fall of Scharfenberg, Friedrich had managed to save himself by jumping into the ditch of manure outside the castle walls. It had been such a humiliating departure that the memory of it alone almost sent him out of his mind daily. Since then, his thoughts had gone around in circles all the time. That memory had suddenly forced everything he had dreamed of for so long into the background: the Norman treasure that would have allowed him to cut his ties with his father, an independent life as the proud lord of a castle. He could keep his hatred under control only by killing hares and game birds with his crossbow from up here now and then. That at least brought him relief for a few hours. But Friedrich knew that every time he aimed at a rabbit, pheasant, partridge, or grouse, it was a very different target that he really had in mind.

Agnes . . .

His humiliation had begun with her, and only with her would it end. Agnes had left him, in the company of that wretched minstrel, and then she had obviously given away the secret of the escape tunnel to the peasants. She had done it even though they were alike in so many respects. She was the first woman for whom he had felt something like affection. Friedrich knew he wouldn't rest until he had her in his arms again. He spent nights on end imagining what he would do to her then.

Where are you, Agnes? Where are you?

So far, all the messengers he had sent out had returned empty-handed. They had found no trace of either Agnes or the minstrel.

"Well, maybe you'll be lucky and won't have to recapture your castle for yourself." His father's words suddenly brought him back to the present. The old man was standing beside him, looking out at the landscape baking in the heat. "I hear that the elector of the Palatinate is hunting the peasants like hares. This nightmare won't last much longer." He nodded grimly. "I'm thinking of mounting a punitive expedition in my own lands. There's at least one rabble-rouser to be hanged in every provincial hole. The wounds must be cauterized before they begin to fester." Ludwig von Löwenstein-Scharfeneck broke off and seemed to be thinking. Then he looked watchfully at his son. "Well, why not? Think you can do it?"

"Do what?" Friedrich replied, somewhat irritated. His mind had been wandering back to his gloomy train of thought again.

"I'll need a hard man to lead my punishment squad. One who'll shrink from nothing and feel no sympathy for children weeping because their fathers are hanging from the village linden tree, their tongues blue and hanging out. I also want to raise the rents again. It's going to be difficult to squeeze any more out of those stubborn blockheads." The old count scrutinized his son. "At least it would give you something to think about, and you could show what you're made of." He suddenly smiled, showing the blackened stumps of his teeth. "I tell you what—if you help me, you can have the men for your own purposes later. Take the fifty men I'd be giving you anyway for the punishment squad, and use them to get your own damned ruins back. How about it?"

Friedrich von Löwenstein-Scharfeneck did not reply at once. He was watching another falcon in flight, and that one name was still throbbing in his mind, again and again.

Agnes. Agnes. Agnes . . .

"Yes, why not?" he said in a deliberately casual tone. "A little diversion would do me no harm." He glanced disparagingly at his father. "And after that you'll really give me the landsknechts to storm Scharfenberg and Trifels?"

Ludwig von Löwenstein-Scharfeneck nodded. "The landsknechts, a dozen arquebuses, and a couple of my culverins. I give you my word." He held out his hand. "Shake hands on it, and show me at last that you're worthy to bear my name."

Friedrich shook hands and smiled contentedly. He suddenly felt strangely relaxed. He would get his castle back, he would again go searching for the treasure he so longed to find, and someday he would also find Agnes. But first there was hard if not completely unpalatable work to be done.

Work for which emotions were entirely out of place.

A week later, a dozen horses were towing a broad sailboat up the Rhine. The sun, high in the sky, made the water glitter like diamonds. Boatmen with necks burned red waved from the many skiffs, barges, and rafts going the other way. It seemed that the terrible war now coming to an end was taking place only on land, where you were still reminded of it by burning villages, the ruins of castles, and trees with corpses hanging from them. Here on the river, however, peace reigned.

Under an awning in the middle of the ship, three travelers dozed in the shade. The two men and the young woman wore expensive but not showy clothing. A brand-new sword belt with its sword dangled by the mast, with a lute of polished maple wood leaning beside it. The crystal carafe of Palatinate wine that stood on a small table between the travelers sparkled in the midday light.

Deep in thought, Agnes reached for her glass and sipped. When she realized how strong the wine was, she put it aside again. She needed all the powers of her mind to make sense of what had happened to her. Her life had changed so much that she sometimes thought she was a completely different person: no longer Agnes von Erfenstein, daughter of the castellan of Trifels, but some kind of shadow being, more likely to have sprung from an old book than from reality.

After the fire in the library at St. Goar, she, Mathis, and Melchior had left the town in a hurry. First, the master of a raft, although he was suspicious, had taken them on board and upstream to Bingen, then they had continued on another vessel to Mainz, which Melchior had visited several times before. He had taken them to see a rich spice merchant who had paid the minstrel over two hundred guilders for one of the books that he had rescued and offered them passage on one of his ships in the bargain. They had stocked up with new clothes and provisions, and the ship was now on its way to the old imperial city of Worms, where its cargo would be unloaded and they would spend the night at a good inn.

Yawning, Melchior rose to his feet, went over to his new lute, and plucked a few strings. The tone was soft and warm.

"A really lovely instrument," said the minstrel. "Expensive, but worth its price. Like a good woman. I am certainly going to win the laurel wreath at the singers' contest in the Wartburg with it." He looked at Agnes with a twinkle in his eyes. "Especially with a ballad in which the identity of a woman who is the last legitimate descendant of the Staufers is revealed. I very much hope you will both accompany me."

"Forget it!" Agnes snapped. "I'm tired of all this nonsense. It's enough to know where I come from at last, and who my real parents were. At least my nightmares have stopped since that dreadful fire in the library of St. Goar."

"But remember, you do have a responsibility," Melchior told her. "Especially in these dreadful times. Think of what Father Domenicus said to you just before he died. You could be the figure who unites the empire. You and the Holy Lance."

"Holy Lance," murmured Agnes. "I don't want to hear any more about that. How is a single lance supposed to unite an empire?"

"A lance which, incidentally, we still can't locate," said Mathis, stretching out where he sat and yawning. Surreptitiously, Agnes looked at him. Over the last few days, the sun had turned his face and neck brown, and strong muscles stood out under his new shirt of fine linen. Mathis had also taken to wearing a pointed beard. The war, and their long journey, had turned the pale youth of the past into a fine figure of a man.

"What's more, I still have no idea what's so special about this lance," Mathis went on morosely. He glanced at Agnes, but she immediately lowered her eyes. "Whenever we were about to talk about it these last few days, you've dismissed the subject. Why?"

"Because . . . because all these stories to do with my past are getting me down," Agnes exclaimed. "Can't you understand that? Until a week ago I was still an ordinary woman, the daughter of a castellan in the Palatinate, no more. And now, all of a sudden, I'm supposed to be saving the entire German Empire. It's too much for me." She sighed. "But yes, let's talk about it now. I'm sure our minstrel friend will be able to tell us something about the famous Holy Lance."

Melchior von Tanningen cleared his throat. "Yes, indeed." He propped his lute against the mast and sat down cross-legged in front of Agnes and Mathis.

"The lance has a long history," he began. "According to legend, it is the very spear that the Roman centurion Longinus used to pierce the side of the Savior on the cross. The blood that then flowed from Jesus cured Longinus of severe eye trouble, so he had himself baptized and later died a martyr in Caesarea. He is said to have buried the blood of Christ first."

"I do remember reading about the lance somewhere," Agnes said thoughtfully. "Oh, of course. In the legend of the Holy Grail. Old King Amfortas guarded both the lance and the Grail itself in the Grail Castle."

Melchior nodded. "As the lance bore the Savior's blood, it is venerated to this day and immortalized in stories. In fact all that was preserved of it was the iron head of the spear, about the length of a man's forearm, and it also has a nail from the cross in it. The relic is considered the most sacred of the German imperial insignia. I've read about it in several books, and the rest of the insignia as well."

"The imperial insignia, did you say?" Agnes looked at him in surprise. "The holy objects necessary for the coronation of the emperor?"

"Yes. Why do you ask?"

"Father Tristan told me about the imperial insignia some while ago, because they were kept at Trifels Castle for several centuries. And now I do remember that he mentioned the Holy Lance." Agnes frowned. "But if it is really so sacred, couldn't it be that Constanza and Johann simply took it with them when they escaped?"

Melchior von Tanningen smiled knowingly. He picked up his lute and struck a few soft chords as he went on: "The lance is the most powerful of all those relics, more powerful than the imperial cross, sword, and orb combined. It is said that anyone carrying it in battle is invincible. King Otto threw back the Hungarians at the battle of Lechfeld with it, and it has brought glorious victories to other commanders as well. Without the Holy Lance, no one can be crowned Holy Roman Emperor."

"But if Constanza and Johann stole the lance long ago and hid it somewhere, then how have coronations been carried out ever since?" asked Mathis, baffled.

"How do you think?" The minstrel looked inquiringly at them. "What would you have done in the Habsburgs' place?"

"I . . . I would have forged it?" Agnes suggested.

"That's probably what happened." The minstrel struck a dramatic final chord and put the lute down again. "If what Father Domenicus said is true, then the theft had major consequences for the empire. Its loss would have made all coronations since the time of Albrecht von Habsburg null and void. Meaning that no Habsburg ever occupied the throne legitimately, and that includes the present emperor, Charles V."

For some time no one said anything, and only the sound of the river running by was to be heard, along with the boatmen's shouting. Melchior grinned mischievously and finally turned to Agnes.

"Now do you understand what power that relic could have in the hands of the right person? If you and the Holy Lance appear with me at the Wartburg, in the presence of all the princes, dukes, counts, and barons, who are already shaken out of their sense of security by the war, a storm will arise and sweep the Habsburgs away from the imperial throne. That much is certain."

Agnes laughed quietly. "And how do you see that happening? Even if we do find this relic—am I to walk into the Wartburg with you saying I'm a descendant of the Staufers and, incidentally, this is the Holy Lance? We'd be ridiculed, and probably burned at the stake for heresy."

"Don't underestimate the power of stories." Melchior poured some of the deep red wine into his goblet and clicked his tongue appreciatively. "We also have the ring, and most important of all the deed, certified by Emperor Frederick himself. With my ballad, all that would convey a strong message to the princes. They've never been really close to Emperor Charles anyway. It is difficult to rule a large, disunited empire such as that of the German lands from Spain."

Now Mathis spoke up. "Do you mean Agnes could lay claim to the imperial throne?" He shook his head incredulously. "Are you serious?"

Melchior shrugged his shoulders. "Not Agnes personally, as a woman. But at the side of a powerful prince . . ."

"Oh, let's have no more of this," Agnes interrupted furiously. "I'm not to be sold off like a filly at the horse market. Not even to a prince." She looked angrily at Mathis. "To the devil with the Staufers and this Holy Lance. I'd have expected a little more sympathy from you, at least."

"But I didn't . . ." Mathis began. However, Agnes had turned away and gone to the ship's rail. She stared discontentedly at the river, sparkling in the sun. Far above her, some of the boatmen clambered around in the rigging, while back in the stern, the steersman shouted his orders, but she perceived it all as though divided from it by a wall. She was both irate and confused. At heart, she did not know what to do next. She couldn't return to Trifels if she didn't want to expose herself to the power of her vengeful husband. And as for accompanying Melchior to this singers' contest, to tell everyone that she was a descendant of the Staufers, that was out of the question. So far they had decided only to travel up the Rhine, without any other definite destination in mind. Clearly Melchior and Mathis wanted to give her time to come to terms with her situation. For the minstrel, the search for the Holy Lance was surely the high point of their adventures together, and he fervently hoped to have it with him at the Wartburg. As for Mathis, was he with her because he loved her, or only for the sake of a rusty old lance?

All at once she heard footsteps behind her and felt a strong hand on her shoulder. It was Mathis. He now leaned over the rail beside her, looking out at the water. They were passing a small village with a church and several houses thatched with reeds. All at once, Agnes longed for a quiet life, far from war, castles, and old tales of chivalry.

."I . . . I'm sorry if I hurt your feelings," Mathis hesitantly began. "This is all rather too much for me as well. The last year has been eventful enough for an entire lifetime, if not two." He chuckled. Then, taking her hand, he pressed it. "Believe me, if there's anything I think worth fighting for, it's not that damned lance, it's you."

Agnes smiled to herself, but she still did not look at him. Mathis and she had come very close to one another during the last week. Only yesterday they had made love, hidden behind some casks, and it had been wonderful. As time passed, Agnes's fear of men had receded. The face of Barnabas seldom appeared in her dreams now, and she no longer flinched at any touch, however hesitant. Mathis had taken great trouble to be gentle and considerate with her, and her love for him had grown more and more. All the same, she was not quite sure of him yet.

"I like to hear you say that," she replied at last. "Although I can't really imagine you growing old beside me without fighting, or at least standing up for freedom and justice. You wouldn't be the Mathis I know." She sighed, and looked at him at last. "Why can't we leave these tedious old stories behind us? Get off this ship somewhere and start a new life. So much has changed in the country now. So many people have died, so many have left their old homes. A young smith with a woman beside him must be needed somewhere. It wouldn't have to be guns that you forged."

Mathis smiled. "Never fear, I'm cured of guns. I'd rather turn to horseshoes and plowshares." His expression suddenly changed as he stared sadly at another village on the bank, where several thatched roofs were burning. Smoke drifted through the air to them. Three dead men hung from the branches of a willow right above the river.

"It's so damned unjust," Mathis said angrily, striking the rail with his hand. "*We* ought to have won the war. How much longer will the poor have to suffer under the lash of their masters?"

"Perhaps the peasants' time simply has not yet come," Agnes suggested. "Now that there are more and more books, more and more people will learn to read. They'll find out a great deal that they don't yet know, and then the nobility and gentry won't find it so easy to lord over ordinary folk."

"Oh, come now, the great and powerful simply have better weapons and more skillful leaders, that's all. If only we'd been better united, maybe under Florian Geyer, fighting for a common cause. We could have—"

Mathis suddenly stopped and frowned, as he always did when he was thinking hard.

"That lance," he finally murmured. "Melchior said it could unite the princes. Why wouldn't that hold true for the peasants as well?"

Agnes looked at him imploringly. "Please, Mathis, don't start along that line of argument again."

"No, listen to me. You say you don't want to be the plaything of any kind of powers. That's your right. But the lance makes a difference. It could be a strong symbol to unite the peasants. Suppose the knight Florian Geyer were to gather them together one last time. They would all follow him. A divine lance promising victory, a victory over injustice, over usury and serfdom, what greater symbol could there be?" Mathis had talked himself into a frenzy. "Agnes, please! Don't think only of yourself, think of what you can achieve." He grasped her shoulder. "Those dreams of yours. Didn't they tell you anything about the whereabouts of the lance?"

"I don't know," Agnes replied. "I do remember dreaming of their flight. Johann was carrying the child . . . and Constanza had a bundle of fabric with her . . ."

"The lance was in it!" Mathis exclaimed. "I'm sure it was. Try to remember, Agnes. Did your mother say anything about where the two of them hid it?"

"I was only five, Mathis, have you forgotten?" Bitterly, she turned away from him. "And anyway, didn't I say I don't want to hear any more about it? First you say you love me, and you don't want to forge weapons anymore, and now you think of nothing but this lance."

"It's not the lance itself, it's justice I'm thinking of. Try to understand, Agnes. You may be the only one who can still change the course of this war. I'm only asking you to search your memory, that's all."

Agnes hesitated. She felt like simply jumping into the water, diving into the cool current, and leaving everything behind her. But she could also understand Mathis to some extent. She, too, had seen much injustice and suffering during these last few months. Even if she didn't think that a mere lance, however holy, could make any difference to that, she appreciated Mathis's good intentions.

"Very well," she said at last. "I'll try to remember. But that's all I can say. I can't promise you anything."

"Thank you. That's all I ask." Mathis gave her a boyish smile and ran his hand through her hair, which, as so often, was already tousled. "Never forget that I love you, Agnes. Not as a figure from legend, the heiress of the Staufers, but as the stubborn girl I used to play hide-and-seek with in the castle cellars."

He pressed her hand, and she felt hot tears running down her cheeks.

In spite of her hopes, however, her dreams did not return to her on either of the following two nights. Her sleep was sound and deep, and by day, the closer they came to Trifels, the more strongly she felt a strange uneasiness. She knew it was dangerous to seek out the place where her vengeful husband was, presumably, still set on retribution. On the other hand, she felt magically attracted to the castle itself. When the ship put in at the cathedral city of Speyer, which meant that they were just under thirty miles from Annweiler, Agnes knew that she must make up her mind.

With Mathis beside her, she sat quietly on the pier in the river harbor, looking at the skyline of the city, dominated by the cathedral towers. Melchior had gone to buy provisions at one of the inns. So close to Trifels Castle, and thus within the sphere of influence of the Scharfenecks, they all three thought it too dangerous to risk being seen in the streets for longer than necessary.

"I've been thinking a great deal about the two of us these last few days," Mathis said at last. Hands clasped, he looked down into the black, stinking water of the harbor basin.

"And?" Agnes prompted him. "What conclusion did you come to?"

Silence reigned again, and only now did Agnes notice how quiet it was in this usually lively harbor quarter. She thought of her last visit to Speyer, just under a year ago, with her father. At that time, the self-confidence of the citizens had been almost palpable. Now there was a gloomy atmosphere; the people hurrying past kept their heads bent, as if they feared being taken away at any moment by the henchmen of the elector of the Palatinate or the bishop of Speyer.

"Even if we don't find the Holy Lance, I must go back to Trifels," Mathis went on at last, sighing. "I won't be able to stay long, while I'm still a wanted man. But I must at least see my mother and my little sister one last time. If they're still alive," he added gloomily. He looked at Agnes, waiting for her reaction. Suddenly he was once again like the little boy who was never quite sure of himself and whom she had loved so much when they were children.

"Would you come with me?" he asked at last. "When all this is finished with, then . . . then we can go wherever you like. I promise."

Agnes compressed her lips. She was still at a loss to think where she could turn in these unsettled times, times when she had both lost and won so much. The only home she knew was Trifels Castle, but that was barred to her forever, and, unlike Mathis and Melchior, she had never learned a trade that would enable her to earn a living elsewhere.

Except healing the sick, she thought. *At least Father Tristan taught me how to tend the sick.*

"I don't know, Mathis. It will be very dangerous for both of us to go back," she began. "I have no family to say goodbye to. Maybe I'd do better to wait here for you."

"And then you'll vanish again without a trace, and I'll have to spend months searching for you?" Mathis smiled. "I don't think that's such a good idea."

Now Melchior von Tanningen appeared at the end of the quay, carrying some steaming pies and a jug of wine.

"I've been finding out what I could in the town," he said, already munching as he reached them. Sketching a bow, he handed Agnes one of the appetizingly fragrant pastries. "The area around Annweiler seems to be one of the last places where the peasants of the Palatinate are still holding out. Our old friend Shepherd Jockel is apparently still in charge there."

"And Trifels?" asked Agnes, so eager for news that she forgot to eat. "How about Trifels?"

"It's Jockel's den. He rules the place with a strong hand—probably one reason why the peasants don't dare to surrender. And one of the innkeepers told me that young Count Friedrich has fled to his father's castle near Heilbronn. That sounds like he survived the storming of Scharfeneck Castle uninjured."

"Well, at least we're rid of him, then," said Mathis, hungrily eating his pie. "His lordship the count can stagnate in Heilbronn for all I care, so long as he doesn't come back to the Wasgau." He finished the pie, wiped his mouth, and looked expectantly at the others.

"Well, what do you think?" he began. "The news could be worse. Maybe it will be possible to talk to Jockel and get inside the castle. After all, I was his deputy once . . ."

"Forget it, Mathis!" Agnes snapped. "That man is crazy and he loves bloodshed. Were you thinking of giving him the Holy Lance if we find it?"

"We? Can I believe my ears?" Melchior applauded enthusiastically. "Then you are still on our side, noble lady? That's excellent!"

"Wait, I . . . I didn't say that," replied Agnes. "I only meant—"

"Your dreams," Mathis said. "Maybe they'll come back as we get closer to Trifels. It could be that familiar scenes will help you to re-member." He took her hand. "We'll never find the Holy Lance with-out you, Agnes. Constanza and Johann could have hidden it anywhere around the area. It's like looking for a needle in a haystack. Think of all the poor peasants we could help." She still kept silent, and in the end he sighed deeply. "Very well, what do you think of this as a plan? We go close to Trifels, I try to find news of my mother and my sister, and if we're still no farther along, we give up. Agreed? Then we will begin a new life, I promise you."

"Word of honor?"

Mathis put his hand to his broad chest. "My word as a friend and as a man of honor."

"Then . . . yes. Agreed."

Agnes hesitantly nodded, and half an hour later they were taking their leave of the river boatmen and setting off together in the direction of Annweiler.

But Agnes still feared that her return could be a terrible mistake. She felt as if she were on the rim of a whirlpool that was slowly but inexorably dragging her down into the depths.

"I already miss the ship," grumbled Mathis as they made their way through the forest on paths trodden by game animals. This was their second day since arriving at Speyer, and it was already quite late in the afternoon. They had avoided the few villages they passed, eating only the cold pies from the city and drinking water from the brooks. Mathis, cursing, swatted at the myriad mosquitoes whirring through the air. Burs and thorns from bramble bushes kept catching on his shirt. "I miss the wine, too," he added. "The heat here's enough to kill a man of thirst."

"I thought you never wanted to be a pampered nobleman?" Melchior replied with a smile. "Careful, because you're beginning to act like one."

Mathis laughed. "Well, they say in your circles that clothes make the man, don't they? Maybe it's just as well that the thorns are tearing my new hose before I turn into a pot-bellied minstrel forever chattering away."

Agnes observed the two men who were so different, both of whom she had come to be so fond of, each in his own way. They came from different worlds, yet something linked them—a passion for life and complete commitment to their ideals. These were things that she lacked. And now they both wanted her to decide for one side or the other, the princes or the peasants.

She couldn't do it.

The closer they came to Trifels Castle, the more feverish Agnes felt. The sultry air in the forest, the whine of mosquitoes, the soft marshy woodland floor that made walking difficult, it all made her terribly tired. Even as a child she had felt, at times, that Trifels itself was calling to her. And now, once again, she heard an inner voice. But it did not, as in the past, sound friendly and soothing. It frightened her.

Welcome, Agnes. I have missed you. Where have you been for so long?

Soon after they passed Annweiler, when the glowing red globe of the sun had just sunk over the city, her exhaustion was so great that she could not go on.

"I think I'll have to lie down for a little while," she said. Her legs suddenly felt as soft as wax. She just managed to sit down on the ground before everything went black before her eyes.

Welcome, Agnes . . .

She shook herself, and the blackness went away.

"Are you all right?" asked Mathis, concerned. "Do you feel feverish?"

Agnes breathed deeply. "No, no. It's just all been rather too much for me today." She smiled encouragingly at the two men. "Suppose I rest for a little while, and you two go on to scout out Trifels? I'm sure I'll feel better tomorrow. And by then, maybe I'll have remembered something."

Mathis frowned. "You think we should leave you here on your own? I don't know about that . . ."

"Think of the dreams, Master Wielenbach," the minstrel said. "We want the lady to dream, don't we? And fevered dreams can be particularly graphic. A little sleep won't harm her, either. It's been a long walk today."

"Very well," said Mathis, still unsure. "We'll be back in two hours' time at the latest. But don't move from here, understand?"

"Yes, my big, strong man." In spite of her weariness, Agnes managed to smile. "I'll be good, I promise."

Mathis nodded, and soon he and Melchior von Tanningen had disappeared into the forest ahead.

For a little while Agnes could hear the twigs cracking under their feet, and then there was no sound but the birds twittering in the evening twilight. She closed her eyes. A sense of peace pervaded her body, and almost at once she fell into a deep, leaden slumber.

✦ ✦ ✦

A stone chamber like the inside of a cube. A constant flickering illuminates the room, but only faintly. It comes from a single lighted candle end propped on a stone. Beeswax drips to the floor, hissing, and a sorrowful voice echoes through the walls, singing the old Occitanian lullaby.

Coindeta sui, si cum n'ai greu cossire . . .

It takes Agnes a little while to realize that she herself is the singer. She is standing in front of one of the walls with a piece of charcoal in her hand, using it to draw a picture on the rock. It is too dark to see anymore. Agnes knows only that she can use three colors. Those are all she has.

Black charcoal. Green moss. Red blood.

She found the charcoal on the floor of her dungeon, and the slippery moss comes from the niche beside the opening, where she saw the sun for the last time.

The blood is her own.

A wave of unspeakable agony goes through her body, as if only now has she become aware of what has happened to her. The pain is so strong that it takes her breath away. They burned her breasts with red-hot pincers, they dislocated her left arm on the rack, they drove nails into her flesh, and they pulled out several of her fingernails.

But she said nothing.

Now she sings quietly. Sometimes a whimper of complaint comes from her vocal cords, which are exhausted by all her screaming. She goes on paint-

ing her picture with the bleeding stumps of her hands, while the pain crawls back into its lair again. It makes way for other sensations, and they are almost as strong.

Hunger and thirst.

Agnes's lips are cracked, her tongue is a thick, swollen lump in her mouth, her stomach a yawning, endlessly deep hole.

She is so exhausted that sometimes she leans against the wall and drops off to sleep for a few moments. But she must not fall over, must not really sleep yet, she must go on painting before the last candle has burned down.

She did not betray her child. Neither the child nor the lance. That is all that matters. The Hohenstaufen line will not die out. And she has given her son the ring and the deed that, between them, will make him the rightful ruler of the empire someday. The Holy Lance will help him to put their joint enemies to flight once and for all. With the lance, they will scatter the armies of the Habsburgs like dust in the wind.

The family of tanners taking care of the boy knows the words. The words that reveal the hiding place of the Holy Lance. They will tell him where it is when he is old enough to understand.

The place where enmity is no more.

Humming quietly, Agnes goes on with her picture. It gives her strength and consolation. The picture shows the place where enmity is no more. She repeats that phrase again and again, like a quiet prayer.

As she adds the final stroke with her bleeding hand, the last colored line, the candle goes out.

Forever.

✦ ✦ ✦

Agnes cried out and opened her eyes. All was black around her. For an endless moment she thought that she was still in that eerie tomb. Had she been walled up alive? But then she heard the quiet sounds of the forest, she felt the familiar prickle of pine needles under her shoulders, and suddenly she knew where she was again.

She was close to Trifels Castle, and she had been dreaming.

The dream had been as graphic as her dreams in the castle last year. Once again she had been Constanza, but this time she had shared the Staufer descendant's final moments. Agnes cautiously stretched her hands, almost expecting that they would still hurt from the torture. What pain the woman must have suffered. What a dreadful, lonely death, walled up somewhere in Trifels Castle. The strange phrase that Constanza had kept murmuring was still going through her own head.

The place where enmity is no more.

Had Constanza already, in her imagination, been in paradise? Or had she really been describing the hiding place of the Holy Lance?

Agnes was so deep in thought that she did not hear the footsteps until they were very close. Joyfully, she got to her feet.

"Mathis? Melchior?" she whispered. "Is that you? I've—"

Rough hands pushed a couple of branches aside, and Agnes stopped short in shock. A broad-shouldered peasant, with a dripping nose and popping eyes, was staring down at her as though she were some strange bird.

"Ho, so I was right after all," he muttered. "It *was* a scream we heard just now."

Then the peasant turned around. "Joseph, Andreas, Simon!" he bellowed, and to Agnes his voice was like a slap square in her face. "Come see the pretty thing I've found. Won't Jockel be surprised."

With Melchior von Tanningen, Mathis was stealing through the brushwood on the sloping ground below Trifels Castle. They had decided to approach it from the north side, where the slope was steepest and therefore not so well guarded.

Cautiously, Mathis made his way through the undergrowth where he and Agnes used to play as children. Trifels Castle was very close now. He could already see the staterooms through the leaves, with lights flickering in some of the holes that had been windows. All at once Mathis felt strong nostalgia for the place where he had spent his childhood. He thought of his dead father, but also of his mother and his sister, Marie, who would be nine now. Their poor little house was only a stone's throw away. He had such a strong wish simply to go straight to them, to see whether they were all right. But the danger of being found by Jockel's men was too great. First they must find out how the land lay, especially as Mathis could hear voices and laughter quite close. He got down on the ground, with its smell of pine needles and damp earth, and crawled the last few yards to the place where the forest came to an end, meeting the broad road that led up to the castle. Beside him, Melchior did the same.

When Mathis finally put his head above the bushes, the sight he saw hit him like a blow.

Not far from the well tower, campfires were burning at regular intervals, with men in colorful clothes sitting around them, talking, laughing, and passing wine jugs around. There must be over fifty mercenaries. Many spears were driven into the ground. Among them Mathis saw several medium-weight guns, with piles of stone balls in front of them. Soldiers' songs wafted through the air to the forest. No doubt about it, Trifels Castle was under siege.

"So Friedrich von Löwenstein-Scharfeneck has decided to reclaim his castle after all," said Melchior, who had crawled out of the brushwood with Mathis. "Look at that!"

He pointed to a banner rammed into the ground; it had a crowned lion rampant on it. Mathis knew that coat of arms from the siege of the Ramburg a year ago, and now he also saw the red and blue tent standing beside it. A slight figure was emerging from the tent at that very moment, barking out a few orders. The voice could be heard all the way to the outskirts of the forest, and it caught Mathis's attention.

"Damn it all, that really is the count," he whispered. "Now it will be twice as difficult to get into Trifels and look for any clues to the hiding place of the Holy Lance."

"Twice as difficult, or maybe downright impossible," replied Melchior, looking thoughtfully at the tent, weighing their chances. "We could have taken on a few peasants at a pinch, but a whole troop of landsknechts? These men don't look as though this is their first siege."

Mathis narrowed his eyes so as to make out more details in the firelight. Sure enough, all the landsknechts were armed with long daggers, spears, and short swords. He saw some long two-handed swords as well. The artillery also looked impressive. The besiegers had three falconets, a large culverin, and one of the large cannon known as nightingales, which fired balls of up to fifty pounds. The storming of the castle clearly had not begun yet, for Mathis saw several unfinished fieldworks near Trifels, but the smithy and several of the surrounding buildings had been burned down. He could only hope that his mother and sister had reached safety in time.

For a while, Mathis studied the little army camp in silence, and then he nodded firmly. "Well, that's it, then," he said quietly. "We can't get into Trifels, and obviously Agnes can't help us there. Thinking that dreams and childhood memories could tell us where to find the Holy Lance was a crazy idea anyway." He shook his head. "Now I'm going to try to find my family to say goodbye to them, and then Agnes and I will be off somewhere else. I ought to have done that long ago."

Melchior von Tanningen smiled ironically, but for the first time there was a trace of uncertainty in his eyes. "Throwing your ideals overboard so soon? Only a day ago, you were convinced that with the aid of the Holy Lance and Florian Geyer this war could yet be won. And suddenly all that's worth nothing?"

"It was a mistake. I see that now." Mathis stood up. "All I really want to win is Agnes."

Without another word, he turned away and went back into the forest, pushing branches and twigs aside angrily and marching down the slope, not even looking to see whether Melchior was following him. Thoughts raced through his head like dark clouds in a hurricane. How had he let himself be carried away by the idea that an old lance was more important than the only girl he had ever loved? Agnes had positively begged for the two of them to go away together, but no, he had thought of nothing but his sublime ideals. He'd go down on his knees and beg her to forgive him.

With his head bent, Mathis went on through the forest. He had been walking for about half an hour when, suddenly, he heard a scream. It came from the very direction where he and Melchior had left Agnes.

Mathis felt his heart racing. He began to run as he heard another shrill scream. This time he was sure that it had been Agnes. He remembered how she had been dragged on board that boat in Albersweiler, and then disappeared into the darkness.

Oh God, not again. Please let me get to her this time before it's too late.

Mathis was sorry now that he had set off in such a hurry, without Melchior von Tanningen. He could only hope that the minstrel was not too far behind him. He was going faster and faster. Several times he stumbled over roots and thorn bushes in the darkness, recovered himself, and ran on, until he could suddenly see two figures beyond the trees not far away. In the moonlight, they were bending over something that kicked and struck out like a captured animal.

"Agnes, Agnes!" cried Mathis, beside himself. Without another thought he ran toward the two men and flung himself on them. One of the pair, a sturdy peasant in a torn doublet, fell to the ground.

"What the devil?" he growled, but Mathis had already smashed both fists into his face. Whimpering and bleeding, the man lay there, while Mathis snatched up a stick from the ground and ran at the second peasant with it, shouting. For a moment the man hesitated, and then he turned and disappeared among the pines in the darkness.

Panting, Mathis turned to Agnes, who was cowering in a dip in the ground for protection and had her hands in front of her face. When he touched her, she flinched as if from a whiplash.

"It's me, Agnes," he said softly. "Everything will be all right. This time I reached you, this time . . ."

There was a crunching sound right behind him. Before Mathis could spin around, something hit him on the back of the head and a thousand stars exploded in his head.

He collapsed sideways like a felled tree. The last thing he saw was a dark outline rushing at him.

"Go to hell, traitor!" cried a voice.

Then a tied leather shoe hit him in the face.

Count Friedrich von Löwenstein-Scharfeneck was sitting at table, a leg of wild boar larded with bacon in front of him, listening to the singing of the landsknechts outside his tent. He loved their warlike songs about wine, women, the lust to kill, and a short but satisfactory life. They were full of hatred, which was the strongest emotion he knew. He used his knife to cut the sinews of the meat while, with relish, he summoned up his latest memories.

His men had fallen on the counties of Löwenstein and Scharfeneck like the Four Horsemen of the Apocalypse. They had burned down half the houses in every village and hanged five men chosen by lot. The landsknechts had trampled down the fields with their horses and taken away the seed corn and the last cows as feudal dues, while the children and women screamed, flinging themselves to the ground and begging for mercy.

No mercy had been shown.

That sense of absolute power had allowed Friedrich to forget his anger with Agnes for a while. With every order he gave, with every blow or kick, Friedrich was also striking at his own father, who all his life had made him feel that he was the last in a long line of Scharfenecks, and not much was to be expected of him: a motherless boy who grew up surrounded by dusty books in which great men fought great battles.

Now he was fighting a battle of his own. He was no chivalrous hero, no King Arthur, but a rampaging avenger, and that was at least as good.

If not even better.

Lost in thought, Friedrich von Löwenstein-Scharfeneck carved up the leg of wild boar. He cut it smaller and smaller, until it was in tatters. Meanwhile he thought of what he would do to the peasants when he had finally recaptured Trifels. Yesterday he had taken back Scharfenberg Castle in short order. There had been few guards posted, and the state in which Friedrich had found his expensive furnishings and tapestries had not improved his temper.

Now was the time to take his revenge. His father had kept his word and given him fifty landsknechts and the artillery for another month. More than enough time to take Trifels, where he already knew the terrain only too well after searching for the Norman treasure. Tomorrow morning they would begin the attack. They would storm the makeshift castle gates, climb the low dilapidated walls on the east side with siege ladders, and then make short work of the peasants.

Friedrich would spare only Shepherd Jockel, their leader, for later. The hunchback would have to pay for that brief but shameful moment of his flight from Trifels, and pay with a different sort of pain.

His fork scooped up a few more of the fibrous pieces of meat. Friedrich von Löwenstein-Scharfeneck put one in his mouth and began to chew. Maybe he could contrive to keep some of the landsknechts on at Trifels as mercenaries. Then he could send out a punishment squad into the district from that base, a squad of which the peasants would tell tales for a long time to come. They would never rise against their masters again.

"Forgive me for disturbing you, Excellency."

Annoyed, the count looked up from his meal and saw one of his deputies at the entrance to the tent. The man with the big nose had been a good bloodhound these last few weeks, but now there was a spark of something like fear in his eyes.

"What is it?" asked Friedrich curtly.

"You have a visitor, Excellency. A guest."

"I don't intend to receive guests today. The man would have to come from the emperor himself."

The landsknecht cleared his throat. "Well, that's it," he hesitantly replied. "He does come from the emperor. There's a letter and a seal to prove it. I think you . . . you should see him."

"How dare you . . ."

At that moment a figure pushed past the guard and entered the tent. With a slight bow, the man finally stood in front of the count. When Friedrich recognized him, he didn't know at first whether to have him broken on the wheel or offer his humble salutations.

Friedrich von Löwenstein-Scharfeneck might be a little crazy, but he was not stupid.

He therefore decided on the latter course of action.

Mathis was awoken by a kick and a torrent of cold water. His head was still ringing from the blow that the peasant had struck him. With difficulty, he tried to open his eyes, but they were gummed up with something. It took him a moment to realize that it was his own congealed blood.

With a low groan, he passed his hand over his swollen face. At least he could now manage to peer through narrow slits and see where he was. Clearly he was in the Knights' House at Trifels, its floor covered with dirty rushes. In the light of several torches and braziers, he vaguely saw about a dozen peasants standing around him in a circle, staring down at him. Agnes was nowhere to be seen, nor was Melchior. The minstrel had hopefully managed to disappear in the forest.

Someone was lounging in the background on a chair made of woven strips of willow, near the smoking hearth, but the man was too far off for Mathis to see him. Mathis tried to stand up, but he immediately collapsed again.

Where is Agnes? Where . . . ?

"Help that dog back on his feet and bring him here so that I can see his treacherous face."

Hearing that cutting voice, Mathis knew at once who the man in the chair was. Two peasants seized him and dragged him over to the throne made of fur and willow on which Shepherd Jockel sat with his legs crossed.

"Well, well, so we meet again," said the peasant leader, thoughtfully examining his dirty fingernails. "Homesick, were you?" Only now did he look into Mathis's bloodshot eyes. "What did the count say to get you to show him secret passages into the castle, eh?"

"Where ... is ... Agnes?" Mathis gasped, without answering Jockel's question. A glance out of the window showed him that it was still dark night. The campfires of the besiegers shone on the other side of the wall.

Shepherd Jockel raised his eyebrows. "The count's whore? I've already had her thrown into the dungeon. You're going there too, while I decide what to do with you. You *traitor!*" He jumped up and pointed at the stooped figure of Mathis, who still had to be held up by the two peasants. "This man left us to join the enemy," he proclaimed. "He's killed dozens of you, and now he's come back to tell the count how to get into this castle."

"That ... that's not ... true." Mathis began, but Shepherd Jockel kicked him in the stomach, so that he collapsed, groaning.

"Do you see what I do with traitors?" Jockel went on in a calmer voice. "I know there are some of us who want to give up. They don't believe that victory is within reach. But I've sent for troops. It won't be long now. Bands of peasants will soon be hurrying to our aid from all over the Palatinate, indeed all over the empire. This is Trifels, the center of the Holy Roman Empire! We'll set out from here to the last battle, and we'll yet win this war."

"It's ... lost," Mathis groaned.

Jockel, startled, looked at him. "*What* did you say?"

"The ... war ... is lost."

For a while, the peasant leader seemed to be deprived of speech. Then, finally he struck out at Mathis like a man deranged.

"You accursed traitor," he said furiously. "Sowing lies and discord. I distrusted you all along, and I was right. You were always on the side of the lords and masters. That little whore corrupted you. Tell me what the count is planning to do out there, or—"

"I ... don't ... know," Mathis managed to gasp. "By God, I really don't know." Jockel's blows had struck him in the face, the stomach, and the loins. The pain was so savage that he was on the point of losing consciousness.

"The oath of a traitor." Jockel looked around at a dozen or so peasants who watched the spectacle with a mixture of fright and obsequiousness. "Of course he knows. And I know how to get it out of him." He smiled unpleasantly. "Bring the two of them in. We'll celebrate a delightful reunion."

Some of the peasants hurried out, and soon returned with two trembling figures whose heads were wrapped in cloth. Jockel snatched the ragged fabric away, and Mathis groaned aloud.

The two were his mother and his little sister, Marie.

They both looked reasonably well, although there were bruises on Martha Wielenbach's face. Her skirt and bodice were torn, like someone had been pulling at her clothes. Marie's face was red and swollen with tears, and her nose was running. She looked as though she had been crying for hours.

"Mathis!" his mother sobbed. "Dear Mathis, you're alive! But for God's sake, why—"

"Hold your tongue, woman," Jockel barked. "So far we've treated the pair of you well. At least as well as anyone can treat the family of a traitor. You've had food and drink. But that could come to an end . . ."

He paused, and winked at Mathis.

"You always were a stubborn bastard, Mathis," he went on, in an almost friendly tone. "Clever, but stubborn. So how am I to hurt you if you do nothing but keep your mouth shut or lie to me? I have a better idea." He went over to little Marie, who was whimpering, and ran his hand through her matted hair. "I'll give you until tomorrow to change your mind, Mathis. If you're still as obstinate then, I'll hang your little sister from the battlements until she's black and blue in the face. Then it will be your mother's turn, and you'll have to watch her slowly choke to death." He looked pityingly at Martha Wielenbach, who was weeping bitterly with her hands over her face. "I am afraid that war sometimes calls for cruel measures," Jockel said pompously. "But those who want paradise on earth must walk through hell at times to get there." He sat down on his throne again and snapped his fingers.

"Now, take this fellow away. I feel sick to my stomach at the sight of him."

Agnes crouched deep down in the keep, staring at the darkness. The shivering fits that had been attacking her since she was captured had begun to die down now, but her breath still came fast and uneven. She had tried to weep, but her throat was constricted. Was this to be the end? Had she traveled so far only to die in the dungeon of her own castle?

Buried alive, like Constanza, she thought. *Why did I come here?*

Trying to take her mind off her predicament, Agnes massaged her joints and the place where her feet were bound. Her limbs hurt from being tied up by the peasants and then dragged through the undergrowth. With her and Mathis, who had been knocked unconscious, they had taken secret ways past the ranks of landsknechts and then, finally, into the castle. Seeing one of the banners waving above the attackers' camp, in the light of their campfires, she had been horrified to realize that it was under siege by her husband's men. She had not seen Mathis since; she still did not know what the peasants were doing to him, or whether he was even alive.

Agnes closed her eyes and thought of the few happy moments they had spent with one another since their reunion in the army camp near Ingolstadt. It looked as if those moments were the end of their time together.

Above her there was a square stone shaft with a stone slab over the top of it. At a height of twelve feet, narrow strips of moonlight fell in through two slits in the east wall of the keep. Agnes remembered standing up above on the other side of those slits, more than a year ago, talking to Mathis through them. He had been imprisoned in this dark, dank hole for over two weeks. After only about an hour, she felt that her rib cage was constricted as if all the stones of the keep were weighing down on her. She also had a clammy sensation, a steady throbbing that could lead up to a fainting fit. On her brief visit to

Mathis in here last year, she had felt the same, just as she had in Speyer Cathedral, when she and her father visited the corpulent merchant Jakob Gutknecht. Agnes shook herself to drive away the wave of faintness.

What in heaven's name does this castle want from me?

All at once she heard a scraping noise up above, the stone slab was pushed aside, and the broad face of a peasant showed at the opening. He shone a torch down into the depths below.

"Hey there, count's whore," he shouted. "Ready to hold your first audience in your wonderful throne room? Here comes the handsome prince. But don't touch him or he'll fall to pieces entirely."

There was laughter, and then two of the peasants let down a figure hanging lifeless as a puppet in a loop of rope. Blood dripped on Agnes.

The man's face was so badly beaten that it took her a moment to realize that it was Mathis. His clothing was torn, his head lolled forward. He looked like a hanged man.

"You murderers!" Agnes yelled up to the two peasants. "What have you done to him?"

"Never fear, he's still alive. Jockel is keeping him for later." Suddenly the moon-faced peasant raised his voice in a threatening tone that echoed through the walls. "But if his lordship your husband thinks he can storm Trifels, we'll make short work of the pair of you. Then we'll see what his whore and her fancy man are worth to the count."

He laughed and spat into the shaft. Then he let go of the rope, so that Mathis fell like a stone for the last few feet. He groaned softly as they put the slab back in place.

"My God, Mathis! What have they done to you?" Agnes crawled toward him and cradled his head in her lap. Her eyes were well enough accustomed to the darkness now for her to see his face more clearly.

Mathis's lips were split, and his nose and mouth covered with congealed blood. Agnes cautiously felt his skull and his cheekbones, but apart from a large lump on the back of his head she could find no major cause for anxiety. The peasants had been rough with Mathis, but at least he would survive.

Or he'll survive these injuries, she thought in fear. *But not what they're going to do to us later. Unless we can find some way out . . .*

She reached for a bucket containing a little clouded, stinking water and washed Mathis's face. He was quaking with pain and cold. With difficulty, he looked up at her.

"I'm so sorry, Agnes," he said hoarsely. "Why didn't I listen to you? We never ought to have come back to Trifels." Mathis coughed and spat out a broken tooth. "I . . . I love you. But now it's too late."

"At least we are together," said Agnes softly, stroking his hair, encrusted as it was with blood and dirt. "It probably had to be this way. It was Trifels, you see. It called to me."

"What do you mean?"

"I dreamed of it again, Mathis. Of Trifels and Constanza. Just before the peasants found me. Your idea really did work." Quietly, she told Mathis about her dream, about Constanza walled up in the castle, and the strange phrase that she could not get out of her head.

"The place where enmity is no more," she murmured at last. "I wonder what Constanza meant by that?"

Mathis coughed again. "Never mind what it means, we'll never find out now, or at least not in this life."

"You're forgetting that my hated husband is at the gates of this castle," Agnes pointed out. "He may not exactly love me ardently, but if we hold out here for a little while, then—"

"Agnes, listen to me." Mathis laboriously sat up. "My mother and my sister are up there. Jockel is threatening to execute them if I don't tell him what your husband's plans are. He thinks I know about a hidden tunnel of some kind. But I know no such thing. I am dreadfully sorry for getting us into this situation. Believe me, I don't care about my own life, but I do care about the lives of my family." He looked pleadingly at her with his swollen eyes. "You may curse me, Agnes, but if you know anything, maybe a second escape tunnel, a hidden crawl space, any kind of damned mouse hole, then tell me now, for the sake of my mother and my sister."

"By God, I wish I could help them, but I don't know any other way out." Agnes stared into the void. Once again, she felt close to fainting. "All I know is that Constanza was walled up alive somewhere in Trifels Castle." She hesitated. "And, strange as it sounds, I feel that the place can't be far from here."

Mathis laughed in desperation. "What a comfort. Imprisoned where your ancestress —"

Suddenly he stopped short, thunderstruck. He straightened up until he could drag himself on his knees to the western wall of the dungeon, where he immediately began searching frantically in the straw.

"What are you doing?" asked Agnes.

"Looking for something. Something I found when I was in here before, but I quite forgot it later." Without any more explanation, he went on feeling the floor and the wall. At last he stopped. "Ah, here it is!"

Mathis had pushed the straw aside, and now he pointed to a spot on the wall. When he tapped it, the stone made a suspiciously hollow sound.

"A stone was set into the wall here," he excitedly explained. "And if I remember correctly, there was a Latin inscription on it." He felt for it and finally nodded, satisfied. "Here it is."

With her heart beating unsteadily, Agnes got close to the wall and knelt in front of it. It was still dark in the dungeon, but Mathis gently took her hand and guided it until she could feel the words engraved on the stone. After passing her fingers over it a couple of times, Agnes thought she knew what it said.

ALBERTUS FACIEBAT LEONES EXPULSOS ESSE . . .

"Albertus caused the lions to be banished," she murmured. "What in God's name does that mean?"

"I don't know. All I know is that a stone was set into the wall of the dungeon here, and the space behind it presumably goes on farther." Mathis knocked again at the stone block. His excitement obviously helped him to forget his pain for a while. "When you said just now that Constanza was buried alive somewhere near here, it came back to me. I wanted to blow the block out of place with gunpowder, don't you remember? Why didn't we think of it before? This is the dungeon of Trifels Castle. Way back in the past, Barbarossa's son Henry kept his captives here. There may well be a passage leading from here to another chamber."

"*Albertus faciebat leones expulsos esse,*" said Agnes, repeating the words of the inscription quietly. She shrugged her shoulders. "That word *faciebat* often occurs on memorials, so that people will know who set them up. Maybe some stonemason was immortalizing himself here, or . . ." Agnes stopped in amazement. She felt herself begin to tingle all over with excitement.

Can it really be true? Is it as simple as that? Or am I beginning to dream in broad daylight?

"Of course." she said. "It really does refer to Constanza. The lions, it's the lions that stand for her."

"The lions?" Mathis asked, baffled.

"Well, the lions are on the Hohenstaufen coat of arms. Do you see? It's a riddle." The words were tumbling out of Agnes now, as she went on interpreting the inscription. "The lions, meaning the Staufers, were banished to Trifels, with Constanza as their last legitimate descendant."

"But then who is Albertus?"

Agnes smiled. "Albertus is the Latin form of Albrecht. And if I remember what Father Tristan told me correctly, Albrecht was the German king of the Habsburg family who ordered Constanza to be put to death. So Albrecht was making sure that the Hohenstaufen lion would be banished behind these walls for ever. *Albertus faciebat leones expulsos esse* . . ." She reverently stroked the block. "My ancestress's grave is behind this stone," she whispered. "I'm sure of it. We really have found the place."

Agnes closed her eyes, feeling a strange sense of peace come over her. All at once she was sure she had finally come to the end of her long journey. The fever that had been troubling her for two days was making her shiver, and once again a soft voice purred inside her head.

The voice of Trifels.

The circle is closing, Agnes. It all began here at Trifels Castle, and this is where it will all end. Even though it is not the end you would have wished for, is it?

Agnes turned away, with a laugh of desperation. "How ironic. We really have found the entrance to Constanza's grave, but we can't reach her. We'll never be able to move this stone."

"Not us, but maybe someone else will." Mathis twisted his battered face into a grin, showing a wide gap between his teeth. "For instance, Jockel and his men."

Agnes looked at him, baffled. "Jockel? Why would he want to help us?"

"Well, if we tell Jockel about our discovery, he'll certainly want to know what's just beyond this dungeon. He'll begin digging. At least we'll gain a little time that way." Gingerly, Mathis leaned back against the slab. "And in our situation, time is very, very valuable."

About an hour later, Shepherd Jockel stood in the dungeon, thoughtfully feeling the edges of the stone slab. He had let himself down into the depths with three of his peasants, all of them carrying picks and shovels. A few lanterns cast light on the interior of the cell, so that the stone and its inscription were now clearly in view.

"A walled-up escape tunnel, eh?" Jockel grinned at Mathis. "So you obviously did think of something after all. I knew you wouldn't let your family down."

"Are my mother and my sister all right?" Mathis asked without responding to Jockel's suggestion. He and Agnes had decided not to tell the peasants the true purpose of the tunnel. A noblewoman's grave would be of far less interest to the rebels than the possibility of escaping Count Scharfeneck and his landsknechts at the last moment. By now, even a fanatic like Jockel would have realized that he could not hold the castle.

"Your family are all right, at least so long as you're not trying to fool us." Jockel looked at him sharply. "Here, how did you know about this slab?"

"I was imprisoned here once before, you know," Mathis replied truthfully. "I couldn't move the block out of place at the time, but now it's different." He indicated the three peasants standing expectantly in the background with their tools. "What are you waiting for?"

Jockel signaled to the men, and they began loosening the masonry and plaster around the slab. It soon became clear that the heavy stone, about the thickness of a man's arm, was set deep into the ground where it met the floor. Above it there was a small slit now walled up with bricks. When the peasants broke out the upper bricks, damp, musty air blew through into Mathis's face.

The crack that Father Domenicus mentioned, he thought. *The crack through which Constanza could be heard moaning and singing until she died. The dean was right.*

"This is hard work, Jockel," grumbled one of the peasants, tugging at the slab. It was the moon-faced man who had let Mathis down into the dungeon a few hours ago. "This thing won't shift from the ground, not without a hell of a lot of digging."

"Then for God's sake, dig," Jockel hissed. "Or do you want the landsknechts cutting your throats a couple of hours from now?"

"But you said other bands of peasants were coming to help us."

"So they are. But meanwhile it wouldn't be a bad idea to . . . er, have another plan up our sleeve. It's all to do with the trade of warfare. You wouldn't understand that."

Muttering, the peasants went on with their work, while Jockel glanced suspiciously at Agnes. For some time now the castellan's daughter had been leaning back against the opposite wall as she sat hunched on the floor, her eyes closed. Mathis was not sure whether it was because of the fever that had clearly been troubling Agnes for some time. Since they had been down in this dungeon, though, she had seemed to be in another world.

"What's the matter with her?" Jockel asked Mathis. "Is my lady the countess sick? Doesn't she fancy the air down here?"

"You can see yourself that she isn't at all well," Mathis replied. "She has a fever, and she's in pain. I expect your stupid peasants were too rough with her."

Jockel gave a thin-lipped smile. "That's nothing compared to the pain I'll inflict on her if her husband really dares to storm Trifels. We sent a message to the landsknechts' camp. The count knows his whore is here. And he knows what we'll do to her if he lifts so much as a finger against us."

Mathis did not reply but looked solicitously at Agnes. Did her fainting fits and her absence of mind have anything to do with the fact that they were approaching the grave of her ancestress? Was such a thing possible?

The next half hour passed in silence. The peasants dug, breathing heavily, driving their picks deep into the ground, until there was a hole over three feet deep beside the stone block. At last it could be shifted slightly.

"Get it out," Jockel ordered, rubbing his hands together, positively quaking with excitement. "Let's see what's behind it."

Puffing and panting, the peasants raised the heavy block and finally let it crash to the ground, where it broke into several pieces. A low-roofed passage came into view where it had stood. The musty smell was so strong now that the men covered their faces with their hands.

"Aha, welcome to the gates of hell," Jockel grinned. "The way this passage smells, no one's used it for a long time. All the better."

Only a moment later, a muted clap of thunder shook the dungeon. The peasants cried out and looked fearfully up to where the noise had come from.

"Holy Mother Mary—the devil!" Moonface screamed. "We've woken the devil!"

"Don't worry," Jockel reassured them. "It's only the guns of the besiegers. Sounds like the storming of the castle has begun." He tried to smile and did not entirely succeed. "But Trifels Castle has held out against worse, right? So come on. We don't have much time left."

But he looked anxiously up at the shaft, for screams and more firing could now be heard. It sounded like some of the landsknechts were already inside the lower bailey. The hunchback was about to start along the dark tunnel when a clear, loud voice stopped him in his tracks.

"Get back, all of you. I will be the first to enter this passage."

Astonished, Mathis looked around at Agnes, who approached the entrance with new self-confidence. She seemed to have awoken from a long sleep.

"If we must walk this way, I go first," she said firmly. "I owe it to my forebears."

"Forebears? What nonsense are you talking?" Jockel looked at her, taken aback. "And how do you think you're speaking to me anyway, woman?" He raised his hand to strike her. "I'll teach you what it means to arouse the wrath of the peasants, you . . ." But he stopped, and smiled unpleasantly, "Well, I don't know. Maybe it's really better for our princess to go first. That passage looks damned old. It can't hurt to have someone go ahead in case it falls in." He seized Agnes by the chin and pulled her to him. "But don't forget, countess, I'm right behind you. One false step, and this passage is your grave."

"Isn't it my grave already?" Agnes replied quietly. Then she freed herself from him and disappeared into the darkness. Jockel and Mathis followed her, with the three peasants carrying lanterns after them.

As Mathis, stooping, went along the low-roofed passage, he thought again of the self-confidence that Agnes had just shown. Almost as if someone else were speaking through her. What in the world, he wondered, was going on? Painfully, he hit his head on an overhanging rock and staggered on. The tunnel ran straight for about thirty feet then turned sharp right before finally widening out. Here, parts of the walls and roof were supported by rotting wooden props and joists, and a few rats scurried away between Mathis's feet. Soon they stood at the entrance to another chamber; its extent could not be made out easily in the darkness. The thunder of the guns resounded from somewhere above them.

"Get on with it, bring up those lanterns," Jockel called to his men. "Or are you going to wait until the whole place falls in?"

When the peasants had finally brought their lanterns to the front of the party, Mathis held his breath. This room was far larger than the dungeon, more of a great hall. Water dripped from the high ceiling, and Mathis guessed that they were underneath the well tower. The floor was weathered marble. But it was the walls that were truly extraordinary. All four of them bore the remnants of a huge fresco. Although the paintings were faded, Mathis could tell that they depicted German kings and emperors. There were about two dozen of them, each with a crown on his head and dressed in richly decorated robes whose colors had flaked off long ago. Some held a sword, others a scepter, a Bible, or an imperial orb. The whole place was like a vast underground mausoleum.

One of the rulers in particular caught Mathis's eye. He was very tall, with a long, red beard, and his right hand held a mighty spear. The man's name was written clearly above his flowing hair.

Fridericus Barbarossa Imperator.

"Emperor Redbeard and the Holy Lance," Mathis whispered, staring at the portrait, fascinated. He shook his head in astonishment. "Who'd have thought? So the legend is true, or at least the kernel of it. Barbarossa really does sleep under Trifels Castle."

"Damn it, what's all this?" That was Shepherd Jockel's agitated voice. "Where have we ended up? This is no escape tunnel, it's more like a crypt. Speak up, countess. Where have you brought us?"

He made for Agnes, who was kneeling in front of one wall with several bleached bones directly before her. They bore a distant resemblance to the figure of a human being. Tiny scraps of fabric and matted hair still clung to them. Agnes picked the bones up and passed them through her fingers. She was so absorbed in her thoughts that she seemed not to hear the shouting of the peasant leader.

"I want to know where we are," Jockel demanded.

He struck Agnes a blow that knocked her sideways, but she did not cry out. Instead, she slowly straightened up and looked Jockel so firmly in the face that he involuntarily flinched back. The cannon still rumbled overhead.

"This is the grave of my ancestress Constanza, the daughter of Enzio, grandson of the great Emperor Frederick II," Agnes said, pointing to the verdigris-tinged bones before her. She was like a woman in a trance, and her dreamy voice clearly terrified the three peasants in the background. "She was tortured and walled up alive here at Trifels. Kneel down and pray before her bones. We must give her a worthy burial."

For a split second it looked as though the peasants really would kneel down reverently. But then Jockel's bleating laugh was heard.

"I *piss* on your ancestors, count's whore," the peasant leader said. "I piss on you and the airs you put on. We're not your inferiors any-more; that time is over." He kicked the pale bones, scattering them in all directions. "I don't need a burial chamber, I need a passage to get me out of here." He seized Agnes by the throat so violently that she began to retch, but her gaze was still as steady and fearless as before. "Tell me, does that passage exist?" Jockel screeched. "Tell me, before I hurt you more than anyone has ever hurt you before."

"There's no passage, but there is something else," Mathis inter-jected. "A sacred object, and very valuable. We hoped to discover where to find it down here. Let us go free, and you can have it."

"What?" Jockel let go of Agnes, who fell to the floor, gasping, and lay there dazed. The peasant leader stared suspiciously at Mathis. "What are you talking about?"

The three other peasants still had not moved from the side of the room. They didn't seem to know what frightened them more: the roar of the guns above them, or the secret chamber and this woman talking to them like a spirit.

"It's the Holy Lance," said Mathis, turning to Jockel and raising his hands to placate him. "Give me a little time, and I'll explain everything."

"I'll give you until the next cannonball strikes up there, so hurry. And by God, don't you try to put one over on me."

Mathis took a deep breath and then quickly told Shepherd Jockel the whole story. He left out how he and Agnes had come by this knowledge, as well as that Agnes was a direct descendant of the Staufers. The Holy Lance would mean more to Jockel than this ancient story. Meanwhile Agnes crouched by the wall of the chamber as if in a stupor.

"Is this lance really so powerful?" Jockel asked.

Mathis nodded. "It is the most powerful relic in Christendom, and said to make its bearer invincible. Many battles have been won with it in the past. And so, maybe, the peasants will win their own battles in the near future," he added conspiratorially. "How does that sound, Jockel? You leading a peasant army, with the Holy Lance in your hand? You might be able to decide the outcome of the war for our side after all."

He paused, watching Jockel, and seeing the greed in his eyes. Mathis did not know whether the hunchback really believed the lance would make him leader of all the peasants—but at least Jockel was thoughtfully biting his lip. He glanced at his three companions, who were staring at him as if he were the Messiah in person, and finally brought out an answer.

"Well, well, that does sound interesting," Jockel hesitantly began. He jumped when another stone cannonball hit the staterooms of the castle above them. "But I don't see any lance here. Only a few bones and faded old paintings. So where is this powerful weapon?"

"You fool, weren't you listening? Constanza and Johann hid it." Agnes said. She had risen and stood upright in the middle of the room, with the scattered bones of her ancestress around her. Mathis swallowed at the sight of her. It was as if the discovery of Constanza's grave had turned her into someone else. Agnes suddenly seemed much older and more mature, and she looked like a queen personified. Even Jockel was so surprised that at first he did not answer.

"This is the secret chamber where the imperial insignia were hidden in times of trouble in the past," Agnes went on, and her voice echoed from the walls. She spread out her arms, pointing to all the crowned and bearded men on the walls. "Charlemagne, Ludwig the German, Otto the Great, Barbarossa, the Carolingians, Ottonians, the Salians, the Guelphs, and the Staufers—all were crowned German kings and emperors with the imperial insignia. My mother told me about this room, and my memory of it has come back to me at last." She gazed into a void as she went on in her dreamlike state. "When Johann of Brunswick and Constanza fled because of the supposed conspiracy against the German king, and it turned out that the Holy Lance had disappeared along with them, the imperial insignia were removed from Trifels Castle. This once magnificent hall stood empty, robbed of its treasures. Later, when the Habsburgs' henchmen captured Constanza, they thought it particularly and horribly apt to wall up the last descendant of the Staufers here, surrounded by all the rulers whose successor she should really have been. But Constanza withstood them, and she took her secret to her grave."

"Then there is no clue here to the whereabouts of the lance?" Mathis asked quietly.

Agnes smiled. "I said she took her secret to the grave. This is her grave, and here is the clue." She pointed to a drawing below the painting of Barbarossa, a drawing that Mathis had not noticed at first. Unlike the other pictures, this one was very simple, more like a child's drawing. Basically, it consisted of only a few lines, and the colors had long since faded. Long ago, the drawing might have been red, green, and black. All the same, you could still see what it showed. Mathis thought he recognized it as a building with towers and a dome. Scrawled under it were a few words that finally trailed away.

The place where enmity is no more . . .

At that moment several cannonballs crashed into the castle above them, and the ceiling rattled. Small stones and some larger chunks of rock fell to the floor, and in one corner a rent suddenly gaped in the wall. The peasants screamed and ran along the passage back to the dungeon.

"Damn you, wait!" Cursing, Jockel ran after them. As he left the chamber, he turned to his two prisoners. "If you want to see the sun again, come with me," he said. "Devil take it, I want to know where this Holy Lance is. After that, you can go to hell for all I care."

Only a little later they were together up in the Knights' House, with the first light of dawn falling through its windows.

The storming of the castle had begun in earnest. The guns crashed and boomed at regular intervals, and the shouts of the besiegers could be heard as they went on the attack. Mathis ventured a glance through one of the window frames, and saw about two dozen landsknechts running toward the walls with ladders. They were supported by a troop of arquebusiers who kept the peasants on the battlements under fire. The insurgents fought off the landsknechts, but it seemed only a question of time before the castle was finally captured. The cannonballs from the huge nightingale and the almost equally powerful culverin punched holes in the already decrepit masonry like giant fists.

Shepherd Jockel stood motionless at one of the windows, staring at the chaos below him. He might have been turned to stone. He had said not a word since their flight from the dungeon. Some of his men, meanwhile, had tied up Agnes and Mathis and dragged them over to the willow throne. Now the peasants glanced uncertainly at their leader.

"Jockel, what are we to do with the hostages now?" asked Moonface. Naked fear—the fear of death—showed clearly on his face. "Hans says the lower castle gate will probably go down soon. And we can't defend the wall on the eastern side much longer. Maybe you ought to go down yourself and—"

Another blow shook the hall. It was so violent that the peasants threw themselves on the floor, whimpering like little children. In one corner, part of the stone landing of the staircase gave way and fell, crashing down and burying two screaming men under it. A cloud of dust from the shattered stonework spread through the hall.

"You damn cowards!" Jockel bellowed over the noise. He was enveloped in clouds of dust and smoke. "Don't you see that in our hour of need, God has given us a gift?" Jockel's eyes flashed as he turned to his few remaining supporters, arms outspread. "I thought God had abandoned us. But no, it was only a trial sent to test us, and now he is sending us his most powerful relic. The Holy Lance."

He uttered a shrill laugh, and in Jockel's eyes Mathis saw the insanity that had probably always been in him breaking out at last. His laughter suddenly died away. Shepherd Jockel ran to Agnes, who was still bound, and hauled her up by her hair.

"The lance," he said. "Give it to me, count's whore. Tell me, where your ancestors hid it."

"I don't know." Struggling wildly, Agnes tried to break free of Jockel's grasp. The confidence she had shown in the chamber had disappeared, the proud queen turned back into a frightened young woman. "All I know is that Constanza's drawing will take us to it," she added desperately. "The drawing and those words she wrote."

"You lie, whore, the lance is hidden somewhere here. The drawing shows a castle, and what castle can it be but Trifels? So talk. I need the lance now. *Now!*" Jockel let go of Agnes and began knocking at the walls of the Knights' House with his crippled hand. "Aha, there'll be a secret door somewhere, a walled-up niche. Come on, you layabouts, help me search."

Those last words were for the half a dozen peasants who were still in the Knights' House. All the others had run. The last few gawped, open-mouthed, at the dancing dervish who had once been their leader. It was now clear, even to them, that Shepherd Jockel was no longer in his right mind.

"Jockel, stop it," one of them said falteringly. "Whatever it is you're looking for, we don't need it. What we need are your orders. Do we withdraw from the upper bailey, or do we —"

"Aha, there's a hollow space here," Shepherd Jockel laughed, hitting the wall so hard that he left traces of blood on it. "I've found the Holy Lance. Now the battle can begin at last." Over and over he struck the wall like a man possessed.

"Holy Virgin Mary, we're done for," Moonface muttered, making the sign of the cross. "This is the end."

At that moment there was a whistling sound, followed by mighty explosion. The whole hall shook, and Mathis was lifted off his feet by the blast.

The nightingale, he thought. *A thirty-pound ball has breached the east wall.*

Stones, wooden joists, and dust rained down on him. He instinctively crouched down, holding his bound hands over his head to protect it.

"Agnes!" he called into the raging chaos. "Agnes!"

Another beam fell, but before it smashed Mathis to pieces, it suddenly dropped at an angle, catching a fall of stone coming away from the ceiling. Mathis heard a few faint cries, and then, suddenly, there was silence. Somewhere, debris trickled down, but otherwise there was not a sound in the hall.

"Agnes?" Mathis said quietly.

There was no answer. He cautiously sat up and looked at all that was left of what had once been the Knights' House. Half of the ceiling had fallen in, and so had part of the east wall, letting the cool morning wind blow through. Stones and splintered wood lay all over the floor, with lifeless arms and legs showing from under the ruins. On the west wall, where Jockel had been standing, a huge hole gaped wide, with small remnants of bone and splashes of blood around the edge of it. Mathis flinched when he saw a mushy red substance oozing from under a square stone block.

Nothing else was left of Shepherd Jockel.

"Ma . . . Mathis . . . ?"

He spun around when he heard the faint voice of Agnes somewhere in the room. It took Mathis a little while to find her at last in the rubble. She was huddled on the open hearth, the only place in the Knights' House that had been spared from the falling masonry.

"My God, you're alive!"

Laughing and weeping at the same time, Mathis struggled through the wreckage until he finally reached the hearth. Using the sharp edge of a stone, he hastily sawed through the rope tying his wrists, and then, at last, took Agnes in his arms. They were both covered with dust and ashes, looking more like ghosts than human beings.

For a while neither of them said a word. At last Mathis stepped back from Agnes and cut her bonds as well.

"I truly thought—" he began, but Agnes silenced him with a gesture.

"Listen," she whispered excitedly, clinging to him. "I think I know now where the Holy Lance can be found," she went on quietly. "When Jockel was talking, it all came clear to me. It's not here at Trifels, it's somewhere else entirely." A hoarse sound escaped her throat. Mathis could not have said whether it was laughter or tears.

"The drawing," Agnes breathed. "Down in the chamber with the kings and emperors, it seemed so familiar. But it's only now that I'm sure. The way I fainted in the dungeon, that feeling of being watched by my ancestors—I'd felt all that before in another place."

Shaking his head, Mathis held her very close again. "Wake up, Agnes. I couldn't care less where the lance is, understand? You are all I need. For far too long I've been—"

He stopped short, hearing the sound of footsteps behind him. Since he had his back to the flight of stairs, it was Agnes who saw the two newcomers first. She uttered a soft cry.

"Oh, my God, Mathis," she whispered. "Tell me this isn't true. Tell me I'm dreaming."

Trembling, she turned to Mathis.

If this was a dream, it was something of a nightmare.

· 23 ·

Trifels Castle, 24 June, Anno Domini 1525

AGNES, SEEING THE COUNT WITH Melchior von Tanningen at
the foot of the stairs to the Knights' House, felt for a moment like she
was still in that trancelike state. The idea that at last she knew where
the Holy Lance was hidden made her see everything else as if through
a clouded lens. But then the daze wore off, and she began to recognize details.

Details that disturbed her more and more.

It was not so much the unpleasant grin on her husband's face or
the nervous twitch at the corners of his mouth that surprised her. Far
more alarming were the changes she saw in Melchior. At first she
thought that the minstrel must be bound. But then she saw his sword,
still hanging from his belt, and she noticed the self-assured glance
and the air of authority with which Melchior stepped forward, as
though he, not the count, were the man of superior rank. She sensed
the silent understanding that clearly existed between the two of
them.

Melchior held his head slightly to one side, smiling as he scrutinized the lovers still standing in front of the hearth in the Knights'
House. Before them towered the ruins of the fallen ceiling, and

a fine cloud of dust from the stonework hovered in the air. After a few moments of silence, the slightly built minstrel sketched a bow.

"Greetings, Lady Agnes," he said in a calm and courteous tone. "Don't let us disturb you. Do continue your conversation. What the two of you were saying just now was very informative."

Mathis's eyes went back and forth between Melchior and Friedrich von Löwenstein-Scharfeneck. He, too, seemed to notice the familiarity of their relationship.

"Melchior, what . . . what's going on?" he asked, still dazed by the violence of the explosion. "I suppose you fell into a trap set by the count's men. You are his prisoner, aren't you?"

The minstrel did not reply. Only a tiny movement of his lips showed that the question amused him. Agnes held her breath. In a fraction of a second, Melchior changed from a good friend to a sinister stranger. Was it possible? She cast her mind back to all the adventures they had had together, all the good moments and the bad ones. She had grown fond of Melchior, with his eccentric, entertaining manner; he had fought for her and had saved her life at St. Goar. And now?

A terrible understanding took possession of her.

This can't be true. Can I really have been so mistaken?

She remembered tiny details that only now, in retrospect, made sense. Melchior's interest in the ring and the old stories; his extensive knowledge of St. Goar and the Holy Lance; his wish to have her with him at a singers' contest in the Wartburg; his skill as a swordsman, something unusual in a minstrel. Once again she looked at Melchior, who now lowered his eyes and shrugged regretfully. Her suspicion turned to certainty.

We've been so stupid. So shockingly stupid.

"It's time I set a few things straight," Melchior finally replied, clearing his throat awkwardly. "There may be a few misunderstandings so far as my connection with His Excellency your husband the count is concerned." Friedrich von Löwenstein-Scharfeneck stood beside him, a malicious smile playing around his lips.

"So we meet again, Agnes," the count said cooly. "And my rival is here as well. It will give me particular pleasure to slit his belly open and pull out his guts while you watch."

But noticing the horror with which Agnes was still scrutinizing the minstrel's graceful form, he turned to Melchior, sighing.

"I'm afraid my dear wife has just suffered a bitter disappointment. Although I must say that you played your part very well, Tanningen. I myself had no idea why the emperor had sent you to me. Would you care to explain?"

"The emperor?" Only now did Mathis seem capable of speech again. His face was white as chalk. "I don't understand."

"I think I do," Agnes said, standing rigid, trying to hide her fear and disillusionment, but all the same trembling slightly. Down in the dungeon another, stronger woman had spoken through her. But here and now, up in the wreck of the Knights' House, she felt small and vulnerable. All the more so because she now knew how much she had been deceived.

"The emperor sent an agent to find me and kill me," she went on. "And that agent's name is Melchior von Tanningen. Isn't that so? If that is indeed your real name."

"Why do you think so poorly of me?" Melchior shook his head, and briefly Agnes had the impression that he meant it. But then she thought, once again, what a consummate actor the minstrel must be.

He played with us as if we were puppets.

"Of course Melchior von Tanningen is my real name," he said, sighing. "And I do indeed come from a family of Franconian knights. The count can confirm it. I am a man of honor. This whole business is . . . extremely regrettable."

The new lute of polished maple wood was still slung over his shoulders. Only now did he take it off, strike a sad chord, and then carefully put it down in a corner.

"Yes, indeed, extremely regrettable," he repeated.

All this time Friedrich von Löwenstein-Scharfeneck's eyes had been resting on Agnes. He did not seem to have heard the minstrel at all.

"I've waited so long for this moment," said the count quietly, as if to himself. "I saw you in my dreams, Agnes. Beautiful as a blood-red sunrise, screaming and writhing in pain. And now I finally have you here before me." He grinned. "We will spend some wonderful last hours together."

Agnes felt the fear of death seize upon her. Friedrich had always been odd, but obviously the experiences of the last few months had brought out his true nature. All the same, she did not move a muscle. She was the mistress of Trifels, and although her husband might be out of his mind with hatred, he was not going to see her weep.

However difficult that might be for her.

"The last thing I do in my life will be to curse your name, Friedrich," she finally replied. "You murdered my father. You'll roast in hell for all eternity for that."

"I think we ought to shelve both your interests at the moment," said Melchior, frowning, as he turned to the count. "Apart from which, it was always my opinion that the lady was not a suitable wife for you, Scharfeneck. A genuine member of the house of Hohenstaufen. You could hardly expect to aim so high."

For a moment Friedrich seemed about to answer back, but then he merely sighed deeply. "I'm not going to quarrel with you, Tanningen. We'll stick to our agreement. You get the lance, I get my wife. What I do with her then is entirely my own business."

Melchior smiled, although a certain sadness played around his lips. "You are right, count, it's your own business. That's what we agreed."

"I might have guessed that you weren't a real minstrel," Mathis said. His first confusion had been followed by deep embitterment. He glared at Melchior. "You were always far better with the sword than the lute."

Melchior pouted. "You wound me, Master Wielenbach. I may not be a genuine minstrel, but my playing wasn't as bad as all that. Very well, it wouldn't be up to the standards of the Wartburg, but I invented the contest myself."

"You did *what*?" asked Mathis, startled.

"Do you still not understand?" Agnes asked him. "Everything that Melchior ever told us was a lie. The Wartburg contest, his love of old ballads, our friendship." Gathering her torn skirts around her, she clambered over several of the fallen beams until she was finally close to Melchior. Her fear and desperation were turning to deep hatred. Hatred for Melchior, and for herself for being taken in for so long.

"It wasn't that black-skinned devil in St. Goar who was sent by the Habsburgs to find and kill the last Staufer descendant," she said. "It was our pleasant and amusing friend Melchior." She pointed to the minstrel with derision, and then spat full in his face. "He made his way into Scharfenberg Castle as long ago as last year to spy out the land. Presumably my husband knew all about it from the first. It was always Trifels that Friedrich wanted, anyway, not me."

"I must defend your husband. He knew that I had been sent by the emperor, and he was instructed to employ me as a minstrel, that's true. But he had no idea of my real task." With an expression of regret, Melchior wiped the saliva from his cheek. "In fact, at first I didn't know what it was myself. There was a rumor that a young woman descended from the Staufers was living in these parts. I was to investigate the story, and if that young woman really existed, track her down and eliminate her before the French could get their hands on her. I admit, I was close to giving up. I spent so many months searching the archives, gleaning what information I could, and yet I found nothing." He sighed and looked sadly at Agnes. "But in the end, you yourself gave me the vital clue. When you told me, just before your flight from here, about the secret that you hoped to find out at St. Goar, I knew that I was on the right track at last. And it really could not have been foreseen that the true Holy Lance would be another reward." There was a weary smile on Melchior's lips. "I wonder whether the emperor has any idea that the lance kept in Nuremberg is only a forgery. One way and another, I have certainly earned my own weight in gold."

"But . . . but then what about that black devil at St. Goar?" Mathis asked, still bewildered. "I thought that *he* had been sent to kill Agnes by the Habsburgs."

"I assume that he was an agent of the French," Agnes said. "He'd have handed me over to the royal house of France. Alive. Isn't that so, Melchior?"

Melchior waved that away. "The fact is that no one had taken any interest in the last members of the Staufer line for a long time. Over ten years ago, there was another attempt to investigate those concerned and dispose of them. As you know, it failed. But then, last year, the French got wind of the rumors." His eyes were bright as he looked at Agnes. "You would have been a good match for the King of France, noble Countess von Löwenstein-Scharfeneck, especially now, when his wife has recently died. Even though he was captured after the battle of Pavia, Francis will still have his eye on the imperial throne once the Habsburgs set him free, as they presumably soon will. A wife descended from the Staufers at his side would indeed have lent him a certain credibility." He sighed sadly. "And once the French had sent their man here, naturally the emperor could not sit idle. After all, his throne was in danger."

Melchior's sword hand played with the hilt of his valuable weapon. "He was a good fighter, that French agent. We knew one another from several previous . . . well, let's say . . . encounters. Although I still don't think much of those newfangled handguns. We've seen where that can lead." Again, the supposed minstrel bowed slightly to Agnes, as if preparing to dance. "At this point, may I ask you for the signet ring, my lady? After all, you will soon have no more use for it."

Agnes flinched away, instinctively reaching for the ring on her finger. The journey had begun with it and was obviously to end with it as well. But must she really part from it now? She tried to take it off, but it fit so tightly, like it had grown into her flesh.

"I would be very sorry if you were to lose your finger as well as the ring," Melchior said. "I am inconsolable, but I fear I must insist on your handing that ring over. Along with the imperial deed, it is proof that I have carried out my mission to the satisfaction of all concerned."

Agnes tugged at the ring again, but it refused to leave her. It had become a part of her, although it had brought her nothing but misfortune. Ever since it had come into her possession, she had been tormented by nightmares and had gone through abysmal experiences. Her life had changed so much that she sometimes thought she was not the same person she had been only a year ago—and yet she valued the ring. It was like a curse.

Go away, she thought. *Go away and leave me in peace.*

The ring suddenly came loose, with a slight sucking sound, and dropped to the floor, clinking. Melchior picked it up and put it in a pocket of his doublet.

"Thank you," he said, smiling. "I think we'll all feel a bit better now."

Once again there were footsteps on the stairs. This time they belonged to three of Scharfeneck's landsknechts. Their garments were smeared with soot and blood, and they were sweating heavily under their uniform coats, but the light of satisfaction showed in their eyes. Only now did Agnes notice that no more sounds could be heard in the castle courtyard.

Outside, all was silent as the grave.

"We've routed the peasants out of hiding and made short work of them," reported a broad-shouldered man with a prominent scar on his face. "They're hanging from the battlements as a deterrent, every last man. Just as you ordered, Your Excellency." He looked down, uneasily. "Except for their leader, that Shepherd Jockel. We're still searching for him. I suppose the cowardly dog has made off."

"You can stop searching," Agnes said, pointing to the large slab of stone around which a pool of blood had formed. "Another power is sitting in judgment on Shepherd Jockel now. Your work is finished."

"A pity," said the count quietly. "A real pity. I'd have liked to watch the dog die, after he so shamefully turned me out of my castle." He scrutinized Mathis and Agnes, taking stock of the situation. "But at least I have substitutes for him."

"Remember the emperor's orders, Scharfeneck," Melchior von Tanningen warned him. "We agreed that you would not take the lady until we had found the Holy Lance. If I understood the conversation just now correctly, my lady the countess has found Constanza's grave here at Trifels, and is now the only one to know where the relic is." He looked encouragingly at Agnes. "Well? You were just about to tell your friend something. Wouldn't you like to go on?"

Agnes bit her lip. To her, although not to the count and Melchior, the lance was of no importance. Yet she was aware that her knowledge of its hiding place was the one thing that now kept her alive. It was for that alone that Melchior had not killed her already. If she told what she knew at this point, presumably she and Mathis would die at once. But if she kept her mouth shut, there were means of inflicting great pain on her to make her talk.

Constanza kept silent, she thought. *Will I be as strong as she was?*

After a moment of silence, Friedrich von Löwenstein-Scharfeneck snapped his fingers and pointed to Mathis. "Roland, Hans, Marten, take this fellow and hang him from the top of the staterooms, head down," he ordered. "Then we'll see if my dear wife has anything to say."

The three men moved toward Mathis, who stood there like he'd turned to stone, seized him, and dragged him over to the wall that had fallen in.

"No!" Agnes cried. "I'll tell you. But in return you must let Mathis go."

"Are you out of your mind? The man with whom you've been unfaithful to me all this time?" Friedrich laughed. "The devil I will! But I tell you what I'll do: talk now, and he can stay alive until we have the Holy Lance in our hands. My word of honor as a nobleman. After all, I don't want you collapsing in tears before we find the lance."

"Never fear, I'm not going to collapse," Agnes replied, straightening her back again. "I will be strong. I'll direct you to the place, but only if—"

"What, *another* condition?" the count snarled.

"I want Constanza's bones buried in the graveyard of Trifels Castle. She's the one who has given us the information. We . . . we owe it to her."

Melchior nodded. "A reasonable suggestion, I think. After all, we don't want an avenging ghost after us. Not that I really believe in such things, but you never know. Besides, Constanza was a true descendant of the house of Hohenstaufen. What do you say, Scharfeneck?"

"Very well." Friedrich cast his eyes up. "We'll bury her bones. But she'll have to do without a sermon. We're certainly not letting any priest in on the secret." He grabbed Agnes by her dress and pulled her close to him. "Now, talk. Where is that damned lance?"

Agnes did not speak for a while; her eyes fixed on the distance. Not until Friedrich had let go of her again did she slowly nod.

"So be it," she said at last. "I will tell you the place. So that there will be peace at last. Peace for Constanza, and peace for me."

As Melchior, Friedrich, and Mathis sat on some of the ruinous rocks, and the three landsknechts guarded the entrance, Agnes described the walled-up chamber and the secret it contained. She spoke softly of the Latin inscription in the dungeon, the faded paintings of the kings and emperors—and the ancient story that the pictures told.

"At the time, presumably the Habsburgs erased the knowledge of that underground chamber from all written records," she said thoughtfully. "No one was ever to know about Constanza's grave. It was common knowledge that the imperial insignia were kept here at Trifels for almost two hundred years, but until today no one was aware of the existence of that room. No one apart from Constanza's descendants, who passed on the knowledge from generation to generation of their family." She hesitated. "I suppose my mother told me about it all those years ago, but I was too young to remember. The story didn't come back to me until I was down there in the dungeon."

"That accounts for your fainting fits," Mathis said. "Do you remember, you were already suffering from them when you visited me in the dungeon a year ago?"

Agnes nodded. "And that was probably where the voice came from —the voice that I thought I heard as a child. I believed the castle was speaking to me, but it could have been a memory of my mother's stories. Although the strange thing is that—"

"Never mind all that nonsense," Friedrich interrupted. "We want to know where the lance is. That's all that interests us."

For a moment, Agnes closed her eyes. She was so tired, so inexpressibly tired. But it would not be much longer until this nightmare would come to an end.

And I will go home to my mother. Home to my foster father. Home to Constanza.

"Shepherd Jockel put me on the right track," she finally said. "He was convinced that the Holy Lance was hidden somewhere here at Trifels. He saw the drawing of the towers down in the chamber with the kings and emperors, and he immediately thought of a castle. I expect he was thinking that Trifels had two towers at some time in the past, but it never had more than one. And in addition, Johann and Constanza must have hidden the lance somewhere when they were escaping, so it can't have been in this castle."

"I can follow you so far," said Melchior, who had been listening all this time with interest. "But what does the drawing show, then?"

Agnes smiled faintly, then knelt down and drew, in the dust, the exact outline of the drawing that she had seen down in the crypt.

"It's not a castle," she explained. "Do you see the cupola with the pointed roof in the middle of it? It's a large church, or rather a cathedral. Even down there I had an idea of what cathedral it was. But the building that I immediately thought of has four towers and two cupolas. Like Jockel, however, I made the mistake of forgetting that

Constanza drew that sketch when she was at the end of her strength, and in almost absolute darkness. The cathedral is shown from directly in front. That's why there is not more of it to be seen." Agnes looked expectantly at the others. "I for one know of only a single cathedral which looks like that from the front. I visited it with my father only last year."

"Speyer Cathedral." Mathis said softly, and stared in astonishment at the drawing on the floor. "Of course. We passed it only a few days ago. It really does look exactly like that from the front. And also, the knight Johann was caught by his pursuers in Speyer. It's perfectly possible for him to have hidden the lance in the cathedral first. But that saying—"

"The place where enmity is no more," Agnes said. "At first I thought it simply meant the cathedral, as a place of peace. But then I remembered all the kings and emperors depicted in the walled-up chamber here below Trifels. The Salians, the Guelphs, the Staufers, and the Habsburgs. Many were sworn enemies, each wanting the crown for his own family, his dynasty. But there's only one place where all that enmity is no more." She paused before going on. "And that place is in the middle of Speyer Cathedral."

For a moment there was profound silence, while what Agnes had just said echoed through the ruined Knights' House. It was Melchior von Tanningen who finally turned to the others, laughing.

"The imperial vault." The minstrel enthusiastically clapped his hands, a strange gesture here among all the ruins and the dead men. "Magnificent! There really couldn't have been a better hiding place. The place where enmity is no more. Why didn't I think of that myself?"

Agnes nodded. "When Johann and Constanza separated during their flight, the Guelph must have told his wife what he meant to do with the lance. At that time, the imperial vault in Speyer Cathedral was already famous far beyond the borders of the Palatinate."

"The imperial vault?" The count looked at Melchior and Agnes, irritated. "I don't understand . . ."

"Well, the tombs of eight German kings and emperors stand in Speyer Cathedral," Agnes explained. "There are Salians among them, as well as Staufers and Habsburgs. For instance, Philipp, Barbarossa's son, and Emperor Rudolf von Habsburg."

"As well as their wives, and several bishops," Melchior added. "Once they were enemies, now they lie peacefully side by side. I think there are about twenty tombs in all. This means a great deal of dirty work." He glanced at the three landsknechts, and signed to them to come closer.

"Young Master Wielenbach will accompany us on our journey," Melchior said amiably. "Make sure he doesn't get any stupid ideas." Smiling, he turned to Mathis. "We have traveled a long way together, but everything comes to an end. I'm glad that you are still willing to help us, all the same. As I see it, there'll be some digging to be done at Speyer."

"Of his own grave, for instance," retorted the count, turning and marching down the steps to the castle courtyard.

It was a strange company of mourners that stood in the graveyard of Trifels Castle about three hours later, to see Constanza's bones consigned to the earth.

Agnes stood with Mathis, the count, and Melchior von Tanningen by a hollow that had been hastily dug, with a small, iron-bound chest lying in it. Philipp von Erfenstein's grave, with a plain little tombstone, lay right beside. A few landsknechts, ordered to guard the two prisoners, lounged about by the wall of the graveyard. The soot-blackened walls of the castle rose in the background, breached in many places. The staterooms looked like a giant's broken tooth. Agnes could hardly picture this ruin as her old home anymore.

As if in a trance, she stared at the chest that had once held her books. She had had it brought from her former bedchamber. The famous book on falconry, like most of the library, had been destroyed when the peasants attacked. Now the chest served as a coffin for the bleached bones of her ancestress. Two landsknechts had brought up Constanza's remains from the underground chamber. Soon after they had left the hall, with its pictures of the emperors, there had been rumbling and shaking, and the passage had finally filled up with rubble. Agnes smiled sadly. Now Barbarossa and the rest of the German kings and emperors could at least sleep in peace under Trifels Castle.

The hidden chamber was sealed forever, along with the mystery that it contained.

"*In nomine Patris et Filii et Spiritus Sancti. Amen.*"

Murmuring the valedictory prayer for Constanza, Agnes sprinkled a handful of earth on the chest. Beside her, Mathis picked up a shovel and slowly began filling in the grave. The young smith visibly bore the marks of the last hours: he limped, his face was badly bruised, and congealed blood still clung to the corners of his mouth. And yet there was an aura of peace and fearlessness about him that Agnes admired. He seemed to have resigned himself to his fate.

And so have I, she thought. *We will go to Speyer and die there together. Like Johann and Constanza so long ago.*

She knelt down, made the sign of the cross, and passed her hand one last time over the fresh grave mound.

Rest in peace, Constanza. I'll be following you very soon.

"Right, there we are," the count said abruptly. Clapping his hands, he signed to the landsknechts by the graveyard wall. "Tie these two to their saddles, and then let's be off as fast as we can. The sooner we are back, the better."

The men seized Agnes and Mathis and dragged them over to a group of horses standing in the lower bailey. In passing, Agnes looked up at the distorted bodies of the peasants still hanging from the battlements. Many of them had been wounded by the heavy gunfire first, or cut down by the landsknechts' swords. Their shirts were torn and drenched with blood. They swung back and forth in the mild summer wind, while the first crows and ravens came down to settle on them.

"So perish all who rebel against authority," Friedrich announced to his men. "May the peasants never again venture to raise their hands against their rightful lords and masters. Let them hang there until their bones fall to the earth."

He swung himself up on his fine steed, while Agnes and Mathis were tied to a couple of decrepit nags. Three men were going to travel to Speyer with them, the three who had already reported to the Knights' House, as well as Melchior von Tanningen and the count. The rest of the soldiers were staying at the castle until Friedrich returned. Clearly the count did not want too many of them knowing where the relic was hidden. But Agnes was under no illusions. Melchior von Tanningen on his own would probably have been enough to guard and eventually kill her and the injured Mathis.

The little group moved away and soon left the ruined walls of Trifels behind. Their path went over the trampled fields and into the forest until they met the river Queich below the Sonnenberg and followed its course eastward. The few other travelers whom they met during the next few hours looked aside in alarm. People knew that a company including three heavily armed landsknechts and two bound prisoners could bode no good.

At first they had ridden in silence most of the time, the count and Melchior von Tanningen at their head, the soldiers bringing up the rear. But now the minstrel fell back until he was level with Agnes and Mathis.

"Will you permit me to speak to you?" he asked, turning to the castellan's daughter.

Agnes shrugged. By now her hatred for the deceiver had turned to cold contempt. "I am your prisoner, Tanningen," she said coolly. "You can do as you like with me, so speak, but don't expect me to listen."

Melchior nodded and rode on in silence. He had left his lute behind at the castle, and instead of colorful clothing he now wore black hose and a black velvet doublet, his sword with its filigree basket hilt was in a leather sheath beside his saddle. Agnes noticed how sinewy and muscular Melchior really was; the loose clothing he often wore had concealed it well.

"Even if you don't listen to me, I will speak, all the same," Melchior began again. "Believe me, none of this has turned out as I intended. I didn't want the commission. In the past, yes, such work was an adventure, and I had no scruples. But I have changed, truly." He sighed. "I know it will not interest you, but my family really does have a small castle in Franconia. We are deep in debt, just as your father was. I was offered a choice: leave the castle or accept this last commission."

Agnes smiled mockingly. "I can hardly hold back my tears of sympathy."

"Spare me your sarcasm." Melchior looked pleadingly at her. "Agnes, on my honor, I think highly of you. When I took on the task of tracking down a woman descended from the Staufers, I thought she would be some insipid, uneducated tradesman's daughter, or a stupid peasant girl. It was most unfortunate that the peasant girl turned out to be a beautiful and intelligent lady of the nobility."

"Never mind the excuses," replied Agnes. "Whether she was a peasant girl or a lady, you were hired to murder an innocent human being."

"I know this will be hard to understand, but sometimes the life of a single person stands in the way of the good of the whole empire. Which weighs more heavily in the balance." Melchior looked into the distance, where two birds of prey circled in the sky above the fields. Finally he turned back to Agnes. "I told you that the young, inexperienced Charles V is not too steady in the saddle as emperor yet, and there are not a few German princes who would like to be rid of him. In that, at least, I told you no lies. Can you imagine what would have happened if King Francis had in fact laid hands on you, along with the ring and the deed?"

"I don't want to imagine it."

"There would have been a great war," Melchior went on, undeterred. "As soon as he was released from captivity, King Francis would have made you his wife. With a queen of the house of Hohenstaufen at his side, he could probably have brought some of the German princes over to him, particularly if he had also been in possession of the Holy Lance. The Germans are avid for symbols, and they love their Staufers, who are considered the last great rulers of the empire."

"Thank you, Tanningen, I'm sure I'll die in a happier frame of mind now."

Mathis, who up to this point had been riding beside them in silence, glanced disparagingly at the supposed minstrel. "I, too, have always been anxious to give my life for an emperor who lets his subjects live in want and famine," he remarked. Then he spat scornfully in front of Melchior.

Melchior von Tanningen sighed again. Then he looked ahead to where Friedrich von Löwenstein-Scharfeneck was riding.

"Master Wielenbach, believe me, if it were up to me, then you at least would go free," he whispered, turning to Mathis. "I like you. Why do you think I helped you to escape from Geyer's castle when it was under siege? Why did I tend you when you lay in bed so sick with fever?"

"Probably because you thought I might yet be useful to you," Mathis replied bitterly.

The minstrel smiled. "Well, I'll admit that my reasons were not entirely selfless. But I am not pretending when I say I like you." He looked forward with a movement of his head. "Unfortunately, I must go along with that deranged murderer ahead of us." He shook his head. "You have an extraordinarily unpleasant husband there, noble lady. And all those stories of treasure. He's obsessed by the idea."

"I think you two go very well together," replied Agnes. "A lunatic and an assassin without a shred of conscience. When I'm gone, and that will be soon, the pair of you are welcome to marry. You have my blessing."

She kicked her horse in the side to make it break into a faster trot. Mathis followed her, watched by the landsknechts, who stuck close to them.

"Why talk like that, Agnes?" he said quietly. "You must never give up, never."

"Oh, and what else am I to do? Hope that my husband may forgive you and me and wish us well?"

Mathis lowered his voice to such a whisper that she could barely hear it. "Up in the Knights' House this morning, I picked up a dagger that one of the dead peasants had with him. I have it in my boot. These idiotic landsknechts didn't notice when they searched me. They think I'm limping." He smiled surreptitiously. Out of the corner of his eye, he watched the three soldiers. "Once we reach Speyer, I'll find a moment when I can cut the ropes binding us, and we'll try to get away together. They'd soon lose sight of us among all the people in the city."

Agnes felt her heart thudding. A tiny glimmer of hope showed on the horizon, but it was too small to give her any real confidence. "And suppose they catch us all the same?" she faltered.

Mathis looked at her grimly. "Then I'll cut the count's throat with my dagger. I don't intend to give your husband the pleasure of watching me die."

He stared darkly at the trees and thickets that stood like green ramparts to the right and left of the path.

· 24 ·

Speyer, 27 June, Anno Domini 1525

SPEYER CAME INTO SIGHT on the evening of the second day, after they had spent the previous night in a rundown village tavern,
where Mathis heard that the peasants' war in the Palatinate was over
at last. Thousands of rebels had been cut down, stabbed, or burned
by the elector's troops in the distant city of Pfedderheim.

The struggle also seemed to be approaching its end for Mathis and
Agnes. During the journey at least one of the landsknechts had been
with them all the time, preventing any possibility of flight.

When they finally reached Speyer, just after darkness fell, the city
gates were already closed. However, a brusque command from the
count was enough to get them opened again. The watchmen eyed the
strange group suspiciously but did not venture to ask questions.

Their way took them first to the bishop's palace, on the left of the
cathedral. While the count, his prisoners, and the landsknechts waited
outside the magnificent building, Melchior von Tanningen went to
the episcopal scriptorium. After a while he returned, whistling cheerfully.

"The emperor's seal still means something in Speyer," he said, showing a limp purse. "Well, the seal and a little hush money. I told the dean of the cathedral that we had come on behalf of Emperor Charles to check that the tomb of his forebear Rudolf von Habsburg was intact. He swallowed the story. However, we ought to complete our search by dawn, before the first of the faithful arrive for early mass, or there could be inconvenient questions."

"If we haven't found anything by then, it's my wife who'll be asked some inconvenient questions," the count snarled. He turned his horse, and they trotted together to the empty square outside the cathedral, where they finally dismounted beside the well, the large stone bowl known as the cathedral font. They entrusted the horses to the care of an alarmed night watchman in return for a few coins.

Inwardly, Mathis cursed their luck. He had been hoping to spend another night at some inn in Speyer, where he and Agnes might have found a chance to escape. But now it looked as if they had only a few hours left.

The sun had long since set, and the broad market street was quiet and empty. Now and then he heard drunken tipplers singing in the distance. Light showed in only a few of the windows of the houses nearby. Melchior brought out the copper key that the dean had lent him, went over to the cathedral, and unlocked the porch of the great west door. Before he went in, Mathis looked up at the towers, now wreathed in mist. He wondered whether this would be the last time he ever saw the sky. Then the door slammed shut, and Melchior bolted it behind them.

"Trust me," Mathis whispered to Agnes as he passed. He wanted to reassure her, but his voice shook. "If those bastards take their eyes off us for just a moment, I'll stab the nearest one, and we'll find somewhere in the cathedral to hide. There are so many niches and altars here, they'll be looking for us until dawn."

He looked cautiously around the nave, which smelled strongly of incense. With all its columns, it resembled a dark forest. Only a little moonlight fell through the tall windows. Both aisles contained altars

with statues of martyrs, contorted in agony, standing on them, looking almost alive in the murky atmosphere. Mathis shivered. In spite
of the warm summer night it felt as cold as a grave here.

And it is a grave, he thought gloomily. *It will soon be my grave, and
the grave of Agnes too. But by God, we'll not be the only ones who fail to leave
the building alive.*

"Mathis, it's madness," replied Agnes quietly. "There are five of
them, have you forgotten?"

"Never mind that. I'd sooner—"

"Hey, no whispering," one of the landsknechts growled, pushing
Mathis so that he stumbled forward. It was the mercenary with the
scar on his face. Mathis knew now that his name was Roland, and he
was the count's right-hand man. He was broadly built and wore
shabby leather armor. His small eyes, sunk deep into their sockets,
wandered over Agnes as if he were caressing her. The two other
landsknechts, Hans and Marten by name, were sinewy young men,
and they, too, stared at her. Mathis felt sick to his stomach.

Several candles flickered on one of the side altars, casting long
shadows that twitched over the walls like gigantic hands. Melchior lit
a torch at one of them, and then they went forward together to the
apse, where a cube-shaped monument as tall as a man stood in front
of the choir screen.

Mathis blinked as he tried to see in the darkness. The monument
was covered by a purple canopy and seemed to be made entirely of
marble. When Melchior strode forward, gilded inscriptions on the
front of it shone in the light of the torch.

"The imperial vault!" the minstrel whispered in awe. "Do you feel
the breath of history? Many Christians think this place is the spiritual
center of Europe, there are so many great men and women buried
here." He leaned forward and began reading aloud in a quiet voice.
"King Konrad II and his wife, Gisela, of Swabia; Henry III; Henry
IV; Philipp of Swabia, of the house of Hohenstaufen; Rudolf von
Habsburg . . ." He stopped suddenly. "Oh, and there's a bishop here,
too, called Konrad of Scharfenberg. Any relation of yours?"

"A cousin three times removed," Friedrich replied. "He actually lived in Scharfenberg Castle. I hope I can avoid desecrating the grave of one of my ancestors. Especially as I hardly think the Holy Lance would be in *his* sarcophagus. Old Konrad wasn't important enough for that." He turned to Agnes. "So where is the lance now, then?"

"I don't know exactly," she replied. Her hands were still bound, and she wearily sat down beside a column. "This is the place where enmity is no more. But precisely where Johann hid the lance I can't say."

"Then I'm afraid we'll just have to search for it." The count snapped his fingers, and tall Marten let a sack full of digging tools slide to the floor. "We'll start with the tombs at the top and slowly work our way down to the lower levels. Try to do it so that we can cover up the mess later. I don't want to have the whole of the Christian Occident cursing me for defiling the vault."

The landsknechts climbed to the top of the tall monument. Then they took some of the picks and shovels that they had brought with them and began cautiously levering out the tombs. Melchior von Tanningen undid Mathis's bonds and put a spade into his hand.

"If I may make so bold, Master Wielenbach?" The minstrel pointed to one of the tombstones. "How would you like to open the tomb of Empress Beatrix of Burgundy? It must surely be an edifying moment to set eyes on the bones of Barbarossa's wife, the mother of Henry VI."

"If it's so edifying, get your own hands dirty, Tanningen," snapped Mathis. "You could always lie down in her tomb yourself."

"Interesting that you say that. Friedrich was suggesting something along those lines for you yesterday." Melchior's face was impassive. "I think there must be worse places to find one's eternal rest." He made an encouraging gesture, and Mathis climbed the monument and silently set to work.

Opening the tomb was not as difficult as he had expected. Mathis worked the spade into the narrow crack at the top, broke away the mortar, and levered the stone sarcophagus out. The heavy stone slab slipped off and fell to the plinth, crashing as it hit the floor. A fine crack appeared on its surface.

"For heaven's sake, be careful," Melchior warned him. "We don't want to destroy the tombs. What will the Bishop of Speyer say if he hears that we've been desecrating the bodies of the noblest figures in the empire?"

"Even if the bishop doesn't hear of it, God will never forgive you," Mathis said.

Melchior nodded, troubled. "You are right. We can only hope that salvaging the holiest of all relics means more to Him than a few brittle bones and one or two lives."

"Curse it, Melchior, I hate you," Mathis burst out, throwing the spade down on the floor of the church. "I never ought to have trusted you. I—"

Roland, beside him, struck him such a violent blow on the back that he fell forward, gasping. "Do your work and hold your tongue," the mercenary said. "Or we'll bury you here alive. You've heard what they're planning to do with you."

Mathis scrambled up, casting Melchior a black look. The minstrel looked back at him penetratingly.

"By all the saints, Mathis, I didn't want it to turn out this way," he whispered, looking cautiously at the other men. "Believe me, if there was any other way out, I'd take it. But the fate of the empire . . ."

"Being doomed to die is bad enough," Mathis said. "At least spare me your pitiful excuses."

He turned away and looked into the sarcophagus that he had just opened. A musty odor rose from it. Before him lay a skeleton in the rags of once magnificent clothing. Dark, dried scraps of flesh clung to the skull, which was adorned with a plain copper circlet for burial.

"Beatrix must have been a great beauty once," sighed Melchior, who had now climbed up on top of the monument with the count and was looking pensively at the remains. His scruples seemed to have died down. "A shame that we are only able to see her in such a condition."

Mathis indicated the empress's bony arms. "She's holding something."

"Yes, indeed, there's something there," Friedrich von Löwenstein-Scharfeneck excitedly leaned forward and snatched a moldering wooden casket from the desiccated figure's hands. "The Holy Lance. We've really found it. It—"

The casket crumbled in his hands. Tiny bones and a small skull fell clattering to the floor.

"Curse it, what's that?" the count asked.

"I'm afraid we ought to have read the funerary inscription more closely," Melchior murmured, staring with narrowed eyes at a small lead plate with writing engraved on it at the front of the sarcophagus. "Her newborn daughter was buried with Beatrix. The baby's name was Agnes. What a charming coincidence, don't you think?"

He glanced at Agnes. She was still crouching on one of the lower steps up to the vault, leaning against a column. She had closed her eyes as if she were asleep.

When she did not answer, Melchior turned to the three landsknechts. "What do the other tombs look like? Have you found anything that could be taken for a lance, or any clue to finding it?"

By now the men had also opened the other sarcophagi on the upper level of the monument. All three contained skeletons, two of which began crumbling to dust a few minutes after the air reached them. One corpse, however, was still so well preserved that Mathis felt as if the dead man were following the desecration of his body with small, evil eyes. According to the inscription, this must be no less than the great Habsburg emperor Rudolf.

The mercenary leader, Roland, shook his head, exhausted, and leaned on his shovel. "We've found nothing. A few grave gifts. Daggers, rings, brooches and so forth. We even found a small, rusty imperial orb. But nothing like a lance."

"It's very small, don't forget," said Melchior. "It's only the point of the weapon, no longer than a man's forearm."

"You heard what my men said," the count told him. "The lance isn't here. And time is running out for us." He turned angrily to Agnes. "You were only trying to fool us. Admit it. Not that that will do you any good now."

"I truly thought the lance was in this place," Agnes said, raising her voice at last. She rubbed her arms as she shivered. The expression in her eyes was empty, as though she were looking at something far away. "It could be in a sarcophagus lower down."

"Where exactly, countess?" Melchior insisted. "We can't pull the whole monument to pieces. We don't have time for that."

"Why would I help you any farther?" whispered Agnes. "I must die anyway."

"But you can choose how," replied the count. "And think of your lover here. You don't want my men burying him alive in one of these coffins, do you?"

Agnes remained obdurately silent. Friedrich was about to go on when Mathis suddenly laughed aloud. He threw his spade away and shook his head, between desperation and amusement. The answer to the puzzle had struck him like a flash of lightning, at the very moment when Friedrich was threatening to bury him in one of the coffins. Now he stared, bewildered, at the work of destruction wreaked among the tombs in front of him.

We could have spared ourselves all this work, he thought. *Why did none of the others think of it? They are all obviously obsessed by the idea of this lance.*

"What in the devil's name is so funny?" snapped Friedrich. "Out with it, fellow. Before I stuff your mouth with a bone to close it."

"You don't frighten me, Scharfeneck," Mathis folded his arms defiantly. "Did you really expect to find the lance in a sarcophagus here? How stupid are you all?"

Melchior von Tanningen frowned. "What do you mean? Explain yourself, Master Wielenbach."

"Well, if I remember correctly, Johann of Brunswick was in flight from his pursuers when he was finally brought to bay in Speyer

Cathedral," Mathis began, with quiet satisfaction. "Even if he did have the lance with him, do you really suppose he'd have had the time to open a sarcophagus at his leisure and hide it there? Just how was he going to do that, if not by calling on the angels to help him?"

For a while all was so still that they could hear nothing but the wind rattling the cathedral windows. Finally, Friedrich von Löwenstein-Scharfeneck angrily kicked the monument. "Damn it, the fellow is right. We're on the wrong trail. If the lance is in the cathedral, then it must be someplace where it could be hidden quickly. But where?"

He let his eyes wander through the huge building and then stared furiously at Agnes.

"Do you know what I think?" he hissed. "You've been lying to us all along. The lance isn't in the vault, it's probably not even in the cathedral. You said all that just to prolong your wretched life a little." He took a step toward her. "But there'll be no more of that."

"The lance is in the cathedral," Agnes insisted. "I simply know it is. I felt it the last time I was here. It must be in this place, there's no doubt of that. It was like it called out to me."

Friedrich looked mockingly at her. "You felt it . . . well, well. Then I recommend you *feel* something else, and quickly." There was an unpleasant grin on his face, and the spark of insanity was back in his eyes. "You heard what I said just now. Unless you have a useful idea, Mathis will soon be keeping the skeleton of Emperor Rudolf company. Alive, or at least until the air in the stone sarcophagus runs out."

In the ensuing silence, Mathis thought he could hear the thudding of his own heart. Rigid with shock, he looked at the remnants of flesh on the face of the mummified Habsburg emperor. Then he straightened his back.

Never. I'll take some of these men to the grave with me first.

"I'm not going to wait much longer." The count grated his teeth. "Where is the lance, Agnes? Tell me, or your lover disappears into eternal darkness. One . . . two . . ."

The dagger pressed against Mathis's heel in the shaft of his boot. Gritting his teeth, he slowly bent down to reach for it.

It was time to die with his head held aloft in pride.

Agnes was paralyzed by horror. She gazed helplessly around the huge cathedral, hoping to find some clue to Johann's hiding place for the lance. Had she been mistaken after all?

But the mysterious phrase in the chamber at Trifels was not the only thing to have put her on that trail. Agnes had remembered going to Speyer with her father and entering the cathedral. She had thought then that someone was calling to her. At the time, she had supposed that someone had followed her into the building, but she was now firmly convinced that she had heard the call of her ancestors entombed here. Just as she had heard Constanza's voice in that underground hall three days ago. Were her forebears trying to tell her something? Was that possible?

The place where enmity is no more . . .

"And three. My patience is exhausted," said Friedrich von Löwenstein-Scharfeneck, bringing her back from her thoughts. The count glanced with malice at Mathis, stooping as he knelt by the monument.

"What do you think, Tanningen?" inquired Friedrich. "How long will that fellow last in the coffin? Two days? Three? Or will the air run out before that? I doubt whether anyone will hear him screaming under that heavy stone slab."

"If you want the lady to think of something, you'd better stop talking like that," Melchior retorted. "How do you expect the poor girl to concentrate?"

"I don't care. All I know is that I'm tired of this game. Either she tells us now where the lance is, or we end this farce in my own way."

Closing her eyes, Agnes tried to blot out everything around her. Maybe then it would be possible to conjure up the voice that she had heard here before. Yet whatever it had been, it did not return. It could be her fear, or simply the presence of the others, but she sensed nothing within her. Only a void filling with panic at ever-increasing speed. Agnes fervently hoped to remember something, anything that her mother had told her back in the past. Scraps of sound flared up in her mind like lightning flashes.

Slip in here under the blanket and listen to me . . . Long, long ago, my child, your ancestors had to run away . . . Johann of Brunswick had a lance with him, a mighty weapon that could defeat all the evil in this world . . . Constanza stayed in Annweiler with her child, and Johann told her he would take that lance to the place where enmity is no more . . .

Where enmity is no more . . . enmity is no more . . . enmity . . .

Agnes blinked and saw Mathis reaching for his boot. She knew at once what he intended to do. Sadly, but at the same time with determination, he looked at her, his eyes dark and gleaming with moisture, like deep wells reflecting torchlight.

Deep, dark wells . . . the place where enmity is no more . . .

At the same moment an image came into her mind, an image that had been buried in some corner of her memory and only now came into view again.

The cathedral font . . .

"I know it!" she cried out. It sounded like a cry of pain. "I know it! I know what those strange words mean." Mathis, astonished, straightened up. Evidently he had decided to wait before mounting his last attack. Friedrich and Melchior were also eyeing her curiously.

"You mean you know where the Holy Lance is?" Melchior asked hopefully.

Agnes shook her head. Her rib cage felt as if she had been running a long, fast race. "Not that, but at least I know that the cathedral is the right place. We were on the wrong track, yet it was also the right one. The place where enmity is no more." She let out a clear, high laugh. "It's not the imperial vault, it's the sanctuary of the entire cathedral."

"The . . . sanctuary of the cathedral?" Friedrich frowned.

"Well, why did Johann come to Speyer at that time?" Agnes swiftly went on. "He could have hidden the lance somewhere else. Did he just want to hide it where Constanza's ancestors were entombed?" Agnes shook her head. "That was something that I didn't understand properly at the time. And Mathis was right. Johann wouldn't have had time to hide the lance in one of the tombs. Only now do I realize why Constanza's husband really wanted to come to the cathedral."

"And why was that?" asked Melchior.

Agnes took a deep breath. "At that time the Bishop of Speyer was a powerful man, almost as powerful as an elector. I read about that in the library at Trifels, and Father Tristan told me about it as well. The bishop had his own sphere of jurisdiction. Those who sought sanctuary with him were safe even from the emperor's henchmen."

"The sanctuary of the cathedral," Melchior groaned. "Of course. As far as I know, the principle still holds good. The border is out in the square in front of the cathedral."

Agnes smiled. "To be exact, at the place where we left our horses. Those who go beyond the cathedral font cannot be brought before any secular court. They are entirely in the hands of the bishop. I was thinking of that when I was here a year ago. Only not in connection with Johann, but for Mathis, who could have asked for sanctuary here as a wanted man." She nodded firmly. "Johann did exactly that, he asked for asylum in the cathedral. This is the place where enmity is no more. He wanted to give the Holy Lance into the bishop's care. As a prince of the church, the bishop would certainly have been interested in acquiring such a precious relic. Johann probably tried to strike a bargain: the Holy Lance in exchange for his life and the lives of his wife and child. And presumably that was why they had taken the lance from Trifels with them—as a pledge."

"But something went horribly wrong," murmured Melchior. "Or Johann would not have been killed in Speyer."

"I suspect that the Habsburgs simply ignored the sanctuary of the cathedral. Or the bishop was bribed by the emperor to hand Johann over. We'll never know." Agnes sighed. "But at least we now know that we need to search a considerably larger area than we thought.

The sanctuary covers the whole cathedral, and the other buildings. The bishop's palace, the deanery, the cloisters, the outside chapels . . . Johann could have hidden the lance anywhere."

"And suppose this Johann of yours didn't hide it at all, but the Habsburgs took it from him?" Melchior persisted.

Agnes shook her head. "After he was dead, the Habsburgs had Constanza tortured for days. They wouldn't have done that if they had found the lance. No, it is somewhere here."

"Forget it, Agnes," Friedrich von Löwenstein-Scharfeneck laughed contemptuously. "This is only another ruse to delay our search. Don't you see?" He turned to Melchior. "She wants us to go on searching as long as possible, until morning comes and she can throw herself into the arms of some priest. You're not falling for this story of hers, are you?"

"It sounds not wholly implausible." Melchior tugged the point of his beard. "The sanctuary of the church is still a popular method of escaping secular justice. It could be true that Johann asked the Bishop of Speyer for asylum. The bishop wielded great influence in the empire. So why not?" He shrugged. "And I don't have a better idea at the moment. In God's name let's search the cathedral and its surroundings, then." He raised a finger in admonition. "But not until dawn, only until four in the morning. If we have found nothing by then, I'll declare our venture over, and you, Scharfeneck . . ." He paused, casting a sad, surreptitious glance at Agnes. "You can finally take your wife."

Friedrich von Löwenstein-Scharfeneck nodded. "Until the hour of four, then. But that will definitely be the end." He looked expectantly at his wife. "Well, where do we begin?"

Once again Agnes closed her eyes and tried to concentrate. Now that she knew she was on the right track, it was easier. She imagined Johann of Brunswick as she had so often seen him in her dreams. Only as an outline at first, then more and more distinctly, a young man emerged from the mists of her memory. He wore an old hauberk and a torn cloak, riding through the night and torrential rain, until at last he reached the walls of a city.

The city of Speyer.

◆ ◆ ◆

The dark walls tower up, wind and rain lash the willows, making their foliage look like the wet hair of giants. Johann knows the city; he has often been here as an envoy from Trifels. So he also knows the small hidden gate north of the harbor, for he has already slipped in through it once before. He hastily drops the reins of his horse, gives the animal a farewell pat, and then wades through reeds and marshy water meadows along the wall, always keeping out of sight of the guards. Sometimes he sinks to his waist in the mire, the sheath of his sword is muddy, his hauberk several times threatens to drag him down. In both hands, Johann holds aloft an object wrapped in a plain gray cloth. Everything else may get wet and dirty, but not the contents of that cloth.

The Holy Lance.

Johann hastily folds back the cloth to check yet again that the lance has come to no harm. It is intact, although the shaft has been missing for many centuries, and only the upper part has been preserved. The head of the lance has been forced apart at some time, so that there is a narrow gap between it and the remains of the shaft, closed again later with silver wire and a silver sleeve.

There is a nail from the cross of Christ in the point of the lance.

Johann knows that he has stolen the most important relic in Christendom. He murmurs a prayer that is carried away on the wind like dead leaves, asking God to forgive him someday for his sacrilege. The young knight has not acted out of greed or avarice, but solely to protect his family. He wants to exchange the lance for life and freedom, for the lives of his wife and his child. Johann wraps up the lance again and nods grimly, while the wind tugs at his wet hair. In a few minutes' time he will have reached the place that offers him sanctuary.

The place where enmity is no more.

At last the small porch, overgrown with creepers and ivy, appears before him. He quietly gives the password, told to him by friends the day before. The door squeals open, and a burly guard admits him silently. On this side of the wall, the storm does not seem to be quite so strong. Johann looks cautiously around. It is dark night. A small church is hunched against the city wall like a scared dog. There is not a human soul in sight in the muddy streets. All the same, he remains watchful. He guesses that his enemies know what is going on. Where would he go if not to Speyer, the bishop's own city? They are sure to be lying in wait for him here, but where?

Bending low, Johann steals along the narrow, musty alleys of the city, where the walls of the houses on opposite sides of the street are sometimes only a little way apart. He avoids the large squares and keeps stopping to listen. He hears the mew of a cat, the shrill laughter of a whore, the muted chime of the cathedral bells. Johann's heart beats wildly. Only a short way to go, and he will be safe. Can it be as easy as that? Is the protecting hand of God himself above him?

At last he sees the empty cathedral square, with its well. A chain is stretched right across the square, on both sides of the cathedral font. Beyond it lies the sanctuary of the cathedral, beyond it he will be safe, in the care of the bishop of Speyer.

Johann says a last quiet prayer, he kisses the Holy Lance in its cloth wrapping, then he runs. The rain lashes his face, the storm roars like a wild animal. One last leap, and he is on the other side of the chain. Johann can hardly believe his good fortune. All he has to do now is rouse the watchman, claim sanctuary, and when the bishop arrives in the morning . . .

He stops short when he sees three mounted men near a side chapel of the cathedral. A fourth man is just leaving the bishop's palace with a priest, and he hurries toward the other three. The priest, in red vestments, stands on the steps to give them his blessing with the sign of the cross and then hurries back through the wind and rain to the palace. Behind Johann, the chain rattles in the wind. Almost at the same time, the four strangers turn to him, and at that moment the knight knows that he has been betrayed.

Johann winces. The men wear dark cloaks, but in the light of a torch he can see the red and white of the coat of arms they wear on their uniforms.

Agents of the Habsburgs, hired assassins sent to kill him.

Johann immediately turns and runs. He is a good swordsman, but there are four of them and they will not fight fair. They are cowardly bloodhounds, not knights, sent out for the sole purpose of eliminating him and taking possession of the Holy Lance. Johann knows that his own life is forfeit, but now he will at least ensure that no Habsburg ever sits rightfully on the imperial throne again.

He will hide the Holy Lance somewhere. He will leave it in the hands of God.

Breathing heavily, he reaches the cathedral, runs in, and hastily looks around. Dark columns, the monument to the dead emperors at the front, beyond the choir screen, altars lying in shadow to the right and the left . . . where can he hide the lance? In only a few moments' time his executioners will be in the cathedral.

Where?

Leaning back against a column, he scans the nave again.

Where?

When he has found the hiding place at last, and left the lance in it, the knight breathes deeply. Then he climbs up on the monument of the imperial vault and draws his long sword. In his mud-spattered shoes, he stands on the tombstone of the man whose family has besmirched the honor of the house of Hohenstaufen forever. Now at least Johann's blood will mark the tomb of Rudolf von Habsburg.

"Constanza," Johann whispers. "For you and for our child."

He kisses his sword and waits for his enemies to attack.

◆ ◆ ◆

Agnes opened her eyes and stared at the monument in front of her. For a moment she thought she still saw Johann standing up there, a silent prayer on his lips, his sword raised, ready to fight. But the picture quickly faded, and instead she saw the three landsknechts, who had begun pushing the stone lid back on top of the sarcophagus. Friedrich, Melchior, and Mathis stood at the foot of the monument with their eyes fixed on her. She felt dizzy and had to lean on the column behind her.

"Well?" Friedrich asked. "Where's the lance? Talk, woman."

"He was here," Agnes gasped. "Johann was here in the cathedral. I saw him."

Melchior, fascinated, pressed his hands together, an expression of childlike astonishment on his face. "Did you see the whites of her eyes?" he murmured. "The countess saw a vision. Like a martyr, like the great Hildegard of Bingen. What a song this adventure would make. A shame that I'll never be able to tell the tale."

"Mere hocus-pocus," the count snapped. "All I want to know is whether she's thought of a possible hiding place. Unlike you, I haven't the slightest wish to spend the next few hours digging up half the city. The sanctuary of the cathedral runs all the way to the eastern city wall."

"He hid the lance here, I'm sure of it," Agnes insisted. "It must be someplace near the monument."

"There's nothing near the monument but pews and columns," retorted Friedrich. "No one can hide anything there. At least, not for long."

Mathis snorted, and looked angrily at the two men beside him. "If you want Agnes to find this lance for you, at least cut her bonds. We can't run away from you anyway."

Melchior took out his dagger and cut Agnes free. She rubbed her hands to get the blood running through them again.

"Thank you," she said quietly, while the minstrel continued to look at her as if she were a ghost.

"A martyr," he repeated monotonously. "A genuine martyr." Something seemed to be working powerfully within him.

Agnes leaned against the column and felt the cold of the stone creeping along her back. Once again, she was overcome by the feverish dizziness that she had sensed before in the dungeon cell at Trifels and in the hall with the pictures of emperors beyond it. Narrowing her eyes, she tried again to imagine Johann standing here in the cathedral over two hundred years ago, maybe leaning against this very column.

Only a few moments, he had only a few moments . . .

Agnes let her eyes wander over the dark altars in the side chapels, the cathedral windows, the many columns reaching all the way to the steps at the south side that led down to the crypt from which she had run headlong last year. Where those steps began there was a small picture at waist height that she noticed only now. It had been hastily executed and showed a female figure. One of the builders of the cathedral might have engraved it there in the past, perhaps as a sign of his love for a girl who, like him, had turned to dust long ago. Could Johann have seen that picture and thought of his wife? A shudder ran through Agnes. Had Constanza loved Johann as she loved Mathis?

Her sense of vertigo was so strong now that she slowly slid down against the column; it was as if the bare stone were comforting her. She felt at one with the cathedral. As in Trifels Castle, she seemed to feel its breath and hear its voice.

Welcome, Agnes . . . Accept my gift . . .

At that moment, her fingers felt a gap in the stone behind her. It was at exactly the place where the curve of the rounded column met the angular base of an arch. Almost by itself, her hand slipped into the gap as she gazed at the picture on the stone.

Only a few moments . . . here . . . he was here . . . Johann was standing by this column . . .

Her fingers felt a piece of fabric, wrapped around something hard. She tugged, but it was wedged tight. She pulled harder, and the thing inside the fabric slowly worked loose.

"What are you doing?" asked her husband, who was pacing impatiently up and down the nave. "Uprooting that column by yourself with the power of the angels? All this drivel about martyrdom has gone to your head."

He stopped as Agnes, with a grunt of release, at last brought the bundle out of the gap. It was stained and dirty with stone dust and mold. Small pieces of stone came loose and crumbled to the floor. The object wrapped in the cloth was about the length of a man's forearm.

An iron point showed at its tip.

"My God," Melchior breathed. "The Holy Lance. This is a sign from God. She has actually found it."

Mathis and the other men had now turned their attention to Agnes. They watched in silence as she knelt down and slowly unfolded the cloth.

It contained the upper part of a lance. The tip was notched and had been broken; wire held it together, and a silver sleeve had been added. There was an inscription engraved on it. Agnes whispered its first words like a magic spell.

"*Clavus Dominicus*. The nail of the Lord."

Melchior von Tanningen knelt down and made the sign of the cross. The three landsknechts beside him looked as if the strangely solemn moment had touched even their dark hearts. Only Friedrich von Löwenstein-Scharfeneck shook his head skeptically.

"Is that supposed to be the genuine Holy Lance?" he rasped. "I'd have expected something fancier. Why the devil didn't Johann take the damned imperial crown instead? At least it has jewels in it."

Melchior looked at him indignantly. "What are you talking about? The Holy Lance is worth many, many times more than all the jewels in the world put together. It symbolizes the most wonderful story ever told."

"Do you think I don't know that? How stupid do you take me for, Tanningen?" Friedrich shrugged his shoulders and heaved a deep sigh. Suddenly his mouth twisted like he was enjoying a poor joke.

"But we didn't have to desecrate the imperial vault just for the sake of a beautiful story," he went on, smiling. "So don't suppose I'm a fool. Because above all, the lance proves that, ever since Johann stole it, the Habsburgs have wrongfully occupied the throne. No lance, no coronation, right? They've resorted to a fake for centuries." He assumed an innocent expression as his hand went to the hilt of his sword. "I've done some thinking over these last two days, and changed my plans accordingly. What do you think the emperor would pay to ensure that the original doesn't fall into the wrong hands?"

Melchior von Tanningen looked at the count in surprise. "I'm afraid I don't understand . . ."

"You don't understand? Then you'd better ask the revered Emperor Rudolf von Habsburg himself," replied Friedrich, giving his men a sign. "We've left the place next to him free for you."

A crossbow clicked, and with an expression of boundless astonishment Melchior stared at the bolt that suddenly protruded from his left shoulder. Marten put the weapon back in the sack of tools, where it had been hidden until now. Beside him Roland casually held another crossbow in his hands.

"You . . . you'll regret this, Scharfeneck . . ." the minstrel gasped, drawing his sword. "You miserable . . . traitor . . ."

"Coming from you, that almost sounds like a compliment, Tanningen." Friedrich von Löwenstein-Scharfeneck raised his hat as if in a final greeting. Then he once again looked greedily at the lance that Agnes was holding, while his three landsknechts drew their short swords.

"Roland, Hans, Marten, put that blue-eyed idiot out of his misery," he ordered. "And then place him and the other idiot in the sarcophagi. It's time to bring this farce to an end."

His face expressionless, Roland aimed the crossbow at the startled Mathis and pulled the trigger.

Hearing the whir of the bolt, however, Mathis instinctively threw himself forward. In contrast to the unsuspecting Melchior, he had seen the weapon a split second earlier, and that saved his life. The bolt ricocheted from a column above him, chipping out a piece of stone before clattering to the floor somewhere in the dark. Cursing, Roland threw the crossbow away; there was no time to reload it. His hand went to his sword belt.

That was what Mathis had been waiting for. He snatched the dagger from his boot and, with a yell, threw himself at his much larger adversary, who was taken by surprise and staggered a few steps back.

You wanted your chance, Mathis told himself. *Here it is, so use it, because you won't get another.*

Out of the corner of his eye, he saw Marten and Hans both fencing with the badly injured Melchior.

"Damn it, what useless fools you are!" Friedrich raged. "You're meant to kill the pair of them, not challenge them to duels."

With all the pent-up fury in him, Mathis thrust with his dagger, but it could not penetrate his adversary's hauberk. The burly landsknecht brushed the dagger aside like a toy and pushed Mathis away from him. Puffing and panting, he drew his short sword, the kind that landsknechts used in close combat. Mathis ducked under it, took a leap, and hit his back painfully on the side of the imperial vault, which cut off his way of retreat. He waited for the next attack, with his dagger in his trembling hand, but he knew that ultimately he had no chance against the longer blade. In addition, and unlike Mathis himself, Roland had learned to kill, and was also far superior to him physically. With an evil grin, the landsknecht raised his arm to strike a mortal blow. Then he ran at Mathis.

"You little bastard," he hissed. "Should have been dead long a—"

At that moment, Mathis threw the dagger.

It was a final act of desperation, but this time fate itself seemed to guide his hand. The blade flew straight as an arrow through the air, burying itself in the base of his opponent's throat, just where the hauberk ended. Carried on by his own impetus, the landsknecht kept running for a moment longer, but then blood streamed from his wound, and he collapsed, gurgling. He reached with both hands for the dagger in his throat, and finally fell over forward, reaching out to Mathis in a last, desperate attempt. Then he lay twitching on the cathedral floor, a large dark pool forming around him.

Paralyzed with horror, Mathis stared at his dying adversary. Beside him, Melchior, now as pale as a corpse, still battled the two other landsknechts. The shaft of the crossbow bolt stuck a finger's length out of the minstrel's shoulder, and a red patch had formed on his elegant velvet doublet. He wouldn't last much longer.

Mathis hesitated. Should he hurry to the aid of the man who had betrayed them so contemptibly? Or should he try to escape with

Agnes? Where was she, anyway? And where, for heaven's sake, was the count? His thoughts were interrupted when he heard Friedrich von Löwenstein-Scharfeneck bellowing in fury somewhere in the nave. In the darkness of the cathedral, Mathis now saw Agnes, carrying the lance, running among the columns to the west door.

Don't go to the western porch, Mathis thought. *They locked that door. You'll run into a trap!*

But Agnes doubled back on her own tracks and ran to a small door on the left of the west porch. The count followed her.

"Agnes!" Mathis cried. "Wait for me!"

In a fraction of a second, he had decided to leave the severely wounded Melchior alone with his two opponents, although he realized that if the minstrel lost the fight, he and Agnes would soon be pursued by two enraged landsknechts. With Friedrich, that made three opponents, all well armed. Nonetheless, Mathis couldn't leave Agnes on her own.

Not with that madman.

He raced to the small door through which Agnes and Friedrich had just disappeared. Steps led up to the second floor, and he heard the furious cries of Friedrich coming from it.

"Stop, you bitch! The lance, give me the lance."

Mathis reached a large hall with a broad table, several chairs, and a pile of ropes in a corner. Mathis assumed that the ropes must belong to the belfry somewhere above him. A tiny door to the right stood open, and he heard hasty footsteps on the other side of it.

"Agnes!" shouted Mathis once more, and his voice echoed through the vault of the cathedral. "Agnes!"

Crossing the hall, he hurried through the door. A narrow wooden staircase led steeply up. At regular intervals he passed windows standing open, the cool night air blowing through them.

Once again he heard footsteps, more muted this time. After more climbing, Mathis came to a chest-high opening that looked out into the night. The decaying wooden staircase went on above him, probably leading to the top of one of the front towers. Mathis listened, but he could hear nothing now. Where had the two of them gone? Through this opening or on up into the tower? Finally he decided to go through the low exit into the fresh air. If Agnes and the count were in the tower, he would presumably have heard their voices.

Gusts of wind ruffled Mathis's hair as he stepped out into a narrow gallery that ran to left and right of him, going all around the cathedral. It had narrow columns at regular intervals, and he clung convulsively to them. The walkway behind them was just wide enough for a single man to walk along it. All the same, Mathis dared not look down for too long. Even a brief glance had been enough to show him that it was some ninety feet above the ground. He looked straight ahead and wondered desperately which way to go, when he heard a scream from his right.

Ducking down, Mathis ran along behind the columns, while the first faint light of the morning sun showed in the east beyond the cupola crossing. The cathedral galleries, towers, and roofs were still in deep darkness.

When Mathis turned a corner, he suddenly saw the count not very far away from him. He was standing by the parapet and looking up, to where a trembling figure stood atop the wall, clinging to one of the slender columns, only a hand's breadth away from the abyss below.

Agnes.

"My God," whispered Mathis. "Don't jump—just don't jump!"

He stared in horror at his love, who was about to fall from Speyer Cathedral.

Agnes was trying to fight down her fear. She gripped the column with one hand, while with the other she held the stained cloth in which the Holy Lance was wrapped. A brief glance showed her that the sloping slate roof was more than fifteen feet below her. She felt nauseated.

When the landsknechts had fallen on Melchior and Mathis, she had initially stayed where she was, standing by the imperial monument, but then Friedrich had suddenly made for her, and she had rushed away without stopping to think. Only just in time did she remember that the west door was locked. So she decided on one of the front two towers of the cathedral, and that way ultimately brought her to this narrow gallery. Friedrich gained on her as she fled. When Agnes could almost feel him breathing down her neck, she had finally jumped up on the parapet, and as she stood there now she held the lance out into the faint morning twilight.

"Don't come a step closer," she gasped, "or I'll let go of it."

The count stopped and looked down, assessing the distance. Finally he shrugged.

"The lance will fall on the roof, where I'll retrieve it later. So let go of it, and then I can devote myself entirely to you." His mouth twisted in an unpleasant smile. "You have no idea how long I've been looking forward to that."

"You're crazy, Friedrich," Agnes pleaded. "Come to your senses. I'm still your wife."

"A wife who has betrayed me. A wife whom I once loved and desired, but who was a great disappointment to me." Friedrich shook his head regretfully. "I hoped for so much from you, Agnes. You were so clever, so well read, almost as much in love with the old stories as I am. I'm sure we could have found the Norman treasure together. We could have—"

"There is no Norman treasure, Friedrich! Can't you see that?" Agnes forced herself a little closer to the abyss. Anything was better than getting within reach of this madman. "It was never more than a dream of yours," she implored him. "Yes, the treasure may once have been at Trifels, but then the Staufers took it back to Apulia. It's probably been scattered to the four winds by now. Come to your senses." She cast him a glance of desperation. "I beg you, take the lance and get out of my life at long last."

The count pouted like a sulky child. "The treasure does exist," he said. "And I'll find it. You can't talk me out of that. Not you and not my miserly father, damn him. The treasure is somewhere at Trifels Castle. But I'll need money to find all the chests containing it, and salvage them, a great deal of money. And the emperor will give me that money in return for the true lance. So hand it over . . ."

He took another step. At that very moment, Agnes saw a figure at the corner of the gallery beginning to rush forward. Agnes cried out in surprise. She saw only too late that it was Mathis, on his way to attack her husband. She slipped on the parapet, damp as it as with morning dew, staggered once, and then fell from the gallery with her arms flailing in the air. The lance slipped out of her hands and fell on the sloping slate roof, where it slowly slid down and was finally caught in the gutter.

Agnes herself had caught hold of the plinth of the column at the very last moment, and was now dangling by one hand above the roof below. She felt her strength gradually draining away from her. Her fingers tingled as though thousands of ants were running over them. In the end, sheer exhaustion made her let go and fall to the hard roof. She tumbled down the rough slate surface toward the gutter.

"Murderer, Murderer!" Mathis shouted from above her.

A gray shadow suddenly rose from one of the towers, came gliding toward her, and she lost consciousness.

What in the world . . .

The last thought to cross her mind was that the shadow seemed strangely familiar.

And it let out a familiar screech.

Mathis ran toward the count, and at the same moment, Agnes fell. Mathis felt as if a dagger were piercing his heart, and then he tackled the count, dragging him down to the floor.

"Murderer, murderer!" he kept shouting, drumming his fists on Friedrich.

For all his slender figure, the count was muscular and very strong. He flung Mathis across the gallery and drew his sword.

"I'd really intended to take my time killing you," Friedrich panted, still breathless from their collision. A thin trickle of blood ran from his split lip, where Mathis's fist had made contact. "Well, too bad, it will have to be a quick death."

He thrust his blade at Mathis, who swerved at the last moment. Blind with hatred, Friedrich kept thrusting, so that Mathis was forced farther and farther back.

I have no weapon left, not even that dagger, he thought desperately. *What a fool I was not to bring the dead landsknecht's sword up here with me.*

Finally all he could do was jump up on the parapet, where he would be out of the reach of the sword at least for a moment. But Friedrich followed him, clambering onto the parapet himself, and now he was on the other side of a column. From there, he tried to strike the fatal blow, but Mathis kept eluding him like a fish, darting back and forth behind the column. He peered down desperately, trying to get a glimpse of Agnes, but the furious count blocked his view.

Oh God, don't let her have fallen all the way to the ground. Then it will all have been for nothing.

"She's dead!" Friedrich gloated, interpreting the expression on his adversary's face correctly. He laughed, derangement like poison in his eyes. "That woman will never torment me in my dreams again. Nor will you! You . . . *Curse it, what's that?*"

As Friedrich prepared to strike the final blow, a shadow suddenly passed along the gallery, a patch of black even darker than the dim light around him. A shrill, inhuman cry rang out, and feathers brushed Mathis in the face. The thing reached the count, who struck out wildly as a screeching, fluttering ball seemed to explode right before his eyes.

"Get away! Get away!" shouted the count. "You come from hell, you damned creature!"

As suddenly as it had come, the startled bird disappeared into the entablature of the gallery again. The whole thing happened so quickly that Mathis didn't know whether it was really a living creature or a ghost.

But the count was screaming in pain. The bird had gone for his face with its talons. He helplessly groped for his eyes, letting go of the column for a brief moment. As he did so he staggered, his right leg stepped into the void, and then his left leg.

"You come from hell!" he screamed again. "From hell!"

For a moment Friedrich seemed to hover in the air, and then he fell like a sack of flour. Only moments later he crashed on the roof below. Mathis saw the count rolling toward the sheer drop, flinging his arms out wildly but finding no handhold. As he slid over the edge, his fingers reached one last time for the gutter, winding around the leaden pipe like white worms.

For a split second the scratched and bloody face of Friedrich von Löwenstein-Scharfeneck appeared above the gutter, twisted into a grimace of madness and deathly fear.

Then the darkness swallowed him up.

Agnes was lying on the roof, dazed, when some large object struck it not far away from her. She heard a high scream, and then, suddenly, there was silence.

Friedrich, she thought. *That was Friedrich. He's dead.*

Curiously, she felt no relief. She thought of the shadow, the inhuman screech above her, the furious bellowing of her husband.

You come from hell, you damned creature . . .

Could it be true? After so many months?

She cautiously raised her head and tried to get her bearings. She was lying on the lower part of the roof, her limbs hurt from the impact when she fell, but the slight slope had ensured that she made a fairly soft landing. Nothing seemed to be broken. She tried to crawl farther up the slope, only to find herself sliding a considerable way down it. The morning dew had turned the slate slick. Agnes tried to push herself up again, only to slide back once more. Her feet could find no support, small stones rolled past her, and soon both her legs were dangling over the abyss. She desperately clawed at the wet slate, but she could feel sweat and the dew covering her hands with a slippery film.

"Don't move!" Mathis called from above her. "I'll be right back."

She heard footsteps hastily running away. Panic arose in her, like a small, gnawing animal. What in heaven's name was Mathis planning to do? Again, she slipped a little closer to the edge. She tried to become one with the slate underneath her, pressing close to the stone like a lizard, but it was no use. Once again she lost a hand's breadth of support, as her own weight inexorably dragged her farther down.

"Mathis, Mathis," she shouted desperately. "Where are you? I'm falling!"

Seconds became an eternity. Was this to be the end of her? After all that she had gone through? Had she really escaped from Black Hans, Barnabas, Shepherd Jockel, and finally her deranged husband, only to fall to her death from the roof of Speyer Cathedral? Agnes could almost have laughed in desperation, but she was unable to utter a sound. Fear was choking her.

At last, when she had given up hope, she heard footsteps again, and a moment later the end of a rope slapped down on the roof beside her.

"Grab hold of it, quick!" Mathis ordered.

"I . . . I can't," sobbed Agnes, whose voice had come back by now. "If I let go I'll fall."

"You must! Take it first in one hand, then the other. Trust me, it'll be all right."

Agnes gritted her teeth. Finally she took her right hand off the slates of the roof and reached for the rope. At the same moment she slipped the last little way toward the abyss.

"Nooooo . . ."

Her fingertips slipped over the rough stone, leaving a trail of blood, but she felt no pain, only the naked fear of death. Suddenly she felt a projection, and clutched it convulsively. It was the leaden gutter.

It shifted, and then gave way with a grating sound. Two hooks tore free from the cornice, and the gutter to the left of her came loose, so that Agnes was now dangling over the drop. The rope was only about a foot away from her.

"For heaven's sake, Agnes!" Mathis shouted above her. "Take hold of the rope."

Agnes looked down into the depths far below. The light of dawn was growing now, but the ground was still hidden by lingering mist, gray and wavering. The rooftops of some of the chapels emerged from it, and far in the east the morning sun shone on the Rhine with an almost unearthly radiance.

It won't hurt, thought Agnes. *It won't hurt at all. Only a short fall, a hollow thud . . .*

"Damn it, Agnes, grab the rope. If you won't do it for yourself, then do it for me. I love you!"

It was Mathis's voice that brought her back to reality. She saw the rope directly in front of her, seeming to point like a warning finger. Agnes closed her eyes, screamed with fear through the morning mists . . .

And jumped.

The rope was so wet that she slid down it for a moment, and her heart skipped a beat. But then she clutched it firmly with her bleeding fingers, and her fall came to an abrupt halt. She swung gently back and forth, like a bell, while the gutter stuck out beside her in the milky twilight. At the same moment there was a tug, and she felt herself being drawn steadily upward. Soon she was back on the slate roof.

"Now make a loop and tie the rope around your waist," Mathis said reassuringly. "There's only a little way to go, and then you'll be safe."

Trembling, Agnes did as he said. She made a loop with her bleeding fingertips, slipped it around her, and let him haul her up. At last she reached the gallery, where she collapsed, gasping. Mathis took her in his arms and held her so close to him that he robbed her of breath.

"That's the third time I've nearly lost you," he whispered. "Never leave me again. Do you hear, Agnes? Never again."

He laid her gently down on the floor and kissed her. Only now did she feel the pain in her grazed fingertips, but it was almost pleasant. It showed that she was still alive.

They lay like that for a long time on the floor of the narrow gallery, while the first birds began to sing. It was Agnes who finally spoke again, in a faltering voice.

"I saw a flying shadow and heard a screech," she said softly. "It sounded like Parcival's cry in the old days." She paused hopefully. "Mathis, do you think . . . was that Parcival?"

Mathis shook his head. "Surely not. It must have been a kestrel that we disturbed up here, or maybe an owl or a jackdaw. Who knows? It all happened so fast that I didn't get a good look at it."

"I thought Parcival . . ."

"Had come back to you?" Mathis frowned thoughtfully. "Agnes, Speyer is a long way from Trifels. I do think Parcival was fond of you. So far as we can ever tell with animals. But would he have flown so far to defend his mistress?" He shrugged his shoulders, and laughed quietly. "Why not? Let's say it was Parcival. It's a good story, anyway. And . . ."

He trailed off as they heard slow, dragging footsteps.

Is this nightmare never going to end? Agnes thought desperately.

Cautiously, Mathis got to his feet and picked up a stone that had broken away from the gallery during his fight. With the chunk of stone in his hand, he waited for the new arrival.

Now they heard gasping breath, and a hacking cough quickly becoming louder. At last a man came around the corner of the gallery. He tottered rather than walked, clutching the columns, forcing himself on step by step. Blood dripped from him to the floor.

It was Melchior von Tanningen.

The slightly built minstrel was near death. The crossbow bolt was still in his shoulder, but his doublet also showed patches of red spattered across it. His right hand, still clutching his sword of Toledo steel, hung limp at his side. Nonetheless, he was smiling.

"Ah, so I have found you in the end, Lady Agnes," he said, attempting and failing to sketch a slight bow. He fell forward on his knees, coughing up blood. Laboriously, he hauled himself up again by one of the columns.

"I was afraid I might have to rid you of your appalling husband," he went on faintly. "But thank God, I see you have done that for yourself. How very kind of you . . ." Briefly, he closed his eyes, while blood continued to seep from his wounded shoulder. "Not that I would have feared a fight. But at the moment I . . . don't feel quite fit for it."

"The count is dead," Mathis said coolly. "And so, obviously, are the two men you were fighting."

Melchior nodded. "Irritating . . . gnats. They stung me. If it hadn't been for the bolt . . ."

"Maybe we ought to thank you," Mathis interrupted him. "After all, you made sure that Agnes had a chance to get away. But somehow I can't feel much gratitude."

"You . . . still don't understand, Master Wielenbach." Melchior's face was as white as the stone behind him. "The . . . empire was in danger. I . . . I had no choice. But I owe you both an apology, all the same. I ought never to have allied myself to that madman. My eyes were opened at last only here in the cathedral. Your vision . . ." He smiled at Agnes, and made the sign of the cross. "I was privileged to witness a divine vision. Now I can die in peace."

Agnes took a step back. "I really don't know whether it was a vision," she hesitantly replied. "It may just have been chance. The lance was hidden in that gap. Someone could have found it before me."

Melchior shook his head. "It was a vision. A sign from God. No doubt of that." Breathing with difficulty, he searched a pocket of his blood-stained doublet and finally brought out a crumpled, rolled-up document. "Your ancestral family tree, Lady Agnes," he said. "Take it. Your fate, and the fate of the whole empire, now lie in the hands of

God alone. The family tree will guide you and tell you what to do." Once again the minstrel reached into his pocket. He took out the signet ring, and handed it and the document to Agnes. "Here, take this, too. It seems that the ring has brought me only misfortune. I never should have taken it from you. Can you forgive me?"

Agnes took the parchment and the ring, which felt strangely cold in her fingers.

"I forgive you," she finally replied.

"Thank you. You are very kind." Melchior clutched one of the columns and gazed longingly at her. "The Holy Lance . . . might I see it once again?"

"We don't have it," Mathis intervened. "We don't want it, either. A little while ago I still thought that I could change the world with it. But that's all over." He pointed disparagingly toward the slate roof below them. "It's lying there, somewhere in the gutter, where it will soon be covered with leaves, dust, and bird droppings. May it rot there for the next three hundred years. It's all the same to me."

Melchior stared at him, open-mouthed. "But . . . the . . . Holy Lance," he whispered. "It must not . . ."

At that moment they heard a screech in the distance. It came closer, and finally a large bird appeared above the cupola, crossing in the light of the morning sun. Its wings were spread wide, and it swooped down to the roof below them at a steep angle. The dew on the roof reflected the sunlight into Agnes's eyes, and she saw nothing but radiance below her. It was like a glittering sea into which the bird plunged. Suddenly it surfaced again, but it was still difficult to make the creature out clearly. A moment or so later, it was above them.

It carried a gray bundle the length of a man's forearm in its talons.

"The Holy Lance," Mathis breathed. "That bird has actually snatched up the Holy Lance."

One last time, the bird circled above them, and then it finally turned away, screeching once more as if in farewell, a falcon's familiar cry. This time, Agnes felt sure of herself.

"That was Parcival," she said quietly, but firmly. "Parcival put us on the trail of the lance all that time ago, and now he is taking it away again."

Clinging to the parapet, Mathis leaned far out to see more, but the bird had already disappeared behind the towers.

"Nonsense," he replied. "That's . . . not possible. It was larger than your falcon, more like a buzzard or an eagle. I expect it's going to use it to build its nest, or thinks it's something to eat. What you're saying could happen only in stories." He looked out over the rooftops of the city, to where swamps, cultivated fields, and forests reached far away. "I wonder where it will take the lance?" he murmured. "Maybe its eyrie is in some ruined castle."

Agnes smiled. "Not Trifels, I hope. I've had enough adventures. And as long as the forged lance is kept in Nuremberg, no one will miss it."

She turned to Melchior von Tanningen, who had collapsed on the floor of the gallery. The minstrel huddled against the wall, his empty, glazed eyes staring into the distance where the bird had disappeared. There was an expression of utter peace on his face.

"He's dead," Mathis said after placing his hand on the minstrel's breast to feel for a heartbeat. "It's a miracle that he made his way up here at all, wounded as he was." He shook his head, and then gently closed Melchior's eyes. "What was he? A friend? A traitor? I could never entirely make him out."

"At least he was a good storyteller," Agnes replied sadly. "I hope he saw the falcon, so that he could know how his story ended." She sighed. "All stories come to an end some time."

"How about ours?" Mathis hesitantly asked.

"Ours? Ours has only just begun." She hesitated. "And it's a story that will be played out in the future and not the past."

With determination, Agnes took the crumpled old sheet of parchment, and tore it into dozens of pieces, throwing them into the wind. The scraps of parchment drifted away like snowflakes and finally disappeared behind the cupola of the cathedral.

Then she took Mathis by the hand, and they went along the gallery together to the eastern end, where the shining globe of the sun stood in the sky above the river Rhine, announcing the beginning of a new day.

Agnes smiled. It was going to be the first good day in a long time.

EPILOGUE

A village somewhere on the Upper Rhine, May, Anno Domini 1526

THE MIDDAY SUN, GOLDEN AS stalks of wheat, shone down on the newly thatched reed roofs of the little hamlet, and barley was ripening in the surrounding fields. Agnes reclined on a small bench outside the village smithy, hearing the hammer come down on the anvil at regular intervals. It was a reassuring sound, in spite of its volume. There was something monotonous and soporific about it that, along with the warm sunlight, always made her eyes close.

Peace, thought Agnes, lost in reverie. *That sound means peace.*

It had been almost a year since she and Mathis had left Trifels forever. They had finally found a new home in a village on the Rhine. Exactly as Mathis had said, many parts of the country in south Germany were so devastated that the survivors were glad of any newcomer who would help to repair the damage. Almost all of this once pretty place, with its church, its inn, and some two dozen peasant houses, had been burned down by the landsknechts of the Swabian League. The former smith had joined the Palatinate Band of peasants, and never came home, so Mathis took his place. Together with the villagers, he and Agnes had felled trees in the nearby wood; rebuilt the houses to look better than before; dug up the burned, trampled fields and sowed fresh seed; and rounded up the runaway live-stock wandering in the woods. The first of the cows had calved again in spring. Agnes smiled sadly. Life went on. It did not mourn the many dead who found their last resting place in the nearby graveyard.

The old priest had run away from the peasant hordes last year, and the new one was a young monk who had left his monastery and joined the Lutherans. His sermons were mild and full of imagery, and in many ways he almost reminded Agnes of Father Tristan.

The hammering stopped, and soon Mathis appeared at the door of the smithy. He reached for a jug of water that sat on the window sill, drank deeply, and then plopped down on the bench beside her.

"The horseshoes are ready," he said, wiping the sweat off his fore-head. "You can tell old Answin to come and fetch them. But I'll need a little longer for his harrow." He grinned. "It'll be ready for the next early sowing season at the latest, though."

Agnes laughed. "Don't say that, with all the work you've already taken on."

"You're right. I shudder to think of all the hatchets, picks, and horseshoes that I still have to forge."

Groaning, Mathis stretched his limbs. Now that people had re-built their villages, new tools were in demand everywhere. The young smith earned a good living, and he had kept his vow never to forge firearms again. Agnes contributed a few guilders to their household budget with her knowledge of healing. By now people were coming from the neighboring villages to consult her. She had a growing rep-utation as a skillful healer, and although they were not rich, there was a hot meal on the table every day.

Tired but happy, Agnes leaned against the man she had loved since childhood. Now, at last, they could be together. Mathis had grown stronger over the last year, and a wild sandy beard grew on his face, hiding the scar on his right cheek left after the storming of the Ramburg. In bed at night, Agnes sometimes teasingly called him her Barbarossa. Then they would make love, and the dark thoughts went away for a while. Things improved as the months went by, but it was taking some time. A troubled expression came over Agnes's face, and Mathis looked at her in concern.

"You were dreaming again last night, weren't you?" he asked. "I heard you cry out in your sleep."

She shook her head. "It . . . it was nothing too bad. The usual. I sometimes still see the dead on the battlefields, raising their arms and pleading with me, and I can't help them." She sighed. "At least Constanza leaves me alone now, and Trifels has stopped calling to me."

Mathis smiled. "It's probably given up hope that you will move back in, as a descendant of the Staufers."

"Yes, it looks rather like that." Suddenly Agnes felt somber. The castle had been her home, the castle and the stories that haunted its walls. Now those stories were in the past. A new life had begun, but sometimes the old one came back, knocking and asking Agnes to let it in.

"How's our little emperor?" asked Mathis, to give her something else to think about. He caressed her belly, which had grown visibly rounder during the last few months.

"Why not empress?" Agnes banished her dark thoughts and smiled. "What gives you men the right to want a male successor to the throne all the time?"

Mathis's eyes twinkled as he looked at her. "Well, who's going to wield the hammer in this smithy when I'm old and feeble? Besides, I'd like a great many children. I don't mind if we have a few daughters among them." He put his head on one side. "Well, maybe one."

Laughing, Agnes hit his broad chest. They had married in the spring, when they could simply no longer conceal their good news. Fortunately the local steward was a kindly old man who gave his permission at once. In return, Mathis had made him some particularly fine carpenters' nails and horseshoes.

The wedding itself had been a splendid village festival, although they had only a small cask of wine, a few loaves of bread, some cheeses, and a ham given by the steward for their celebration. But after all the

horror and death, people were so glad of any diversion that a simple
fiddle and a tambourine were enough to have them dancing on the
tables of the new inn.

"Agnes! Agnes!"

Excited cries came from the outskirts of the wood. Looking up,
Agnes saw little Marie hurrying over the fields to them. Close behind
her came Mathis's mother, Martha Wielenbach, desperately trying to
keep the child from treading down the ears of barley. But Marie was
much too excited to listen to her mother. At last the two of them, out
of breath, arrived at the smithy.

"I've told her a dozen times not to run through the fields," Martha
Wielenbach panted. "But she's like her big brother. She just won't
listen."

Mathis raised a threatening finger, but he was grinning. "Marie, I
warn you, listen to your mother or you won't be allowed to help
change your little nephew's diapers."

"Or your little niece's diapers, for goodness' sake," Agnes shook
her head, laughing. "You still don't understand, do you, you stubborn
creature?"

After their escape from Trifels Castle, little Marie and Mathis's
mother had stayed for a while with a distant cousin near Annweiler.
But several months ago, Mathis had sent a message asking them to
come and join him and Agnes, and since then they had been a little
family.

A family that is soon going to be larger, thought Agnes, and a warm
sensation went through her.

"Agnes, look!"

Marie excitedly held out her two hands, which she had cupped
together. A baby bird nested in them, chirping furiously. With its soft
white feathers, it looked like a ball of wool with a beak.

"Why, he's a falcon!" Agnes said in astonishment. "I do believe he's
a saker falcon. Where did you find him?"

Marie gestured behind her. "In the wood, in the burned-out ruins
of the monastery. He must have fallen out of his nest." She looked

pleadingly at Agnes. "May I keep him? Please? Mother says I have to ask you."

"Me?" Agnes frowned. It was still difficult for Martha Wielenbach not to think of Agnes as a countess, daughter of the castellan of Trifels, but simply as her son's wife. This time, however, she was glad to give permission.

"If you look after him well, why not?" Smiling, she stroked the soft down of the frightened chick. "Maybe you can train him when he's bigger."

"The way you trained Parcival. Yes, I'd like that." Little Marie beamed. "I'm going to give him a name." She thought hard. "Galahad!" she finally cried. "I'll call him Galahad. You've told me so many stories about Sir Galahad."

Agnes laughed. "A good choice. Although I don't know how this little bird is going to carry the Holy Grail."

"Oh yes, tell me about the Holy Grail."

"Please, not the Grail again," Agnes groaned. "I'm sure I've told you that story a hundred times already."

Martha Wielenbach cast up her eyes. "I can see it's all decided, and I'm not needed here any longer." She knocked the fir needles off her apron. "So I'll go and sweep out the stable. I've been wanting to do that all day."

"And I'll do some more work on that harrow," said Mathis, standing up. "Or good old Answin really will have to wait until next sowing season for it."

He gave Agnes a last kiss and went into his forge. The monotonous sound of the hammer was soon ringing out of it. When Martha Wielenbach too had left them, Marie sat down beside Agnes. The ten-year-old carefully stroked the little falcon.

"Will you tell me a story now?" she asked hopefully.

Agnes looked at her with a twinkle in her eyes. "All right, as long as it doesn't have to be the Holy Grail or the Red Knight. So what story would you like?"

For a moment Marie thought, then she suddenly pointed to the golden signet ring that Agnes wore on her right hand. "You once said there was a wonderful story about that ring," the child suggested. "Tell me that one."

Agnes hesitated, her face briefly darkening. But then she took the ring off her finger and looked at it thoughtfully. She followed the contours of the bearded face engraved on it. That ring was her last link to her old life. To Trifels Castle, to Parcival, to her dead father. She had been unable to part with it. In silence, Agnes held the ring up to the sun, making it sparkle.

"Well, why not?" she said at last.

Collecting her thoughts, she began in a low tone that sounded like an incantation, a trick that she had once learned from Father Tristan.

"This ring is the ring of a mighty emperor, and his name was Barbarossa. He sleeps under a mountain, and his red beard grows and grows. Once every hundred years, the emperor sends a dwarf into the outside world, to see whether ravens are still flying around the mountain . . ."

Agnes began the story quietly, and Marie listened, open-mouthed, as the sun slowly sank behind the treetops.

It was indeed a wonderful story, and it was not yet over when night fell.

Afterword

I have loved castles for as long as I can remember. It is understandable that I did so as a little boy, but by now I suppose I must say I have a bee in my bonnet about them. When we go to Italy, I give my children a candy for every castle that they spot. Our vacations are full of visits to castles, and at the time of this writing we are soon to go on vacation to a castle in Scotland. The result of all this is that my family are . . . well, let's say not as keen as they might be on castles, which is a pity, because I suppose it means I'll have to go on vacation by myself.

I've spent a long time wondering why these old buildings, usually now in ruins, exert such a powerful attraction on me. I assume I must be a hopeless romantic. To me, a ruined castle is like one of Caspar David Friedrich's paintings—it tells stories of a time now long forgotten. As a child, I could spend hours in such ruined buildings, imagining what went on there in the past. I explored secret passages, treasure chambers, and dark dungeons; I heard the shouting of besiegers, the crash of battering rams, the hiss of catapults. I smelled pitch and sulphur and the smoke of the smithy fires on which legendary magic swords were forged.

A castle is a hoard of stories, true and invented, and this novel is a mixture of fact and fiction. Most of the characters in and around

Trifels Castle are my own inventions, and so are their adventures. Probably this former imperial castle was already being administered from Neukastell after 1509, and the castellan would have been more like a domestic steward.

On the other hand, the historical events framing the story are true, including the political confrontation between Emperor Charles V and King Francis I of France, the latter's capture at the battle of Pavia, and the exchange of hostages on the river Bidasoa. My model and inspiration here was an excellent biography, *Franz I. von Frankreich* (Francis I of France), by Gerd Treffer.

The legendary Norman treasure also existed. Emperor Henry VI brought it back to Trifels as loot from his Sicilian campaign. Later, the treasure presumably went to Lucera in Apulia, to be guarded by the Saracens, whom Frederick II had settled there. No one knows for sure what happened to it after that. Professor Knut Görich, an expert on the Staufer emperors, thinks it was probably used to finance later political business and military campaigns, and so was gradually whittled down to nothing. But who knows, maybe a part of it still lies hidden at Trifels Castle after all . . .

As for the descendants of Enzio, Frederick II's favorite son, the sources mention several possible children. One of them, a daughter, is in fact said to have borne the name Constanza. But her mother was not, to the best of my knowledge, a nun with access to the Staufer who was kept prisoner at Bologna. I have also invented Constanza's later experiences at Trifels, as well as the character of Johann of Brunswick, their child, Sigmund, the Annweiler Brotherhood, and also Barbarossa's signet ring and the legendary deed of descent. On the other hand, the many bloodthirsty battles of the German Peasants' War, and the part played by the leaders Florian Geyer and Götz von Berlichingen, are all recorded history.

For reasons of the story, I have made a few changes to the facts concerning some local events. Eusserthal monastery was not burned down until about two weeks later than in this novel, probably by the

Landau Band of insurgents. As far as I know, there was no separate rising by the peasants of Dahn and Wilgartswiesen.

My opinion is that a historical novel should always represent a dramatic expression of the real background of events. Did the international political powers of the time really send agents to find a descendant of the Staufers? Presumably not. But what matters is that, particularly in the fifteenth and sixteenth centuries, there was indeed a nostalgic longing for the emperors of the house of Hohenstaufen that had died out so long ago. In written works of the time, Barbarossa and his grandson Frederick II merge into a kind of messianic figure who will restore peace and justice to the world.

One reason why Francis I did not win the election for Holy Roman Emperor over Charles V was his lack of German roots. So the idea that he might have hoped to acquire the necessary legitimacy by marrying a descendant of the Staufers is not as far-fetched as all that. But this is where history ends and the realm of fantasy begins ...

Probably no other castle in Germany offers so much material for historical novels as Trifels. Once, the former imperial castle was something like the center of the German Empire. It was from here that Emperor Henry VI set out against the Normans and came back with the legendary treasure that plays a major part in my novel. It is also where Barbarossa's more sinister son kept King Richard the Lionheart of England prisoner, and where the sacred imperial insignia was housed for almost two centuries. And the mountain on which the castle stands, like the legendary Kyffhäuser range of hills, is thought to be a possible location, according to myth, of Barbarossa's resting place, where he has slept for nearly a thousand years, waiting to help Germany in the hour of its greatest need.

Whether Trifels was stormed in the Peasants' War, however, is a matter of controversy. It was long past its heyday at the time. Then, early in the seventeenth century, the building was struck by lightning and burned down. In the nineteenth century Trifels was rebuilt, and in the twentieth century it went through more reconstruction. Today you can visit the restored Trifels, though it is thought to bear little resemblance to the original medieval castle.

Only in the twentieth century was the *idea* of Trifels revived, if in an unedifying context. The National Socialists planned to convert the ruined building into a Nazi place of pilgrimage, probably on the direct instructions of Adolf Hitler. The war put an end to this deranged notion, but in particular the so-called Imperial Hall, included in the Nazi-era plans for the castle, derives from the Nazi architectural style. This large space was designed to be a hall of fame and the scene of Nazi Party rallies, and the chamber above the chapel was to be a solemn place of initiation. Anyone walking through the halls of Trifels today should therefore remember that German history does not consist solely of knights, minstrels, and damsels in castles.